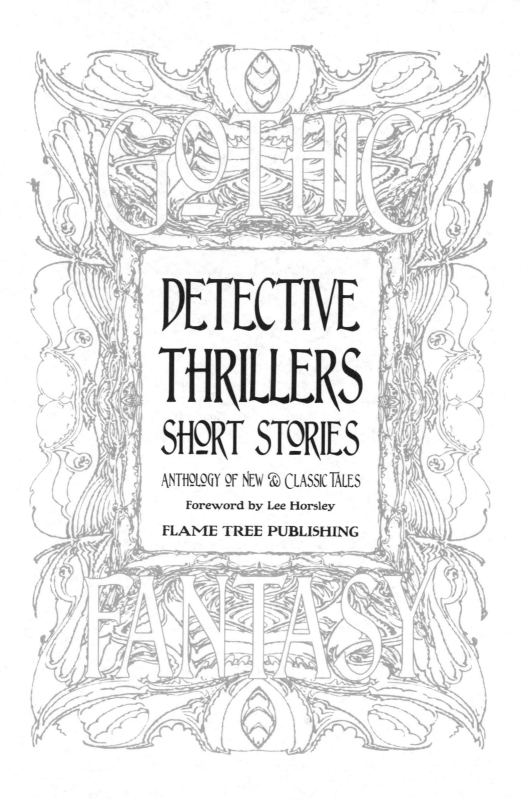

GOTHIC

DETECTIVE THRILLERS

SHORT STORIES

ANTHOLOGY OF NEW & CLASSIC TALES

Foreword by Lee Horsley

FLAME TREE PUBLISHING

FANTASY

This is a FLAME TREE Book

Publisher & Creative Director: Nick Wells
Project Editor: Gillian Whitaker
Editorial Board: Josie Karani, Taylor Bentley, Catherine Taylor

Publisher's Note: Due to the historical nature of the classic text, we're aware that there may be some language used which has the potential to cause offence to the modern reader. However, wishing overall to preserve the integrity of the text, rather than imposing contemporary sensibilities, we have left it unaltered.

FLAME TREE PUBLISHING
6 Melbray Mews, Fulham,
London SW6 3NS, United Kingdom
www.flametreepublishing.com

First published 2020

20 22 24 23 21
1 3 5 7 9 10 8 6 4 2

ISBN: 978-1-78755-780-2

The cover image is created by Flame Tree Studio based on artwork by Slava Gerj and Gabor Ruszkai.

A copy of the CIP data for this book is available from the British Library.

Printed and bound in China

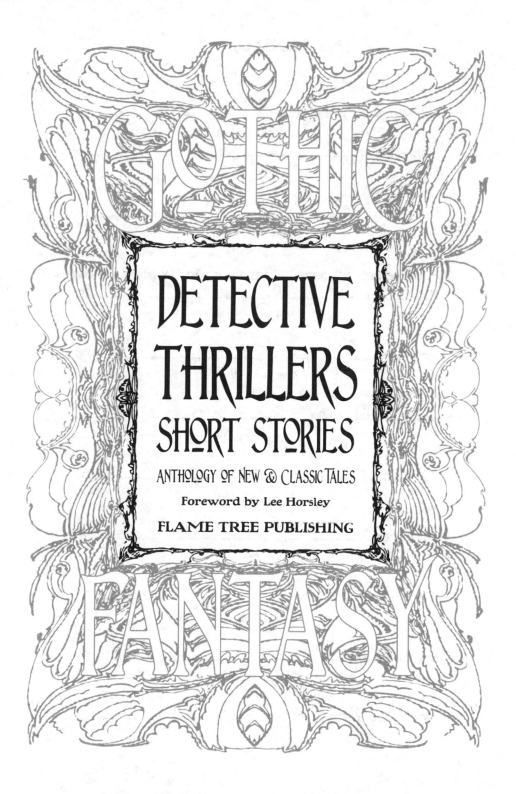

GOTHIC

DETECTIVE
THRILLERS
SHORT STORIES
ANTHOLOGY OF NEW & CLASSIC TALES

Foreword by Lee Horsley

FLAME TREE PUBLISHING

FANTASY

Contents

Foreword: Detective Thrillers Short Stories

"SOMETIMES," Race Williams says, "one hunk of lead is worth all the thought in the world." The hero of the detective thriller doesn't always come out with guns blazing, but even the most thoughtful of detectives has to be ready for action in a treacherous world. In *The Adventures of Sherlock Holmes*, Mycroft, according to his brother, only detects 'from an armchair', whereas Sherlock ventures out, exposing himself to danger. In 'The Final Problem', he confronts his greatest adversary, Moriarty, declaring, "If I were assured of your eventual destruction I would, in the interests of the public, cheerfully accept my own." As readers of such stories, we simultaneously want to discover the secrets of the plot and to experience the acute suspense generated by an atmosphere of fear and anxiety.

In late Victorian and Edwardian British crime writing, there was a growing popular audience for adventures that combined mystery with hazardous exploits. The stories of writers like Conan Doyle, Buchan and Le Queux are often set against a background of war, with Britain feared to be vulnerable to invasion. The protagonist must stand against threats posed by international adversaries – secret agents, German spies, Russian nihilists and a sensational array of other sanguinary foreigners. Le Queux begins 'The Woman with a Blemish' amidst the horrors of the Russo-Turkish wars, during which his narrator encounters a mysterious woman driven by 'the desire for revenge, the mad, insatiable craving for blood.' Even London is not safe from her. Conan Doyle's 'The Adventure of the Bruce-Partington Plans' starts with the theft of vital submarine plans. Holmes, hampered by thick London fog, must identify the foreign agent responsible and recover this 'most jealously guarded of all government secrets.' In Buchan's story of a strange spiritualist, 'Dr Lartius', those working secretly in the service of Britain use every stratagem at their disposal to prevent 'the Boche' from prevailing during the grim closing stages of World War I.

The heroes of these stories sometimes resort to disguise and deception in order to protect the innocent and save the country. There was at the same time, however, a vogue for anti-heroes, for stories in which the virtuous investigator's tricks of the trade are replaced by far more thoroughgoing forms of trickery. Some of the most successful turn-of-the-century crime writers inverted the Holmesian model to produce tales of miscreants. Conan Doyle's brother-in-law, E. W. Hornung, dedicated the stories of *Raffles, The Amateur Cracksman*, to Doyle: 'To A. C. D. This Form of Flattery.' Guy Boothby and Arthur Morrison, too, offered readers the thrill of following the careers of incorrigible scoundrels. Boothby's Simon Carne is a master of disguise, travelling from India to London to pull off a succession of daring robberies. His aim, he says in 'An Imperial Finale', is to secure his fame: "I think they'll say that, all things considered, I have won the right to call myself 'A Prince of Swindlers.'" Morrison introduced the wonderfully subversive Horace Dorrington in 'The Narrative of Mr. James Rigby'. He is a 'private inquiry agent' who has done 'much *bona fide* business', but who is utterly unscrupulous, willing to murder, steal and defraud without compunction. In the second story in the series, 'The Case of Janissary', his thwarting of an intended murder ends in his explaining to the would-be killers that he won't hand them over to the police but will instead take them into his service: "I may as well tell you that I'm a bit of a scoundrel myself."

Both the heroes and anti-heroes of British crime and adventure stories have clear affinities with the men of action who, from the 1920s on, dominate American hard-boiled detective fiction in the pages of pulp magazines like *Black Mask* and *Dime Detective*. Drawn to trouble, they are in the main trying to achieve some sort of rough justice, but they can be difficult to distinguish from the culprits they're pursuing. The first of the hard-boiled detectives, Carroll John Daly's Race Williams, identifies himself as 'a halfway house between the cops and the crooks', an independent, frequently endangered, often solitary figure. Many other cynical, case-hardened investigators followed in Race's bold footsteps – for example, the two-fisted Irish operative Jack Cardigan, created by Frederick Nebel in the 1930s. There were a few hard-boiled women as well – like Patricia Seaward, a tough dame who went into action alongside Cardigan in several of Nebel's stories, and Cleve F. Adams' Violet McDade, a one-time circus fat lady who was as intrepid, two-fisted and straight-talking as any man. But women were more often cast as dangerous adversaries, the *femmes fatales* who joined the gangsters, crooked cops and unscrupulous tycoons threatening to corrupt life in every large American city. For Raymond Chandler, whose Philip Marlowe is probably the best-known of all the tough guy detectives, the 'smell of fear' generated by such stories was evidence of their serious response to the moral failures of post-war American society: 'Their characters lived in a world gone wrong... The law was something to be manipulated for profit and power. The streets were dark with something more than night.'

Detective Thrillers offers readers an absorbing selection of stories that blend mystery and adventure. Our fascination with such stories goes considerably beyond our pleasure in seeing individual mysteries solved. Those editing the dozens of serial publications that flourished between the 1890s and 1950s were keenly aware of the fact that readers' anxieties about the survival of their heroes (and indeed anti-heroes) can keep them hooked for story after story. Conan Doyle's intention had been to kill off Holmes in 'The Final Problem'. But so intense was audience pressure to revive him that Doyle at last relented, revealing, a decade later, that Holmes had cunningly escaped an untimely death at Reichenbach Falls. Courageous and resolute, the protagonists of mystery adventures survive because it is in their nature to survive untold perils – but also because their audiences expect it of them.

Lee Horsley

Publisher's Note

Tales of mysteries, murders and undercover secret operations are irresistible to fans of crime fiction, and there's nothing quite like a charismatic detective – or memorable villain – to capture the imagination. In this book we've chosen a range of stories from the birth of the genre to the interpretation of its form in the current day.

Once again, our call for submissions for the new short stories was met with a great response, and we're delighted to present the successful authors and their modern detectives alongside the likes of Sherlock Holmes, Max Latin, iconic PI Race Williams, the 'Island Detective' Jo Gar, and Cleve F. Adams's wonderfully feisty Violet McDade. Atmospheric, high-action and fast-paced: this anthology proves to be, we hope, a gripping collection of new and old tales in celebration of this exciting genre.

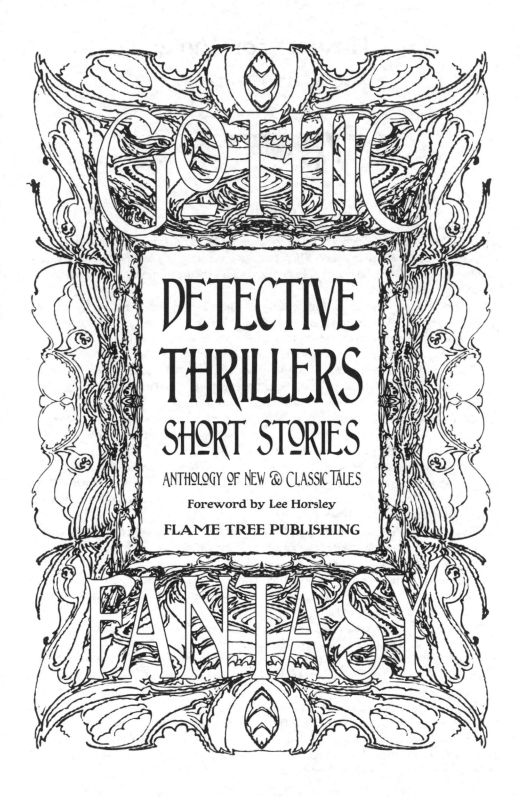

GOTHIC

DETECTIVE THRILLERS SHORT STORIES

ANTHOLOGY OF NEW & CLASSIC TALES

Foreword by Lee Horsley

FLAME TREE PUBLISHING

FANTASY

Flowers for Violet
A Violet McDade Story
Cleve F. Adams

Chapter I

VIOLET MCDADE in a night club is as conspicuous as an elephant in an aquarium. It isn't altogether her prodigious size, nor is it her atrocious taste in clothes. Rather, it is a combination of these things added to the manner of a precocious child bent on attracting attention. She was attracting it, beyond a doubt.

The floor show at the Green Kitten was pretty good; exceptional, in fact. The crowded supper room didn't even know it was there. All eyes were centered on that great lummox who is my partner. Or, at least, that's the way I felt. I was never so embarrassed in my life.

I said, "Violet McDade, if you ask another man to dance with me I'll – I'll scream!"

"Go ahead," she said. "People will just think you're drunk." She waved a pudgy, beringed fist at the second drink I'd had in the last hour, her fat nose crinkled in disgust. "There you go, soppin' up liquor, spoilin' the effect of all the swell contacts I'm makin'."

"Contacts!" I said. "All the contacts we've made tonight have been on my feet. I've danced with fat men, lean men, in fact every man in the room who has been unfortunate enough to pass our table. I'm sick of it. I'm going home!"

"Trouble with you" – she sniffed – "trouble with you, Nevada, is you don't realize what contacts mean to a couple of female dicks like you and me. Look, here comes Stephen Wright, the assistant district attorney. I'm going to hornswoggle him into dancin' with you and after that – well, after that mebbe I'll go home, too."

Wright seemed in a great hurry to get back to his table. His cold eyes missed her smirk of recognition and she calmly stuck out a foot, tripped him. He stopped then. Square, granite face aflame with wrath, he righted himself, muttered an ungracious apology.

She beamed. "Think nothin' of it, Stevie. Meet my partner, Nevada Alvarado. Senator Hymes will wait for you. Fact is, it looks like you're both waitin' for somethin'. Couldn't be your new boss, the district attorney, could it?"

He glared at her, made as if to pass on, thought better of it and pulled out a chair. "Why should you think Alvin Foss is coming here tonight?"

"A little birdie told me," she said easily. "Or maybe it was a stool pigeon. Tell you the truth, that's the real reason I'm here myself. I'm kind of keepin' an eye on Rose Donelli in case her husband gets into trouble."

Something flamed in the depths of those cold eyes opposite. He said, "Why should Mike Donelli have any trouble with Alvin Foss? The Green Kitten is a licensed club."

"There's things upstairs that the license don't cover, Stevie. Mike's real business is gamblin'. He's in the rackets up to his ears, and I got a idea" – she winked owlishly – "I got an idea that a certain state senator's dough is behind him."

Wright said, "You're talking wildly, woman. Perhaps too wildly." He let that sink in, rose. His eyes on a distant table, where sat State Senator Hymes, he bowed absently. "I'll bid you ladies a very good evening." He went away.

Mike Donelli, very genial, very hearty, came in through the arch which led to the stairs, paused beside us just as Rosita was announced. Rosita was Rose Donelli. She did a whirlwind number, clad mostly in brilliants, and was the big drawing card of the Green Kitten – the supper room part of it, I mean. I hadn't known about the other diversions upstairs until just now. Violet, eyes on Rose, addressed Donelli. "Why don't you get out o' the rackets, Mike? Rose is too nice a kid to be mixed up in – well, in things that'll likely make her a widow before she's twenty."

He was watching his wife. His smooth, round face was a little troubled. "You think a lot of Rose, don't you, Violet?"

"No, you ape, I don't. I think she's an empty-headed little tramp. I think she was a sap for marrying a guy like you. But" – Violet's little greenish eyes got that far-away look which somehow always brought a lump to my throat – "but Rose's mother was damn white to me back in the old days when she was tops and I was doin' the fat lady in the same circus. I – I kind of owe Rose somethin' for that."

Mike looked at her then. The lines about his mouth softened. "You're a good egg, Violet McDade. And for your information I'll tell you that I'm trying to get out. It – isn't easy." Dark eyes swept the great, crowded room, dwelt on Rosita's exit, caught sight of something which made his lips tighten suddenly. He left us hurriedly. Turning, I saw District Attorney Alvin Foss enter the lobby, go directly to Senator Hymes' table and, ignoring the senator, speak crisply to Stephen Wright.

Violet said, "I better have a word with Rose. Pay the check and I'll meet you out in the lobby." She waddled away toward the rear of the orchestra platform.

It was raining outside, not heavily, just enough to freshen the air and I breathed it gratefully after the smoke fog I'd been inhaling for what had seemed ages. The doorman signaled Sweeney, Violet's diminutive chauffeur, and presently the great limousine rolled up to the curb.

We got in. The door slammed, and I prepared to unburden my mind of several things I'd been meaning to tell the great gooph. I might as well have saved my breath. She was asleep. It was, I think, a little after one when we reached home. I kicked off my mistreated slippers, donned mules and started to mix myself a nightcap before getting ready for bed, had got as far as the ice cubes when the doorbell rang.

Violet, plumped down on the chaise longue, opened an eye sleepily. "See who it is, Mex."

"See who it is, yourself!" I snapped. The bell rang again, insistently. Violet grunted, got up and waddled into the hall. Surprise, then dismay, registered in the rumble of her voice. The front door slammed, the chain rattled. The elephant returned, ushering in Rose Donelli.

I set my glass down, prepared for anything. Or so I thought at the time.

"Mike Donelli," announced Violet cheerfully, "has just shot a guy." She went to the windows, eased one of the drapes aside and peered out into the night. And I? Well, I just stood staring at the girl. Still in her spangles with nothing but a sheer negligee to cover her, feet bare, face pale and hair disordered, she essayed a wan smile in my direction, failed miserably and tumbled in a heap at my feet.

There was the rasp of gears from the street, sound of a car getting underway. There followed an instant of silence, then the roar of a second motor, coming up very fast. Tires shrieked down the block. And Violet said, "Douse the lights!" She dropped the drape, swiveled, to see me rooted above the prone figure of Rose Donelli. "Well, for cryin' out loud, don't stand there gawking like she was a .ghost or something! I said, douse the lights!"

As if in a daze, I moved to the wall switch, clicked it. The dim glow from my bedroom door showed me Violet stooping, lifting the girl as she would a feather. Breathing imprecations against some unknown, the creature strode into my room. I followed.

Violet laid the girl on the bed, said, "O.K., revive her." Just like that. Busy with smelling salts and a wet towel I watched the lummox pawing through my wardrobe and inquired with exaggerated calm what she was looking for.

"Something for Rose to wear!" she snarled. "You can't take her to a hotel lookin' like that!"

"Oh, so I'm taking her to a hotel?"

"Of course. She can't go back to the Green Kitten 'cause she's scared Mike'll kill her, too. She accidentally busted in on this party just after the guy got the one-way ticket. Mike and a couple other bums locked her up, but she got away."

"And came here. Thoughtful of her. Very. But now she's here, why can't she stay here?"

Violet glared at me over a piece of my very best lingerie. "Because, you nit-wit, she didn't get away as clean as she thought she did. A couple of mugs just went by in a car and likely they're havin' a talk with her taxi driver. I'm kind of expecting them back."

I started to shiver. Since becoming Violet McDade's partner I'd been led into practically everything except a gang war. It looked as if my education was about to be completed. Rose Donelli chose this moment to sit up.

Violet said, "O.K., kid, everything's going to be all right. Nevada will rustle you some duds and then we'll find you a place to sleep." She left us, went out into the living room again. She didn't turn on the lights. I helped the girl as best I could. She said, "Sorry to be such a nuisance, Miss Alvarado. Murders are pretty horrible things, aren't they? Especially when your own husband commits them." Her teeth started to chatter. "Mike's been so darned good to me that I guess I've sort of shut my eyes to a lot of things. But tonight, when I actually saw him with that gun in his hands, with that awful look on his face, I – I lost my head. I'm still scared silly."

"Did you," I asked, "recognize the dead man? Or the other two who were with your husband? There is no doubt, I suppose, that the man was really dead?"

"He was dead right enough! No one could live with his face shot away, could he?" She got the jitters at that, communicated them to me. After a little: "No, I don't know who he was, but the other two I've seen around with Mike. One had very white hair, I remember."

"You're still crazy about Mike, aren't you?" Her "yes" was smothered in a sob. And right after that the whole world exploded. The floor rocked, buckled beneath my feet. Numbed, I stood there, watching with a sort of dispassionate interest as window glass shattered, slashed through sheer hangings. The lights went out, blinked on again just long enough for me to catch a glimpse of Rose's terror-stricken face, then something very heavy – probably the ceiling – crashed down upon us both.

Chapter II

I AWOKE with a terrible roaring in my ears, a hissing, crackling roar that could be but one thing: fire! I opened my eyes, discovered that I was hanging over someone's shoulder. Fire was licking up at the skirts of the someone, and the stench of smoke was thick in my nostrils. Those skirts could belong to no one but Violet McDade. She was carrying me somewhere. I passed out again.

Fresh air brought me around the second time – fresh air tainted with smoke, but that terrible heat was gone, and the flames. No, the flames were still there, gnawing greedily at the base of a door through which we'd evidently just come. I was lying on the floor in almost pitch darkness, and Violet, cursing under her breath, was tugging at something heavy.

I sat up. The room reeled dizzily, steadied. My eyes picked out Violet's bulk heaving at a fallen ceiling joist. Lath and plaster littered the floor, what was left of the furniture. And I discovered another form beneath that massive beam. Bridget, our housekeeper!"

"Violet, is – is Bridget dead?"

"Nope. Give me a lift with this damn timber, will you?" Our combined strength managed to raise one end and Violet wedged it with something. She said, "Bridget, can you hear me?"

"Who couldn't?" The voice was very weak, husky, but it was the sweetest sound I ever expect to hear. "Am I dyin', Mac?"

"Hell, no," said Violet grumpily. "Nothin' wrong with you except a couple of broken ribs and a crack on the dome. Now, look, Bridget, I've turned in the alarm and the fire boys'll be here 'most any minute. In case it gets too hot for you, we've raised the timber so you can crawl out. But stick if you can."

"She'll do no such thing, Violet McDade!"

"I will too," said Bridget. "If Mac wants me to stick, I'll stick. I'd go to hell for her and she knows it!"

"Sure I do," said Violet. "But this time you don't have to. All you do is let 'em drag you out and act kind of hysterical, 'cause Nevada and me is buried up ahead in the ruins. Get it?"

I said, "I'll be no party to it!"

And Violet's great arms infolded me, lifted me, carried me, struggling and kicking, through a rear door. The flames, mounting skyward, cast a lurid glow over the back yard and the limousine waiting in the alley behind the garage, but there was no sign of the neighbors. They must have all been out in front. I opened my mouth to scream and Violet clapped a hand over it.

"Shut up, you sap! Shut up and quit kickin'. You want to catch the lice that done this to us, or you want to give 'em a bigger and better chance? Bridget's all right!"

Sirens wailed around the corner behind us. I was suddenly assured of Bridget's safety; and the promise of vengeance was sweet. I stopped struggling. Little Sweeney opened the car door for us; I got a flash of a huddled figure on the floor of the tonneau; then we were inside and the great car was rolling down the alley, into a cross street.

"Is – is Rose all right, too?"

"Sure." Violet leaned over, tucked the robe clumsily about the still form. "Still out, but O.K."

"By the way," I demanded, "where were you when the bomb landed? I thought you were in the living room."

"Me, I was out in the garage waking Sweeney, so you and him could take Rose and park her somewhere. Lucky for you I was, too. You and the kid would have been a couple of roasts by this time if anything had happened to me. Just like I'm always tellin' you – without Vi McDade you wouldn't be worth the powder to blow you to hell."

"I guess you're right," I said, and suddenly found myself crying on her shoulder. She patted my knee awkwardly, stopped that as if embarrassed, and began her ominous sleeve-gun practice. Her left arm, flexing up and down, kept digging in my ribs. It hurt like the very devil but I didn't have the heart to tell her so. Rose Donelli heaved a tremulous sigh, sat up.

"Violet?" she queried. "Violet, is that you?"

"In the flesh."

"What – what happened?"

"Friends of your dear husband tossed a pineapple through our front window. I told you not to marry that guy."

Rose covered her face with her hands. Then, with a sudden fierce little gesture said: "Mike never ordered that. Mike wouldn't – couldn't do such a cowardly thing! But there, I've been enough trouble to you. Let me out here." She struggled to rise. "Let me out and forget that you ever saw me!"

Violet lifted her to the seat. "Look," she said, "look, Rosie, Mike gunned somebody out. You happened to bust in at the wrong time and stumbled into him and his two friends. Naturally, your runnin' away would make 'em all kind of nervous. Far as I'm concerned it's dead open and shut. You can believe Mike's the curly-haired boy who wouldn't rub us all out to save his own skin. Me, I'm for not lettin' you stick your neck out. Not till I've paid off a couple of debts I owe, anyway." She clamped her jaws shut on this last, lapsed into a brooding silence.

Sweeney tooled the car into Wilshire Boulevard, pulled up before the Lancaster. And it wasn't till we'd actually entered the lobby that I fully realized the enormity of our position. Violet – well, I've seen her look worse, though her eyes were red-rimmed, her moon face grimed with smoke and soot.

But Rose and I resembled nothing so much as a couple of plasterers after a hard day. There was a bluish welt on my forehead; blood from a nasty cut in my cheek had streaked down, dried in a pool at the base of my neck. Rose's face and arms were scarred with deep scratches; her dress – my dress, rather – was positively charred all down one side of her.

A full-length mirror in one of the great pillars told me all this – and more. My shoes were not mates. I cursed Violet under my breath for this added indignity, remembered suddenly that she had done exceedingly well to find me any shoes at all, remembered that but for her I'd be beyond the need of shoes.

She, the pachyderm, was at the desk, trying to convince the clerks we were respectable. Beside her, the tiny Sweeney in his outrageous uniform looked a solemn, wizened midget. It was no go with the clerks. Even the sight of the enormous roll Violet always carries had no effect. The Lancaster, you see, was our newest, smartest hostelry.

One of the desk men beckoned a house detective, evidently with the purpose of having us ejected. Mortified? I was petrified. And then, wonder of wonders, the dick recognized Violet. They fell on each other's necks like long-lost buddies.

"Hi, Mac!" he cried.

"Hello, yourself," she said. Then: "Look, Elmer, tell these dumb apes at the counter who I am, will you? Our house just burned down and we got to get a roof over our heads."

Elmer addressed the chief clerk in an undertone. The fellow eyed Violet with a new respect. Still a little doubtful he finally capitulated.

"How many rooms will you need?"

Violet said, "Four of your best, all in a row."

He raised an eyebrow, stared hard at Sweeney's uniform. "Four, madam? Did you say four of our best? We have a servant's annex, you know."

Violet bridled. "Sweeney ain't no servant! Sweeney's as good as I am and probably a damn sight better. So we want four rooms just like I told you. Servant's annex!" She snorted.

And I thought of poor Bridget lying back there in the wreckage. A servant undoubtedly. An Irish cook who called her employer 'Mac' and was not always civil to me. But a servant ready to risk her very life for Violet McDade. I resolutely put Bridget from my mind and trailed rather forlornly after the others as they were escorted to the elevators.

One thing I'll say for the Lancaster. They may be snobbish; they may rob you of your eyeteeth when it comes to charges, but you can get almost anything you want, night or day. In half an hour's time we were all fairly presentable, and Violet was just finishing with her hair when I entered her room.

"What do you intend doing, Violet?"

"Doing?" she snarled. "I'm going to get the two guys that tossed that pineapple and tear 'em limb from limb. Now you, of course, don't mind – now – petty annoyances like having your cook half murdered and your house burned down around your ears, so you can stay here and play nurse to Rose until I get back."

"Oh, I can, can I? Well, if you think I've got any love for Rose Donelli you're crazy. She's the one that caused all the trouble. Sweeney can stay here if she has to be nursed. And I've got a gun that's aching for a target as much as yours are!" I bethought myself to feel for the little .32 I carry just above my right knee. It wasn't there. I'd noticed its absence before but had forgotten it.

Violet opened her purse, produced the gun. "I kind of thought you might be wantin' it," she said. "After you got the shock out of your system. O.K. then, me proud senorita, we'll let Sweeney guard Rose while we go gunnin' for her husband."

Sweeney demurred. "Gosh, Mac, I ain't no hand with women. Besides, I'd like to take a cut at them bozos, myself."

Rose Donelli must have heard the argument. She came through the adjoining bath, stared from one to the other of us with suspicion.

"You're intending to pin that bombing on Mike? You're – you're going to hurt him?"

"Not much," said Violet grimly. "I'm going to put about six slugs in his middle is all."

Rose was upon her like a raging cat. "You're not! You're not! You're not!" Small fists beat against Violet. "You've other enemies! I tell you Mike wouldn't do such a thing!" Her wild eyes sought the telephone. "I'll warn him, that's what I'll do. Let me go!"

Violet calmly slapped her down, nodded to Sweeney. "Take care of her, runt. Don't let anyone get to her or I'll skin you."

We went down to the lobby. The after-theater supper crowd was just breaking up and I realized with a start that it was only a little after two – scarcely an hour since we'd left the Green Kitten. In that short hour our home had been demolished and Bridget, poor old soul, had sustained injuries that might well keep her in the hospital for months.

My heart crawled up into my throat, jiggled there uncertainly, and then dropped like a plummet at sight of a familiar figure between us and the doors – Lieutenant Belarski! Belarski whom Violet didn't like and who certainly didn't like Violet. She'd bested him too many times.

She saw him at the same instant. "Well, for cryin' out loud! Of all the dicks in the city we would have to run into that rat, Belarski!"

He spotted us, advanced unhurriedly, a sardonic grin on his lean, dark face. "Well, well, well!" he said. "Fancy meeting you here!" His grin vanished. Clutching Violet's cloak in his two hands, he snarled: "Who did it?"

"Who did what?" she inquired innocently.

"Don't stall!" he grated. "You know damn well what I'm talking about. Who bombed your house? Why did you run out on your cook, carefully coaching her in a pack of lies before you left? I'll tell you why, you fat imitation of a female shamus! You were trying to give the law a run around till you could find the mugs that did the job."

"That's what you think," said Violet. "Take your hands off me before I flatten you!" Her voice suddenly lost its belligerence, her shoulders sagged. "O.K., Belarski, you're a smart dick. I figured we'd got away clean." She eyed him appraisingly. "Anybody else know we're still alive?"

He grinned again, wolfishly. "No," he said. "The cook put it over for the rest of the boys, even for the reporters. They're still waiting for the embers to cool so they can look for your remains. But it happens that I know you, know that any job you're interested in smells to high heaven. So I found a neighbor who thought she'd seen you leave the back way, and put a quick check on the hotels. Who tossed that pineapple?"

"O.K.," she said. "I admit I was goin' after the mugs, myself. Nobody, I says, is going to do my work for me. I figured that bein' dead would maybe give us a little edge, see what I mean?"

Belarski's dark eyes got cunning. "Yes, I see what you mean. With half an eye I could see you've got a damned good idea of who you're looking for. So open up and maybe I won't take you down to headquarters yet. Maybe I'll just leave you in your rooms under guard until I make the collar."

Violet looked relieved. "Now you're talkin'. That's what I call bein' a pal, Belarski. One of the men in the blue sedan that passed our house just before the blow-off – one of them guys looked like Broken-nose Murphy. You 'member? I helped put him away a few years back."

"So that's it!" Belarski positively beamed. "Well, I think I can locate Broken-nose!" He swiveled, signaled to a detective lounging against a pillar. The fellow came up. "Hammel, escort these two – ah – ladies to their rooms. See that they stay there until I get back." Violet winked broadly, linked her arm in that of the fat detective. "Sarge, you look like you're going to be interestin' company. Come on, Nevada, let's show the sarge our suite." We entered an elevator, leaving Belarski staring after us with a look of indecision on his hatchet face.

Chapter III

THE DOOR to my room was locked. So, too, were all the others. Sweeney evidently was taking no chances. And wrangling voices from within told me that Rose Donelli wasn't being too docile. Violet knocked, and after a moment Sweeney's wizened face appeared in a cautious crack.

Violet said, "Open up, you lug, we've got company." She stepped back politely, let the burly sergeant enter first. And the moment the man's eyes rested on the bound figure of Rose Donelli he knew something was wrong.

"Rosita! Rose Donelli!" He turned accusing eyes on Violet. "So you crossed Belarski, huh? Ten to one Mike Donelli is behind all this, and you sent the lieut kiting after poor old Broken-nose Murphy. Lemme at that phone!"

Violet hit him with a hamlike fist – once. He went down like a poled ox. Violet said, "There, Sweeney, is another charge for you. You ought to be able to take care of two as easy as one." And as Sweeney looked doubtful, she added: "Well, be seein' you," and waddled to the door.

Rose Donelli screamed. Sweeney, a look of long-suffering patience on his face, clapped a hand over her mouth. And Violet came back to stare down gloomily at the figure on the bed.

"Look, Rose, you came to me 'cause you was scared to death of your own husband. Now, like all women, you've changed your mind and think he's a curly-haired angel or somethin'. You want to help him, huh? Well, neither you nor all the Belarskis in the world is going to keep me from gettin' to Mike Donelli!" She strode to the door.

Under a full head of steam she sailed through the lobby below only to halt before the news stand as if she'd run into something solid. It wasn't solid, but it was startling. A boy had just deposited a stack of extras on the case. Other boys screamed: "District Attorney Foss Murdered!" A boxed-in account gave the place as an alley near Pico and Central; the time of death as approximately one o'clock, and the cause as a large-caliber bullet which had entered the back of his head and, emerging, practically obliterated his face. I thought of Rose's description. It fitted. But Pico and Central was a long, long way from the Green Kitten.

We went out into the night and I climbed under the wheel of the limousine. "Violet," I said, "Alvin Foss was at the Green Kitten at one o'clock. We saw him. Do you suppose he is the one—"

"That Mike shot? Why not? Alvin Foss has been threatenin' to raise hell with places like Mike's ever since he was elected. Maybe he got tired waitin' for Steve Wright, his assistant, to do something. Maybe he decided to do it himself and Mike had to plug him. The only thing is – well, in the back of the head don't sound like Mike's way of doing things. And in his own office, too."

"They could have carried the body away easily enough; planted it in that alley where the rain would obliterate any traces. I mean, the police could never prove that Foss wasn't killed right where he was found." I remembered something Rose had said. "Violet, I believe Senator Hymes was there when it happened! Rose said there was a man with white hair."

"Yeah, and she said there was another guy, too, maybe with green hair. Maybe the two of 'em left Mike Donelli to get rid of the body while they tailed Rose and bombed our house. Which reminds me, I want to find a phone."

I obediently parked before the first all-night café we came to, and she got out, went inside. She emerged presently with a curious look on her moon face. "I located Rose's taxi driver," she said.

"You did! What did he say?"

"He didn't say nothin', Mex. 'Cause why? 'Cause he's deader'n a mackerel. Them bozos caught up with him, found out where he'd dumped Rose, and slugged him – for keeps. Why do you reckon they'd do that?"

"I – I don't know," I said faintly. "Unless he knew them, would be able to identify them."

"Or the car they was drivin', huh?"

"You told Belarski it was a blue sedan!"

She stared at me in disgust. "I must be improving," she said. "Or you're dumber than I thought. You think I'd tell that guy the truth about anything?"

We drove on. It was raining again and the street lamps made pale blobs of reflected light against the glistening pavement. The clock on the dash said 2:15 as we approached the neon sign of the Green Kitten. A car was pulling into the curb ahead of us, a tan touring car with a khaki-colored top. It looked like one of the county cars, and as passed it I saw the familiar insignia on the front door.

Two men got out, nodded to the doorman, pushed on through into the foyer. I parked a little way down the block. Violet, with a prodigious grunt, heaved her bulk to the sidewalk.

"Don't lock the car," she said. "We may need it in a hurry. She strode away down the curb like a man going to a fire; and, despite her clothes, despite her ridiculous, tent-like opera cloak, she looked like a man, a veritable mountain of a man, masquerading in woman's garb. I followed as best I could, caught up with her for the sole reason that she'd stopped beside the county car and was deliberately removing her cloak.

The doorman stepped forward. "May I help you?"

"Yeah," she grunted. "Yeah, you can help me by minding your own business." She had the cape off by this time and seemed bent on arranging its folds so that they draped over the car's right door. Satisfied, apparently, by the effect thus obtained she once more donned the garment. Peeling a bill from her roll she tendered it to the man.

"Look, general, the two dicks that just went inside. Were they here before – say, around one o'clock?"

He shook his head.

"Well, then, is Mike Donelli still here?"

"No ma'am," he said. "Mike came out and got in his car at ten after one. I ain't seen him since, but he's sure to be back before closing time."

"Swell," said Violet, "my partner will wait for him. Me, I got business down the street a ways." She gave me an encouraging shove toward the entrance, hunched over against the driving rain, and disappeared in the darkness.

Well, I managed to get past the check girl with a casual nod, flashed a glance into the main supper room as I passed. State Senator Hymes was still at his table. There were two girls there now. And over against the far wall, partially obscured by the crowd on the dance floor, I saw Assistant District Attorney Stephen Wright. With him were the two men who had gotten out of the tan car. Wright, I thought, looked worried, but there was no sign of excitement such as should have attended a shooting in the club. And apparently news of the district attorney's death hadn't spread this far. Possibly the two detectives had come to notify Wright.

The colored orchestra was blaring away as if nothing had changed. Perhaps it hadn't – for them. I thought of our house, of Bridget, went up the broad, carpeted stairs hoping, yes, praying that the doorman had lied, that Mike Donelli was in and that I'd get to him before Violet did.

People passed me on the stairs, in the hall above. I was barely conscious of them. The door to the gambling salon stood wide, inviting. I paused there a moment, didn't see Donelli, and went on to his private suite. As I touched the knob a man stepped from the shadows. "Mr. Donelli isn't in just now."

"I know. He's down below. I'm to wait for him." He looked at me searchingly, evidently was of two minds. I decided for him and with an assurance I certainly didn't feel twisted the knob, went in. The great room was empty. I waited, heart pounding, to see if the man would follow me. He didn't. I went on through into Mike's bedroom and, beyond that, into what must have been Rose's. No one there, either.

Back in the combination office and living room, I looked around for signs of the shooting. There were none – or so I thought till I noticed from the impressions in the thick carpeting that the desk had been moved. The thing was very ornate, heavy as the devil. I couldn't budge it.

Dropping to my knees I crawled about, searching for something, I hardly knew what. And then, just inside the knee hole I found it. A little smear that the left-hand pedestal didn't quite cover. Unmistakably blood. Not much, but the spot was still moist, sticky and gave me a pretty good idea that there was a lot more under that pedestal. Well, that was that. Rose Donelli had actually seen something.

I heard the door open, stood up confusedly. A man came in, his face shadowed by a pulled-down hat brim. It wasn't the fellow I'd left in the hall. It wasn't Donelli. It was – yes, it was one of the men from downstairs, from that tan car outside, a county dick.

"I thought this was a private office!" I said. "What happened to the man outside?"

"Why – uh – he was called away on business, ma'am. I just thought I'd" – his eyes, studiously avoiding mine, roamed over the entire room – "that is, I wanted to see Mr. Donelli."

"Well," I said, "he isn't here. And when he gets here he's going to be very busy, so perhaps—" I let the suggestion hang in mid-air. It didn't hang long. Or maybe it's hanging yet. I wouldn't know, because at that moment the door opened again, and in walked Lieutenant Belarski. I nearly passed out.

He closed the door behind him quietly enough, passed the county dick with barely a flicker of recognition, planted himself squarely in front of me. His dark, narrowed eyes were hot and his jaws were clamped so tightly that the skin at the corners of his mouth showed gray. He said nothing for a moment, just stared at me with a glare so baleful, so ominous, that I sagged against the desk, weak with fright.

At last he said, "Well, Miss Alvarado, we meet again."

I said, "How true." And even though my voice was quivery I managed a flippant, "And how is Mrs. Belarski?"

His control broke then. "By Heaven!" he rasped. "By Heaven, where is that she-devil partner of yours?" His hands snaked out, clutched my shoulders, dug in hard. "I found Broken-nose Murphy. And you know where I found him? In jail! Right where the McDade woman knew he was all the time. You tell me where that fat fool is or I'll break every bone in your body!"

"I'm lookin' at you, Belarski," said a hoarse voice from the bedroom door. And there was Violet, very composed, very dirty, rust streaks all down the front of her, but her two .45s held unwaveringly on the irate lieutenant. "Yep," she went on, "I'm here, so mebbe you better unhand the senorita, huh?"

He took his hands away, made a half-hearted movement toward his gun, thought better of it. The county dick, over by the door, was staring at Violet as if she were a ghost.

"You – you mean to tell me, lieutenant, that these two dames are the private dicks, McDade and Alvarado?"

"Not only telling you," said Belarski. "I'm telling the whole cock-eyed world! But they won't be private dicks much longer. They'll be occupying cells next to that runty chauffeur of theirs!"

Violet grunted. "You got Sweeney?"

"I've got Sweeney! I've got him booked for kidnapping an officer. And that's what you two will be booked for."

"What happened to Rose Donelli?"

Belarski cursed luridly. "I had her, too, but the little spitfire got away. Oh, don't worry, we'll pick her up! And with what we can wring out of the three of you we'll find out what this case is all about."

Violet said, "The guy behind you could mebbe give you the low-down, Belarski, if he would." The lights clicked out as Belarski whirled. There was a sudden burst of flame, another. I heard a body fall to the floor, the soft thud of hurried feet on the thick carpet.

By the time I had my own gun out, the lights were on again. Violet was at the switch. The county dick was gone. And Lieutenant Belarski lay on the floor, almost at my feet, a thin trickle of blood oozing from under his hat brim.

Violet knelt beside him, lifted the hat. With a vast sigh she replaced it, stood up. "Just a crease, Mex. And that's about the first lucky thing that's happened to me tonight. If Belarski had got it for keeps I wouldn't have a damn thing left to live for."

I stared. "I thought you hated him!"

"I do, you sap! But an enemy like him keeps you on your toes, keeps you from stagnatin'." She tilted her head, poised in a listening attitude. There was no sound from without. How had the county dick got away? How, for that matter, had Violet got in? The three-room suite was a solid unit, no other door but the one from the office into the hall.

She read my mind. "The fire escape in Rose's bedroom, ninny. He knew about it, too, which proves somethin' or other." She brushed rather aimlessly at the rust streaks on her cloak, looked down at the prone Belarski. "Rose escaped by the fire ladder, so did the dick. More'n likely the corpse went down that way, too, the hall and stairs bein' full of people most of the time. Point is, who helped him?"

"Couldn't we," I demanded, "do our wondering in some other place? Belarski isn't going to stay put all night."

She nodded absently, took pencil and paper from the desk and scribbled a note. This she fastened with a paper clip to Belarski's coat lapel. The scrawl said:

> Honest, Belarski, I never done it.
> I never fired a single shot in this room and neither did the Mex.
> Be seeing you.

Chapter IV

SHE TIPTOED to the door, opened it cautiously. The man who had accosted me was still missing. We negotiated the corridor, noting no sign whatsoever that the shot had been heard, descended the stairs. The crowd in the supper room was thinning out and a hurried glance through the great archway told me that Senator Hymes had gone; so, too, had the assistant district attorney.

Violet halted, caught the eye of the head waiter. He came over and she whispered to him for a moment. I saw a bill change hands. Impatiently I waited as she was led away, back toward what must have been the kitchens. And then the lummox was waving at me from out on the sidewalk. She'd gone clear around the building!

I went out vowing I'd give her a piece of my mind. But I didn't. Not then, anyway, for she had again buttonholed the doorman.

"So Senator Hymes and Steve Wright ain't been out of the club all night till just now, huh?"

"That's right, miss."

"Thanks a lot, fella. If you ever get into trouble just look me up."

I said, "Yes, Miss McDade could give you a lot of new ideas. If we're not at home, try the county jail." I departed hastily for our car, fully intending to leave her, but Violet moves rather swiftly at times. She was beside me when I meshed the gears.

"What do you mean, if we're not at home? We ain't got no home – nor no housekeeper if we did have a home. We can't go back to the hotel because Belarski will have that sewed up. Where the hell can we go?"

"You just mentioned one place. I think that's where we're pointing!" I found myself weeping. The tears ran down my nose, dripped off onto my hands at the wheel. "Have – have you forgotten that little Sweeney's in jail?"

"How could I?" she grumbled. "You never let me have a minute's peace, you cry baby. Like I'm always tellin' you, when the going gets tough you lay down on me."

I stopped crying then. I was so furious I could have killed her. "Listen to me, you hippopotamus, you're everything Belarski ever called you! You're a menace to society. I'm darned sick of being played for a sucker to help out some of your so-called friends. What did

Rose Donelli ever do for you? Why should I take the rap for helping her? Did I ever ask you to help one of my friends?" I shook a fist under her fat nose. "Did I?"

She reached over, steadied the wheel. "Come to think of it, you never did, Nevada. I – I guess maybe I've been expectin' too much of you. But if you didn't have such damn high-class friends, if ever any one of 'em did get in a jam I expect maybe I'd be around, huh?"

Never a word about going into that flaming room after me tonight; not a hint that she'd saved my life a dozen times in the past. Violet McDade is – well, just Violet McDade. I suddenly felt very small.

"I'm sorry, Violet. I'm a – a cat."

"'Course you are," she acknowledged comfortably. "A regular hell-cat. So let's forget it and concentrate on our problem. You see, Mex, we're in what they laughingly call a predicament. Havin' lied to Belarski so I'd get first shot at Mike Donelli; havin' bopped his helper, the sarge; havin' left Belarski with a bullet crease in his head; all them things is – now – mere details. The real facts of the matter is that poor Sweeney's in jail, we've lost Rose, and we ain't yet met up with Mike Donelli. Our results, to date, is null and void."

"And apt to remain so." But I was feeling more cheerful for some unknown reason. The tears may have helped. "You've stated our position with admirable clarity. Is there supposed to be a solution?"

"There's always an answer," she affirmed. "An answer to everything. Maybe you ain't got it, maybe I ain't. But it's there, Mex. 'Member that time we got Sweeney out of jail down in San Juan Batista?"

"Violet McDade, you're thinking of trying that trick again! You couldn't be – not even you!

"Nope," she said, "nope, I'm afraid it wouldn't work in the States of America. 'Fraid we'll have to use a little – now – *finesse* in Sweeney's case. Meantime, let's forget him and think of Rose. Thinking of Rose reminds me that we'd better turn around and get to the Green Kitten."

"Belarski," I reminded her, "is at the Green Kitten."

"I hope so," she said. "I hope he's still there and that Rose runs right into his arms. I'd a lot rather Belarski had her than some others I know." She cursed the girl under her breath.

I turned right at the next cross street, headed back in the general direction of the Green Kitten. I wasn't pushing the car too hard. It was still raining, but the rain had nothing to do with my caution. Personally, I was hoping that Belarski had collared Rose and her husband, too. I only got half my wish.

We were just in time to see Belarski escorting Rose out the front door and into his car. I cut the lights, skidded into the nearest alley, halted with my heart in my throat. Belarski's car passed the alley doing fifty.

Violet grunted, "Well, that's a relief. Back out and let's buzz the doorman again."

The doorman was indignant. "You again! Mike's been raising merry hell with me about you and one thing and another!"

"Mike's been here, huh?"

He spat disgustedly. "Yeah, and gone again. He comes busting in, goes upstairs, and right after that Rosita. She goes upstairs too. Couple of minutes later he comes tearing down, cussing somebody about a pineapple job. He's got a rod in his fist, this time, and he offers to slap me down if I don't tell him all I know. Which is practically nothin', but—"

"Save it," Violet advised. "Mike plenty mad, huh? You know she was goin' this time?"

"So help me," said the fellow earnestly, "if you was to give me another fifty bucks I couldn't tell you."

We got back in the car and rode aimlessly for a while, Violet apparently sunk in a stupor. I should have known better. Presently she straightened. "Why," she demanded, "why would the bombing of our house make Mike Donelli mad? Because it failed? Why'd he leave Rose to the – now – tender mercies of Belarski, when all the time his main idea must have been to shut her up?"

"You tell me," I suggested wearily.

"All right, I will!" But she didn't. For just at that moment I discovered that we were being tailed. My cry of dismay brought a snort from Violet.

"Hell, I've known it for fifteen minutes. The only reason we went back to the Green Kitten this last time is because they missed us before. I wanted to give 'em another chance."

"Who?"

"The mugs that tossed the pineapple, I'm hopin'. This damn rain has rubbed out what little chance I had of pinning the job on anybody. And all the actors are hopping around like fleas. I'm going to let 'em light on me for a change."

The car was about two blocks behind us. It showed no lights, which is probably why I hadn't noticed it before.

Violet said, "Give 'em a few whirls around the block and let's make sure." So I did. I turned corners till I was dizzy, wove in and out of dark streets, decided finally that we'd lost our shadow. And was proved wrong the minute we turned into the boulevard again. The car was still there and coming up fast. There were no other machines in sight either way. At this hour in the morning the thoroughfare was as deserted as a county road in the sticks.

"What do we do now, run for it?"

"For a ways," said Violet, peering back. "Just enough to get 'em going good. When I give you the word, slam on your brakes."

I fed gas for all I was worth. We might as well have been standing still. That car behind certainly had something under its hood that we didn't have. In less time than it takes to tell it we were doing seventy, our limit. And the other car crept up on us steadily. I could make out its color now and the fact that it held two men. It was less than fifty yards behind us when Violet said, "O.K."

Well, we did have brakes – and good tires. We stopped right now. The shock threw me hard against the wheel; I heard Violet go "Oo-o-m-ph!" The other car slid by us, rocking crazily, brakes grinding. A double burst of orange flame cut across our hood; there was a rattling, tearing sound as metal ricocheted off metal and into glass. The windshield developed a sudden case of smallpox, but held. And the open car righted itself, whirled on two wheels, started back.

Violet grunted, "I expect we'll be safer outside, Mex. Not that I want to be safe. This is the first sign of action I've seen tonight." Which would have struck me as extremely funny at any other time. She opened the door on the curb side, floundered out. I followed, reaching for my gun. I got it, came up behind the hood just as the touring car slid to a halt.

The driver opened his door. "We must have got 'em, Logan, but we've got to make sure this time. Darker than hell, ain't it?"

I shot him. Shot again and again at that vague blur which was his face. Shot until the hammer of my gun clicked on an empty chamber. I saw him slump, slide into the street. And Violet's voice, quite calm, said: "Drop the rod, fella. You're covered."

She was evidently talking to the man on the off side. I couldn't see him. I couldn't see her, either. But he could. Or thought he could for he didn't drop his gun. He used it. The darkness suddenly became a bedlam of sound, of stabbing tongues of flame that looked two feet long from where I crouched. As swiftly as it had all begun, it was over. Silence descended like a pall, broken by Violet, slightly petulant.

"Where the hell are you, Nevada? I can't make out what this guy's sayin'. Must be a Greek or something."

I rounded the two cars, saw her on her knees beside a huddled form. The man wasn't a Greek. His voice just sounded that way because of the blood welling from his graying lips. He was one of the two county detectives I'd seen talking to Stephen Wright; not the one who had shot Belarski in the office, but the other.

Violet McDade isn't much good as a nurse. She can shoot people but after she's done it she's rather helpless when it comes to patching them up. Not that anyone could have done much for this chap; he was about through. I found my handkerchief, wiped some of the blood away, lifted his head. His eyes opened a little and he coughed, horribly.

Violet said, "You're the guys that tossed that pineapple. Who gave you your orders?"

He just looked at her. Thick lips curled in a mirthless smile and he said – his words, too, were thick, mushy: "Wouldn't you like to know?" He died in my arms.

In the near distance now there was the crescendo of sirens; in the other direction headlights were coming up, too close for comfort. Violet said, "Let's be on our way, Mex."

A swift look at the driver told us that for once my shooting had been excellent. He was dead. We were on our way. Where, I didn't know, nor did I care. I was content to go anywhere away from there, grateful for the cool freshness of the rain, for – yes, for being alive instead of lying as were those two behind us. Did I feel badly for having just killed a man? Not then. Perhaps I would later, but now I was pleasantly numb.

Chapter V

VIOLET'S VOICE, seeming to come from a long way off, impinged on my consciousness. "I got to make a couple of phone calls, Nevada, if you can tear yourself away from your meditations."

I sat up straight. "I'm not meditating, you elephant, I'm resting."

"Rest tomorrow, or next week. If you think we're through because we rubbed out a couple of blots on the county's – now escutcheon, you're silly. Let's find a phone."

We found the phone – in a bar that was still doing business. The place reeked, and there were a couple of drunks. I ordered a drink, downed it and immediately felt better. Violet emerged from the phone booth as I was lighting my first cigarette in hours.

"There you go," she complained. "There you go, carousin' again. No wonder I can't get nowhere with drunkards and cigarette fiends for partners." She led the way outside, climbed under the wheel herself. "Can't afford to let you drive with the taint of liquor on your breath."

I actually giggled. "No," I said, "imagine being arrested for drunken driving with our spotless record. Belarski undoubtedly has forgotten all about the other minor crimes you've committed tonight – this morning, rather. Poor Sweeney."

She said, "Shut up!" and clamped down hard on the accelerator. Fifteen minutes of silence after that, and we wheeled into Gramercy Park Lane. The Lane is pretty exclusive, great stone arches at either end of the block-long street frowning on anything less than a millionaire – or a state senator. I remembered that this was where Senator Hymes lived.

As we whirled through one arch I saw headlights bearing down on the other. Violet, seemingly bent on destruction, hurled the limousine straight into their path. Brakes squealed, not ours, at first.

A thickset figure detached itself from the coupe, crossed the sidewalk on the run and disappeared into a tree-lined drive. Violet took the turn on two wheels, rocked into the drive and applied the brakes just back of the running man. The front bumper caught him, staggered him, but he didn't fall. One up-flung arm ended in a gun. He swiveled, cat-like, and I recognized his face in headlights' glare. He was Mike Donelli.

"Drop the rod, Mike," said Violet and as he hesitated, "Drop it," she urged, very low, almost as if she were afraid of being overheard. "A guy we both know is plenty dead because he didn't drop his when I told him." He dropped the gun.

"Come over here, Mike. Over by the left-hand door. You can let your hands down."

He let his half-raised hands fall to his sides, came slowly around the left front fender. His broad face, always ruddy, genial, looked positively haggard now.

"What is this, a gag, Violet McDade?"

"In a way," she said. And crowned him with one of her guns. The movement was so swift, so utterly unexpected that even I was stunned. I barely caught the flash of her down-swooping arm before the blow landed. Mike's eyes crossed, he started to sag. Violet leaned out the window and supported him.

"Get out the other side, stupid!" she hissed. "If I let him fall he'll get all mussed up."

"You've just mussed him considerably," I said. "And anyway, I thought that was what you intended to do all along. You were, I believe, going to put six slugs in his middle or some such a matter."

"Don't argue!" she snarled. "Can't a lady change her mind?"

I got out, sighing a little, and between us we managed to get him into the tonneau, fixed him nice and comfy. "Do you mind, sweet Violet, explaining your unwonted solicitude?"

"I'm savin' him," she said. And led the way majestically up the drive.

Senator Hymes answered the bell in person. I thought he was going to faint when he saw Violet. His long face, bleak as a winter's day, under waving white hair, turned a sickly yellow; myriad tiny lines appeared in the skin as if the flesh beneath had suddenly shrunk.

He said, "I – I don't believe I can see you. I'm – uh – in conference."

"Right ungrateful, I calls it," said Violet. "Here I just saved your life – ours and Stevie Wright's – by stopping Mike Donelli."

"You – you stopped Donelli! You mean you – killed him?"

"Nope," said Violet, "just stopped him from becoming a murderer." She shouldered her way past the agitated Solon, held the door wide.

A voice from down the hall said, "Bring them in, senator, bring the ladies right in. I'm sure we're both very glad to see them." Stephen Wright, the assistant district attorney stood in the shadows beside an open door. There was a gun in his hand. He gestured with it impatiently.

"This way, ladies. Hurry please. My nerves are not at their best and this gun might go off."

"Like it did once before tonight, huh? Or did Senator Hymes bump Alvin Foss?"

I felt Hymes sag against me, tremble violently. He said, as Wright lifted the gun, "No, Stephen, not here! Don't do – don't do anything you'd be sorry for."

"My sentiments, exactly," Violet approved, and waddled toward the man with the gun. "We're all friends, ain't we?" She leered at Wright. "You know us private dicks can always be fixed – if the price is right. So let's talk it over and forget our past mistakes, huh?"

"Mistakes?" said Wright. He stood there, gun poised steadily until we'd entered the room, then followed us in and closed the door.

I rubbed one knee surreptitiously against the other, felt my gun in its holster, realized with a terrible sinking in the pit of my stomach that I'd emptied the weapon into the county detective. I wondered if Violet's .45s was empty, too.

She was saying: "Yep, it was a mistake to have your two dicks bomb our house tryin' to get Rose Donelli."

"My two dicks?"

"Yours. In a way you was smarter than Mike Donelli when Rose got away. You knew she was a friend of mine 'cause I told you so myself. You knew I was a dick and you put two and two together, figured she might run to me. Now Mike, of course, knew of other places she might run and wasted a lot of time lookin' there first. You, bein' a very efficient guy, just phoned your office and gave Logan and the other guy their instructions."

"She knows!" moaned Senator Hymes. "She knows, Stephen! She's got to Logan!"

"Shut up!" said Wright. "I've heard about this she-devil. She'll talk you into hell if you let her." His eyes rested with cold malice on Violet. "Why do you think this – ah – Logan was connected with me?"

"Well," she said, "I'll tell you. Just after Rose broke the news to me I took a peek out our front window. I thought I recognized one of the county's cars, but couldn't be sure because it was travelin' dark and somebody had, thoughtfullike, tossed a coat over the door insignia. It was just an idea of mine. I couldn't prove it because again the boys was very thoughtful. They took care of the taxi driver, too, so he'd never mention taking Rose out to our neighborhood.

"Later on one of the lugs stumbled into me and Nevada in Mike's office, knew the pineapple had failed, reports that sad fact to you, and you tell him to try again. Which he done with a sawed-off shotgun. I called the sheriff's office later and he says that car was assigned to the district attorney's office. And that reminds me, Stevie, the death of Foss makes you the new district attorney."

"I'm the new district attorney," said Wright grimly. "And I intend to remain in office if I have to kill a dozen, including you."

"Pshaw!" said Violet. "I never realized how much it meant to you, Stevie. Not until I got to thinkin' that a guy must be pretty desperate to shoot a man in the back of the head. And only a fella that would do that would resort to bombin' helpless women without givin' 'em a chance. Didn't sound like Mike Donelli, but still you can't ever tell, I says. Wasn't really until I find out how surprised Mike is about the pineapple business that I figure him for a – now – innocent bystander. Did he take the gun away from you, or from the senator here?"

"Not from me!" screamed Hymes.

Wright shot him. Even as the old man started to sag Wright turned the gun on Violet. And Violet just stood there; stood perfectly still without lifting her arms. Her guns must be empty!

"Fortunately," said Wright, "the family is away. I think that I shall enjoy sending you flowers, Violet McDade." His finger whitened on the trigger; his lips grew taut. I made a dive for my gun intending to throw it. And Violet, wrist flicking like a striking rattler, shot him just as the door burst open.

Belarski snarled, "You promised, you she-devil! You promised not to kill him!"

"And I didn't," said Violet calmly. "He'll live to hang, but, hell, I couldn't wait any longer for you. His remark about sending me flowers kind of got me nervous."

"You mean," I gasped, "you mean that you sent for Belarski?"

"She phoned me," Belarski snapped, "phoned me and guaranteed a pinch if I'd forget about Sweeney and Rose and Mike and Heaven knows who else!"

Stephen Wright sat up, stared about the room uncertainly. Then: "I – I guess I won't be sending you flowers, after all, Violet McDade."

"You wouldn't have, anyway," said Violet gloomily. "You send pineapples. I'm sorry I made the deal with Belarski, sorry I promised not to hurt you – much. There's a little old lady down in the receiving hospital, an old lady I'm kind of crazy about. The killin' of Alvin Foss and" – an overlarge foot stirred the limp form of State Senator Hymes – "and this guy don't mean a thing to me. My family does." She scowled at Belarski as he clipped the cuffs on Wright. "You sure got the best of the bargain this time, you mug!"

"I suppose," Belarski said, "that I should send you flowers!"

She brightened. "Now that," she said, "that would be kind of sweet of you, Belarski!"

Parameters of Social Dispersion in Domestic Lawn Populations

B. Morris Allen

"THEY'VE been here. I can smell them." The gnome-catcher wrinkled her formidable nose, nostrils expanding like bat wings. "In fact…"

I sniffed tentatively. Paperwhites, a hint of apple blossom, the chemical reek of geranium. No gnomes.

"What do they smell like?" I asked with a smile. For all their reputation, goblins look more droll than dreadful, and this gnarled creature doubly so.

The catcher rounded on me with hard, wide eyes. Her eyebrows arched like pampas grass, pale tufts swept back across her temples to merge with the graying hair on her head and ears. Maybe *in* the ears; I tried not to look. "You questioning my nose?" she asked. She twitched it at me threateningly. Goblins are famously sensitive, which is why they make such good trackers.

"No, no. Not at all. I'm sure it's a fine nose. I can see that it is." The nose was as hairy as the ears. "A truly masterful nose." The gnome-catcher was in high demand. I wasn't going to jeopardize weeks of careful solicitation, let alone my sizeable, non-refundable deposit. "If you say they've been here, they have been."

She was just over waist-high to me, but somehow managed to give the impression of looking down. Her chin bobbed as if slowly chewing something over. "Okay," she nodded, with just a flash of fearsome teeth.

"I've just never had stray gnomes come by before," I offered. "My own gnomes don't seem to smell much." They smelled of iris and jasmine and phlox, but I could hardly mention that to this grim, weathered creature.

She snorted, generating a flurry of patterns in her generous beard. I found it hard to take my eyes off the dance of curls. "Shows how much you know." I could see I'd taken the right tone, though. "Your average garden gnome smells mostly of clay, tinged with a little salt, and just a touch of beer."

"Ah."

"Lager," she added with distaste. "That's your average, of course. Each gnome smells different. Your English-descended gnome will have more of a bitter tinge, while a pureblood Swiss gnome will have more of a fruit scent." She looked up to check that I was following, and I nodded. "Not that a Swiss gnome would survive around here, of course. They need fresh mountain air." We looked around at my low-lying suburban neighborhood, and I nodded again.

"Mine are…um …" I'd gotten the originals online, then accreted more as gifts. Some I didn't recall getting at all.

"Mutts, yeah. I can see that. You wouldn't catch a pureblood around these parts, not even the Italians."

"Well!" Diplomacy was one thing. Insulting my gnomes was another. Especially out here in the garden where the gnomes could hear it.

She seemed to sense that she'd gone too far, and gave a little shrug. "No, that's a good thing. Those purebloods are sensitive critters. Don't last long even in the right habitat. Your mutt gnome, now, he'll last for years, and be loyal to boot." It seemed that was as close to an apology as I'd get.

"You may be right. I had one Irish gnome – a present from an ex. He was the first one to go." I motioned toward a bed of white alyssum sprinkled with orange marigolds. There was a bare patch in the middle. "He used to…" My eyes welled up, and it was hard to go on. "He used to stand right there. Shoulder-high in alyssum." The tears spilled over their retaining lids and flowed down my cheeks like cold trickles of rain. "With marigolds for shade. On…on hot days, I'd fill that calla lily for him to drink from." The lily blossom was torn and soiled, the stem bruised, even crumpled in places.

I felt a soft hand on my hip. "Don't you worry, Mr. Huderven. I'll find him." Her hand squeezed my ample flesh and let go. "I've never failed yet. Give me a week, and your gnomes will be back home, none the worse for their little adventure."

* * *

I was on my patio when she called three days later. I'd been sitting under the little 'Gnome place like Home' sign, lost in a reverie of happier days, sitting in the sun surrounded by my gnomes, watching them pop in and out of sight between blinks, too shy to move when observed. The harsh ring was startling, and my tea slopped onto the cute little wrought-iron table as I fumbled with the phone.

"Hello? Hilda? I mean, Ms. Archuslart? Is there news?" At a distance of space and memory, she seemed less grumpy, more helpful.

Her voice was grave. "There is, Mr. Huderven. I'm afraid it's not good." She paused so long that my hand began to tremble. I thought of setting the phone down, putting her on speaker. But if it were the news I feared, I couldn't let the other gnomes hear. I'd been keeping up a brave front so far, and I had to keep on, for their sake. They look cheery, but gnomes are a lot more sensitive than people think. And they gossip.

"Did you find them? Are they…?"

"Oh, I found them all right. They weren't very careful. Found them the first day." She paused again. "But it's what I feared it might be. We're not just talking about a few strays here, Mr. Huderven. Not just some gnomes out on a lark. Or even a blue jay. I'm afraid it's worse. Your gnomes didn't run off, Mr. Huderven. They were taken. And not by strays."

"You don't mean…"

"I do."

"A…pack of…of wild gnomes?" My heart shrank in my chest. I'd heard what wild gnomes could get up to, trying to adjust their habits to a growing urban footprint.

"Not wild, Mr. Huderven. These aren't gnomes native to the Northwest. No, I'm afraid it's worse. Your gnomes have been taken by a feral group – a spray, to use the technical term. Gnomes that for some reason lost their way. Some get confused in a new location, and can't find their way home. Some are abandoned, if you can believe it." I could hear the anger in her voice, and felt its equal in my own heart. I'm not a member of the Gnomadic Welfare Society for nothing. "However it happens, these are gnomes that were once tame, but now have taken to the wilderness. And there's nothing wilder than a gnome with no home. That's what makes them so dangerous." There was a dark current in her voice that said she'd seen the danger up close.

"But still," I sputtered, trying to think of another possibility. Trying not to think of my sweet domestic gnomes, mistreated by some savage, tatty band with worn surfaces. "Wild gnomes around here?"

"*Not* wild, Mr. Huderven. Feral. Big difference, and it'll make getting yours back that much harder."

"Yes, right. Feral. A spray of feral gnomes." I gathered my tattered emotions together, and spoke as firmly as I could. "What can we do?"

"Well, the important thing is to get your gnomes out as soon as we can. The longer they spend with the spray, the harder it will be to reorient them. Stockhold syndrome, you know."

"I…Are you saying these gnomes are Swedish?" Surely Scandinavian gnomes would be better behaved.

"Stock*hold*, with a 'd'. The longer your gnomes are held, the more they'll start to resemble their captors and forget their home."

"Is…are they changing already? D – Danny-boy?"

"He's alright so far, Mr. Hunderven. Just a bit tattered around the clover. Nothing a bit of home rest can't fix. But the sooner we get him out the better."

"Yes. Yes, of course. What can I do?"

"For now, just sit tight. I wanted to let you know it's going to be a harder job than I thought, and riskier. I'll do my best, Mr. Hunderven, but you need to know it's dangerous. They may not all make it."

I shuddered. I'd lost gnomes before to age, even accident. But this… "I understand. But please…please do what you can." My voice cracked, half whisper, half prayer.

"I will, Mr. Hunderven. I always do my best for the client." There was a brief silence. "And I understand, Mr. Hunderven. I really do. If anyone can get your gnomes out safe, I will."

* * *

I ushered the last of the guests out the door, and turned to survey the mess. Half-dipped bowls of hummus and baba ghanouj sat on every table, with empty platters scattered here and there. The only carrots left were on the floor, with florets of cauliflower crumbled into the carpet by the loveseat. I started gathering dishes, wondering whether it had been worth it. What I had meant as a distraction had quickly turned to a council of war, with all my friends offering opinions unasked. Navi had started it, asking after Danny-boy, and hinting that she'd never let her gnomes wander. Shawkhan had quickly asserted that he brought his in every night – not a great feat when all he had was one gaudy French gnome with an upturned nose. They'd gone round and round, until finally, when even Tanya offered an opinion, I'd kicked them out. Tanya, who'd never owned a gnome in her life, and who'd made fun of mine just this spring. Tanya, with her "Oh, they're so *decorative!*" and her "Can't you just buy new ones?" As if gnomes were all the same, and you could just replace them like plates. Some people just aren't gnome people.

I piled the dirty dishes in the sink, and ran some water to let them soak. I looked out the window as the water ran. In the side garden, I'd set up a little…(my mind shied away from the word 'memorial')…tribute to my missing friends. A little painted pot of gold for Danny-boy. A miniature grindstone for Hans-im-Glück, the happy-go-lucky German-American gnome. A piece of driftwood for Chena, the Alaskan taken from outside her cute little igloo.

I'd kept the tribute inside for the first few days, but after Hilda called, I realized I couldn't keep the news from the rest of the group forever. Even if all my gnomes came back, it would be obvious something had happened. It might even be, Hilda had said, that the three would never be quite the same again. It was only fair to let the other gnomes know what was happening. Seeing the tribute might even help keep them careful, in case the feral spray came around again. Gnomes have minds of their own, but you can guide them, if you're subtle.

I'd felt helpless, setting up the tribute. Keeping my hands busy, trying not to think about my poor gnomes, out in the wilds, with wild companions. Now, though, after the fiasco of the party, my blood was up. Hilda had advised me to stay at home. Why should I? Why sit on my hands waiting? I was a healthy adult. Middle-aged, sure, but still hardy, still able, and only a little bit paunchy. Why shouldn't I take part? Why shouldn't I pitch in to save my friends, my family?

I felt a surge of relief as I resolved to take matters into my own hands, an awareness that, for once, I was doing the right thing.

* * *

"You think this is a joke?" Hilda's very gobliny teeth were showing a little more than I cared for.

I shook my head. In the face of Hilda's vigorous rejection, my confidence shrank a bit. This wasn't going quite how I had anticipated.

"You think just anybody can do what I do? You think this is just a walk in the park? Do you?" For a very small person, she had an awfully loud whisper.

"Well, no." I looked around the park. We were crouched on dank soil beneath a purple rhododendron. "Of course not."

"When I agreed to let you come watch, did you not understand me? Do you not know what '*watch*' means?"

"No. I mean, I do. I do know. I just thought…"

"Maybe if you *actually* thought, you'd get it straight."

I looked down. There was a slug wandering over a fallen leaf nearby, glossy brown on glossy green, and a trail of glossy slime behind. Glimy. "I'm sorry. I just want to help. I…I have to help." One or two smidgeons of resolve filtered back in. "I have to do *some*thing. These are my gnomes. I owe it to them." It had seemed a lot more reasonable back in my snug little kitchen, and I had felt a lot braver.

She shook her head, and a few long hairs escaped her camouflage kerchief to waft back and forth. "What you owe them is the best help you can offer. That's me. Now shut up and let me do my job." She stared hard at me. "One more word about you 'helping' and you go back to the van. Got it?"

I nodded glumly. It seemed possible that derring-do might not be quite my cup of tea after all.

"Or I call this off entirely. I'll report this spray to the authorities and let them clean it up. Good luck getting your gnomes back then."

My shoulders slumped, and I gave it up. The city was notorious for its lack of caution with escaped gnomes. Some had been returned scratched, or even chipped. I'd heard of one gnome returned with one arm and the tip of his hat completely broken off. I shuddered at the thought of it happening to Chena, the most delicate of the three.

"Okay, then." Hilda moderated her whisper a little. "All you have to do is watch, and take the occasional picture." Photography had been part of the deal to let me come along – something to spice up her website. I'd told her I was an expert, and what's the difference between expert and novice, really? Some pictures turn out, some don't. No one controls it.

"Got it." I waved the little point-and-shoot as if I knew exactly what to do with it. I'd already found the power switch and the take-a-picture button. I'd sealed the deal with Hilda by calling it a 'shutter release', which I was pretty sure was the technical term for part of the camera.

"Okay. The spray is camped out in that grove of azalea." She pointed left. "I'm going to circle around behind, come up through the camellia. I should be able to grab one or two of yours before the others know what's going on." She hitched at her broad belt, with its three soft pouches. Gnome-sized, they extended down to her ankles. "After that, just hope."

"Wait. What if...you said the spray had been near other humans recently. Maybe..."

"*No.*" She relented a bit at my obvious tension. "Believe me, it never turns out well. Yes, there are misguided people who try to care for strays. They'll leave out bits of clothing, or little tubs of cement and paint. The ferals use it to patch themselves up. But they never really trust the humans. Those fools are just as likely to have basement windows broken as they are to have weeds pulled. Ferals take advantage, they don't take care." She reached up and pressed my shoulder down hard. "Stay here. Take pictures. Don't worry."

With that, she was off, a soundless wraith vanishing into the shrubs of the park. She was surprisingly lithe for such a stocky figure. Every now and then, I thought I saw a bush shake, but it might just have been the wind. I hoped the spray would think so.

I turned on the camera, and, with a little experimentation, managed to zoom in on the azaleas. The spray was there, no question. Every now and then, I could catch a red hat against the orange, yellow, and green of the flowers and leaves – just the colors for an Irish runaway. Kidnapee. Captive.

After what seemed an hour, there was a commotion in the grove. The branches shook violently back and forth, and I could hear grunts and cries. Even through the leaves, I could see red hats gathered into a mass around a hairy central tuft. The shaking grew to a tumult, and just as I feared the branches would break, I saw a small figure fly out of the grove toward me with a despairing "*Run!*" It was Hilda's voice, and it sounded grim.

I started up, but recalled Hilda's admonition. *Stay here,* she'd said. As I crouched, uncertain, I saw the figure that had come out. It was Hans – face grinning just above the long grass of the park. He had escaped! Hilda had rescued him. But at what cost?

I blinked and he was closer. He was coming to me! I alternated looking at the ground and looking up, seeing Hans come closer at every step. Within moments, he was by my right knee, devil-may-care smile twinkling beneath his feathered hat. I gathered him into my arms and hugged him tight. He smelled funny, and after a moment, I relaxed my grip, holding him out and turning him every which way to look for injury. He looked fine, thank goodness, and I blessed Hilda for her courage.

Hilda! Whether it was Hans' safe return, or the strange odor that clung to him, something burst within me. My friends were in danger, and by golly, I was going to do something about it, risk or none. I'd sat back my entire life, letting caution guide me, and that time was done.

"In you go," I said to Hans, laying him into my knapsack with its clutch of soft hand towels. "I'll get this family back together. Trust me." He just grinned in his carefree way, but I took it for encouragement as I zipped him in and settled him at my back.

I rose to my full height, bursting through the rhododendron at chest-level. I pushed through to the grass, and with a steady gait, loped toward the azalea grove. I felt free at last, caution thrown to the winds, committed no matter what.

I must have looked a grim sight to the gnomes, a juggernaut of determination thundering toward them over the lawn – nemesis made flesh and seeking vengeance. Gnomes scattered to all sides, hats popping up here and there as they fled. I kept my eye open for Chena's distinctive off-white skin, and Danny's clover-hung cap. There! To the left of the grove, huddled together for comfort. I stared fixedly at them, hoping that, despite their obvious fear, gnome modesty would keep them from moving if I watched.

Whether through modesty or luck, they stayed put. I like to think that they saw and recognized me, though gnome eyesight isn't the best over long distances. In any case, even though I lost sight of them briefly as I forced my way into the grove, they stuck around until I was able to gather them in my arms. They were dirty, but otherwise unharmed. Tears of joy clouded my vision as I quickly stashed them in the safety of the knapsack with their friend.

Family secure at last, I sank to my knees, arms tight around the bag. The world was right again, the ugly adventure over.

"Hghh!" The grunt came from the right, and I turned quickly, fearing that the spray had returned. My burst of confidence faded, and I knew I'd never be able to stand up to them all. Best to get out while I could.

"*Hbhsfsth!*" There was a familiar undertone to the grunt this time, a hint of goblin. Hilda! I slung the knapsack on my back and crawled toward the noise. Sure enough, it was Hilda, tied to azalea trunks with braided grass, and gagged with her own beard. She seemed to be trying to chew her way free.

I had to do some chewing myself, to free her arms and legs. I didn't look forward to removing her gag, but once her hands were free, she was able to remove that on her own with a tool from her belt. I wished I'd known it was there, as I sat picking grass stems out of my teeth.

"Thanks," she said grudgingly. "I owe you one." A humbled goblin is a rare sight, and one I could do without seeing again. The hanks of spit-soaked beard dangling from her upper lip haunted my sleep for days.

I looked away and shrugged. My gnomes were safe, and that was all that mattered. I looked forward to getting them home, and having a calming drink of tea. Maybe even a stiff glass of juice. I wasn't tired, I realized. If anything, I was energized. I hadn't had this much excitement in years.

"Come on," said Hilda. "Let's get out of here before they come back." She rolled her shoulders and pushed through the grove to the grass. "I underestimated them," she admitted as we jogged back to her van. "Most gnomes fear a goblin; even a hob like me. This group, though, they're tough. They've been feral a long time, and some of them have gone bad."

As we settled in the van, and Hilda started the short drive home, I peeked into my knapsack. The gnomes had wrapped the towels around themselves; napping, maybe, after their big excitement. I worried about how they'd adjust to quiet home life again. I stroked Chena's smooth cheek, and she seemed to hum a little, the way she did when her igloo needed freshening. Hans, grinning even in his sleep, seemed to wink. Danny, at the far edge of the bag, was hidden in a thick fold of towel, and I let him be. "Soon," I whispered into the bag. "Soon, we'll all be home, and life can go back to normal." If there's anything more normal than a garden full of smiling gnomes, I don't know what it is.

* * *

A week later, I was sitting on my little patio, a tall glass of juice on the iron table before me. Chena had been a little quiet at first, but she'd been pleased with a new piece of driftwood, and she was slowly shaping it into a fine carving, more seal-like every morning. Hans had just winked and gone on with life, wheeling his new little grindstone around the garden at night, constantly offering to trade with the other gnomes for something less useful.

Danny, though… He just wasn't the same. He'd taken his little pot of gold readily enough, but it had vanished one dark night, leaving him with dirt on his cheeks, and a dour countenance. What had he suffered, I wondered, in the grip of those filthy, feral gnomes? What foul deeds had been done to him? I'd started to despair that he'd ever recover his happy, smiling insouciance, his ability to let troubles pass over him without a trace.

"I'll get them," I promised him with a whisper. "I'll see those foul creatures tamed, Danny. Just you wait."

"Why wait?" The voice from behind sent me surging forward into my table, juice flying as I twisted and fell simultaneously.

"Oh," I said, when I'd finished my fall to the hard stone floor and my heart slumped back out of my throat. "Hilda. Good to see you." It was, in a way. Even reliving my adventure around the office water cooler hadn't offered quite the frisson of excitement that my life now seemed to lack. I climbed painfully to my feet, wondering just how many frissons I really needed, and whether it wasn't dangerous to get too many at once.

"Look," she said, eyebrows fluttering like flags. "I been digging into that spray."

It seemed to explain the mud on her hands. "Yes?" I said cautiously.

"I found something." She shivered, and I was startled to see what looked like fear in her eyes. "They're not just feral," she said.

I winced. Danny had been in their hands. Not just wild, but feral, and not just feral, but …

"Dark gnomes," she said at last, with a grimace. "The worst of the worst." She paused. "If I don't stop this spray, no gnome in the city will be safe." Hilda looked up at me, calculation in her eyes. "You weren't entirely useless last time." A vision of beard-smudged lip passed before me, along with a faint taste of grass. "Want to help?"

I looked around at my little garden, my little family, and thought of hapless Hans, still smiling despite it all, fragile Chena, working so hard to forget. And most of all, Danny, sweet Danny, still fighting demons and memories, with no certainty that he would win.

"Well," I said. "Why not?" There was a little space at the back of the fridge where a jar of frissons might store nicely.

Patience

Donald J. Bingle

CLIFFORD HURLING used more dental floss than anyone else on the moon.

Flipping open the plastic lid on the Johnson & Johnson waxed variety, he grabbed the loose end of the string and spooled off precisely fourteen inches, using the metal tab to cut it and hold the end for the next night. Wrapping an end several times lightly around one finger, he looped the middle part of the floss around the spout of his tube of BriteWhite toothpaste, at the lower edge of the cap, where a residue of the paste always squeezed out a bit when he closed it. A thin film of congealing paste clung to the floss as he drew the string tight.

Dropping the tube back onto the metal sink, he crossed over to the bookshelf and pulled down a postcard his sister had sent him years ago from home. A small packet of white sand, labeled 'Genuine Sand from Cocoa Beach, Florida', was taped to the card. He gazed at the picture of the sun rising behind the gantries of the launch pads at Kennedy Space Center on Cape Canaveral as he efficiently loosed the open end of the plastic packet from the tape, opened it, and dropped the center of the loop of floss into the white sand. He smiled as he remembered, for the thousandth time, that his dentist always told him that his Extra-Whitening toothpaste was too abrasive on his teeth. He pulled the floss out and carefully closed the packet and re-affixed the tape.

Finally, he looped both ends of the floss more tightly around his index fingers. Folded pieces of cardboard from a paperback novel cover kept the floss from cutting into his fingers. Then he set to work. Not too fast. He had plenty of time. He would be at this for hours. Rhythmic and methodical, he started to work the floss back and forth.

* * *

The phone rang shrilly in the dark room. Swenson slapped at the alarm clock twice before the sound fully registered, then woke up, swearing vociferously. It didn't matter. No one shared his bed to be disturbed or offended. Finally he found the light, and – after being assaulted by its brightness – found the offending phone and snatched it from its cradle.

"Do you know what time it is?" he growled by way of greeting. He didn't care if his voice had an edge to it.

"Seventeen hundred Lunar Standard Time," responded the smooth, slightly professorial voice at the other end. Swenson did not recognize the caller's voice as it continued. "Let's see, in Tallahassee it would be…oh dear…that would be four…" The voice faltered and seemed flustered for a moment, then it regained its composure and confidence. "My apologies. This can wait until later."

"Look, buddy-boy. If you got the balls to call me at this hour, it better not be able to wait until morning. I'm up now, so spit it out. What's the emergency?"

"No emergency, Detective Swenson. The file jacket indicates that you are to be notified immediately in the event of any unusual development. I was just following the instructions."

"What file? What development? Maybe you'd better start from the beginning. Who is this, anyway?"

"I'm Corporal Pancek at the Lunar Correctional Facility. It seems that your prisoner, Clifford Hurling, has escaped."

A loud 'clank' reverberated through thousands of miles of optic cable and satellite wave transmissions to assault Pancek's ears as Swenson's phone hit the wall. The line remained open, however, and Pancek listened to Swenson's swearing receding as the Detective threw on some clothes and headed into the office.

Pancek disconnected the lunar end of the call. He didn't understand the problem. The prisoner's file said he was incarcerated for something to do with substandard electronic components – hardly the type of thing that should have gotten him a stint in the moon's finest prison facility. Usually only the hard cases came up here. Besides, where could Hurling go?

* * *

Swenson was waiting for the captain when he arrived at the station house at 6:30 a.m. He pounced before the man could pour himself a cup of coffee.

"I have to go to the moon."

"Excuse me?" replied the captain, unimpressed that Swenson was on the premises a good three hours ahead of his normal schedule.

"Hurling's escaped. There's no telling what he might do."

"Hurling, hmmm… Hurling… Oh, the fraud case that you were following so closely when I first got transferred here. I don't see why the Bureau of Prison's incompetence should entitle you to a joy ride to the moon. Just because some fools in the legislature want to waste the taxpayers' money by putting a prison facility up there, doesn't mean I have to waste any more money sending you up because a minor-league crook wandered out of the facility."

"He's not a minor-league crook, Captain. He's a stone-cold killer."

The captain's eyes narrowed in thought and minor consternation. "I thought it was some procurement scam or something with NASA…"

"They plea-bargained it to that. They didn't want any publicity."

The captain waited silently for Swenson to continue the explanation. Finally, he did.

"Actually, he was the guy behind the Nassau incident."

"Jesus…" exhaled the captain.

Everybody knew about the Nassau incident. It was the worst public-relations disaster for NASA since the Challenger explosion, not to mention the thousands of dead in the Bahamas when a NASA booster rocket went haywire and crashed into the outskirts of the town, leveling buildings and setting up the closest thing to a firestorm since Dresden, Tokyo, Hiroshima, and Nagasaki.

"No wonder they sent him to the lunar jail – if word ever got out that his faulty components caused the Nassau incident, a mob would storm the prison and lynch him for sure."

"It's worse than that, boss. It wasn't a faulty component. Almost nobody knows this – and NASA will have both our butts if this gets out – but…" Swenson's voice hardened to steel. "Hurling planned the whole thing. The damn chip was programmed to direct the rocket exactly where it landed. The guy's a cold-blooded killer – a thousand times over."

"Sure, and he's behind the Kennedy assassination, too. C'mon, Swenson, get a grip. Those chips and components in the space program go through hundreds, thousands, of tests. You just can't slip something in at the last second that sends a rocket careening off course."

"That's the thing, Captain. The guy's patient. He designed the component years beforehand, set it up so that it would pass the tests and only change its behavior when it was in actual flight – altered the telemetry coordinates or gimbals or somesuch rocket science. I gotta go to the moon and catch him. They don't know what they're dealing with."

"I don't know. I think you're overreacting. I mean, the place is isolated from even the other moon outposts. There's nowhere to go. Check in with the warden and keep track, but I need you here. We have a few unsolved murders to take care of, you know."

"A few..." Swenson shook his head wearily in exasperation. "You just don't get it. This guy is in jail for fraud, but he's one of the biggest mass murderers ever. Heck, if it wasn't for those terrorists that released sarin at the Pro-Bowl in 2034, this guy would probably have the record. And he wants it. I questioned him. You can tell... Kept asking for the final 'collateral damage' count all through questioning."

"You're being paranoid, Swenson. Check in with the moon and keep me informed, but don't spend too much time on it."

* * *

"I assure you, Detective Swenson, that no one has ever successfully escaped from the Lunar Correction Facility and that Clifford Hurling will be caught momentarily." The warden was irritated. Swenson wasn't sure if it was from his phone call or the fact that the warden's monotonous, but well-paid, job with a nice view had been interrupted by something so mundane as a prison break.

"How'd he get out, anyhow? Living in a vacuum, you'd think you guys would be careful about closing the door." He hated bureaucrats. They never volunteered anything. They always made you seem like a hard case just for asking for the basic facts.

"He cut through the bars."

The street-wise detective whistled lowly between his teeth. "You guys in the habit of leaving hacksaws lying around up there?"

"No... it appears... it appears he used dental floss."

"Criminy! He cut through steel bars with dental floss?"

"He seems to have accelerated the abrasion with a mixture of toothpaste and silica."

"Sand? You guys have a beach in that jail?"

"I don't really see how this is constructive, Detective. He had a small packet of beach sand among his personal effects. Nobody thought it could do any harm."

"How many bars did he cut though?"

"Three – well, three and a half. He appears to have started the project in another cell before he was moved. We found the other bar on a closer inspection after the break-out."

"Are you housing those guys in chicken wire cages or something? How long does something like that take?"

"Well, our bars are somewhat more light-weight than standard fare in a state facility," the warden sniffed haughtily. "No need to boost extra weight all the way to the moon, you know."

"You're avoiding the question. How long has this been in the works?"

"He was transferred from the old cell five and a half years ago. Our records show he first put in a toiletries request for dental floss and abrasive toothpaste three weeks after his arrival – almost seven years ago."

Swenson paused at the sheer audacity of it. Seven years of meticulous, but monotonous work, abrading the bars without being noticed, then covering his work so as to keep it secret. "You have to get this guy, fast, do you understand, warden? You cannot take any chances. If there is any risk of him getting away, you have to shoot to kill." His voice involuntarily became more shrill than he intended. "Shoot to kill, you hear me?"

"I don't think that is in any way…"

"Shoot to kill, I said!"

There was a brief moment of silence before the warden responded, condescendingly. "Those of us living in pressurized environments amidst a vacuum generally avoid the use, even the availability, of projectile weaponry. You see, Detective, explosive decompression can result from any puncture…"

But Swenson wasn't listening anymore. He didn't care if it took his life savings. He had to get to the moon.

* * *

Thirty-six hours and $687,000 later, plus tips, Swenson demonstrated his own version of explosive decompression in the warden's office.

"What do you mean, you think he stole a rocket?" Swenson might have weighed one-sixth as much on the moon, but his voiced boomed even heavier in the close confines of the pressurized and compartmentalized facility.

"An ore freighter, actually. Used to carry ore from the asteroid belt to the moon for construction. Heavy metals mostly. Much cheaper and more plentiful than bringing things up from earth. They can move a great deal of mass, not quickly, but inexpensively."

"Thanks for the economics lesson, warden, but what happens when this guy plows that craft into Mexico City or Hong Kong from high orbit?"

"Ohh…" whimpered the warden. "Perhaps we ought to call in NASA-Lunar HQ."

* * *

Jason Petterlie, the resident rocket scientist at NASA-Lunar, was unimpressed with Swenson's concerns.

"You just don't understand. First off, it's a deep-space craft – not designed to land where there's an atmosphere. It's not even streamlined. All, or at least everything but the reactor, would burn off in the atmosphere. The reactors are designed to avoid irradiating the countryside if they accidentally reenter the earth's atmosphere. Shaped shielding, automatic ejection of the core so it burns up at high altitude, that kind of thing. Someone could have the minor remains of the thing fall through their roof, I suppose – a few hundred pounds at the most – but the odds are…" he looked at the two concerned officials smugly, "… astronomical."

Swenson was unimpressed. "What about if it's full of cargo?"

The technician brushed away his concern. "It's not. It's empty. Supplies for six crewmen for several months, but no ore. Even if it did have cargo, ore is loose rock – it would behave just like any other small particulate matter once the hull ablated away. Good meteor shower – no damage."

Swenson's mind raced. "The lunar colony, then, or one of the other near-space outposts."

"In theory, I suppose. But he's not headed in that direction. If he was, we'd send up a laser mining ship and shoot him down."

"You mean you know where he is! Shoot the bastard down, then."

"This isn't Buck Rogers, Detective. We don't have fighters patrolling the solar system looking for alien ships to blast. It could be done, but it would be expensive. Besides, it is completely unnecessary. He's boosted to a moderate rate of speed. It is inefficient for him to change course, and we'd see it coming if he did. Besides, Detective, he's headed out of the solar system."

"What about the mining colonies in the asteroid belt? Won't he have to go by them?"

"Well," the technician paused to tap out a few commands in the air on his virtual data-pad. A three-dimensional hologram of the solar system popped up on the tabletop with outposts and trajectories highlighted, "the orbital dynamics don't put him near anything at all on the way out. The portion of the asteroid belt he'll near in a couple months is not populated. He might skim by a few rocks when he gets to the Oort Cloud, but that's about it."

The tech turned off the projection, the science lesson over. "Look, he probably just got stir-crazy and headed away from the moon without any thought to where he was going."

"Thank you, Dr. Petterlie," interrupted the warden, once more confident. "We will worry no more about it."

Swenson wished that were true, but the mealy-mouthed warden didn't speak for him.

* * *

The ore ship was not elegant, but compared to the cramped facilities in prison, it was roomy. Equipped for six, Clifford had plenty of food, air, and water – the hydroponics room even had a few scrawny tomato plants. His only company was the crew vid-cube collection (mostly action movies and porn) and a couple of cockroaches. He preferred the cockroaches to the porn, but he did not have much time for either.

He had things to do.

Fortunately, the nav-computer was first rate. And once he was up to speed, he didn't need to expend fuel until he wanted to stop or change vectors. He could coast while he finished his calculations.

* * *

As the months went by, the guys at the station house grew bolder and bolder about teasing Swenson for blowing his retirement money on a 'working' trip to the moon. He hadn't even taken in the sights in Lunar City or visited the low-grav brothel in the port district. They laughed at him and 'mooned' him in the locker room. Even the captain, initially sympathetic, found an excuse to pass him over on the next round of promotions.

Still, every week Swenson checked in with Petterlie, the confident technician at NASA-Lunar.

"No, Detective. There's no change at all. For all we know, he's not even alive. His course is unchanged. There is no answer to our periodic hails. We can tell his computer and life support systems are operating, but that's about it. He probably committed suicide or is gibbering away while he looks out at the vast reaches of space. I really do have better things to do with my time than chat with you, Detective."

"Just tell me, right away, if anything happens."

Petterlie tapped at his virtual data-pad again. "We'll lose him for a few weeks about the time he arrives at the Oort Cloud – it's on the other side of the sun from us at that point."

"Isn't that dangerous? Could we set up a relay station to monitor him from another vector?"

"Detective! He's hundreds of millions of miles away on a ship that takes a week to even stop. Don't you have criminals down there on earth to catch?"

* * *

Hurling finished the computer work with months to spare, but there was some detail to adjust as he got closer. The rest of his time he spent in a painstaking effort to train the cockroaches, but to no avail.

"Too stupid to learn, yet smart enough to survive. That's evolution."

A week out of the core of the loosely-defined and scattered Oort Cloud, he started the burn to stop. Hurling turned his attention to locating the right real estate.

* * *

"I told you he was alive. He's up to something." If the Detective gripped the phone any tighter, the plastic would be sure to break.

"I didn't say he was dead. I said he could be dead."

"So, what does this burn mean?"

"He's probably just going to settle the ship down on the biggest chunk of rock he can find and declare it his own personal planet or something. Or maybe he put the ship on scouting auto-pilot and it has located a potential ore body. He could still be dead for all we know."

"You've got to send someone to shoot him down…"

"You police and your guns…"

The line went dead.

* * *

Petterlie ducked Swenson's calls for the next month. If he'd had the money, Swenson would have gone back to the moon just to strangle the scrawny tech's neck.

Then finally, Petterlie called him. "There's been a development, Detective."

"I told you…"

"Well, yes. Right as his position on the other side of the sun became visible to our instruments, they indicated that he was in the midst of another burn. We don't know when it started, an asteroid was blocking our view. We probably wouldn't have seen the end of the burn, but the solar flares have died down unexpectedly early, possibly giving credence to the Wyzinski theory as to their source of periodicity…"

"Yeah, yeah. Whatever." The guy was a geek, a geek that couldn't stay on the subject, at least not on Swenson's subject. "You're avoiding something. What else is there?"

"We received a long-range signal this morning."

"You waiting to engrave it on a Hallmark Card and mail it to me?" Why couldn't some people ever get to the point?

"It reads: 'In a game with a real pro, the cockroaches win.'" The technician cleared his throat. "I told you he was probably gibbering to himself."

A vise gripped Swenson's chest. It suddenly made sense. The damn rocket scientist was going for the record. He didn't want those terrorist psychos from the Pro-Bowl to best his numbers. And though he was no scientist, Swenson knew how Hurling was going to do it.

"Sweet Jesus, Petterlie. The bastard's pushing a rock."

The technician felt suddenly lightheaded, even for lunar gravity. An asteroid six or seven miles across falling toward the Earth was the type of calamity that had befallen the dinosaurs at the end of the Cretaceous, not to mention the similar event exterminating the trilobites and the gorgons before that, ending the Paleozoic Era. Impacts like that typically were believed to have caused the extinction of seventy to ninety percent of species existing at the time of the collision. It was the type of event that could wipe out humanity completely…efficiently.

Petterlie started analyzing the data even before the surly Detective asked him to.

* * *

Properly motivated, and with more than a year's notice, even much-maligned NASA managed to track and destroy the ten-mile wide asteroid nudged onto a collision path with Earth. There were much congratulations and backslapping and bottles of champagne (from Oregon these days).

Swenson finally got his promotion.

Petterlie was similarly slated for rapid advancement.

The warden, on the other hand, was quietly cashiered.

After sending the rock on its way, the ore ship drifted in space. Computer-enhanced analysis of the end of its burn suggested that it had run out of fuel, rather than ending the burn with a fuel shut off.

Most of the world did not even know of the danger it had faced, but even those who did stopped worrying. Except for Swenson. He awoke one night with a start and called Petterlie.

"How much fuel did it take to send that rock?"

A day later, he received the reply. "About twenty percent of what Hurling had left when he got to the belt."

There was a long pause. "Damn it. Don't you see, Petterlie? He sent more than one. I know it. Deep down in my bones, I know it. There are more rocks headed for us."

The tech contemplated a moment. He had to admit it was a possibility. "It could be," he said evenly.

"How many?" pressed the Detective. "How many could he have sent?"

"Two, maybe four, depending on how far apart they were, how big they are, and how much juice it took to nudge their orbits."

"Good God, four…" muttered Swenson in awe.

"But we've scanned the area," continued the scientist. "Nothing else is headed directly for us – well, directly in the sense of an intersecting elliptical orbit now moving toward our orbital path, that is."

"He's a rocket scientist, Petterlie, just like you. What would you do?"

Petterlie bristled at the 'just like you' remark, but thought quietly for almost a minute. Swenson showed unusual patience and left the line open without uttering any rude comments.

"I'd send something on an elliptical orbit away from us, to arrive later, when we weren't looking."

"Bingo. The bastard's still after the record. He wants to be the biggest mass murderer of all time."

"But he's failed, Swenson. Don't you see? You've caught him. We're onto his game. We know what he's done. We'll watch the skies. We've been warned. Whether it's next year or five years from now, you have my word. I'll make sure we're watching."

"Don't you understand, Petterlie? The man cut through three steel bars with dental floss and sand. Years it took him. He's patient. It won't be next year or the year after. Those rocks are coming decades, centuries, millenia from now."

Tears welled in Detective Swenson's eyes as he continued – tears his squad mates had never seen. "Who's going to remember your warning two thousand years from now? You're clever, Petterlie, but you're not Nostradamus. What about fifty thousand or a million years from now?" The tears stopped as his anger took over again. "He's right, you know. He's got the record. Cockroaches will be the only survivors and there's not a damn thing we can do about it."

Petterlie strained against the logic of it, but somehow he knew the Detective was right. "I guess," he said quietly, "we'll just have to wait and see."

* * *

Hurling reviewcd the nav-computer logs one last time. Everything was in motion, just as it should be. One or two of his 'projects' might miss or be detected, but almost certainly not all of them. One would hit – it was just a matter of time and sophisticated orbital mechanics. He would die knowing he had the record, a record that could never be broken.

He had thought of bleeding the air from the ship to commit suicide, but that wouldn't have been fair to the cockroaches. He wondered how long the insects could live on the remaining provisions (which he took care to conveniently open) and, of course, his body. As the future rulers of Earth, the species deserved some respect, he believed.

Instead of suicide by decompression, he had raided the medical supplies and cooked up something sufficiently lethal to take. It wasn't really that hard.

It wasn't rocket science.

An Imperial Finale

Guy Boothby

OF ALL the functions that ornament the calendar of the English social and sporting year, surely the Cowes week may claim to rank as one of the greatest, or at least the most enjoyable. So thought Simon Carne as he sat on the deck of Lord Tremorden's yacht, anchored off the mouth of the Medina River, smoking his cigarette and whispering soft nothings into the little shell-like ear of Lady Mabel Madderley, the lady of all others who had won the right to be considered the beauty of the past season. It was a perfect afternoon, and, as if to fill his flagon of enjoyment to the very brim, he had won the Queen's Cup with his yacht, *The Unknown Quantity*, only half an hour before. Small wonder, therefore, that he was contented with his lot in life, and his good fortune of that afternoon in particular.

The tiny harbour was crowded with shipping of all sorts, shapes, and sizes, including the guardship, his Imperial Majesty the Emperor of Westphalia's yacht the *Hohenszrallas*, the English Royal yachts, steam yachts, schooners, cutters, and all the various craft taking part in England's greatest water carnival. Steam launches darted hither and thither, smartly equipped gigs conveyed gaily-dressed parties from vessel to vessel, while, ashore, the little town itself was alive with bunting, and echoed to the strains of almost continuous music.

"Surely you ought to consider yourself a very happy man, Mr. Carne," said Lady Mabel Madderley, with a smile, in reply to a speech of the other's. "You won the Derby in June, and today you have appropriated the Queen's Cup."

"If such things constitute happiness, I suppose I must be in the seventh heaven of delight," answered Carne, as he took another cigarette from his case and lit it. "All the same, I am insatiable enough to desire still greater fortune. When one has set one's heart upon winning something, beside which the Derby and the Queen's Cup are items scarcely worth considering, one is rather apt to feel that fortune has still much to give."

"I am afraid I do not quite grasp your meaning," she said. But there was a look in her face that told him that, if she did not understand, she could at least make a very good guess. According to the world's reckoning, he was quite the best fish then swimming in the matrimonial pond, and some people, for the past few weeks, had even gone so far as to say that she had hooked him. It could not be denied that he had been paying her unmistakable attention of late.

What answer he would have vouchsafed to her speech it is impossible to say, for at that moment their host came along the deck towards them. He carried a note in his hand.

"I have just received a message to say that his Imperial Majesty is going to honour us with a visit," he said, when he reached them. "If I mistake not, that is his launch coming towards us now."

Lady Mabel and Simon Carne rose and accompanied him to the starboard bulwarks. A smart white launch, with the Westphalian flag flying at her stern, had left the Royal yacht and was steaming quickly towards them. A few minutes later it had reached the companion ladder, and Lord Tremorden had descended to welcome his Royal guest. When they reached the deck together, his Majesty shook hands with Lady Tremorden, and afterwards with Lady Mabel and Simon Carne.

"I must congratulate you most heartily, Mr. Carne," he said, "on your victory today. You gave us an excellent race, and though I had the misfortune to be beaten by thirty seconds, still I have the satisfaction of knowing that the winner was a better boat in every way than my own."

"Your Majesty adds to the sweets of victory by your generous acceptance of defeat," Carne replied. "But I must confess that I owe my success in no way to my own ability. The boat was chosen for me by another, and I have not even the satisfaction of saying that I sailed her myself."

"Nevertheless she is your property, and you will go down to posterity famous in yachting annals as the winner of the Queen's Cup in this justly celebrated year."

With this compliment his Majesty turned to his hostess and entered into conversation with her, leaving his *aide-de-camp* free to discuss the events of the day with Lady Mabel. When he took his departure half an hour later, Carne also bade his friends goodbye, and, descending to his boat, was rowed away to his own beautiful steam yacht, which was anchored a few cables' length away from the Imperial craft. He was to dine on board the latter vessel that evening.

On gaining the deck he was met by Belton, his valet, who carried a telegram in his hand. As soon as he received it, Carne opened it and glanced at the contents, without, however, betraying very much interest.

An instant later the expression upon his face changed like magic. Still holding the message in his hand, he turned to Belton.

"Come below," he said quickly. "There is news enough here to give us something to think of for hours to come."

Reaching the saloon, which was decorated with all the daintiness of the upholsterer's art, he led the way to the cabin he had arranged as a study. Having entered it, he shut and locked the door.

"It's all up, Belton," he said. "The comedy has lasted long enough, and now it only remains for us to speak the tag, and after that to ring the curtain down as speedily as may be."

"I am afraid, sir, I do not quite take your meaning," said Belton. "Would you mind telling me what has happened?"

"I can do that in a very few words," the other answered. "This cablegram is from Trincomalee Liz, and was dispatched from Bombay yesterday. Read it for yourself."

He handed the paper to his servant, who read it carefully, aloud:

TO CARNE, PORCHESTER HOUSE, PARK LANE, LONDON. — BRADFIELD LEFT FORTNIGHT SINCE. HAVE ASCERTAINED THAT YOU ARE THE OBJECT. TRINCOMALEE.

"This is very serious, sir," said the other, when he had finished.

"As you say, it is very serious indeed," Carne replied. "Bradfield thinks he has caught me at last, I suppose; but he seems to forget that it is possible for me to be as clever as himself. Let me look at the message again. Left a fortnight ago, did he? Then I've still a little respite. By Jove, if that's the case, I'll see that I make the most of it."

"But surely, sir, you will leave at once," said Belton quickly. "If this man, who has been after us so long, is now more than half way to England, coming with the deliberate intention of running you to earth, surely, sir, you'll see the advisability of making your escape while you have time."

Carne smiled indulgently.

"Of course I shall escape, my good Belton," he said. "You have never known me neglect to take proper precautions yet; but before I go I must do one more piece of business. It must be something by the light of which all I have hitherto accomplished will look like nothing. Something really great, that will make England open its eyes as it has not done yet."

Belton stared at him, this time in undisguised amazement.

"Do you mean to tell me, sir," he said with the freedom of a privileged servant, "that you intend to run another risk, when the only man who knows sufficient of your career to bring you to book is certain to be in England in less than a fortnight? I cannot believe that you would be so foolish, sir. I beg of you to think what you are doing."

Carne, however, paid but small attention to his servant's entreaties.

"The difficulty," he said to himself, speaking his thoughts aloud, "is to understand quite what to do. I seem to have used up all my big chances. However, I'll think it over, and it will be strange if I don't hit upon something. In the meantime, Belton, you had better see that preparations are made for leaving England on Friday next. Tell the skipper to have everything ready. We shall have done our work by that time; then head for the open sea and freedom from the trammels of a society life once more. You might drop a hint or two to certain people that I am going, but be more than careful what you say. Write to the agents about Porchester House, and attend to all the other necessary details. You may leave me now."

Belton bowed, and left the cabin without another word. He knew his master sufficiently well to feel certain that neither entreaties nor expostulations would make him abandon the course he had mapped out for himself. That being so, he bowed to the inevitable with a grace which had now become a habit to him.

When he was alone, Carne once more sat for upwards of an hour in earnest thought. He then ordered his gig, and, when it was ready, set out for the shore. Making his way to the telegraph office, he dispatched a message which at any other, and less busy, time, would have caused the operator some astonishment. It was addressed to a Mahommedan dealer in precious stones in Bombay, and contained only two words in addition to the signature. They were:

'Leaving – come.'

He knew that they would reach the person for whom they were intended, and that she would understand their meaning and act accordingly.

The dinner that night on board the Imperial yacht *Hohenszrallas* was a gorgeous affair in every sense of the word. All the principal yacht owners were present, and, at the conclusion of the banquet, Carne's health, as winner of the great event of the regatta, was proposed by the Emperor himself, and drunk amid enthusiastic applause. It was a proud moment for the individual in question, but he bore his honours with that quiet dignity that had stood him in such good stead on so many similar occasions. In his speech he referred to his approaching departure from England, and this, the first inkling of such news, came upon his audience like a thunder-clap. When they had taken leave of his Majesty soon after midnight, and were standing on deck, waiting for their respective boats to draw up to the accommodation ladder, Lord Orpington made his way to where Simon Carne was standing.

"Is it really true that you intend leaving us so soon?" he asked.

"Quite true, unfortunately," Carne replied. "I had hoped to have remained longer, but circumstances over which I have no control make it imperative that I should return to India without delay. Business that exercises a vital influence upon my fortunes compels me. I am therefore obliged to leave without fail on Friday next. I have given orders to that effect this afternoon."

"I am extremely sorry to hear it, that's all I can say," said Lord Amberley, who had just come up. "I assure you we shall all miss you very much indeed."

"You have all been extremely kind," said Carne, "and I have to thank you for an exceedingly pleasant time. But, there, let us postpone consideration of the matter for as long as possible. I think this is my boat. Won't you let me take you as far as your own yacht?"

"Many thanks, but I don't think we need trouble you," said Lord Orpington. "I see my gig is just behind yours."

"In that case, goodnight," said Carne. "I shall see you as arranged, tomorrow morning, I suppose?"

"At eleven," said Lord Amberley. "We'll call for you and go ashore together. Goodnight."

By the time Carne had reached his yacht he had made up his mind. He had also hit upon a scheme, the daring of which almost frightened himself. If only he could bring it off, he told himself, it would be indeed a fitting climax to all he had accomplished since he had arrived in England. Retiring to his cabin, he allowed Belton to assist him in his preparations for the night almost without speaking. It was not until the other was about to leave the cabin that he broached the subject that was occupying his mind to the exclusion of all else.

"Belton," he said, "I have decided upon the greatest scheme that has come into my mind yet. If Simon Carne is going to say farewell to the English people on Friday next, and it succeeds, he will leave them a legacy to think about for some time after he has gone."

"You are surely not going to attempt anything further, sir," said Belton in alarm. "I *did* hope, sir, that you would have listened to my entreaties this afternoon."

"It was impossible for me to do so," said Carne. "I am afraid, Belton, you are a little lacking in ambition. I have noticed that on the last three occasions you have endeavoured to dissuade me from my endeavours to promote the healthy excitement of the English reading public. On this occasion fortunately I am able to withstand you. Tomorrow morning you will commence preparations for the biggest piece of work to which I have yet put my hand."

"If you have set your mind upon doing it, sir, I am quite aware that it is hopeless for me to say anything," said Belton resignedly. "May I know, however, what it is going to be?"

Carne paused for a moment before he replied.

"I happen to know that the Emperor of Westphalia, whose friendship I have the honour to claim," he said, "has a magnificent collection of gold plate on board his yacht. It is my intention, if possible, to become the possessor of it."

"Surely that will be impossible, sir," said Belton. "Clever as you undoubtedly are in arranging these things, I do not see how you can do it. A ship at the best of times is such a public place, and they will be certain to guard it very closely."

"I must confess that at first glance I do not quite see how it is to be managed, but I have a scheme in my head which I think may possibly enable me to effect my purpose. At any rate, I shall be able to tell you more about it tomorrow. First, let us try a little experiment."

As he spoke he seated himself at his dressing table, and bade Belton bring him a box which had hitherto been standing in a corner. When he opened it, it proved to be a pretty little cedar-wood affair divided into a number of small compartments, each of which contained crepe hair of a different colour. Selecting a small portion from one particular compartment, he unraveled it until he had obtained the length he wanted, and then with dexterous fingers constructed a moustache, which he attached with spirit gum to his upper lip. Two or three twirls gave it the necessary curl, then with a pair of ivory-backed brushes taken from the dressing table he brushed his hair back in a peculiar manner, placed a hat of uncommon shape upon his head, took a heavy boat cloak from a cupboard near at hand, threw it round his shoulders, and, assuming an almost defiant expression, faced Belton, and desired him to tell him whom he resembled.

Familiar as he was with his master's marvellous power of disguise and his extraordinary faculty of imitation, the latter could not refrain from expressing his astonishment.

"His Imperial Majesty the Emperor of Westphalia," he said. "The likeness is perfect."

"Good," said Carne. "From that exhibition you will gather something of my plan. Tomorrow evening, as you are aware, I am invited to meet his Majesty, who is to dine ashore accompanied by his *aide-de-camp*, Count Von Walzburg. Here is the latter's photograph. He possesses, as you know, a very decided personality, which is all in our favour. Study it carefully."

So saying, he took from a drawer a photograph, which he propped against the looking-glass on the dressing table before him. It represented a tall, military-looking individual, with bristling eyebrows, a large nose, a heavy grey moustache, and hair of the same colour. Belton examined it carefully.

"I can only suppose, sir," he said, "that, as you are telling me this, you intend me to represent Count Von Walzburg."

"Exactly," said Carne. "That is my intention. It should not be at all difficult. The Count is just your height and build. You will only need the moustache, the eyebrows, the grey hair, and the large nose, to look the part exactly. Tomorrow will be a dark night, and, if only I can control circumstances sufficiently to obtain the chance I want, detection, in the first part of our scheme at any rate, should be most unlikely, if not almost impossible."

"You'll excuse my saying so, I hope, sir," said Belton, "but it seems a very risky game to play when we have done so well up to the present."

"You must admit that the glory will be the greater, my friend, if we succeed."

"But surely, sir, as I said just now, they keep the plate you mention in a secure place, and have it properly guarded."

"I have made the fullest inquiries, you may be sure. It is kept in a safe in the chief steward's cabin, and, while it is on board, a sentry is always on duty at the door. Yes, all things considered, I should say it is kept in a remarkably secure place."

"Then, sir, I'm still at a loss to see how you are going to obtain possession of it."

Carne smiled indulgently. It pleased him to see how perplexed his servant was.

"In the simplest manner possible," he said, "provided always that I can get on board the yacht without my identity being questioned. The manner in which we are to leave the vessel will be rather more dangerous, but not sufficiently so to cause us any great uneasiness. You are a good swimmer, I know, so that a hundred yards should not hurt you. You must also have a number of stout canvas sacks, say six, prepared, and securely attached to each the same number of strong lines; the latter must be fifty fathoms long, and have at the end of each a stout swivel hook. The rest is only a matter of detail. Now, what have you arranged with regard to matters in town?"

"I have fulfilled your instructions, sir, to the letter," said Belton. "I have communicated with the agents who act for the owner of Porchester House. I have caused an advertisement to be inserted in all the papers tomorrow morning to the effect that the renowned detective, Klimo, will be unable to meet his clients for at least a month, owing to the fact that he has accepted an important engagement upon the Continent, which will take him from home for that length of time. I have negotiated the sale of the various horses you have in training, and I have also arranged for the disposal of the animals and carriages you have now in use in London. Ram Gafur and the other native servants at Porchester House will come down by the midday train tomorrow, but before they do so, they will fulfil your instructions and repair the hole in the wall between the two houses. I cannot think of any more, sir."

"You have succeeded admirably, my dear Belton," said Carne, "and I am very pleased. Tomorrow you had better see that a paragraph is inserted in all the daily papers announcing the fact that it is my intention to leave England for India immediately, on important private business. I think that will do for tonight."

Belton tidied the cabin, and, having done so, bade his master goodnight. It was plain that he was exceedingly nervous about the success of the enterprise upon which Carne was embarking so confidently. The latter, on the other hand, retired to rest and slept as peacefully as if he had not a care or an anxiety upon his mind.

Next morning he was up by sunrise, and, by the time his friends Lords Orpington and Amberley were thinking about breakfast, had put the finishing touches to the scheme which was to bring his career in England to such a fitting termination.

According to the arrangement entered into on the previous day, his friends called for him at eleven o'clock, when they went ashore together. It was a lovely morning, and Carne was in the highest spirits. They visited the Castle together, made some purchases in the town, and then went off to lunch on board Lord Orpington's yacht. It was well-nigh three o'clock before Carne bade his host and hostess farewell, and descended the gangway in order to return to his own vessel. A brisk sea was running, and for this reason to step into the boat was an exceedingly difficult, if not a dangerous, matter. Either he miscalculated his distance, or he must have jumped at the wrong moment; at any rate, he missed his footing, and fell heavily on to the bottom. Scarcely a second, however, had elapsed before his coxswain had sprung to his assistance, and had lifted him up on to the seat in the stern. It was then discovered that he had been unfortunate enough to once more give a nasty twist to the ankle which had brought him to such grief when he had been staying at Greenthorpe Park on the occasion of the famous wedding.

"My dear fellow, I am so sorry," said Lord Orpington, who had witnessed the accident. "Won't you come on board again? If you can't walk up the ladder we can easily hoist you over the side."

"Many thanks," replied Carne, "but I think I can manage to get back to my own boat. It is better I should do so. My man has had experience of my little ailments, and knows exactly what is best to be done under such circumstances; but it is a terrible nuisance, all the same. I'm afraid it will be impossible for me now to be present at his Royal Highness's dinner this evening, and I have been looking forward to it so much."

"We shall all be exceedingly sorry," said Lord Amberley. "I shall come across in the afternoon to see how you are."

"You are very kind," said Carne, "and I shall be immensely glad to see you if you can spare the time."

With that he gave the signal to his men to push off. By the time he reached his own yacht his foot was so painful that it was necessary for him to be lifted on board — a circumstance which was duly noticed by the occupants of all the surrounding yachts, who had brought their glasses to bear upon him. Once below in his saloon, he was placed in a comfortable chair and left to Belton's careful attention.

"I trust you have not hurt yourself very much, sir," said that faithful individual, who, however, could not prevent a look of satisfaction coming into his face, which seemed to say that he was not ill-pleased that his master would, after all, be prevented from carrying out the hazardous scheme he had proposed to him the previous evening.

In reply, Carne sprang to his feet without showing a trace of lameness.

"My dear Belton, how peculiarly dense you are today," he said, with a smile, as he noticed the other's amazement. "Cannot you see that I have only been acting as you yourself wished I should do early this morning — namely, taking precautions? Surely you must see that, if I am laid up on board my yacht with a sprained ankle, society will say that is quite impossible for me to be doing any mischief elsewhere. Now, tell me, is everything prepared for tonight?"

"Everything, sir," Belton replied. "The dresses and wigs are ready. The canvas sacks, and the lines to which the spring hooks are attached, are in your cabin awaiting your inspection. As far as I can see, everything is prepared, and I hope will meet with your satisfaction."

"If you are as careful as usual, I feel sure it will," said Carne. "Now get some bandages and make this foot of mine up into as artistic a bundle as you possibly can. After that help me on deck and prop me up in a chair. As soon as my accident gets known there will be certain to be shoals of callers on board, and I must play my part as carefully as possible."

As Carne had predicted, this proved to be true. From half-past three until well after six o'clock a succession of boats drew up at his accommodation ladder, and the sufferer on deck was the recipient of as much attention as would have flattered the vainest of men. He had been careful to send a letter of apology to the illustrious individual who was to have been his host, expressing his sincere regrets that the accident which had so unfortunately befallen him would prevent the possibility of his being able to be present at the dinner he was giving that evening.

Day closed in and found the sky covered with heavy clouds. Towards eight o'clock a violent storm of rain fell, and when Carne heard it beating upon the deck above his cabin, and reflected that in consequence the night would in all probability be dark, he felt that his lucky star was indeed in the ascendant.

At half-past eight he retired to his cabin with Belton, in order to prepare for the events of the evening. Never before had he paid such careful attention to his make-up. He knew that on this occasion the least carelessness might lead to detection, and he had no desire that his last and greatest exploit should prove his undoing.

It was half-past nine before he and his servant had dressed and were ready to set off. Then, placing broad-brimmed hats upon their heads, and carrying a portmanteau containing the cloaks and headgear which they were to wear later in the evening, they went on deck and descended into the dinghy which was waiting for them alongside. In something under a quarter of an hour they had been put ashore in a secluded spot, had changed their costumes, and were walking boldly down beside the water towards the steps where they could see the Imperial launch still waiting. Her crew were lolling about, joking and laughing, secure in the knowledge that it would be some hours at least before their Sovereign would be likely to require their services again.

Their astonishment, therefore, may well be imagined when they saw approaching them the two men whom they had only half an hour before brought ashore. Stepping in and taking his seat under the shelter, his Majesty ordered them to convey him back to the yacht with all speed. The accent and voice were perfect, and it never for an instant struck any one on board the boat that a deception was being practised. Carne, however, was aware that this was only a preliminary; the most dangerous portion of the business was yet to come.

On reaching the yacht, he sprang out on the ladder, followed by his *aide-de-camp*, Von Walzburg, and mounted the steps. His disguise must have been perfect indeed, for when he reached the deck he found himself face to face with the first lieutenant, who, on seeing him, saluted respectfully. For a moment Carne's presence of mind almost deserted him; then, seeing that he was not discovered, he determined upon a bold piece of bluff. Returning the officer's salute with just the air he had seen the Emperor use, he led him to suppose that he had important reasons for coming on board so soon, and, as if to back this assertion up, bade him send the chief steward to his cabin, and at the same time have the sentry removed from his door and placed at the end of the large saloon, with instructions to allow no one to pass until he was communicated with again.

The officer saluted and went off on his errand, while Carne, signing to Belton to follow him, made his way down the companion ladder to the Royal cabins. To both the next few minutes seemed like hours. Reaching the Imperial state room, they entered it and closed the door behind. Provided the sentry obeyed his orders, which there was no reason to doubt he would do, and the Emperor himself did not return until they were safely off the vessel again, there seemed every probability of their being able to carry out their scheme without a hitch.

"Put those bags under the table, and unwind the lines and place them in the gallery outside the window. They won't be seen there," said Carne to Belton, who was watching him from the doorway. "Then stand by, for in a few minutes the chief steward will be here. As soon as he enters you must manage to get between him and the door, and, while I am engaging him in conversation, spring on him, clutch him by the throat, and hold him until I can force this gag into his mouth. After that we shall be safe for some time at least, for not a soul will come this way until they discover their mistake. It seems to me we ought to thank our stars that the chief steward's cabin was placed in such a convenient position. But hush, here comes the individual we want. Be ready to collar him as soon as I hold up my hand. If he makes a sound we are lost."

He had scarcely spoken before there was a knock at the door. When it opened, the chief steward entered the cabin, closing the door behind him.

"Schmidt," said his Majesty, who was standing at the further end of the cabin, "I have sent for you in order that I may question you on a matter of the utmost importance. Draw nearer."

The man came forward as he was ordered, and, having done so, looked his master full and fair in the face. Something he saw there seemed to stagger him. He glanced at him a second time, and was immediately confirmed in his belief.

"You are not the Emperor," he cried. "There is some treachery in this. I shall call for assistance."

He had half turned, and was about to give the alarm, when Carne held up his hand, and Belton, who had been creeping stealthily up behind him, threw himself upon him and had clutched him by the throat before he could utter a sound. The fictitious Emperor immediately produced a cleverly constructed gag and forced it into the terrified man's mouth, who in another second was lying upon the floor bound hand and foot.

"There, my friend," said Carne quietly, as he rose to his feet a few moments later, "I don't think you will give us any further trouble. Let me just see that those straps are tight enough, and then we'll place you on this settee, and afterwards get to business with all possible dispatch."

Having satisfied himself on these points, he signed to Belton, and between them they placed the man upon the couch.

"Let me see, I think, if I remember rightly, you carry the key of the safe in this pocket."

So saying, he turned the man's pocket inside out and appropriated the bunch of keys he found therein. Choosing one from it, he gave a final look at the bonds which secured the prostrate figure, and then turned to Belton.

"I think he'll do," he said. "Now for business. Bring the bags, and come with me."

So saying, he crossed the cabin, and, having assured himself that there was no one about to pry upon them, passed along the luxuriously carpeted alley way until he arrived at the door of the cabin, assigned to the use of the chief steward, and in which was the safe containing the magnificent gold plate, the obtaining of which was the reason of his being there. To his surprise and chagrin, the door was closed and locked. In his plans he had omitted to allow for this contingency. In all probability, however, the key was in the man's pocket, so, turning to Belton, he bade him return to the state room and bring him the keys he had thrown upon the table.

The latter did as he was ordered, and, when he had disappeared, Carne stood alone in the alleyway waiting and listening to the various noises of the great vessel. On the deck overhead he could hear someone tramping heavily up and down, and then, in an interval of silence, the sound of pouring rain. Good reason as he had to be anxious, he could not help smiling as he thought of the incongruity of his position. He wondered what his aristocratic friends would say if he were captured and his story came to light. In his time he had impersonated a good many people, but never before had he had the honour of occupying such an exalted station. This was the last and most daring of all his adventures.

Minutes went by, and as Belton did not return, Carne found himself growing nervous. What could have become of him? He was in the act of going in search of him, when he appeared carrying in his hand the bunch of keys for which he had been sent. His master seized them eagerly.

"Why have you been so long?" he asked in a whisper. "I began to think something had gone wrong with you."

"I stayed to make our friend secure," the other answered. "He had well-nigh managed to get one of his hands free. Had he done so, he would have had the gag out of his mouth in no time, and have given the alarm. Then we should have been caught like rats in a trap."

"Are you quite sure he is secure now?" asked Carne anxiously.

"Quite," replied Belton. "I took good care of that."

"In that case we had better get to work on the safe without further delay. We have wasted too much time already, and every moment is an added danger."

Without more ado, Carne placed the most likely key in the lock and turned it. The bolt shot back, and the treasure chamber lay at his mercy.

The cabin was not a large one, but it was plain that every precaution had been taken to render it secure. The large safe which contained the Imperial plate, and which it was Carne's intention to rifle, occupied one entire side. It was of the latest design, and when Carne saw it he had to confess to himself that, expert craftsman as he was, it was one that would have required all his time and skill to open.

With the master key, however, it was the work of only a few seconds. The key was turned, the lever depressed, and then, with a slight pull, the heavy door swung forward. This done, it was seen that the interior was full to overflowing. Gold and silver plate of all sorts and descriptions, enclosed in bags of wash-leather and green baize, were neatly arranged inside. It was a haul such as even Carne had never had at his mercy before, and, now that he had got it, he was determined to make the most of it.

"Come, Belton," he said, "get these things out as quickly as possible and lay them on the floor. We can only carry away a certain portion of the plunder, so let us make sure that that portion is the best."

A few moments later the entire cabin was strewn with salvers, goblets, bowls, epergnes, gold and silver dishes, plates, cups, knives, forks, and almost every example of the goldsmith's art. In his choice Carne was not guided by what was handsomest or most delicate in workmanship or shape. Weight was his only standard. Silver he discarded altogether, for it was of less than no account. In something under ten minutes he had made his selection, and the stout canvas bags they had brought with them for that purpose were full to their utmost holding capacity.

"We can carry no more," said Carne to his faithful retainer, as they made the mouth of the last bag secure. "Pick up yours, and let us get back to the Emperor's state room."

Having locked the door of the cabin, they returned to the place whence they had started. There they found the unfortunate steward lying just as they had left him on the settee. Placing the bags he carried upon the ground, Carne crossed to him, and, before doing anything else, carefully examined the bonds with which he was secured.

Having done this, he went to the stern windows, and, throwing one open, stepped into the gallery outside. Fortunately for what he intended to do, it was still raining heavily, and in consequence the night was as dark as the most consummate conspirator could have desired. Returning to the room, he bade Belton help him carry the bags into the gallery, and, when this had been done, made fast the swivel hooks to the rings in the mouth of each.

"Take up your bags as quietly as possible," he said, "and lower them one by one into the water, but take care that they don't get entangled in the propeller. When you've done that, slip the rings at the other end of the lines through your belt, and buckle the latter tightly."

Belton did as he was ordered, and in a few moments the six bags were lying at the bottom of the sea.

"Now off with these wigs and things, and say when you're ready for a swim."

Their disguises having been discarded and thrown overboard, Carne and Belton clambered over the rails of the gallery and lowered themselves until their feet touched the water. Next moment they had both let go, and were swimming in the direction of Carne's own yacht.

It was at this period of their adventure that the darkness proved of such real service to them. By the time they had swum half a dozen strokes it would have needed a sharp pair of eyes to distinguish them as they rose and fell among the foam-crested waves. If, however, the storm had done them a good turn in saving them from notice, it came within an ace of doing them an ill service in another direction. Good swimmers though both Carne and Belton were, and they had proved it to each other's satisfaction in the seas of almost every known quarter of the globe, they soon found that it took all their strength to make headway now. By the time they reached their own craft, they were both completely exhausted. As Belton declared afterwards, he felt as if he could not have managed another twenty strokes even had his life depended on it.

At last, however, they reached the yacht's stern and clutched at the rope ladder which Carne had himself placed there before he had set out on the evening's excursion. In less time than it takes to tell, he had mounted it and gained the deck, followed by his faithful servant. They presented a sorry spectacle as they stood side by side at the taffrail, the water dripping from their clothes and pattering upon the deck.

"Thank goodness we are here at last," said Carne, as soon as he had recovered his breath sufficiently to speak. "Now slip off your belt, and hang it over this cleat with mine."

Belton did as he was directed, and then followed his master to the saloon companion ladder. Once below, they changed their clothes as quickly as possible, and having donned mackintoshes, returned to the deck, where it was still raining hard.

"Now," said Carne, "for the last and most important part of our evening's work. Let us hope the lines will prove equal to the demands we are about to make upon them."

As he said this, he took one of the belts from the cleat upon which he had placed it, and, having detached a line, began to pull it in, Belton following his example with another. Their hopes that they would prove equal to the confidence placed in them proved well founded, for, in something less than a quarter of an hour, the six bags, containing the Emperor of

Westphalia's magnificent gold plate, were lying upon the deck, ready to be carried below and stowed away in the secret place in which Carne had arranged to hide his treasure.

"Now, Belton," said Carne, as he pushed the panel back into its place, and pressed the secret spring that locked it, "I hope you're satisfied with what we have done. We've made a splendid haul, and you shall have your share of it. In the meantime, just get me to bed as quickly as you can, for I'm dead tired. When you've done so, be off to your own. Tomorrow morning you will have to go up to town to arrange with the bank authorities about my account."

Belton did as he was ordered, and half an hour later his master was safely in bed and asleep.

It was late next morning when he woke. He had scarcely breakfasted before the Earl of Amberley and Lord Orpington made their appearance over the side. To carry out the part he had arranged to play, he received them seated in his deck chair, his swaddled up right foot reclining on a cushion before him. On seeing his guests, he made as if he would rise, but they begged him to remain seated.

"I hope your ankle is better this morning," said Lord Orpington politely, as he took a chair beside his friend.

"Much better, thank you," Carne replied. "It was not nearly so serious as I feared. I hope to be able to hobble about a little this afternoon. And now tell me the news, if there is any."

"Do you mean to say that you have not heard the great news?" asked Lord Amberley, in a tone of astonishment.

"I have heard nothing," Carne replied. "Remember, I have not been ashore this morning, and I have been so busily engaged with the preparations for my departure tomorrow that I have not had time to look at my papers. Pray what is this news of which you speak with such bated breath?"

"Listen, and I'll tell you," Lord Orpington answered. "As you are aware, last night his Imperial Majesty the Emperor of Westphalia dined ashore, taking with him his *aide-de-camp*, Count Von Walzburg. They had not been gone from the launch more than half an hour when, to all intents and purposes, they reappeared, and the Emperor, who seemed much perturbed about something, gave the order to return to the yacht with all possible speed. It was very dark and raining hard at the time, and whoever the men may have been who did the thing, they were, at any rate, past masters in the art of disguise.

"Reaching the yacht, their arrival gave rise to no suspicion, for the officers are accustomed, as you know, to his Majesty's rapid comings and goings. The first lieutenant met them at the gangway, and declares that he had no sort of doubt but that it was his Sovereign. Face, voice, and manner were alike perfect. From his Majesty's behaviour he surmised that there was some sort of trouble brewing for somebody, and, as if to carry this impression still further, the Emperor bade him send the chief steward to him at once, and, at the same time, place the sentry, who had hitherto been guarding the treasure chamber, at the end of the great saloon, with instructions to allow no one to pass him, on any pretext whatever, until the chief steward had been examined and the Emperor himself gave permission. Then he went below to his cabin.

"Soon after this the steward arrived, and was admitted. Something seems to have excited the latter's suspicions, however, and he was about to give the alarm when he was seized from behind, thrown upon the floor, and afterwards gagged and bound. It soon became apparent what object the rascals had in view. They had caused the sentry at the door of the treasure chamber to be removed and placed where not only he could not hinder them in their work, but would prevent them from being disturbed. Having obtained the key of the room and safe from the chief steward's pocket, they set off to the cabin, ransacked it completely, and stole all that was heaviest and most valuable of his Majesty's wonderful plate from the safe."

"Good gracious!" said Carne. "I never heard of such a thing. Surely it's the most impudent robbery that has taken place for many years past. To represent the Emperor of Westphalia and his *aide-de-camp* so closely that they could deceive even the officers of his own yacht, and to take a sentry off one post and place him in such a position as to protect them while at their own nefarious work, seems to me the very height of audacity. But how did they get their booty and themselves away again? Gold plate, under the most favourable circumstances, is by no means an easy thing to carry."

As he asked this question, Carne lit another cigar with a hand as steady as a rock.

"They must have escaped in a boat that, it is supposed, was lying under the shelter of the stern gallery," replied Lord Amberley.

"And is the chief steward able to furnish the police with no clue as to their identity?"

"None whatever," replied Orpington. "He opines to the belief, however, that they are Frenchmen. One of them, the man who impersonated the Emperor, seems to have uttered an exclamation in that tongue."

"And when was the robbery discovered?"

"Only when the real Emperor returned to the vessel shortly after midnight. There was no launch to meet him, and he had to get Tremorden to take him off. You can easily imagine the surprise his arrival occasioned. It was intensified when they went below to find his Majesty's cabin turned upside down, the chief steward lying bound and gagged upon the sofa, and all that was most valuable of the gold plate missing."

"What an extraordinary story!"

"And now, having told you the news with which the place is ringing, we must be off about our business," said Orpington. "Is it quite certain that you are going to leave us tomorrow?"

"Quite, I am sorry to say," answered Carne. "I am going to ask as many of my friends as possible to do me the honour of lunching with me at one o'clock, and at five I shall weigh anchor and bid England goodbye. I shall have the pleasure of your company, I hope."

"I shall have much pleasure," said Orpington.

"And I also," replied Amberley.

"Then goodbye for the present. It's just possible I may see you again during the afternoon."

The luncheon next day was as brilliant a social gathering as the most fastidious in such matters could have desired. Everyone then in Cowes who had any claim to distinction was present, and several had undertaken the journey from town in order to say farewell to one who had made himself so popular during his brief stay in England. When Carne rose to reply to the toast of his health, proposed by the Prime Minister, it was observable that he was genuinely moved, as, indeed, were most of his hearers.

For the remainder of the afternoon his yacht's deck was crowded with his friends, all of whom expressed the hope that it might not be very long before he was amongst them once more.

To these kind speeches Carne invariably offered a smiling reply.

"I also trust it will not be long," he answered. "I have enjoyed my visit immensely, and you may be sure I shall never forget it as long as I live."

An hour later the anchor was weighed, and his yacht was steaming out of the harbour amid a scene of intense enthusiasm. As the Prime Minister had that afternoon informed him, in the public interest, the excitement of his departure was dividing the honours with the burglary of the Emperor of Westphalia's gold plate.

Carne stood beside his captain on the bridge, watching the little fleet of yachts until his eyes could no longer distinguish them. Then he turned to Belton, who had just joined him, and, placing his hand upon his shoulder, said:

"So much for our life in England, Belton, my friend. It has been glorious fun, and no one can deny that from a business point of view it has been eminently satisfactory. You, at least, should have no regrets."

"None whatever," answered Belton. "But I must confess I should like to know what they will say when the truth comes out."

Carne smiled sweetly as he answered:

"I think they'll say that, all things considered, I have won the right to call myself 'A Prince of Swindlers.'"

The Game Played in the Dark

Ernest Bramah

"IT'S A FUNNY thing, sir," said Inspector Beedel, regarding Mr. Carrados with the pensive respect that he always extended towards the blind amateur, "it's a funny thing, but nothing seems to go on abroad now but what you'll find some trace of it here in London if you take the trouble to look."

"In the right quarter," contributed Carrados.

"Why, yes," agreed the inspector. "But nothing comes of it nine times out of ten, because it's no one's particular business to look here or the thing's been taken up and finished from the other end. I don't mean ordinary murders or single-handed burglaries, of course, but" – a modest ring of professional pride betrayed the quiet enthusiast – "real First-Class Crimes."

"The State Antonio Five per cent. Bond Coupons?" suggested Carrados.

"Ah, you are right, Mr. Carrados." Beedel shook his head sadly, as though perhaps on that occasion someone ought to have looked. "A man has a fit in the inquiry office of the Agent-General for British Equatoria, and two hundred and fifty thousand pounds' worth of faked securities is the result in Mexico. Then look at that jade fylfot charm pawned for one-and-three down at the Basin and the use that could have been made of it in the Kharkov 'ritual murder' trial."

"The West Hampstead Lost Memory puzzle and the Baripur bomb conspiracy that might have been smothered if one had known."

"Quite true, sir. And the three children of that Chicago millionaire – Cyrus V. Bunting, wasn't it? – kidnapped in broad daylight outside the New York Lyric and here, three weeks later, the dumb girl who chalked the wall at Charing Cross. I remember reading once in a financial article that every piece of foreign gold had a string from it leading to Threadneedle Street. A figure of speech, sir, of course, but apt enough, I don't doubt. Well, it seems to me that every big crime done abroad leaves a fingerprint here in London – if only, as you say, we look in the right quarter."

"And at the right moment," added Carrados. "The time is often the present; the place the spot beneath our very noses. We take a step and the chance has gone for ever."

The inspector nodded and contributed a weighty monosyllable of sympathetic agreement. The most prosaic of men in the pursuit of his ordinary duties, it nevertheless subtly appealed to some half-dormant streak of vanity to have his profession taken romantically when there was no serious work on hand.

"No; perhaps not 'for ever' in one case in a thousand, after all," amended the blind man thoughtfully. "This perpetual duel between the Law and the Criminal has sometimes appeared to me in the terms of a game of cricket, inspector. Law is in the field; the Criminal at the wicket. If Law makes a mistake – sends down a loose ball or drops a catch – the Criminal scores a little or has another lease of life. But if *he* makes a mistake – if he lets a straight ball pass or spoons towards a steady man – he is done for. His mistakes are fatal; those of the Law are only temporary and retrievable."

"Very good, sir," said Mr. Beedel, rising – the conversation had taken place in the study at The Turrets, where Beedel had found occasion to present himself – "very apt indeed. I must remember that. Well, sir, I only hope that this 'Guido the Razor' lot will send a catch in our direction."

The 'this' delicately marked Inspector Beedel's instinctive contempt for Guido. As a craftsman he was compelled, on his reputation, to respect him, and he had accordingly availed himself of Carrados's friendship for a confabulation. As a man – he was a foreigner: worse, an Italian, and if left to his own resources the inspector would have opposed to his sinuous flexibility those rigid, essentially Britannia-metal, methods of the Force that strike the impartial observer as so ponderous, so amateurish and conventional, and, it must be admitted, often so curiously and inexplicably successful.

The offence that had circuitously brought 'il Rasojo' and his 'lot' within the cognizance of Scotland Yard outlines the kind of story that is discreetly hinted at by the society paragraphist of the day, politely disbelieved by the astute reader, and then at last laid indiscreetly bare in all its details by the inevitable princessly 'Recollections' of a generation later. It centred round an impending royal marriage in Vienna, a certain jealous 'Countess X.' (here you have the discretion of the paragrapher), and a document or two that might be relied upon (the aristocratic biographer will impartially sum up the contingencies) to play the deuce with the approaching nuptials. To procure the evidence of these papers the Countess enlisted the services of Guido, as reliable a scoundrel as she could probably have selected for the commission. To a certain point – to the abstraction of the papers, in fact – he succeeded, but it was with pursuit close upon his heels. There was that disadvantage in employing a rogue to do work that implicated roguery, for whatever moral right the Countess had to the property, her accomplice had no legal right whatever to his liberty. On half-a-dozen charges at least he could be arrested on sight in as many capitals of Europe. He slipped out of Vienna by the Nordbahn with his destination known, resourcefully stopped the express outside Czaslau and got away across to Chrudim. By this time the game and the moves were pretty well understood in more than one keenly interested quarter. Diplomacy supplemented justice and the immediate history of Guido became that of a fox hunted from covert to covert with all the familiar earths stopped against him. From Pardubitz he passed on to Glatz, reached Breslau and went down the Oder to Stettin. Out of the liberality of his employer's advances he had ample funds to keep going, and he dropped and rejoined his accomplices as the occasion ruled. A week's harrying found him in Copenhagen, still with no time to spare, and he missed his purpose there. He crossed to Malmo by ferry, took the connecting night train to Stockholm and the same morning sailed down the Saltsjon, ostensibly bound for Obo, intending to cross to Revel and so get back to central Europe by the less frequented routes. But in this move again luck was against him and receiving warning just in time, and by the mysterious agency that had so far protected him, he contrived to be dropped from the steamer by boat among the islands of the crowded Archipelago, made his way to Helsingfors and within forty-eight hours was back again on the Frihavnen with pursuit for the moment blinked and a breathing-time to the good.

To appreciate the exact significance of these wanderings it is necessary to recall the conditions. Guido was not zigzagging a course about Europe in an aimless search for the picturesque, still less inspired by any love of the melodramatic. To him every step was vital, each tangent or rebound the necessary outcome of his much-badgered plans. In his pocket reposed the papers for which he had run grave risks. The price agreed upon for the service was sufficiently lavish to make the risks worth taking time after time; but in order to consummate the transaction it was necessary that the booty should be put into his employer's hand. Halfway across Europe that employer was waiting with such patience as she could maintain, herself watched and shadowed at every step. The Countess X. was sufficiently exalted to be personally immune from the high-handed methods of her country's secret service, but every approach to her was tapped. The problem was for Guido to earn a long enough respite to enable him to communicate his position to the Countess and for her to go or to reach him by a trusty hand. Then the whole fabric of intrigue could fall to pieces, but so far Guido had been kept successfully on the run and in the meanwhile time was pressing.

"They lost him after the *Hutola*," Beedel reported, in explaining the circumstances to Max Carrados. "Three days later they found that he'd been back again in Copenhagen but by that time he'd flown. Now they're without a trace except the inference of these 'Orange peach blossom' agonies in *The Times*. But the Countess has gone hurriedly to Paris; and Lafayard thinks it all points to London."

"I suppose the Foreign Office is anxious to oblige just now?"

"I expect so, sir," agreed Beedel, "but, of course, my instructions don't come from that quarter. What appeals to *us* is that it would be a feather in our caps – they're still a little sore up at the Yard about Hans the Piper."

"Naturally," assented Carrados. "Well, I'll see what I can do if there is real occasion. Let me know anything, and, if you see your chance yourself, come round for a talk if you like on – today's Wednesday? – I shall be in at any rate on Friday evening."

Without being a precisian, the blind man was usually exact in such matters. There are those who hold that an engagement must be kept at all hazard: men who would miss a death-bed message in order to keep literal faith with a beggar. Carrados took lower, if more substantial, ground. "My word," he sometimes had occasion to remark, "is subject to contingencies, like everything else about me. If I make a promise it is conditional on nothing which seems more important arising to counteract it. That, among men of sense, is understood." And, as it happened, something did occur on this occasion.

He was summoned to the telephone just before dinner on Friday evening to receive a message personally. Greatorex, his secretary, had taken the call, but came in to say that the caller would give him nothing beyond his name – Brebner. The name was unknown to Carrados, but such incidents were not uncommon, and he proceeded to comply.

"Yes," he responded; "I am Max Carrados speaking. What is it?"

"Oh, it is you, sir, is it? Mr. Brickwill told me to get to you direct."

"Well, you are all right. Brickwill? Are you the British Museum?"

"Yes. I am Brebner in the Chaldean Art Department. They are in a great stew here. We have just found out that someone has managed to get access to the Second Inner Greek Room and looted some of the cabinets there. It is all a mystery as yet."

"What is missing?" asked Carrados.

"So far we can only definitely speak of about six trays of Greek coins – a hundred to a hundred and twenty, roughly."

"Important?"

The line conveyed a caustic bark of tragic amusement.

"Why, yes, I should say so. The beggar seems to have known his business. All fine specimens of the best period. Syracuse – Messana – Croton – Amphipolis. Eumenes – Evainetos – Kimons. The chief quite wept."

Carrados groaned. There was not a piece among them that he had not handled lovingly.

"What are you doing?" he demanded.

"Mr Brickwill has been to Scotland Yard, and, on advice, we are not making it public as yet. We don't want a hint of it to be dropped anywhere, if you don't mind, sir."

"That will be all right."

"It was for that reason that I was to speak with you personally. We are notifying the chief dealers and likely collectors to whom the coins, or some of them, may be offered at once if it is thought that we haven't found it out yet. Judging from the expertness displayed in the selection, we don't think that there is any danger of the lot being sold to a pawnbroker or a metal-dealer, so that we are running very little real risk in not advertising the loss."

"Yes; probably it is as well," replied Carrados. "Is there anything that Mr. Brickwill wishes me to do?"

"Only this, sir; if you are offered a suspicious lot of Greek coins, or hear of them, would you have a look – I mean ascertain whether they are likely to be ours, and if you think they are communicate with us and Scotland Yard at once."

"Certainly," replied the blind man. "Tell Mr. Brickwill that he can rely on me if any indication comes my way. Convey my regrets to him and tell him that I feel the loss quite as a personal one… I don't think that you and I have met as yet, Mr. Brebner?"

"No, sir," said the voice diffidently, "but I have looked forward to the pleasure. Perhaps this unfortunate business will bring me an introduction."

"You are very kind," was Carrados's acknowledgment of the compliment. "Any time… I was going to say that perhaps you don't know my weakness, but I have spent many pleasant hours over your wonderful collection. That ensures the personal element. Goodbye."

Carrados was really disturbed by the loss although his concern was tempered by the reflection that the coins would inevitably in the end find their way back to the Museum. That their restitution might involve ransom to the extent of several thousand pounds was the least poignant detail of the situation. The one harrowing thought was that the booty might, through stress or ignorance, find its way into the melting-pot. That dreadful contingency, remote but insistent, was enough to affect the appetite of the blind enthusiast.

He was expecting Inspector Beedel, who would be full of his own case, but he could not altogether dismiss the aspects of possibility that Brebner's communication opened before his mind. He was still concerned with the chances of destruction and a very indifferent companion for Greatorex, who alone sat with him, when Parkinson presented himself. Dinner was over but Carrados had remained rather longer than his custom, smoking his mild Turkish cigarette in silence.

"A lady wishes to see you, sir. She said you would not know her name, but that her business would interest you."

The form of message was sufficiently unusual to take the attention of both men.

"You don't know her, of course, Parkinson?" inquired his master.

For just a second the immaculate Parkinson seemed tongue-tied. Then he delivered himself in his most ceremonial strain.

"I regret to say that I cannot claim the advantage, sir," he replied.

"Better let me tackle her, sir," suggested Greatorex with easy confidence. "It's probably a sub."

The sportive offer was declined by a smile and a shake of the head. Carrados turned to his attendant.

"I shall be in the study, Parkinson. Show her there in three minutes. You stay and have another cigarette, Greatorex. By that time she will either have gone or have interested me."

In three minutes' time Parkinson threw open the study door.

"The lady, sir," he announced.

Could he have seen, Carrados would have received the impression of a plainly, almost dowdily, dressed young woman of buxom figure. She wore a light veil, but it was ineffective in concealing the unattraction of the face beneath. The features were swart and the upper lip darkened with the more than incipient moustache of the southern brunette. Worse remained, for a disfiguring rash had assailed patches of her skin. As she entered she swept the room and its occupant with a quiet but comprehensive survey.

"Please take a chair, Madame. You wished to see me?"

The ghost of a demure smile flickered about her mouth as she complied, and in that moment her face seemed less uncomely. Her eye lingered for a moment on a cabinet above the desk, and one might have noticed that her eye was very bright. Then she replied.

"You are Signor Carrados, in – in the person?"

Carrados made his smiling admission and changed his position a fraction – possibly to catch her curiously pitched voice the better.

"The great collector of the antiquities?"

"I do collect a little," he admitted guardedly.

"You will forgive me, Signor, if my language is not altogether good. When I live at Naples with my mother we let boardings, chiefly to Inglish and Amerigans. I pick up the words, but since I marry and go to live in Calabria my Inglish has gone all red – no, no, you say, rusty. Yes, that is it; quite rusty."

"It is excellent," said Carrados. "I am sure that we shall understand one another perfectly."

The lady shot a penetrating glance but the blind man's expression was merely suave and courteous. Then she continued:

"My husband is of name Ferraja – Michele Ferraja. We have a vineyard and a little property near Forenzana." She paused to examine the tips of her gloves for quite an appreciable moment. "Signor," she burst out, with some vehemence, "the laws of my country are not good at all."

"From what I hear on all sides," said Carrados, "I am afraid that your country is not alone."

"There is at Forenzana a poor labourer, Gian Verde of name," continued the visitor, dashing volubly into her narrative. "He is one day digging in the vineyard, the vineyard of my husband, when his spade strikes itself upon an obstruction. 'Aha,' says Gian, 'what have we here?' and he goes down upon his knees to see. It is an oil jar of red earth, Signor, such as was anciently used, and in it is filled with silver money.

"Gian is poor but he is wise. Does he call upon the authorities? No, no; he understands that they are all corrupt. He carries what he has found to my husband for he knows him to be a man of great honour.

"My husband also is of brief decision. His mind is made up. 'Gian,' he says, 'keep your mouth shut. This will be to your ultimate profit.' Gian understands, for he can trust my husband. He makes a sign of mutual implication. Then he goes back to the spade digging.

"My husband understands a little of these things but not enough. We go to the collections of Messina and Naples and even Rome and there we see other pieces of silver money, similar, and learn that they are of great value. They are of different sizes but most would cover a lira and of the thickness of two. On the one side imagine the great head of a pagan deity; on the other – oh, so many things I cannot remember what." A gesture of circumferential despair indicated the hopeless variety of design.

"A biga or quadriga of mules?" suggested Carrados. "An eagle carrying off a hare, a figure flying with a wreath, a trophy of arms? Some of those perhaps?"

"*Si, si bene*," cried Madame Ferraja. "You understand, I perceive, Signor. We are very cautious, for on every side is extortion and an unjust law. See, it is even forbidden to take these things out of the country, yet if we try to dispose of them at home they will be seized and we punished, for they are *tesoro trovato*, what you call treasure troven and belonging to the State – these coins which the industry of Gian discovered and which had lain for so long in the ground of my husband's vineyard."

"So you brought them to England?"

"*Si*, Signor. It is spoken of as a land of justice and rich nobility who buy these things at the highest prices. Also my speaking a little of the language would serve us here."

"I suppose you have the coins for disposal then? You can show them to me?"

"My husband retains them. I will take you, but you must first give *parola d'onore* of an English Signor not to betray us, or to speak of the circumstance to another."

Carrados had already foreseen this eventuality and decided to accept it. Whether a promise exacted on the plea of treasure trove would bind him to respect the despoilers of the British Museum was a point for subsequent consideration. Prudence demanded that he should investigate the offer at once and to cavil over Madame Ferraja's conditions would be fatal to that object. If the coins were, as there seemed little reason to doubt, the proceeds of the robbery, a modest ransom might be the safest way of preserving irreplaceable treasures, and in that case Carrados could offer his services as the necessary intermediary.

"I give you the promise you require, Madame," he accordingly declared.

"It is sufficient," assented Madame. "I will now take you to the spot. It is necessary that you alone should accompany me, for my husband is so distraught in this country, where he understands not a word of what is spoken, that his poor spirit would cry 'We are surrounded!' if he saw two strangers approach the house. Oh, he is become most dreadful in his anxiety, my husband. Imagine only, he keeps on the fire a cauldron of molten lead and he would not hesitate to plunge into it this treasure and obliterate its existence if he imagined himself endangered."

"So," speculated Carrados inwardly. "A likely precaution for a simple vine-grower of Calabria! Very well," he assented aloud, "I will go with you alone. Where is the place?"

Madame Ferraja searched in the ancient purse that she discovered in her rusty handbag and produced a scrap of paper.

"People do not understand sometimes my way of saying it," she explained. "*Sette*, Herringbone—"

"May I—?" said Carrados, stretching out his hand. He took the paper and touched the writing with his fingertips. "Oh yes, 7 Heronsbourne Place. That is on the edge of Heronsbourne Park, is it not?" He transferred the paper casually to his desk as he spoke and stood up. "How did you come, Madame Ferraja?"

Madame Ferraja followed the careless action with a discreet smile that did not touch her voice.

"By motor bus – first one then another, inquiring at every turning. Oh, but it was interminable," sighed the lady.

"My driver is off for the evening – I did not expect to be going out – but I will phone up a taxi and it will be at the gate as soon as we are." He despatched the message and then, turning to the house telephone, switched on to Greatorex.

"I'm just going round to Heronsbourne Park," he explained. "Don't stay, Greatorex, but if anyone calls expecting to see me, they can say that I don't anticipate being away more than an hour."

Parkinson was hovering about the hall. With quite novel officiousness he pressed upon his master a succession of articles that were not required. Over this usually complacent attendant the unattractive features of Madame Ferraja appeared to exercise a stealthy fascination, for a dozen times the lady detected his eyes questioning her face and a dozen times he looked guiltily away again. But his incongruities could not delay for more than a few minutes the opening of the door.

"I do not accompany you, sir?" he inquired, with the suggestion plainly tendered in his voice that it would be much better if he did.

"Not this time, Parkinson."

"Very well, sir. Is there any particular address to which we can telephone in case you are required, sir?"

"Mr Greatorex has instructions."

Parkinson stood aside, his resources exhausted. Madame Ferraja laughed a little mockingly as they walked down the drive.

"Your man-servant thinks I may eat you, Signor Carrados," she declared vivaciously.

Carrados, who held the key of his usually exact attendant's perturbation – for he himself had recognized in Madame Ferraja the angelic Nina Brun, of the Sicilian tetradrachm incident, from the moment she opened her mouth – admitted to himself the humour of her audacity. But it was not until half-an-hour later that enlightenment rewarded Parkinson. Inspector Beedel had just arrived and was speaking with Greatorex when the conscientious valet, who had been winnowing his memory in solitude, broke in upon them, more distressed than either had ever seen him in his life before, and with the breathless introduction: "It was the ears, sir! I have her ears at last!" poured out his tale of suspicion, recognition and his present fears.

In the meanwhile the two objects of his concern had reached the gate as the summoned taxicab drew up.

"Seven Heronsbourne Place," called Carrados to the driver.

"No, no," interposed the lady, with decision, "let him stop at the beginning of the street. It is not far to walk. My husband would be on the verge of distraction if he thought in the dark that it was the arrival of the police – who knows?"

"Brackedge Road, opposite the end of Heronsbourne Place," amended Carrados.

Heronsbourne Place had the reputation, among those who were curious in such matters, of being the most reclusive residential spot inside the four-mile circle. To earn that distinction it was, needless to say, a cul-de-sac. It bounded one side of Heronsbourne Park but did not at any point of its length give access to that pleasance. It was entirely devoted to unostentatious little houses, something between the villa and the cottage, some detached and some in pairs, but all possessing the endowment of larger, more umbrageous gardens than can generally be secured within the radius. The local house agent described them as "delightfully old-world" or "completely modernized" according to the requirement of the applicant.

The cab was dismissed at the corner and Madame Ferraja guided her companion along the silent and deserted way. She had begun to talk with renewed animation, but her ceaseless chatter only served to emphasize to Carrados the one fact that it was contrived to disguise.

"I am not causing you to miss the house with looking after me – No. 7, Madame Ferraja?" he interposed.

"No, certainly," she replied readily. "It is a little farther. The numbers are from the other end. But we are there. *Ecco!*"

She stopped at a gate and opened it, still guiding him. They passed into a garden, moist and sweet-scented with the distillate odours of a dewy evening. As she turned to relatch the gate the blind man endeavoured politely to anticipate her. Between them his hat fell to the ground.

"My clumsiness," he apologized, recovering it from the step. "My old impulses and my present helplessness, alas, Madame Ferraja!"

"One learns prudence by experience," said Madame sagely. She was scarcely to know, poor lady, that even as she uttered this trite aphorism, under cover of darkness and his hat, Mr. Carrados had just ruined his signet ring by blazoning a golden "7" upon her garden step to establish its identity if need be. A cul-de-sac that numbered from the closed end seemed to demand some investigation.

"Seldom," he replied to her remark. "One goes on taking risks. So we are there?"

Madame Ferraja had opened the front door with a latchkey. She dropped the latch and led Carrados forward along the narrow hall. The room they entered was at the back of the house, and from the position of the road it therefore overlooked the park. Again the door was locked behind them.

"The celebrated Mr. Carrados!" announced Madame Ferraja, with a sparkle of triumph in her voice. She waved her hand towards a lean, dark man who had stood beside the door as they entered. "My husband."

"Beneath our poor roof in the most fraternal manner," commented the dark man, in the same derisive spirit. "But it is wonderful."

"The even more celebrated Monsieur Dompierre, unless I am mistaken?" retorted Carrados blandly. "I bow on our first real meeting."

"You knew!" exclaimed the Dompierre of the earlier incident incredulously. "Stoker, you were right and I owe you a hundred lire. Who recognized you, Nina?"

"How should I know?" demanded the real Madame Dompierre crossly. "This blind man himself, by chance."

"You pay a poor compliment to your charming wife's personality to imagine that one could forget her so soon," put in Carrados. "And you a Frenchman, Dompierre!"

"You knew, Monsieur Carrados," reiterated Dompierre, "and yet you ventured here. You are either a fool or a hero."

"An enthusiast – it is the same thing as both," interposed the lady. "What did I tell you? What did it matter if he recognized? You see?"

"Surely you exaggerate, Monsieur Dompierre," contributed Carrados. "I may yet pay tribute to your industry. Perhaps I regret the circumstance and the necessity but I am here to make the best of it. Let me see the things Madame has spoken of, and then we can consider the detail of their price, either for myself or on behalf of others."

There was no immediate reply. From Dompierre came a saturnine chuckle and from Madame Dompierre a titter that accompanied a grimace. For one of the rare occasions in his life Carrados found himself wholly out of touch with the atmosphere of the situation. Instinctively he turned his face towards the other occupant of the room, the man addressed as 'Stoker', whom he knew to be standing near the window.

"This unfortunate business *has* brought me an introduction," said a familiar voice.

For one dreadful moment the universe stood still round Carrados. Then, with the crash and grind of overwhelming mental tumult, the whole strategy revealed itself, like the sections of a gigantic puzzle falling into place before his eyes.

There had been no robbery at the British Museum! That plausible concoction was as fictitious as the intentionally transparent tale of treasure trove. Carrados recognized now how ineffective the one device would have been without the other in drawing him – how convincing the two together – and while smarting at the humiliation of his plight he could not restrain a dash of admiration at the ingenuity – the accurately conjectured line of inference – of the plot. It was again the familiar artifice of the cunning pitfall masked by the clumsily contrived trap just beyond it. And straightway into it he had blundered!

"And this," continued the same voice, "is Carrados, Max Carrados, upon whose perspicuity a government – only the present government, let me in justice say – depends to outwit the undesirable alien! My country; O my country!"

"Is it really Monsieur Carrados?" inquired Dompierre in polite sarcasm. "Are you sure, Nina, that you have not brought a man from Scotland Yard instead?"

"*Basta!* He is here; what more do you want? Do not mock the poor sightless gentleman," answered Madame Dompierre, in doubtful sympathy.

"That is exactly what I was wondering," ventured Carrados mildly. "I am here – what more do you want? Perhaps you, Mr. Stoker—?"

"Excuse me. 'Stoker' is a mere colloquial appellation based on a trifling incident of my career in connection with a disabled liner. The title illustrates the childish weakness of the criminal classes for nicknames, together with their pitiable baldness of invention. My real name is Montmorency, Mr. Carrados – Eustace Montmorency."

"Thank you, Mr. Montmorency," said Carrados gravely. "We are on opposite sides of the table here tonight, but I should be proud to have been with you in the stokehold of the *Benvenuto.*"

"That was pleasure," muttered the Englishman. "This is business."

"Oh, quite so," agreed Carrados. "So far I am not exactly complaining. But I think it is high time to be told – and I address myself to you – why I have been decoyed here and what your purpose is."

Mr Montmorency turned to his accomplice.

"Dompierre," he remarked, with great clearness, "why the devil is Mr. Carrados kept standing?"

"Ah, oh, heaven!" exclaimed Madame Dompierre with tragic resignation, and flung herself down on a couch.

"*Scusi,*" grinned the lean man, and with burlesque grace he placed a chair for their guest's acceptance.

"Your curiosity is natural," continued Mr. Montmorency, with a cold eye towards Dompierre's antics, "although I really think that by this time you ought to have guessed the truth. In fact, I don't doubt that you have guessed, Mr. Carrados, and that you are only endeavouring to gain time. For that reason – because it will perhaps convince you that we have nothing to fear – I don't mind obliging you."

"Better hasten," murmured Dompierre uneasily.

"Thank you, Bill," said the Englishman, with genial effrontery. "I won't fail to report your intelligence to the Rasojo. Yes, Mr. Carrados, as you have already conjectured, it is the affair of the Countess X. to which you owe this inconvenience. You will appreciate the compliment that underlies your temporary seclusion, I am sure. When circumstances favoured our plans and London became the inevitable place of meeting, you and you alone stood in the way. We guessed that you would be consulted and we frankly feared your intervention. You were consulted. We know that Inspector Beedel visited you two days ago and he has no other case in hand. Your quiescence for just three days had to be obtained at any cost. So here you are."

"I see," assented Carrados. "And having got me here, how do you propose to keep me?"

"Of course that detail has received consideration. In fact we secured this furnished house solely with that in view. There are three courses before us. The first, quite pleasant, hangs on your acquiescence. The second, more drastic, comes into operation if you decline. The third – but really, Mr. Carrados, I hope you won't oblige me even to discuss the third. You will understand that it is rather objectionable for me to contemplate the necessity of two able-bodied men having to use even the smallest amount of physical compulsion towards one who is blind and helpless. I hope you will be reasonable and accept the inevitable."

"The inevitable is the one thing that I invariably accept," replied Carrados. "What does it involve?"

"You will write a note to your secretary explaining that what you have learned at 7 Heronsbourne Place makes it necessary for you to go immediately abroad for a few days. By the way, Mr. Carrados, although this is Heronsbourne Place it is *not* No. 7."

"Dear, dear me," sighed the prisoner. "You seem to have had me at every turn, Mr. Montmorency."

"An obvious precaution. The wider course of giving you a different street altogether we rejected as being too risky in getting you here. To continue: To give conviction to the message you will direct your man Parkinson to follow by the first boat-train tomorrow, with all the requirements for a short stay, and put up at Mascot's, as usual, awaiting your arrival there."

"Very convincing," agreed Carrados. "Where shall I be in reality?"

"In a charming though rather isolated bungalow on the south coast. Your wants will be attended to. There is a boat. You can row or fish. You will be run down by motor car and brought back to your own gate. It's really very pleasant for a few days. I've often stayed there myself."

"Your recommendation carries weight. Suppose, for the sake of curiosity, that I decline?"

"You will still go there but your treatment will be commensurate with your behaviour. The car to take you is at this moment waiting in a convenient spot on the other side of the park. We shall go down the garden at the back, cross the park, and put you into the car – anyway."

"And if I resist?"

The man whose pleasantry it had been to call himself Eustace Montmorency shrugged his shoulders.

"Don't be a fool," he said tolerantly. "You know who you are dealing with and the kind of risks we run. If you call out or endanger us at a critical point we shall not hesitate to silence you effectively."

The blind man knew that it was no idle threat. In spite of the cloak of humour and fantasy thrown over the proceedings, he was in the power of coolly desperate men. The window was curtained and shuttered against sight and sound, the door behind him locked. Possibly at that moment a revolver threatened him; certainly weapons lay within reach of both his keepers.

"Tell me what to write," he asked, with capitulation in his voice.

Dompierre twirled his mustachios in relieved approval. Madame laughed from her place on the couch and picked up a book, watching Montmorency over the cover of its pages. As for that gentleman, he masked his satisfaction by the practical business of placing on the table before Carrados the accessories of the letter.

"Put into your own words the message that I outlined just now."

"Perhaps to make it altogether natural I had better write on a page of the notebook that I always use," suggested Carrados.

"Do you wish to make it natural?" demanded Montmorency, with latent suspicion.

"If the miscarriage of your plan is to result in my head being knocked – yes, I do," was the reply.

"Good!" chuckled Dompierre, and sought to avoid Mr. Montmorency's cold glance by turning on the electric table-lamp for the blind man's benefit. Madame Dompierre laughed shrilly.

"Thank you, Monsieur," said Carrados, "you have done quite right. What is light to you is warmth to me – heat, energy, inspiration. Now to business."

He took out the pocket-book he had spoken of and leisurely proceeded to flatten it down upon the table before him. As his tranquil, pleasant eyes ranged the room meanwhile it was hard to believe that the shutters of an impenetrable darkness lay between them and the world. They rested for a moment on the two accomplices who stood beyond the table, picked out Madame Dompierre lolling on the sofa on his right, and measured the proportions of the long, narrow room. They seemed to note the positions of the window at the one end and the door almost at the other, and even to take into account the single pendent electric light which up till then had been the sole illuminant.

"You prefer pencil?" asked Montmorency.

"I generally use it for casual purposes. But not," he added, touching the point critically, "like this."

Alert for any sign of retaliation, they watched him take an insignificant penknife from his pocket and begin to trim the pencil. Was there in his mind any mad impulse to force conclusions with that puny weapon? Dompierre worked his face into a fiercer expression and touched reassuringly the handle of his knife. Montmorency looked on for a moment, then, whistling softly to himself, turned his back on the table and strolled towards the window, avoiding Madame Nina's pursuant eye.

Then, with overwhelming suddenness, it came, and in its form altogether unexpected.

Carrados had been putting the last strokes to the pencil, whittling it down upon the table. There had been no hasty movement, no violent act to give them warning; only the little blade had pushed itself nearer and nearer to the electric light cord lying there…and suddenly and instantly the room was plunged into absolute darkness.

"To the door, Dom!" shouted Montmorency in a flash. "I am at the window. Don't let him pass and we are all right."

"I am here," responded Dompierre from the door.

"He will not attempt to pass," came the quiet voice of Carrados from across the room. "You are now all exactly where I want you. You are both covered. If either moves an inch, I fire – and remember that I shoot by sound, not sight."

"But – but what does it mean?" stammered Montmorency, above the despairing wail of Madame Dompierre.

"It means that we are now on equal terms – three blind men in a dark room. The numerical advantage that you possess is counterbalanced by the fact that you are out of your element – I am in mine."

"Dom," whispered Montmorency across the dark space, "strike a match. I have none."

"I would not, Dompierre, if I were you," advised Carrados, with a short laugh. "It might be dangerous." At once his voice seemed to leap into a passion. "Drop that matchbox," he cried. "You are standing on the brink of your grave, you fool! Drop it, I say; let me hear it fall."

A breath of thought – almost too short to call a pause – then a little thud of surrender sounded from the carpet by the door. The two conspirators seemed to hold their breath.

"That is right." The placid voice once more resumed its sway. "Why cannot things be agreeable? I hate to have to shout, but you seem far from grasping the situation yet. Remember that I do not take the slightest risk. Also please remember, Mr. Montmorency, that the action even of a hair-trigger automatic scrapes slightly as it comes up. I remind you of that for your own good, because if you are so ill-advised as to think of trying to pot me in the dark, that noise gives me a fifth of a second start of you. Do you by any chance know Zinghi's in Mercer Street?"

"The shooting gallery?" asked Mr. Montmorency a little sulkily.

"The same. If you happen to come through this alive and are interested you might ask Zinghi to show you a target of mine that he keeps. Seven shots at twenty yards, the target indicated by four watches, none of them so loud as the one you are wearing. He keeps it as a curiosity."

"I wear no watch," muttered Dompierre, expressing his thought aloud.

"No, Monsieur Dompierre, but you wear a heart, and that not on your sleeve," said Carrados. "Just now it is quite as loud as Mr. Montmorency's watch. It is more central too – I shall not have to allow any margin. That is right; breathe naturally" – for the unhappy Dompierre had given a gasp of apprehension. "It does not make any difference to me, and after a time holding one's breath becomes really painful."

"Monsieur," declared Dompierre earnestly, "there was no intention of submitting you to injury, I swear. This Englishman did but speak within his hat. At the most extreme you would have been but bound and gagged. Take care: killing is a dangerous game."

"For you – not for me," was the bland rejoinder. "If you kill me you will be hanged for it. If I kill you I shall be honourably acquitted. You can imagine the scene – the sympathetic court – the recital of your villainies – the story of my indignities. Then with stumbling feet and groping hands the helpless blind man is led forward to give evidence. Sensation! No, no, it isn't really fair but I can kill you both with absolute certainty and Providence will be saddled with all the responsibility. Please don't fidget with your feet, Monsieur Dompierre. I know that you aren't moving but one is liable to make mistakes."

"Before I die," said Montmorency – and for some reason laughed unconvincingly in the dark – "before I die, Mr. Carrados, I should really like to know what has happened to the light. That, surely, isn't Providence?"

"Would it be ungenerous to suggest that you are trying to gain time? You ought to know what has happened. But as it may satisfy you that I have nothing to fear from delay, I don't mind telling you. In my hand was a sharp knife – contemptible, you were satisfied, as a weapon; beneath my nose the 'flex' of the electric lamp. It was only necessary for me to draw the one across the other and the system was short-circuited. Every lamp on that fuse is cut off and in the distributing-box in the hall you will find a burned-out wire. You, perhaps – but Monsieur Dompierre's experience in plating ought to have put him up to simple electricity."

"How did you know that there is a distributing-box in the hall?" asked Dompierre, with dull resentment.

"My dear Dompierre, why beat the air with futile questions?" replied Max Carrados. "What does it matter? Have it in the cellar if you like."

"True," interposed Montmorency. "The only thing that need concern us now—"

"But it is in the hall – nine feet high," muttered Dompierre in bitterness. "Yet he, this blind man—"

"The only thing that need concern us," repeated the Englishman, severely ignoring the interruption, "is what you intend doing in the end, Mr. Carrados?"

"The end is a little difficult to foresee," was the admission. "So far, I am all for maintaining the *status quo*. Will the first grey light of morning find us still in this impasse? No, for between us we have condemned the room to eternal darkness. Probably about daybreak Dompierre will drop off to sleep and roll against the door. I, unfortunately mistaking his intention, will send a bullet through—Pardon, Madame, I should have remembered – but pray don't move."

"I protest, Monsieur—"

"Don't protest; just sit still. Very likely it will be Mr. Montmorency who will fall off to sleep the first after all."

"Then we will anticipate that difficulty," said the one in question, speaking with renewed decision. "We will play the last hand with our cards upon the table if you like. Nina, Mr. Carrados will not injure you whatever happens – be sure of that. When the moment comes you will rise—"

"One word," put in Carrados with determination. "My position is precarious and I take no risks. As you say, I cannot injure Madame Dompierre, and you two men are therefore my hostages for her good behaviour. If she rises from the couch you, Dompierre, fall. If she advances another step Mr. Montmorency follows you."

"Do nothing rash, *carissima*," urged her husband, with passionate solicitude. "You might get hit in place of me. We will yet find a better way."

"You dare not, Mr. Carrados!" flung out Montmorency, for the first time beginning to show signs of wear in this duel of the temper. "He dare not, Dompierre. In cold blood and unprovoked! No jury would acquit you!"

"Another who fails to do you justice, Madame Nina," said the blind man, with ironic gallantry. "The action might be a little high-handed, one admits, but when you, appropriately clothed and in your right complexion, stepped into the witness-box and I said: 'Gentlemen of the jury, what is my crime? That I made Madame Dompierre a widow!' can you doubt their gratitude and my acquittal? Truly my countrymen are not all bats or monks, Madame." Dompierre was breathing with perfect freedom now, while from the couch came the sounds of stifled emotion, but whether the lady was involved in a paroxysm of sobs or of laughter it might be difficult to swear.

* * *

It was perhaps an hour after the flourish of the introduction with which Madame Dompierre had closed the door of the trap upon the blind man's entrance.

The minutes had passed but the situation remained unchanged, though the ingenuity of certainly two of the occupants of the room had been tormented into shreds to discover a means of turning it to their advantage. So far the terrible omniscience of the blind man in the dark and the respect for his markmanship with which his coolness had inspired them, dominated the group. But one strong card yet remained to be played, and at last the moment came upon which the conspirators had pinned their despairing hopes.

There was the sound of movement in the hall outside, not the first about the house, but towards the new complication Carrados had been strangely unobservant. True, Montmorency had talked rather loudly, to carry over the dangerous moments. But now there came an unmistakable step and to the accomplices it could only mean one thing. Montmorency was ready on the instant.

"Down, Dom!" he cried, "throw yourself down! Break in, Guido. Break in the door. We are held up!"

There was an immediate response. The door, under the pressure of a human battering-ram, burst open with a crash. On the threshold the intruders – four or five in number – stopped starkly for a moment, held in astonishment by the extraordinary scene that the light from the hall, and of their own bull's-eyes, revealed.

Flat on their faces, to present the least possible surface to Carrados's aim, Dompierre and Montmorency lay extended beside the window and behind the door. On the couch, with her head buried beneath the cushions, Madame Dompierre sought to shut out the sight and sound of violence. Carrados – Carrados had not moved, but with arms resting on the table and fingers placidly locked together he smiled benignly on the new arrivals. His attitude, compared with the extravagance of those around him, gave the impression of a complacent modern deity presiding over some grotesque ceremonial of pagan worship.

"So, Inspector, you could not wait for me, after all?" was his greeting.

Dr. Lartius

John Buchan

> *The idols have spoken vanity, and the diviners have seen a lie, and have told*
> *false dreams; they comfort in vain; therefore they went their way as a flock.*
> **Zechariah x. 2.**

IN THE EARLY SPRING Palliser-Yeates had 'flu, and had it so badly that he was sent to recruit for a fortnight on the Riviera. There, being profoundly bored, he wrote out and sent to us this story. He would not give the name of the chief figure, because he said he was still a serving soldier, and his usefulness, he hoped, was not exhausted. The manuscript arrived opportunely, for some of us had just been trying, without success, to extract from Sandy Arbuthnot the truth of certain of his doings about which rumour had been busy.

Chapter I

IN THE second week of January 1917, a modest brass plate appeared on a certain door in Regent Street, among modistes and hat-makers and vendors of cosmetics. It bore the name of Dr. S. Lartius. On the third floor were the rooms to which the plate was the signpost, a pleasant set, newly decorated with powder-blue wallpapers, curtains of orange velveteen, and sham marqueterie. The milliners' girls who frequented that staircase might have observed, about eleven in the morning, the figure of Dr. Lartius arriving. They did not see him leave, for they had flown to their suburban homes long before the key turned of an evening in the doctor's door.

He was a slim young man of the middle height, who held himself straighter than the usual run of sedentary folk. His face was very pale, and his mop of hair and fluffy beard were black as jet. He wore large tortoiseshell spectacles, and, when he removed them, revealed slightly protuberant and very bright hazel eyes, which contrasted oddly with his pallor. Had such a figure appeared on the stage, the gallery experts, familiar with stage villains, would have unhesitatingly set him down as the anarchist from Moscow about to assassinate the oppressive nobleman and thereby give the hero his chance. But his clothes were far too good for that part. He wore a shiny top-hat and an expensive fur coat, and his neat morning coat, fine linen, unobtrusive black tie and pearl pin suggested the high finance rather than the backstairs of revolution.

It appeared that Dr. Lartius did a flourishing business. Suddenly London had begun to talk about him. First there were the people that matter, the people who are ever on the hunt for a new sensation and must always be in the first flight of any fad. Lady A told the Duchess of B about a wonderful new man who really had Power – no ordinary vulgar spiritualist, but a true Seeker and Thinker. Mr. D, that elderly gossip, carried the story through many circles, and it grew with the telling. The curious began to cultivate Dr. Lartius, and soon the fame of him came to the ears of those who were not curious, only anxious or broken-hearted; and because the last were a great multitude, and were ready to give their all for consolation, there was a busy coming and going all day on Dr. Lartius's staircase.

His way with his clients was interesting. He had no single method of treatment, and varied his manner according to the motives of the inquirer. The merely inquisitive he entertained with toys. "I am no professor of an art," he told them laughingly. "I am a student, groping on the skirts of great mysteries." And to the more intelligent he would propound an illustration. "Take the mathematics of the Fourth Dimension," he would say. "I can show you a few simple mechanical puzzles, which cannot be explained except by the aid of abstruse mathematics, and not always then. But these puzzles tell you nothing about the Fourth Dimension, except that there is a world about us inexplicable on the rule of three dimensions. It is the same with my toys – my crystal ball, my pool of ink, my star-maps, even those superinduced moods of abstraction in which we seem to hear the noise of wings and strange voices. They only tell me that there is more in earth and heaven than is dreamed of in man's philosophy."

But his toys were wonderful. The idle ladies who went there for a thrill were not disappointed. In the dusky room, among the strange rosy lights, their hearts seemed to be always fluttering on the brink of a revelation, and they came away excited and comforted, for Dr. Lartius was an adept at delicate flattery. Fortune-telling in the ordinary sense there was none, but this young man seemed to have an uncanny knowledge of private affairs, which he used so discreetly that even those who had most reason to desire secrecy were never disquieted. For such entertainments he charged fees – high fees, as the fur coat and the pearl pin required. "You wish to be amused," he would say, "and it is right that you should pay me for it."

Even among the idle clients there was a sprinkling of the earnest. With these he had the air of a master towards initiates; they were fellow-pilgrims with him on the Great Road. He would talk to them by the hour, very beautifully, in a soft musical voice. He would warn them against charlatans, those who sought to prostitute a solemn ritual to purposes of vulgar gain. He would unroll for them the history of the great mystics and tell of that secret science known to the old adepts, which had been lost for ages, and was now being recovered piecemeal. These were the most thrilling hours of all, and the fame of Dr. Lartius grew great in the drawing rooms of the Elect. "And he's such a gentleman, my dear – so well-bred and sympathetic and unworldly and absolutely honest!"

But from others he took no fees. The sad-faced women, mostly in black, who sat in his great velvet chair and asked broken questions, found a very different Dr. Lartius. He was no longer fluent and silver-tongued; sometimes he seemed almost embarrassed. He would repeat most earnestly that he was only a disciple, a seeker, not a master of hidden things. On such occasions the toys were absent, and if some distracted mother sought knowledge that way she was refused. He rarely had anything definite to impart. When Lady H.'s only son was about to exchange from the cavalry to the Foot Guards and his mother wanted to know how the step would affect his chances of survival, she got nothing beyond the obvious remark that this was an infantry war and he would have a better prospect of seeing fighting. Very rarely, he spoke out. Once to Mrs. K., whose boy was a prisoner, he gave a very full account of life in a German prison-camp, so that, in the absence of letters, her imagination had henceforth something to bite on. Usually his visitors were too embarrassed to be observant, but one or two noted that he was uncommonly well informed about the British Army. He never made a mistake about units, and seemed to know a man's battalion before he was told it. And when mothers poured out details to him – for from the talk of soldiers on leave and epistolary indiscretions a good deal of information circulated about London – he now and then took notes.

Yet, though they got little from him that was explicit, these visitors, as a rule, went away comforted. Perhaps it was his gentle soothing manner. Perhaps, as poor Lady M. said, it was that he seemed so assured of the spiritual life that they felt that their anxieties were only tiny eddies on the edge of a great sea of peace. At any rate, it was the afflicted even more than the idly curious who spoke well of Dr. Lartius.

Sometimes he had masculine clients – fathers of fighting sons, who said they came on their wives' behalf, elderly retired Generals who preferred spiritualism to golf, boys whose nerves were in tatters and wanted the solace which in other ages and lands would have been found in the confessional. With these last Dr. Lartius became a new man. He would take off his spectacles and look them in the face with his prominent lustrous eyes, and talk to them with a ring in his pleasant voice. It was not what he said so much, perhaps, as his manner of saying it, but he seemed to have a singular power over boys just a little bit loose from their moorings. "Queer thing," said one of these, "but one would almost think you had been a soldier yourself." Dr. Lartius had smiled and resumed his spectacles. "I am a soldier, but in a different war. I fight with the sword of the spirit against the hidden things of darkness."

Towards the end of March the brass plate suddenly disappeared. There was a great fluttering in the dovecotes of the Elect when the news went round that there had been trouble with the police. It had been over the toys, of course, and the taking of fees. The matter never came into court, but Dr. Lartius had been warned to clear out, and he obeyed. Many ladies wrote indignant letters to the Home Secretary about persecution, letters which cited ominous precedents from the early history of the Christian Church.

But in April came consolation. The rumour spread that the Seekers were not to lose their guide. Mr. Greatheart would still be available for the comforting of pilgrims. A plate with the name of Dr. S. Lartius reappeared in a quiet street in Mayfair. But for the future there would be no question of fees. It was generally assumed that a few devout women had provided a fund for the sustenance of the prophet.

In May his fame was greater than ever. One evening Lady Samplar, the most ardent of his devotees, spoke of him to a certain General who was a power in the land. The General was popular among the women of her set, but a notorious scoffer. Perhaps this was the secret of his popularity, for each hoped to convert him.

"I want you to see him yourself," she said. "Only once. I believe in him so firmly that I am willing to stake everything on one interview. Promise me you will let me take you. I only want you to see him and talk to him for ten minutes. I want you to realise his unique personality, for if you once feel him you will scoff no more."

The General laughed, shrugged his shoulders, but allowed himself to be persuaded. So it came about that one afternoon in early June he accompanied Lady Samplar to the flat in Mayfair. "You must go in alone," she told him in the anteroom. "I have spoken about you to him, and he is expecting you. I will wait for you here."

For half an hour the General was closeted with Dr. Lartius. When he returned to the lady his face was red and wrathful.

"That's the most dangerous fellow in London," he declared. "Look here, Mollie, you and your friends have been playing the fool about that man. He's a German spy, if there ever was one. I caught him out, for I trapped him into speaking German. You say he's a Swiss, but I swear no Swiss ever spoke German just as he speaks it. The man's a Bavarian. I'll take my oath he is!"

It was a very depressed and rather frightened lady who gave him tea a little later in her drawing room.

"That kind of sweep is far too clever for you innocents," she was told. "There he has been for months pumping you all without your guessing it. You say he's a great comfort to the mourners. I daresay he is, but the poor devils tell him everything that's in their heads. That man has a unique chance of knowing the inside of the British Army. And how has he used his knowledge? That's what I want to know."

"What are you going to do about it?" she quavered.

"I'm going to have him laid by the heels," he said grimly, as he took his departure. "Interned – or put up against a wall, if we can get the evidence. I tell you he's a Boche pure and simple – not that there's much purity and simplicity about him."

The General was as good as his word, but in one matter he was wrong. The credentials of the prophet's Swiss nationality were good enough. There was nothing for it but to deport him as an undesirable, so one fine morning Dr. S. Lartius got his marching orders. He made no complaint, and took a dignified farewell of his friends. But the Faithful were not silent, and the friendship between Lady Samplar and the General died a violent death. The thing got into the papers, Dr. Lartius figured in many unrecognisable portraits in the press, and a bishop preached a sermon in a City church about the worship of false gods.

Chapter II

AS DR. LARTIUS, closely supervised by the French police, pursued his slow and comfortless journey to the Swiss frontier, he was cheered by several proofs that his fame had gone abroad and that he was not forgotten. At Paris there were flowers in his dingy hotel bedroom, the gift of an unknown admirer, and a little note of encouragement in odd French. At Dijon he received from a strange lady another note telling him that his friends were awaiting him in Berne. When he crossed the border at Pontarlier there were more flowers and letters. The young man paid little attention to such tributes. He spent the journey in quiet reading and meditation, and when he reached Berne did not seem to expect anyone to greet him, but collected his luggage and drove off unobtrusively to a hotel.

He had not been there an hour when a card was brought to him bearing the name of Ernst Ulrici, Doctor of Philosophy in the University of Bonn.

"Dr. Lartius," said the visitor, a middle-aged man with a peaked grey beard and hair cut en brosse. "It is an honour to make your acquaintance. We have heard of your fine work and your world-moulding discoveries."

The young man bowed gravely. "I am only a seeker," he said. "I make no claim to be a master – yet. I am only a little way on the road to enlightenment."

"We have also heard," said the other, "of how shamelessly the British Government has persecuted learning in your person."

The reply was a smile and a shrug. "I make no complaint. It is natural that my studies should seem foolishness to the children of this world."

Dr. Ulrici pressed him further on the matter of Britain, but could wake no bitterness.

"There is war today," he said at last. "You are of German race. Your sympathies are with us?"

"I have no nationality," was the answer. "All men are my brothers. But I would fain see this bloodshed at an end."

"How will it end?" came the question.

"I am no prophet," said Dr. Lartius. "Yet I can tell that Germany will win, but how I can tell I cannot tell."

The conversation lasted long and explored many subjects. The German led it cunningly to small matters, and showed a wide acquaintance with the young man's science. He learned that much of his work had been done with soldiers and soldiers' kin, and that in the process of it he had heard many things not published in the newspapers. But when he hinted, ever so delicately, that he would be glad to buy the knowledge, a flush passed over the other's pale face and his voice sharpened.

"I am no spy," he said. "I do not prostitute my art for hire. It matters nothing to me which side wins, but it matters much that I keep my soul clean."

So Dr. Ulrici tried another tack. He spoke of the mysteries of the craft, and lured the young man into the confession of hopes and ideals. There could be no communion with the dead, he was told, until communion had first been perfected with the spirits of the living. "Let the time come," said Dr. Lartius, "when an unbroken fellowship can be created between souls separated by great tracts of space, and the key has been found. Death is an irrelevant accident. The spirit is untouched by it. Find the trait d'union between spirits still in their fleshly envelope, and it can be continued when that envelope is shed."

"And you have progressed in this affair?" asked Ulrici, with scepticism in his tone.

"A few stages," said the other, and in the ardour of exposition he gave proofs. He had clients, he said, with whom he had established the mystic catena. He could read their thoughts even now, though they were far away, share in their mental changes, absorb the knowledge which they acquired.

"Soldiers?" asked the German.

"Some were soldiers. All were the kin of soldiers."

But Ulrici was still cold. "That is a great marvel," he said, "and not easy to believe."

Dr. Lartius was fired. "I will give you proofs," he said, with unwonted passion in his voice. "You can test them at your leisure. I know things which have not yet come to pass, though no man has spoken to me of them. How do I know them? Because they have come within the cognisance of minds attuned to my own."

For a moment he seemed to hesitate. Then he spoke of certain matters – a little change in the method of artillery barrages, a readjustment in the organisation of the British Air Force, an alteration in certain British commands.

"These may be trivial things," he said. "I do not know. I have no technical skill. But they are still in the future. I offer them to you as proofs of my knowledge."

"So?" said the other. "They are indeed small things, but they will do for a test…"

Then he spoke kindly, considerately, of Dr. Lartius's future.

"I think I will go to Munich," said the young man. "Once I studied at the University there, and I love the bright city. They are a sympathetic people and respect knowledge."

Dr. Ulrici rose to take his leave. "It may be I am able to further your plans, my friend," he said.

Late that night in a big sitting room in another hotel, furnished somewhat in the style of an official bureau, Ulrici talked earnestly with another man, a heavy, bearded man, who wore the air of a prosperous bagman, but who was addressed with every token of respect.

"This Lartius fellow puzzles me. He is a transparent fanatic, with some odd power in him that sets him above others of his kidney. I fear he will not be as useful to us as we had hoped. If only we had known of him sooner and could have kept him in England."

"He can't go back, I suppose?"

"Impossible, sir. But there is still a chance. He has some wild theory that he has established a link with various people, and so acquires automatically whatever new knowledge they gain. Some of these people are soldiers. He has told me things – little things – that I may test this power of his. I am no believer in the spiritualist mumbo-jumbo, but I have lived long enough not to reject a thing because it is new and strange. About that we shall see. If there is anything in it there will be much. Meantime I keep closely in touch with him."

"What is he going to do?"

"He wants to go to Munich. I am in favour of permitting it, sir. Our good Bavarians are somewhat light in the head, and are always seeking a new thing. They want a little ghostly consolation at present, and this man will give it them. He believes most firmly in our German victory."

The other yawned and flung away the end of his cigar. "The mountebank seems to have some glimmerings of sense," he said.

Chapter III

SO IT CAME ABOUT that in August of the year 1917 Dr. Lartius was settled in comfortable rooms off the Garmischstrasse in the Bavarian capital, and a new plate of gun-metal and oxidised silver, lettered in the best style of art nouveau, advertised his name to the citizens of Munich.

Fortune still attended the young man, for, as in London, he seemed to spring at once into fame. Within a week of his arrival people were talking about him, and in a month his chambers were crowded. Perhaps his friend Ulrici had spoken a word in the right place. It was the great season before Caporetto, and Dr. Lartius spoke heartening things to his clients. Victory was near and the days of glory; but when asked about the date of peace he was coy. Peace would come, but not yet; for the world there was another winter of war.

His methods were the same as those which had captured Lady Samplar and her friends. To the idly curious he showed toys; to the emotional he spoke nobly of the life of the spirit and the locked doors of hidden knowledge which were now almost ajar. Rich ladies, bored with the dullness of the opera season and the scarcity of men, found in him a new interest in life. To the sorrowful he gave the comfort which he had given to his London circle – no more. His personality seemed to exhale hope and sympathy, and mourners, remembering his pleasant voice and compelling eyes, departed with a consolation which they could not define.

That was for the ordinary run of clients; but there were others – fellow-students they professed themselves – to whom he gave stronger meat. He preached his doctrine of the mystic community of thought and knowledge between souls far apart, and now and then he gave proofs such as he had given to Ulrici. It would appear that these proofs stood the test, for his reputation grew prodigiously. He told them little things about forthcoming changes in the Allied armies, and the event always proved him right. They were not things that mattered greatly, but if he could disclose trivialities some day his method might enable him to reveal a mighty secret. So more than one Generalstabschef came to sit with him in his twilit room.

About once a month he used to go back to Berne, and was invariably met at the station by Ulrici. He had been given a very special passport, which took him easily and expeditiously over the frontier, and he had no trouble with station commandants. In these visits he would be closeted with Ulrici for hours. Occasionally he would slip out of his hotel at night for a little, and when Ulrici heard of it he shrugged his shoulders and laughed. "He is young," he would say with a leer. "Even a prophet must have his amusements." But he was wrong, for Dr. Lartius had not the foibles he suspected.

The winter passed slowly, and the faces in the Munich streets grew daily more pinched and wan, clothing more shabby and boots more down at heel. But there was always comfort for seekers in the room in the Garmischstrasse. Whoever lost faith it was not Dr. Lartius. Peace was coming, and his hearers judged that he had forgotten his scientific detachment from all patriotisms and was becoming a good German.

Then in February of the New Year came the rumour of the great advance preparing in the West. The High Command had promised speedy and final victory in return for a little more endurance. Dr. Lartius seemed to have the first news of it. "It is Peace," he said, "Peace before winter"; and his phrase was repeated everywhere and became a popular watchword. So, when the news came at the end of March of the retreat of the French and English to the gates of Amiens, the hungry people smiled to each other and said, "He is right, as always. It is Peace." Few now cared much about victory, except the high officers and the very rich, but on Peace all were determined.

April passed into May, and ere the month was out came glorious tidings. Ludendorff had reached the Marne, and was within range of Paris. About this time his closest disciples marked a change in Dr. Lartius. He seemed to retire into himself, and to be struggling with some vast revelation. His language was less intelligible, but far more impressive. Ulrici came up from Berne to see him, for he had stopped for some months his visits to Switzerland. There were those who said his health was breaking, others that he was now, in very truth, looking inside the veil. This latter was the general view, and the fame of the young man became a superstition.

"You tell us little now about our enemies," Ulrici complained.

"*Mystica catena rupta est*," Dr. Lartius quoted sadly. "My friends are your enemies, and they are suffering. Their hearts and nerves are breaking. Therefore the link is thin and I cannot feel their thoughts. That is why I am so sad, for against my will the sorrow of my friends clouds me."

Ulrici laughed in his gross way. "Then the best omen for us is that you fall into melancholia? When you cut your throat we shall know that we have won."

Yet Ulrici was not quite happy. The young prophet was in danger of becoming a Frankenstein's monster, which he could not control. For his popular fame was now a thing to marvel at. It had gone abroad through Germany, and to all the fighting fronts, and the phrase linked to it was that of 'Peace before winter'. Peace had become a conviction, an obsession. Ulrici and his friends would have preferred the word to be 'Victory'.

In the early days of July a distinguished visitor came from Berlin to the Garmischstrasse. He was an Erster Generalstabsoffizier, high in the confidence of the Supreme Command. He sat in the shaded room and asked an urgent question.

"I am not a Delphian oracle," said Dr. Lartius, "and I do not prophesy. But this much I can tell you. The hearts of your enemies have become like water, and they have few reserves left. I am not a soldier, so you can judge better than I. You say you are ready to strike with a crushing force. If you leave your enemies leisure they will increase and their hearts may recover."

"That is my view," said the soldier. "You have done much for the German people in the past, sir. Have you no word now to encourage them?"

"There will be peace before winter. This much I can tell, but how I know I cannot tell."

"But on what terms?"

"That depends upon your armies," was the oracular reply.

The staff officer had been gazing intently at the speaker. Now he rose and switched on the electric light.

"Will you oblige me by taking off your glasses, sir?" he asked, and there was the sharpness of command in his voice.

Dr. Lartius removed his spectacles, and for some seconds the two men looked at each other. "I thank you," said the soldier at last. "For a moment I thought we had met before. You reminded me of a man I knew long ago. I was mistaken."

After that it was noted by all that the melancholy of Dr. Lartius increased. His voice was saddened, and dejection wrapped him like a cloud. Those of the inner circle affected to see in this a good omen. "He is *en rapport* with his English friends," they said. "He cannot help himself, and their despair is revealed in him. The poor Lartius! He is suffering for the sins of our enemies." But the great public saw only the depression, and as August matured, and bad news filtered through the land, it gave their spirits an extra push downhill.

In those weeks only one word came from the Garmischstrasse. It was "Peace – peace before winter." The phrase became the universal formula whispered wherever people spoke their minds. It ran like lightning through the camps and along the fronts, and in every workshop and tavern. It became a passion, a battle-cry. The Wise Doctor of Munich had said it. Peace before winter – Peace at all costs – only Peace.

In September Ulrici was in communication with a certain bureau in Berlin. "The man is honest enough, but he is mad. He has served his purpose. It is time to suppress him." Berlin agreed, and one morning Ulrici departed from Berne.

But when he reached the Garmischstrasse he found the flamboyant plate unscrewed from the door and the pleasant rooms deserted.

For a day or two before Dr. Lartius had been behaving oddly. He gave out that he was ill, and could not receive, but he was very busy indoors with his papers. Then late one evening, after a conversation on the telephone with the railway people, he left his rooms, with no luggage but a small dressing-case, and took the night train for Innsbruck. His admirable passport franked him anywhere. From Innsbruck he travelled to the Swiss frontier, and when he crossed it, in the darkness of the September evening and in an empty carriage, he made a toilet which included the shaving of his silky black beard. He was whistling softly and seemed to have recovered his spirits. At Berne he did not seek his usual hotel, but went to an unfrequented place in a back street, where, apparently, he was well known. There he met during the course of the day various people, and their conversation was not in the German tongue.

That night he again took train, but it was westward to Lausanne and the French border.

Chapter IV

IN THE EARLY DAYS of November, when the Allies were approaching Maubeuge and Sedan, and the German plenipotentiaries were trying to dodge the barrage and get speech with Foch, two British officers were sitting in a little room at Versailles. One was the General we have already met, the quondam friend of Lady Samplar. The other was a slim young man who wore the badges of a lieutenant-colonel and the gorget patches of the staff. He had a pale face shaven clean, black hair cut very short, and curious, bright, protuberant hazel eyes. He must have seen some service, for he had two rows of medal ribbons on his breast.

"Unarm, Eros," quoted the General, looking at the last slip on a pile of telegrams. "'The long day's task is done.' It has been a grim business, and, Tommy, my lad, I think you had the most difficult patch of the lot to hoe… It was largely due to you that the Boche made his blunder on 15th July, and stretched his neck far enough to let Foch hit him."

The young man grinned. "I wouldn't like to go through it again, sir. But it didn't seem so bad when I was at it, though it is horrible to look back on. The worst part was the loneliness."

"You must have often had bad moments."

"Not so many. I only remember two as particularly gruesome. One was when I heard you slanging me to Lady Samplar, and I suddenly felt hopelessly cut off from my kind… The other was in July, when von Mudra came down from Berlin to see me. He dashed nearly spotted me, for he was at the Embassy when I was in Constantinople."

The General lifted a flamboyant plate whereon the name of Dr. S. Lartius was inscribed in letters of oxidised silver. "You've brought away your souvenir all right. I suppose you'll have it framed as a trophy for your ancestral hall. By the way, what did the letter S stand for?"

"When I was asked," said the young man, "I said 'Sigismund'. But I really meant it for 'Spurius' – the chap, you remember, who held the bridge with Horatius."

The Vanishing Prince

G.K. Chesterton

THIS TALE BEGINS among a tangle of tales round a name that is at once recent and legendary. The name is that of Michael O'Neill, popularly called Prince Michael, partly because he claimed descent from ancient Fenian princes, and partly because he was credited with a plan to make himself prince president of Ireland, as the last Napoleon did of France. He was undoubtedly a gentleman of honorable pedigree and of many accomplishments, but two of his accomplishments emerged from all the rest. He had a talent for appearing when he was not wanted and a talent for disappearing when he was wanted, especially when he was wanted by the police. It may be added that his disappearances were more dangerous than his appearances. In the latter he seldom went beyond the sensational – pasting up seditious placards, tearing down official placards, making flamboyant speeches, or unfurling forbidden flags. But in order to effect the former he would sometimes fight for his freedom with startling energy, from which men were sometimes lucky to escape with a broken head instead of a broken neck. His most famous feats of escape, however, were due to dexterity and not to violence. On a cloudless summer morning he had come down a country road white with dust, and, pausing outside a farmhouse, had told the farmer's daughter, with elegant indifference, that the local police were in pursuit of him. The girl's name was Bridget Royce, a somber and even sullen type of beauty, and she looked at him darkly, as if in doubt, and said, "Do you want me to hide you?" Upon which he only laughed, leaped lightly over the stone wall, and strode toward the farm, merely throwing over his shoulder the remark, "Thank you, I have generally been quite capable of hiding myself." In which proceeding he acted with a tragic ignorance of the nature of women; and there fell on his path in that sunshine a shadow of doom.

While he disappeared through the farmhouse the girl remained for a few moments looking up the road, and two perspiring policemen came plowing up to the door where she stood. Though still angry, she was still silent, and a quarter of an hour later the officers had searched the house and were already inspecting the kitchen garden and cornfield behind it. In the ugly reaction of her mood she might have been tempted even to point out the fugitive, but for a small difficulty that she had no more notion than the policemen had of where he could possibly have gone. The kitchen garden was enclosed by a very low wall, and the cornfield beyond lay aslant like a square patch on a great green hill on which he could still have been seen even as a dot in the distance. Everything stood solid in its familiar place; the apple tree was too small to support or hide a climber; the only shed stood open and obviously empty; there was no sound save the droning of summer flies and the occasional flutter of a bird unfamiliar enough to be surprised by the scarecrow in the field; there was scarcely a shadow save a few blue lines that fell from the thin tree; every detail was picked out by the brilliant daylight as if in a microscope. The girl described the scene later, with all the passionate realism of her race, and, whether or no the policemen had a similar eye for the picturesque, they had at least an eye for the facts of the case, and were compelled to give up the chase and retire from the scene. Bridget Royce remained as if in a trance, staring at the sunlit garden in which a man had just vanished like a fairy. She was still in a sinister mood, and the miracle took in her mind a character of unfriendliness and fear, as if the fairy were decidedly a bad fairy. The sun upon the glittering garden depressed her more than the darkness, but she continued to stare at it. Then the world itself went half-witted and she screamed. The scarecrow moved in the sunlight. It had stood with its back to her in a battered old black hat and a tattered garment, and with all its tatters flying, it strode away across the hill.

She did not analyze the audacious trick by which the man had turned to his advantage the subtle effects of the expected and the obvious; she was still under the cloud of more individual complexities, and she noticed most of all that the vanishing scarecrow did not even turn to look at the farm. And the fates that were running so adverse to his fantastic career of freedom ruled that his next adventure, though it had the same success in another quarter, should increase the danger in this quarter. Among the many similar adventures related of him in this manner it is also said that some days afterward another girl, named Mary Cregan, found him concealed on the farm where she worked; and if the story is true, she must also have had the shock of an uncanny experience, for when she was busy at some lonely task in the yard she heard a voice speaking out of the well, and found that the eccentric had managed to drop himself into the bucket which was some little way below, the well only partly full of water. In this case, however, he had to appeal to the woman to wind up the rope. And men say it was when this news was told to the other woman that her soul walked over the borderline of treason.

Such, at least, were the stories told of him in the countryside, and there were many more – as that he had stood insolently in a splendid green dressing gown on the steps of a great hotel, and then led the police a chase through a long suite of grand apartments, and finally through his own bedroom on to a balcony that overhung the river. The moment the pursuers stepped on to the balcony it broke under them, and they dropped pell-mell into the eddying waters, while Michael, who had thrown off his gown and dived, was able to swim away. It was said that he had carefully cut away the props so that they would not support anything so heavy as a policeman. But here again he was immediately fortunate, yet ultimately unfortunate, for it is said that one of the men was drowned, leaving a family feud which made a little rift in his popularity. These stories can now be told in some detail, not because they are the most marvelous of his many adventures, but because these alone were not covered with silence by the loyalty of the peasantry. These alone found their way into official reports, and it is these which three of the chief officials of the country were reading and discussing when the more remarkable part of this story begins.

Night was far advanced and the lights shone in the cottage that served for a temporary police station near the coast. On one side of it were the last houses of the straggling village, and on the other nothing but a waste moorland stretching away toward the sea, the line of which was broken by no landmark except a solitary tower of the prehistoric pattern still found in Ireland, standing up as slender as a column, but pointed like a pyramid. At a wooden table in front of the window, which normally looked out on this landscape, sat two men in plain clothes, but with something of a military bearing, for indeed they were the two chiefs of the detective service of that district. The senior of the two, both in age and rank, was a sturdy man with a short white beard, and frosty eyebrows fixed in a frown which suggested rather worry than severity.

His name was Morton, and he was a Liverpool man long pickled in the Irish quarrels, and doing his duty among them in a sour fashion not altogether unsympathetic. He had spoken a few sentences to his companion, Nolan, a tall, dark man with a cadaverous equine Irish face, when he seemed to remember something and touched a bell which rang in another room. The subordinate he had summoned immediately appeared with a sheaf of papers in his hand.

"Sit down, Wilson," he said. "Those are the depositions, I suppose."

"Yes," replied the third officer. "I think I've got all there is to be got out of them, so I sent the people away."

"Did Mary Cregan give evidence?" asked Morton, with a frown that looked a little heavier than usual.

"No, but her master did," answered the man called Wilson, who had flat, red hair and a plain, pale face, not without sharpness. "I think he's hanging round the girl himself and is out against a rival. There's always some reason of that sort when we are told the truth about anything. And you bet the other girl told right enough."

"Well, let's hope they'll be some sort of use," remarked Nolan, in a somewhat hopeless manner, gazing out into the darkness.

"Anything is to the good," said Morton, "that lets us know anything about him."

"Do we know anything about him?" asked the melancholy Irishman.

"We know one thing about him," said Wilson, "and it's the one thing that nobody ever knew before. We know where he is."

"Are you sure?" inquired Morton, looking at him sharply.

"Quite sure," replied his assistant. "At this very minute he is in that tower over there by the shore. If you go near enough you'll see the candle burning in the window."

As he spoke the noise of a horn sounded on the road outside, and a moment after they heard the throbbing of a motor car brought to a standstill before the door. Morton instantly sprang to his feet.

"Thank the Lord that's the car from Dublin," he said. "I can't do anything without special authority, not if he were sitting on the top of the tower and putting out his tongue at us. But the chief can do what he thinks best."

He hurried out to the entrance and was soon exchanging greetings with a big handsome man in a fur coat, who brought into the dingy little station the indescribable glow of the great cities and the luxuries of the great world.

For this was Sir Walter Carey, an official of such eminence in Dublin Castle that nothing short of the case of Prince Michael would have brought him on such a journey in the middle of the night. But the case of Prince Michael, as it happened, was complicated by legalism as well as lawlessness. On the last occasion he had escaped by a forensic quibble and not, as usual, by a private escapade; and it was a question whether at the moment he was amenable to the law or not. It might be necessary to stretch a point, but a man like Sir Walter could probably stretch it as far as he liked.

Whether he intended to do so was a question to be considered. Despite the almost aggressive touch of luxury in the fur coat, it soon became apparent that Sir Walter's large leonine head was for use as well as ornament, and he considered the matter soberly and sanely enough. Five chairs were set round the plain deal table, for who should Sir Walter bring with him but his young relative and secretary, Horne Fisher. Sir Walter listened with grave attention, and his secretary with polite boredom, to the string of episodes by which the police had traced the flying rebel from the steps of the hotel to the solitary tower beside the sea. There at least he was cornered between the moors and the breakers; and the scout sent by Wilson reported him as writing under a solitary candle, perhaps composing another of his tremendous proclamations. Indeed, it would have been typical of him to choose it as the place in which finally to turn to bay. He had some remote claim on it, as on a family castle; and those who knew him thought him capable of imitating the primitive Irish chieftains who fell fighting against the sea.

"I saw some queer-looking people leaving as I came in," said Sir Walter Carey. "I suppose they were your witnesses. But why do they turn up here at this time of night?"

Morton smiled grimly. "They come here by night because they would be dead men if they came here by day. They are criminals committing a crime that is more horrible here than theft or murder."

"What crime do you mean?" asked the other, with some curiosity.

"They are helping the law," said Morton.

There was a silence, and Sir Walter considered the papers before him with an abstracted eye. At last he spoke.

"Quite so; but look here, if the local feeling is as lively as that there are a good many points to consider. I believe the new Act will enable me to collar him now if I think it best. But is it best? A serious rising would do us no good in Parliament, and the government has enemies in England as well as Ireland. It won't do if I have done what looks a little like sharp practice, and then only raised a revolution."

"It's all the other way," said the man called Wilson, rather quickly. "There won't be half so much of a revolution if you arrest him as there will if you leave him loose for three days longer. But, anyhow, there can't be anything nowadays that the proper police can't manage."

"Mr. Wilson is a Londoner," said the Irish detective, with a smile.

"Yes, I'm a cockney, all right," replied Wilson, "and I think I'm all the better for that. Especially at this job, oddly enough."

Sir Walter seemed slightly amused at the pertinacity of the third officer, and perhaps even more amused at the slight accent with which he spoke, which rendered rather needless his boast about his origin.

"Do you mean to say," he asked, "that you know more about the business here because you have come from London?"

"Sounds funny, I know, but I do believe it," answered Wilson. "I believe these affairs want fresh methods. But most of all I believe they want a fresh eye."

The superior officers laughed, and the redhaired man went on with a slight touch of temper:

"Well, look at the facts. See how the fellow got away every time, and you'll understand what I mean. Why was he able to stand in the place of the scarecrow, hidden by nothing but an old hat? Because it was a village policeman who knew the scarecrow was there, was expecting it, and therefore took no notice of it. Now I never expect a scarecrow. I've never seen one in the street, and I stare at one when I see it in the field. It's a new thing to me and worth noticing. And it was just the same when he hid in the well. You are ready to find a well in a place like that; you look for a well, and so you don't see it. I don't look for it, and therefore I do look at it."

"It is certainly an idea," said Sir Walter, smiling, "but what about the balcony? Balconies are occasionally seen in London."

"But not rivers right under them, as if it was in Venice," replied Wilson.

"It is certainly a new idea," repeated Sir Walter, with something like respect. He had all the love of the luxurious classes for new ideas. But he also had a critical faculty, and was inclined to think, after due reflection, that it was a true idea as well.

Growing dawn had already turned the window panes from black to gray when Sir Walter got abruptly to his feet. The others rose also, taking this for a signal that the arrest was to be undertaken. But their leader stood for a moment in deep thought, as if conscious that he had come to a parting of the ways.

Suddenly the silence was pierced by a long, wailing cry from the dark moors outside. The silence that followed it seemed more startling than the shriek itself, and it lasted until Nolan said, heavily:

"'Tis the banshee. Somebody is marked for the grave."

His long, large-featured face was as pale as a moon, and it was easy to remember that he was the only Irishman in the room.

"Well, I know that banshee," said Wilson, cheerfully, "ignorant as you think I am of these things. I talked to that banshee myself an hour ago, and I sent that banshee up to the tower and told her to sing out like that if she could get a glimpse of our friend writing his proclamation."

"Do you mean that girl Bridget Royce?" asked Morton, drawing his frosty brows together. "Has she turned king's evidence to that extent?"

"Yes," answered Wilson. "I know very little of these local things, you tell me, but I reckon an angry woman is much the same in all countries."

Nolan, however, seemed still moody and unlike himself. "It's an ugly noise and an ugly business altogether," he said. "If it's really the end of Prince Michael it may well be the end of other things as well. When the spirit is on him he would escape by a ladder of dead men, and wade through that sea if it were made of blood."

"Is that the real reason of your pious alarms?" asked Wilson, with a slight sneer.

The Irishman's pale face blackened with a new passion.

"I have faced as many murderers in County Clare as you ever fought with in Clapham Junction, Mr. Cockney," he said.

"Hush, please," said Morton, sharply. "Wilson, you have no kind of right to imply doubt of your superior's conduct. I hope you will prove yourself as courageous and trustworthy as he has always been."

The pale face of the red-haired man seemed a shade paler, but he was silent and composed, and Sir Walter went up to Nolan with marked courtesy, saying, "Shall we go outside now, and get this business done?"

Dawn had lifted, leaving a wide chasm of white between a great gray cloud and the great gray moorland, beyond which the tower was outlined against the daybreak and the sea.

Something in its plain and primitive shape vaguely suggested the dawn in the first days of the earth, in some prehistoric time when even the colors were hardly created, when there was only blank daylight between cloud and clay. These dead hues were relieved only by one spot of gold – the spark of the candle alight in the window of the lonely tower, and burning on into the broadening daylight. As the group of detectives, followed by a cordon of policemen, spread out into a crescent to cut off all escape, the light in the tower flashed as if it were moved for a moment, and then went out. They knew the man inside had realized the daylight and blown out his candle.

"There are other windows, aren't there?" asked Morton, "and a door, of course, somewhere round the corner? Only a round tower has no corners."

"Another example of my small suggestion," observed Wilson, quietly. "That queer tower was the first thing I saw when I came to these parts; and I can tell you a little more about it – or, at any rate, the outside of it. There are four windows altogether, one a little way from this one, but just out of sight. Those are both on the ground floor, and so is the third on the other side, making a sort of triangle. But the fourth is just above the third, and I suppose it looks on an upper floor."

"It's only a sort of loft, reached by a ladder, said Nolan. "I've played in the place when I was a child. It's no more than an empty shell." And his sad face grew sadder, thinking perhaps of the tragedy of his country and the part that he played in it.

"The man must have got a table and chair, at any rate," said Wilson, "but no doubt he could have got those from some cottage. If I might make a suggestion, sir, I think we ought to approach all the five entrances at once, so to speak. One of us should go to the door and one to each window; Macbride here has a ladder for the upper window."

Mr. Horne Fisher languidly turned to his distinguished relative and spoke for the first time.

"I am rather a convert to the cockney school of psychology," he said in an almost inaudible voice.

The others seemed to feel the same influence in different ways, for the group began to break up in the manner indicated. Morton moved toward the window immediately in front of them, where the hidden outlaw had just snuffed the candle; Nolan, a little farther westward to the next window; while Wilson, followed by Macbride with the ladder, went round to the two windows at the back. Sir Walter Carey himself, followed by his secretary, began to walk round toward the only door, to demand admittance in a more regular fashion.

"He will be armed, of course," remarked Sir Walter, casually.

"By all accounts," replied Horne Fisher, "he can do more with a candlestick than most men with a pistol. But he is pretty sure to have the pistol, too."

Even as he spoke the question was answered with a tongue of thunder. Morton had just placed himself in front of the nearest window, his broad shoulders blocking the aperture. For an instant it was lit from within as with red fire, followed by a thundering throng of echoes. The square shoulders seemed to alter in shape, and the sturdy figure collapsed among the tall, rank grasses at the foot of the tower. A puff of smoke floated from the window like a little cloud. The two men behind rushed to the spot and raised him, but he was dead.

Sir Walter straightened himself and called out something that was lost in another noise of firing; it was possible that the police were already avenging their comrade from the other side. Fisher had already raced round to the next window, and a new cry of astonishment from him brought his patron to the same spot. Nolan, the Irish policeman, had also fallen, sprawling all his great length in the grass, and it was red with his blood. He was still alive when they reached him, but there was death on his face, and he was only able to make a final gesture telling them that all was over; and, with a broken word and a heroic effort, motioning them on to where his other comrades were besieging the back of the tower. Stunned by these rapid and repeated shocks, the two men could only vaguely obey the gesture, and, finding their way to the other windows at the back, they discovered a scene equally startling, if less final and tragic. The other two officers were not dead or mortally wounded, but Macbride lay with a broken leg and his ladder on top of him, evidently thrown down from the top window of the tower; while Wilson lay on his face, quite still as if stunned, with his red head among the gray and silver of the sea holly. In him, however, the impotence was but momentary, for he began to move and rise as the others came round the tower.

"My God! It's like an explosion!" cried Sir Walter; and indeed it was the only word for this unearthly energy, by which one man had been able to deal death or destruction on three sides of the same small triangle at the same instant.

Wilson had already scrambled to his feet and with splendid energy flew again at the window, revolver in hand. He fired twice into the opening and then disappeared in his own smoke; but the thud of his feet and the shock of a falling chair told them that the intrepid Londoner had managed at last to leap into the room. Then followed a curious silence; and Sir Walter, walking to the window through the thinning smoke, looked into the hollow shell of the ancient tower. Except for Wilson, staring around him, there was nobody there.

The inside of the tower was a single empty room, with nothing but a plain wooden chair and a table on which were pens, ink and paper, and the candlestick. Halfway up the high wall there was a rude timber platform under the upper window, a small loft which was more like a large shelf. It was reached only by a ladder, and it seemed to be as bare as the bare walls. Wilson completed his survey of the place and then went and stared at the things on the table. Then he silently pointed with his lean forefinger at the open page of the large notebook. The writer had suddenly stopped writing, even in the middle of a word.

"I said it was like an explosion," said Sir Walter Carey at last. "And really the man himself seems to have suddenly exploded. But he has blown himself up somehow without touching the tower. He's burst more like a bubble than a bomb."

"He has touched more valuable things than the tower," said Wilson, gloomily.

There was a long silence, and then Sir Walter said, seriously: "Well, Mr. Wilson, I am not a detective, and these unhappy happenings have left you in charge of that branch of the business. We all lament the cause of this, but I should like to say that I myself have the strongest confidence in your capacity for carrying on the work. What do you think we should do next?"

Wilson seemed to rouse himself from his depression and acknowledged the speaker's words with a warmer civility than he had hitherto shown to anybody. He called in a few of the police to assist in routing out the interior, leaving the rest to spread themselves in a search party outside.

"I think," he said, "the first thing is to make quite sure about the inside of this place, as it was hardly physically possible for him to have got outside. I suppose poor Nolan would have brought in his banshee and said it was supernaturally possible. But I've got no use for disembodied spirits when I'm dealing with facts. And the facts before me are an empty tower with a ladder, a chair, and a table."

"The spiritualists," said Sir Walter, with a smile, "would say that spirits could find a great deal of use for a table."

"I dare say they could if the spirits were on the table – in a bottle," replied Wilson, with a curl of his pale lip. "The people round here, when they're all sodden up with Irish whisky, may believe in such things. I think they want a little education in this country."

Horne Fisher's heavy eyelids fluttered in a faint attempt to rise, as if he were tempted to a lazy protest against the contemptuous tone of the investigator.

"The Irish believe far too much in spirits to believe in spiritualism," he murmured. "They know too much about 'em. If you want a simple and childlike faith in any spirit that comes along you can get it in your favorite London."

"I don't want to get it anywhere," said Wilson, shortly. "I say I'm dealing with much simpler things than your simple faith, with a table and a chair and a ladder. Now what I want to say about them at the start is this. They are all three made roughly enough of plain wood. But the table and the chair are fairly new and comparatively clean. The ladder is covered with dust and there is a cobweb under the top rung of it. That means that he borrowed the first two quite recently from some cottage, as we supposed, but the ladder has been a long time in this rotten old dustbin. Probably it was part of the original furniture, an heirloom in this magnificent palace of the Irish kings."

Again Fisher looked at him under his eyelids, but seemed too sleepy to speak, and Wilson went on with his argument.

"Now it's quite clear that something very odd has just happened in this place. The chances are ten to one, it seems to me, that it had something specially to do with this place. Probably he came here because he could do it only here; it doesn't seem very inviting otherwise. But the man knew it of old; they say it belonged to his family, so that altogether, I think, everything points to something in the construction of the tower itself."

"Your reasoning seems to me excellent," said Sir Walter, who was listening attentively. "But what could it be?"

"You see now what I mean about the ladder," went on the detective; "it's the only old piece of furniture here and the first thing that caught that cockney eye of mine. But there is something else. That loft up there is a sort of lumber room without any lumber. So far as I can see, it's as empty as everything else; and, as things are, I don't see the use of the ladder leading to it. It seems to me, as I can't find anything unusual down here, that it might pay us to look up there."

He got briskly off the table on which he was sitting (for the only chair was allotted to Sir Walter) and ran rapidly up the ladder to the platform above. He was soon followed by the others, Mr. Fisher going last, however, with an appearance of considerable nonchalance.

At this stage, however, they were destined to disappointment; Wilson nosed in every corner like a terrier and examined the roof almost in the posture of a fly, but half an hour afterward they had to confess that they were still without a clue. Sir Walter's private secretary seemed more and more threatened with inappropriate slumber, and, having been the last to climb up the ladder, seemed now to lack the energy even to climb down again.

"Come along, Fisher," called out Sir Walter from below, when the others had regained the floor. "We must consider whether we'll pull the whole place to pieces to see what it's made of."

"I'm coming in a minute," said the voice from the ledge above their heads, a voice somewhat suggestive of an articulate yawn.

"What are you waiting for?" asked Sir Walter, impatiently. "Can you see anything there?"

"Well, yes, in a way," replied the voice, vaguely. "In fact, I see it quite plain now."

"What is it?" asked Wilson, sharply, from the table on which he sat kicking his heels restlessly.

"Well, it's a man," said Horne Fisher.

Wilson bounded off the table as if he had been kicked off it. "What do you mean?" he cried. "How can you possibly see a man?"

"I can see him through the window," replied the secretary, mildly. "I see him coming across the moor. He's making a beeline across the open country toward this tower. He evidently means to pay us a visit. And, considering who it seems to be, perhaps it would be more polite if we were all at the door to receive him." And in a leisurely manner the secretary came down the ladder.

"Who it seems to be!" repeated Sir Walter in astonishment.

"Well, I think it's the man you call Prince Michael," observed Mr. Fisher, airily. "In fact, I'm sure it is. I've seen the police portraits of him."

There was a dead silence, and Sir Walter's usually steady brain seemed to go round like a windmill.

"But, hang it all!" he said at last, "even supposing his own explosion could have thrown him half a mile away, without passing through any of the windows, and left him alive enough for a country walk – even then, why the devil should he walk in this direction? The murderer does not generally revisit the scene of his crime so rapidly as all that."

"He doesn't know yet that it is the scene of his crime," answered Horne Fisher.

"What on earth do you mean? You credit him with rather singular absence of mind."

"Well, the truth is, it isn't the scene of his crime," said Fisher, and went and looked out of the window.

There was another silence, and then Sir Walter said, quietly: "What sort of notion have you really got in your head, Fisher? Have you developed a new theory about how this fellow escaped out of the ring round him?"

"He never escaped at all," answered the man at the window, without turning round. "He never escaped out of the ring because he was never inside the ring. He was not in this tower at all, at least not when we were surrounding it."

He turned and leaned back against the window, but, in spite of his usual listless manner, they almost fancied that the face in shadow was a little pale.

"I began to guess something of the sort when we were some way from the tower," he said. "Did you notice that sort of flash or flicker the candle gave before it was extinguished? I was almost certain it was only the last leap the flame gives when a candle burns itself out. And then I came into this room and I saw that."

He pointed at the table and Sir Walter caught his breath with a sort of curse at his own blindness. For the candle in the candlestick had obviously burned itself away to nothing and left him, mentally, at least, very completely in the dark.

"Then there is a sort of mathematical question," went on Fisher, leaning back in his limp way and looking up at the bare walls, as if tracing imaginary diagrams there. "It's not so easy for a man in the third angle to face the other two at the same moment, especially if they are at the base of an isosceles. I am sorry if it sounds like a lecture on geometry, but—"

"I'm afraid we have no time for it," said Wilson, coldly. "If this man is really coming back, I must give my orders at once."

"I think I'll go on with it, though," observed Fisher, staring at the roof with insolent serenity.

"I must ask you, Mr. Fisher, to let me conduct my inquiry on my own lines," said Wilson, firmly. "I am the officer in charge now."

"Yes," remarked Horne Fisher, softly, but with an accent that somehow chilled the hearer. "Yes. But why?"

Sir Walter was staring, for he had never seen his rather lackadaisical young friend look like that before. Fisher was looking at Wilson with lifted lids, and the eyes under them seemed to have shed or shifted a film, as do the eyes of an eagle.

"Why are you the officer in charge now?" he asked. "Why can you conduct the inquiry on your own lines now? How did it come about, I wonder, that the elder officers are not here to interfere with anything you do?"

Nobody spoke, and nobody can say how soon anyone would have collected his wits to speak when a noise came from without. It was the heavy and hollow sound of a blow upon the door of the tower, and to their shaken spirits it sounded strangely like the hammer of doom.

The wooden door of the tower moved on its rusty hinges under the hand that struck it and Prince Michael came into the room. Nobody had the smallest doubt about his identity. His light clothes, though frayed with his adventures, were of fine and almost foppish cut, and he wore a pointed beard, or imperial, perhaps as a further reminiscence of Louis Napoleon; but he was a much taller and more graceful man that his prototype. Before anyone could speak he had silenced everyone for an instant with a slight but splendid gesture of hospitality.

"Gentlemen," he said, "this is a poor place now, but you are heartily welcome."

Wilson was the first to recover, and he took a stride toward the newcomer.

"Michael O'Neill, I arrest you in the king's name for the murder of Francis Morton and James Nolan. It is my duty to warn you—"

"No, no, Mr. Wilson," cried Fisher, suddenly. "You shall not commit a third murder."

Sir Walter Carey rose from his chair, which fell over with a crash behind him. "What does all this mean?" he called out in an authoritative manner.

"It means," said Fisher, "that this man, Hooker Wilson, as soon as he had put his head in at that window, killed his two comrades who had put their heads in at the other windows, by firing across the empty room. That is what it means. And if you want to know, count how many times he is supposed to have fired and then count the charges left in his revolver."

Wilson, who was still sitting on the table, abruptly put a hand out for the weapon that lay beside him. But the next movement was the most unexpected of all, for the prince standing in the doorway passed suddenly from the dignity of a statue to the swiftness of an acrobat and rent the revolver out of the detective's hand.

"You dog!" he cried. "So you are the type of English truth, as I am of Irish tragedy – you who come to kill me, wading through the blood of your brethren. If they had fallen in a feud on the hillside, it would be called murder, and yet your sin might be forgiven you. But I, who am innocent, I was to be slain with ceremony. There would be long speeches and patient judges listening to my vain plea of innocence, noting down my despair and disregarding it. Yes, that is what I call assassination. But killing may be no murder; there is one shot left in this little gun, and I know where it should go."

Wilson turned quickly on the table, and even as he turned he twisted in agony, for Michael shot him through the body where he sat, so that he tumbled off the table like lumber.

The police rushed to lift him; Sir Walter stood speechless; and then, with a strange and weary gesture, Horne Fisher spoke.

"You are indeed a type of the Irish tragedy," he said. "You were entirely in the right, and you have put yourself in the wrong."

The prince's face was like marble for a space then there dawned in his eyes a light not unlike that of despair. He laughed suddenly and flung the smoking pistol on the ground.

"I am indeed in the wrong," he said. "I have committed a crime that may justly bring a curse on me and my children."

Horne Fisher did not seem entirely satisfied with this very sudden repentance; he kept his eyes on the man and only said, in a low voice, "What crime do you mean?"

"I have helped English justice," replied Prince Michael. "I have avenged your king's officers; I have done the work of his hangman. For that truly I deserve to be hanged."

And he turned to the police with a gesture that did not so much surrender to them, but rather command them to arrest him.

This was the story that Horne Fisher told to Harold March, the journalist, many years after, in a little, but luxurious, restaurant near Piccadilly. He had invited March to dinner some time after the affair he called 'The Face in the Target', and the conversation had naturally turned on that mystery and afterward on earlier memories of Fisher's life and the way in which he was led to study such problems as those of Prince Michael. Horne Fisher was fifteen years older; his thin hair had faded to frontal baldness, and his long, thin hands dropped less with affectation and more with fatigue. And he told the story of the Irish adventure of his youth, because it recorded the first occasion on which he had ever come in contact with crime, or discovered how darkly and how terribly crime can be entangled with law.

"Hooker Wilson was the first criminal I ever knew, and he was a policeman," explained Fisher, twirling his wine glass. "And all my life has been a mixed-up business of the sort. He was a man of very real talent, and perhaps genius, and well worth studying, both as a detective and a criminal. His white face and red hair were typical of him, for he was one of those who are cold and yet on fire for fame; and he could control anger, but not ambition. He swallowed the snubs of his superiors in that first quarrel, though he boiled with resentment; but when he suddenly saw the two heads dark against the dawn and framed in the two windows, he could not miss the chance, not only of revenge, but of the removal of the two obstacles to his promotion. He was a dead shot and counted on silencing both, though proof against him would have been hard in any case. But, as a matter of fact, he had a narrow escape, in the case of Nolan, who lived just long enough to say 'Wilson' and point. We thought he was summoning help for his comrade, but he was really denouncing his murderer. After that it was easy to throw down the ladder above him (for a man up a ladder cannot see clearly what is below and behind) and to throw himself on the ground as another victim of the catastrophe.

"But there was mixed up with his murderous ambition a real belief, not only in his own talents, but in his own theories. He did believe in what he called a fresh eye, and he did want scope for fresh methods. There was something in his view, but it failed where such things commonly fail, because the fresh eye cannot see the unseen. It is true about the ladder and the scarecrow, but not about the life and the soul; and he made a bad mistake about what a man like Michael would do when he heard a woman scream. All Michael's very vanity and vainglory made him rush out at once; he would have walked into Dublin Castle for a lady's glove. Call it his pose or what you will, but he would have done it. What happened when he met her is another story, and one we may never know, but from tales I've heard since, they must have been reconciled. Wilson was wrong there; but there was something, for all that, in his notion that the newcomer sees most, and that the man on the spot may know too much to know anything. He was right about some things. He was right about me."

"About you?" asked Harold March in some wonder.

"I am the man who knows too much to know anything, or, at any rate, to do anything," said Horne Fisher. "I don't mean especially about Ireland. I mean about England. I mean about the whole way we are governed, and perhaps the only way we can be governed. You asked me just now what became of the survivors of that tragedy. Well, Wilson recovered and we managed to persuade him to retire. But we had to pension that damnable murderer more magnificently than any hero who ever fought for England. I managed to save Michael from the worst, but we had to send that perfectly innocent man to penal servitude for a crime we know he never committed, and it was only afterward that we could connive in a sneakish way at his escape. And Sir Walter Carey is Prime Minister of this country, which he would probably never have been if the truth had been told of such a horrible scandal in his department. It might have done for us altogether in Ireland; it would certainly have done for him. And he is my father's old friend, and has always smothered me with kindness. I am too tangled up with the whole thing, you see, and I was certainly never born to set it right. You look distressed, not to say shocked, and I'm not at all offended at it. Let us change the subject by all means, if you like. What do you think of this Burgundy? It's rather a discovery of mine, like the restaurant itself."

And he proceeded to talk learnedly and luxuriantly on all the wines of the world; on which subject, also, some moralists would consider that he knew too much.

Under Cover

Carroll John Daly

Chapter I

SOME CASES come directly to the office; others I go out and get – a few come by mail. This one did, but the main item had been overlooked. Good clients say what they want to say on the face of a check; this lad had wind enough but was short on figures. I leaned back in my office chair and read the note again. The spelling at least was refreshing.

Just a desire to meet me that night on the lonely road behind the golf links at Van Cortlandt – the hour, one-thirty a.m. Now, the thing itself was childish. I have as many enemies as a shad has eggs. This was one of them, trying what he thought was an original idea. The warning of great secrecy was in the note – also the promise of a liberal amount of jack. But the backwoods spoiled it – might as well have been a back room on the Avenue. I was onto the duck who wrote that note the minute I lamped it.

There was the hint too that I mightn't have the guts to come. Now, clients in trouble don't hire me thinking I'll lay down on them. They need me bad – this lad blurbed that the whole thing was simple and I need have no fear of personal danger. What a poor fish he was! I started to crumple up the note and toss it in the basket – and the phone rang.

"Race Williams? This is a friend. Someone is planning to kill you tonight, Race Williams – watch your step." There was a decided click, and the one-sided conversation was over. But the note stayed in my hand – was straightened out and read again.

Food for thought that – others knew about that note. At least one other did. For all I knew half the underworld of the city might be on. Someone was making open threats of gunning for me. The crooks that feared me would stand by and see if I made good. If I showed the white feather in one instance I'd have to knock off half the town to establish my reputation all over again. What did I do? As they say in the movies – there was a lapse of time; midnight came and went.

It was twelve-thirty when I rolled up Broadway, driving my big touring. Simply big-heartedness on my part. If some bird really wanted the opportunity to bump me off – why – of course I'd be willing to give it to him. In all fairness, however, I must admit that I figured the chances were very much against him.

You know the place – that lonely stretch of flat park far across from Broadway – the other side of the railroad tracks and beyond the links – never a better place for a little shooting.

It wasn't one when I first passed the spot – but I flashed by, doing in the neighborhood of sixty miles an hour. I turned up the hill at the end of the road – came back on the road above – parked the car – and dropped silently down the thickly wooded hill. There was much to think of. Suppose after all the letter writer had been sincere – and the telephone call a fake! But I shook my head. A little careful study would do the trick. I'm not strong on thinking things out – besides, I find they never go according to schedule – action was what I wanted – and action was what I'd get.

Not a soul in sight – there, across the road, lay the great stretch of park – a dull moon piercing the slight mist that enveloped it. Far down toward the city, a half mile perhaps, was the still smouldering fires of the city's garbage dump – a sore eye to that vast expanse of beautiful country – a sore smell too when the wind was right.

And he came – the distant hum of an engine – then silence as he shut the motor off and drifted the few hundred feet remaining. Just the purr of great tires softly rolling over the dirt road. The lights dimmed, to disappear entirely as the car swung around the bend, rolled slowly up and stopped within fifty feet of where I was hiding – crouched in the bushes.

Dimly I made out the single figure that stepped from the car and peered up and down the road. Would he have a friend? I expected a half dozen of them – but, no – just the one man, for he made no attempt to communicate with anyone hidden in the back seat. Five minutes more I waited – not a sound – no hum of another approaching motor – and I did my stuff. Suddenly stepped into the road and shot my flashlight full upon this duck's pan.

I didn't know him. Oh, I knew his breed all right – the prison pallor still stood out on his blanched cheeks – but he hadn't done his stretch through any effort of mine. It was a map one never forgets – a 'before using' sort of a phiz, if you get what I mean. The kisser was enough, but he gave himself away besides that. The half unconscious way he reached for his gun – and the stupid, foolish leer to his eyes as he caught himself and brought out a handkerchief that had done service in the family for many years. If this bird was to have a widow within the next few minutes – why, the dear old girl would owe me a vote of thanks. He was the kind of a lad you'd put out and wonder why you didn't do it before.

"Mr. Williams, I believe." And the way he got it off was a scream. Like amateur night up in Harlem. And when I flattered him for his powers of observation, he broke right into his story.

It was some yarn and no mistake. He should have been on the stage. There was the lost paper and the rich uncle, and the poor mother who had died bringing him up. That last crack I could believe. And he readily admitted being in jail – a false charge by the uncle, who was holding his rightful inheritance from him. Just one thing was needed to make him a millionaire – that bit of paper. And he knew where it was. Of course he couldn't get it himself. He was wanted by the police – who would see him enter his uncle's house. But it was easy for me, and I would receive his undying gratitude – to say nothing of a few hundred thousand bucks. He sure was liberal.

Before he got through he turned on the water works and wept all over the road. All he needed was a cup and a half dozen shoelaces. For the first time I fully appreciated the meaning of the word 'unique'.

This sob-sister finished up with one burst of glory that set me thinking. Perhaps after all he wasn't bent on bumping me off – just a decoy – and what a decoy!

"I want to talk it over wid ya – have papers to show ya. I'm tellin' the truth, the whole truth and nothing but the truth – so help me Gawd." That last was an inspiration. He must have used it many times – or listened to the court clerk get it off for his benefit.

"Why didn't you get a lawyer?" I just had to say something or bust right out laughing. He was so sincere – so childish – in his innocent belief that I swallowed his story. And all this behind the hardest, crudest face I'd looked at in many a moon. Give him a gun and a chance to use it, and he'd probably make a creditable showing, but his gift of gab wouldn't fool a six year old.

"I did hire a mouth-piece," he shook his head in a comical way that was meant to be sad, "but he sold me out." And those were the first words so far that I could actually believe – but then – I'd believe most anything of a lawyer.

"Where do you want to take me?" I asked. In a way I didn't mind finding out just who was staging this little party. A thick outfit, no doubt – but it's a good thing to know who your enemies are. Stupid or shrewd – it makes little difference – some of the dumbest crooks I know are the best in handling a rod or a knife.

He was all excited, was old Sob-Sister, when I showed a fatherly interest in him – even stirred up an imaginary friend who'd stake him to a thousand dollars to hand over to me as a starter. The way this gopher raised money was hot stuff. But I made him precede me to the car, and I could see that his feelings were hurt. He sure wanted to get a good look at my back for a few seconds.

"I tell ya what, Mr. Race Williams." And there was almost a tear in his eye. "Your lack of trust in me hurts, but I guess I deserve it. I ain't had the opportunities that should-a been comin' to me. You see here an orphan what was wronged. So – youse sit in the back of the car. I'll drive and youse can watch me." Then with the first gleam of intelligence he had shown since we met, "You didn't have a car with ya – or a friend maybe?" For the first time also an anxious note crept into his voice.

I marked my bird then – nothing less than a hired murderer. He was going to take a chance, and self-preservation shot to the top.

"No – I didn't have a car." That was a lie. "And I didn't bring a friend. I didn't need to." That was the truth and his chance to crawl out. I knew from his itching fingers that things were going to happen any minute now. Don't ask me why. Live as close to death as I have for as many years, and you do *know*.

I was tired of the whole thing. This business of being dragged into the night by a common thug. As soon as we got in the car I'd stick a gun in his back and get the truth out of him. He never worked this out alone. There wasn't any sense in that. I never saw him before – someone was paying him for the job. I nodded grimly as I started toward the back of the car, Sob-Sister just to one side of me. I'd give this baby something to cry about if he didn't speak up like a little man. In five minutes more I'd have the name and address of the party who'd sent this jail-bird gunning for me.

Then he made his move – God! he swung like lightning. I honestly believe that if he had pulled a gun he'd have gotten me.

I threw myself flat on the step of the car – swung about, jerked out my gun and let drive. The long knife in his right hand grazed my cheek as the shot broke the stillness. He pitched forward, half on top of me, and rolled into the road. Old Sob-Sister was as flat as the distant stretch of desolate park.

There wasn't any need to hold a post mortem. He didn't cry out – call down vengeance upon that imaginary uncle who had wronged him. I'm onto most of the tricks known to corpses – this one was as stiff as King Tut.

A hurried search through the dead man's pockets at first revealed nothing – and then I whistled. You'd never guess what I found – the torn corner of a thousand dollar bill. Think that one out. I did in a way, as I shoved it deep into my pocket.

As I said before, it was a lonely spot. I made it just that much lonelier – beat it through the woods – grabbed my car – and cutting back over the country road, slipped down the Bronx and into the heart of the city. Was the thing dead – the incident closed? I thought so then, but the game was just beginning. Take it from me.

Chapter II

IF YOU LOST a diamond ring in China you certainly wouldn't expect to find it inside a watermelon you happened to buy in Chicago. And what's more, you wouldn't. In crime you never can tell what strange links make up the chain – a single, well-balanced piece of work that all fits in together some place. And it does – sometimes!

The next day the incident of that case is brought suddenly back to me and then dropped entirely. What brought it back is another letter in the mail. This time the spelling is better, and there's a good-sized check to back it up. This looks like real business and gives me an invitation to call at a distant city – a big one – let us call it Rosedale, though the inhabitants would have my head for so defaming the town. The letter ended – 'I would like to discuss with you a matter of the gravest importance.' There was a timetable and a note too that the writer's car and chauffeur would meet all trains.

That was better. There was the check for one thing, and the time to look up the party, who turned out to be a well-known banker in Rosedale. Dough-heavy, a member of the Common Council, vice-president of the Board of Education, and that sort of stuff. His label – Charles Philip Preston – also lent the air of smug respectability to the whole outfit.

It must be about nine o'clock the following evening when I hit Rosedale. Not suspicious this time. The car is there to meet me, and a liveried chauffeur to ask the wrong people if they're on the way to Mr. Preston's house. Not being in a hurry I wait my turn, and sure enough he spots me. I slip him my bag and tag on his heels to the waiting car. There I take care of my own bag. I carry my tools with me.

Charles Philip Preston lives up to his name. He's tall and thin, and lets a black cord run from his glasses to some place in the back of his frock coat. He hasn't got sideboards, but the nearest thing to them – and it would be downright lying to call them whiskers. Too high up for whiskers – too low down for hair – take your choice. They looked like moss. But his check was too big to start off by laughing at him, so I just slip easily into a chair in the library and watch him do the slow marathon up and down the room. This lad has something on his chest – never a doubt about that – but you couldn't exactly say that he was nervous – nor worried either. His dignity wouldn't permit that. Sometimes he'd stick his left hand across his vest – and he'd look like the Common Council – then the hand would slip behind his back and you'd see the Board of Education slipping into the picture. Finally both hands would get into the tails of his coat some place and you wouldn't be sure whether it was Preston the Banker or Preston the Deacon of the church. He was one pompous duck. There wasn't any Mrs. Preston, which was probably lucky for her.

"Mr. Williams – Mr. Race Williams." He was slightly static after so much walking, but I get him clear enough. "I was doubtful at first – very doubtful – about bringing you into this matter. Mr. Morrison insisted on it. I shook my head and waited – Mr. Morrison threatened to desert me. Then came this last letter. My life has been threatened."

He came out with the final shot like the end of the world was here. He didn't expect me to believe it – didn't half believe it himself, I guess. He was so sure of himself – so wrapped up in his own importance. That anyone would have the effrontery to threaten him seemed beyond belief.

I took a slant at the letter which he handed over. He was threatened sure enough. In plain words and with no fancy thrills the writer told him his days were numbered. Within a week he would be shot down – nothing could save him.

"You have not paid the money, and you die." It was signed with the black hand. The thing was old to me. Some kill; some just bluff – the chances were ten to one in his favor, I thought. Killing him wouldn't produce the money. But he was shooting off his trap again.

"I would have none of it – but Mr. Morrison believed in these letters – this last one especially. Mr. Morrison spoke very feelingly about the matter. I must not think of myself – but the community – they look to me for guidance – I must take steps against a blackmailer who would – who would – but you see for yourself." His hand shot out and a shiny fingernail pointed to the letter. "Mr. Morrison—" This time I cut in.

"Who the hell is Mr. Morrison?" I couldn't have helped it if the case depended on it. I was already heartily sick of that Morrison guy.

He stopped walking – his hands became useful things for the first time and stayed at his side. Then he blurted it out.

"You – you in your profession, and haven't heard of Mr. Richard Morrison – impossible! Why, he's a detective – a private detective. The very flower of the profession."

I could have laughed right in his face. Of course Morrison believed the whole story. Why wouldn't he? I never met a private dick yet who was worth his salt – that is, damn few of them. Mr. Morrison sure had laid it on thick in this case. At length I get the story.

Charles Philip Preston started in one Monday morning reading his mail. One of the letters was a threat that he would be killed unless he came across with fifty thousand berries. Like the good and indignant citizen he was he turned it all over to the Chief of Police. At first this gang threatened to divulge some very personal matters that most men would go to any length to keep secret. But Preston was a queer duck. He wouldn't cough up under any circumstances – went right to the police with each letter. And they, dear souls, spent their time arresting half the strangers that came into town. It was great fun for a while and I guess that Preston liked it at first himself. His map decorated the front page, with the glowing caption:

LEADING CITIZEN SCOFFS AT THREATS OF DEATH!

Looked good in print, didn't it? And then along came Detective Morrison. Just arrived at Rosedale on another case. Saw the paper and wrote a letter to the press, commending the magnificent attitude of Rosedale's esteemed citizen – and found himself shaking hands with Charles Philip himself. After that all was gravy. Richard Morrison extended his stay and I dare say his pocket book – though what he brought me into the graft for is more than I knew.

"It's like this—" Charles Philip came down at last to the real business of the evening, "Morrison believes in these threats – wants me to have you here – sort of keep an eye on me."

"Can't he do that himself?" Somehow I didn't relish the business. Don't like to play in on a case where a private dick is running things.

Charles Philip smiled – the real banker this time.

"Mr. Morrison works with the brain. He tells me a disappointed blackmailer is sometimes so desperate that he will shoot a man down on the street. You are a good shot – you might circumvent such a disaster."

I was just about to tell him I wouldn't touch his case until Morrison got the gate – but I stopped and let him talk.

Something black had suddenly bobbed up over the back of a great armchair in the corner – something black and sinister – just a flash and it was gone. I looked at Charles Philip's face. He hadn't seen it. Had nothing to do with it either. He was still singing his own praises and occasionally glorifying Morrison.

I didn't listen to him now – I watched. This man wouldn't stoop to having someone listen to our conversation. He didn't know that another was in that room. But I did – one hand slipped behind me – the other slid the revolver into my lap – hidden beneath my coat. Was the blackmailer actually in the house? Stranger things than that have happened in real life – in my life too for that matter. And then a real scare – would a gun suddenly slip from behind that chair? Would a man actually attempt to assassinate Charles Philip before I was financially interested in the case? It would be a fine mess if I happened to kill this lad without putting a price on him. Two men in two nights – and nothing in it but a half column of newspaper bunk! Why, I'd be soon getting into the amateur class – an out and out Simon pure.

So I broke right in on Mr. Charles Philip.

"What's in the thing for me?" I piped, snappy-like – time was precious.

The eagerness in my voice made him start. Before, he was busy trying to talk me into it. Now, when I was ripe for it, he became speechless. And me – my eyes were glued to that chair. Any second the hidden figure might dig a hole and chuck my money into it. So I made my own price. Even in the excitement I didn't overcharge. Fair's fair. I gave him a square deal. He was just talking something about so much a day when I horned in with the proposition.

"Twenty-five hundred dollars if I get this man for you – double if I have to kill him in the very act of jumping you over the hurdles. Quick, man! What do you say?" Damn it, I had seen the chair move.

"I'll see what Morrison says." He crossed toward the door, passing between me and the chair, and I almost had to be a contortionist to keep my eye out and my gun ready.

"Never mind Morrison – what do you say?" I was up and had him by the shoulder.

"But he'll explain just what you are to do – of course I'll pay your price." That last a little stiffly, I thought, as he added, "Morrison must be upstairs now."

"Then you're on about the twenty-five hundred, and five thousand if I have to kill this duck?" I wanted to at least have his verbal contract. I have a way of my own for collecting debts.

"Of course – of course." He seemed annoyed, and then as he reached the door and I kept my eye on that chair, "Funny – Morrison told me you might be very difficult to handle – interest, rather. That's why he had me speak to you first – said you didn't like detectives, though I always half thought – or was led to understand that you were a—"

"Beat it and get Morrison." I was tired of his guff. And the map on him when he suddenly swung and left the room! It would take time to forget it. I suppose no one ever shot a line like that at him. This time there wasn't a good yip in him as he went to fetch Morrison.

Chapter III

NOW FOR IT. I turned squarely and faced that chair. How easy to put a bit of lead through it! And another thought! Was it Morrison that was lurking there? A little sinking feeling in that. I was counting on the twenty-five hundred at least. It would be like a detective to hide behind a chair and listen in.

The flash of black came again. Why didn't that lad stick a gun out and try a little shooting? Double or quits would suit me. And the black wasn't a gun – hair, I thought. But there was little time to waste – twenty-five hundred was better than nothing. If it was Morrison—! I shrugged my shoulders – pulled my gun squarely now and stepped over to the chair.

"Come out of there." My voice was low but sharp. "Come with your hands first – and empty. Now!" I stood back and waited. Not a sound – then the soft scraping of feet – but no figure. I tried again. Relieved too. It couldn't be Morrison.

"I'll count five," I said slowly, "then – I'll drive a bit of lead through the chair. One – " I don't believe in wasting time – and I never bluff. Them that know Race Williams, know that. It might be tough on the furniture – on the fine Persian rug too. I should have made an agreement about that.

I reached "Four" – not a movement – no hands – no sound of a body coming erect – and then. Believe it or not – there was a laugh – a suppressed giggle from behind that chair. It took the wind out of my sails – I won't deny that. But I was mad. The laugh was feminine. I stepped forward and saw my five grand fly out of the window.

Before I reached the chair she stood up – a Kid – twelve, at the most – her little bobbed head looked over the top – great black eyes smiled out at me. And she put out her hand.

"Race Williams." One gold tooth made her smile the more fetching. "I know it ain't right to call you by your first name. Papa would be real cockey about that – but then, he's cockey about everything. You see, I feel like I know you – read so much about you. Won't you take my hand? Ain't you – don't you like Kids?"

I gulped and took it. She sure was a bagful of cute tricks. How near death she was she never knew – and only laughed when I told her.

"You're nice-looking," she said suddenly. "I never knew just how you looked – you have an eye like father's, too, when you're mad. But you don't look like him (a minute's pause) and don't act like him neither."

I was glad of that, and smiled a bit. Her next chirp was another shock.

"Father sure does put on the dog." She shook her head knowingly. "But you mustn't mind that. He's good to me."

She sure did know her old man.

"Have you heard everything we said – your father and I?" It was a foolish question, I guess – but piercing little black eyes were on me.

"All of it." Then she laughed – hesitated a moment as the laugh disappeared with the gold tooth. "You won't tell, will you? Mr. Morrison's a snitch."

"I won't tell," I took the outstretched hand now and held it, "if you promise not to do it again."

"Oh, I don't believe you'd tell anyway." She sort of jerked up her head. "Besides, it's great fun – do you think they'll try to kidnap me?" And her eyes flashed – thrilled at the prospect. Queer little duck – looked you straight in the eye.

"Tell me all about yourself." She sort of cuddled up to me. "Mr. Morrison tells me lots of stories – but there's fairies and giants in them. I can't fall for that anymore. I think he's a misprint, and—"

And that was all. Charles Philip Preston sailed into the room – and behind him came a big man – a clean-shaven, stout sort of chap – one of these boys who looks as if he just stepped out of a band box. A couple of band boxes was Morrison's order. Damned if he didn't sport a white carnation in his button hole. His voice was as high as Charles Philip's was low. They'd have made a great team in a church choir. I didn't like Morrison.

While Morrison mitted me, Charles Philip eyed his daughter, stretching out a hand and catching her as she went to slip from the room. "How long have you been here?" he asked sternly – and I saw his eyes slip toward the chair. She had played that game before then.

"Just a few minutes. Ask Mr. Williams. He'll tell you just when I came in – and how." Get that? She wouldn't lie to the old geezer – she left that part to me. Girls learn the game young, I guess. But why spoil her party – and worry her father? So I lied like a gentleman.

"She came in looking for you, I guess." But the guess was for the child alone. I saw her father bend down and kiss her – saw her run from the room – caught too the kiss she turned and threw to me just before the old man closed the door. It's kind of nice to have a child around – you can't get away from that.

You'd think this Morrison was booked to be our next president the way Charles Philip paraded him off. Every word he spoke had the ring behind it – "Come, Richard, show the gentleman how clever you are."

"He's the flower of the profession – the cream of them all." Charles Philip patted him on the back. "Tell Mr. Williams just what you expect of him." And Morrison did.

"I've heard of you often, Mr. Williams," and the Flower of the Profession smiled down at me. "Admired you too – and this case is one after your own heart – and one that will try even your far-famed marksmanship. The Chief of Police and myself have agreed that you are the only man for it." Somehow there seemed an unnatural ring to his voice.

"You want me to lay someone out?" I didn't like this lad and didn't mind showing it. It had been like shaking hands with a sea lion – cold and clammy.

"No – no – let us hope not." He stroked his chin. "But Mr. Preston is threatened by a desperate character. One who would shoot him down perhaps in the crowded street. We want you to walk behind him – be ready – shoot at the first attempt on our esteemed friend's life. The Chief of Police thinks the idea a good one. And see the advertisement in it for you, my friend." A huge hand stretched out and fell upon my shoulder. This lad wasn't all soft flesh – his ham-like fist rested there like a cobble stone.

There was more talk of course – there always is. Morrison divided the credit of such a brilliant thought between Charles Philip and the Chief of Police – and Charles Philip laid it all up to 'the flower of the profession.' All agreed that I was the only man capable of handling it.

Get the whole of it now. The thing's good. If it worked out the advertisement would be worth thousands to me. That was true enough. I'm hired to walk about fifty feet behind the threatened banker. I must drop the man, when he made attempt to get Charles Philip. Imagine it! Of course there would be a day rate to that. A good one too, for in my way of thinking the thing never would be pulled. Richard Morrison had a soft job and wanted to cash in on it. Not liking him, I tossed a wrench into the works.

"Here's a man who writes, threatening death if he don't get money. He don't get it. Blooey – he decides to kill the banker. He'll collect a lot for that! It don't sound right." I certainly didn't get the why or how of that.

"When you have studied the ways of blackmailers as long as I, Mr. Williams, you will understand better." And before I could cut in on him and flatten his wind he turned to Charles Philip. "Get those letters for Mr. Williams – all of them, from the first about the money."

Charles Philip out of the room, the 'flower of the profession' took a decided change. Hard gray eyes stared into mine – his face took on heavy lines. I knew that I was in for some real dirt at last – and I was.

"It's more than money, Mr. Williams. I, like you, scoffed at the idea of actual killing, with Mr. Preston so well protected – but the Chief of Police, an old friend of the family, got at the real truth. Not a word to a soul now – least of all to Mr. Preston. He don't suspect, I know." He leaned forward and tapped me on the knee as his voice lowered to the soft notes of a flute. As for me, I suspected some old-time feud or such rot. But, no – here it is.

"We suspect a depositor in the bank – one who made bad investments and from a disordered mind holds the bank responsible. A real blackmailer don't kill his victim until he has played his last card. This is vengeance – maniacal vengeance. We know this from information the Chief of Police got from Mr. Preston."

I whistled softly – such a thing had the ring of truth – and if it was Preston was in real danger. I have heard of such birds – had one gun for me once. They're bad customers and you can kiss the Book on that. I nodded in understanding.

"You want me to shoot such a man." That part I didn't like.

"It would be your duty as a public spirited citizen, if you happened to be by when the attack was made. Now – we simply want you always to be by – to capture this man if possible – to kill him if necessary. After all, the man may be anything but mad – just seeking vengeance. We must save Mr. Preston."

I didn't like Mr. Richard Morrison, the Flower of the Profession. Neither did I like the grating sound of his voice – like a sleigh being pulled over dry pavement. But he stated a clear case. A policeman couldn't do the trick. It's mighty tricky shooting to get your man in a crowd and not stretch out some innocent bystander. And a maniac killed our president not so many years ago. Now I shrugged my shoulders. They wanted pretty shooting and they'd get it. That the law was behind me helped matters too. Most times my best work is kept secret. Besides, nothing might ever come of this. Just a nut idea.

Charles Philip blew in with the letters. As a matter of form and to show the proper interest, I read them over. Nothing unusual in the batch – the regular run of black hand letters. Bad English, bad spelling – yet true to form. Still, some nuts are mighty shrewd at certain things.

The Flower of the Profession sat there with his hands clasped across his ample front, nodding and smiling. He was about forty; a mighty powerful man, with a jowl that hung down when he wasn't watching it. A chap that had worked up from the bottom – yet I didn't like him.

There was a handshake all around – each praised the other to the sky – both smiled at me, and a butler with a surprised look and a vacant stare showed me to my room. I don't know if the Flower of the Profession and the beneficent banker kissed each other goodnight, but I heard that mutual admiration society break up as I shoved Butts out of the room and got ready to hit the hay.

No one seemed to be worried that anything would happen during the night. It seemed decided that any gun-play that took place would come off as a grand circus-act on some main thoroughfare. If not, I guess they felt I wasn't needed in the house. How could Charles Philip fear violence in his own home with the Flower himself sleeping in the next room? A laugh there – I bet a good crook could steal that bum detective's vest without his knowing it. He had found a good ear to blow his horn into – that was all.

Chapter IV

I SLEEP WELL – none better – and yet you couldn't drop your breath around me without my hearing it – so, I awoke with a start, jerked up in bed and listened. Unmistakably something had gone against my door. Not like someone trying to get in exactly. Just a dull thud, as if something had been placed against it – dropped down, or tossed there.

My gun was in my hand before I was half awake even. I dare say if the necessity arose I could take a pretty fair shot at a fellow without being fully awake. But now – barefooted I crossed noiselessly to the door. It was locked of course, but I had seen to that before I went to bed – just oiled the lock and hinges slightly. Try it sometime – it works wonders, and you never can tell when you might use it.

No hurry, you understand. The door opened without a sound – I tried to peer out into the darkness of the old house. Not a ray of light – the jet blackness of deep sleep. Something stirred there by my feet. I jerked my flash from my bathrobe pocket – held my gun ready and let the light blaze forth.

Again the Kid! But this time there was no laugh – just a sort of sigh as the light fell on her face. She half turned, pulled a little bare arm over her face to shut out the light, and slept on. Slept – that's it. Like a dog she was curled up before my door – fast asleep. Why? Oh – I know lots of life but I didn't guess the riddle of that. I haven't been much with children since – but that's in the old forgotten days.

At first I thought she had been hurt, as I bent down and lifted her in my arms – but, no – there was a folded blanket and a pillow beneath her head. She was parked before my door for the night. I was going to pipe out for her old man – this was his party, not mine. Then I thought better of it. The Kid had listened around a lot – perhaps she had something to tell me. But why fall asleep over it? Did she think I might come out for a midnight walk? I half shrugged my shoulders – and carried her inside. Then I jerked on the lights.

Kids are funny – you'd almost think she had been hit on the head the time it took to bring her around – twice she half sat up – once she smiled, murmured "Race" and passed out again. You could-a burnt the house down around her and she'd of slept on. At last I got her awake, and she was a most surprised young lady.

First, she wanted to make a dash from the room – then she didn't, but came back and looked straight up at me.

"I forgot and called you 'Race' again – but I always think of you as that, and—"

"I don't mind," I told her. "Now—" I lowered my voice to pretended secrecy, "what do you want to tell me?"

"Me! Tell you?" And her black eyes got as big as a couple of buckets. "What put that into your head?"

"Well – you were outside my door." And then when she didn't answer, "I know you like to listen in – but surely you didn't expect me to talk to myself."

She didn't turn red or anything – just smiled, like there was nothing insinuating in my remark. Then she walked toward the door – her little bare feet peeping out from beneath the long robe that trailed behind her on the floor.

"Won't you tell me why you were there?" I opened the door for her. "I'll have to tell your father if you don't. Besides catching cold, something might happen to you—" I didn't know her name.

"Dorothy." She filled in the blank. "And you won't tell father – you'd laugh at me if you knew why I was there. I – I—" And damned if she didn't suddenly clutch at me – dig her little head against my chest and burst out crying.

Then the truth came out. For the first time I realized how stupid I was. Poor little kid – she was frightened. That talk of threats of death, which so pleasantly thrilled her in the daytime, sent the fear through her little body at night. I guess it ain't children alone who have different thoughts in daytimes. One of the coldest and cruelest crooks I ever knew slept with the light turned full on. It's just human nature. Nothing frightens me, but then – I ain't strong for walking under ladders.

Poor little kid – she clung tightly to me and I had to lift her and carry her to her room on the floor above. No wonder she couldn't sleep – a big comfortable room all right, but far away from everybody. And when I placed her on her bed I had to unwind her arms about my neck.

As they say in certain circles – 'comes it another shock'. Her room is just covered with pictures – mostly cuttings from the newspapers. I've had many a thrill in my day, but maybe I didn't get one then – when my own face looked out at me from over the bed, on the walls, and fairly littered the tiny dresser in the corner. No movie idol ever had a more sincere worshiper, I guess.

I was in that house for a deadly purpose – playing a game that was booked to end in death. Ready to save the life of a prosperous banker – and I'll bet I sat there for upwards of an hour, holding a little hand and promising not to leave her.

She went to sleep all right – there was a smile on her face too, and when I left her and turned out the light, the gold tooth stood out like a beacon. It was the tell-tale mark with her. When you saw it she was happy – when it disappeared behind childish red lips, things were not so good. Despite her precocious little nature and sophisticated air, one could read her like an open book. Look at a child asleep sometime – Man! it will put thoughts into your mind that you never had before. At least, it did into mine. I've lived hard, but I sure felt a new sort of softness. Truth is truth too. As I looked at those pictures I never felt more flattered. The Flower of the Profession could have his Charles Philip Preston, Charles Philip could have his Richard Morrison, but I – yep, I swelled with pride. I had my Dorothy. To hell with both of them!

I was humming softly to myself as I passed down the stairs. Not listening particularly for anything – just naturally walking lightly, my flash picking out the steps before me and occasionally blazing off in the depths beneath, as it slipped around a bend and shone down the wide pit to the bottom floor nearly two flights below. A real old-fashioned house this one. I could picture a great Christmas tree stretching up above the second floor.

I turned into the darkness of my own room – stretched and yawned by the open window, and stared out into the night. A bright moon – but distant in the heavens as it streaked the lawn with uneven ribbons of light that wavered with the swinging branches of the trees.

A figure – striped by the moon like a convict. A crouching, running figure that disappeared in the thickness of great trees. But I had seen it all right – a mean, sneering face, with a deep cut across the center of the upper lip. Someone had run away from the house, which was set back from the broad, well-shaded street. This threat to kill in broad daylight was not to be taken too seriously. I knew I'd recognize that mug if I saw it again.

I turned from the window – took one step – and was back by the window again. A dull thud had come from below – an unmistakable thud. Someone had closed a window. For a moment I watched the lawn – then bent far out – not a soul was in sight. But someone below had closed a window. That meant just one thing. It wasn't a departing figure – but one who still was in that house. Not Dorothy this time. She was tucked safely up in bed. I had seen to that personally. One man had run from the house. Why? I couldn't answer that question. One man had stayed behind. Why? I gripped my gun the tighter and again sought the hall. I wanted that question answered.

No flash this time. I knew the stairs – stretched out a hand, found the banister, and started down. I thought that I heard a board creak far below in the darkness; then I pulled a creak of my own – the worn stairs gave up their dead. I cursed softly. I should have listened first – let the intruder come up to me. Now – I had sounded my warning. Listen as I would – stand there as patiently as I might, not another sound from below.

Five, ten minutes passed. Slowly I went down again, keeping close to the wall where the steady tread of feet had not so loosened the old boards. But there were creaks – I couldn't get away from that. It would take a remarkably lucky shot to find me in that blackness though. One shot, mind you! And then I'd decorate that hall with enough lead to make it a war relic.

I reached the last step – sent forth one dismal wail and stood on the thick rug in the main hall. So much for that. Give me one cue – just the slightest noise – and I'd have my flash doing its stuff.

A window stood out like a lighthouse on a sea of darkness. One of those old-time windows, with the stained glass and a lass with a flower in her hand, doing her trick in the center of the faded colored glass. Through the white robe of that figure the moon sent a generous strip of light, that cut the darkness like a knife.

A half hour I stood there, trying to detect the slightest sound. If I had any nerves I'd blame it on that, and think I hadn't heard that window plop down in the first place. But I was sure of myself. I had played at this game before – alone in a darkened house, with pretty tough birds – bent on murder.

Creak. Another lad was hitting the boards and they were playing him false. I perked up considerable – things were going to break. Another wait – again the creak. Coming nearer. I set my lips grimly. There was someone in the darkness after all, and that someone was coming to me – slowly making his way toward the stairs. Well – he'd have to run me down or cross the light. I drew a bead on that stretch of moonlight and waited.

He'd have to make it snappy now, for the ribbon of light was getting smaller and smaller until it looked like a string. Another creak – and I spotted my man. Just the dimmest flash of something blurred across the tiny stretch. But that was enough. I stepped out – stuck my gun and flash forward at the same time.

We both got the idea together, for my light shot into a large white face just as the blinding rays of another torch shone upon me. My gun was pressed against his face – his against my chest. It was a nice party all around. There was a nervous laugh as the gun lowered from my stomach and the flash dropped, to make a circle on the floor. But my flash was steady on the great jowls and blinking gray eyes of Richard Morrison. And my gun too was still sticking close against the kisser of the Flower of the Profession. What was on my mind is a different story. You'd think I had nothing to do but run around that old house and play hide and seek with – first, the child; then, the great detective himself. Maybe it was in my mind to croak him – I don't like detectives anyway.

He was talking now and, I thought, half edging his gun up again. But of a certainty he had had a shock, and the flute-like tones of his voice were about a note and a half off key.

"It's me – Richard Morrison." He was in a hurry to get it all out. Like 'last words' sort of stuff. "I came down here – heard a noise – saw a figure ducking across the lawn. Then—"

"You closed the window and stood on the inside," I added. That sounded like the truth.

"Why – yes. How did you know?" He seemed surprised. "I was about to pursue the figure when I heard the step upon the stairs. I didn't know it was you, and waited."

Well, what was the good! I guess his story was true enough. But he was ducking to get up them stairs – call me. He was good on thinking things up – not on action. Any dick worth his salt would have ducked out and after that bird on the lawn. This lad simply wanted a soft berth. He had got me hired to do the dirty work.

I didn't say nothing – I couldn't. His voice wasn't right but I got to admit that his hand didn't tremble and the same ruddy hue stood out on his fat round cheeks. Cherub-like he looked – that is, his face. When I dropped my gun and followed him up the stairs, he looked more like a bear, with his great brown bathrobe wrapped tightly about him.

He got his wind back as we reached the landing.

"I always like to look the house over at night. Feel it a duty." His chest came out like a dozen pouter pigeons. "You are to be commended for your ready assistance and your keen sense of hearing – while asleep." And he looked back at me over his shoulder as he snapped on the light in the hall above.

Was there suspicion in his eyes? I don't think so. More a keen, scrutinizing, searching look as he hunted for something in my face. Besides, I had no desire to give the Kid away. Why? You can search me – I don't know.

I didn't get up again that night. I dare say if I did I'd of poked my gun against Charles Philip's face. Everybody but the old butler and him had come near tasting lead. The Kid part worried me. If I had of stretched out the Flower of the Profession I dare say I wouldn't have lost much sleep over it.

Chapter V

THE NEXT DAY was Sunday and Charles Philip and the Flower of the Profession went on with the mutual admiration society. I could have listened all day but I didn't. The Chief of Police blew in, and he was a little runt with a lisp, that filled out the trio nicely. He didn't stay long – just shook hands with me and finished up arrangements. Nothing to it. I was simply to follow Charles Philip back and forth to the bank on Monday morning.

They wanted me to go out in the garage behind the house and show my stuff with a gun but I wouldn't. Charles Philip, who was most insistent that I do a few tricks, was also the loudest in disclaiming all fear for his life "in this public-spirited attempt to abolish crime from Rosedale."

As for me, I did a trick over the hills with little Dorothy. And she wasn't twelve, but would be eleven on the first of the month. She wanted a pony and cart for her birthday, but her father thought that was a waste of money. He told her about the starving children in Russia and took her bank with the dollar and eight cents to send to them. He sure was a big-hearted lad. And the poor Kid fell for it all, even trying to get me interested in starving Russia. But I'd been to Russia myself – damned near starved there too.

But most of all she was worried about her father. And acted for a bit like he was already planted; then she perked up, and if it wasn't for her age I'd have suspected her of simply laying on the apple-sauce like her older sisters.

"But you won't let anyone hurt my daddy, will you Race?" She bit her lips and fought back the tears. "I'd like to hear you promise that. Then I'd know everything is all right."

"I won't let anyone hurt him." I told her and meant it. "Nor you either," I added.

"Maybe he'll be so happy that you're here that he'll buy me that pony and cart."

I nodded at that. He could well afford it. Three cars were parked back in that big garage and he wouldn't come through with a couple of hundred for a pony. A dollar and eight cents for the starving Russians! Big-heartedness and good training it may be. But I've always looked on it as pretty small potatoes. He wouldn't dare come that game on a waiter – not him.

Monday morning came and the parade was on. I had hard work to keep from laughing right out loud at breakfast. Richard Morrison, the Flower, was decked out like a lily, and his face was long and serious. He was simply pulling his stuff, to match the dignity of Charles Philip.

A dozen times before breakfast Charles Philip had a look out the window. You'd think half the gunmen in the country were out there ready to serenade him with lead before he got half a block. Everybody connected with the case was doing as he wished. He scorned threats – defied 'the viciousness of human depravity', and yet down in his heart I think he was surprised that the governor of the state hadn't heard of it and called out the militia.

Charles Philip was dressed like he was going to his own funeral. Long frock coat and all that goes with it. Everything but the high hat. His sky piece was of that queer mongrel breed – a cross between a derby and a stove pipe. Not so high as a dicer and not round on top like a derby – the thing that judges often wear, if you get what I mean. There ain't no name for it that I ever heard.

It was his habit for years to walk the mile and a half to the bank. His father had done it before him. But, though he threw his chest out and gripped his cane tightly, I'd of made a bet that he'd of broken his right leg for a chance to ride in a closed car that morning.

And Morrison cautioned me in the doorway. Just before the parade began.

"I'm sure it will happen today." His face was very serious. "Keep an eye out and shoot to kill." There was an earnestness to his voice that was not to be laughed off. If he had a hunch or secret information or something, I don't know.

"We must face the thing squarely and be done with it. Watch his every movement – close up near him when you reach the business district – watch every face. I can't walk with you – because – I might – would no doubt be recognized."

With the parting warning that he would be watching some place in town, the great detective ducked across the street, slid into a waiting car and was whisked away.

Charles Philip's step never faltered as he trod down the steps of the great front porch. He even stopped for a word with the gardener. You could see him raise his eyes and lamp the big mansion across the street, in hopes that some other great man of Rosedale saw and understood. The dear old soul was scared stiff – there ain't no two ways about that. But give him credit! He was facing the music. Already he had convinced himself that when he entered his house again he would enter feet first. Never a martyr faced the lions with a weaker heart and a stauncher stride than Charles Philip. He was the Banker, the Board of Education, and the Common Council all rolled into one.

Less than fifty feet behind him came yours truly. I didn't take much stock in the whole thing but I was earning my money – hands sunk deep in the pockets of my light overcoat, wrapped around heavy forty-fives. I smiled to myself – if anyone was bent on laying out Charles Philip – why, he'd need a machine gun. And that's that. Dorothy waved to me from the window. I half caught her eye – but I didn't look back. If Charles Philip happened to see me he'd faint right on the street.

Charles Philip never turned to see if I followed. He must have felt that the eyes of the world were on him, and wanted to strut his stuff. I skipped once – got into step and crossed the street a good fifty feet to the rear. Every cop we passed was on. Serious they looked too. Richard Morrison, the Flower of the Profession, sure had laid it on thick. Well – it was good stuff and great advertising, even if nothing came of it. So I wiped off my grin – jerked forward my slouch hat and made the whole affair smack of tragedy. Just one thing I couldn't do. That was – keep in step with Charles Philip. Not that I couldn't see his legs pattering along all right – but he jerked too much. I'm no dancing master.

We hit the business section – not so many people at first – then crowds. Charles Philip grew a bit nervous – tugged his hand under his winged collar, and tried to look in shop windows with the hope of getting a slant at me. He was having a tough time of it.

As for me, I stepped faster. The street was thick with people – all hurrying about their business. Thirty feet now – I swung along behind him, trying to keep daylight between me and the back of Charles Philip's neck. About three blocks from the bank I glanced across the street and saw the Chief of Police in plain clothes. Even at that distance the whiteness of his face showed up. He didn't like the whole thing. Would rather have tucked Charles Philip up in bed until the scare blew over. The Flower of the Profession sure had a way of putting it over. He couldn't fool me with—

And there he was – the Flower himself, in person. He had suddenly gripped me by the shoulder. I heard his voice – caught the excited note in it.

"Faster, man – faster." He fairly hissed the words. "See that figure there – the one just ahead of Mr. Preston – those stooped shoulders!"

And I didn't see anything – nothing suspicious anyway. But I kept my eyes peeled ahead and increased my gait. Of course the Flower was only trying to work up an interest. If he could get me excited – why, we'd drag the affair out for a month or so – with the lurking enemies just ducking off before—

"There – there – watch, man. Quick!" The words in my ear were almost a screech.

Two women passed suddenly in front of me. Then I got it. A shabby, round-shouldered man lurched from the curb – there was no hesitation – no threat. A gun just flashed from beneath his coat and thudded up against the back of Charles Philip Preston.

Them that know me know that I'm a quick shot. There's no horse radish about that. Oh – I fired – but I'm not supernatural. I can control my own bullets to the fraction of an inch. I did then. I'll lay a bet more than one lady had her hair singed when my guns spoke.

But the man had fired too – I saw the shoot of flame – the tiny streak of smoke. Did I hit my man? He shot into the air like a jack-in-the-box and stretched his length upon the sidewalk. He'd never make his confession in this world.

At first there wasn't anybody on the street. They lit out for doorways. The Chief of Police and myself reached the body together, Richard Morrison close on our heels.

And what of Charles Philip, you ask? Yep, he went down – I thought he was dead sure; this lad had snapped his gun plunk against his back. The Chief and Morrison lifted him and carried him to the drug store on the corner. For a moment I was alone with the dead. He was clutching something in his left hand. Quickly I pulled it from his fingers and as quickly shoved it into my pocket. But not before I had recognized it as the torn corner of a thousand dollar bill.

After that the police and the crowds. Brave men brought their aid to the stricken – bent over to get a look at the dead man's face, and a slant at the wicked-looking automatic that he still held in his hand.

"You'll be Race Williams?" A burly Captain of Police laid a hand upon my shoulder. Then he gasped. "Two shots, eh – drilled him right behind the ear." Behind the ear was right. Some shooting. You couldn't have put the width of your little finger between those two shots. And remember they slipped through a crowded street and copped off my man. I'm not conceited, you understand, but I do take a little pride in my work.

Just one thing bothered me as I stood up and walked toward the drug store. Had Charles Philip kicked off? Not that I was attached to the old dear – but it hurt my feelings to think that I let that corpse put it over on me. But imagine it – never a word – just a shot.

Chapter VI

I PUSHED through the crowd to the back of the drug store in time to see Charles Philip and the Flower of the Profession duck out the rear and jump a taxi. Good enough, I sighed with relief. Charles Philip was walking on his own feet. He must have had a hide like a rhinoceros – that baby with the gat couldn't have missed. If I hadn't of shot to kill, friend corpse would have emptied the cannon in his back.

I too slipped out the back way and trotted slowly off towards the Preston house. Was the lad who did the shooting crazy? I didn't think so. He had the face of the underworld rat. The worst breed of gunman. I tried to recollect every detail before I fired. I was almost certain that a big car slipped slowly along by the curb. And the driver had a cut lip. That was the get-away car – a well-planned murder then. But I shrugged my shoulders – it had nothing to do with me. Five thousand smackers should be waiting for me at the Preston house. Between you and me and the corner speak-easy I don't know anyone that needed five grand more than I did.

Before I reached the house though, I climbed up on a wall by a deserted street and examined that torn end of the thousand dollar bill. Now, where did that fit into the picture? I compared it with the other – the one from the Sob-Sister's pocket. Both corners had been torn from different bills. On both halves the serial numbers stood out – nothing in common between the two bills – except that both had been found on the persons of tough eggs who were bent on murder.

I shoved both the bill corners into my pocket – hopped from the wall, and whistling softly trotted along to Preston's. You got to admit it was fast work – easy money – and yet earned money. Time isn't what counts – it's results.

Charles Philip wasn't home. No one was there but the old butler. "No – Mr. Preston wasn't hurt none – just shook up considerable."

That – and the news that he and the Flower had gone to the police station to see the Chief and the coroner was the best I could get. What do you make of that – and me just saving his life and looking for tears of gratitude?

I hung around for about an hour, and then shot down to see the Chief of Police. He was a nervous little duck and seemed to look on me as if I were a problem in solid geometry. He thought I had left town, and hoped I had. Before I could get the lowdown on the thing, the coroner blew in. He was full of bull and veiled threats, and finally on the advice of the Chief paroled me in the Chief's custody. They were a couple of flustered gentlemen, so I put a few questions of my own.

"I tell you, Williams," the Chief gripped my hand. "I respect you and don't see how you could have done any less than you did. But the thing won't look well in print – that is, when the rival paper gets hold of it. You see, the man you killed wasn't armed."

"Wasn't what?" You could have knocked me down with a load of brick.

"Well – his gun held blanks – nothing more. Mr. Preston was simply scorched. The man who shot at him must have been crazy. Mr. Preston was sorry you didn't hit him in the leg."

"He was, was he?" I was a bit mad now. Things evidently weren't going right and they wanted to pass the buck to me. "I suppose he wanted me to take the man by the hand and lead him away. Besides, I saw that fellow's face – he wasn't goofy – just an out-and-out crook. Where's Preston now? And where's that detective – the Flower of the Profession – who you have taken to your bosom?"

"It's too bad." The Chief shook his head. "But you were in the right. Just slip out and get back to the city. The paper is going to run a story about Preston hiring a gunman. It won't do either of you any good."

"It won't, eh – and what about my money? Did this Preston mention that to you?"

The coroner broke in this time – his mouth was full of cigar, but I would have caught his words if it had been full of mud.

"You run along – I dare say Mr. Preston will take care of you. Not as handsome as if the gun was really loaded. The blanks make things look—"

"Mr. Coroner," I put an eye on him that must have kept him awake for a week, "Mr. Preston made a bargain with me – that it was verbal makes no difference. He'll pay me what he owes me, and pay me today. I'm not interested in what kind of a humor he's in."

I think they would have liked to arrest me. But they knew I'd stir up an odor that would cost one of them his job. I was a deputy sheriff – acting in accordance with my instructions straight from the Chief of Police. And Preston? He was the biggest man in town. He had them all buffaloed. Had them – but not me. And right then I got to wondering if after all there wasn't something deeper in the whole thing. Had Preston really wanted a certain party killed, and sucked us all in? But how did he get that lad to shoot with blanks? It had me guessing.

I always get paid – this time I would too. My gun didn't carry any blanks. We'd see if Preston didn't feel more like paying up after I had talked turkey to him. With that in mind I shot straight out to the Preston house again.

I can't say that I was made welcome by the butler. In fact, if the truth must be told, I had to push my way in. But the butler became downright obliging – served me dinner and everything – that is, after he picked himself up off the floor.

Charles Philip wouldn't be back until late in the evening, and Butts had been instructed to help in packing my bag. I would hear from the Banker in the city.

"We won't trouble him like that." I smiled pleasantly. "I'll wait for him." And wait I did. Little Dorothy was no place about. So I spent my time reading in the library.

I guess it was close to ten o'clock when the doorbell rang. I stepped to the hall as old Butts passed through it. Just a word in his ear.

"You needn't bother to mention that I'm waiting here." I put an eye on the good and faithful – then, in way of a little pleasantry, I added, "I killed one man today."

Butts lacked a sense of humor but held a great respect for human life. As I stepped back into the library I heard him greet the master of the house – and the name of Race Williams was not on his lips.

There was the hurried step of childish feet upon the stairs. A low, complaining voice from Charles Philip – and a high pitch, falsetto laugh as Richard Morrison's soft notes reassured him on some point. As for me, I lit a butt and waited. Luck was with me – the two sailed into the room together.

I'll give Morrison credit for grinning broadly when he saw me. Not so Charles Philip – all his dignity scattered to the four winds. Surprised and mad – that was it. Fear hadn't come yet. That was to follow. Charles Philip blustered when he spoke.

"I gave orders that you were to leave town – go back to New York where you came from. I don't want you here – don't want you strutting about the streets, fresh from – from killing a man. A man whom the papers claim I hired you to kill."

"Yeah? Well, didn't you?" I stared straight at the pompous duck, but I had an eye for Morrison too.

It was Morrison who cut in as Charles Philip started in to talk.

"I can't blame you, Mr. Williams." He nodded seriously enough at me. "You are an unfortunate man – nothing more. That the bullets were fake was hardly – hardly your fault." And he got it out like it was actually my fault. "I think it best that you do as Mr. Preston suggests – leave the city."

"I have no desire to stay in Rosedale." I guess my dignity matched the banker's as I half bowed. "I have completed a task – and I am here to be paid for it."

Charles Philip became slightly excited.

"By God – I believe you staged the whole affair – an enemy you wanted to kill – I—"

I took one step forward.

"You can't crawl out of it with that." And I half wondered where he got the flukey idea. "The man is dead – you are alive. I want my five thousand – and I want it now."

Morrison knew what was coming. I saw his hand steal toward his coat pocket. And I gave him his chance – let him get his gun half out. It always looks better in such affairs. Half out was all though. He might have done better if he was really bent on making a draw. But he just wanted to slip the gun into his hands and shine at the crucial moment. Now – his time to shine had passed – he was looking down the round black mouth of my forty-five – and the hammer was rising and falling gently. One of my regular stunts.

A nice picture we made there – the three of us. And I could see only one thing. Charles Philip was trying to beat me out of my five grand – Morrison was strong to help him – and I was set on collecting. How congenial we had been twenty-four hours before – money sure can make trouble! But Charles Philip was speaking. And though his dignity was still there – his voice had a wheeze to it.

"Mr. Morrison has the check. After he investigates fully he shall pay you – not before."

"Ah!" I breathed easier. Morrison claimed to know my reputation – admire my tactics. He'd get an eyeful now.

"You don't appreciate the esteem with which Mr. Morrison regards me." I smiled easily. "He trusts in me absolutely and will turn over that check to me – now." Oh, the rest of the yarn is too long to bother with details at a time like this. Morrison was a sensible man. That I nearly knocked out one of his teeth calculating the distance from my gun to his mouth is of minor importance. He came across with the check.

"I think you have earned it." He tried to be gracious – though he'd have liked to have bitten my left ear off.

There was some wind from Charles Philip – loose talk about stopping payment on the check; and then, I thought in some shame, he blurted out:

"It isn't as if you saved my life – but you shot down an unarmed man. I hope that you were honest – but I think you crooked and—"

Charles Philip's age might have protected him. There's some talk I won't stand. I half leaned toward him. What was on my mind I don't rightly know. But a little figure dashed into the room – stepped between us and threw two arms about my neck. They had me then if they wanted to – the two of them. But I guess we all three were a bit knocked over. Just a soft cheek against mine – two wet, childish lips – then great black eyes that blazed in anger.

"How can you say such things, father – he promised me to save you. And the other night, when I was alone – forgotten and—" There was a burst of tears, a soft, yielding little body, and a great silence – broken only by Dorothy's sobs.

Somehow I got her arms from about my neck – half led her from the room – watched her up the stairs. The case was closed – the check in my pocket – my bag there by the vestibule door, and Butts eyeing me from near the dining room. Not another word – I just turned and passed into the night. Still, I won't take too much credit myself. If it hadn't of been for the Kid, I dare say I'd have clouted the old man a smack in the mouth.

And this silly talk of my framing the whole thing – getting a lad to plug at Charles Philip with empty shells. A strange fancy that, and one he never thought out himself. Then who put it into his head? Suppose – but, oh, what the hell – the thing was too deep for me. I had my five grand and the case was closed. But was it? There were still the torn corners of the thousand dollar bills to account for. Gad – it would almost look like someone was getting paid to be bumped off by me. On the surface it all looked straight enough. But what was under cover?

Through it all one bright spot stood out. Dorothy! Only those who never have been kissed by a little child can understand how I felt about that. And I'm not ashamed to admit it either.

Chapter VII

A COUPLE of days later the thing still stuck in my crop. Not only the newspaper notice that Richard Morrison had sailed for Europe on the *Albertania,* but he had had the bad taste to send me a wireless when he was two days out. Why? You can search me. And the thing read funny.

> *Much thanks for your many courtesies.*
> *Richard Morrison*

There – laugh that one off. I couldn't.

Now for something new on you. I went and pulled a stunt I hadn't pulled in years. Perhaps I was getting sentimental – 'blood thicker than water' business when I thought of that Kid – but I skipped far out in the Westchester hills and visited my brother, Balcome Williams. Never heard of him before? Of course you didn't. I never told you – he's a queer duck and we ain't got much in common. But he's got the greatest analytical mind in the world. Would make a great detective if he hadn't gone in for chemistry, got a hold of a bit of money, and become so fat and lazy.

Balcome is my elder brother but there are times when he nearly turns my stomach – this was one of them. He didn't get up to greet me – just laid there in the great chair before the open fire, sipping tea and feeding bits of sardines to a fat, hairy, brown cat that stretched off on his ample stomach.

"Oh, Race! Yes, it is Race!" His eyes half opened and closed again. "You have come to see me – there, take my hand – it is fatiguing, these brotherly visits – but it isn't often." He sighed again. It was like shaking hands with a jellyfish as I lifted up his mushy fin. And all the time he was talking softly – half to the cat and half to me.

"You haven't come to excite me, I hope. There's a bit of sardine, my pretty. You've been killing a man up in Rosedale, I see. Be careful of papa's vest, my brown pearl. An unarmed man – in the prize ring they would call it a set up. There now, a bit of cracker and—" The thing went on – a sad jumble – when I butted in.

"I've come to make a call on you – not that damned cat." I half made a pass at the suddenly arched back of the animal.

"There – stop it." A slight interest seemed to blaze in his eyes – not anger exactly – he wouldn't make the effort for that. "You haven't changed – at least not for the better, Race." And he shook his huge head slowly from side to side. "Only last week I read of a corpse up Van Cortlandt way. The brotherly touch was there."

"You know of that!" I sure got a start. I wondered if others were on – if the police net was quietly making ready to drag me in.

"Tut, tut!" He waved a pudgy hand a few inches in the air. "You are fortunate in living in an age of incompetence. I suspected you at once. Knew, the minute you walked in the door. Why not tell me the whole case, let me see what you play with there in your pocket – and be gone."

"I have nothing to ask you." I jerked my hand from my pocket and let the torn corners of the thousand dollar bills drop back.

A moment's pause while he stroked the cat.

"A detective from Paris was here yesterday – crossed all the way from France to see me. But it did not interest me – this case. Too bad, for it was simple of solution. I could have cleared the thing up in ten minutes – but I was bored. Now, you – you will sit there and fidget and watch the windows and look for death." A lone sigh now before he continued.

"I hate death – but you will be killed some day. I am your brother and I suppose I shall go to the funeral. It will be expected of me. You have made no will of course. That would be like you. Let us hope you die after a successful case."

"I have no intention of dying yet," I told him – and meant it. "And I'd rather be out in the open, meeting an enemy face to face, than stretched off here with a mangy cat that—"

"You would live to be old indeed," he broke right in upon me, not listening to what I said, I guess, "if you used your head instead of your hands." A yawn that showed great white, even teeth – another great gap in his face, and then – "The clock behind me on the bookcase, Race – will you be so good as to tell me the time?"

Yep – damned if he wasn't too lazy to turn around. Well, I told him – and got up and started for the door. The unpleasant duty was over. Each time I returned I expected to see the great carcass rotted away. But he stopped me in the doorway – half straightened in his chair – dumped the cat unceremoniously to the floor.

"They have been making a fool of you, eh?" There was no sneer, more of a laugh in his voice, or rather a smile, if you get what I mean. "Come, the thing may interest me – out with what's on your mind. I know that you visited me for a purpose. I would think you a fool if you hadn't. What could you and I have in common?"

Perhaps he was right. I never go to anyone for help though. I fight my own battles. But this case was dead – finished. I had been paid. It might give me a laugh to see my dead brother try to explain the coincidence of those thousand dollar bills, that unloaded gun, and Charles Philip's desire to shut down on the check. Well, I'd knock some of the conceit out of him with that yarn. So I spun it to him – all of it – from the first letter at my office to the final parting with Dorothy. Richard Morrison's going to Europe, I didn't mention – didn't think of it as important.

"And now," I finished, "how do you explain such a coincidence of the two torn pieces of separate thousand dollar bills?" And I chucked the torn corners onto his lap – if you could call it a lap.

"My dear boy," his great lips slipped back, stretching almost across his face, "let us not call the thing a coincidence. Practical men would laugh. Such coincidence is not in life. First, we must connect up the corner of the bill in Van Cortlandt park with the other corner by the little drug store in Rosedale.

"Of a certainty a link joins them." His eyes half closed as he went on. "A part of a bill – men have done it with waiters – head waiters – giving them half a twenty when they first visit the hotel, and matching it with the other half when they leave. Just the promise of something for a service rendered. To kill you, the first one maybe – I—" And his voice sunk to a whisper, to die off to nothing.

He was still so long that I thought he slept – and then the room suddenly vibrated with his laugh. He just flung back his head and roared.

"My poor, dear, gullible brother," he finally explained between great gusts of mirth. "The man with the fingers of a genius, the eyes of a vulture and the brains of a little child! You have been beaten at your own game. Someone wanted certain parties killed, and that someone arranged for you to do it. The first was a simple matter. He sent an inferior gunman – one who would surely bungle the job and who did bungle it. You were picked as one who shoots to kill. Easy – so our hidden foe is dispossessed of one undesirable who learned too much of his secrets.

"The second was more intricate – yet you shot the man down. Clever – very clever. For this man under cover did not want Charles Philip Preston hurt – thus the fake bullets in the gun. You were very easy, my boy – very easy."

And damn it, the thing rang with truth – an impossible truth. Would one dare to trick me like that, and who? I had it though.

"Charles Philip Preston," I gasped.

"Not so fast." Balcome shook his head. "You must learn of him first. Is the bank sound – has he got a past? But, no – he could not have so handled it."

"But we have our clues laid out before us. The night before the shooting – one visited the Preston house, you say? Nothing was stolen – he brought a message then, and—"

"But Preston hinted that I framed the whole thing," I cut in. "He—"

"The man who hinted at it got the idea from someone else – and—" he pointed to a huge volume that lay beneath a table in the corner of the room. "That book – there."

I stretched out and lifting the dust-covered volume, gave it to him. It was a directory of detective agencies. I watched Balcome turn the pages, noted the closely written sheet in the back that had been filled in with Balcome's tiny letters. Somehow, I thought that I knew before he spoke. Richard Morrison was the man!

"I know his name," Balcome started – then after a moment's thought, "I shall not tell you. The thing is not finished, but just beginning. This man has tricked you like a child. The great Race Williams and – but I cannot tell you. For if you crossed such a man you would die. Think of it – he made you do his bidding – killing his enemies, and did not spend a single cent – another paid you for this last—"

"Did you find his name in that book?" I busted in.

"No," he shook his head. "I found him because his name was *not* in that book. Do not try to guess – I shall not tell you his name."

I was mad clean through. What he told me rang with truth. Besides, Balcome was always right – but now – I tried him again.

"You see," it was hard to smile, "I know who you think it is. But the case is ended. For Mr. Richard Morrison is on his way to Europe."

"The case is not ended. Such a man plays for a big game." Big white teeth looked up at me. "And the man I refer to is not on his way to Europe." And damned if he didn't flop back and refuse to utter another word – either about the case or about commonplace things. I left him there – his huge carcass filling the large chair – his red cheeks puffed out – and the cat again perched upon his stomach.

Balcome had been right. I could see that now – explain the torn bills. Someone had used me to further his own ends. But was Richard Morrison, the Flower of the Profession, that man? Yet Richard Morrison was three days out to England, and Balcome said that *the man* was not on his way to Europe. Past interviews with my brother swept back. Balcome never had been wrong yet. Yet, to me the case was ended. I shrugged my shoulders as I sped back to the city. I'm not a detective and I didn't have any desire to hunt around Europe trying to get at the truth from Richard Morrison. Not me! Yet it was hard to believe that any man had dared use me to blow off his enemies.

Balcome could be wrong, even though I had never known him to be. What more could there be to the case? Home – in my slippers – I picked up the evening paper and glanced through it. The case was over, eh? Five minutes later I was frantically pacing the room. Not much space in a great New York daily was given over to it. But there it was. Dorothy Preston had been kidnapped.

Chapter VIII

A CASE! The money there would be in it to find her! No – strange, but nothing like that was in my head. Here was something new to me, and the memory of those childish arms and – but – I had said that both my guns were at her service.

I guess I spent the best part of an hour trying to get Charles Philip Preston on the wire. I wouldn't have taken a nickel. I kept jamming the telephone hook with one hand and clutching at my gun with the other. I was ready to do a bit of gunning for pleasure – for the love of the sport, so to speak.

A full hour I wasted to find out that Charles Philip wouldn't even speak to me. Old Butts finally came to the phone. Not much to hear from him. Dorothy had gone out for a walk and disappeared. There had been letters demanding money. Preston had wired for Richard Morrison, but it would take him at least two weeks to get back in the country. I jammed up the receiver.

I couldn't think. Somehow it seemed the biggest thing of my life. And the feeling that Dorothy would be counting on me – the pictures in her room – the poor frightened child in the hands of – who? It couldn't be Richard Morrison, for he was on his way to Europe. Who then – the lad with the cut lip, who visited the house that night? If I only knew the name of the boy who had duped me! I tried getting Balcome on the phone. Finally his lazy voice reached me. Balcome never guessed – never lied. If he didn't know he simply said that the case didn't interest him. He could do the thinking. I'd furnish the action. His slow drawl was maddening.

"I can't tell you this man's name, Race. It would be murder. And as I expect to inherit what you leave – why, I couldn't have that on my conscience. This man has played with you – you are no match for him. Give it up and stick to the rats in the underworld. I—"

"If you don't tell me as you have doped it out I'll come to your place and bust every window in the house." Childish that – certainly – but then, you don't know Balcome – he hates to be disturbed. And I – if I thought for a moment it would bring results, I'd do it – willing. Balcome knew that and it was a long time before he answered. Then—

"I'll help you out – only be sure to appoint me executor of your will – this two per-cent eats into the money so. If you wish to find this child – keep your eyes open. Remember the man with the cut lip. Watch for him and follow him."

"But how in the name of common sense will I find him?"

"He will find you. This man who works under cover got rid of two confederates by having you kill them. He decided there were too many close to him aware of his criminal life. He won't trust many – and he'll have you watched – sooner or later this split-lipped man will turn up. Watch for him – follow him!"

"I'll cut his heart out. But I must act at once."

"Yes, yes – the latest paper says that this Charles Philip is counting on the police and determined to give up nothing. Pressed too closely they might harm the child. So—" His voice trailed off and I knew that he was talking to the cat.

"But the name of the man – this one who duped me and now holds the child."

"Ah – that. Is it possible you don't know? Why, Richard Morrison, of course – and don't forget to have the executor of your will serve without bond." There was a click as the receiver hung up.

Fool – he was wrong. Richard Morrison was over halfway to England. Had he guessed wrong, or was he simply laughing at me? After all, Balcome could not be infallible. He simply sat there in his chair and doped the whole thing out. Or did he really fear for my life and was hiding the real name? That was it. He didn't tell me the truth.

It didn't take me long to get out Westchester way when I couldn't get an answer to my continued clicking of the phone. I'd threaten, plead, beg – anything to save little Dorothy. How simple other cases had been, when there was just money involved. And this one – there seemed no way to turn.

The house was in darkness – not even Balcome's old servant was there. I went through it from cellar to attic. He had skipped out – guessed that I was coming. And there, on the library table, was an envelope addressed to me. I quickly tore it open – not a word of where he had gone. Just the line –

The Flower of the Profession will no doubt lay a lily in your hand. Watch out for if he thinks you are on the case he will trap you.

Under ordinary circumstances I could have laughed. Balcome prided himself on never missing out on a case that 'interested' him. And it was true that he was consulted often by the biggest detective agencies in the country. Richard Morrison, on the high seas, could have nothing to do with the kidnapping of Dorothy Preston in Rosedale.

But the advice about following the man who followed me would be good. I'd add something to that myself. And I didn't get over a block from Balcome's house when I knew that someone was getting my smoke. Good! Of course, knowing that I was in the Preston case before, these crooks would keep an eye on me, and they didn't know that I had spotted Split-Lip in the moonlight.

I didn't look back – just watched the car behind in my mirror. Balcome certainly had called the cards. Now, if I did what was in my head – stick this lad up – shove a gun down his throat and find out all he knew – I might be led straight to Dorothy. Then again, this fellow might know nothing and I would lose the chance of seeing who he met – of turning the tables and following him. But how to do that! I'm not so good at shadowing – not so bad either – but to follow a party who is already following you! Well – it may be done, but I have never learned the trick.

When I slowed down, the car behind slowed down – when I gathered speed, the car too picked up. It's mighty hard, under the best of conditions, to spot a lad's map in the mirror of a moving car. And conditions were not of the best. It was tough on me. Here was plenty of desolate country road – nothing to suddenly block the road and stick up the lad behind me. Yet – but look at the whole thing. Wasn't this the worst case I ever tackled? And the incentive to win! A little child who admired and trusted in me. The leader of a gang who had made a monkey out of me – led me around like a puppet on a string while he simply kept under cover.

And think! Man! I couldn't seem to think at all. Before I had made up my mind to do anything I was back in the city – the blue car behind me mingling with many other cars. One thing I did learn – there was but one man in the car behind, and as I got held up by traffic I discovered that he didn't have a split lip.

It was hard to keep an eye on the car behind now as I pulled up before my house and stepped out. Several cars were coming down the street – the blue one not among them. But across the street and directly beneath the light, a man loitered. For the high-class gang that Balcome reckoned them to be, they were pulling off their shadow show in rather shabby style.

It didn't take me a minute to duck into my apartment – part the curtains at the front window and look out. The blue car came slowly down the street. There was a man in the back seat this time – must have picked him up along Broadway. It didn't stop across the street, but the man in the rear seat climbed out while the one on the sidewalk jumped aboard the slowly moving car. Then the car continued down the street. Not very clever that – in fact, rather stupid. The house was being watched pretty openly. For the moment I suspected some private detective agency. Who would be having me spotted? Charles Philip Preston maybe. Suspecting that I had had a hand in the kidnapping of—

I whistled softly – Balcome had certainly called the trick to the very card. The newcomer before the house passed directly beneath the light. It was the same face that I had seen in that stretch of moonlight on the Preston grounds in Rosedale. I nodded grimly – the cut lip stood out plainly. So, I sat by the darkened window and played absently with a forty-five.

Intently I watched the man across the street. Balcome was right – thinking was not for me. In every movement where intrigue was needed, this unknown foe had tricked me. I had killed at his bidding. Certainly my line was action, so action it would be. One more slant at the lad across the street and I ducked out my side window and dropped into the alleyway between the two houses. The night was dark – the gun in my hand for use, not ornament. They had played fast and loose with me long enough. I'd save Dorothy if I had to shoot a straight line to the leader of this gang.

Split-Lip would be the first victim. Crouched at the foot of the eight stone steps, I kept my eyes on him. I'd see where he went – follow him. If he led me to the gang, all right. I'd walk in, and we'd see who'd come out alive. The leader could use that fertile brain of his and I'd use those gifted fingers that Balcome sneered at. If this fellow, Split-Lip, saw that I followed him and tried to get away – why, I'd stop him with a bit of lead and get all the information that he had. Good – the black nose of my heavy artillery kept him covered.

Twice he killed a butt and gave me a good clear look at his twisted kisser. Queer that – did they think I didn't have any sense at all? Then he decided that I was in for the night, for after consulting his watch and stretching himself he turned and started slowly down the street. That was my cue – a quick glance up and down the deserted thoroughfare, and I followed, holding close to the shadows of the building. He never looked back – I licked my lips. Innocent he was – never dreaming that two would play at the same game.

Chapter IX

AND WHAT of Balcome now? He'd see what happened to cheap crooks who ran up against me. Trap me, eh? Put a lily in my hand? We'd see about that – I'd scatter lilies from Harlem to the Battery to save little Dorothy, and that ain't maybe. As I dogged my man I half sighed – it was too bad that Richard Morrison – the Flower of the Profession – wasn't the kidnapper and the real crook that had toyed with me while he kept under cover. It would come under the head of pleasure to stretch him so cold you could skate on his chest.

And Split-Lip never looked back. Steadily he went along – not too fast – not too slow either – just a lovely night for a walk. We'd go bye-bye together. I hoped he enjoyed it as much as I did. If he led me to where Dorothy was kept, well and good – good for him, I mean. If he didn't I'd have to make him chew the end of my gun. If he suddenly made a run for it or ducked into a doorway, I'd open up, and interview him later at the hospital if he didn't wind up in the morgue.

All along something told me I wasn't playing my game. I wasn't getting action. But I'd meet trick with trick. Not for a moment did I agree with Balcome – that the leader of this gang was too clever for me. Only the end could tell – would tell.

Just around the corner was the blue car – the big touring. And a man waited at the wheel. Cagey work that. I stayed close against the building, my cap shading my face, while Split-Lip slowly approached the big car. The man at the wheel was peering back – more careful, more watchful than Split-Lip. Two to tackle now – but I didn't mind that. The more, the merrier – in a pinch I dare say two men would tell me twice as much as one.

Split-Lip said something to his companion – they both laughed. Then the man at the wheel gave his attention to starting the car. Neither turned around. The hum of the racing motor – the sudden grind as the car slipped into gear – and I dashed from the corner – shot off the gutter into the street – ducked low and raced to the slowly moving machine. Not much trouble to that – this car was built for me – ample room to swing up and push myself snugly into the generous circle of the spare tire on the rear. And we were off – speeding easily up the street.

The route was a good one – not many cars on the streets – few in Central Park, where the car swerved, ever gathering speed. Good enough – they couldn't travel too fast for me. And Balcome – I laughed. If he could see the way I was playing the game now! But my laugh hadn't much mirth in it. I was thinking of little Dorothy. This would be a grim, bloody trail – and there would be death at the end of it. I was sure of that – and satisfied too. I wondered if the child was being mistreated. And the more I thought of it the harder it was for me to keep from climbing into the car and burying a hunk of lead in the back of Split-Lip's thick neck.

Out of Central Park up at One-Hundred and Tenth Street – across town and over to Broadway. Once we hummed by a car – for a moment the dim lights of the machine behind turned into a blaze of light as the brights shot forth. The horn tooted once. Did they make out my figure slunk well into the circle of the tire? It didn't matter. The lights dimmed again, to die off far behind. Nothing else to bother me. These boys were so sure of themselves! I chuckled. The leader, who kept so well under cover, may have had brains – but they weren't reflected in the lieutenants that he employed. I didn't mind his brains – the more he had the easier it would be to shoot them out. Not a pretty thought that – but it was in my mind just the same.

A few blocks below One-Hundred and Eighty-first Street and not far from St. Nicholas Avenue the car turned into a side street, stopped by a lot where a building was being erected, and directly across the street from a large apartment house.

I couldn't have picked a better place myself. It was dark. Just across the sidewalk was a large tool-house. Before the men in the front had fairly brought the cart to a stop I had dropped from the rear and was stretching my legs in the shadow of the rude shanty.

Leisurely the two climbed from the car and stood talking a moment on the sidewalk. Somewhere a clock struck two – the street was silent and deserted.

Just a lone line of lights stretching up to the top window of the six story apartment across the street. That would be the hall lights. If you wanted quiet you couldn't have found more of it way out in the country.

The door of the apartment house across the street opened – a shadow stood in the semi-darkness – looked up and down the street – spotted the car, and closing the door ran quickly across the road. I made out the brass buttons of the elevator boy – a light-colored negro, I thought. He joined the others – there was a whispered greeting and the three walked toward the shanty. I drew quickly back. They slipped around the sides of the tool-house, driving me to the back of it. Fine! I could catch most everything they said. At least enough – enough to set my heart beating – the hot blood pounding through my body. Things were going to break!

"Did everything go as planned?" was the first crack out of the box – this came from the giant negro, and there was no drawl to his voice. Nothing to distinguish him from these others – these creatures of the night.

One of the others jumped him with a "Shs!" I think it was Split-Lip. Then he had a question to put.

"The boss is coming tonight – yes?" Split-Lip sort of asked and answered his own question.

"Absolutely." I could feel rather than see the elevator boy nod his head vigorously.

"With the Kid?" the third man of the party and driver of the car shot in.

"'The Kid' is right. At two-thirty, I'm to run them up in the elevator to the third floor."

"Will they come through the front door?" There was a surprised note in Split-Lip's voice.

"You never can tell." The elevator boy chuckled. "Maybe the rear – maybe through the ground apartment – maybe through the basement. How they come I don't know – but the third floor is where they go. That am certain."

I guess they all nodded at that. Me too – and Balcome claimed that coincidence was not of life. What would you call my horning in on that conversation? If it wasn't coincidence, what was it? After that the conversation didn't interest me so much. It was mostly of money and if the 'boss' had left certain envelopes. And he had. If the huge negro was trying to held out on them, I don't know. I had thought out my plan – was itching to get on the third floor. I'd sure surprise that party when they tripped gayly out of the elevator. There would be no mistake about that. One thing now – I just wanted the others to beat it.

Right – they were all very obliging young men. They muttered something about the 'boss' being in a bad humor if he found them there – got off a wise crack about me being safely tucked in bed – and climbed into the car. The elevator boy stood and watched them slide away down the street. Then he turned, and crossing the street passed into the hallway of the apartment.

Dimly I saw his massive shoulders disappear down the long hall. A moment's wait – a careful look up and down that side street – even a peep at the darkened windows of the house itself – and I ran across the street. One thing in mind. When the elevator of that house reached the third floor I'd be there to greet it.

Chapter X

IT WAS in my mind to stick up the negro – knock him out for an hour and meet the party when they came. But how were they coming? The front door? Maybe! Through the ground floor apartment? Perhaps! From the basement? Who can tell! One thing only was certain. I was bent on reaching the third floor. That was the only sure hangout for me.

There was an iron gate protecting the alleyway which led to the rear. The work of a second only to hop that. And the cellar door was easy to find. And it wasn't locked. Why, the whole thing was simple. And Dorothy would sleep home the next night.

I turned my flash loose long enough to locate the cellar steps. And all the time I watched my step. I never take unnecessary chances and it would be no surprise to me if a lad jumped me in that cellar. The surprise would be for him. Whenever I cut loose with my flash, my gun was ready and my back plunk up against the wall.

These steps didn't lead directly into the apartment – but up to a door that gave entrance both to the court and the building itself. Still, the door had a nice bit of glass just below my chin, and I was looking from darkness into light. I turned the knob softly. It too was unlocked. But I didn't go in yet – just stood there, watching and waiting.

I guess I was fifteen minutes at that door before I saw the elevator boy. Then his back came into view as he sauntered down the long hallway toward the front door. He never stopped till he reached the door, then turned once – paused a minute and looked at his watch. With that he pulled a pack of cigarettes from his pocket – lit one and passed out, closing the great glass doors behind him. I could see the outline of his body against the glass. Was he watching for the approach of the 'boss', or was he just killing a butt – and time?

I only had a short run once the door was open – still, for the fraction of a minute I would be in the light, that was a chance I had to take – and I took it. I didn't need to be careful closing the door behind me. Thick glass separated me from the broad shoulders of the colored lad in the front. No danger of his hearing me. It was his turning and seeing me that I feared.

I don't think he saw me; at least he didn't turn. But as I slipped from view of the front doors and got around between the elevator and the telephone switch-board I waited a few minutes. Would he come to investigate? If he did I'd have to change my plans – rock him to sleep with the butt of my gun and wait for the arrival of the 'boss'. Of course that would not be so good. If they missed the elevator boy my surprise party would not be complete. They might even change their plans entirely. For all I knew, the negro might have to signal them if everything was jake.

I guess it was a full five minutes before I heard the front door open and the negro's slow step on the marble floor. He was humming to himself. I backed up the stairs until I reached the first turn. There I waited. But he suspected nothing. I heard him flop into the chair by the switch-board – suspected that he put his feet up and took it easy. Not another sound from him – not any sound from me.

Another wait – the buzz of the telephone – and the low voice of the elevator boy. Boy! – that's what I call him, but he was a good six feet-three or more, and had had his first shave long before the war. His voice barely reached me.

"Everything is a'right, boss – I jus' this minute looked out the front door. Not a thing to worry about. Yes, sah, it is goin' as planned."

He was right – as planned – but as I planned. I'd have been a fine cluck too if I had interfered with the boy. The 'boss' was checking up on things. Nothing to bother me now – my rubber soles made no noise as I climbed those stairs. Each hall I gave the once over. Not only to the third floor but right to the roof. I'd eliminated all danger of a trap. And what's more, I found the door leading to the roof unlocked – believe me, I put the hook on that. Everything was quiet. Here was a respectable apartment. The police would never think of looking here for the kidnapped child. There was danger, of course, that one of the tenants might walk in at the critical moment, but I guess these crooks would attend to that. No one would see the child come – just slip her straight into the elevator and whisk her to the third floor. I wondered how they would keep her quiet there. And I clenched my teeth – gagged probably.

Returning to the third floor I took my place before the elevator shaft – gun drawn – ready in my hand. There would be no slip-up this time. When that elevator door swung open I'd meet that little gathering with a gun in either hand. After that it was up to them. But if any of them got mussy there'd be a bunch of tenants moving out in the morning. And what's more, I was going to get a look at the leader's face.

Fifteen minutes, I must have laid against that elevator door, waiting. I wasn't neglecting the possibility of an apartment door opening behind me. No – I was ready for that. Ready for anything.

No more time for thought. There came a gentle hum from below. Then louder and louder. The elevator was coming up.

The light now – shone clearly through the stained glass of the door – and the poor fish of an elevator boy was nervous. He was having a devil of a time with that elevator. Not high enough. It was a good two feet below the landing. But I guess the others didn't care or couldn't wait. Someone was fumbling with the elevator door.

A final glance behind me – and I braced myself squarely before the slowly moving door. A fraction of an inch it opened. Enough! I quickly reversed a gun – stuck the butt forward – gave a quick jerk and shot the door open.

Dorothy was there. I didn't see her at first, of course – her little figure was held by a man in the rear – a man whose hat was pulled far down over his face – whose collar was turned up almost to his nose, and who wore a black mask that hid his eyes. I was a bit surprised too, for besides this man and the elevator boy, the driver of the blue car made up the party.

It was the elevator boy that I watched mostly. For the car was well below the landing. I was afraid that he would shoot on the power and dash down again. But nothing to worry about there. His hands fell to his side – to jump immediately above his head as his bulging eyes rolled and rolled from one gun to the other.

I didn't have to speak. Every hand went up – even to that masked figure in the back. And Dorothy – I think that she tried to cry out – but, poor kid, she couldn't. Her face was white and frightened, and her eyes were red with weeping. Besides that, a thick towel was wrapped about her mouth.

The masked figure didn't try to reach for a gun. I half wished that he had. There would have been real pleasure in planting a few posies on his grave. But I did the talking.

"Come, Dorothy – it's Race Williams. You remember my promise to you. No one can harm you now – come." Silly talk? I suppose so. But there was a lump in my throat that was new to me. If I ever got a thrill out of anything, this was the time. I'd have that mask off the leader just as soon as the kid was out of the car. It looked like a job for the police. These ducks had no guts at all. It's always that way when a man might get a little pleasure out of what's always been a business.

Dorothy stepped forward – from beneath the cruel gag came a glad little cry – the soft, shrill, hurt note of a wounded bird. I stretched out my left arm to fold her into it – when the thing happened. Oh, I saw the shadow all right, the curve of the arm – the flash as it shot down. Did I shoot? – No. Because I didn't know it in time – I couldn't see when I was first struck – all blurred before me – Dorothy was too close to risk a shot in my dazed condition. Before I dropped into unconsciousness I knew the truth. That elevator wasn't meant to come all the way to the third floor. A figure lying on top of that car had leaned over and crowned me – brought a hunk of lead pipe straight down upon my head. I might have guessed but I didn't. I had been a fool. Balcome was right. This leader was playing with me. And – then came blackness.

Chapter XI

BALCOME was right. This was not coincidence. Before I was fully conscious or even aware of where I was, the whole thing flashed before me as if in a dream. This 'boss' had tricked me again. Taken me in like a helpless infant. It was planned that I should follow Split-Lip – planned that I should overhear the conversation behind the little tool house. Even the flashing light of the car behind us upon the road was planned – and the warning note of the horn told that I was safely clinging to the rear tire. The doors of the apartment were open for me. Each step that I took I was led into – and finally trapped on that third floor. Trapped where no one would interfere – where my own assurance would be my downfall. What the movies call a mastermind – this man under cover. I'd have given much to see his face. Race Williams was a flop. Me – who'd always claimed that crooks were like children. I was beaten at every move. I had to admit that as I opened my eyes.

I couldn't be sure if I was in the apartment house or not. I thought that I had been carried some place, had a hazy recollection of a ride through the night – the rising and falling motion of a boat or a car. What did it matter?

Darkness – no motion now. I was not on a ship. I stretched my arms and legs. That was good – I was not bound then. Until I stretched I could not be sure, so numb was my body. I sat up – located the dull breaking of day through a barred window. My guns – I was convinced that they weren't there before I looked. And they weren't. Everything was gone – even my watch. Everything but the two closely folded corners of the thousand dollar bills, which had been tucked away in my watch pocket. A laugh in that.

With the help of the distant light in the sky I groped around the room – reached the window – felt of the thick steel bars. They were new and strong – besides, even if they could have been jerked out, there was hardly room for a child to slip through that tiny window.

I was still alive – on my feet – and with a chance. You laugh at that, eh? I was alive and a prisoner – but the game had not been fully played yet.

There wasn't much light yet. I located the door – tapped on it lightly. Not enough to disturb the household, but enough to assure me that it was not only locked but that it was reinforced with steel or iron. Nice prospect – you said it. My head still buzzed. I had made an awful mess of things. But I had to make the best of it. Perhaps I should have run around the house, banging my head against the wall – but I didn't. I just took off my coat – rolled it up – picked out a soft spot on the floor, and using the coat as a pillow, curled up in the corner. And I slept too – don't make any mistake about that.

The sun was shining into the room when I awoke. Just a chair or two but no bed. It wasn't the sun that disturbed me – it was the ring of a key and the heavy snap of a strong lock. The door opened. I had two visitors.

The driver of the blue car held a tray in his hand, and I caught the whiff of hot coffee, to say nothing of the aroma of toast. And behind this lad stood Split-Lip. A gun was directed full upon me – I looked straight into the black nose of a heavy automatic. I nodded at that. If they had no respect for my brains, they had some for my brawn. Both grinned. It was Split-Lip who spoke.

"Breakfast." He grinned. I could see that he was taking in the deep scar above my forehead. I hadn't seen it but I knew it was there. Explain that? Well – it felt like the Black Hole of Calcutta.

There was no use in being up-stage. I had no hard feeling against the boys. They were doing their duty as they saw it. I might as well be sociable – perhaps learn something. So I did the polite.

"What's the game, boys?" I asked, as I stuck my nose in the coffee and took a taste of the toast. The coffee was strong and the toast a bit burnt, but then, I'm easy-going and didn't make any complaint.

They watched me sip my coffee without a word. I tried to entertain them – especially get Split-Lip, with the gun, interested. But he never made a peep – just waved me back once, when I got about ten feet from him. He was taking no chances. The boys could be dumb when they wanted to – this was one of the times. And it came to me that I could be dumb when I didn't want to. I noticed too, that though the door of my room was left open while they stood there, the passage did not lead to safety. There was another door across a little ante-room without, and that door was closed. Locked? I couldn't tell, but I thought so. It looked like this man under cover had not only knocked me down, but was bent on walking all over me.

I thought of Dorothy then – and, believe me, if it wasn't for that door in the room beyond, I'd of tackled the two of them. Crazy? Sure! but I'd of had a try at it.

The coffee was good and refreshing. I'd need my strength – if I'd get a chance to use it. When the slim meal was over I bowed the boys out. I had thought this guy behind the whole show easy to handle – now I understood. His orders were strictly obeyed. When he wanted them to talk, they talked – when he wanted them to act, they acted.

They had hardly closed the door behind them and turned the key in the lock, when I was across that room – on my knees, with my eye screwed to the keyhole. What did I want to find out? I'm not exactly sure. See if they both passed out the door of the other room or if one stayed in there. But I found out nothing. They turned the key and left it in the lock. I could plainly see the heavy barrel of it, blocking my vision.

How simple if I had my tools along! Just a strong pair of the right kind of pliers or nippers – I'd turn that key in a minute. Insert the slender steel nippers in the lock – grip the barrel of the key and make a quick turn. Then – but what the hell! I had nothing – nothing but the torn corners of two thousand-dollar bills. Was I superstitious when I thought of them? Two men had died with those corners in their pockets! Was the handwriting on the wall for Race Williams?

I'm not afraid of dying – but I wasn't stuck on it just then either. And I'd like to slip out with a gun in either hand and a party to shoot at. Preferably this bird who kept under cover. And Dorothy – but I tried to keep that childish face from my mind. It wasn't pleasant to think of. What a flat tire I thought myself!

A thorough search of the room disclosed nothing. There was the window and the chair to stand upon and look out. I was high up in the house – somewhere off in the country. Long Island, would be my guess, though it might have been Connecticut. Across a great desolate stretch of long grass and burning sand I could see Long Island Sound. It wasn't rough enough for the ocean – too big for a lake, and – But the question wasn't where I was, but how I'd get away. And was Dorothy there?

There was a closet too – empty, but for some papers spread out upon the floor. They were old and stuck to the floor, so I squatted down by the closet door and read them over. Believe me, it's tough work getting a thrill out of a paper nearly two years old – besides, the print would rise up and fall down, where the paper didn't stick to the floor. Little mountains and valleys-like, to read over.

Then I tried pacing the room. I got thinking of Balcome and wondering if his Sherlock Holmes brain could dope a way out of this mess. A door slammed – the outer door. I pushed the closet door closed – slipped into a chair – crossed my legs easily and waited. Who would be coming now? The key turned – the door to the room opened – Split-Lip and the driver of the blue car stood on either side of the door. You'd think the king himself was coming. And he did. The masked figure of the elevator – the man who had duped me – stepped into the room. The door closed behind him – the two others remained upon the outside. I was alone with the man I most wanted to see.

Chapter XII

TALL – yes; and broad. The color of his hair and eyes was hidden by the mask and the peaked cap that came down over his forehead. It might have been Richard Morrison. The Flower of the Profession didn't have a stoop to his shoulders, but that could easily be counterfeited. They might have been the same – there was enough in common between the two figures – if I hadn't gotten that wireless and knew that Richard Morrison was nearing the coast of England. But I'd wait until he talked.

"The great Race Williams, eh." And I started, for somehow I half thought it was Morrison before. But here was a low tone – not the guarded notes of a feigned voice – nor the chesty effect that comes even when a clever man disguises his voice. There was a natural ring to its low clear depths.

I bowed my acknowledgment. I'd be as much at ease as he. And I noticed too that he carried no gun – but I remembered the two men who stood behind that closed door, and that he had but to raise his voice to have me showered with lead.

"Sit down – sit down." He paced up and down the room while he talked. "Really, I am sorry to see you like this, and with that cut upon your forehead. I owe you something – two men there were – bothered me greatly. I dislike death – and to kill them would make others, my friends, distrust me. But you – you were obliging. But now – really, Mr. Williams, I expected more of you – you disappointed me – greatly."

I knew that he eyed me through the slits in his mask – and I knew too that he was proud of his accomplishments. Was he simply coming to gloat over me? And he was – he couldn't hide that. Conceited – yes. And he had a right to be. It almost turned my stomach the way he sang his praises. The temptation to give him a smack in the snoot was strong – but I resisted – perhaps he would talk about Dorothy. But, no – he explained each move in the method he had used to trap me. Just as I had guessed at it after it had happened.

Suddenly he paused – swung about and stood still, facing me. "You see, these men were paid money – the one to kill you; the other to kill Preston – given the corner of a bill in good faith – a thousand-dollar bill. These bits of money were not found on the bodies. Do you know anything about them?"

Ah – my chance at last. This bird had been clever. Well, I'd show him something. Here was the time to dicker for my freedom. He wanted those bills for some reason. Perhaps there was a way for the bank to trace them.

"The corners of those bills are well taken care of." I put a hard eye on him. "If I do not turn up by night – tonight, those bills will be traced to their original owner."

Did he wilt up? No – damn it – he laughed.

"My dear Williams – you amuse me – more and more every day. Come—" he stretched forth a hand. "Those corners – in your watch pocket – give them to me."

I half drew back. He turned and pointed to the door. What was the use? He had beaten me again. Not that it mattered. Just pride – nothing more. I guess this last wasn't nearly as bad as what went before. I dug into my pocket, produced the torn bills and stretched them out to him. For a moment our hands met – his was cold and clammy. I clutched it a second and let it drop. For the moment I could have sworn that I again held the cold, fish-like hand of Richard Morrison, and yet—

I half circled before him – placing my body between him and the door. Did he suspect my purpose? Did I know what my purpose was? The temptation to tear that mask from his face was almost irresistible. Suddenly there was a loud pounding upon the door.

My hidden enemy raised his hand – looked full at me a moment – then called, "Come in."

The door opened. Split-Lip half entered the room. The other man stood behind him. Far distant came a cry – a pitiful cry. By God! A shriek of agony. Was it Dorothy?

"It's the Kid again, boss." Split-Lip sneered. "Ed's been sort of stirring her up for the dictograph record. She won't do nothin' but holler – won't send no message over it to her father – like you wanted her to."

"She won't." The masked figure nodded grimly. "Take the whip and beat her till she does – her father must deal with us tonight." And then in sudden frenzy, I thought, "Damn that Kid – and that nigger. He's too soft-hearted. Here – I'll give the little slut something to cry about."

Self-possession – that boasted calmness of mine – that lack of passion I prided myself with. All went – the masked figure never reached that door. Just a lunge forward – Split-Lip and the other were thrust aside and I had the leader by the throat. I could have torn his mask off easily enough. But I didn't think of that. Fingers of steel sunk into his throat – just a curse that died on his lips.

It was useless though – I had failed again – as usual, it seemed. As we went to the floor together the others were on me. Oh, they couldn't have dragged me off. I'd of strangled him to death before that. But the heavy pounding of a gun on my head ended the fray. They pulled my locked fingers from his throat – and he wasn't dead. I could hear him gasp for air – great sucking sounds as his fingers clutched beneath his collar. A minute more – perhaps less than that – would have turned the trick. Certainly, I was having no luck, in this case – the breaks were all against me.

I sat there in the corner – the blood streaming down my face. There wasn't much power left in me – just enough to struggle to a sitting position and lean back against the wall. One thing now – the thing I had neglected when I had that second's chance. I wanted to get a look at this crook's face – a desire as strong as the previous one to choke him to death.

What they would do with me now I didn't know – didn't care. Split-Lip was helping his master – half holding him against the wall while he gasped for breath. The other kept his eyes on me – a gun drawn – pointed at me. He was waiting for the order to shoot, I guess – and he looked willing enough. It was in my mind to cry out to these men – let them know that it was the 'boss' who had brought about the death of the two I had killed. At least I might cause confusion in the camp of the enemy – but I didn't. I sat there silent.

I got a real surprise – the masked figure had recovered and was going to stay in that room with me – yes, alone with me. I staggered to my feet. The other two retired, closed the great door but did not lock it. This mastermind and I faced each other. He was the first to speak.

"Race Williams," he began slowly, "you have dared to lay a hand on me. Not an act of courage that. An irresistible impulse – nothing more. I did not intend to kill you – now I shall give you a chance to live – or a chance to die. I can read your mind like an open book – as you sprawled there upon the floor you thought of death and thought too that you would like to know who I am."

I nodded.

"Well—" he laughed, "we'll see if you have the stuff in you – my fine braggart. While you don't know who I am you may live. If you do know who I am you will surely die. Come—" He spread his hands far apart and stood facing me. "If you wish you may remove my mask. But I'm giving it to you straight, if you do you'll die!"

Melodramatic – certainly – but the life I lead is nine-tenths melodrama. There is plenty of melodrama in real life if you know how to find it. He was speaking again as he faced me – arms still flung apart.

"Go ahead and take it off – if you have the guts!"

Well, I had been so many kinds of a damn fool lately, that it didn't really matter. I just stepped across the room – reached up – and without bothering to untie the cords that held it jerked the mask from his face. I knew it – and yet I didn't know it and couldn't understand it then. But the man who faced me was Richard Morrison, the Flower of the Profession. Balcome was right.

He must have read the surprise in my face – it ain't often I show anything – but I did then. I'll admit it. Everything I did was wrong.

"It was easy, you see," he explained. "My natural walk is slightly stooped – my natural voice is low. Until you met me masked, you never met the real Richard Morrison – every act of mine was feigned – my walk studied – my voice a work of years."

Like a child with a new toy, he was – so proud of all he had pulled. It was really the Chief of Police of Rosedale who suggested bringing me into the case. Richard Morrison had planned to milk Charles Philip Preston – and then he delayed things while he used me to bump off undesirable colleagues. It was he who gave Charles Philip the impression that I had pulled the game myself. It was he who switched the gun on the poor fool who shot at Preston. He let that boob think that I was working with them and would cover his retreat into the get-away car that would be driven by Split-Lip. His idea after the shooting was to get rid of me – and keep me out of the case when he finally pulled the grand stunt – getting the ransom for Dorothy's return.

"Really," for a moment he used the shrill voice that I had heard at Rosedale, "I was thinking seriously of hanging the crime on you when I came back from Europe. Europe – that was quite a touch. Another man traveled in my name, and now Mr. Preston will receive a wireless *from me,* advising him to pay this ransom – assuring him that I shall recover the money upon my return. It is all so simple – you are such a child."

"If I was such a child, why did you take all the trouble you did to capture me – bring me here?" I couldn't help but ask.

"Because you went to see your brother. If you told him all, he would see the truth. He is one man I respect. Alone, he would not bother me. He is too lazy – but with his brains and you to act upon his ideas, I thought it better to have you with me."

"What are you going to do with the child, Dorothy Preston?"

"That, my friend, will be a touch of genius. Mr. Preston is close – very tight – but we plan a surprise for him at his office this afternoon. A dictograph record. He will hear her cry – plead with him to save her – and get the full benefit of her shrill screams of agony. I assure you she will do it well – a little touch of pathos and sentiment makes of my business a work of art."

My hands clenched but I said nothing. Fleeting through my head was – well, a hope at least.

"Preston will come to us tonight, I think – so you live until then – he may not bring enough money. It may help things for him to see you helpless here – he at least believes you are a desperate man. No doubt it will lend local color. But come he must – or the child dies – that is the message he will receive. And he will come – and alone."

"And then the girl – Dorothy – will be returned to him?" I watched that round face – those mean gray eyes – closely.

"That—" Morrison, the Flower of the Profession, grinned. "That is where the joke on Preston comes in. I will have future business with him – and – unfortunately the child recognized me. The mask slipped – and she has seen my face." He walked to the door – tapped – and it opened.

"You and the child have seen my face – therefore—" A shrug of huge shoulders and he was gone. As for me, I stood there helpless.

Chapter XIII

AND DOROTHY was going to die. Tortured first – tortured now – tortured so that her pitiful little pleas for help would reach her father. The dictograph! Clever – diabolical – that was the word for it. And me – she counted on me – knew that I was here. God! For a gun and the chance to use it! Madly I paced the room – the sun went down, but not before I had located the electric switch and snapped up the lights.

Self condemnation, pacing and cursing were futile. That wasn't the thing. Balcome said I had no brains – now, if I did have any, now was the time to use them. Look at my brother – he just sat there in his room, closed his eyes, and in less than five minutes explained the whole case to me. Even knew the name of this leader – Mr. Richard Morrison – the Flower of the Profession. And what of Morrison when I was dead – and Dorothy was dead?

He'd strut around as before – ostensibly return from Europe – probably blackmail Charles Philip Preston again – milk him dry with other schemes. After the death of Dorothy – the death of Dorothy – that was it.

I clenched my hands until the nails tore into icy flesh. But I won my battle against emotion – my first taste of real emotion. Brawn wouldn't do now – brains must start the ball rolling – get me out of that room. I tried to reason, like Balcome. He always said that simplicity was the keynote in detective work, as it was in all great arts. He called it an art – but think as I would—

And it came out of nothing. A chance – a hope – perhaps a sure thing. I ducked to the little closet – flung open the door and knelt upon the floor. It took time, easing that old paper from the closet floor. But I did it – and there beneath the paper, evidently shoved under one of the rises, were the other parts of the thousand dollar bills! Funny that – I wasn't looking for them – never would have found them if I had been. Probably they were slipped there by Morrison in the presence of the men who were now dead – killed by me. Poor, dear thugs – they hoped to match them up with the torn corners. Well – if my plan worked out there would be other dead ones. I shoved the bills into my pocket. There might be a future for Race Williams yet.

A careful search about the floor revealed a split section of wood in one corner. It was tough work, but I finally was able to tear off a long thick sliver. With my nails I pared this down to about the length and thickness of a slate pencil. Good! I nodded and put out the lights. Then I went to the door and listened – a good ten minutes and not a sound – from the generous crack beneath the door no light showed.

Now for it. Never have I spent such a heart-stopping five minutes – and in my life I've spent some real five minutes, and no mistake about that. It was careful work to keep that old worn paper flat as I shoved it beneath the door – it curled up and it crumpled but I got it well stretched out in the little room beyond. Then to it. I was working according to Balcome's plan – at least, the keynote of the whole thing was simplicity.

My stick of wood slipped into that keyhole and pressed against the key – too bad it wasn't nippers but – the key gave against pressure easily enough – I never doubted that, once I had thought of the plan. But when it fell where would it land – on the paper? Certainly – but would it bounce? I guess for a full minute I had the key out of that keyhole – just hanging, ready to drop. Then I let it go. I had had enough hard luck. This time – *clink* – I heard it hit the floor – heard it bounce too. Was it on the paper? Slowly I started to haul in my paper. Would the key be on it? On the level – I'd have been willing – yes, glad to be killed at sunrise if that key would only drift to me from beneath the crack. If it did – well, I might die before sunrise – but there'd be others coming with me, and you can kiss the book on that.

I'd pull a bit – then feel along the paper; pull a bit more – and feel again. I must have pretty near reached the end of the paper when my groping, anxious fingers touched the key. Man! I could have shouted. Race Williams was coming back into his own – and this was the first step. It didn't take me long to slip the key in the lock and open the great door and slip out. Then I locked it again and left the key in the lock.

I stood erect – in the darkness of that little ante-room. Slow work locating the door. It was locked, of course – and a man must have stood against it – for I could have sworn that I heard heavy breathing. There was nothing to do now but wait. Sooner or later a man with a gun would enter that room – a struggle in the dark. That would be the deciding moment – the few seconds that would tell if I was to live or die. Would I get that gun?

Hours passed – I had no way of telling the time. I heard the purr of a motor. Had they brought Preston to the house? Would he come alone? Would they let him bring someone with him? Hardly. No doubt they would get him to come in, someway. Mean he might be, but I knew that he had a great love for his motherless child.

Very late, I guessed the time was. I was leaning against the wall, crouched in one corner close to the door. Suddenly a blaze of light dazzled me, from an electric bulb in the center of the room. The button was outside, I guess.

Close back in the corner by the door I had a chance to examine the tiny room in the sudden light. No windows – no chairs either. I had half an idea of trying the key trick over again if that fellow on the outside of the door beat it. And then my hopes in that direction exploded entirely, this door was made of thin steel, like a bank door – not just wood reinforced with steel, like the other. And this door fitted close to the floor. I doubt if the paper would shove under it, let alone the key. Besides, they'd hear it drop out there in the hall.

A grating noise close to my head – I backed against the wall and waited – would the door be opened? No – a thin slip of steel in the top of the door shot slowly back – like the ones in speak-easies and gambling houses. I didn't dare look – with arms outstretched I was flattened against the wall like a bat – the opening wasn't big enough for a man to get his head in. But one was looking things over. Evidently satisfied, he snapped back the slide. There was a dull plink – and the light went out. I waited now in darkness.

Fifteen minutes passed – then the blinding light again, and again the sliding panel. But this time, before the steel panel slipped back I distinctly heard the screams of a child – a scream of agony. And what could I do – I must wait. Wait for what? That was the hell of it!

No – I couldn't wait – the Kid might – oh, anything might happen while I stood there clenching my hands together. Great stuff for a man of action! I can't say there was anything clever about the plan I decided on to hurry things. It isn't what you do that counts – it's the results those efforts or those thoughts bring.

The ceiling of the room was low – I could almost reach it – reach to the light easily enough. I reached up and unscrewed the electric light bulb. What would this man at the door do if he found the room in darkness the next time he pressed the button and looked in? He'd no doubt come in to investigate. Would he call the others? If he thought the thing queer, he might. I held the bulb in my hand a moment. Suppose he shot the rays of an electric torch into the room and missed the bulb? Suspicion would come then, and he'd call for help. Good enough – I stuck the bulb back in the socket – just turned it enough to hold it in the fixture, but not enough to make the connection. Nothing might come of it but at least I was doing something.

It seemed like a longer wait this time. But at length came the tiny click, and this time no light responded. Then the creak of the sliding panel. A moment's wait – a half muffled exclamation – and several sharp clicks as he pressed the button in the hall without.

So far so good – he was uncertain – deciding what to do. Then a movement – steps without. He was going for help – but, no – just a backward step, I guess – and he was again by the door. He had thought it out as I had hoped. The globe had become loose or had burnt out. I held myself flat against the corner of the door. Then I smacked my lips. Came a glare of light – a circle that shot full upon the unlit globe in the center of the room. Things were looking up – the old brains were hitting on all six cylinders again.

The light disappeared – silence – the man was thinking. What had he to fear? He had seen across the room – noted that the key was still in the lock. Just something wrong with the bulb – perhaps his fault, he thought. He should have put in a new one. At least that's how I doped it out. And then the cheerfulest sound since I had first read in the paper of Dorothy's kidnapping. Simply the grating of a key in a lock. My friend without was going to investigate alone – for I had heard no voice, and my trained ears had counted but a single footfall in that hall.

I stepped back – trying to make my body give naturally with the swing of the door as it would come inward. What was going on below – surely someone in such a house would hear a struggle. I must see my man – then strike but one deciding blow. Never a crook longed for a pair of brass knuckles or a blackjack more than I did at that moment. I'd of kissed this lad then for sure.

I can hit a mean blow – know just where to push a man over too – but to sing a lad clean into dream-land with a single wallop of your fist is some accomplishment. You've got to have the breaks. And the way things were going lately I could hardly count on them. Strategy – I guess that would have to turn the trick.

A little light came with the darkness. Not much – enough though to make out the dull outline of a body slipping through the crack. Just hard luck – this baby wasn't sticking his head in first and playing hide and seek. And the light – the flash came as his body eased through the opening. It didn't shine on me. This lad was careful but the light fell where his thoughts of danger were – directly on the key in the door across the room – that door that had led to my prison of a short time before. If I ever prayed I did it then.

"Stick 'em up – high!" Man! I put all the viciousness of a life close to crime in those words. "If you cry out – or move – I'll kill you." And I meant that. We'd die together perhaps, but he'd die sure, before his friends could reach him. Just a semi-darkened room – with a splash of light that wavered slightly across from us now. Nothing of drama in the situation, and yet – to my way of thinking there was a moment of tenseness that had never been equaled. At least not in my life. What would the man do? Then my first sigh of relief.

His hands went up – Man! I could have kissed him – and when I reached up, took the light from his grasp and slipped the gun from his outstretched right hand, I loved him like a brother. There was no passion or hatred or thoughts of vengeance when I crashed the butt of that gun down upon his head. I even felt a bit sorry as his limp body flopped into my arms. It was gently I let him slip to the floor – I was almost tempted to make a pillow out of his coat, but he looked so comfortable there that I didn't let my sentiment run away with me.

The light disclosed the face of the driver of the car. A search in his pockets brought out another gun. Two guns – two fine guns – I had no more than felt them when I knew that they were mine. How they had fallen into his hands I didn't know – didn't care. I was getting the breaks now – the fates were being kind to me. I'd been belly-aching about getting my hands on a couple of guns – now I had two of the best – my own.

There was nothing to tie this lad up with – and nothing needed. When I kiss a lad on the dome like that, he slips out for many hours. This chap had gone bye-bye for the rest of that night. Pretty birds would sing to him while I sought his friends below.

Chapter XIV

SOMEWHERE – far below in the old house – a door closed softly. That was my cue. I slipped out the door – locked it and dropped the key in my pocket. It had been mighty close in that room and now the blood had started flowing from the cut over my eyes and was dripping down across my face. But that would simply add a little color to the events which were sure to follow. We'd see how this mastermind stood to the gaff when he faced Race Williams in action. Was I going to kill? I'm no murderer, and I wouldn't shoot any lad down in cold blood. But something told me that this Richard Morrison was going to die – and by my hands.

A light at one end of the hall – not a soul in sight – plainly the stairs showed up in the semi-darkness as I broke my guns open to be sure they were fully loaded. How many men would be below? What do you care if I don't? I wanted to shine before two persons. I wanted Dorothy to live and know that I had kept my promise and saved her. And I wanted Richard Morrison to know that I had saved her, and take his knowledge to hell with him. A bad spirit, you think. None better to take into gun-play.

I stuck the flash in my hip pocket. I didn't expect to need it – both my hands were busy with forty-fives. So, I started down the stairs.

Another piercing scream of a child in pain. It went to my heart all right – sent cold blood up and down my spine. But it didn't make me dash down those stairs – didn't make my feet go the fraction of an inch faster. There must be no possibility of failure now.

No one stayed my passage – no one guarded the hall below, nor the great double-doored front entrance which led to freedom. It was easy too to locate the room from which the sound came. Great dark curtains were tightly drawn, but the light shone through. Silently – slowly – steadily – I crossed to those curtains – bent slightly – glued my eye to the crack and peered into the room.

Hard to see at first – the giant negro, the elevator boy of the previous night, stood before the curtains – his arms folded – a gun stuck up, scratching his left cheek, as he took in the scene before him. And there by a long table was the masked figure of Richard Morrison. Across from him, strapped in a straight-backed chair, was Charles Philip Preston. But right then he wasn't the Common Council, the dignified Board of Education, nor yet the portly banker. Just a broken down old man – who begged and pleaded with the masked Richard Morrison. A changed man – if the straps would have permitted it he would have been on his knees – for he, like me, had his eyes glued to the fireplace – and the barefooted figure of Dorothy, who was held tightly by Split-Lip, her little body close to the licking tongues of the flames from huge logs.

"Simplicity itself." I heard Richard Morrison's low voice as he addressed Charles Philip. "You see, I knew you would be interested the minute you got that dictograph record."

"But the child – my child – don't do it – I shall pay you all that you ask – my check – anything – the money where you wish it put." It was hard to feel pity for Charles Philip, but I guess I did.

"So." Richard Morrison's voice was cold – I could swear that Charles Philip shivered. "You were to bring fifty thousand dollars, and you have but ten. Tomorrow we shall have the rest – you shall leave it where I designate. Until then the child stays with me – don't think that we make idle threats." Morrison turned to Split-Lip, by the fire. "Just another scream or two for Mr. Preston – I fear that he is not sufficiently convinced." There was a wave of Richard Morrison's hand – not indifference – for later his hands came together, rubbing back and forth with a certain appreciation of this little child's suffering. Just a natural cruel streak in the man – the outgrowth of those abnormal children who torture dumb animals.

Now I came straight up in the doorway. Weak from loss of blood – slightly blinded with the trickle of red that still came down my face? I don't know. Race Williams was his own man again.

No need to pity little Dorothy further. That brute, Split-Lip, still held her tightly – was pushing her forward, close to those blazing logs – even kicking those bruised little bare legs. And the show was on. This was the moment I was waiting for.

They say that the negro's head is as hard as rock. Perhaps it is – I won't pose as an authority on that. But that kinkey black head before and just above me would have had to be as hard as the Rock of Gibraltar. Man! I sure put all my strength into the blow I struck. The remembrance of Split-Lip's statement that the former elevator boy had been making Dorothy scream for the dictograph record didn't make me ease up any on the wallop.

The giant black crashed to the floor like an earthquake had struck him. It's an even money bet that before he reached the carpet his soul was already pounding at the gates of hell. Don't know – care less. At the best, he was sure of six months in the hospital. This was action and I know my stuff.

Split-Lip never got a chance to shoot. It was in his mind all right – in his frightened eyes and trembling lips as he frantically clutched at his gun. He tried to hold the child as a shield, but his bulk was too large behind her frail little body.

Two shots – one that drove him to one side of Dorothy – the other that crashed between his eyes. He shot straight up in the air – half turned – and doubling up, tumbled on the stones of the fireplace – clutching fingers falling about burning logs. But that didn't worry him.

Now for the 'mastermind' – the lad who had laid so long under cover. His time had come and he knew it. Like all his breed he wasn't there when the pinch came. He was seeing death – sure and certain – and he didn't like the smell of it. Richard Morrison had come to his feet. Those wonderful brains of his were still working, but his legs were trembling and the fingers that held his blazing guns didn't have the real artistic touch to them. This lad was great on murder – but not there in a battle of death – where one man stays upon the floor and the other walks out into the sunlight. That takes more than brains.

Oh – I got pinked slightly below the knee and a bit of a sear along the cheek. All this of course before I gave him my attention. God! He fell straight back against the wall as my guns turned on him. He knew – just the tightening of a finger, a roar and a blinding flash – and he'd turn up his heels and do his trick.

And Dorothy – she darted across the room – straight between me and the crouching figure that held his still smoking gun – afraid to use it now that he looked down the barrels of two well directed smoke-wagons.

I shouted to Dorothy to stand back – Preston called in a high, weird voice – Morrison half straightened and raised his gun. Then it happened. His gun spoke – there was a dull thud – a stifled cry that turned to a moan, and little Dorothy bumped against me – half clung to my coat a moment. Then slumped to the floor.

Did Richard Morrison try to fire again? Maybe, but he didn't. There was nothing between us now. I fired twice – just a single report though. Funny the way Morrison took it. The tiny specks of white that were fast becoming a vivid red appeared in the center of that black mask – almost one hole – at least the two seemed to merge into one crimson gash. He didn't fall at once. He dropped his gun and raised his hand – a hand that tore off his mask. Then he stood there – hands half stretched out before him as if in pleading – but the gray eyes that rolled in their sockets were glassy and sightless. Richard Morrison opened and clenched his hands – a tiny bit of crumpled yellow paper fell to the floor. Funny that – I knew it to be the torn corners of the two thousand-dollar bills. Then the curtain was pulled down – Richard Morrison leaned back against the wall and slid slowly to the floor – his feet sticking out straight before him. No need to guess there – Richard Morrison was already storming the gates of hell.

One of his feet pushed the torn corners of the bills till they lay at my feet. I picked them up and shoved them in my pocket. Only one thing then – the little figure at my feet. I bent down beside her – lifted her cold little hand – felt of her hot head. A gasp. I thought – just a spasmodic something. Had I killed Morrison too late? And then Dorothy opened her eyes.

Fear – horror – and the eyes changed – a sudden brightening to them. Again two little arms stole up and about my neck. She was bleeding from a wound just below the shoulder. And I – well – like the old Indian legend – our blood intermingled. Did she faint – or cry out – or grow hysterical? Nope, she just wrapped herself into my arms and went to sleep. Dorothy wasn't going to pull any little Eva stuff yet.

I didn't have any time for Charles Philip. He was straining at the cords that held him, making an awful squawk. But he undid himself, I guess. I know that as I started from the room with the sleeping child in my arms I heard him mutter:

"Richard Morrison – the Flower of the Profession."

I half swung in the doorway. Charles Philip was turning from the dead man in repugnance. As for me, there was a certain sense of satisfaction. Death had wiped out the stain upon me. Richard Morrison and I had fought our battles. It was ended now. I was still upon my feet and he was dead.

"The Flower of the Profession?" I muttered half aloud, for of a certainty my head was light. "He's the last rose of Summer then." And I walked from the room humming the notes of that once popular song.

No one stopped us – and we found a high-powered car out front. I don't rightly remember it all, but I heard later that I would not let the child out of my arms, and drove the eighteen miles to the hospital at Jamaica with Dorothy still clinging about my neck.

One thing I do remember though – just before I decided to bunk at the hospital for the rest of that day anyway, Charles Philip was plucking at my sleeve.

"I offered a reward of five thousand dollars," he was saying. "It's yours for—"

And I turned on him, mad as hell. Why? Search me. I always need money, but somehow I couldn't take a cent for this. It wasn't my weakness from loss of blood – nor the buzzing in my head – nor yet the desire to drop down on the nearest bed. It was something different – something stronger. I don't know just what the hell it was anyway.

One of the two thousand-dollar bills I left at the hospital – and the other thousand I blew in on the swellest pony and cart you ever set your lamps on. Was I a bit goofy, you think? Maybe. But I'll tell you this – the first time I breezed down Fifth Avenue, there was a swing to my arms and a certain jauntiness to my gait that were new to me. I was on my way to go pony riding with a certain young lady up in Rosedale. If I could stand her old man I'd probably stay for dinner. The song I was humming was – 'The Last Rose of Summer'.

Don't Give Your Right Name

Norbert Davis

Chapter I
An Autograph Addict

GUITERREZ was leaning against the wall beside the front door of his restaurant with his tall chef's hat pushed down over one eye and his hands folded under the bib of his apron. He looked disgusted. There was nothing unusual about that. He always did. He had his reasons, and one of them was getting out of a taxi in front of the restaurant now.

"Hello, you crook," said Guiterrez. "How are you, you chiseler? Have you burned down any orphan asylums or robbed any starving widows today?"

"Not yet," said Max Latin. "But the night is young."

He was a tall man, thin and high-shouldered, and he had the assured, sleek self-confidence of a champion racehorse. His eyes were as cold and smooth as green glass, tipped a little at the corners.

Guiterrez was counting on his fingers. "It seems incredible to me, but you ain't been pinched for three weeks. How does that happen? Did you catch the mayor sleeping with somebody else's wife?"

"No," said Latin. "But I have hopes. What's on the menu tonight?"

"Tonight," Guiterrez answered, "Guiterrez is featuring steamed ragout *à la supreme à la Guiterrez.*"

"Is it good?"

Guiterrez snorted. "Good! It's marvelous! I cooked it, didn't I?" He opened the restaurant door and yelled loudly: "Dick! Here's that thief of a Latin! Be sure you mark the level of the brandy bottle before you give it to him – and with an indelible pencil!"

Latin went on inside, and Guiterrez poked a cigarette into the corner of his mouth and leaned against the wall again. The red neon tubing that bordered the doorway gave his face a satanically dissipated cast.

Another taxi pulled up at the curb, and two men and a woman got out of it. The men were very young and broad-shouldered and husky. They were hatless, and they had crew haircuts. One was blond and the other was brunet. They wore dress overcoats with the collars turned up and white scarfs. They were unmistakably college boys weekending in the city.

"Are you sure this is the place you want to go?" the blond one asked doubtfully.

"It looks dirty," the brunet observed.

"It don't only look dirty," Guiterrez told him. "It is. You won't like it."

The two men stared at him and then decided to ignore him.

The woman said: "I'm certain this is the place. It has an international reputation. The food is divine." She must have been younger, in years, than even her escorts were. Only in years, though. She had a lusciously curved young body very much on display in a striptease-black evening gown with a cut-out middle section. She wore a silver fox cape and the diamond bracelet on her left wrist was a good four inches wide. Her hair was dead black, and she wore it in a long sleek bob. Her brown eyes were sultry and languorous, and her mouth was a red, moist invitation.

"This is Guiterrez's restaurant, isn't it?" she asked Guiterrez.

"Yup," said Guiterrez. "I run the dump." He leered at her knowingly. "And how are you getting along with your work, baby?"

The two men looked at each other and then started ominously for Guiterrez.

Guiterrez pushed the door open behind him and called: "Hey, Dick!"

A wizened little waiter wearing a black, grease-stained coat and an apron so big that he had wrapped it around himself three times and still had plenty left over appeared instantly. Without saying a word, he took a butcher knife with a blade over a foot long from under the apron and handed it to Guiterrez.

The two college men stopped short, eyeing the long shimmering blade uneasily. Guiterrez commenced to clean his fingernails with it. Dick, the waiter, watched with a sort of idle interest.

The girl laughed throatily. "Bruce! Bill! Behave yourselves! He's just ribbing you. Aren't you, Mr. Guiterrez?"

"Sure," Guiterrez answered. "I'm one of these here humorists. I'm funny as hell all day long."

The two college men decided they saw the joke. They laughed in a rather pained way.

The girl said: "I've been wanting to try some of your wonderful food for a long time, Mr. Guiterrez. Everybody in town is talking about it."

"Yeah," said Guiterrez. "You got any room in the joint for these people, Dick?"

"I got one table left," Dick said. "But I was savin' it for a big spender. These birds look like cheapskates to me."

Guiterrez nodded. "Yeah. They probably are. But just think what you can watch while you're servin' them." He pointed the butcher knife at the girl.

"You got something there," Dick agreed, popping his eyes admiringly. "Come on, gorgeous. I'll give you and your two poodles my personal attention."

The girl swept her magnificently inviting body through the door with the two college men trailing uncertainly behind her.

Guiterrez spat his cigarette butt into the gutter and sighed drearily. Running feet pattered along the walk, and a youth as skinny and tall as a beanpole staggered up and leaned against the wall beside Guiterrez, panting in exhausted gasps.

"Gobble-glip-glip," he said unintelligibly, pointing toward the door of the restaurant. "Glip?"

"I think it'll rain myself," Guiterrez answered.

The skinny youth fought for breath. "Did – did they go – in there?"

"Which they?" Guiterrez asked.

"Lily Trace. She had – two guys – with her."

"Who?" said Guiterrez.

The skinny youth got his breath back with a desperate gasp. "Lily Trace! The most glamorous girl in the world! Her pictures are in all the papers and magazines all the time!"

"She did look a little familiar, at that," Guiterrez observed. "Yeah, she just went in to eat. Is she a friend of yours?"

"Friend!" the skinny youth echoed, aghast. "No! All her friends are millionaires and people like that! She has a penthouse apartment that rents for a thousand dollars a month and twenty-four fur coats and a hundred thousand dollars worth of diamonds!"

"How'd she get all that?" Guiterrez asked, interested. "Buy it?"

"No!" said the skinny youth scornfully. "Her admirers present her with every luxury she desires."

"They do, do they?" said Guiterrez. "For free?"

"Of course! All she has to do is smile at them, and they grant her slightest wish."

"Is that a fact?" Guiterrez asked. "Well, you live and learn, I always say. What do you want with her?"

The skinny youth looked at him doubtfully, and then backed away a little, getting ready to run. "I want her autograph, is all."

"So," said Guiterrez. "You're one of them cookies, are you?"

He didn't sound very hostile, and the skinny youth relaxed. He was wearing a ragged sport coat and baggy sport slacks and white shoes that were unbelievably soiled. His small, high-crowned hat had the brim tipped up jauntily in front. His face was pale and bony, spotted with enormous freckles, and he had a desperately serious do-or-die air.

"Sure," he said. "I'm an autograph collector. I specialize in celebrities who aren't in the theater or on the radio or in the movies or like that. I've got over ten thousand famous names in my collection. It's very valuable."

"I wouldn't doubt it," said Guiterrez. "You don't go for actors or actresses, huh?"

The skinny youth was scornful. "Naw. That's cornfed stuff. They're too easy. I pick the hard babies. I'm well known for that. The tougher they are, the better I like it. My name's Steamer. You ever heard of me?"

"Not until now," Guiterrez admitted. "How do you propose to get Lily Trace's autograph?"

"I'll wait here until she comes out and then ask her. If she refuses I'll think up some other gag. I've got lots of them on tap. You don't mind me waitin' here, do you? I mean, lots of guys get tough if they catch us autograph hunters hanging around their joints. They claim we pester the customers and keep 'em from comin' again."

"Is that so?" Guiterrez said thoughtfully. "Pester the customers, huh?"

"Oh, I won't," said Steamer. "Honest."

"Oh, yes, you will," said Guiterrez.

Steamer started to edge away again. "Huh?"

Guiterrez got him by the arm. "Listen, jitterbug. Here's a buck. That's for you if you go inside and start annoying customers in a big way."

"Why?" Steamer asked, still doubtful.

"On account of I hate my customers," Guiterrez explained. "I hate each and every one of them personally."

"Well, why?" Steamer repeated blankly.

Guiterrez scowled ferociously. "Because I sweat and slave over a hot stove all day long to cook them the most beautiful food in the whole world! And what do they do with it? Sit in there and poke it down their gullets like a bunch of pigs at a swill box!"

"They pay for it, don't they?" Steamer inquired.

"Is money everything?" Guiterrez demanded. "No! I'm an artist! I've got a soul!"

"What ought they to do with your food?" Steamer asked curiously.

"Appreciate it! Sit there and savor each mouthful gracefully and gratefully! It's genius they're eating! The genius of Guiterrez!"

"Oh," said Steamer.

"Come along," said Guiterrez.

He opened the door and pushed Steamer into the restaurant. It was a long bare room with a high, smoke-stained ceiling. There were booths along the walls, and the center space was packed with round spindle-legged tables. It was late now for the dinner hour, but the place was full and overflowing.

Diners were hunched over the tables, eating with ferocious concentration, as though they were afraid that if they paused for a breath the food would be snatched from them. They were quite right about that. A mangy horde of waiters prowled around, ready to pounce at the first signs of slackening interest. You had to fight for your food at Guiterrez's.

The noise was terrific. The waiters dropped trays now and then just because they were tired of carrying them. They screamed threats at each other and the customers and orders at the cook. They conducted profane political arguments the length of the room, digressing occasionally to discuss the manners and looks of the diners. A jukebox howled jive from a corner, and the cash register had a bell like a fire gong attached to it.

"Wow!" said Steamer in an awed voice.

Guiterrez shouted in his ear. "Nobody with any brains would eat in a joint like this, would they? I ask you. But look at 'em! I can't get rid of 'em!"

Dick, the small waiter in the big apron, came up and said to Guiterrez: "What's with you now, stupid? You want I should feed this starving fugitive from a rat race?"

"No," said Guiterrez. "He's an annoyer. He collects autographs. Get to work, Steamer."

"Can I get Lily Trace's first?" Steamer asked.

"Sure," Guiterrez said. "She's over there at the side—" He stopped, staring at a small table near the door. "Since when am I running a flophouse here? Who's that sleeping beauty?"

There was only one man at the table. He was slumped down in his chair, head resting in his folded arms. His thinnish blond hair was crumpled and sticky with perspiration, and there was a loose pink roll of fat over the back of his collar.

"He's drunk," said Dick.

"Do tell," said Guiterrez. "I would never have guessed it." He raised his voice to an indignant shout. "So he's drunk! So throw the bum out, you bum!"

"He's got dough," said Dick. "He waves it. I charged him double for the dinners and he didn't kick."

"How many dinners did he have?" Guiterrez demanded.

"Only one. He's got a dame with him. She had one, too. Also he had fifty or sixty drinks. The dame has been tryin' to get him to blow, but he don't want to. She went back to telephone. I think she's calling for help."

"Maybe I could wake him up," said Steamer. "Sometimes when you ask a guy for his autograph, he concentrates and gets sort of sober. Shall I try?"

"Sure," said Guiterrez.

Steamer went over and tapped the drunk politely on the shoulder and began to talk in a low, insistent voice in his ear. For about a minute he got no results. Then the man rolled his head back and forth in vague awareness. Steamer kept on talking and tapping confidentially.

The man heaved himself back in his chair. "Huh?" He had a round, heavily jowled face and eyes that were glassily bloodshot. His clothes were expensively tailored. "What you say?"

Steamer slid a piece of paper in front of him and poked a pencil into the vaguely fumbling fingers all in one deft, practiced motion.

"Your name, sir. Your autograph, please."

"Oh," said the man. He scowled at the pencil as though he had never seen one before. He maneuvered it around until he got the point headed in the right direction and made a groping, careful scrawl on the piece of paper.

"Thank you," said Steamer.

He pocketed the slip of paper and headed for Lily Trace's table.

"The kid's good," said Dick. "Maybe we should try being more polite to the suckers, huh?"

"Don't be a Communist," said Guiterrez. "The guy's waked up now. Where's his dame?"

"She's coming. The skinny one, there."

The girl was thin to the point of emaciation, and her eyes were enormous in the white stillness of her face. Her lips were a thin, bright-red streak. She looked like a drawing of one of those impossibly elongated fashion manikins, and her sport clothes had the same slick, professional lines. She walked with a beautiful, practiced grace.

"Come on, Don," she said with determination. "Please."

"One drink," said the man. "Only one. Honest. Then we'll go right away."

"Now!" said the girl.

"One drink!" said the man stubbornly. He looked inquiringly at Dick and raised a finger.

"We're fresh out of everything but Mickey Finns," said Dick. "Be happy to serve you one of them, though."

"Eh?" said the man blankly.

The girl jerked at his arm. "Oh, come on! Please, Don! We *can't* stay here any longer! You can have a drink when we get home."

"Two?" asked the man cleverly.

"A dozen! A hundred!"

"O.K.," said the man. He got unsteadily to his feet. "How much I owe, waiter?"

Dick whipped a bill out of his pocket. "Well, you had two *de luxe* dinners—" He stopped in midsentence, looking at the girl. He drew a deep breath and put the bill away again. "But you paid for them. Don't you remember?"

"Sure, sure. Tip for you."

The man dropped a crumpled bill on the table. The girl picked it up and calmly put it in the pocket of her sport coat, watching Dick as she did it. Dick smiled in a painfully polite way.

The girl took a firm hold on the man's arm and steered him carefully toward the door and out through it. Dick went back to where Guiterrez was standing.

"See that?" he asked. "A man can't even chisel an honest dollar anymore. That dame is pure poison. I'd hate to have her get behind me if she had a knife around anywhere."

"She don't need a knife," said Guiterrez. "She's got fingernails she could cut your throat with. Where'd that autograph bug go?"

"I dunno," said Dick, looking around.

"Must have got Lily Trace's signature and beat it out the side door, I guess," Guiterrez said, shrugging. "Well, there goes a buck, but it wasn't a very good idea, anyway."

"Naturally not," Dick observed. "If you thought of it. Why don't you go back and do some cooking?"

"I'm not in the mood," Guiterrez answered sourly. "I want to be alone."

Chapter II
Hired to Steal

MAX LATIN was sitting in his special booth, the last one in the line, near the metal swing door that led into the kitchen. Dick stopped beside him and produced a bottle of brandy and a small glass from under his voluminous apron. He pulled the cork out of the bottle with his teeth and put it down beside the glass on the table.

"Screwball is having one of his fits again," he observed.

"Guiterrez?" Latin asked, pouring brandy.

"Yeah. He wants to be alone. So do I – with hot hips over there. Only I'm afraid she comes higher than a gumdrop or a shiny apple."

Latin looked across the room. "I'm afraid so. That's Lily Trace. She's on the expensive side."

"I wonder if she ever gives a benefit performance – for charity and like that?" Dick said speculatively.

"I wouldn't count on it."

"I wish I had more money and less brains," said Dick gloomily. "I got to go to work. Holler if you want me."

Latin sipped at his brandy, enjoying himself. He had the lazy, relaxed air of a sleepy cat.

A smoothly clipped voice said: "Are you Mr. Max Latin, the private inquiry agent?"

"Yes," said Latin, looking up.

The man beside the booth was very tall, taller even than Latin. He had even young-old features that were as cold and sharp as chiseled steel. His eyes were a faded, smooth blue, very light against the tan of his face. He was wearing a dark business suit, and he carried a topcoat over his arm.

"My name is Caleb Drew," he said. "I was informed that you were in the habit of conducting your – ah – business from this restaurant."

"This booth is my office," Latin answered.

"I have a friend who would like to talk to you. If you'll pardon me for a second."

Caleb Drew walked across to Lily Trace's table. She smiled up at him in excellently simulated surprise. The two college boys stood at attention and were introduced to Drew. Lily Trace made a gesture inviting him to sit down. He shook his head and nodded toward Latin's booth.

Lily Trace clapped her hands delightedly. The college boys scowled. Lily Trace got up and took Caleb Drew's arm and let him guide her toward Latin's booth. The college boys sat down glumly and glowered at each other.

"This is Mr. Max Latin," Drew said. "Mr. Latin, this is Lily Trace."

Dick, the waiter, came up and put his elbows on the back of the booth and stared dreamily at Lily Trace. "Latin," he said, "how do you do it, anyway?"

"Get me a couple of glasses," Latin ordered. "Sit down, Miss Trace – Mr. Drew."

Dick took two small glasses from under his apron and put them down on the table. "You go settin' up drinks with that brandy, and Guiterrez will cloud up and rain all over you. That stuff costs sixteen smackers a bottle."

"Go away," said Latin.

"Don't say I didn't warn you," said Dick, obeying. "Call me before the dame leaves, will you? I want to watch her wiggle out of that booth."

Drew said: "The help around here is a little bit – forward."

"I've noticed that," Latin said idly. "Have some brandy?"

"I never drink," said Lily Trace, smiling.

Drew nodded. "Thanks."

Latin poured him a drink. "You wanted to see me, Miss Trace?"

"Yes," said Lily Trace frankly. "I really did want to see you. I like to meet famous people, and you are one of them."

Latin sipped at his brandy. "I've got a long police record, if that's what you mean."

"A lot of arrests," said Drew. "No convictions."

"Bribing juries is an expensive habit," Latin told him. "And with me, time is money. Now you've met me, and we're all happy here together, so what's next?"

"I'd like you to do some work for me," Lily Trace stated. "Some confidential work."

"All my work is confidential – and expensive."

"I'm paying," Drew said.

"Go into your spiel, then," Latin invited.

Lily Trace lowered her voice to a husky, confidential murmur. "I want you to help me steal some jewelry."

"O.K.," said Latin. "Where and when?"

Lily Trace laughed admiringly. "Oh, I like the way you said that! You're so casual. You'd think you went around stealing things all the time!"

"I do," said Latin.

"Oh," said Lily Trace, surprised.

Drew said: "You'd better let me handle this, Lily. You're a little out of your weight class here, I think."

Lily Trace didn't like that last. She studied Latin with narrowed, speculative eyes. She took a deep breath and stretched the cloth of the front of her dress. Latin sipped his brandy. He was not impressed. Lily Trace chewed on her lower lip, slightly at a loss.

"This is no gag, Mr. Latin," Drew said in his smooth voice. "At least, not the kind you think. Lily doesn't mean for you to actually steal any jewels, of course. She wants it to appear that hers have been stolen."

Latin looked at her. "Insurance?"

"Of course not!" said Drew. "There's no crooked work involved at all."

"Then I don't want to be involved, either."

"Now just a moment," Drew said, losing some of his smooth veneer. "Let me explain, please. Lily wants some more publicity – of the undercover, confidential sort that's so hard to get. Cryptic little hints by columnists and that sort of thing. You know what I mean."

"I've got a rough idea."

"She's not going to report her jewels stolen, and they aren't going to be. But she wants the rumor to get around that they have been – wants people whispering behind their hands about it. You're just the man to handle that."

"I'm listening."

Drew coughed. "Your – ah – reputation…"

"It smells high," said Latin.

"Yes," said Drew, relieved. "She wants to use it. She wants you to put out feelers – inquiries – as though you were trying to buy back her jewelry secretly from the imaginary thieves who stole it."

"Compounding a felony," Latin defined.

"Yes," said Lily Trace eagerly. "But it'll work. Really it will. I know. Everybody will be running around and whispering and pointing and wondering. There'll be hints about it in all the gossip columns. It'll be one of those secrets because they know, and I'll just get all kinds of publicity!"

"And maybe some more jewelry," Latin added.

"Nothing like that is intended," Drew said coldly. "Miss Trace is not accepting any more presents from her admirers. She and I are going to be married."

"Felicitations," said Latin. "My price for this little job of work is one thousand dollars – in advance."

Drew stared at him. "That seems excessive—"

"Unless I have to argue about it," Latin continued in the same tone. "Then the price goes up. It costs money to argue with me."

Drew's face looked white and stiff. He took his wallet from his pocket and carefully counted out ten one-hundred dollar bills.

"I judged you'd want cash." He dropped a card on the bills. "There's my address and phone number, if you want to get in touch with me."

"Very thoughtful of you," Latin commented. "You'll be hearing of and from me. You'd better get the jewelry out of sight somewhere. As soon as the police hear that I'm nosing around, they'll come and see you. They might be a little on the rough side. They're mad at me now for one reason or another."

"That will be taken care of," Drew promised.

He helped Lily Trace out of the booth. The two college boys sprang to attention and settled back into despair again as Lily Trace waved to them gaily and went on out of the restaurant with Drew.

Dick came out of the kitchen and leaned over the back of the booth. "Latin," he murmured. "There's a stiff out in the alley. Is it one of yours?"

Latin looked up at him silently.

"No joke," said Dick. "Guiterrez fell over it and grabbed a handful of blood. He don't want to be alone anymore."

Latin slid out of the booth. "Come on."

Guiterrez was holding his hands under the hot water faucet in the sink. He took them out and wiped them on a dish towel and looked at them. They were as clean and pink as a new baby's. Guiterrez shuddered and shoved them under the hot water faucet again.

"That's the kind of thing I run into around here," he muttered savagely. "My customers not only stuff themselves like hogs – they go out in my alley and die on me. Why don't they go home first if they want to die?"

"You sure it isn't just a stray drunk?" Latin asked.

Guiterrez looked at him soberly. "I'm sure. It's a guy, and he's awful dead, Latin. In that dark stretch between the side door and the mouth of the alley. Just beyond where we set the garbage cans."

"Wait here," Latin ordered.

He went out the side door and closed it behind him. The darkness was like a living thing, a heavy menacing weight that pressed coldly against his face. The mouth of the alley, half a block away, was a narrow high rectangle with the streetlights feeble and yellow beyond it.

Latin moved slowly and cautiously forward. His knee thrust against the side of a garbage can, rattled the galvanized lid, and the echoes chased themselves hollowly away from him. He touched a limp, yielding weight with the toe of his shoe.

In the street an auto horn blatted flatly, and gears clashed. Latin took a match from his pocket and snapped it on his thumbnail. Shadows jiggled and swooped weirdly around him, and then the yellow flame steadied as he cupped it in his hands.

The man was lying sprawled on his face with his head pillowed in a slick pool of blood. He looked very flat and thin and deflated. His throat had been cut.

The match flickered out, and Latin struck another. The dead man's clothes had a messy, pulled-around look to them. All his pockets had been turned inside out, the linings hanging like multiple tags pinned helter-skelter to him.

Latin leaned closer to look at his face and then blew out the match. He made his way cautiously back to the side door and went into the restaurant kitchen.

Guiterrez was letting the water from the cold water tap run over his hands. Dick was leaning against the asbestos-covered side of the steak broiler, picking his teeth with a curved paring knife.

"Did you look at him?" Latin asked.

"Oh, no," said Guiterrez. "I felt him. That convinced me that I didn't want to know him any better."

Latin said: "He's just a kid – maybe twenty at the best. Skinny and tall – freckled face. Wearing dirty white shoes and checked slacks and a sport coat."

Guiterrez stared at Dick, his eyes widening. "The jitterbug!"

Dick nodded. "Must be."

"Do you know him?" Latin inquired.

Guiterrez said: "He told me his name was Steamer. He's one of these dopey autograph collectors. He wanted to get Lily Trace's signature. He saw her go in the joint, and he was gonna wait outside. I told him to go on in and brace her inside and pester some of the other customers while he was at it. I think maybe that wasn't such a hot idea."

"He had something somebody wanted," Latin said. "He's been rolled. A nice thorough job."

"Rolled!" Guiterrez repeated, startled. "Why, hell, anybody could tell just by lookin' at him that he wouldn't be carrying any dough."

"Something else, then," said Latin.

The second cook pushed Dick out of the way and threw steaks in the broiler like a man dealing out meaty, thick cards. The steaks sizzled and smoked and spattered. Guiterrez looked at them and shivered. He put his hands back under the water faucet.

"Did Steamer pester any customers?" Latin asked.

Guiterrez shook his head. "He gypped me. He got Lily Trace's signature and hopped it."

"The drunk," Dick said.

Guiterrez nodded. "Oh, yeah. There was a drunk sleepin' on one of the tables. The kid woke him up by pretendin' he wanted the guy's autograph."

"Did you know the drunk?"

"Nope," said Guiterrez. "He's been here before, though. Quite a while ago, as I remember."

Latin nodded at Dick, and Dick went out through the swing door into the front part of the restaurant. A waiter yelled some unintelligible gibberish through the order slot, and the pastry chef said: "Go to hell. That ain't on the menu."

Guiterrez began to wipe his hands slowly and carefully. "I don't feel so good now, Latin. I'm afraid I pulled that kid into this. I shoulda kept my big mouth shut."

"Forget it," Latin said absently. He was frowning, his greenish eyes narrowed thoughtfully.

Dick came back into the kitchen. "The drunk's been here before – two or three times. But nobody knows his name or anything about him. The dame he had with him called him Don. She's never been here except tonight. The drunk is a big spender. Steamer got his autograph and Lily Trace's. Nobody else's. Then two college cutups beefed with Steamer when he braced Lily Trace. They're just leavin' now."

"Have they got a car?" Latin asked.

"No."

"Go out and tell the taxi driver who picks them up to keep track of them and telephone me here."

"O.K.," said Dick, going out again.

"Get me a tablecloth," Latin said to Guiterrez. "A big one."

"What're you gonna use that for?" Guiterrez asked.

"A shroud."

Guiterrez stared at him, his face paling.

Latin said: "If the cops find that body there, they'll pinch me on suspicion. They couldn't prove anything, but they could hold me for a couple of days. I don't want to be in jail right at the moment."

"You're gonna move him?" Guiterrez asked shakily.

"Yes. Afterwards, I want you to get some ashes out of the broiler – a lot of them – and spread them over the blood and stamp them down."

"Oh-oh," said Guiterrez.

Dick came back through the swing door. "Benny Merkle was the driver that picked up the college guys. I told him what you said."

Latin nodded. "All right. I'm going over and get my car now. You go out in the alley and see that nobody else falls over Steamer. Wait there until I come back with the car."

"O.K., chum," Dick said casually.

Chapter IIII
Death of a Dick

DETECTIVE INSPECTOR WALTERS, Homicide, had a yellowish gaunt face and a sourly cynical nature. He had been chasing murderers of one sort or another for twenty years, and he had gotten to the point where he didn't believe what he heard even when he was talking to himself. He sat in Latin's booth and watched Latin sip delicately at a small glass of brandy.

"It's good," said Latin. "Want some?"

"No," said Walters.

It was late now, and the restaurant was almost empty. A half-dozen waiters were playing craps on a table near the cash register.

Guiterrez came out of the kitchen and said: "Listen, Latin. I've told you before I don't like cops hanging around here all the time. People are gonna think I'm running a bookie joint or a hook shop. You know what kind of a reputation cops have. They stink a place up."

Before Walters could think of an answer, Guiterrez went on up to the front of the restaurant and shouldered his way into the crap game.

Walters drew a deep breath and said: "A guy got killed tonight, Latin."

"Only one?" Latin observed. "Hitler must be slipping."

"This guy wasn't in Europe," Walters said patiently. "And Hitler didn't kill him."

"Who did?" Latin inquired.

"That's a coincidence," Walters said. "I was just about to ask you that."

"Me?" Latin said, surprised. "Now listen, Walters, this is getting to be a nuisance. Just because you find a body somewhere—"

"Not somewhere. On the front steps of the morgue."

"That was thoughtful of the guy."

"He didn't put himself there. Somebody else did."

"Not guilty," said Latin. "I don't even know where the morgue is, and besides, I haven't been out of this place all night. You can ask Guiterrez or Dick or any of the waiters."

"Let's not clown around," said Walters wearily. "I know you own this joint and that all these birds work for you. They'd swear black was white if you gave them the nod."

"Prove it," Latin invited.

"I can't. Besides, I've got other things to do. This is just a confidential chat. Do you know anything about this bird that got biffed?"

"Who was he?" Latin asked.

"He called himself Steamer Morgan. He was a private detective and a good one – that is, if there are any good ones."

Latin put his glass down. "A private detective?"

"Yeah. Not a crook like you are, though. At least, he didn't go around talking about it as much if he was. He specialized in getting evidence in civil cases."

"Divorces?" Latin inquired.

"No. Accident cases and damage suits. He was plenty expert – knew a lot about law. He had a swell front for it. He looked like a kid, and he went around acting like a jitterbug and a sort of a screwy young punk. The last type of guy you'd suspect of being a detective. He's sneaked up on an awful lot of smarties with that act. And when he got evidence – it was the kind that held in court."

"Was he working on a case?"

Walters shrugged. "I think so. I'm trying to find out now. He worked undercover and on his own. He didn't keep any records. Somebody searched him before they left him at the morgue. Nothing in his pockets at all."

Dick came up to the booth carrying a portable telephone. "One of your crummy friends wants to talk to you."

Latin plugged the phone in on the concealed connection behind the drape at the back of the booth. "Latin speaking," he said into the mouthpiece.

"This here is Benny Merkle, Mr. Latin. I'm the taxi driver that picked up them two guys from your joint a while back. Dick said you wanted to know where they went and such."

"Yes," said Latin. "Go ahead."

"They called each other Bruce and Bill. They didn't use no last names. I drove 'em from your joint to a very swanky dive called the Chateau Carleton on Vandervort Road. They don't live there. They waked up the janitor and laid down a pound note to get in."

"What then?" Latin asked.

"I waited around, and in about ten minutes they came boiling out again. One of 'em had a bloody nose and the other had a big bump on his noggin. They was plenty mad at some dame they called Lily."

"What did they do next?"

"They had me drive 'em to a liquor store, and they bought a fifth of Scotch. It was good Scotch. They gave me a couple of drinks. Then they asked me if I knew where they could – I mean, they told me to drive 'em over to Katie Althouse's place on Barker Street. They went in there, and they both picked out a girl by the name of Priscilla."

Latin was smiling. "What does she look like?"

"Priscilla? Well, she's sort of dark and kinda built in a big way. She's got black hair she wears in a long bob, and she makes up her mouth in a smear."

Latin chuckled. "All right, Benny. Did you wait for them?"

"Yeah. I took 'em home. They was kinda tired and pretty drunk. I put 'em to bed at the Milton Hotel. I'm there now. You want I should ask some questions about 'em?"

"No," said Latin. "Let it go. Thanks a lot, Benny. Drop in and say hello to the cashier here tomorrow."

Latin put the telephone back in its cradle. He was still grinning.

"Let me laugh, too," Walters invited.

Latin said: "Lily Trace came in here tonight with a couple of college boys. She ditched them and then bounced them when they tried to call on her later. They got mad and went over to Katie Althouse's place and picked out a girl who looked like Lily Trace. As long as they couldn't get the real article they were going to take a substitute."

"They must be dopes," said Walters.

"They've got some fancy company."

Walters nodded. "I don't get it. This café society is away over my head. In my time gals like Lily Trace stayed down by the stockyards and hung red lanterns over their doors. They didn't have their pictures in the society pages waltzing with all the town's best bankrolls."

"Do you know where she came from?"

"No, but I'll make you a bet I can guess how. You want to watch your step with her, sonny."

"What?" said Latin.

Walters said: "Look, Latin. I like you in spite of all your fancy tricks, and I think maybe you're even halfway honest now and then. This little deal you've got on with Lily Trace is going to backfire right in your face if you don't watch your step."

"What deal?" Latin asked casually.

"It didn't fool me any, but some of the boys have got a mad on with you. Especially the district attorney's office. About twenty tips have come in tonight that Lily Trace had a lot of jewelry stolen and that you're dickering either for the guys who lifted it or for her or for both. I knew it was phoney because there were too many tips, but the district attorney's boys aren't that subtle."

"Thanks, Walters," said Latin. "I'll take care of it. I know something about Steamer's death. I don't know who killed him, but I'll find out and let you know."

Walters got up. "Better hurry a little. I can't hold the district attorney's boys off you forever, and anyway I like to see results for my efforts."

Latin poured himself another drink. "Find out what Steamer was working on if you can."

"Find out yourself. You know more crooked lawyers than I do."

Walters stopped at the crap game to exchange insults with Guiterrez and then went on out of the restaurant. Latin finished up his glass of brandy and lit a cigarette. After a while, he took the card Caleb Drew had given him out of his pocket and looked at it.

It was outsize, made of thick parchment. Engraved on it in jet-black old English letters was the name 'Caleb Drew IV' and under that 'Investment Counsellor'. In the lower left corner was an address Latin recognized as belonging to the Teasdale Building in the downtown financial district and a telephone number. In the lower right-hand corner there was another telephone number.

Latin dialed that number, and after the first ring a voice said politely in his ear: "Gravesend Manor."

"May I speak to Mr. Caleb Drew?" Latin asked.

"He's not in, sir."

"Do you mean that he's not home or that he's asleep?"

"He's not here, sir. He hasn't been in for the last two or three days. Do you wish to leave a message?"

"No, thanks."

Latin hung up and dialed Information. When a courteously long-suffering feminine voice answered, he said: "Will you give me the number of Miss Lily Trace? She lives at the Chateau Carleton on Vandervort Road."

"One moment, please." The line hummed emptily to itself, and then the long-suffering voice said: "There's no telephone listed under that name, sir."

"You mean it's a hidden number?"

"There's no telephone listed under that name, sir."

"All right," said Latin. "Is there switchboard service at the Carleton?"

"No, sir."

"Goodbye," said Latin. He hung up and poured himself another very small portion of brandy. He didn't drink it. He scowled at it thoughtfully for a while and then dialed still another number.

This time the telephone at the other end rang a long time before the connection snapped and a hoarse, blurred voice said: "Abraham Moscowitz, Attorney, speaking."

Latin said: "This is Latin, Abe."

"O.K. I'm coming." The line clicked and was dead.

Latin swore to himself and dialed the same number again. "O.K., O.K.," said Moscowitz's blurred voice. "Don't get ants in your pants. I said I'm coming. Give me a chance to put on my shoes first, will you?"

"I'm not in jail," Latin told him.

"What?" said Moscowitz incredulously. "You mean those police bums got the nerve to hold you without booking you? Get off the phone so I can call the mayor! I'll fix 'em!"

"Shut up," said Latin. "I'm not even arrested. I want to ask you some questions about law."

"Law?" said Moscowitz. "I don't know anything about law. I'm an attorney."

"Did you ever do any business with a private detective named Steamer Morgan?"

"Nope," said Moscowitz. "He's too ignorant. He won't even commit perjury. Can you imagine a private detective that won't commit perjury? What good is he as a witness?"

"Who does he work for?"

"Baldwin and Frazier, mostly. They are a couple of old dodos with hay in their hair. Sometimes they win a case by accident, but not very often."

"What kind of cases?"

"They got a whole bunch of corporate accounts they inherited from their grandpappies."

"Anything in court now that's hot?"

"They got half-a-dozen appeals floating around here and there. Stockholders' suits. They're always suing for an accounting."

"What does that mean?" Latin asked.

"Oh, that's when the stockholders find out there's no dough in the treasury and they want to find out who spent it and what for. I always say, as long as it's gone – who cares? Some sharpshooter is always rapping suckers for their nickels. It doesn't make much difference who he is or how he does it – they won't get their money back."

"Ever hear of a girl named Lily Trace?"

"*Whee!*"

"Aside from that, do you know anything about her?"

"Nope. I never met her except in my dreams."

"How about a gent named Caleb Drew?"

"Never heard of him."

"He's going to marry Lily Trace."

"Marry her?" Moscowitz repeated, startled. "Say, now there's a smart guy! I never thought of that. A marriage license only costs two bucks, and mink coats come a lot higher than that – even wholesale."

"Goodbye," said Latin. He put the telephone back in its cradle and downed the small drink of brandy. He got up out of the booth and went through the metal swing door into the kitchen.

After a moment Guiterrez followed him. He was carrying Latin's hat and topcoat. Without a word he helped Latin into the coat.

Latin took a stubby hammerless Smith and Wesson revolver out of the waistband of his trousers and dropped it into the side pocket of the topcoat. He took his hat from Guiterrez and put it on carefully.

Guiterrez cleared his throat. "Be a little careful, huh?" he suggested uneasily.

Latin winked at him and went out the back door.

The Gravesend Manor Apartment Hotel was a somber, heavily dignified building in the massive style of a medieval European castle. It had a lobby like a baronial hall, long and narrow, with ornamental beams that were smooth and dark and oily against the high white ceiling. Latin walked down a length of deep red carpet to the small desk in the corner.

"I'd like to speak to Caleb Drew," he said.

The desk clerk was a small, plump man with a benign smile and white hair that floated around his head like a halo. He looked like a casket salesman.

"I'm sorry, sir," he said, as though he really meant it. "He's not in now."

"It's rather important that I see him," said Latin. "Do you expect him soon?"

"No, sir. That is, I have no idea when he'll return."

Latin nodded and frowned as though he were masticating on some weighty problem. Finally he leaned confidentially on the desk.

"May I have your name?"

"Mr. Hammersley, sir," the clerk said, looking faintly surprised.

"Mr. Hammersley, I'm Detective Inspector Walters of the Homicide detail. May I speak to you in confidence?"

"Oh, of course," said Hammersley, impressed.

"Have you ever heard of a man named Max Latin?"

"That person!" said Hammersley. "Oh, yes indeed! I follow the crime news with – ah – considerable interest. A hobby of mine, you might say. This Latin seems to be a very reprehensible sort of a character – always getting arrested for something or other. He's a private detective, isn't he, sir?"

"That's what he claims," said Latin. "But I know him well, and in my opinion he's nothing but a crook. We're very anxious to prove that. He's in trouble right now over the matter of an unexplained murder."

"Murder!" Hammersley repeated, blinking.

"Yes. He has homicidal tendencies. Now, we have heard it rumored that he's done some sort of work for Mr. Drew in the past. Not connected with this business, of course, but we think that Latin might try to get in touch with Mr. Drew, knowing how influential Mr. Drew is, to try to persuade him to lend Latin his influence or even some money."

"I understand," said Hammersley eagerly.

"Have you seen Latin around here? He looks a little bit like me."

"No, I haven't. I'm certain I'd have noticed him if he'd been here. I can recognize his type easily."

"Be sure and notify headquarters if you see him. But I think – knowing the sly, crafty nature of the man – that he will probably attempt to get in touch with Mr. Drew by telephone. I know this is a very unusual request, but will you tell me if Mr. Drew has received any telephone calls this evening while he's been out? I'm sure Gravesend Manor would want to cooperate with the authorities, and this man Latin is really a menace."

"In the circumstances," said Hammersley, "anything we can do…" He fluttered through some telephone call slips and put several on the desk in front of Latin. "You can see that if he did call, he didn't leave his name."

"Oh, he wouldn't use his own name," Latin said, going through the slips. "How about these five calls? They're all from the same person."

"Oh, no," said Hammersley. "They don't have anything to do with Latin."

"I hate to seem inquisitive, but I'd like to be sure—"

"They're all from Miss Mayan. Miss Teresa Mayan. She's Mr. Drew's secretary. She called here repeatedly early this evening, as you see. She said she had to get in touch with Mr. Drew in regard to an important business matter."

"Oh, yes," said Latin. "I wonder. Perhaps she could tell me something about Mr. Drew's business dealings with Latin. It's something I don't like to speak about over the telephone. Do you know where she lives?"

"Yes. At Hadley House. It's on First and Drexel."

"Thank you, Mr. Hammersley," said Latin. "We of the police department appreciate the help of conscientious citizens like you are."

"It was nothing at all," Hammersley said, embarrassed and pleased. "Don't mention it."

Chapter IV
Target for Teresa

HADLEY HOUSE went in for the modernistic. It was all as sleek and streamlined as a pursuit plane. Latin got out of the mirror-studded, chromium-lined elevator at the fourth floor and walked down a long hall that had pale blue walls and a dark blue ceiling. He knocked on the door numbered 412.

Teresa Mayan opened it. Latin had never seen her before, but he recognized her at once from the descriptions Guiterrez and Dick had given him. She was the girl who had been with the drunk called Don at the restaurant.

She was wearing a black satin hostess coat that rustled luxuriously when she moved, and her face looked pale and still and thoughtful above it. She was not at all surprised to see Latin. She nodded casually and said: "Come on in."

Latin stepped into the square, low-ceilinged living room and watched her move in her gracefully indolent way to the liquor cabinet in the corner. She poured whiskey out of a squat decanter into two tall, silver-rimmed glasses, fizzed a shot of soda into each. She gave Latin one of the glasses and pointed to the divan.

"Sit down."

Latin sat down slowly, holding the glass in both hands, and watched her. He couldn't quite figure out this approach and he said: "Were you expecting someone – I mean, now?"

"Yes," said Teresa Mayan. "You."

"Do you know who I am?" Latin asked.

She nodded. "I recognized you – from your picture. It's quite a remarkable likeness."

"Picture?" Latin repeated slowly and thoughtfully.

Teresa Mayan smiled at him. "You're quite a clever little lad, but that surprised you, didn't it? You didn't know I had a camera with me, did you?"

"No," said Latin honestly. "I didn't."

"A good one, too. A very good one. Wait." She walked through the doorway that led into the bedroom and came out carrying a large flat square of cardboard. "Be careful. It's still wet."

She lowered the cardboard so that he could see the wet photographic print lying on it. Latin looked and closed his eyes slowly and then looked again.

It was a remarkably good picture of him. Very effective, too. He *was* kneeling down, holding a match in front of him, and the match flame made his features look white and sharp and clear. It also revealed plainly the body that was lying on the ground in front of him, the slick shine of the pool of blood, the pale loosened features of Steamer Morgan, and even a couple of shadowy garbage cans.

"I've got a title for it," said Teresa Mayan. "I'm going to call it 'Caught in the Act'. I think that sort of explains it, don't you?"

"Sort of," Latin agreed. His face looked white and a little strained.

"The camera is specially made for candid shots," Teresa Mayan explained. "Has a beautiful lens. Very fast, very sensitive. A match in a dark alley like that was just right for it."

"I can see that," said Latin.

"I developed the print myself. I have knockdown darkroom equipment here."

"Very handy," said Latin.

"Yes, it is. I got it for Don. I've been keeping him amused by letting him take nude candid shots of me." She smoothed the front of her housecoat. "I make a good nude model if you like them long and limber."

"Oh," said Latin.

Teresa Mayan laughed at him.

"Still a little at sea, aren't you? I'll tell you how it was. I know that you own that restaurant and that you hang around there all the time and that you're a sharpshooter. It's not as big a secret as you seem to think. And I knew that the dope who runs it for you – Guiterrez – saw me tonight when he fell over the body in the alley. He covered it up – pretending he didn't know there was anyone around and acted scared out of his pants – but he didn't fool me. I knew he recognized me, and I knew you'd find out who I was someway or other and come around and try to blackmail me. I was right, wasn't I?"

"It looks that way," Latin admitted.

"So I acted to protect myself," said Teresa Mayan. "You played right along with me by moving the body. Now I've got more on you than you have on me." She indicated the picture with a forefinger that had a bloodred glistening nail two inches long and pointed like a dagger. "I only developed one negative. I've got a lot more."

"Where?" Latin asked.

"Not here," she said, smiling coolly. "Now you put that print in your pocket and run along home. Take a look at it any time you get more smart ideas about shaking me down."

"O.K.," said Latin glumly. He put his glass down on the coffee table and got up. "I don't suppose it would do any good to tell you that I didn't have any such ideas in mind at all when I came over here?"

Teresa Mayan stood and laughed at him in a lightly amused way.

"O.K.," said Latin again.

He took one catlike step toward her and hit her. His fist didn't travel more than six inches, and it landed with a sharp smack on the hinge of her jaw just below her ear. Teresa Mayan whirled around with a graceful rustle of silk, fell across the divan, and rolled off on the floor. She lay motionless, face down.

Latin dropped instantly on one knee and one hand, like a football linesman getting ready to charge. He was holding the stubby Smith and Wesson in his other hand, and he peered tensely over the top of the divan at the door into the bedroom.

Nothing happened. There was no sound, no movement in the apartment. A minute dragged past, then another. Latin came up out of his crouch and slid into the bedroom and flicked the light switch.

The room was severely modernistic. The bed was low and wide. It had no foot, and the head was one huge mirror. There were a good many pictures of Teresa Mayan on the walls. As she had said, she made a very good nude model if you like them long and limber.

Latin looked in the closet and in the bathroom. He went back through the living room and tried the kitchen. The portable developing outfit was on the tile sideboard next to the sink. Its light-proof hood was raised now, and there were trays and round bottles of developing fluid lined up behind it. The camera was there, too. A pocket-sized German miniature. The back of it was open. There was no film in it and none anywhere around that Latin could see.

Silk rustled in the living room, and Latin jumped for the doorway. Teresa Mayan was still lying in a limp, graceful heap on the floor.

Latin walked over and looked down at her. "The trouble with you is that you've been to too many movies. You're not dealing with Charlie Chan now. I want that negative. Where is it?"

She didn't move.

Latin leaned over and picked her up effortlessly and bounced her on the divan. She pulled herself slowly up to a sitting position. There was a little red spot on her cheek where Latin had hit her, and she rubbed it slowly and gently, watching him with eyes that were glistening, narrow slits.

"This isn't going to hurt me worse than it does you," Latin told her conversationally. "In fact, I just love to bat people around. You tell me where that film is or you're going to be in the market for some store teeth. You got yourself into this by being too smart. Guiterrez actually didn't see you in the alley. He really was scared out of his pants. I didn't come around here to blackmail you. I didn't know who you were or that you were anywhere near that alley. I wanted to find Caleb Drew, and I thought he'd probably check in here sooner or later."

Teresa Mayan said: "What do you want him for?"

"I'm working for him."

"You're a liar."

"Certainly. That's why he hired me. I'm supposed to be negotiating for the return of some of Lily Trace's jewelry that hasn't been stolen."

Her eyes looked as lidless and deadly as a snake's. "Why?"

"She wants publicity. I was going to tell Caleb Drew that if she wanted to get it from what I was doing, she'd have to keep her own big mouth shut. If she doesn't quit sounding off everyone will know it's a phoney. Now I want that film. I don't think it's going to convict me of murder or anything like that, but it can make me plenty of trouble. Where is it?"

"Then what happens?"

"We'll talk about that after I get the film."

"It's in the top drawer of the desk over there."

The desk was against the wall next to the door into the bedroom. Latin went over to it and opened the top drawer. He leaned down to look into it, and the bullet that had been meant for the back of his head missed by about an inch and buried itself in the wall in front of his face.

Latin didn't turn around or straighten up. He dived headfirst through the door into the bedroom. As he hit the floor and rolled, he flipped his arm up and shoved the door hard. The sound of its slam was like an echo of the bursting smash of the shot.

Latin rolled on over and came up to his knees, cursing himself soundlessly. Teresa Mayan wasn't wearing anything under the hostess coat, and it didn't have any pockets large enough to hide a gun. But he should have known she would have one cached around somewhere. Probably it had been poked back of the cushions on the divan.

Another report smacked out, and the bullet made a neat white hole in the door about six inches below the knob. It would have taken Latin right in the middle of the face had he been trying to look through the keyhole.

Latin didn't like that, either. Teresa Mayan could call her shots. He knew just as well as if he could see her that she was kneeling in back of the divan, using its top for a rest. From the sound of its reports, he judged she was using a .25 caliber automatic. That meant she had at least five more shots. Under the circumstances, Latin had no slightest urge to open the door.

This was like a motion picture script that had gone haywire. The heroine besieged in the bedroom protecting her honor. Only Latin wasn't a heroine, and he didn't have any honor.

He tilted his head, listening intently. There were faint, hurried sounds of motion in the living room. The subdued swish of silk, the muffled tap of a high heel. Latin got up and slid along the wall beside the door. He paused again to listen. If she wasn't on a direct line with the doorway, he had some chance of getting out and finding cover before she could hit him.

He reached slowly and cautiously for the knob and then stiffened rigidly as a latch clicked. It wasn't the bedroom door, though. It was the front door. It slammed with a final, solid thud.

Latin jerked the bedroom door open and slammed it back against the wall. He was afraid of a trick, and he didn't show himself in the doorway. He stayed flat beside it.

Voices came to him very faintly, mumbling from the hall just outside the apartment. Among them, Teresa Mayan's sounded quite clear and loud.

"Shots? Yes, I heard them plainly."

Latin came into the living room and walked across to the front door and put his ear against the panel. It sounded like there were a dozen people in the hall, all talking at once. Teresa Mayan's voice came again.

"You'd better keep watch here in the hallway. There might be a prowler around. Of course, he couldn't be in my apartment, but I'd feel safer if you'd just watch my door for a little while. It's silly, I know, but I'm so easily frightened by just the thought of things like that."

Another voice said: "Oh, I'll be watching, Miss Mayan."

Latin said some more things to himself. If he stepped out of the apartment now, there was sure to be a beef. That was the last thing he wanted at the moment. He was cornered.

After thinking it over, he shrugged casually and looked around the front room. The satin hostess coat lay on the floor in an untidy pile. Latin studied it for a second, puzzled, and then he understood. Teresa Mayan's tailored gabardine sport coat had been lying across one of the chairs. It was gone now.

She hadn't been able to get at any of her clothes in the bedroom. The hostess coat was too bulky to fit under the sport coat. She had discarded it and put on the sport coat in its place. As a costume, it was a trifle sketchy, but it would get by. She had been wearing plain black suede bedroom slippers. They were a little exotic for street wear, but she probably didn't intend to do any walking.

Latin shook his head ruefully. He braced one of the chairs under the doorknob and began to search the living room. He found some packets of love letters that made very interesting reading, but their writers had signed them with nicknames that didn't mean anything to him.

He went on into the bedroom. He uncovered an astonishing array of underclothing, all very expensive, lots of costume jewelry, and a great many more pictures of Teresa Mayan. She evidently was quite proud of her own anatomy.

He didn't find any film negative, and he moved to the bathroom. He opened the lid of the big wicker clothes hamper and stood there, rigid with surprise, staring down into the face of the man squatting inside it.

After a long time, Latin took his handkerchief from his pocket and wiped his forehead. The face of the man in the clothes hamper was a mottled bluish-red, and his eyes bulged horribly. He was dead.

Latin left him there. He went back into the living room hurriedly and picked up the drink Teresa Mayan had poured for him. He lifted it to his lips and then froze, staring down into it with a sort of fascinated horror. He was thinking of the round, brown bottles of developing fluid on the drainboard in the kitchen.

"Good God," he said in a whisper. He poked one finger in the whiskey and touched the end of it gingerly with the tip of his tongue. He put the drink down very quickly.

He remembered hearing somewhere that some sort of cyanide derivative was used in developing film. Teresa Mayan evidently also used it for a mixer. Latin's whiskey was laced with it.

"Good God," he said again, thinking of the blue face of the man in the clothes hamper.

He revised his estimate of Teresa Mayan upward ten notches. She had put the cyanide in the drink while he was in the bedroom. She had known he'd hear what she said out in the hall and that he wouldn't want to dash out and start an argument with the other tenants. He'd wait for a while, and while he was waiting, what would be more natural than to take a drink? And two bodies were just as easy to dispose of as one.

"Yes, indeed," said Latin to himself.

He went over to the telephone stand in the corner and dialed the number of Guiterrez's restaurant. The instrument at the other end got time to ring only once, and then Guiterrez's voice bellowed in his ear: "We're closed!"

"This is Latin."

"I said we're closed! We don't serve no more tonight! You come around here and start a beef, and I'll have you *arrested!*"

"Are the cops there looking for me?" Latin asked. "Are they listening to you?"

"*Yes,* you heard me! I said I'll have you *arrested,* or maybe even *murder* you!"

"Is it Walters?" Latin inquired.

"So you got a pull with the cops, have you? All right, I'll have the *district attorney's men* pinch you! And don't think they won't!"

"Thanks," Latin said. "I'll keep undercover."

He put the telephone back in its cradle and returned to the bathroom. He searched the man with the blue face and found from the contents of his wallet that his name was Donald K. Raleigh. Going into the living room, he picked up the telephone and dialed another number.

After about ten rings a hollow, tired voice said: "This is Abraham Moscowitz, the attorney who never sleeps."

"It's Latin again, Abe."

"I'm putting on my shoes right now."

"Never mind. I'm not in jail – yet. How do you feel about murder, Abe?"

"I can take it or leave it alone. Why don't you? I mean leave it alone."

"It follows me around and comes when I whistle – sometimes even when I don't. The district attorney's men are looking for me to ask me about killing Steamer Morgan."

"So you're eliminating competition now, eh? You'd better watch out for the feds. Murder is considered an unfair trade practice in some industries, I understand."

"I didn't kill Steamer. They don't even think I did. They want to hold me while they ask me about some jewels I'm not negotiating to buy back from some thieves who didn't steal them."

"That makes as much sense as a Supreme Court decision. Call me back in the morning."

"Wait a minute," Latin requested. "You mentioned that Steamer worked for a law firm named Baldwin and Frazier. Do they have any case on now involving a man named Donald K. Raleigh?"

"Raleigh," Moscowitz repeated thoughtfully. "Raleigh… Oh, yeah. The Cataract Power Company case. It's been banging around in the courts for three years. It's got whiskers as long as Frazier and Baldwin have. Raleigh is the president of Cataract Power."

"What's the case about?"

"The same old story. There ain't no dough in the treasury and no kilowatts in the powerhouse and no customers to buy any even if there were. So the suckers want to know why. I could tell them for free. Raleigh's grandpappy and his pappy were smart men in a steal. They could grab the power rights on a river and pay off in confederate money and make the chumps like it, but he can't. He's a rumdumb. I don't think he stole the company dough – that is, intentionally. He probably spent it trying to crossbreed giant pandas and teddy bears or trying to corner the paperweight market."

"Why has the case been dragging on so long?"

"Well, naturally Raleigh doesn't want to go to jail. He will if he ever testifies. He's too stupid to lie convincingly. Even to the juries they hatch up in this state – and do we have some dillies! So the first time Baldwin and Frazier jumped him, he fixed the judge and got the case dismissed. So Baldwin and Frazier appealed that decision and got it reversed and started over with another judge that he couldn't fix. So now Raleigh is too sick to appear in court. He's been sick for six months or so. Maybe he really is, I don't know."

"He looked pretty bad the last time I saw him," Latin observed. "In fact, I think somebody may start a rumor that I murdered him."

"Did you?"

"No."

"Well, then what are you calling me for?" Moscowitz snarled. "If I've told you once, I've told you twenty times that I won't defend an innocent client! That's too hard work. If you want me to keep you out of jail, don't get pinched for things you didn't do!"

"O.K. I'll go murder somebody else right away."

"Now you're talking. Be sure you do it in front of some nice, honest witnesses. It's cheaper to buy them before than to bribe them afterwards."

"Goodbye," said Latin.

Chapter V
Lily Takes a Licking

THE FIRST thin red rays of the sun hit the casement windows in the tall spire of the Chateau Carleton and reflected in a million jewel-like pinpoints. Now, in the dawn, the streets were hushed and quiet and empty, and Latin was all alone as he walked past the front of the building and turned down the side street beyond it.

A garbage can bonged against some obstruction and raised dismal, clanking echoes, and then a man came out of the alley behind the apartment building rolling the can along expertly in front of him. He deposited it at the curb beside three more like it and paused to wipe his forehead with a luridly pink bandana.

Two men crossed the street toward him. They were Bruce and Bill, the college men. They were wearing their overcoats and white scarfs, and each carried a cellophane-wrapped florist's box under his arm. They didn't look so healthy this morning, but they were up and around.

Latin slowed to a saunter, watching. Bruce and Bill came up to the janitor and halted, standing at attention.

"Will you let us in the building?" Bruce asked.

"We want to see Miss Lily Trace," Bill added.

The janitor eyed them sourly. "You got a nerve, you two. After the hell you raised last night."

"We came to apologize for that," Bruce said.

Bill held out a ten dollar bill wordlessly.

"Well..." said the janitor uncertainly. "Why don't you wait until some decent hour to do your apologizing?"

"Miss Trace will be up," Bruce said.

"She told us she always waits up to see the sun rise," Bill explained.

"Well, all right," said the janitor, taking the bill. "But no fighting and hollering, remember. Come on and – what do *you* want?"

"I'm with these gentlemen," said Latin.

Bruce and Bill looked at him in surprise.

"I'm Miss Trace's agent," Latin explained.

"Her business agent?" Bruce asked.

Latin nodded casually. "Sort of. Lead on, MacDuff!"

"The name is MacGillicuddy," the janitor corrected.

He piloted them along the alley and down a flight of cement steps into the shadowy reaches of the apartment basement. He opened the door of the express elevator and pointed to the control panel.

"It operates itself. Just punch the buttons."

Bruce and Bill and Latin got in the elevator, and Bill pushed the button numbered 7. The elevator rose with ponderous, quiet dignity.

Bruce cleared his throat. "I hope Miss Trace won't be too angry at us. We behaved very rudely to her last night. We were drunk."

"How'd you like Priscilla?" Latin asked.

Bruce and Bill looked at each other, startled.

"The taxi driver who took you to Kate's is a friend of mine," Latin explained.

"Oh," said Bruce.

"We enjoyed her very much – I think," said Bill.

Latin nodded. "I'll tell her the next time I see her. She'll be interested to know that she looks like Lily Trace."

There was a pained silence until the elevator stopped gently. Bill slid the door back and then followed Latin and Bruce down the hall. Bruce stopped in front of the door numbered 702 and reached for the gilt knocker.

Latin pushed his hand away. "Listen!"

Inside the apartment there was a rumbling thump, and then the sharp smash of breaking glass. A woman screamed in a choked, furious way.

Latin tried the door. It was locked. He slammed his shoulder against the panel. The door was thick and as solid as a stone wall. It bounced him right back.

The woman screamed again. Bruce and Bill shoved Latin to one side and hit the door together, grunting in concert. They hit hard and expertly, shoulders down, but the door was equal to them. It didn't even squeak.

Latin caught Bill by the shoulder and pulled him back. "Down that hall and around to the side! There must be a back door or a terrace to this apartment! Quick!"

Bill went down the hall at a run. Latin hammered on the door with both fists.

"Open up! Open the door!"

There was another final thump and then silence. On the other side of the door someone whimpered softly. Latin rattled the knob fiercely while Bruce breathed on the back of his neck.

The lock snapped. Latin kicked the door wide open and jumped into the apartment, crouching, the stubby revolver poised in his right hand.

"Oh, my God!" Bruce whispered.

Lily Trace was sitting down on the floor with her back against the wall and her rounded, bare legs spread out asprawl in front of her. Her hair was pulled down over her forehead, and she glared through it at them like a cornered animal. She had been wearing a black silk nightgown, but there wasn't much left of it.

"That bitch!" she said breathlessly. She was holding both hands up to her right cheek. She took the hands away, revealing four red furrows that ran from under her eye down past the corner of her mouth. She looked at the blood on her fingers and said many more things, all obscene. The room looked like someone had tried to cage a stray typhoon in it.

Bill came staggering through the rear door of the living room. He was bent painfully double, and his face was white and sick-looking.

"She – kicked me. I tried to stop her—"

He sat down on the side of an overturned chair and rocked back and forth.

Lily Trace had pulled the remnants of her nightgown from her shoulders and was gingerly examining four more parallel red gashes that ran from her collarbone down between her breasts to her hip like a fantastic slanted bandolier. She looked up and nodded at Latin.

"Forget the jewelry gag, Latin. Get that dame for me. I'll pay anything extra it costs."

"What do you want me to do with her when I get her?" Latin asked.

"Light a cigarette," said Lily Trace. "And stick it in her eye. Or better yet – hold her until I can get there and do it myself." She wasn't fooling.

"I'll see what I can do," said Latin. "Want me to call you a doctor now?"

Lily Trace's mouth was swollen, and she grinned at him lopsidedly. "Hell, no. I've been beaten up worse than this – but not lately. The Gold Dust Twins, here, will help me patch myself up. You get out and locate that dame for me."

Latin liked her suddenly, better than he would have thought possible a half hour before. He nodded and grinned at her.

"I'll find her. I'll get in touch with you when I do. Put your face together again carefully. It's too nice to spoil."

"Well, thanks, kid," said Lily Trace. "See you soon."

Latin chuckled and went out into the hall. Three or four sleepy, awed tenants watched him as he got into the freight elevator and closed the door behind him. He punched the button for the basement and rode downward.

The janitor was nowhere in sight in the cellar, and Latin walked through it and up the flight of cement steps into the alley.

"Tweet-tweet," said a hoarse voice.

Latin stopped instantly. Inspector Walters sauntered over to him and took hold of his arm in a friendly way.

"This is another one of those coincidences," he greeted. "I was just thinking about you. I was saying to myself: 'I wonder what my old pal Latin is doing with himself these days.' And here you are. Funny, eh?"

"No," said Latin. "I thought you were going to keep the district attorney's office off my neck."

"That was before a cop reported that he spotted Steamer Morgan hanging around your joint. Where were you all night – if the answer won't shock me too much?"

"I was cornered in an apartment with a house dick and three old maids watching the door. I had to wait until they got tired and went away. I've got your murderer cornered for you now."

"That's a matter of indifference to me," said Walters. "On account of I've got *you* cornered. The district attorney's dopes were too dumb to look under those ashes in your alley, but I wasn't. Let's see you work yourself out of that hold."

"Come along," Latin invited.

Mr Hammersley was still on duty when Latin and Inspector Walters entered the enormous, austere lobby of the Gravesend Manor.

"How do you do, Inspector Walters," he said cordially.

Walters's mouth opened in surprise, but before he could make any reply, Latin said smoothly: "Good morning, Mr. Hammersley. This man is one of my subordinates. It has become very important that I see Mr. Drew at once. Is he in?"

"Why, yes," said Hammersley, "but he left strict instructions that he was not to be disturbed for any reason. He said he wouldn't answer the phone or the doorbell."

"I'm very sorry," Latin said firmly, "but we must see him. Will you give me the passkey to his apartment? You can trust my discretion."

"I'm sure I can," Hammersley agreed, handing over a tagged passkey. "Mr. Drew has apartment 404. Have the police apprehended that Latin person as yet?"

"Oh, yes," said Latin. "He's in custody right now."

He led the way to the elevator, with Walters following a step behind him.

"Impersonating an officer," Walters said grimly. "I don't mind that so much. What gets me is that you impersonated *me* – and then introduced me as my own subordinate!"

The elevator stopped at the fourth floor, and they walked down a shadowed hallway to the dark, fumed oak door that had the small silvered numerals, 404, placed in a neat slant across its middle panel.

"We'll give him a try," said Latin.

He rang the doorbell and then knocked loudly on the door with his fist. There was no answer. After waiting a moment, Latin fitted the passkey in the lock and opened the door.

The living room was square and low-ceilinged, furnished in massive, heavy mahogany. From the doorway at the left came the spattering thunder of a shower.

Latin, with Walters still right behind him, looked in the living room closet, in the bedroom and its closet, and into the kitchenette that was fitted up as a bar. He came back into the living room and pushed the bathroom door wider.

Steam misted the mirror and the chrome fittings of the sink and toilet and billowed in misty clouds against the moisture-beaded ceiling. On the far side of the room there was a sunken bathtub completely enclosed now with a slickly wet shower curtain. Water splashed noisily behind it.

Latin raised his voice: "Drew!"

The curtain shivered and billowed, and then Drew put his head around the edge of it, wiping soap and water out of his eyes.

"What the devil… Oh, it's you. I didn't hear the doorbell. Who's that with you?"

"Inspector Walters, Homicide," said Walters.

Drew's eyes widened. "Oh. Well – well, make yourselves at home. I'll be out in just a second."

Latin and Walters went back into the living room. In the bathroom, the sound of the shower stopped abruptly, and then Drew came out into the living room, wrapping himself in a woolly white bathrobe. He looked puzzled and worried.

"Are you in trouble, Latin?"

"Somewhat," Latin admitted. "That's what I wanted to talk to you about."

"Oh," said Drew vaguely. "Well, would you like a drink? I've got some of your favorite brandy."

"Is the bottle open?" Latin asked.

Drew shook his head. "No. I seldom drink brandy."

"I'll take some," said Latin, "if I can watch you open the bottle."

"Why, yes," said Drew in amazement.

He found it in the cupboard behind the kitchenette bar. With Latin watching, he cut through the foil seal and worked out the cork.

"What did you want?" Drew asked.

Latin had the brandy in an inhaler a little smaller than a goldfish bowl. He sniffed at it appreciatively, took a sip, and rolled it around on his tongue.

"We're looking for Teresa Mayan," he said, swallowing. "Do you know her?"

"Of course," said Drew. "She's my secretary."

"She used to be your mistress, didn't she?"

"Sort of," Drew admitted.

"But she isn't now?"

Drew coughed. "Well, now and then…"

Latin nodded. "Yeah. Have you seen her lately?"

"Not for the last few days. I haven't been to my office."

"She tried to get you last night – on the phone."

"Yes," said Drew. "She wanted me to sign some important letters."

"Did she bring them over here?"

"No."

"Has she been here?"

"No," said Drew, irritated. "She hasn't been here, and she isn't here now. Look around if you don't believe me."

"We have," said Walters glumly. "Don't ask me why, though. I'm just a subordinate."

Latin said: "Did Teresa kick up a row when you gave her the old brush-off?"

Drew controlled his temper. "Yes, she did. A hell of a row, if you must know."

"But you still hire her?"

Drew shrugged. "She's a good secretary and she knows a lot about my business."

"Do you know a man named Donald K. Raleigh?" Latin asked.

Drew eyed him in silence for a long moment and then said slowly: "Yes. I know of him. I don't know him personally. He's president of the Cataract Power Company. He moved in with Teresa after I moved out. That's why she hasn't been bothering me lately."

"Did you know Raleigh was in legal trouble?"

"Just a stockholders' suit," Drew said. "It doesn't mean anything. I understand from what Teresa has said that he's stalling them. They'll get tired pretty soon."

"Those stockholders," Latin said, "got hold of a couple of lawyers who don't get tired and who – believe it or not – are also honest. Raleigh was pretending he was too sick to appear in court. The lawyers hired a private detective to follow him and prove he wasn't. The private detective got the goods on him last night. He got pictures of him eating and drinking in Guiterrez's restaurant, and he got Raleigh's signature on a dated menu from that restaurant. Evidence like that, you can't skid around."

"Ah-ha!" Walters said, suddenly seeing the light. "So Steamer pulled his autograph collecting gag once too often!"

"Yes," said Latin. "Raleigh was too drunk to know the difference. But Teresa Mayan was with him, and she wasn't. She spotted Steamer, so Steamer ended up in the alley with his throat cut and his pockets empty."

"No!" Drew protested instantly. "Teresa wouldn't—"

"Raleigh was plenty scared when he sobered up enough to understand, after they got back to Teresa's apartment," Latin went on. "Teresa scared him some more. I don't know what she told him. It probably was convincing, and he was pretty dumb and pretty fuddled anyway. She told him he'd have to beat it – skip the country. He had assets hidden around here and there. She got his power of attorney, so she could cash in on them and send them to him."

Latin smiled thinly. "She didn't mean to do it, of course. She didn't even give him a chance to go anywhere. She put some cyanide in his farewell drink of whiskey and dumped him into the dirty clothes hamper. She had decided to move back in on you, Drew."

Drew was staring at him, fascinated. "I – I don't believe… Why, Teresa wouldn't—"

"She went over and beat up Lily Trace to warn Lily to keep her hands off."

Drew's face whitened. "Lily!" He turned and jumped for the telephone.

"She's all right," Latin said, heading him off. "A little battered and bruised, but that's all. You better not call her now. I don't think she'd be in very good humor. After all, she knows who beat her up and why."

"Oh," said Drew uncertainly.

"All I want to know," said Walters, "is where is this here Teresa Mayan?"

"I can't figure that out," Latin said slowly. "I was sure she'd come here. She wouldn't risk going back to her own apartment until she got some reinforcements or found out what happened to me. She ought to be here now."

"Well, she ain't," said Walters.

Latin was frowning at Drew, his eyes narrowed and calculating. He looked at Drew's water-damp hair, at the bathrobe. He glanced toward the bathroom door in the same calculating way and then back to Drew again. He cleared his throat.

"May I have some more brandy?"

"Surely," said Drew. "Try it with some soda. I'll get some ice…"

He reached down under the little shelf that served as a bar. Latin stepped silently forward and picked up the brandy bottle by its neck and swung it in a glistening arc.

There was a sodden smack as the bottle hit Drew's head. He bounced backward into some shelves loaded with glasses and brought them down around him in a ringing, shattering crash.

"They make these thick," Latin said, examining the brandy bottle. "It didn't even crack."

"Talk," Walters ordered dangerously. "Real fast, pal."

"Look in the bathroom," Latin said. "In the tub."

Walters went into the bathroom and came out again almost instantly. "There's a dame in there. She's dead. Drowned."

"Teresa Mayan," said Latin. "Drew was behind her all the time. She was crazy about him. She spotted Steamer at Guiterrez's or on the way there, and she telephoned Drew from the restaurant. He took care of Steamer – with her help. He fed Raleigh a cyanide drink – again, with her help. He planned all this just like I outlined it, only he was going to get the dough – not Teresa. She would do anything he said, but she wouldn't stand for Lily Trace. When she found out about that, she went on a rampage. She smacked Lily around, and she must have told Drew she'd squeal on him if he didn't quit looking in that direction. Drew had maneuvered all this business with Raleigh just to get enough money to get Lily. He wouldn't throw the prize away after he'd won the game, so he dunked Teresa in the bathtub.

"He had it all figured out that she was to take the blame for everything and then throw herself in the river for remorse over her evil deeds."

Walters had a small round tin in his hand. "She was only wearing a sport coat, and this was the only thing in the pockets. I wonder what it is?"

"Open it and see what's inside," Latin suggested.

Walters unscrewed the cover of the tin. He reached in and pulled out a long string of 36-millimeter film.

"Pictures!" he exclaimed. "Now why would she be carrying these around with her?"

"We'll never know," said Latin, pouring himself a drink. "Because that was undeveloped film, and when you exposed it to the light, you ruined it."

The Frame-Up

Richard Harding Davis

WHEN THE VOICE over the telephone promised to name the man who killed Hermann Banf, District Attorney Wharton was uptown lunching at Delmonico's. This was contrary to his custom and a concession to Hamilton Cutler, his distinguished brother-in-law. That gentleman was interested in a State constabulary bill and had asked State Senator Bissell to father it. He had suggested to the senator that, in the legal points involved in the bill, his brother-in-law would undoubtedly be charmed to advise him. So that morning, to talk it over, Bissell had come from Albany and, as he was forced to return the same afternoon, had asked Wharton to lunch with him uptown near the station.

That in public life there breathed a man with soul so dead who, were he offered a chance to serve Hamilton Cutler, would not jump at the chance was outside the experience of the county chairman. And in so judging his fellow men, with the exception of one man, the senator was right. The one man was Hamilton Cutler's brother-in-law.

In the national affairs of his party Hamilton Cutler was one of the four leaders. In two cabinets he had held office. At a foreign court as an ambassador his dinners, of which the diplomatic corps still spoke with emotion, had upheld the dignity of ninety million Americans. He was rich. The history of his family was the history of the State. When the Albany boats drew abreast of the old Cutler mansion on the east bank of the Hudson the passengers pointed at it with deference. Even when the search lights pointed at it, it was with deference. And on Fifth Avenue, as the 'Seeing New York' car passed his town house it slowed respectfully to half speed. When, apparently for no other reason than that she was good and beautiful, he had married the sister of a then unknown Upstate lawyer, everyone felt Hamilton Cutler had made his first mistake. But, like everything else into which he entered, for him matrimony also was a success. The prettiest girl in Utica showed herself worthy of her distinguished husband. She had given him children as beautiful as herself; as what Washington calls 'a cabinet lady' she had kept her name out of the newspapers; as Madame L'Ambassatrice she had put archduchesses at their ease; and after ten years she was an adoring wife, a devoted mother, and a proud woman. Her pride was in believing that for every joy she knew she was indebted entirely to her husband. To owe everything to him, to feel that through him the blessings flowed, was her ideal of happiness.

In this ideal her brother did not share. Her delight in a sense of obligation left him quite cold. No one better than himself knew that his rapid-fire rise in public favor was due to his own exertions, to the fact that he had worked very hard, had been independent, had kept his hands clean, and had worn no man's collar. Other people believed he owed his advancement to his brother-in-law. He knew they believed that, and it hurt him. When, at the annual dinner of the Amen Corner, they burlesqued him as singing to 'Ham' Cutler, 'You made me what I am today, I hope you're satisfied', he found that to laugh with the others was something of an effort. His was a difficult position. He was a party man; he had always worked inside the organization. The fact that whenever he ran for an elective office the reformers endorsed him and the best elements in the opposition parties voted for him did not shake his loyalty to his own people. And to

Hamilton Cutler, as one of his party leaders, as one of the bosses of the 'invisible government',"
he was willing to defer. But while he could give allegiance to his party leaders, and from them
was willing to receive the rewards of office, from a rich brother-in-law he was not at all willing to
accept anything. Still less was he willing that of the credit he deserved for years of hard work for
the party, of self-denial, and of efficient public service the rich brother-in-law, should rob him.

His pride was to be known as a self-made man, as the servant only of the voters. And now
that ambition, now that he was district attorney of New York City, to have it said that the office
was the gift of his brother-in-law was bitter. But he believed the injustice would soon end. In
a month he was coming up for re-election, and night and day was conducting a campaign
that he hoped would result in a personal victory so complete as to banish the shadow of his
brother-in-law. Were he re-elected by the majority on which he counted, he would have the
party leaders on their knees. Hamilton Cutler would be forced to come to him. He would be
in line for promotion. He knew the leaders did not want to promote him, that they considered
him too inclined to kick over the traces; but were he now re-elected, at the next election, either
for mayor or governor, he would be his party's obvious and legitimate candidate.

The re-election was not to be an easy victory. Outside his own party, to prevent his
succeeding himself as district attorney, Tammany Hall was using every weapon in her armory.
The commissioner of police was a Tammany man, and in the public prints Wharton had
repeatedly declared that Banf, his star witness against the police, had been killed by the police,
and that they had prevented the discovery of his murderer. For this the wigwam wanted his
scalp, and to get it had raked his public and private life, had used threats and bribes, and with
women had tried to trap him into a scandal. But 'Big Tim' Meehan, the lieutenant the Hall had
detailed to destroy Wharton, had reported back that for their purpose his record was useless,
that bribes and threats only flattered him, and that the traps set for him he had smilingly
side-stepped. This was the situation a month before election day when, to oblige his brother-in-
law, Wharton was uptown at Delmonico's lunching with Senator Bissell.

Downtown at the office, Rumson, the assistant district attorney, was on his way to lunch
when the telephone-girl halted him. Her voice was lowered and betrayed almost human interest.

From the corner of her mouth she whispered: "This man has a note for Mr. Wharton – says if
he don't get it quick it'll be too late – says it will tell him who killed 'Heimie' Banf!"

The young man and the girl looked at each other and smiled. Their experience had not
tended to make them credulous. Had he lived, Hermann Banf would have been, for Wharton,
the star witness against a ring of corrupt police officials. In consequence his murder was more
than the taking off of a shady and disreputable citizen. It was a blow struck at the high office
of the district attorney, at the grand jury, and the law. But, so far, whoever struck the blow had
escaped punishment, and though for a month, ceaselessly, by night and day 'the office' and the
police had sought him, he was still at large, still 'unknown'. There had been hundreds of clues.
They had been furnished by the detectives of the city and county and of the private agencies,
by amateurs, by newspapers, by members of the underworld with a score to pay off or to gain
favor. But no clue had led anywhere. When, in hoarse whispers, the last one had been confided
to him by his detectives, Wharton had protested indignantly.

"Stop bringing me clues!" he exclaimed. "I want the man. I can't electrocute a clue!"

So when, after all other efforts, over the telephone a strange voice offered to deliver the
murderer, Rumson was skeptical. He motioned the girl to switch to the desk telephone.

"Assistant District Attorney Rumson speaking," he said. "What can I do for you?"

Before the answer came, as though the speaker were choosing his words, there was a pause.
It lasted so long that Rumson exclaimed sharply:

"Hello," he called. "Do you want to speak to me, or do you want to speak to me?"

"I've gotta letter for the district attorney," said the voice. "I'm to give it to nobody but him. It's about Banf. He must get it quick, or it'll be too late."

"Who are you?" demanded Rumson. "Where are you speaking from?"

The man at the other end of the wire ignored the questions.

"Where'll Wharton be for the next twenty minutes?"

"If I tell you," parried Rumson, "will you bring the letter at once?" The voice exclaimed indignantly:

"Bring nothing! I'll send it by district messenger. You're wasting time trying to reach me. It's the *letter* you want. It tells—" the voice broke with an oath and instantly began again: "I can't talk over a phone. I tell you, it's life or death. If you lose out, it's your own fault. Where can I find Wharton?"

"At Delmonico's," answered Rumson. "He'll be there until two o'clock."

"Delmonico's! That's Forty-fort Street?"

"Right," said Rumson. "Tell the messenger—" He heard the receiver slam upon the hook. With the light of the hunter in his eyes, he turned to the girl.

"They can laugh," he cried, "but I believe we've hooked something. I'm going after it." In the waiting room he found the detectives. "Hewitt," he ordered, "take the subway and whip up to Delmonico's. Talk to the taxi-starter till a messenger-boy brings a letter for the D.A. Let the boy deliver the note, and then trail him till he reports to the man he got it from. Bring the man here. If it's a district messenger and he doesn't report, but goes straight back to the office, find out who gave him the note; get his description. Then meet me at Delmonico's."

Rumson called up that restaurant and had Wharton come to the phone. He asked his chief to wait until a letter he believed to be of great importance was delivered to him. He explained, but, of necessity, somewhat sketchily. "It sounds to me," commented his chief, "like a plot of yours to get a lunch uptown."

"Invitation!" cried Rumson. "I'll be with you in ten minutes."

After Rumson had joined Wharton and Bissell the note arrived. It was brought to the restaurant by a messenger-boy, who said that in answer to a call from a saloon on Sixth Avenue he had received it from a young man in ready-to-wear clothes and a green hat. When Hewitt, the detective, asked what the young man looked like, the boy said he looked like a young man in ready-to-wear clothes and a green hat. But when the note was read the identity of the man who delivered it ceased to be of importance. The paper on which it was written was without stamped address or monogram, and carried with it the mixed odors of the drug-store at which it had been purchased. The handwriting was that of a woman, and what she had written was: "If the district attorney will come at once, and alone, to Kessler's Café, on the Boston Post Road, near the city line, he will be told who killed Hermann Banf. If he don't come in an hour, it will be too late. If he brings anybody with him, he won't be told anything. Leave your car in the road and walk up the drive. Ida Earle."

Hewitt, who had sent away the messenger-boy and had been called in to give expert advice, was enthusiastic.

"Mr. District Attorney," he cried, "that's no crank letter. This Earle woman is wise. You got to take her as a serious proposition. She wouldn't make that play if she couldn't get away with it."

"Who is she?" asked Wharton.

To the police, the detective assured them, Ida Earle had been known for years. When she was young she had been under the protection of a man high in the ranks of Tammany, and, in consequence, with her different ventures the Police had never interfered. She now was proprietress of the road-house in the note described as Kessler's Café. It was a place for joy-riders. There was a cabaret, a hall for public dancing, and rooms for very private suppers.

In so far as it welcomed only those who could spend money it was exclusive, but in all other respects its reputation was of the worst. In situation it was lonely, and from other houses separated by a quarter of a mile of dying trees and vacant lots.

The Boston Post Road upon which it faced was the old post road, but lately, through this back yard and dumping-ground of the city, had been relaid. It was patrolled only and infrequently by bicycle policemen. "But this," continued the detective eagerly, "is where we win out. The road-house is an old farmhouse built over, with the barns changed into garages. They stand on the edge of a wood. It's about as big as a city block. If we come in through the woods from the rear, the garages will hide us. Nobody in the house can see us, but we won't be a hundred yards away. You've only to blow a police whistle and we'll be with you."

"You mean I ought to go?" said Wharton.

Rumson exclaimed incredulously: "You got to go!"

"It looks to me," objected Bissell, "like a plot to get you there alone and rap you on the head." "Not with that note inviting him there," protested Hewitt, "and signed by Earle herself."

"You don't know she signed it?" objected the senator.

"I know her," returned the detective. "I know she's no fool. It's her place, and she wouldn't let them pull off any rough stuff there – not against the D.A. anyway."

The D. A. was rereading the note. "Might this be it?" he asked. "Suppose it's a trick to mix me up in a scandal? You say the place is disreputable. Suppose they're planning to compromise me just before election. They've tried it already several times."

"You've still got the note," persisted Hewitt. "It proves why you went there. And the senator, too. He can testify. And we won't be hundred yards away. And," he added grudgingly, "you have Nolan."

Nolan was the spoiled child of 'the office'. He was the district attorney's pet. Although still young, he had scored as a detective and as a driver of racing-cars. As Wharton's chauffeur he now doubled the parts.

"What Nolan testified wouldn't be any help," said Wharton. "They would say it was just a story he invented to save me."

"Then square yourself this way," urged Rumson. "Send a note now by hand to Ham Cutler and one to your sister. Tell them you're going to Ida Earle's – and why – tell them you're afraid it's a frame-up, and for them to keep your notes as evidence. And enclose the one from her."

Wharton nodded in approval, and, while he wrote, Rumson and the detective planned how, without those inside the road-house being aware of their presence, they might be near it.

Kessler's Café lay in the Seventy-ninth Police Precinct. In taxi-cabs they arranged to start at once and proceed down White Plains Avenue, which parallels the Boston Road, until they were on a line with Kessler's, but from it hidden by the woods and the garages. A walk of a quarter of a mile across lots and under cover of the trees would bring them to within a hundred yards of the house.

Wharton was to give them a start of half an hour. That he might know they were on watch, they agreed, after they dismissed the taxi-cabs, to send one of them into the Boston Post Road past the road-house. When it was directly in front of the café, the chauffeur would throw away into the road an empty cigarette-case.

From the cigar-stand they selected a cigarette box of a startling yellow. At half a mile it was conspicuous.

"When you see this in the road," explained Rumson, "you'll know we're on the job. And after you're inside, if you need us, you've only to go to a rear window and wave."

"If they mean to do him up," growled Bissell, "he won't get to a rear window."

"He can always tell them we're outside," said Rumson – "and they are extremely likely to believe him. Do you want a gun?"

"No," said the D.A.

"Better have mine,'" urged Hewitt.

"I have my own," explained the D.A.

Rumson and Hewitt set off in taxi-cabs and, a half-hour later, Wharton followed. As he sank back against the cushions of the big touring-car he felt a pleasing thrill of excitement, and as he passed the traffic police, and they saluted mechanically, he smiled. Had they guessed his errand their interest in his progress would have been less perfunctory. In half an hour he might know that the police killed Banf; in half an hour he himself might walk into a trap they had, in turn, staged for him. As the car ran swiftly through the clean October air, and the wind and sun alternately chilled and warmed his blood, Wharton considered these possibilities.

He could not believe the woman Earle would lend herself to any plot to do him bodily harm. She was a responsible person. In her own world she was as important a figure as was the district attorney in his. Her allies were the man 'higher up' in Tammany and the police of the upper ranks of the uniformed force. And of the higher office of the district attorney she possessed an intimate and respectful knowledge. It was not to be considered that against the prosecuting attorney such a woman would wage war. So the thought that upon his person any assault was meditated Wharton dismissed as unintelligent. That it was upon his reputation the attack was planned seemed much more probable. But that contingency he had foreseen and so, he believed, forestalled. There then remained only the possibility that the offer in the letter was genuine. It seemed quite too good to be true. For, as he asked himself, on the very eve of an election, why should Tammany, or a friend of Tammany, place in his possession the information that to the Tammany candidate would bring inevitable defeat. He felt that the way they were playing into his hands was too open, too generous. If their object was to lead him into a trap, of all baits they might use the promise to tell him who killed Banf was the one certain to attract him. It made their invitation to walk into the parlor almost too obvious. But were the offer not genuine, there was a condition attached to it that puzzled him. It was not the condition that stipulated he should come alone. His experience had taught him many will confess, or betray, to the district attorney who, to a deputy, will tell nothing. The condition that puzzled him was the one that insisted he should come at once or it would be 'too late'.

Why was haste so imperative? Why, if he delayed, would he be 'too late'? Was the man he sought about to escape from his jurisdiction, was he dying, and was it his wish to make a death-bed confession; or was he so reluctant to speak that delay might cause him to reconsider and remain silent?

With these questions in his mind, the minutes quickly passed, and it was with a thrill of excitement Wharton saw that Nolan had left the Zoological Gardens on the right and turned into the Boston Road. It had but lately been completed and to Wharton was unfamiliar. On either side of the unscarred roadway still lay scattered the uprooted trees and boulders that had blocked its progress, and abandoned by the contractors were empty tar-barrels, cement-sacks, tool-sheds, and forges. Nor was the surrounding landscape less raw and unlovely. Toward the Sound stretched vacant lots covered with ash heaps; to the left a few old and broken houses set among the glass-covered cold frames of truck-farms.

The district attorney felt a sudden twinge of loneliness. And when an automobile sign told him he was '10 miles from Columbus Circle', he felt that from the New York he knew he was much farther. Two miles up the road his car overhauled a bicycle policeman, and Wharton halted him.

"Is there a road-house called Kessler's beyond here?" he asked.

"On the left, farther up," the officer told him, and added: "You can't miss it Mr. Wharton; there's no other house near it."

"You know me," said the D.A. "Then you'll understand what I want you to do. I've agreed to go to that house alone. If they see you pass they may think I'm not playing fair. So stop here."

The man nodded and dismounted.

"But," added the district attorney, as the car started forward again, "If you hear shots, I don't care how fast you come."

The officer grinned.

"Better let me trail along now," he called; "that's a tough joint."

But Wharton motioned him back; and when again he turned to look the man still stood where they had parted.

Two minutes later an empty taxi-cab came swiftly toward him and, as it passed, the driver lifted his hand from the wheel, and with his thumb motioned behind him.

"That's one of the men," said Nolan, "that started with Mr. Rumson and Hewitt from Delmonico's."

Wharton nodded; and, now assured that in their plan there had been no hitch, smiled with satisfaction. A moment later, when ahead of them on the asphalt road Nolan pointed out a spot of yellow, he recognized the signal and knew that within call were friends.

The yellow cigarette-box lay directly in front of a long wooden building of two stories. It was linked to the road by a curving driveway marked on either side by whitewashed stones.

On verandas enclosed in glass Wharton saw white-covered tables under red candle-shade and, protruding from one end of the house and hung with electric lights in paper lanterns, a pavilion for dancing. In the rear of the house stood sheds and a thick tangle of trees on which the autumn leaves showed yellow painted fingers and arrows pointing, and an electric sign, proclaimed to all who passed that this was Kessler's. In spite of its reputation, the house wore the aspect of the commonplace. In evidence nothing flaunted, nothing threatened. From a dozen other inns along the Pelham Parkway and the Boston Post Road it was no way to be distinguished.

As directed in the note, Wharton left the car in the road. "For five minutes stay where you are," he ordered Nolan; "then go to the bar and get a drink. Don't talk to anyone or they'll think you're trying to get information. Work around to the back of the house. Stand where I can see you from the window. I may want you to carry a message to Mr. Rumson."

On foot Wharton walked up the curved driveway, and if from the house his approach was spied upon, there was no evidence. In the second story the blinds were drawn and on the first floor the verandas were empty. Nor, not even after he had mounted to the veranda and stepped inside the house, was there any sign that his visit was expected. He stood in a hall, and in front of him rose a broad flight of stairs that he guessed led to the private supper-rooms. On his left was the restaurant.

Swept and garnished after the revels of the night previous, and as though resting in preparation for those to come, it had an air of peaceful inactivity. At a table a *maître d'hôtel* was composing the menu for the evening, against the walls three colored waiters lounged sleepily, and on a platform at a piano a pale youth with drugged eyes was with one hand picking an accompaniment. As Wharton paused uncertainly the young man, disdaining his audience, in a shrill, nasal tenor raised his voice and sang:

"And from the time the rooster calls
I'll wear my overalls,

And you, a simple gingham gown.
So, if you're strong for a shower of rice,
We two could make a paradise
Of any One-Horse Town."

At sight of Wharton the head waiter reluctantly detached himself from his menu and rose. But before he could greet the visitor, Wharton heard his name spoken and, looking up, saw a woman descending the stairs. It was apparent that when young she had been beautiful, and, in spite of an expression in her eyes of hardness and distrust, which seemed habitual, she was still handsome. She was without a hat and wearing a house dress of decorous shades and in the extreme of fashion. Her black hair, built up in artificial waves, was heavy with brilliantine; her hands, covered deep with rings, and of an unnatural white, showed the most fastidious care. But her complexion was her own; and her skin, free from paint and powder, glowed with that healthy pink that is supposed to be the perquisite only of the simple life and a conscience undisturbed.

"I am Mrs. Earle," said the woman. "I wrote you that note. Will you please come this way?"

That she did not suppose he might not come that way was obvious, for, as she spoke, she turned her back on him and mounted the stairs. After an instant of hesitation, Wharton followed.

As well as his mind, his body was now acutely alive and vigilant. Both physically and mentally he moved on tiptoe. For whatever surprise, for whatever ambush might lie in wait, he was prepared. At the top of the stairs he found a wide hall along which on both sides were many doors. The one directly facing the stairs stood open. At one side of this the woman halted and with a gesture of the jewelled fingers invited him to enter.

"My sitting room," she said. As Wharton remained motionless she substituted: "My office."

Peering into the room, Wharton found it suited to both titles. He saw comfortable chairs, vases filled with autumn leaves, in silver frames photographs, and between two open windows a business-like roller-top desk on which was a hand telephone. In plain sight through the windows he beheld the garage and behind it the tops of trees. To summon Rumson, to keep in touch with Nolan, he need only step to one of these windows and beckon. The strategic position of the room appealed, and with a bow of the head he passed in front of his hostess and entered it. He continued to take note of his surroundings.

He now saw that from the office in which he stood doors led to rooms adjoining. These doors were shut, and he determined swiftly that before the interview began he first must know what lay behind them. Mrs. Earle had followed and, as she entered, closed the door.

"No!" said Wharton.

It was the first time he had spoken. For an instant the woman hesitated, regarding him thoughtfully, and then without resentment pulled the door open. She came toward him swiftly, and he was conscious of the rustle of silk and the stirring of perfumes. At the open door she cast a frown of disapproval and then, with her face close to his, spoke hurriedly in a whisper.

"A man brought a girl here to lunch," she said; "they've been here before. The girl claims the man told her he was going to marry her. Last night she found out he has a wife already, and she came here today meaning to make trouble. She brought a gun. They were in the room at the far end of the hall. George, the waiter, heard the two shots and ran down here to get me. No one else heard. These rooms are fixed to keep out noise, and the piano was going. We broke in and found them on the floor. The man was shot through the shoulder, the girl through the body. His story is that after she fired, in trying to get the gun from her, she shot herself – by accident. That's right, I guess. But the girl says they came here to die together – what the newspaper call a 'suicide pact' – because they couldn't marry, and that he first shot her, intending to kill her and then himself. That's silly. She framed it to get him. She missed him with the gun, so now she's trying to get him with this murder charge. I know her. If she'd been sober she wouldn't have shot him; she'd have blackmailed him. She's that sort. I know her, and—"

With an exclamation the district attorney broke in upon her. "And the man," he demanded eagerly; "was it *he* killed Banf?"

In amazement the woman stared. "Certainly *not*!" she said.

"Then what *has* this to do with Banf?"

"Nothing!" Her tone was annoyed, reproachful. "That was only to bring you here."

His disappointment was so keen that it threatened to exhibit itself in anger. Recognizing this, before he spoke Wharton forced himself to pause. Then he repeated her words quietly.

"Bring me here?" he asked. "Why?"

The woman exclaimed impatiently: "So you could beat the police to it," she whispered. "So you could *hush it up*!"

The surprised laugh of the man was quite real. It bore no resentment or pose. He was genuinely amused. Then the dignity of his office, tricked and insulted, demanded to be heard. He stared at her coldly; his indignation was apparent.

"You have done extremely ill," he told her. "You know perfectly well you had no right to bring me up here; to drag me into a row in your road-house. 'Hush it up!'" he exclaimed hotly. This time his laugh was contemptuous and threatening. "I'll show you how I'll hush it up!" He moved quickly to the open window.

"Stop!" commanded the woman. "You can't do that!" She ran to the door.

Again he was conscious of the rustle of silk, of the stirring of perfumes.

He heard the key turn in the lock. It had come. It was a frame-up. There would be a scandal. And to save himself from it they would force him to 'hush up' this other one. But, as to the outcome, in no way was he concerned. Through the window, standing directly below it, he had seen Nolan. In the sunlit yard the chauffeur, his cap on the back of his head, his cigarette drooping from his lips, was tossing the remnants of a sandwich to a circle of excited hens. He presented a picture of bored indolence, of innocent preoccupation. It was almost too well done.

Assured of a witness for the defense, he greeted the woman with a smile. "Why can't I do it?" he taunted.

She ran close to him and laid her hands on his arm. Her eyes were fixed steadily on his. "Because," she whispered, "the man who shot that girl – is your brother-in-law, Ham Cutler!"

For what seemed a long time Wharton stood looking down into the eyes of the woman, and the eyes never faltered. Later he recalled that in the sudden silence many noises disturbed the lazy hush of the Indian-summer afternoon: the rush of a motor-car on the Boston Road, the tinkle of the piano and the voice of the youth with the drugged eyes singing, "And you'll wear a simple gingham gown," from the yard below the cluck-cluck of the chickens and the cooing of pigeons.

His first thought was of his sister and of her children, and of what this bomb, hurled from the clouds, would mean to her. He thought of Cutler, at the height of his power and usefulness, by this one disreputable act dragged into the mire, of what disaster it might bring to the party, to himself.

If, as the woman invited, he helped to 'hush it up', and Tammany learned the truth, it would make short work of him. It would say, for the murderer of Banf he had one law and for the rich brother-in-law, who had tried to kill the girl he deceived, another. But before he gave voice to his thoughts he recognized them as springing only from panic. They were of a part with the acts of men driven by sudden fear, and of which acts in their sane moments they would be incapable.

The shock of the woman's words had unsettled his traditions. Not only was he condemning a man unheard, but a man who, though he might dislike him, he had for years, for his private virtues, trusted and admired. The panic passed and with a confident smile he shook his head.

"I don't believe you," he said quietly.

The manner of the woman was equally calm, equally assured.

"Will you see her?" she asked.

"I'd rather see my brother-in-law," he answered.

The woman handed him a card.

"Doctor Muir took him to his private hospital," she said. "I loaned them my car because it's a limousine. The address is on that card. But," she added, "both your brother and Sammy – that's Sam Muir, the doctor – asked you wouldn't use the telephone; they're afraid of a leak."

Apparently Wharton did not hear her. As though it were 'Exhibit A', presented in evidence by the defense, he was studying the card she had given him. He stuck it in his pocket.

"I'll go to him at once," he said.

To restrain or dissuade him, the woman made no sudden move. In level tones she said:

"Your brother-in-law asked especially that you wouldn't do that until you'd fixed it with the girl. Your face is too well known. He's afraid someone might find out where he is – and for a day or two no one must know that."

"This doctor knows it," retorted Wharton.

The suggestion seemed to strike Mrs. Earle as humorous. For the first time she laughed. "Sammy!" she exclaimed. "He's a lobbygow of mine. He's worked for me for years. I could send him up the river if I liked. He knows it." Her tone was convincing. "They both asked," she continued evenly, "you should keep off until the girl is out of the country, and fixed." Wharton frowned thoughtfully.

And, observing this, the eyes of the woman showed that, so far, toward the unfortunate incident the attitude of the district attorney was to her most gratifying. Wharton ceased frowning. "How fixed?" he asked. Mrs. Earle shrugged her shoulders.

"Cutler's idea is money," she said; "but, believe me, he's wrong. This girl is a vampire. She'll only come back to you for more. She'll keep on threatening to tell the wife, to tell the papers. The way to fix her is to throw a scare into her. And there's only one man can do that; there's only one man that can hush this thing up – that's you."

"When can I see her?" asked Wharton.

"Now," said the woman. "I'll bring her." Wharton could not suppress an involuntary "Here?" he exclaimed.

For the shade of a second Mrs. Earle exhibited the slightest evidence of embarrassment.

"My room's in a mess," she explained; "and she's not hurt so much as Sammy said. He told her she was in bad just to keep her quiet until you got here."

Mrs. Earle opened one of the doors leading from the room. "I won't be a minute," she said. Quietly she closed the door behind her.

Upon her disappearance the manner of the district attorney underwent an abrupt change. He ran softly to the door opposite the one through which Mrs. Earle had passed, and pulled it open. But, if beyond it he expected to find an audience of eavesdroppers, he was disappointed. The room was empty, and bore no evidence of recent occupation. He closed the door, and, from the roller-top desk, snatching a piece of paper, scribbled upon it hastily. Wrapping the paper around a coin, and holding it exposed to view, he showed himself at the window. Below him, to an increasing circle of hens and pigeons, Nolan was still scattering crumbs. Without withdrawing his gaze from them, the chauffeur nodded. Wharton opened his hand and the note fell into the yard. Behind him he heard the murmur of voices, the sobs of a woman in pain, and the rattle of a door-knob. As from the window he turned quickly, he saw that toward the spot where his note had fallen Nolan was tossing the last remnants of his sandwich.

The girl who entered with Mrs. Earle, leaning on her and supported by her, was tall and fair. Around her shoulders her blonde hair hung in disorder, and around her waist, under the kimono Mrs. Earle had thrown about her, were wrapped many layers of bandages. The girl moved unsteadily and sank into a chair.

In a hostile tone Mrs. Earle addressed her.

"Rose," she said, "this is the district attorney." To him she added: "She calls herself Rose Gerard."

One hand the girl held close against her side, with the other she brushed back the hair from her forehead. From half-closed eyes she stared at Wharton defiantly.

"Well," she challenged, "what about it?"

Wharton seated himself in front of the roller-top desk.

"Are you strong enough to tell me?" he asked.

His tone was kind, and this the girl seemed to resent.

"Don't you worry," she sneered, "I'm strong enough. Strong enough to tell all I know – to you, and to the papers, and to a jury – until I get justice." She clinched her free hand and feebly shook it at him. "*That's* what I'm going to get," she cried, her voice breaking hysterically, "justice."

From behind the armchair in which the girl half-reclined Mrs. Earle caught the eye of the district attorney and shrugged her shoulders.

"Just what *did* happen?" asked Wharton.

Apparently with an effort the girl pulled herself together.

"I first met your brother-in-law—" she began.

Wharton interrupted quietly.

"Wait!" he said. "You are not talking to me as anybody's brother-in-law, but as the district attorney."

The girl laughed vindictively.

"I don't wonder you're ashamed of him!" she jeered.

Again she began: "I first met Ham Cutler last May. He wanted to marry me then. He told me he was not a married man."

As her story unfolded, Wharton did not again interrupt; and speaking quickly, in abrupt, broken phrases, the girl brought her narrative to the moment when, as she claimed, Cutler had attempted to kill her. At this point a knock at the locked door caused both the girl and her audience to start. Wharton looked at Mrs. Earle inquiringly, but she shook her head, and with a look at him also of inquiry, and of suspicion as well, opened the door.

With apologies her head waiter presented a letter.

"For Mr. Wharton," he explained, "from his chauffeur."

Wharton's annoyance at the interruption was most apparent. "What the devil—" he began.

He read the note rapidly, and with a frown of irritation raised his eyes to Mrs. Earle.

"He wants to go to New Rochelle for an inner tube," he said. "How long would it take him to get there and back?"

The hard and distrustful expression upon the face of Mrs. Earle, which was habitual, was now most strongly in evidence. Her eyes searched those of Wharton.

"Twenty minutes," she said.

"He can't go," snapped Wharton.

"Tell him," he directed the waiter, "to stay where he is. Tell him I may want to go back to the office any minute." He turned eagerly to the girl. "I'm sorry," he said. With impatience he crumpled the note into a ball and glanced about him. At his feet was a wastepaper basket. Fixed upon him he saw, while pretending not to see, the eyes of Mrs. Earle burning with suspicion. If he destroyed the note, he knew suspicion would become certainty. Without an instant of hesitation, carelessly he tossed it intact into the wastepaper basket. Toward Rose Gerard he swung the revolving chair.

"Go on, Please," he commanded.

The girl had now reached the climax of her story, but the eyes of Mrs. Earle betrayed the fact that her thoughts were elsewhere. With an intense and hungry longing, they were concentrated upon her own wastepaper basket.

The voice of the girl in anger and defiance recalled Mrs. Earle to the business of the moment.

"He tried to kill me," shouted Miss Rose. "And his shooting himself in the shoulder was a bluff. *That's* my story; that's the story I'm going to tell the judge" – her voice soared shrilly – "that's the story that's going to send your brother-in-law to Sing Sing!"

For the first time Mrs. Earle contributed to the general conversation.

"You talk like a fish," she said.

The girl turned upon her savagely.

"If he don't like the way I talk," she cried, "he can come across!"

Mrs. Earle exclaimed in horror. Virtuously her hands were raised in protest.

"Like hell he will!" she said. "You can't pull that under my roof!" Wharton looked disturbed.

"Come across?" he asked.

"Come across?" mimicked the girl. "Send me abroad and keep me there. And I'll swear it was an accident. Twenty-five thousand, that's all I want. Cutler told me he was going to make you governor. He can't make you governor if he's in Sing Sing, can he? Ain't it worth twenty-five thousand to you to be governor? Come on," she jeered, "kick in!"

With a grave but untroubled voice Wharton addressed Mrs. Earle.

"May I use your telephone?" he asked. He did not wait for her consent, but from the desk lifted the hand telephone.

"Spring, three one hundred!" he said. He sat with his legs comfortably crossed, the stand of the instrument balanced on his knee, his eyes gazing meditatively at the yellow treetops.

If with apprehension both women started, if the girl thrust herself forward, and by the hand of Mrs. Earle was dragged back, he did not appear to know it.

"Police headquarters?" they heard him ask. "I want to speak to the commissioner. This is the district attorney."

In the pause that followed, as though to torment her, the pain, in her side apparently turned, for the girl screamed sharply.

"Be still!" commanded the older woman. Breathless, across the top of the armchair, she was leaning forward. Upon the man at the telephone her eyes were fixed in fascination.

"Commissioner," said the district attorney, "this is Wharton speaking. A woman has made a charge of attempted murder to me against my brother-in-law, Hamilton Cutler. On account of our relationship, I want you to make the arrest. If there were any slip, and he got away, it might be said I arranged it. You will find him at the Winona apartments on the Southern Boulevard, in the private hospital of a Doctor Samuel Muir. Arrest them both. The girl who makes the charge is at Kessler's Café, on the Boston Post Road, just inside the city line. Arrest her too. She tried to blackmail me. I'll appear against her."

Wharton rose and addressed himself to Mrs. Earle.

"I'm sorry," he said, "but I had to do it. You might have known I could not hush it up. I am the only man who can't hush it up. The people of New York elected me to enforce the laws." Wharton's voice was raised to a loud pitch. It seemed unnecessarily loud. It was almost as though he were addressing another and more distant audience. "And," he continued, his voice still soaring, "even if my own family suffer, even if I suffer, even if I lose political promotion, those laws I will enforce!" In the more conventional tone of everyday politeness, he added: "May I speak to you outside, Mrs. Earle?"

But, as in silence that lady descended the stairs, the district attorney seemed to have forgotten what it was he wished to say.

It was not until he had seen his chauffeur arouse himself from apparently deep slumber and crank the car that he addressed her.

"That girl," he said, "had better go back to bed. My men are all around this house and, until the police come, will detain her."

He shook the jewelled fingers of Mrs. Earle warmly. "I thank you," he said; "I know you meant well. I know you wanted to help me, but" – he shrugged his shoulders – "my duty!"

As he walked down the driveway to his car his shoulders continued to move.

But Mrs. Earle did not wait to observe this phenomenon. Rid of his presence, she leaped, rather than ran, up the stairs and threw open the door of her office.

As she entered, two men followed her. One was a young man who held in his hand an open notebook, the other was Tim Meehan, of Tammany. The latter greeted her with a shout.

"We heard everything he said," he cried. His voice rose in torment. "An' we can't use a word of it! He acted just like we'd oughta knowed he'd act. He's *honest*! He's so damned honest he ain't human; he's a – gilded saint!"

Mrs. Earle did not heed him. On her knees she was tossing to the floor the contents of the wastepaper basket. From them she snatched a piece of crumpled paper.

"Shut up!" she shouted. "Listen! His chauffeur brought him this." In a voice that quivered with indignation, that sobbed with anger, she read aloud:

> "*As directed by your note from the window, I went to the booth and called up Mrs. Cutler's house and got herself on the phone. Your brother-in-law lunched at home today with her and the children and they are now going to the Hippodrome.*
>
> "*Stop, look, and listen! Back of the bar I see two men in a room, but they did not see me. One is Tim Meehan, the other is a stenographer. He is taking notes. Each of them has on the ear-muffs of a dictagraph. Looks like you'd better watch your step and not say nothing you don't want Tammany to print.*"

The voice of Mrs. Earle rose in a shrill shriek.

"Him – a gilded saint?" she screamed; "You big stiff! He knew he was talking into a dictagraph all the time, and he double-crossed us!"

Diamonds of Death

Ramon Decolta

THE ROOM was in a cheap hotel, a few blocks from Market Street. The room had two windows, one of which faced the Bay. Jo Gar, his small body sprawled on the narrow bed, shivered a little. San Francisco was cold; he thought of the warm winds of Manila and the difference of the bays. He sighed and said softly to himself:

"Four diamonds – if I had them I could return to the Islands. I do not belong away from them—"

The telephone bell on the wall jangled; Jo Gar stared towards the apparatus for several seconds, then rose slowly. He was dressed in a gray suit that did not fit him too well, and his graying hair was mussed. He unhooked the receiver and said:

"Yes."

A pleasant voice said: "Inspector Raines, of the customs office. I have information for you."

Jo Gar said: "That is good – please come up."

He hung up the receiver and stood for several seconds looking towards the door. One of his three bags had been opened, the other two he had not unlocked. The *Cheyo Maru*, bringing him from Honolulu, had arrived three hours ago, and there had been much for the Island detective to do. In the doing of it he had gained little. Perhaps, he thought, Inspector Raines had done better.

He took from one of his few remaining packages a brown-paper cigarette, lighted it. His gray-blue eyes held a faint smile as he inhaled. Down the hall beyond the room there was the slam of the elevator's door, and footfalls. A man cleared his throat noisily. Jo Gar put his right hand in the pocket of his gray suit at his right side, went over and seated himself on the edge of the bed, facing the door. A knock sounded and the Philippine Island detective called flatly:

"Please – come in."

The door opened. A middle-aged man entered, dressed in a dark suit with a light coat thrown across his shoulders. The sleeves of the man's suit were not within the coat sleeves; it was worn as a cape. Raines had sharp features, pleasant blue eyes. His lips were thick; he was a big man. He said:

"Hello, Señor Gar."

Jo Gar rose and they shook hands. Raines' grip was loose and careless; he looked about the room, tossed a soft, gray hat on a chair. Jo Gar motioned towards the other chair in the room, and the inspector seated himself. He kept the coat slung across his shoulders.

Jo Gar said slowly, almost lazily:

"Something was found?"

The inspector frowned and shook his head. He took from his pocket a small card. His picture was at one corner of the card, which was quite soiled. There was the printing of the Customs Department, some insignia that Gar merely glanced at, a stamped seal – and the statement that Albert Raines was a member of the San Francisco customs office.

Raines said: "The chief thought I'd better show you that right away, as we hadn't seen each other."

The Island detective smiled. "Thank you," he replied, and handed the card back. "Something was found?"

Raines shook his head. "Not a thing," he said. "We held her up for two hours, and we searched everything carefully. We even searched the child – the child's baggage. We gave her a pretty careful questioning. For that matter – everybody on the boat got about three times the attention we usually give. And we didn't turn up a stone."

Jo Gar sighed. Raines said grimly: "If the diamonds were on that boat – they got past us. And that means you're in a tough spot, yes?"

The Island detective said: "I think that is very much – what it means."

Raines said in a more cheerful tone: "Well, the chief said you recovered six of the stones, between Manila and San Francisco – that's not at all bad."

Jo Gar smiled gently: "I was – extremely fortunate," he said. "But the woman in black – I had hopes that the four diamonds—"

Raines said quickly: "So had we. When we got your coded wire telling us that you suspected her of the murder of the man you recovered five stones from, but that you couldn't prove a thing against her, we figured we might be able to help. We weren't. But we did as you requested – when she left the dock we had a man follow her."

The Island detective said: "Good – she went to a hotel?"

Raines shook his head. "Don't suppose you've ever been out around the Cliff House, Señor Gar. It's a spot out on a bunch of jagged rocks, about an hour from town. A sort of amusement park has grown up around it. Seals fool around in the rocks and the tourists go for it strong. The woman took a cab, and our man took another. She went to the amusement park near the Cliff House."

Jo Gar's gray-blue eyes widened slightly.

"She spent more than three weeks on the *Cheyo Maru*," he breathed slowly. "And when she landed and had been cleared after an exhaustive customs examination, she went to an amusement park. Strange."

Raines made a grunting sound. "Damn' strange," he said. "Took all the baggage, which included a trunk we'd gone very carefully through. And the child."

Jo Gar narrowed his eyes and looked beyond the inspector. He said quietly:

"In Manila we have an amusement park that is quite large. After entering the main gate there are many places one can go."

Raines nodded. "It's like that here. Only this park has several entrances, and you can drive through a section of it. The cab went in one entrance, stopped for a while near a merry-go-round – went out another. Then it went to a house and stopped. The luggage was taken inside, and the woman and child went in. Our man stayed around a short time, but nothing else happened."

The Island detective said: "You have the address?"

Raines nodded. He took from his pocket a small slip of paper, on which were scrawled some words, handed it to Jo Gar.

The Island detective read: "'141 West Pacific Avenue.'"

Raines nodded. "That's it – Cary said it was a frame house, set back a short distance from the road. The section isn't much built up out there."

Jo Gar nodded. "It is very good of you to bring me this information," he stated.

Raines made a swift gesture with both hands. "That's all right," he said. "Cary has another job just now, or he'd have come along to tell you about it. Looks queer to me."

The Island detective spoke slowly. "It is not *necessary* to drive through the amusement park, in order to reach this address?" he asked.

Raines said: "Hell, no – that's what seems funny. That woman was trying to hide where she was going. Maybe she figured she *might* be followed."

Jo Gar nodded. "I think you are right," he said.

Raines got to his feet, held out his right hand.

"Sorry the office couldn't get something on her at the pier," he apologized. "But you know where she is – and you know she acted funny getting there."

Jo Gar smiled and shook the inspector's hand. He sat down on the bed again as Raines took his hat. When Raines reached the door, he said:

"Luck on those other four." He grinned and went out. Going along the corridor he whistled. The elevator door slammed.

Jo Gar got to his feet with remarkable speed for him. He got his coat and hat, was out of the room quickly. He used the stairs instead of the elevator. When he reached the small lobby he saw Raines light a cigar, go outside and raise a hand. A cab pulled close to the curb. When it started away the Island detective hailed another parked some feet from the hotel entrance. He said to the driver:

"Follow that machine, please – but do not move too close to it. When it halts, halt some distance away."

The driver looked at Jo curiously but nodded his head. The two cabs moved from one street to another. There was a great deal of traffic, but Jo's driver was skillful. For perhaps ten minutes the two cabs moved through the city, apparently keeping in the heart of it. Finally the leading cab curved close to a building that had a large clock set in granite stone. It halted. Unfamiliar as Jo was with San Francisco, he recognized the building as a railroad station of considerable importance. There were many porters about, and cabs were everywhere.

As his own cab pulled close to the curb Jo watched Raines alight and pay his driver. The inspector hurried into the station, and when he was out of sight Jo paid up and left his cab. He pulled his hat low over his eyes, straightened his small body a little, went into the station. Almost instantly he saw Raines. The man was at a luggage checking counter; as Jo watched from a safe distance he saw Raines handed two large-sized valises. A porter picked them up; Raines gestured towards another clock inside the station and said something. The porter hurried away, followed by the inspector.

Jo Gar followed, being careful not to be seen. When Raines and his porter went through a train gate, the Island detective halted near it, a peculiar smile on his face. After a few minutes the colored porter came back through the gate. Jo beckoned to him.

"The gentleman whose luggage you just carried to the train – I think he was a friend of mine. You saw his ticket?"

The porter shook his head slowly: "He tol' me his car and seat number – didn't show no ticket," he replied.

Jo Gar frowned. "How did you know what train to take him to?" he asked slowly.

The porter grinned. "That's right," he said. "He wanted the Chicago train."

The Island detective drew a sharp breath. He handed the porter a quarter, walked slowly back into the station's waiting room.

"Mr. Raines had barely time to make his train," he breathed softly. "Yet he was very kind to me – and said nothing about leaving on such a journey."

He took a cab back to his hotel, found everything in his room in perfect order. He called the customs office and after considerable inquiry was told that Inspector Raines had left for his hotel some hour or so ago. He said:

"Yes, he has been here. I wondered if he had returned."

There was a pause, questions were asked at the other end, and he was informed that Raines was not expected to return for special night work, but that he would be on duty in the morning. Jo Gar thanked his informant and hung up the receiver.

He sat on the edge of the small bed and watched a light sign flash in the distance. A ferry boat was a glow of moving light, on the Bay waters. The air seemed very cold. Jo Gar decided that the real Inspector Raines had met with injuries, and that a certain person had impersonated him, had told him an untrue story about a certain woman in black – and had then departed from the city of San Francisco. He decided that he was expected to go to the house at 141, West Pacific Avenue, that he was supposed to believe the woman had acted suspiciously in going there.

He said softly and slowly: "I have the six diamonds – they have the four. I am in a strange city, and a card with a seal on it was expected to make a great impression. But one man's picture can replace another's – very easily—"

He rose and looked at his wristwatch. It was almost eight o'clock. He inspected his Colt automatic, slipped it back into a pocket of his coat. The phone bell rang, and when he lifted the receiver and gave his name he was told that the customs office was calling, and that Inspector Raines had been found unconscious in an alley not far from the piers. He was still unconscious and it was not certain that he would live. He had apparently been struck over the head with a blunt instrument. The customs office felt that Señor Gar should know why he had failed to arrive, and also that all passengers on the *Cheyo Maru* had been passed through the office. One had been followed as requested, but her cab had been lost in traffic. The office was very sorry.

Jo Gar said: "I am very sorry to hear of Inspector Raines' injuries. I will call at the office tomorrow. Thank you for calling."

He hung up the receiver, went to the window that faced the Bay and the distant, lighted ferry boat. His gray-blue eyes were smiling coldly. He thought: They did *not* expect Inspector Raines to be found so soon. They *did* expect me to go immediately to the address the impostor gave me. They might easily have escaped with the four diamonds, but they chose to lead me to them. They wish the six in my possession, being very greedy. But I am warned, directly and indirectly.

The Island detective turned away from the window and moved towards the room door. He breathed very softly:

"Just the same – I shall go directly to the address given me."

Jo Gar left his cab a square from 141 West Pacific Avenue. He had picked the driver with care; the man was husky in build and young. He had a good chin and clear eyes, and he said his name was O'Halohan. Somewhere in the Islands Jo had read that the Irish were fighters.

He said now: "I am a detective – and I'm going inside of the house at 141. Here is a ten-dollar bill. In about five minutes I want you to drive to the front of the house and blow your horn twice. After that just stay in your seat. Wait about ten minutes – then blow your horn again, twice. If I do not come to a window or the door, and call to you – go to the police and tell them I went into the house and was prevented from coming out. That is all – is it clear?"

The driver nodded. "I got a gun," he said. "And a permit to carry it. Suppose, after the second time I blow my horn, you don't show. Why not let me come in and *get* you out?"

The Island detective smiled narrowly. "You are young and strong, but neither of those qualities might be of too great value. Neither of us might come out."

The driver said: "If it looks that bad – what you goin' in alone for?"

Jo Gar continued to smile. He said patiently:

"I have an idea it will be better that way. You must follow my instructions."

The driver nodded. "You're doing the job," he muttered. "I'll be down there in five minutes, and make the horn racket. I'll give it to you again in ten. Then if you don't show I'll head for the police."

The Island detective nodded. "That is the way," he said. "Don't get out of the car."

The driver said: "Supposing I hear you yelling for help – I still stick inside?"

Jo said grimly: "You will not hear me calling for help, Mister O'Halohan. My visit is not at all complicated. After you blow your horn twice – the second time, I will either give you instructions, or you will go for the police."

The driver said: "You win."

Jo Gar half closed his almond-shaped eyes. "It may be very important to me – that you do just as I have instructed. You are sure you understand?"

The driver nodded; his eyes met Jo Gar's squarely.

"It ain't anything tough," he stated.

Jo Gar spoke very quietly. "It is extremely simple."

He half turned away from the cab, and heard the driver say harshly:

"Yeah – if it works."

The Island detective moved along the broken pavement of the sidewalk, a thin smile on his browned face.

"It will be just as simple," he said in a low tone, a half whisper, "if it *doesn't* work. But much more final – for me."

Number 141 was a rambling one-story house in not too good condition. There were no streetlights near it; tall trees rose on either side. The nearest house to it was almost a square distant; opposite was a lot filled with low brush. The section was quiet and pretty well deserted, but less than a half mile away there was the flare of colored lights in the sky. And at intervals Jo Gar could hear distant and faint staccato sounds – the noise of shooting gallery rifles.

He did not hesitate as he reached the front of the house. A yellowish light showed faintly beyond one of the side windows. The pavement that ran to a few steps was broken and not level.

Out of the corners of his gray-blue eyes, as he moved towards the steps, Jo saw that the lights of the cab had been dimmed – their color did not show on the street in front of the place. A cold wind made sound in the trees as he reached the steps, moved up them. His right hand was in the right pocket of his coat, gripping the butt of the automatic.

He stood for a few seconds, his eyes on the number plate, which seemed new and had been placed in a position easily seen. The house was old, the section of San Francisco was not too good – but the number plate was in excellent condition.

The Island detective's lips curved just a little. But the smile that showed momentarily on his face was not a pleasant one. He had a definite feeling that this house marked the end of the trail. He thought of the ones who had died in Manila, when Delgada's jewelry store had been robbed – he thought of the men who had died since then. A vision of Juan Arragon's brown face flashed before his eyes.

He touched the index finger of his left hand to a button near the number plate, heard no sound within the house. One hand at his side, the other in his right pocket – he stood in the cold wind and waited. He had come to this house, but he had not been tricked. He was gambling – gambling his life, in a strange country, against his chances of recovering the four missing Von Loffler diamonds, against the final chance of facing the one who had planned the Manila crime.

He could not be positive of anything, but he sensed these things. This was to be the finish, one way or the other. He would return to Manila – or he would never leave this house alive. He felt it, and he was suddenly very calm. From somewhere within he heard footfalls; there was the sound of a bolt being moved, the door opened very wide.

Jo Gar looked into the eyes of a man who had a smiling face. It was a thin, browned face, and the eyes were small and colorless. The man was dressed in a brown suit, almost the color of his skin. There was nothing striking about the one who had opened the door, unless it was the smallness of his colorless eyes.

The eyes looked beyond the Island detective, to the sidewalk and road. The man moved his head slightly and Jo Gar said:

"I am Señor Gar, a private detective who arrived only today in San Francisco. I arrived on the *Cheyo Maru* – and have come here in search of a woman who was on that boat. She had with her a child—"

He stopped and looked downward at the dull color of black that was the metal of the gun held by the man in the doorway. The man had made only a slight movement with his right hand; the gun's muzzle was less than three feet from Jo's body.

Jo Gar smiled into the smiling eyes of the one in the doorway.

"I have made a mistake?" he asked very quietly.

The one in the doorway shook his head. "On the contrary," he said in a voice that was very low and cold, "you have come to the correct place. I have been – expecting you."

He stepped to one side, and Jo Gar walked into a wide hall. The light was dim, and though there were electric bulbs about, it was furnished by a lamp whose wick was uneven. The place was very cold. It had the air of not having been lived in for a long time, and there was no evidence about showing that it would be lived in.

The thin-faced man said: "The first room on your right, please. Lift your hands slightly."

Jo Gar raised his hands slightly, went through a narrow doorway into a room that seemed even colder than the hall. The light in the room was better – there were two lamps. Blinds were drawn tightly. Beside a small table was a stool that might have been made for a piano.

The one with the gun said in the same, cold voice:

"Sit on the stool, Gar – put your hands on the table. Keep them there."

Hatred crept into his voice as he uttered the last three words. Jo Gar did as instructed. He said quietly:

"I knew that the man you sent to me at my hotel lied. I followed him to the station, and watched him leave the city. I returned to the hotel and the customs office informed me that one of their men, who was coming to me with information of no great importance, had been knocked unconscious. I knew then how the card presented me had been obtained, and that I was expected to believe a story that pointed to suspicious action by a woman I was interested in – and that I was expected to come to this address."

There was hatred showing in the small, colorless eyes of the thin-faced one. He stood almost ten feet away from Jo Gar, facing him.

"But you came, knowing all this."

Jo Gar smiled a little. "When you made that movement and held that gun on me – my fingers were on the trigger of my own gun. I could have shot you down – I did not."

There was a flicker of expression in the standing one's eyes. He said:

"You are very kind, Señor Gar."

Mockery and hatred were in his tone. Jo Gar said slowly:

"No – not kind. I have six diamonds that you would like. I think that you have four I would like. You wanted me here to bargain with me. You wanted me here so that you could trap me, then offer me my life for the six diamonds. You have worked that way, with your accomplices, since the robbery was effected."

The thin-faced one smiled and showed white, even teeth.

"You would risk your life and six diamonds – for the four you say I have?"

Jo Gar smiled gently. "My life is not too important," he said. "I have never regarded it that way. I came here because I knew the one responsible for many deaths would be here."

The thin-faced one said mockingly: "And you were not trapped? You simply wanted to see that person who you hated because of Arragon's death, and because of things done to you?"

The Island detective kept his hands motionless on the table surface. He shook his head.

"No," he replied. "Not exactly. I wanted to see that one taken by the police. And that is practically assured, now."

He watched the facial muscles of the thin-faced one jerk, saw his colorless eyes shift towards the blinds of the windows. His gun hand moved a little, in towards his body. Rage twisted his face, and then he smiled. It was a grotesque, mask-like smile. The brown skin was drawn tightly over the face bones and the lips were pressed together. Jo Gar said:

"I remember you, Raaker. You were in the insurance business in Manila until a few years ago. There was about to be a prosecution, and you left the Islands."

The thin-faced one said with hoarseness in his voice:

"And I have never forgotten you, Señor Gar. You tell me you have come here, not caring about your life – and that the police are outside. Well – I didn't bring you here to get your six diamonds, Gar – Von Loffler's diamonds. I brought you here because I hate you. I want to watch your body squirm on the floor, beside that stool."

Jo Gar said quietly: "That was how you knew about the Von Loffler diamonds – that Dutch Insurance Company. You stayed out of Manila, Raaker – you couldn't risk coming back. You hired men. Some of them tricked you – and each other. The robbery was successful, but you lost slowly. All the way back from Manila, Raaker, you lost. You used men and women, and they tried to kill me – too many times. They were killed – there were many deaths. Those were diamonds of death, Raaker – and you only got four of them. The woman in black brought them to you – I think she was the only one who was faithful."

Raaker was breathing heavily. He made a sudden movement with his left hand, plunging it into a pocket. When it came out four stones spilled to the surface of the small table. Three of them only rolled a few inches, but one struck against a finger of the Island detective's left hand. Raaker said fiercely:

"I hate you, Gar. You drove me from the Islands, with your evidence. I hated Von Loffler, too. He took all his properties away from me, because he learned that I was gambling, because he was afraid of the insurance. So I learned about the stones, where they were. And I planned the robbery. I stayed here – and got reports. I tried to direct. But you were on that boat—"

He broke off, shrugged. "You are going to die, Gar. So I can talk. The woman came to me with the diamonds. Four of them. And by the time she brought them to me here – she hated me. She had seen too much death. She's gone away, with her child – and you'll never find her, Gar. She killed a man on the *Cheyo Maru,* and that made her hate me all the more. She had to kill him, before he could talk – to you!"

Jo Gar said steadily: "I don't think – I *want* to find her, Raaker. I know now who planned the crime, who caused the deaths. And you are caught, Raaker—"

There was the sound of brakes beyond the room, the low beat of an idling engine. Two sharp blasts from a horn came into the room. Raaker jerked his head sharply, then turned his eyes towards Jo Gar again. The Island detective made no movement. He smiled with his lips pressed together. Raaker said:

"What's – that?"

His voice was hoarse. Jo Gar parted his lips. He said:

"A signal from the police – that the house is properly covered."

Raaker sucked in a deep breath. "I'll get more than one of them – as they come in!" he muttered.

Jo Gar shook his head. "I do not think you will, Raaker. They will not come in. It is easier to wait for *you* – to go *out*."

Raaker smiled twistedly, but there was fear in his eyes.

"They'll come in, all right," he breathed. "I'll get you first – when they come. *You* won't see them come in, Gar."

Jo Gar smiled. "They will not come in," he said softly. "If I do not go out, within the next ten minutes, they will unload the sub-machine-guns and the smoke bombs. They will know I am dead – and that there is a killer in the house. The smoke bombs – and the tear gas bombs – *they* will come in."

Raaker said hoarsely. "—! How I hate you, you little half-breed—"

He jerked the gun slightly. The Island detective looked him in the eyes, still smiling.

"That is true," he said. "You *do* hate me – and there *is* the blood of the Spanish and the Filipino in my veins. But I am not a criminal – a thief and a killer."

Raaker turned his head slightly and listened to the steady beat of the cab engine. Then his eyes came back to the small figure of Gar, went to the four glittering diamonds on the table. He said thickly:

"With the others – over two hundred thousand dollars – I would have been fixed—"

His voice broke. Jo Gar said quietly: "Yes, you could have had things easy, Raaker. If I had not taken the same boat that your accomplices took – if things had turned out differently in Honolulu—"

Raaker stared at him, his little eyes growing larger. He said slowly:

"Where are – the other six stones?"

Jo Gar smiled. "In the vaults of the customs office," he replied. "You did not think I would bring them here?"

Raaker's body swayed a little. The wind made noise in the trees beyond the house, and he stiffened. Jo Gar said in a voice that was hardly more than a whisper:

"If you had had even the courage of a certain type of criminal – and had gone to the Islands yourself, you might have had the diamonds now. If you had not used others—"

Raaker said fiercely: "Damn the diamonds – I've got *you*! They brought you here—"

Jo Gar half closed his almond-shaped eyes. "And they've brought the San Francisco police here," he said steadily. "They've brought tear gas and sub-machine-guns – and they're bringing death here, Raaker."

Raaker's eyes held rage again. He was losing control of himself. He made a swift motion with his left hand, shaking fingers pointing towards the four stones on the table.

"Look at them – damn you!" he gritted. "Look at the four you couldn't – reach! Look at them—"

Jo Gar looked into the eyes of Raaker. He shook his head.

"I've seen the *others*," he stated quietly. "I've seen many diamonds, Raaker."

Raaker laughed wildly. He backed towards a wall of the room.

"You'll never see diamonds again," he said in a fierce tone. "Never, Gar!"

He raised his gun arm slowly. From the cab outside there came the sharp sound of a horn, silence – and then another blast.

Jo Gar never took his eyes from the eyes of Raaker. He was smiling grimly.

He said very slowly: "Machine-gun bullets, Raaker. And choking, blinding gas. They'll be waiting for *you* – after you get through squeezing that trigger."

Raaker cried out in a shrill tone: "Damn you – Gar – that won't help *you* any—"

There was a sudden engine hum as the cab driver accelerated the motor. Yellow light flashed beyond the house, along the road. O'Halohan was going for the police, starting his cab. For a second Raaker twisted his head towards the sound and the light. He was thinking of machine-guns – and tear gas –

Jo Gar was on his feet in a flash. The table went forward, over. The Island detective leaped to the right as Raaker cried out hoarsely, and the first bullet from his gun crashed into the table wood.

The second bullet from the gun ripped the cloth of Gar's coat, and his right hand was coming up, with the Colt in it, when the cloth ripped. He squeezed the trigger sharply but steadily. There was the third gun crash and Raaker screamed, took a step forward. His gun hand dropped; he went to his knees, stared at Gar for a second, swaying – then fell heavily to the floor.

Jo Gar went slowly to his side. He was dead – the bullet had caught him just above the heart. One diamond lay very close to his curved fingers; it was as though he were grasping for it, in death.

The other three Jo found after a five-minute search. Then he went from the room into the hall, and out of the house. The cab was out of sight; in the distance there was still colored light in the sky. The shooting gallery noise came at intervals. Jo Gar found a package in his pocket, lighted one of his brown-paper cigarettes.

He said very softly, to himself: "I have all – of the diamonds. Now I can go home, after the police come. I hope my friend Juan Arragon – knows."

He stood very motionless on the top step that led to the small porch, and waited for the police to come. And he thought, as he waited, of the Philippines – of Manila – and of his tiny office off the *Escolta*. It was good to forget other things, and to think of his returning.

The Adventure of the Bruce-Partington Plans

Arthur Conan Doyle

IN THE THIRD WEEK of November, in the year 1895, a dense yellow fog settled down upon London. From the Monday to the Thursday I doubt whether it was ever possible from our windows in Baker Street to see the loom of the opposite houses. The first day Holmes had spent in cross-indexing his huge book of references. The second and third had been patiently occupied upon a subject which he had recently made his hobby – the music of the Middle Ages. But when, for the fourth time, after pushing back our chairs from breakfast we saw the greasy, heavy brown swirl still drifting past us and condensing in oily drops upon the window-panes, my comrade's impatient and active nature could endure this drab existence no longer. He paced restlessly about our sitting room in a fever of suppressed energy, biting his nails, tapping the furniture, and chafing against inaction.

"Nothing of interest in the paper, Watson?" he said.

I was aware that by anything of interest, Holmes meant anything of criminal interest. There was the news of a revolution, of a possible war, and of an impending change of government; but these did not come within the horizon of my companion. I could see nothing recorded in the shape of crime which was not commonplace and futile. Holmes groaned and resumed his restless meanderings.

"The London criminal is certainly a dull fellow," said he in the querulous voice of the sportsman whose game has failed him. "Look out this window, Watson. See how the figures loom up, are dimly seen, and then blend once more into the cloud-bank. The thief or the murderer could roam London on such a day as the tiger does the jungle, unseen until he pounces, and then evident only to his victim."

"There have," said I, "been numerous petty thefts."

Holmes snorted his contempt.

"This great and sombre stage is set for something more worthy than that," said he. "It is fortunate for this community that I am not a criminal."

"It is, indeed!" said I heartily.

"Suppose that I were Brooks or Woodhouse, or any of the fifty men who have good reason for taking my life, how long could I survive against my own pursuit? A summons, a bogus appointment, and all would be over. It is well they don't have days of fog in the Latin countries – the countries of assassination. By Jove! Here comes something at last to break our dead monotony."

It was the maid with a telegram. Holmes tore it open and burst out laughing.

"Well, well! What next?" said he. "Brother Mycroft is coming round."

"Why not?" I asked.

"Why not? It is as if you met a tram-car coming down a country lane. Mycroft has his rails and he runs on them. His Pall Mall lodgings, the Diogenes Club, Whitehall – that is his cycle. Once, and only once, he has been here. What upheaval can possibly have derailed him?"

"Does he not explain?"

Holmes handed me his brother's telegram.

> *Must see you over Cadogan West. Coming at once.*
> *MYCROFT.*

"Cadogan West? I have heard the name."

"It recalls nothing to my mind. But that Mycroft should break out in this erratic fashion! A planet might as well leave its orbit. By the way, do you know what Mycroft is?"

I had some vague recollection of an explanation at the time of the Adventure of the Greek Interpreter.

"You told me that he had some small office under the British government."

Holmes chuckled.

"I did not know you quite so well in those days. One has to be discreet when one talks of high matters of state. You are right in thinking that he is under the British government. You would also be right in a sense if you said that occasionally he *is* the British government."

"My dear Holmes!"

"I thought I might surprise you. Mycroft draws four hundred and fifty pounds a year, remains a subordinate, has no ambitions of any kind, will receive neither honour nor title, but remains the most indispensable man in the country."

"But how?"

"Well, his position is unique. He has made it for himself. There has never been anything like it before, nor will be again. He has the tidiest and most orderly brain, with the greatest capacity for storing facts, of any man living. The same great powers which I have turned to the detection of crime he has used for this particular business. The conclusions of every department are passed to him, and he is the central exchange, the clearinghouse, which makes out the balance. All other men are specialists, but his specialism is omniscience. We will suppose that a minister needs information as to a point which involves the Navy, India, Canada and the bimetallic question; he could get his separate advices from various departments upon each, but only Mycroft can focus them all, and say offhand how each factor would affect the other. They began by using him as a short-cut, a convenience; now he has made himself an essential. In that great brain of his everything is pigeon-holed and can be handed out in an instant. Again and again his word has decided the national policy. He lives in it. He thinks of nothing else save when, as an intellectual exercise, he unbends if I call upon him and ask him to advise me on one of my little problems. But Jupiter is descending today. What on earth can it mean? Who is Cadogan West, and what is he to Mycroft?"

"I have it," I cried, and plunged among the litter of papers upon the sofa. "Yes, yes, here he is, sure enough! Cadogan West was the young man who was found dead on the Underground on Tuesday morning."

Holmes sat up at attention, his pipe halfway to his lips.

"This must be serious, Watson. A death which has caused my brother to alter his habits can be no ordinary one. What in the world can he have to do with it? The case was featureless as I remember it. The young man had apparently fallen out of the train and killed himself. He had not been robbed, and there was no particular reason to suspect violence. Is that not so?"

"There has been an inquest," said I, "and a good many fresh facts have come out. Looked at more closely, I should certainly say that it was a curious case."

"Judging by its effect upon my brother, I should think it must be a most extraordinary one." He snuggled down in his armchair. "Now, Watson, let us have the facts."

"The man's name was Arthur Cadogan West. He was twenty-seven years of age, unmarried, and a clerk at Woolwich Arsenal."

"Government employ. Behold the link with Brother Mycroft!"

"He left Woolwich suddenly on Monday night. Was last seen by his fiancée, Miss Violet Westbury, whom he left abruptly in the fog about 7:30 that evening. There was no quarrel between them and she can give no motive for his action. The next thing heard of him was when his dead body was discovered by a plate-layer named Mason, just outside Aldgate Station on the Underground system in London."

"When?"

"The body was found at six on Tuesday morning. It was lying wide of the metals upon the left hand of the track as one goes eastward, at a point close to the station, where the line emerges from the tunnel in which it runs. The head was badly crushed – an injury which might well have been caused by a fall from the train. The body could only have come on the line in that way. Had it been carried down from any neighbouring street, it must have passed the station barriers, where a collector is always standing. This point seems absolutely certain."

"Very good. The case is definite enough. The man, dead or alive, either fell or was precipitated from a train. So much is clear to me. Continue."

"The trains which traverse the lines of rail beside which the body was found are those which run from west to east, some being purely Metropolitan, and some from Willesden and outlying junctions. It can be stated for certain that this young man, when he met his death, was travelling in this direction at some late hour of the night, but at what point he entered the train it is impossible to state."

"His ticket, of course, would show that."

"There was no ticket in his pockets."

"No ticket! Dear me, Watson, this is really very singular. According to my experience it is not possible to reach the platform of a Metropolitan train without exhibiting one's ticket. Presumably, then, the young man had one. Was it taken from him in order to conceal the station from which he came? It is possible. Or did he drop it in the carriage? That is also possible. But the point is of curious interest. I understand that there was no sign of robbery?"

"Apparently not. There is a list here of his possessions. His purse contained two pounds fifteen. He had also a check-book on the Woolwich branch of the Capital and Counties Bank. Through this his identity was established. There were also two dress-circle tickets for the Woolwich Theatre, dated for that very evening. Also a small packet of technical papers."

Holmes gave an exclamation of satisfaction.

"There we have it at last, Watson! British government – Woolwich. Arsenal – technical papers – Brother Mycroft, the chain is complete. But here he comes, if I am not mistaken, to speak for himself."

A moment later the tall and portly form of Mycroft Holmes was ushered into the room. Heavily built and massive, there was a suggestion of uncouth physical inertia in the figure, but above this unwieldy frame there was perched a head so masterful in its brow, so alert in its steel-grey, deep-set eyes, so firm in its lips, and so subtle in its play of expression, that after the first glance one forgot the gross body and remembered only the dominant mind.

At his heels came our old friend Lestrade, of Scotland Yard – thin and austere. The gravity of both their faces foretold some weighty quest. The detective shook hands without a word. Mycroft Holmes struggled out of his overcoat and subsided into an armchair.

"A most annoying business, Sherlock," said he. "I extremely dislike altering my habits, but the powers that be would take no denial. In the present state of Siam it is most awkward that I should be away from the office. But it is a real crisis. I have never seen the Prime Minister so upset. As to the Admiralty – it is buzzing like an overturned beehive. Have you read up the case?"

"We have just done so. What were the technical papers?"

"Ah, there's the point! Fortunately, it has not come out. The press would be furious if it did. The papers which this wretched youth had in his pocket were the plans of the Bruce-Partington submarine."

Mycroft Holmes spoke with a solemnity which showed his sense of the importance of the subject. His brother and I sat expectant.

"Surely you have heard of it? I thought everyone had heard of it."

"Only as a name."

"Its importance can hardly be exaggerated. It has been the most jealously guarded of all government secrets. You may take it from me that naval warfare becomes impossible within the radius of a Bruce-Partington's operation. Two years ago a very large sum was smuggled through the Estimates and was expended in acquiring a monopoly of the invention. Every effort has been made to keep the secret. The plans, which are exceedingly intricate, comprising some thirty separate patents, each essential to the working of the whole, are kept in an elaborate safe in a confidential office adjoining the arsenal, with burglar-proof doors and windows. Under no conceivable circumstances were the plans to be taken from the office. If the chief constructor of the Navy desired to consult them, even he was forced to go to the Woolwich office for the purpose. And yet here we find them in the pocket of a dead junior clerk in the heart of London. From an official point of view it's simply awful."

"But you have recovered them?"

"No, Sherlock, no! That's the pinch. We have not. Ten papers were taken from Woolwich. There were seven in the pocket of Cadogan West. The three most essential are gone – stolen, vanished. You must drop everything, Sherlock. Never mind your usual petty puzzles of the police-court. It's a vital international problem that you have to solve. Why did Cadogan West take the papers, where are the missing ones, how did he die, how came his body where it was found, how can the evil be set right? Find an answer to all these questions, and you will have done good service for your country."

"Why do you not solve it yourself, Mycroft? You can see as far as I."

"Possibly, Sherlock. But it is a question of getting details. Give me your details, and from an armchair I will return you an excellent expert opinion. But to run here and run there, to cross-question railway guards, and lie on my face with a lens to my eye – it is not my metier. No, you are the one man who can clear the matter up. If you have a fancy to see your name in the next honours list—"

My friend smiled and shook his head.

"I play the game for the game's own sake," said he. "But the problem certainly presents some points of interest, and I shall be very pleased to look into it. Some more facts, please."

"I have jotted down the more essential ones upon this sheet of paper, together with a few addresses which you will find of service. The actual official guardian of the papers is the famous government expert, Sir James Walter, whose decorations and subtitles fill two lines of a book of reference. He has grown grey in the service, is a gentleman, a favoured guest in the most exalted houses, and, above all, a man whose patriotism is beyond suspicion. He is one of two who have a key of the safe. I may add that the papers were undoubtedly in the office during working hours on Monday, and that Sir James left for London about three o'clock taking his key with him. He was at the house of Admiral Sinclair at Barclay Square during the whole of the evening when this incident occurred."

"Has the fact been verified?"

"Yes; his brother, Colonel Valentine Walter, has testified to his departure from Woolwich, and Admiral Sinclair to his arrival in London; so Sir James is no longer a direct factor in the problem."

"Who was the other man with a key?"

"The senior clerk and draughtsman, Mr. Sidney Johnson. He is a man of forty, married, with five children. He is a silent, morose man, but he has, on the whole, an excellent record in the public service. He is unpopular with his colleagues, but a hard worker. According to his own account, corroborated only by the word of his wife, he was at home the whole of Monday evening after office hours, and his key has never left the watch-chain upon which it hangs."

"Tell us about Cadogan West."

"He has been ten years in the service and has done good work. He has the reputation of being hot-headed and imperious, but a straight, honest man. We have nothing against him. He was next Sidney Johnson in the office. His duties brought him into daily, personal contact with the plans. No one else had the handling of them."

"Who locked up the plans that night?"

"Mr. Sidney Johnson, the senior clerk."

"Well, it is surely perfectly clear who took them away. They are actually found upon the person of this junior clerk, Cadogan West. That seems final, does it not?"

"It does, Sherlock, and yet it leaves so much unexplained. In the first place, why did he take them?"

"I presume they were of value?"

"He could have got several thousands for them very easily."

"Can you suggest any possible motive for taking the papers to London except to sell them?"

"No, I cannot."

"Then we must take that as our working hypothesis. Young West took the papers. Now this could only be done by having a false key—"

"Several false keys. He had to open the building and the room."

"He had, then, several false keys. He took the papers to London to sell the secret, intending, no doubt, to have the plans themselves back in the safe next morning before they were missed. While in London on this treasonable mission he met his end."

"How?"

"We will suppose that he was travelling back to Woolwich when he was killed and thrown out of the compartment."

"Aldgate, where the body was found, is considerably past the station London Bridge, which would be his route to Woolwich."

"Many circumstances could be imagined under which he would pass London Bridge. There was someone in the carriage, for example, with whom he was having an absorbing interview. This interview led to a violent scene in which he lost his life. Possibly he tried to leave the carriage, fell out on the line, and so met his end. The other closed the door. There was a thick fog, and nothing could be seen."

"No better explanation can be given with our present knowledge; and yet consider, Sherlock, how much you leave untouched. We will suppose, for argument's sake, that young Cadogan West *had* determined to convey these papers to London. He would naturally have made an appointment with the foreign agent and kept his evening clear. Instead of that he took two tickets for the theatre, escorted his fiancée halfway there, and then suddenly disappeared."

"A blind," said Lestrade, who had sat listening with some impatience to the conversation.

"A very singular one. That is objection No. 1. Objection No. 2: We will suppose that he reaches London and sees the foreign agent. He must bring back the papers before morning or the loss will be discovered. He took away ten. Only seven were in his pocket. What had become of the other three? He certainly would not leave them of his own free will. Then, again, where is the price of his treason? One would have expected to find a large sum of money in his pocket."

"It seems to me perfectly clear," said Lestrade. "I have no doubt at all as to what occurred. He took the papers to sell them. He saw the agent. They could not agree as to price. He started home again, but the agent went with him. In the train the agent murdered him, took the more essential papers, and threw his body from the carriage. That would account for everything, would it not?"

"Why had he no ticket?"

"The ticket would have shown which station was nearest the agent's house. Therefore he took it from the murdered man's pocket."

"Good, Lestrade, very good," said Holmes. "Your theory holds together. But if this is true, then the case is at an end. On the one hand, the traitor is dead. On the other, the plans of the Bruce-Partington submarine are presumably already on the Continent. What is there for us to do?"

"To act, Sherlock – to act!" cried Mycroft, springing to his feet. "All my instincts are against this explanation. Use your powers! Go to the scene of the crime! See the people concerned! Leave no stone unturned! In all your career you have never had so great a chance of serving your country."

"Well, well!" said Holmes, shrugging his shoulders. "Come, Watson! And you, Lestrade, could you favour us with your company for an hour or two? We will begin our investigation by a visit to Aldgate Station. Goodbye, Mycroft. I shall let you have a report before evening, but I warn you in advance that you have little to expect."

An hour later Holmes, Lestrade and I stood upon the Underground railroad at the point where it emerges from the tunnel immediately before Aldgate Station. A courteous red-faced old gentleman represented the railway company.

"This is where the young man's body lay," said he, indicating a spot about three feet from the metals. "It could not have fallen from above, for these, as you see, are all blank walls. Therefore, it could only have come from a train, and that train, so far as we can trace it, must have passed about midnight on Monday."

"Have the carriages been examined for any sign of violence?"

"There are no such signs, and no ticket has been found."

"No record of a door being found open?"

"None."

"We have had some fresh evidence this morning," said Lestrade. "A passenger who passed Aldgate in an ordinary Metropolitan train about 11:40 on Monday night declares that he heard a heavy thud, as of a body striking the line, just before the train reached the station. There was dense fog, however, and nothing could be seen. He made no report of it at the time. Why, whatever is the matter with Mr. Holmes?"

My friend was standing with an expression of strained intensity upon his face, staring at the railway metals where they curved out of the tunnel. Aldgate is a junction, and there was a network of points. On these his eager, questioning eyes were fixed, and I saw on his keen, alert face that tightening of the lips, that quiver of the nostrils, and concentration of the heavy, tufted brows which I knew so well.

"Points," he muttered; "the points."

"What of it? What do you mean?"

"I suppose there are no great number of points on a system such as this?"

"No; they are very few."

"And a curve, too. Points, and a curve. By Jove! If it were only so."

"What is it, Mr. Holmes? Have you a clue?"

"An idea – an indication, no more. But the case certainly grows in interest. Unique, perfectly unique, and yet why not? I do not see any indications of bleeding on the line."

"There were hardly any."

"But I understand that there was a considerable wound."

"The bone was crushed, but there was no great external injury."

"And yet one would have expected some bleeding. Would it be possible for me to inspect the train which contained the passenger who heard the thud of a fall in the fog?"

"I fear not, Mr. Holmes. The train has been broken up before now, and the carriages redistributed."

"I can assure you, Mr. Holmes," said Lestrade, "that every carriage has been carefully examined. I saw to it myself."

It was one of my friend's most obvious weaknesses that he was impatient with less alert intelligences than his own.

"Very likely," said he, turning away. "As it happens, it was not the carriages which I desired to examine. Watson, we have done all we can here. We need not trouble you any further, Mr. Lestrade. I think our investigations must now carry us to Woolwich."

At London Bridge, Holmes wrote a telegram to his brother, which he handed to me before dispatching it. It ran thus:

> See some light in the darkness, but it may possibly flicker out. Meanwhile, please send by messenger, to await return at Baker Street, a complete list of all foreign spies or international agents known to be in England, with full address.
> – Sherlock.

"That should be helpful, Watson," he remarked as we took our seats in the Woolwich train. "We certainly owe Brother Mycroft a debt for having introduced us to what promises to be a really very remarkable case."

His eager face still wore that expression of intense and high-strung energy, which showed me that some novel and suggestive circumstance had opened up a stimulating line of thought. See the foxhound with hanging ears and drooping tail as it lolls about the kennels, and compare it with the same hound as, with gleaming eyes and straining muscles, it runs upon a breast-high scent – such was the change in Holmes since the morning. He was a different man from the limp and lounging figure in the mouse-coloured dressing-gown who had prowled so restlessly only a few hours before round the fog-girt room.

"There is material here. There is scope," said he. "I am dull indeed not to have understood its possibilities."

"Even now they are dark to me."

"The end is dark to me also, but I have hold of one idea which may lead us far. The man met his death elsewhere, and his body was on the *roof* of a carriage."

"On the roof!"

"Remarkable, is it not? But consider the facts. Is it a coincidence that it is found at the very point where the train pitches and sways as it comes round on the points? Is not that the place where an object upon the roof might be expected to fall off? The points would affect no object inside the train. Either the body fell from the roof, or a very curious coincidence has occurred. But now consider the question of the blood. Of course, there was no bleeding on the line if the body had bled elsewhere. Each fact is suggestive in itself. Together they have a cumulative force."

"And the ticket, too!" I cried.

"Exactly. We could not explain the absence of a ticket. This would explain it. Everything fits together."

"But suppose it were so, we are still as far as ever from unravelling the mystery of his death. Indeed, it becomes not simpler but stranger."

"Perhaps," said Holmes, thoughtfully, "perhaps." He relapsed into a silent reverie, which lasted until the slow train drew up at last in Woolwich Station. There he called a cab and drew Mycroft's paper from his pocket.

"We have quite a little round of afternoon calls to make," said he. "I think that Sir James Walter claims our first attention."

The house of the famous official was a fine villa with green lawns stretching down to the Thames. As we reached it the fog was lifting, and a thin, watery sunshine was breaking through. A butler answered our ring.

"Sir James, sir!" said he with solemn face. "Sir James died this morning."

"Good heavens!" cried Holmes in amazement. "How did he die?"

"Perhaps you would care to step in, sir, and see his brother, Colonel Valentine?"

"Yes, we had best do so."

We were ushered into a dim-lit drawing room, where an instant later we were joined by a very tall, handsome, light-bearded man of fifty, the younger brother of the dead scientist. His wild eyes, stained cheeks, and unkempt hair all spoke of the sudden blow which had fallen upon the household. He was hardly articulate as he spoke of it.

"It was this horrible scandal," said he. "My brother, Sir James, was a man of very sensitive honour, and he could not survive such an affair. It broke his heart. He was always so proud of the efficiency of his department, and this was a crushing blow."

"We had hoped that he might have given us some indications which would have helped us to clear the matter up."

"I assure you that it was all a mystery to him as it is to you and to all of us. He had already put all his knowledge at the disposal of the police. Naturally he had no doubt that Cadogan West was guilty. But all the rest was inconceivable."

"You cannot throw any new light upon the affair?"

"I know nothing myself save what I have read or heard. I have no desire to be discourteous, but you can understand, Mr. Holmes, that we are much disturbed at present, and I must ask you to hasten this interview to an end."

"This is indeed an unexpected development," said my friend when we had regained the cab. "I wonder if the death was natural, or whether the poor old fellow killed himself! If the latter, may it be taken as some sign of self-reproach for duty neglected? We must leave that question to the future. Now we shall turn to the Cadogan Wests."

A small but well-kept house in the outskirts of the town sheltered the bereaved mother. The old lady was too dazed with grief to be of any use to us, but at her side was a white-faced young lady, who introduced herself as Miss Violet Westbury, the fiancée of the dead man, and the last to see him upon that fatal night.

"I cannot explain it, Mr. Holmes," she said. "I have not shut an eye since the tragedy, thinking, thinking, thinking, night and day, what the true meaning of it can be. Arthur was the most single-minded, chivalrous, patriotic man upon earth. He would have cut his right hand off before he would sell a State secret confided to his keeping. It is absurd, impossible, preposterous to anyone who knew him."

"But the facts, Miss Westbury?"

"Yes, yes; I admit I cannot explain them."

"Was he in any want of money?"

"No; his needs were very simple and his salary ample. He had saved a few hundreds, and we were to marry at the New Year."

"No signs of any mental excitement? Come, Miss Westbury, be absolutely frank with us."

The quick eye of my companion had noted some change in her manner. She coloured and hesitated.

"Yes," she said at last, "I had a feeling that there was something on his mind."

"For long?"

"Only for the last week or so. He was thoughtful and worried. Once I pressed him about it. He admitted that there was something, and that it was concerned with his official life. 'It is too serious for me to speak about, even to you,' said he. I could get nothing more."

Holmes looked grave.

"Go on, Miss Westbury. Even if it seems to tell against him, go on. We cannot say what it may lead to."

"Indeed, I have nothing more to tell. Once or twice it seemed to me that he was on the point of telling me something. He spoke one evening of the importance of the secret, and I have some recollection that he said that no doubt foreign spies would pay a great deal to have it."

My friend's face grew graver still.

"Anything else?"

"He said that we were slack about such matters – that it would be easy for a traitor to get the plans."

"Was it only recently that he made such remarks?"

"Yes, quite recently."

"Now tell us of that last evening."

"We were to go to the theatre. The fog was so thick that a cab was useless. We walked, and our way took us close to the office. Suddenly he darted away into the fog."

"Without a word?"

"He gave an exclamation; that was all. I waited but he never returned. Then I walked home. Next morning, after the office opened, they came to inquire. About twelve o'clock we heard the terrible news. Oh, Mr. Holmes, if you could only, only save his honour! It was so much to him."

Holmes shook his head sadly.

"Come, Watson," said he, "our ways lie elsewhere. Our next station must be the office from which the papers were taken.

"It was black enough before against this young man, but our inquiries make it blacker," he remarked as the cab lumbered off. "His coming marriage gives a motive for the crime. He naturally wanted money. The idea was in his head, since he spoke about it. He nearly made the girl an accomplice in the treason by telling her his plans. It is all very bad."

"But surely, Holmes, character goes for something? Then, again, why should he leave the girl in the street and dart away to commit a felony?"

"Exactly! There are certainly objections. But it is a formidable case which they have to meet."

Mr. Sidney Johnson, the senior clerk, met us at the office and received us with that respect which my companion's card always commanded. He was a thin, gruff, bespectacled man of middle age, his cheeks haggard, and his hands twitching from the nervous strain to which he had been subjected.

"It is bad, Mr. Holmes, very bad! Have you heard of the death of the chief?"

"We have just come from his house."

"The place is disorganised. The chief dead, Cadogan West dead, our papers stolen. And yet, when we closed our door on Monday evening, we were as efficient an office as any in the government service. Good God, it's dreadful to think of! That West, of all men, should have done such a thing!"

"You are sure of his guilt, then?"

"I can see no other way out of it. And yet I would have trusted him as I trust myself."

"At what hour was the office closed on Monday?"

"At five."

"Did you close it?"

"I am always the last man out."

"Where were the plans?"

"In that safe. I put them there myself."

"Is there no watchman to the building?"

"There is, but he has other departments to look after as well. He is an old soldier and a most trustworthy man. He saw nothing that evening. Of course the fog was very thick."

"Suppose that Cadogan West wished to make his way into the building after hours; he would need three keys, would he not, before he could reach the papers?"

"Yes, he would. The key of the outer door, the key of the office, and the key of the safe."

"Only Sir James Walter and you had those keys?"

"I had no keys of the doors – only of the safe."

"Was Sir James a man who was orderly in his habits?"

"Yes, I think he was. I know that so far as those three keys are concerned he kept them on the same ring. I have often seen them there."

"And that ring went with him to London?"

"He said so."

"And your key never left your possession?"

"Never."

"Then West, if he is the culprit, must have had a duplicate. And yet none was found upon his body. One other point: if a clerk in this office desired to sell the plans, would it not be simpler to copy the plans for himself than to take the originals, as was actually done?"

"It would take considerable technical knowledge to copy the plans in an effective way."

"But I suppose either Sir James, or you, or West has that technical knowledge?"

"No doubt we had, but I beg you won't try to drag me into the matter, Mr. Holmes. What is the use of our speculating in this way when the original plans were actually found on West?"

"Well, it is certainly singular that he should run the risk of taking originals if he could safely have taken copies, which would have equally served his turn."

"Singular, no doubt – and yet he did so."

"Every inquiry in this case reveals something inexplicable. Now there are three papers still missing. They are, as I understand, the vital ones."

"Yes, that is so."

"Do you mean to say that anyone holding these three papers, and without the seven others, could construct a Bruce-Partington submarine?"

"I reported to that effect to the Admiralty. But today I have been over the drawings again, and I am not so sure of it. The double valves with the automatic self-adjusting slots are drawn in one of the papers which have been returned. Until the foreigners had invented that for themselves they could not make the boat. Of course they might soon get over the difficulty."

"But the three missing drawings are the most important?"

"Undoubtedly."

"I think, with your permission, I will now take a stroll round the premises. I do not recall any other question which I desired to ask."

He examined the lock of the safe, the door of the room, and finally the iron shutters of the window. It was only when we were on the lawn outside that his interest was strongly excited. There was a laurel bush outside the window, and several of the branches bore signs of having been twisted or snapped. He examined them carefully with his lens, and then some dim and vague marks upon the earth beneath. Finally he asked the chief clerk to close the iron shutters, and he pointed out to me that they hardly met in the centre, and that it would be possible for anyone outside to see what was going on within the room.

"The indications are ruined by three days' delay. They may mean something or nothing. Well, Watson, I do not think that Woolwich can help us further. It is a small crop which we have gathered. Let us see if we can do better in London."

Yet we added one more sheaf to our harvest before we left Woolwich Station. The clerk in the ticket office was able to say with confidence that he saw Cadogan West – whom he knew well by sight – upon the Monday night, and that he went to London by the 8:15 to London Bridge. He was alone and took a single third-class ticket. The clerk was struck at the time by his excited and nervous manner. So shaky was he that he could hardly pick up his change, and the clerk had helped him with it. A reference to the timetable showed that the 8:15 was the first train which it was possible for West to take after he had left the lady about 7:30.

"Let us reconstruct, Watson," said Holmes after half an hour of silence. "I am not aware that in all our joint researches we have ever had a case which was more difficult to get at. Every fresh advance which we make only reveals a fresh ridge beyond. And yet we have surely made some appreciable progress.

"The effect of our inquiries at Woolwich has in the main been against young Cadogan West; but the indications at the window would lend themselves to a more favourable hypothesis. Let us suppose, for example, that he had been approached by some foreign agent. It might have been done under such pledges as would have prevented him from speaking of it, and yet would have affected his thoughts in the direction indicated by his remarks to his fiancée. Very good. We will now suppose that as he went to the theatre with the young lady he suddenly, in the fog, caught a glimpse of this same agent going in the direction of the office. He was an impetuous man, quick in his decisions. Everything gave way to his duty. He followed the man, reached the window, saw the abstraction of the documents, and pursued the thief. In this way we get over the objection that no one would take originals when he could make copies. This outsider had to take originals. So far it holds together."

"What is the next step?"

"Then we come into difficulties. One would imagine that under such circumstances the first act of young Cadogan West would be to seize the villain and raise the alarm. Why did he not do so? Could it have been an official superior who took the papers? That would explain West's conduct. Or could the chief have given West the slip in the fog, and West started at once to London to head him off from his own rooms, presuming that he knew where the rooms were? The call must have been very pressing, since he left his girl standing in the fog and made no effort to communicate with her. Our scent runs cold here, and there is a vast gap between either hypothesis and the laying of West's body, with seven papers in his pocket, on the roof of a Metropolitan train. My instinct now is to work from the other end. If Mycroft has given us the list of addresses we may be able to pick our man and follow two tracks instead of one."

* * *

Surely enough, a note awaited us at Baker Street. A government messenger had brought it post-haste. Holmes glanced at it and threw it over to me.

> *There are numerous small fry, but few who would handle so big an affair. The only men worth considering are Adolph Mayer, of 13, Great George Street, Westminster; Louis La Rothière, of Campden Mansions, Notting Hill; and Hugo Oberstein, 13, Caulfield Gardens, Kensington. The latter was known to be in town on Monday and is now reported as having left. Glad to hear you have seen some light. The Cabinet awaits your final report with the utmost anxiety. Urgent representations have arrived from the very highest quarter. The whole force of the State is at your back if you should need it. – Mycroft.*

"I'm afraid," said Holmes, smiling, "that all the Queen's horses and all the Queen's men cannot avail in this matter." He had spread out his big map of London and leaned eagerly over it. "Well, well," said he presently with an exclamation of satisfaction, "things are turning a little in our direction at last. Why, Watson, I do honestly believe that we are going to pull it off, after all." He slapped me on the shoulder with a sudden burst of hilarity. "I am going out now. It is only a reconnaissance. I will do nothing serious without my trusted comrade and biographer at my elbow. Do you stay here, and the odds are that you will see me again in an hour or two. If time hangs heavy get foolscap and a pen, and begin your narrative of how we saved the State."

I felt some reflection of his elation in my own mind, for I knew well that he would not depart so far from his usual austerity of demeanour unless there was good cause for exultation. All the long November evening I waited, filled with impatience for his return. At last, shortly after nine o'clock, there arrived a messenger with a note:

> *Am dining at Goldini's Restaurant, Gloucester Road, Kensington. Please come at once and join me there. Bring with you a jemmy, a dark lantern, a chisel, and a revolver. – S.H.*

It was a nice equipment for a respectable citizen to carry through the dim, fog-draped streets. I stowed them all discreetly away in my overcoat and drove straight to the address given. There sat my friend at a little round table near the door of the garish Italian restaurant.

"Have you had something to eat? Then join me in a coffee and curaçao. Try one of the proprietor's cigars. They are less poisonous than one would expect. Have you the tools?"

"They are here, in my overcoat."

"Excellent. Let me give you a short sketch of what I have done, with some indication of what we are about to do. Now it must be evident to you, Watson, that this young man's body was *placed* on the roof of the train. That was clear from the instant that I determined the fact that it was from the roof, and not from a carriage, that he had fallen."

"Could it not have been dropped from a bridge?"

"I should say it was impossible. If you examine the roofs you will find that they are slightly rounded, and there is no railing round them. Therefore, we can say for certain that young Cadogan West was placed on it."

"How could he be placed there?"

"That was the question which we had to answer. There is only one possible way. You are aware that the Underground runs clear of tunnels at some points in the West End. I had a vague memory that as I have travelled by it I have occasionally seen windows just above my head. Now, suppose that a train halted under such a window, would there be any difficulty in laying a body upon the roof?"

"It seems most improbable."

"We must fall back upon the old axiom that when all other contingencies fail, whatever remains, however improbable, must be the truth. Here all other contingencies *have* failed. When I found that the leading international agent, who had just left London, lived in a row of houses which abutted upon the Underground, I was so pleased that you were a little astonished at my sudden frivolity."

"Oh, that was it, was it?"

"Yes, that was it. Mr. Hugo Oberstein, of 13, Caulfield Gardens, had become my objective. I began my operations at Gloucester Road Station, where a very helpful official walked with me along the track and allowed me to satisfy myself not only that the back-stair windows of Caulfield Gardens open on the line but the even more essential fact that, owing to the intersection of one of the larger railways, the Underground trains are frequently held motionless for some minutes at that very spot."

"Splendid, Holmes! You have got it!"

"So far – so far, Watson. We advance, but the goal is afar. Well, having seen the back of Caulfield Gardens, I visited the front and satisfied myself that the bird was indeed flown. It is a considerable house, unfurnished, so far as I could judge, in the upper rooms. Oberstein lived there with a single valet, who was probably a confederate entirely in his confidence. We must bear in mind that Oberstein has gone to the Continent to dispose of his booty, but not with any idea of flight; for he had no reason to fear a warrant, and the idea of an amateur domiciliary visit would certainly never occur to him. Yet that is precisely what we are about to make."

"Could we not get a warrant and legalise it?"

"Hardly on the evidence."

"What can we hope to do?"

"We cannot tell what correspondence may be there."

"I don't like it, Holmes."

"My dear fellow, you shall keep watch in the street. I'll do the criminal part. It's not a time to stick at trifles. Think of Mycroft's note, of the Admiralty, the Cabinet, the exalted person who waits for news. We are bound to go."

My answer was to rise from the table.

"You are right, Holmes. We are bound to go."

He sprang up and shook me by the hand.

"I knew you would not shrink at the last," said he, and for a moment I saw something in his eyes which was nearer to tenderness than I had ever seen. The next instant he was his masterful, practical self once more.

"It is nearly half a mile, but there is no hurry. Let us walk," said he. "Don't drop the instruments, I beg. Your arrest as a suspicious character would be a most unfortunate complication."

Caulfield Gardens was one of those lines of flat-faced pillared, and porticoed houses which are so prominent a product of the middle Victorian epoch in the West End of London. Next door there appeared to be a children's party, for the merry buzz of young voices and the clatter of a piano resounded through the night. The fog still hung about and screened us with its friendly shade. Holmes had lit his lantern and flashed it upon the massive door.

"This is a serious proposition," said he. "It is certainly bolted as well as locked. We would do better in the area. There is an excellent archway down yonder in case a too-zealous policeman should intrude. Give me a hand, Watson, and I'll do the same for you."

A minute later we were both in the area. Hardly had we reached the dark shadows before the step of the policeman was heard in the fog above. As its soft rhythm died away, Holmes set to work upon the lower door. I saw him stoop and strain until with a sharp crash it flew open. We sprang through into the dark passage, closing the area door behind us. Holmes led the way up the curving, uncarpeted stair. His little fan of yellow light shone upon a low window.

"Here we are, Watson – this must be the one." He threw it open, and as he did so there was a low, harsh murmur, growing steadily into a loud roar as a train dashed past us in the darkness. Holmes swept his light along the window-sill. It was thickly coated with soot from the passing engines, but the black surface was blurred and rubbed in places.

"You can see where they rested the body. Halloa, Watson! What is this? There can be no doubt that it is a blood mark." He was pointing to faint discolorations along the woodwork of the window. "Here it is on the stone of the stair also. The demonstration is complete. Let us stay here until a train stops."

We had not long to wait. The very next train roared from the tunnel as before, but slowed in the open, and then, with a creaking of brakes, pulled up immediately beneath us. It was not four feet from the window-ledge to the roof of the carriages. Holmes softly closed the window.

"So far we are justified," said he. "What do you think of it, Watson?"

"A masterpiece. You have never risen to a greater height."

"I cannot agree with you there. From the moment that I conceived the idea of the body being upon the roof, which surely was not a very abstruse one, all the rest was inevitable. If it were not for the grave interests involved the affair up to this point would be insignificant. Our difficulties are still before us. But perhaps we may find something here which may help us."

We had ascended the kitchen stair and entered the suite of rooms upon the first floor. One was a dining room, severely furnished and containing nothing of interest. A second was a bedroom, which also drew blank. The remaining room appeared more promising, and my companion settled down to a systematic examination. It was littered with books and papers, and was evidently used as a study. Swiftly and methodically Holmes turned over the contents of drawer after drawer and cupboard after cupboard, but no gleam of success came to brighten his austere face. At the end of an hour he was no further than when he started.

"The cunning dog has covered his tracks," said he. "He has left nothing to incriminate him. His dangerous correspondence has been destroyed or removed. This is our last chance."

It was a small tin cash-box which stood upon the writing desk. Holmes pried it open with his chisel. Several rolls of paper were within, covered with figures and calculations, without any note to show to what they referred. The recurring words, 'water pressure' and 'pressure to the square inch' suggested some possible relation to a submarine. Holmes tossed them all impatiently aside. There only remained an envelope with some small newspaper slips inside it. He shook them out on the table, and at once I saw by his eager face that his hopes had been raised.

"What's this, Watson? Eh? What's this? Record of a series of messages in the advertisements of a paper. *Daily Telegraph* agony column by the print and paper. Right-hand top corner of a page. No dates – but messages arrange themselves. This must be the first:

> "*Hoped to hear sooner. Terms agreed to. Write fully to address given on card.* – *Pierrot.*

"Next comes:

> "*Too complex for description. Must have full report. Stuff awaits you when goods delivered. – Pierrot.*

"Then comes:

> "*Matter presses. Must withdraw offer unless contract completed. Make appointment by letter. Will confirm by advertisement. – Pierrot.*

"Finally:

> "*Monday night after nine. Two taps. Only ourselves. Do not be so suspicious. Payment in hard cash when goods delivered. – Pierrot.*

"A fairly complete record, Watson! If we could only get at the man at the other end!" He sat lost in thought, tapping his fingers on the table. Finally he sprang to his feet.

"Well, perhaps it won't be so difficult, after all. There is nothing more to be done here, Watson. I think we might drive round to the offices of the *Daily Telegraph*, and so bring a good day's work to a conclusion."

* * *

Mycroft Holmes and Lestrade had come round by appointment after breakfast next day and Sherlock Holmes had recounted to them our proceedings of the day before. The professional shook his head over our confessed burglary.

"We can't do these things in the force, Mr. Holmes," said he. "No wonder you get results that are beyond us. But some of these days you'll go too far, and you'll find yourself and your friend in trouble."

"For England, home and beauty – eh, Watson? Martyrs on the altar of our country. But what do you think of it, Mycroft?"

"Excellent, Sherlock! Admirable! But what use will you make of it?"

Holmes picked up the *Daily Telegraph* which lay upon the table.

"Have you seen Pierrot's advertisement today?"

"What? Another one?"

"Yes, here it is:

"Tonight. Same hour. Same place. Two taps. Most vitally important. Your own safety at stake. – Pierrot.

"By George!" cried Lestrade. "If he answers that we've got him!"

"That was my idea when I put it in. I think if you could both make it convenient to come with us about eight o'clock to Caulfield Gardens we might possibly get a little nearer to a solution."

* * *

One of the most remarkable characteristics of Sherlock Holmes was his power of throwing his brain out of action and switching all his thoughts on to lighter things whenever he had convinced himself that he could no longer work to advantage. I remember that during the whole of that memorable day he lost himself in a monograph which he had undertaken upon the Polyphonic Motets of Lassus. For my own part I had none of this power of detachment, and the day, in consequence, appeared to be interminable. The great national importance of the issue, the suspense in high quarters, the direct nature of the experiment which we were trying – all combined to work upon my nerve. It was a relief to me when at last, after a light dinner, we set out upon our expedition. Lestrade and Mycroft met us by appointment at the outside of Gloucester Road Station. The area door of Oberstein's house had been left open the night before, and it was necessary for me, as Mycroft Holmes absolutely and indignantly declined to climb the railings, to pass in and open the hall door. By nine o'clock we were all seated in the study, waiting patiently for our man.

An hour passed and yet another. When eleven struck, the measured beat of the great church clock seemed to sound the dirge of our hopes. Lestrade and Mycroft were fidgeting in their seats and looking twice a minute at their watches. Holmes sat silent and composed, his eyelids half shut, but every sense on the alert. He raised his head with a sudden jerk.

"He is coming," said he.

There had been a furtive step past the door. Now it returned. We heard a shuffling sound outside, and then two sharp taps with the knocker. Holmes rose, motioning us to remain seated. The gas in the hall was a mere point of light. He opened the outer door, and then as a dark figure slipped past him he closed and fastened it. "This way!" we heard him say, and a moment later our man stood before us. Holmes had followed him closely, and as the man turned with a cry of surprise and alarm he caught him by the collar and threw him back into the room. Before our prisoner had recovered his balance the door was shut and Holmes standing with his back against it. The man glared round him, staggered, and fell senseless upon the floor. With the shock, his broad-brimmed hat flew from his head, his cravat slipped down from his lips, and there were the long light beard and the soft, handsome delicate features of Colonel Valentine Walter.

Holmes gave a whistle of surprise.

"You can write me down an ass this time, Watson," said he. "This was not the bird that I was looking for."

"Who is he?" asked Mycroft eagerly.

"The younger brother of the late Sir James Walter, the head of the Submarine Department. Yes, yes; I see the fall of the cards. He is coming to. I think that you had best leave his examination to me."

We had carried the prostrate body to the sofa. Now our prisoner sat up, looked round him with a horror-stricken face, and passed his hand over his forehead, like one who cannot believe his own senses.

"What is this?" he asked. "I came here to visit Mr. Oberstein."

"Everything is known, Colonel Walter," said Holmes. "How an English gentleman could behave in such a manner is beyond my comprehension. But your whole correspondence and relations with Oberstein are within our knowledge. So also are the circumstances connected with the death of young Cadogan West. Let me advise you to gain at least the small credit for repentance and confession, since there are still some details which we can only learn from your lips."

The man groaned and sank his face in his hands. We waited, but he was silent.

"I can assure you," said Holmes, "that every essential is already known. We know that you were pressed for money; that you took an impress of the keys which your brother held; and that you entered into a correspondence with Oberstein, who answered your letters through the advertisement columns of the *Daily Telegraph*. We are aware that you went down to the office in the fog on Monday night, but that you were seen and followed by young Cadogan West, who had probably some previous reason to suspect you. He saw your theft, but could not give the alarm, as it was just possible that you were taking the papers to your brother in London. Leaving all his private concerns, like the good citizen that he was, he followed you closely in the fog and kept at your heels until you reached this very house. There he intervened, and then it was, Colonel Walter, that to treason you added the more terrible crime of murder."

"I did not! I did not! Before God I swear that I did not!" cried our wretched prisoner.

"Tell us, then, how Cadogan West met his end before you laid him upon the roof of a railway carriage."

"I will. I swear to you that I will. I did the rest. I confess it. It was just as you say. A Stock Exchange debt had to be paid. I needed the money badly. Oberstein offered me five thousand. It was to save myself from ruin. But as to murder, I am as innocent as you."

"What happened, then?"

"He had his suspicions before, and he followed me as you describe. I never knew it until I was at the very door. It was thick fog, and one could not see three yards. I had given two taps and Oberstein had come to the door. The young man rushed up and demanded to know what we were about to do with the papers. Oberstein had a short life-preserver. He always carried it with him. As West forced his way after us into the house Oberstein struck him on the head. The blow was a fatal one. He was dead within five minutes. There he lay in the hall, and we were at our wits' end what to do. Then Oberstein had this idea about the trains which halted under his back window. But first he examined the papers which I had brought. He said that three of them were essential, and that he must keep them. 'You cannot keep them,' said I. 'There will be a dreadful row at Woolwich if they are not returned.' 'I must keep them,' said he, 'for they are so technical that it is impossible in the time to make copies.' 'Then they must all go back together tonight,' said I. He thought for a little, and then he cried out that he had it. 'Three I will keep,' said he. 'The others we will stuff into the pocket of this young man. When he is found the whole business will assuredly be put to his account.' I could see no other way out of it, so we did as he suggested. We waited half an hour at the window before a train stopped. It was so thick that nothing could be seen, and we had no difficulty in lowering West's body on to the train. That was the end of the matter so far as I was concerned."

"And your brother?"

"He said nothing, but he had caught me once with his keys, and I think that he suspected. I read in his eyes that he suspected. As you know, he never held up his head again."

There was silence in the room. It was broken by Mycroft Holmes.

"Can you not make reparation? It would ease your conscience, and possibly your punishment."

"What reparation can I make?"

"Where is Oberstein with the papers?"

"I do not know."

"Did he give you no address?"

"He said that letters to the Hôtel du Louvre, Paris, would eventually reach him."

"Then reparation is still within your power," said Sherlock Holmes.

"I will do anything I can. I owe this fellow no particular good-will. He has been my ruin and my downfall."

"Here are paper and pen. Sit at this desk and write to my dictation. Direct the envelope to the address given. That is right. Now the letter:

> "*Dear Sir:*
>
> "*With regard to our transaction, you will no doubt have observed by now that one essential detail is missing. I have a tracing which will make it complete. This has involved me in extra trouble, however, and I must ask you for a further advance of five hundred pounds. I will not trust it to the post, nor will I take anything but gold or notes. I would come to you abroad, but it would excite remark if I left the country at present. Therefore I shall expect to meet you in the smoking-room of the Charing Cross Hotel at noon on Saturday. Remember that only English notes, or gold, will be taken.*

"That will do very well. I shall be very much surprised if it does not fetch our man."

* * *

And it did! It is a matter of history – that secret history of a nation which is often so much more intimate and interesting than its public chronicles – that Oberstein, eager to complete the coup of his lifetime, came to the lure and was safely engulfed for fifteen years in a British prison. In his trunk were found the invaluable Bruce-Partington plans, which he had put up for auction in all the naval centres of Europe.

Colonel Walter died in prison towards the end of the second year of his sentence. As to Holmes, he returned refreshed to his monograph upon the Polyphonic Motets of Lassus, which has since been printed for private circulation, and is said by experts to be the last word upon the subject. Some weeks afterwards I learned incidentally that my friend spent a day at Windsor, whence he returned with a remarkably fine emerald tie-pin. When I asked him if he had bought it, he answered that it was a present from a certain gracious lady in whose interests he had once been fortunate enough to carry out a small commission. He said no more; but I fancy that I could guess at that lady's august name, and I have little doubt that the emerald pin will forever recall to my friend's memory the adventure of the Bruce-Partington plans.

The Final Problem

Arthur Conan Doyle

IT IS WITH a heavy heart that I take up my pen to write these the last words in which I shall ever record the singular gifts by which my friend Mr. Sherlock Holmes was distinguished. In an incoherent and, as I deeply feel, an entirely inadequate fashion, I have endeavoured to give some account of my strange experiences in his company from the chance which first brought us together at the period of the *Study in Scarlet*, up to the time of his interference in the matter of the 'Naval Treaty' – an interference which had the unquestionable effect of preventing a serious international complication. It was my intention to have stopped there, and to have said nothing of that event which has created a void in my life which the lapse of two years has done little to fill. My hand has been forced, however, by the recent letters in which Colonel James Moriarty defends the memory of his brother, and I have no choice but to lay the facts before the public exactly as they occurred. I alone know the absolute truth of the matter, and I am satisfied that the time has come when no good purpose is to be served by its suppression. As far as I know, there have been only three accounts in the public press: that in the *Journal de Genève* on May 6th, 1891, the Reuter's dispatch in the English papers on May 7th, and finally the recent letters to which I have alluded. Of these the first and second were extremely condensed, while the last is, as I shall now show, an absolute perversion of the facts. It lies with me to tell for the first time what really took place between Professor Moriarty and Mr. Sherlock Holmes.

It may be remembered that after my marriage, and my subsequent start in private practice, the very intimate relations which had existed between Holmes and myself became to some extent modified. He still came to me from time to time when he desired a companion in his investigations, but these occasions grew more and more seldom, until I find that in the year 1890 there were only three cases of which I retain any record. During the winter of that year and the early spring of 1891, I saw in the papers that he had been engaged by the French government upon a matter of supreme importance, and I received two notes from Holmes, dated from Narbonne and from Nimes, from which I gathered that his stay in France was likely to be a long one. It was with some surprise, therefore, that I saw him walk into my consulting-room upon the evening of April 24th. It struck me that he was looking even paler and thinner than usual.

"Yes, I have been using myself up rather too freely," he remarked, in answer to my look rather than to my words; "I have been a little pressed of late. Have you any objection to my closing your shutters?"

The only light in the room came from the lamp upon the table at which I had been reading. Holmes edged his way round the wall, and, flinging the shutters together, he bolted them securely.

"You are afraid of something?" I asked.

"Well, I am."

"Of what?"

"Of air-guns."

"My dear Holmes, what do you mean?"

"I think that you know me well enough, Watson, to understand that I am by no means a nervous man. At the same time, it is stupidity rather than courage to refuse to recognise danger when it is close upon you. Might I trouble you for a match?" He drew in the smoke of his cigarette as if the soothing influence was grateful to him.

"I must apologize for calling so late," said he, "and I must further beg you to be so unconventional as to allow me to leave your house presently by scrambling over your back garden wall."

"But what does it all mean?" I asked.

He held out his hand, and I saw in the light of the lamp that two of his knuckles were burst and bleeding.

"It's not an airy nothing, you see," said he, smiling. "On the contrary, it is solid enough for a man to break his hand over. Is Mrs. Watson in?"

"She is away upon a visit."

"Indeed! You are alone?"

"Quite."

"Then it makes it the easier for me to propose that you should come away with me for a week to the Continent."

"Where?"

"Oh, anywhere. It's all the same to me."

There was something very strange in all this. It was not Holmes's nature to take an aimless holiday, and something about his pale, worn face told me that his nerves were at their highest tension. He saw the question in my eyes, and, putting his fingertips together and his elbows upon his knees, he explained the situation.

"You have probably never heard of Professor Moriarty?" said he.

"Never."

"Ay, there's the genius and the wonder of the thing!" he cried. "The man pervades London, and no one has heard of him. That's what puts him on a pinnacle in the records of crime. I tell you Watson, in all seriousness, that if I could beat that man, if I could free society of him, I should feel that my own career had reached its summit, and I should be prepared to turn to some more placid line in life. Between ourselves, the recent cases in which I have been of assistance to the royal family of Scandinavia, and to the French republic, have left me in such a position that I could continue to live in the quiet fashion which is most congenial to me, and to concentrate my attention upon my chemical researches. But I could not rest. Watson, I could not sit quiet in my chair, if I thought that such a man as Professor Moriarty were walking the streets of London unchallenged."

"What has he done, then?"

"His career has been an extraordinary one. He is a man of good birth and excellent education, endowed by nature with a phenomenal mathematical faculty. At the age of twenty-one he wrote a treatise upon the binomial theorem, which has had a European vogue. On the strength of it he won the mathematical chair at one of our smaller universities, and had, to all appearances, a most brilliant career before him. But the man had hereditary tendencies of the most diabolical kind. A criminal strain ran in his blood, which, instead of being modified, was increased and rendered infinitely more dangerous by his extraordinary mental powers. Dark rumours gathered round him in the university town, and eventually he was compelled to resign his chair and to come down to London, where he set up as an army coach. So much is known to the world, but what I am telling you now is what I have myself discovered.

"As you are aware, Watson, there is no one who knows the higher criminal world of London so well as I do. For years past I have continually been conscious of some power behind the malefactor, some deep organizing power which forever stands in the way of the law, and throws its shield over the wrong-doer. Again and again in cases of the most varying sorts – forgery cases, robberies, murders – I have felt the presence of this force, and I have deduced its action in many of those undiscovered crimes in which I have not been personally consulted. For years I have endeavoured to break through the veil which shrouded it, and at last the time came when I seized my thread and followed it, until it led me, after a thousand cunning windings, to ex-Professor Moriarty, of mathematical celebrity.

"He is the Napoleon of crime, Watson. He is the organizer of half that is evil and of nearly all that is undetected in this great city. He is a genius, a philosopher, an abstract thinker. He has a brain of the first order. He sits motionless, like a spider in the centre of its web, but that web has a thousand radiations, and he knows well every quiver of each of them. He does little himself. He only plans. But his agents are numerous and splendidly organized. If there a crime to be done, a paper to be abstracted, we will say, a house to be rifled, a man to be removed – the word is passed to the professor, the matter is organized and carried out. The agent may be caught. In that case money is found for his bail or his defence. But the central power which uses the agent is never caught – never so much as suspected. This was the organization which I deduced, Watson, and which I devoted my whole energy to exposing and breaking up.

"But the professor was fenced round with safeguards so cunningly devised that, do what I would, it seemed impossible to get evidence which would convict in a court of law. You know my powers, my dear Watson, and yet at the end of three months I was forced to confess that I had at last met an antagonist who was my intellectual equal. My horror at his crimes was lost in my admiration at his skill. But at last he made a trip – only a little, little trip but it was more than he could afford, when I was so close upon him. I had my chance, and, starting from that point, I have woven my net round him until now it is all ready to close. In three days – that is to say, on Monday next – matters will be ripe, and the professor, with all the principal members of his gang, will be in the hands of the police. Then will come the greatest criminal trial of the century, the clearing up of over forty mysteries, and the rope for all of them; but if we move at all prematurely, you understand, they may slip out of our hands even at the last moment.

"Now, if I could have done this without the knowledge of Professor Moriarty, all would have been well. But he was too wily for that. He saw every step which I took to draw my toils round him. Again and again he strove to break away, but I as often headed him off. I tell you, my friend, that if a detailed account of that silent contest could be written, it would take its place as the most brilliant bit of thrust-and-parry work in the history of detection. Never have I risen to such a height, and never have I been so hard-pressed by an opponent. He cut deep, and yet I just undercut him. This morning the last steps were taken, and three days only were wanted to complete the business. I was sitting in my room thinking the matter over when the door opened and Professor Moriarty stood before me.

"My nerves are fairly proof, Watson, but I must confess to a start when I saw the very man who had been so much in my thoughts standing there on my threshold. His appearance was quite familiar to me. He is extremely tall and thin, his forehead domes out in a white curve, and his two eyes are deeply sunken in his head. He is clean-shaven, pale, and ascetic-looking, retaining something of the professor in his features. His shoulders are rounded from much study, and his face protrudes forward and is forever slowly oscillating from side to side in a curiously reptilian fashion. He peered at me with great curiosity in his puckered eyes.

"'You have less frontal development than I should have expected,' said he at last. 'It is a dangerous habit to finger loaded firearms in the pocket of one's dressing-gown.'

"The fact is that upon his entrance I had instantly recognised the extreme personal danger in which I lay. The only conceivable escape for him lay in silencing my tongue. In an instant I had slipped the revolver from the drawer into my pocket and was covering him through the cloth. At his remark I drew the weapon out and laid it cocked upon the table. He still smiled and blinked, but there was something about his eyes which made me feel very glad that I had it there.

"'You evidently don't know me,' said he.

"'On the contrary,' I answered, 'I think it is fairly evident that I do. Pray take a chair. I can spare you five minutes if you have anything to say.'

"'All that I have to say has already crossed your mind,' said he.

"'Then possibly my answer has crossed yours,' I replied.

"'You stand fast?'

"'Absolutely.'

"He clapped his hand into his pocket, and I raised the pistol from the table. But he merely drew out a memorandum-book in which he had scribbled some dates.

"'You crossed my path on the fourth of January,' said he. 'On the twenty-third you incommoded me; by the middle of February I was seriously inconvenienced by you; at the end of March I was absolutely hampered in my plans; and now, at the close of April, I find myself placed in such a position through your continual persecution that I am in positive danger of losing my liberty. The situation is becoming an impossible one.'

"'Have you any suggestion to make?' I asked.

"'You must drop it, Mr. Holmes,' said he, swaying his face about. 'You really must, you know.'

"'After Monday,' said I.

"'Tut, tut!' said he. 'I am quite sure that a man of your intelligence will see that there can be but one outcome to this affair. It is necessary that you should withdraw. You have worked things in such a fashion that we have only one resource left. It has been an intellectual treat to me to see the way in which you have grappled with this affair, and I say, unaffectedly, that it would be a grief to me to be forced to take any extreme measure. You smile, sir, but I assure you that it really would.'

"'Danger is part of my trade,' I remarked.

"'This is not danger,' said he. 'It is inevitable destruction. You stand in the way not merely of an individual but of a mighty organization, the full extent of which you, with all your cleverness, have been unable to realize. You must stand clear, Mr. Holmes, or be trodden underfoot.'

"'I am afraid,' said I, rising, 'that in the pleasure of this conversation I am neglecting business of importance which awaits me elsewhere.'

"He rose also and looked at me in silence, shaking his head sadly.

"'Well, well,' said he at last. 'It seems a pity, but I have done what I could. I know every move of your game. You can do nothing before Monday. It has been a duel between you and me, Mr. Holmes. You hope to place me in the dock. I tell you that I will never stand in the dock. You hope to beat me. I tell you that you will never beat me. If you are clever enough to bring destruction upon me, rest assured that I shall do as much to you.'

"'You have paid me several compliments, Mr. Moriarty,' said I. 'Let me pay you one in return when I say that if I were assured of the former eventuality I would, in the interests of the public, cheerfully accept the latter.'

"'I can promise you the one, but not the other,' he snarled, and so turned his rounded back upon me and went peering and blinking out of the room.

"That was my singular interview with Professor Moriarty. I confess that it left an unpleasant effect upon my mind. His soft, precise fashion of speech leaves a conviction of sincerity which a mere bully could not produce. Of course, you will say: 'Why not take police precautions against him?' The reason is that I am well convinced that it is from his agents the blow would fall. I have the best of proofs that it would be so."

"You have already been assaulted?"

"My dear Watson, Professor Moriarty is not a man who lets the grass grow under his feet. I went out about midday to transact some business in Oxford Street. As I passed the corner which leads from Bentinck Street on to the Welbeck Street crossing a two-horse van furiously driven whizzed round and was on me like a flash. I sprang for the footpath and saved myself by the fraction of a second. The van dashed round by Marylebone Lane and was gone in an instant. I kept to the pavement after that, Watson, but as I walked down Vere Street a brick came down from the roof of one of the houses and was shattered to fragments at my feet. I called the police and had the place examined. There were slates and bricks piled up on the roof preparatory to some repairs, and they would have me believe that the wind had toppled over one of these. Of course I knew better, but I could prove nothing. I took a cab after that and reached my brother's rooms in Pall Mall, where I spent the day. Now I have come round to you, and on my way I was attacked by a rough with a bludgeon. I knocked him down, and the police have him in custody; but I can tell you with the most absolute confidence that no possible connection will ever be traced between the gentleman upon whose front teeth I have barked my knuckles and the retiring mathematical coach, who is, I daresay, working out problems upon a blackboard ten miles away. You will not wonder, Watson, that my first act on entering your rooms was to close your shutters, and that I have been compelled to ask your permission to leave the house by some less conspicuous exit than the front door."

I had often admired my friend's courage, but never more than now, as he sat quietly checking off a series of incidents which must have combined to make up a day of horror.

"You will spend the night here?" I said.

"No, my friend, you might find me a dangerous guest. I have my plans laid, and all will be well. Matters have gone so far now that they can move without my help as far as the arrest goes, though my presence is necessary for a conviction. It is obvious, therefore, that I cannot do better than get away for the few days which remain before the police are at liberty to act. It would be a great pleasure to me, therefore, if you could come on to the Continent with me."

"The practice is quiet," said I, "and I have an accommodating neighbour. I should be glad to come."

"And to start tomorrow morning?"

"If necessary."

"Oh, yes, it is most necessary. Then these are your instructions, and I beg, my dear Watson, that you will obey them to the letter, for you are now playing a double-handed game with me against the cleverest rogue and the most powerful syndicate of criminals in Europe. Now listen! You will dispatch whatever luggage you intend to take by a trusty messenger unaddressed to Victoria tonight. In the morning you will send for a hansom, desiring your man to take neither the first nor the second which may present itself. Into this hansom you will jump, and you will drive to the Strand end of the Lowther Arcade, handing the address to the cabman upon a slip of paper, with a request that he will not throw it away. Have your fare ready, and the instant that your cab stops, dash through the Arcade, timing yourself to reach the other side at a quarter-past nine. You will find a small brougham waiting close to the curb, driven by a fellow with a heavy black cloak tipped at the collar with red. Into this you will step, and you will reach Victoria in time for the Continental express."

"Where shall I meet you?"

"At the station. The second first-class carriage from the front will be reserved for us."

"The carriage is our rendezvous, then?"

"Yes."

It was in vain that I asked Holmes to remain for the evening. It was evident to me that he thought he might bring trouble to the roof he was under, and that that was the motive which impelled him to go. With a few hurried words as to our plans for the morrow he rose and came out with me into the garden, clambering over the wall which leads into Mortimer Street, and immediately whistling for a hansom, in which I heard him drive away.

In the morning I obeyed Holmes's injunctions to the letter. A hansom was procured with such precautions as would prevent its being one which was placed ready for us, and I drove immediately after breakfast to the Lowther Arcade, through which I hurried at the top of my speed. A brougham was waiting with a very massive driver wrapped in a dark cloak, who, the instant that I had stepped in, whipped up the horse and rattled off to Victoria Station. On my alighting there he turned the carriage, and dashed away again without so much as a look in my direction.

So far all had gone admirably. My luggage was waiting for me, and I had no difficulty in finding the carriage which Holmes had indicated, the less so as it was the only one in the train which was marked 'Engaged'. My only source of anxiety now was the non-appearance of Holmes. The station clock marked only seven minutes from the time when we were due to start. In vain I searched among the groups of travellers and leave-takers for the lithe figure of my friend. There was no sign of him. I spent a few minutes in assisting a venerable Italian priest, who was endeavouring to make a porter understand, in his broken English, that his luggage was to be booked through to Paris. Then, having taken another look round, I returned to my carriage, where I found that the porter, in spite of the ticket, had given me my decrepit Italian friend as a travelling companion. It was useless for me to explain to him that his presence was an intrusion, for my Italian was even more limited than his English, so I shrugged my shoulders resignedly, and continued to look out anxiously for my friend. A chill of fear had come over me, as I thought that his absence might mean that some blow had fallen during the night. Already the doors had all been shut and the whistle blown, when—

"My dear Watson," said a voice, "you have not even condescended to say good morning."

I turned in uncontrollable astonishment. The aged ecclesiastic had turned his face towards me. For an instant the wrinkles were smoothed away, the nose drew away from the chin, the lower lip ceased to protrude and the mouth to mumble, the dull eyes regained their fire, the drooping figure expanded. The next the whole frame collapsed again, and Holmes had gone as quickly as he had come.

"Good heavens!" I cried, "How you startled me!"

"Every precaution is still necessary," he whispered. "I have reason to think that they are hot upon our trail. Ah, there is Moriarty himself."

The train had already begun to move as Holmes spoke. Glancing back, I saw a tall man pushing his way furiously through the crowd, and waving his hand as if he desired to have the train stopped. It was too late, however, for we were rapidly gathering momentum, and an instant later had shot clear of the station.

"With all our precautions, you see that we have cut it rather fine," said Holmes, laughing. He rose, and throwing off the black cassock and hat which had formed his disguise, he packed them away in a hand-bag.

"Have you seen the morning paper, Watson?"

"No."

"You haven't seen about Baker Street, then?"

"Baker Street?"

"They set fire to our rooms last night. No great harm was done."

"Good heavens, Holmes, this is intolerable!"

"They must have lost my track completely after their bludgeon-man was arrested. Otherwise they could not have imagined that I had returned to my rooms. They have evidently taken the precaution of watching you, however, and that is what has brought Moriarty to Victoria. You could not have made any slip in coming?"

"I did exactly what you advised."

"Did you find your brougham?"

"Yes, it was waiting."

"Did you recognise your coachman?"

"No."

"It was my brother Mycroft. It is an advantage to get about in such a case without taking a mercenary into your confidence. But we must plan what we are to do about Moriarty now."

"As this is an express, and as the boat runs in connection with it, I should think we have shaken him off very effectively."

"My dear Watson, you evidently did not realize my meaning when I said that this man may be taken as being quite on the same intellectual plane as myself. You do not imagine that if I were the pursuer I should allow myself to be baffled by so slight an obstacle. Why, then, should you think so meanly of him?"

"What will he do?"

"What I should do."

"What would you do, then?"

"Engage a special."

"But it must be late."

"By no means. This train stops at Canterbury; and there is always at least a quarter of an hour's delay at the boat. He will catch us there."

"One would think that we were the criminals. Let us have him arrested on his arrival."

"It would be to ruin the work of three months. We should get the big fish, but the smaller would dart right and left out of the net. On Monday we should have them all. No, an arrest is inadmissible."

"What then?"

"We shall get out at Canterbury."

"And then?"

"Well, then we must make a cross-country journey to Newhaven, and so over to Dieppe. Moriarty will again do what I should do. He will get on to Paris, mark down our luggage, and wait for two days at the depot. In the meantime we shall treat ourselves to a couple of carpet-bags, encourage the manufactures of the countries through which we travel, and make our way at our leisure into Switzerland, via Luxembourg and Basle."

At Canterbury, therefore, we alighted, only to find that we should have to wait an hour before we could get a train to Newhaven.

I was still looking rather ruefully after the rapidly disappearing luggage-van which contained my wardrobe, when Holmes pulled my sleeve and pointed up the line. "Already, you see," said he.

Far away, from among the Kentish woods there rose a thin spray of smoke. A minute later a carriage and engine could be seen flying along the open curve which leads to the station. We had hardly time to take our place behind a pile of luggage when it passed with a rattle and a roar, beating a blast of hot air into our faces.

"There he goes," said Holmes, as we watched the carriage swing and rock over the points. "There are limits, you see, to our friend's intelligence. It would have been a *coup-de-maître*[1] had he deduced what I would deduce and acted accordingly."

"And what would he have done had he overtaken us?"

"There cannot be the least doubt that he would have made a murderous attack upon me. It is, however, a game at which two may play. The question now is whether we should take a premature lunch here, or run our chance of starving before we reach the buffet at Newhaven."

We made our way to Brussels that night and spent two days there, moving on upon the third day as far as Strasbourg. On the Monday morning Holmes had telegraphed to the London police, and in the evening we found a reply waiting for us at our hotel. Holmes tore it open, and then with a bitter curse hurled it into the grate.

"I might have known it!" he groaned. "He has escaped!"

"Moriarty?"

"They have secured the whole gang with the exception of him. He has given them the slip. Of course, when I had left the country there was no one to cope with him. But I did think that I had put the game in their hands. I think that you had better return to England, Watson."

"Why?"

"Because you will find me a dangerous companion now. This man's occupation is gone. He is lost if he returns to London. If I read his character right he will devote his whole energies to revenging himself upon me. He said as much in our short interview, and I fancy that he meant it. I should certainly recommend you to return to your practice."

It was hardly an appeal to be successful with one who was an old campaigner as well as an old friend. We sat in the Strasbourg *salle-à-manger*[2] arguing the question for half an hour, but the same night we had resumed our journey and were well on our way to Geneva.

For a charming week we wandered up the valley of the Rhone, and then, branching off at Leuk, we made our way over the Gemmi Pass, still deep in snow, and so, by way of Interlaken, to Meiringen. It was a lovely trip, the dainty green of the spring below, the virgin white of the winter above; but it was clear to me that never for one instant did Holmes forget the shadow which lay across him. In the homely Alpine villages or in the lonely mountain passes, I could still tell by his quick glancing eyes and his sharp scrutiny of every face that passed us, that he was well convinced that, walk where we would, we could not walk ourselves clear of the danger which was dogging our footsteps

Once, I remember, as we passed over the Gemmi, and walked along the border of the melancholy Daubensee, a large rock which had been dislodged from the ridge upon our right clattered down and roared into the lake behind us. In an instant Holmes had raced up on to the ridge, and, standing upon a lofty pinnacle, craned his neck in every direction. It was in vain that our guide assured him that a fall of stones was a common chance in the springtime at that spot. He said nothing, but he smiled at me with the air of a man who sees the fulfilment of that which he had expected.

And yet for all his watchfulness he was never depressed. On the contrary, I can never recollect having seen him in such exuberant spirits. Again and again he recurred to the fact that if he could be assured that society was freed from Professor Moriarty he would cheerfully bring his own career to a conclusion.

"I think that I may go so far as to say, Watson, that I have not lived wholly in vain," he remarked. "If my record were closed tonight I could still survey it with equanimity. The air of London is the sweeter for my presence. In over a thousand cases I am not aware that I have ever used my powers upon the wrong side. Of late I have been tempted to look into the problems furnished by nature rather than those more superficial ones for which our artificial state of society is responsible. Your memoirs will draw to an end, Watson, upon the day that I crown my career by the capture or extinction of the most dangerous and capable criminal in Europe."

I shall be brief, and yet exact, in the little which remains for me to tell. It is not a subject on which I would willingly dwell, and yet I am conscious that a duty devolves upon me to omit no detail.

It was on the third of May that we reached the little village of Meiringen, where we put up at the Englischer Hof, then kept by Peter Steiler the elder. Our landlord was an intelligent man and spoke excellent English, having served for three years as waiter at the Grosvenor Hotel in London. At his advice, on the afternoon of the fourth we set off together, with the intention of crossing the hills and spending the night at the hamlet of Rosenlaui. We had strict injunctions, however, on no account to pass the falls of Reichenbach, which are about halfway up the hills, without making a small detour to see them.

It is, indeed, a fearful place. The torrent, swollen by the melting snow, plunges into a tremendous abyss, from which the spray rolls up like the smoke from a burning house. The shaft into which the river hurls itself is an immense chasm, lined by glistening coal-black rock, and narrowing into a creaming, boiling pit of incalculable depth, which brims over and shoots the stream onward over its jagged lip. The long sweep of green water roaring forever down, and the thick flickering curtain of spray hissing forever upward, turn a man giddy with their constant whirl and clamour. We stood near the edge peering down at the gleam of the breaking water far below us against the black rocks, and listening to the half-human shout which came booming up with the spray out of the abyss.

The path has been cut halfway round the fall to afford a complete view, but it ends abruptly, and the traveller has to return as he came. We had turned to do so, when we saw a Swiss lad come running along it with a letter in his hand. It bore the mark of the hotel which we had just left and was addressed to me by the landlord. It appeared that within a very few minutes of our leaving, an English lady had arrived who was in the last stage of consumption. She had wintered at Davos Platz and was journeying now to join her friends at Lucerne, when a sudden haemorrhage had overtaken her. It was thought that she could hardly live a few hours, but it would be a great consolation to her to see an English doctor, and, if I would only return, *etc*. The good Steiler assured me in a postscript that he would himself look upon my compliance as a very great favour, since the lady absolutely refused to see a Swiss physician, and he could not but feel that he was incurring a great responsibility.

The appeal was one which could not be ignored. It was impossible to refuse the request of a fellow countrywoman dying in a strange land. Yet I had my scruples about leaving Holmes. It was finally agreed, however, that he should retain the young Swiss messenger with him as guide and companion while I returned to Meiringen. My friend would stay some little time at the fall, he said, and would then walk slowly over the hill to Rosenlaui, where I was to rejoin him in the evening. As I turned away I saw Holmes, with his back against a rock and his arms folded, gazing down at the rush of the waters. It was the last that I was ever destined to see of him in this world.

When I was near the bottom of the descent I looked back. It was impossible, from that position, to see the fall, but I could see the curving path which winds over the shoulder of the hills and leads to it. Along this a man was, I remember, walking very rapidly.

I could see his black figure clearly outlined against the green behind him. I noted him, and the energy with which he walked, but he passed from my mind again as I hurried on upon my errand.

It may have been a little over an hour before I reached Meiringen. Old Steiler was standing at the porch of his hotel.

"Well," said I, as I came hurrying up, "I trust that she is no worse?"

A look of surprise passed over his face, and at the first quiver of his eyebrows my heart turned to lead in my breast.

"You did not write this?" I said, pulling the letter from my pocket. "There is no sick Englishwoman in the hotel?"

"Certainly not!" he cried. "But it has the hotel mark upon it! Ha, it must have been written by that tall Englishman who came in after you had gone. He said—"

But I waited for none of the landlord's explanation. In a tingle of fear I was already running down the village street, and making for the path which I had so lately descended. It had taken me an hour to come down. For all my efforts two more had passed before I found myself at the fall of Reichenbach once more. There was Holmes's Alpine-stock still leaning against the rock by which I had left him. But there was no sign of him, and it was in vain that I shouted. My only answer was my own voice reverberating in a rolling echo from the cliffs around me.

It was the sight of that Alpine-stock which turned me cold and sick. He had not gone to Rosenlaui, then. He had remained on that three-foot path, with sheer wall on one side and sheer drop on the other, until his enemy had overtaken him. The young Swiss had gone too. He had probably been in the pay of Moriarty and had left the two men together. And then what had happened? Who was to tell us what had happened then?

I stood for a minute or two to collect myself, for I was dazed with the horror of the thing. Then I began to think of Holmes's own methods and to try to practise them in reading this tragedy. It was, alas, only too easy to do. During our conversation we had not gone to the end of the path, and the Alpine-stock marked the place where we had stood. The blackish soil is kept forever soft by the incessant drift of spray, and a bird would leave its tread upon it. Two lines of footmarks were clearly marked along the farther end of the path, both leading away from me. There were none returning. A few yards from the end the soil was all ploughed up into a patch of mud, and the brambles and ferns which fringed the chasm were torn and bedraggled. I lay upon my face and peered over with the spray spouting up all around me. It had darkened since I left, and now I could only see here and there the glistening of moisture upon the black walls, and far away down at the end of the shaft the gleam of the broken water. I shouted; but only that same half-human cry of the fall was borne back to my ears.

But it was destined that I should, after all, have a last word of greeting from my friend and comrade. I have said that his Alpine-stock had been left leaning against a rock which jutted on to the path. From the top of this boulder the gleam of something bright caught my eye, and raising my hand I found that it came from the silver cigarette-case which he used to carry. As I took it up a small square of paper upon which it had lain fluttered down on to the ground. Unfolding it, I found that it consisted of three pages torn from his notebook and addressed to me. It was characteristic of the man that the direction was as precise, and the writing as firm and clear, as though it had been written in his study.

> *My dear Watson* [it said]:
> *I write these few lines through the courtesy of Mr. Moriarty, who awaits my convenience for the final discussion of those questions which lie between us. He has been giving me a sketch of the methods by which he avoided the English police and kept himself informed of our movements. They certainly confirm the very high opinion which I had formed of his abilities. I am pleased to think that I shall be able to free society from any further effects of his presence, though I fear that it is at a cost which will give pain to my friends, and especially, my dear Watson, to you. I have already explained to you, however, that my career had in any case reached its crisis, and that no possible conclusion to it could be more congenial to me than this. Indeed, if I may make a full confession to you, I was quite convinced that the letter from Meiringen was a hoax, and I allowed you to depart on that errand under the persuasion that some development of this sort would follow. Tell Inspector Patterson that the papers which he needs to convict the gang are in pigeonhole M., done up in a blue envelope and inscribed 'Moriarty'. I made every disposition of my property before leaving England and handed it to my brother Mycroft. Pray give my greetings to Mrs. Watson, and believe me to be, my dear fellow*
> *Very sincerely yours,*
> *Sherlock Holmes.*

A few words may suffice to tell the little that remains. An examination by experts leaves little doubt that a personal contest between the two men ended, as it could hardly fail to end in such a situation, in their reeling over, locked in each other's arms. Any attempt at recovering the bodies was absolutely hopeless, and there, deep down in that dreadful cauldron of swirling water and seething foam, will lie for all time the most dangerous criminal and the foremost champion of the law of their generation. The Swiss youth was never found again, and there can be no doubt that he was one of the numerous agents whom Moriarty kept in his employ. As to the gang, it will be within the memory of the public how completely the evidence which Holmes had accumulated exposed their organization, and how heavily the hand of the dead man weighed upon them. Of their terrible chief few details came out during the proceedings, and if I have now been compelled to make a clear statement of his career, it is due to those injudicious champions who have endeavoured to clear his memory by attacks upon him whom I shall ever regard as the best and the wisest man whom I have ever known.

Footnotes for 'The Final Problem'

   1. Masterstroke.
   2. Dining room.

The Man Who Was Missing

Mignon G. Eberhart

SUSAN DARE waited in the dusk. Above her into the night rose the dim, dark outline of Notre Dame. The heavy doors behind her slowly opened now and then, and closed, as an occasional figure went in or out of the church. Mariette, thought Susan, ought to come soon. Perhaps she herself was a little early at their meeting place, for she hadn't known exactly how to find the French quarter. She hadn't, in fact, known that there was a French quarter in all Chicago.

Yet she hadn't been surprised when Mariette Berne told her that, until times were better, she was living there. She would, of course, have sought her own people. Susan wondered if she would recognize the girl. It had been so long since Susan had been taken in frilly white dresses and huge hair-ribbons to Monsieur Berne's dancing school. Mariette Berne had been then a tiny, dark-eyed wisp of a child; dancing, said the elders approvingly, like a fairy. And now years had passed, and Monsieur Berne's dancing school was no more, and tiny Mariette Berne had grown up and had become a ballet dancer and had telephoned to Susan out of that fragrant past.

If it hadn't been for that past, if the girl's voice hadn't been so soft and appealing, if she hadn't – Come, now, Susan admonished Susan, admit the truth! It's not sentiment that's brought you here. And it's not because a probably fourth-rate artist has taken it into his head to disappear and that he was engaged to marry little Mariette Berne. It's because of the soap on the shaving brush.

A woman came swiftly from the dusk and approached the door of the church. She was tall and slender and, as there was a light above the door, Susan caught an instant's glimpse of a singularly regular face and carefully arranged dark hair. There was something about her – her hat, perhaps, or the sleek lines of her thin light gown – that was not what Susan would have expected to see just there. But at the moment she was only concerned with the fact that the woman could not be Mariette Berne, for she did not hesitate at sight of Susan but went rather hurriedly into the church, and the door closed behind her.

It was terrifically hot. Susan shifted the thin white coat on her arm and was thankful she had worn the thinnest, coolest tailored white silk her summer wardrobe included.

She wished that Mariette would come. And just then she came, emerging from the twilight.

Susan recognized her at once. Her great, soft dark eyes had changed only to hold sorrow. Her hair made a dark cloud for her heart-shaped face, which with maturity had grown beautiful. Her hand met and clung to Susan's.

"Oh, Miss Dare – you will do it, then? You will find André?"

"I'll try," said Susan, wishing the girl's eyes were not so terribly beseeching. "I'll try. But I may not succeed."

"Oh, but you will," cried the girl with soft earnestness. "I know about you. I've read your books – you can solve *any* mystery."

"Look here, my dear," said Susan gently. "Are you sure that you want to know? Can you face it if—"

"If – he's dead, you mean?" breathed the girl. Her hands clasped and unclasped, but there was suddenly a clear, firm strength about her mouth. "I must know," she said in a whisper. "Whatever it is – *I must know.*"

It wasn't what Susan had meant. A voluntary disappearance on the part of the artist had been in her mind.

"You see," added Mariette quite simply, "he would let me know – if he could. If he were alive he would let me know."

After a moment Susan leaned over toward the small dressing case she had brought. "You've told Madame Touseau that you were bringing me?" she asked.

"Yes," said Mariette. "There is a room next to mine. I told her you were a friend of mine. Out of a job." They walked down the steps and off into the mysterious dusk. "But Madame," said Mariette doubtfully, "is very keen."

"Let me see if I have things straight. Madame Touseau owns the house where you live?"

"Yes. There are several roomers. She calls us guests. We have meals there, too, and it is very good cooking. Everything is very clean, and doesn't cost much."

"How many people live there?"

"There's me. And André had a studio in the top floor – the attic. Then there are now, only Mr. Kinder, and Louis Malmin. The maid-of-all-work, Agnes, sleeps out."

"Tell me again," said Susan, "just what happened."

"Well – first you must understand that Madame is very sharp. Nothing at all happens in the house that she does not discover one way or another. I mean, when she says the doors were bolted for the night *after* the guests were all inside the house, and that André did not go out again before the doors were bolted, then that is right. Of course, now, she says that she is not sure. But the doors were bolted on the inside the next morning. I know that."

"Windows?" suggested Susan.

"I don't think so," said Mariette. "His windows are very high, you know, with a straight drop to the street. And in these streets it is well to keep houses locked. That night – that was Wednesday night, two nights ago – André said goodnight to me there in the corridor. I watched him walk up the stairs to his studio in the attic. At the door he turned and waved at me, as he always does. And – that was the last time he was seen. He closed the door and – vanished. Simply dropped out of sight."

They walked on for a few steps in silence. Around them, lining the narrow streets, were tall houses, their shabbiness and their smoke-stained walls hidden by the night.

When Susan spoke, her voice had lowered. "Madame did not want you to call the police?"

"She would not permit it," said the girl slowly. "Madame – is very determined. As you will see."

Madame's changing story bothered Susan. Still, perhaps the woman had honestly not heard André's departure, and then, when it became evident that he had gone, had been obliged to admit her mistake. Yet the door had been bolted on the inside: was that a mistake – or had he gone out some other way? After all, there were windows on the first floor.

"Madame," said Mariette softly, "would be in a rage if she knew that I had told you. She says that André grew tired – of me."

"I expect he could have got out of the house some way if he had wanted to," said Susan, lost in thought.

"Perhaps," said Mariette, in a way that rejected it completely. "But there is the shaving brush, Miss Dare. A man does not put soap on a wet shaving brush and then make up his mind to disappear. And do so taking nothing at all with him. Not even his money."

"Money?"

"Not very much," said Mariette with a sigh. "It was hidden under a brick of the fireplace. I took it," she added with simplicity. "No need to let Madame find it. I will take care of it for him. There's only a little."

"Have you watched the papers?" asked Susan.

"Oh, yes. There's been nothing. No accident – no—" the girl choked and said – "no suicide. Nothing that I could think would be André."

Well, of course, a man would scarcely start to shave, be overcome with a desire to commit suicide in the middle of it, and dash away to hurl himself – where? In the river, perhaps.

And there was something strange, something indecipherable about Mariette's bald little story that caught and held Susan. It might prove to be merely a voluntary disappearance of a man who was important only to himself and to Mariette. Yet its very unimportance was perplexing. Why had he disappeared so suddenly and so completely?

"Had he any enemies?" she asked abruptly. "Did he ever seem to have sums of money?"

"No, no. You are thinking of racketeers. It was nothing like that. André wanted only to paint."

If he had not left of his own free will, then he had been kidnapped. Or murdered. Murder was probably not unknown along that street. But what was the motive?

Quite suddenly Susan thought of Jim Byrne. But he had been out of town for a week following a difficult assignment that had to do with an extradition case then usurping newspaper space. And besides, Jim had not seen the appeal in the girl's soft dark eyes.

"But André has been gone only two nights," Susan said. "Surely you need not—" She never knew what she had intended to say, for the girl whirled suddenly toward her. Her white face and dark eyes looked tragic in the dusk.

"I am afraid," said the girl tensely. "There is something wrong about the house. Something terribly wrong. Something – Here is the house, Miss Dare."

She turned, and Susan looked up at the darkly looming house above them and was conscious of a wish that Jim had returned. Well, she could leave if she wanted to. There was nothing at all to keep her there.

A heavy door, stained with many years of Chicago's smoke, closed behind them, and Susan blinked in the mellow light of a spacious and somewhat elegant entrance hall. The house had been evidently one of the half circle about Chicago of one-time beautiful residences that gave way gradually to the encroachments of warehouses and factories and the steady wave of foreign breadwinners.

Then Mariette was leading her to the wide doorway and into a long crowded living room – crowded with furniture, crowded with plants in pots, crowded with embroidered and laced cushions and footstools and table covers.

There were two people in the room. A woman of perhaps fifty sat under a light, with her sleek, dark hair bent over something like a cushion on her lap. Not far from her a man at a table played some kind of card game.

"Madame," said Mariette, "it is my friend, Miss Dare."

Madame turned, and the light fell strongly upon her. She was dark and heavy and scrupulously neat. Her features were coarse and strong and swarthy. Her eyes were very black, she had a faint mustache across her upper lip, and there were two black marks like warts on one lower eyelid which gave her an extremely sinister look.

She looked Susan up and down. Clearly Madame Touseau's roomers had to pass some test and standard hidden away back in Madame Touseau's Gallic mind. Clearly, too, there was something about Susan which did not altogether please Madame Touseau.

She said something in quick French to Mariette, and Susan caught only Mariette's reply, which was something about a department store and seemed to reassure Madame.

She smiled, disclosing strong yellow teeth.

"You may have one of my rooms," she said. "I'll show you at once. A friend of Mariette's—" She did not finish, and Susan felt that Mariette had vouched for her respectability. The man at the table flipped the cards together with a sigh.

Madame was rolling up intricate white threads. She was an expert lace-maker, for her strong broad hands were inconceivably quick and delicate in their touch. The tiny wooden bobbins clicked faintly against each other as she put down the cushion upon which she worked and which held, firmly pinned, the lace she was making.

"Is it as hot outdoors as it is inside?" said the man at the table, turning to watch and rippling the cards idly.

"Worse," said Mariette. "Miss Dare, this is Mr. Kinder."

Kinder rose and bowed. He was a man of somewhat uncertain age, with a thin face and shoulders and a surprising thickness of body upon long thin legs. His hair was black and he wore a straggly beard, black also. His eyes looked tired and wearily sharp. A small muscle near his mouth twitched as he said something polite to Susan.

Madame said abruptly: "Will you come with me, Miss Dare? I must ask you to sign my guest register. This is not the hotel nor the rooming house, but one is obliged to follow the letter of the law, nevertheless."

She snapped on the light above a long blotter-covered table in the hall, and pulled forward a small ledger.

"Your name, please, and former address. And your occupation. Here is a pen."

Susan sat down slowly in the chair Madame pulled forward and took the pen. Madame was taking no chances – yet perhaps the register was demanded by law and not, as it looked, a ruse to protect herself against unwelcome guests.

Susan looked at the names written on the page Madame placed before her. Looked, and her eyes became thoughtful.

Mariette had not been mistaken then. There was something wrong about the house.

Aware of Madame's brooding regard, Susan slowly wrote her name and address in the space below Louis Malmin. Taking advantage of Mariette's statement that she was out of a job, she left the occupation unnamed.

Madame read it and led the way upstairs.

The room to which she showed Susan was terrifically hot and airless but scrupulously clean. Susan opened the windows as soon as Madame had gone.

The night was hot and still, too, with not a breath of air moving. Away off somewhere she could hear the faint rush and clangor of an elevated train, muffled by heat and distance. Above her was the third-floor studio from which André Cavalliere had so curiously vanished. Tomorrow she would examine it at her leisure.

Mariette, coming quietly to the door, told her definitely of the arrangement of the rooms which Madame had let to her guests. Mariette's own room was beside Susan's, with a vacant room beyond that. Across the back of the house was another vacant room.

"Madame, herself," said Mariette, "has the large room at the front of the house, at the head of the stairs. Across the hall is Mr. Kinder's room: it is the largest and best room, and he pays more than the rest of us. Then beside his room is that of Louis."

"Louis Malmin, is it?"

"Yes. Louis Malmin. An importer of oriental things: he is here for the Century of Progress."

"How long has he been here?"

"Nearly two years. He knows André. André did some silhouettes for him. But they are on good terms."

"Who is Kinder?"

"He was here when I came two years ago. He is a retired salesman. He is not in good health."

"Does he know André?"

"Oh, yes. We are all well acquainted. Madame calls us her family."

Susan had not been strongly impressed with a sense of the sincerity of Madame's sentiment. Still, a tiger could purr for its food and hide the unsheathing of its claws. "It's late," said Susan. "We'll talk in the morning."

But after Mariette had gone, she sat at the window for a long time. Madame, Mariette, Kinder, and Louis Malmin. André Cavalliere who had vanished in that hot, silent house.

Two nights ago, when André Cavalliere had gone to his attic studio and vanished, there had been only four others in the house. Had one of them had something to do with that disappearance?

In the silence of the night it seemed possible.

Down the hall Madame was waiting like a sleeping tiger behind her closed door. Susan felt altogether sure that Madame would know of any sound or movement on the stairway or along the hall. If André Cavalliere had gone out that night, Madame would have known of it. But if he had not gone out, what had happened to him?

It was not a pleasant thought, and it haunted Susan through a long and stifling night. Morning dawned; the air was still hot and misty, and it was an effort to breathe.

While the others were at breakfast in the dining room downstairs Mariette took Susan up to the third floor.

"I took the key," she said, unlocking the low door that led directly from the stairway into the wide, long room which extended, except where it had been walled up under the eaves, over the entire space of the house. The walls and low ceiling, which followed in outline the peaked roof, had been plastered and were hung with a variety of paintings.

At one end was a sort of kitchen, with a small gas plate and a table and some shelves. Along one side and behind a screen was a couch and a mirror and dressing table.

"There," said Mariette, pointing, and Susan bent to look closely at the small congregation of shaving tools – the shaving brush had dried, but little white ribbons of soap clung to it as if they had just been squeezed out of the tube of shaving soap that lay beside it, except that they too had dried. A safety razor was there, also.

It was, of course, exactly what Mariette had already described to her, but as she looked at the bits of white soap and the unused razor blade, Susan found herself convinced: André Cavalliere had not intended to disappear. That much, at least, was certain.

"Have you found something?"

"No more than you told me," said Susan. "Where was the money hidden?"

Mariette led the way quickly to the fireplace at the front of the room. The brick was loose, and it was evident – or would have been evident to a searcher – that it was loose. So probably the money had had nothing to do with the thing. Except to indicate again that André Cavalliere had not intended to disappear. Susan looked thoughtfully about the room. It was evidently here that he had worked and lounged.

There were shabby but comfortable-looking chairs. Easels. A paint-smeared table. Ash trays. A small rug or two, very thin and worn. Queer that the rugs were arranged with so little regard for need or symmetry. One was flung crookedly before the fireplace. One was straight enough below a chair, but the chair had been placed so that it stood at an awkward angle to the rest of the room.

Susan walked over to the chair.

Odd that the chair was placed so carefully in the very center of the rug. Odd—

Someone was coming up the attic stairs.

Madame opened the door; her dark eyes swept keenly over Susan and Mariette.

"So Mariette has been telling you her troubles," she said harshly. "Mariette is a silly girl. The young man has gone. Yes. But it is not for Mariette to find him. He will return if he so desires. Your breakfast," said Madame firmly, "is waiting."

Madame too possessed a key to the studio room, and she locked the door firmly behind them. Susan saw Mariette's slender hand close upon her own key.

And it was as they reached the second floor again that the incident occurred that was, then, so trivial.

And that was the breakfast tray, laden with soiled dishes and a crumpled napkin, which stood upon the bottom step. Madame halted as she saw it, then swept forward, took it up in her wide hands, and looked at Susan and Mariette.

"Mr. Malmin," she said, "had breakfast in his own room this morning. Agnes is very careless. She ought not to have put the tray on the steps."

She turned, and her thin black dress billowed out after her as she went down the steps to the first floor.

As they followed, Susan put out her hand silently toward Mariette who, understanding, gave her the key to the studio.

Madame poured coffee for them and rustled away.

When, an hour later, Susan went to her room again, Madame was sitting in her own room with the door wide open and herself in such a position as to command a view of the entire length of the corridor and the entrance to the narrow third-floor stairway. Susan opened her door, ostensibly to catch any stirring of cool air, and took up a book, and thus entered upon a prolonged and silent duel with the black-eyed Frenchwoman. Mariette came nervously into the corridor now and then, looked at Susan and at Madame, and vanished again.

John Kinder's door remained closed. But once another man, short and stocky and supple, with a dark, hawk-like face, emerged from the room directly opposite Susan's, gave her a quick, keen look, and went down the stairway.

That was, of course, the man Mariette had called Louis Malmin. He looked, Susan was bound to admit, fully capable of accomplishing all the crimes in the Decalogue, alone and unaided. But there was nothing to link him with André. Nothing, indeed, so far, to link André with any of them except Mariette. Unless Madame's vigilance was a clue to – well, to what?

It was late in the afternoon when Susan contrived an errand to take Madame's attention. Although it was actually Mariette who induced the Frenchwoman to examine the money she had taken from André's room. They were downstairs in the living room by that time, and Madame was still vigilant.

"Money!" said Madame. "You took money from his room! How much?"

"I – haven't counted it," said Mariette with unexpected guile. "I thought it was safer with me. Do you want to look at it?"

Madame looked at Susan and looked at Mariette. It was, however, Susan thought, the only bait to which she would have risen.

"Perhaps I'd better see it," she said. "If André Cavalliere does not return, I shall be obliged to claim this money. He owes me – you understand?"

Quietly Susan followed them. When she heard Mariette close the door to her room she hurried along the corridor and, at last, up the steps to the third floor again.

She was always glad that Mariette had not been with her when she moved the chair and looked under the rug.

For under the rug, plain against the old pine floor was a queer, irregular mark. It was not blood – but blood had been there and had been recently and thoroughly washed. Susan sat back on her heels and looked at that mark.

The conclusion, of course, was obvious.

Madame's vigilance took on a new and sinister meaning. That meant, then, that she knew something of the thing that had happened here.

Susan rose.

It did not take long to look carefully over the entire studio, for André Cavalliere had not been widely possessed of this world's goods. Indeed, the only thing of interest Susan found was that André had smoked many cigarettes since the ash trays had been emptied; and that he had sketched everybody in the house in every possible pose.

Susan glanced rapidly through the portfolio crammed with sketches that lay on the broad table. There was Madame – Madame in workaday black; Madame's glossy head bent over her lace; Madame facing her, with lids drooped over her dark eyes. There were sketches of John Kinder, his beard waggish and shaven and church-wardenish in turns. Sketches of Louis Malmin – one apparently a joke on the part of the artist, in which Louis Malmin appeared with a handkerchief tied round his head, huge rings in his ears, a wide knife between his white teeth, and something that was not a joke looking out of his eyes. There were sketches of a woman of great beauty of feature who looked vaguely familiar to Susan. There were sketches of Marietta – many of them. Susan closed the portfolio and put it under her arm.

She must hurry. Mariette could not keep Madame counting money forever.

She paused to replace the rug and the chair. Who had placed them there? Who had scrubbed in cold water that stain below until it was lighter than all the rest of the floor? Who – she bent over and took in her fingers a small object that lay wedged into the cushions of the chair so that only its blunt end had showed, and she stood there a moment, turning it in her fingers slowly. It was a small wooden bobbin. The kind that is used in making lace.

She closed her hand upon it. The attic was growing rapidly darker, and the heat was becoming sultry, as it does before an electrical storm. Madame's hands, strong and broad, making lace assiduously. Madame's hands carrying that breakfast tray. Madame's hands scrubbing out the stain on the floor. She was somehow sure that the Frenchwoman had done that.

Susan decided she'd had enough of the attic and started for the stairway.

The hall below was empty and rather dark. But as she went quietly along it toward her own room a door away down at the end opened, and Madame's figure was silhouetted against the light from a window in the room beyond.

That room was vacant. Why had Susan so strong an impression that there was someone in the room? Was it something about the fleeting glimpse of a turn of Madame's head – a feeling that words had been quickly hushed?

At first Susan thought that, in the sudden dusk of the narrow corridor, Madame did not see her. But she opened her own door and a soft shaft of greenish light from the window beyond struck her face and she saw that black-clad figure hesitate.

There was a small bolt on the door, and Susan fastened it against unexpected interruption before she opened the portfolio and spread the sketches in a wide circle around her on the floor.

Slowly she arranged them so that all the sketches of one person were in a group, and she studied, fascinated, the results of that arrangement.

She had known these people always – she had known those varying expressions familiarly and long. Thus Madame looked when she was pleased; purring and complacent because a new lodger was prompt in paying. So Madame looked when intent on her lace-making. So when she was in festive mood. Thus when she was angry,

Louis Malmin in as many moods; studying them, there was one thing always predominant in the hawk-like, piratical face with its small dark eyes that were just a bit too close set, and that was acquisitiveness. Greed. A subordination of everything else in life to an overmastering need for gain.

Yes, perhaps André Cavalliere's only forte lay in a strange flair for character divination – so that, with one stroke of a pencil, he could place driving greed in Louis Malmin's eyes.

John Kinder, with time at his disposal, had posed exhaustively. Here he was in a dozen aspects, and Susan lingered over each. Here was Mariette, too: Susan looked at those sketches for a long time, and when she had finished was convinced of one thing at least, and that was that the artist had loved Mariette.

He had not of his own volition left her. But then she had known that already. Poor little Mariette.

It was so dark when Susan pulled herself from a reverie into which she had plunged and turned to the last group of pictures that she had to reach up and turn on the single electric globe that hung from the ceiling in order to see the face of the unknown woman. There were only two poses of her, and as the bright light poured garishly down upon it, Susan remembered where she had seen that face with its almost too perfect regularity of feature.

It was certainly that of the woman who had emerged so swiftly from the dusk the previous night while Susan was waiting for Mariette; the woman who had slipped quickly up the steps, fleetingly under the light and into the church of Notre Dame.

Susan frowned and pushed back her soft light hair. Did that entirely account for the familiarity of that perfectly regular face? And if it was a face she had seen somewhere and frequently, whose was it?

She sighed and wished the storm would blow over, and fell to studying the pictures again. She lingered very long over one sketch.

Moments passed while the sky slowly darkened and the hot still house awaited the storm. And by the time Mariette knocked timidly at the door, Susan knew things that she had not known before.

The sound of the knock roused her from a queer, rather terrifying thought that André Cavalliere had left behind him what was, in effect, a record of his death.

For he had been murdered. Susan was sure of that. What should she do?

To inform the police would be, just then, futile. She could say: I think this man was murdered because there's a mark on the floor of his studio that has recently been scrubbed and which I think was blood. Because he has disappeared. Because his sketch portfolio holds certain faces in certain poses. They would say and rightly: Where is the body?

If she knew only a little more – and that little was something that had nothing to do with the blind, fumbling search into currents of thought and feeling around her that was at once Susan's strength and Susan's weakness. She smiled a little wryly. If Jim had been there it would have helped. Without him she must herself confirm instinct – if that was what it was – with reason. With clues. With definite evidence.

"Come in," she said to Mariette's knock, and then remembered the door was bolted and scrambled to her feet to open it.

As Mariette entered, pale as a ghost in her limp white dress, Susan scooped up the sketches, permitting one of the woman of Notre Dame to remain on top.

"Do you know this woman?" she asked Mariette directly.

"No," said Mariette. "But it's one of André's sketches."

"You've never seen her?"

"N-no. That is, there's something vaguely familiar about her. But I'm sure I don't know her. And I never saw this sketch before."

"Has there been any time since you knew André when this woman could have been in the house without your knowing it?"

"Oh, yes. I was on tour for six weeks, last fall. She could have been here then. Louis Malmin was gone at that time, too, on a business trip. And – yes, I remember, that was the time when Mr. Kinder was gone, too. A vacation trip, he said, of about a week. But if she was here then – this woman, I mean – André didn't tell me. You don't mean – you don't think he's gone with her?" Her dark eyes sought Susan beseechingly.

"No, said Susan gently. "He has not gone with her. Has Madame Touseau any family? Any children or – any relatives at all? Or even any intimate friends?"

Mariette shook her head.

"No. Except that I believe she has a niece somewhere in California. But I've never seen her. And Madame keeps very much to herself. She often says her – well, she calls us all guests, you know – are her only family." Mariette hesitated. "I'm afraid," she said, "that Madame knows why you are here. She asked me – oh, a great many questions. She—" Mariette shivered a little in that hot, still room – "*she watches us so.*"

Susan delved into confused thoughts and went back for something, some word that had been spoken, that must be explored.

And she must herself this time, without Jim's help, confirm with hard fact the findings of the queer divining rod of her own consciousness. Of the blind little tentacles of something that was so dangerously like intuition and yet was not quite that either.

The silence lay as heavy as the leaves outside. Then Susan said:

"Mariette – I want you to go out and get me some things, and I don't want Madame to see them when you return."

She paused, glancing at the open transom. Then she crossed to the window and examined the old-fashioned shade and the light rod that held the hem of it flat and straight.

"Bring me," said Susan Dare, "all the movie magazines you can find. And a mirror – a shaving mirror will do, but I'd rather have one of those small make-up mirrors: you've seen them. They have a little standard and are about six inches in diameter. And at dinner tonight when everyone is seated at the table I want you to tell Madame that you are going to inform the police of André's disappearance. Make it emphatic. And again, when I talk of André, follow my lead. Agree with me."

"Yes," said Mariette and was gone.

Susan hid the sketches and opened her door. Madame's door was closed. Probably she had taken up her observation post in the drawing room downstairs. Susan looked about her room, discovered a small push-button bell, and rang it.

Her little plan, however, failed. Either the bell was disconnected or Agnes, the somewhat mysterious servant, was busy in the kitchen. Susan rang several times, but there was still no answer.

Well, the matter of Agnes could wait.

But she must know who was in that supposedly vacant room. Or rather who was not in the room.

But again she failed. For though she managed to approach the closed door to the room at the back of the house without, so far as she knew, having been seen, there was no sound from within. She listened, bending her head to the blank dark panels and holding her breath. But there was no sound at all on the other side of that door. She wanted to knock; she wanted to open the door. But something about the silence and the darkness of the place held her silent, too, and not too certain of herself. After all, a man had been murdered in that house – murdered deliberately and in cold blood. She was as certain of that as she was ever in her whole life certain of anything.

And the murder had been skillfully, carefully concealed. So skillfully and so carefully that there remained no evidence at all to show that it had been done. No evidence but the thin brown mark around that clean spot under the rug. No evidence but the sketches in André Cavalliere's portfolio.

But the murderer had made one mistake.

And that night, if Susan's conclusions were right, there would be an attempt to make that mistake right.

And what could she do then? She would need help – and she must be sure.

There was still no rustle of motion within that room. Susan went quietly back to her own room, took her hat and, boldly this time, went through the hall toward the front and down the stairs.

Madame, bent over her lace, looked up. John Kinder let a card fall from his hand and looked up also. "I'm going out a bit," said Susan. "If Mariette asks for me, won't you tell her I've gone for a little walk?"

Madame's black eyes plunged across the dusk into Susan's.

"The door," said Madame calmly, "is locked. And I have the key. Mariette has just gone out for a little walk, too. But I shouldn't advise Miss Dare to go. Because," said Madame Touseau slowly, "it is about to storm. Mademoiselle would not like to be caught in a storm."

Susan gripped the stair railing. Absurd that her heart had leaped so suddenly to pound in her throat.

She shot a glance at John Kinder. But he had gone placidly back to his card game as if altogether unaware of the threat in Madame's heavy voice.

Susan left the stairway, but Madame reached the door first. Her thick body was an indomitable barrier.

"That gown," said the Frenchwoman, "is too beautiful – too expensive to permit to be ruined. Me, I know the handsome dressmaking. I am not one to be deceived about that – that," she repeated slowly, "or other things. I do not believe Miss Dare wishes the walk in the rain. No."

It was then an open threat. Yet the woman could not keep her jailed for long in that house. She dared not.

Dared not? There was that other thing she had dared.

Susan thought swiftly. It was time for which the woman was playing. She must need time – otherwise her opposition would have taken an entirely different line. Susan restrained a desire to combat the woman openly; for an instant the thought of physical struggle over the key, a mad desire to escape, to be gone from that fetid, silent house with the stain of blood overhead, clutched at Susan as hysteria would clutch.

But the Frenchwoman was stronger. And there was Kinder. And behind Susan quite suddenly on the steps another voice spoke. The words, however, were altogether commonplace.

"Madame Touseau," said Louis Malmin quietly, "may I have dinner a little early tonight?"

As if a puzzle had given itself a jerk so that pieces which had been distorted and confused fell suddenly into a regular and ordinary pattern, so, all at once the queer little scene changed and became regular and ordinary. Susan's breath began to come freely. Madame's dark face was smooth and efficient as she spoke calmly to Louis Malmin.

She had merely advised Susan not to go out in the rain. That was all.

"Will you unlock the door, Madame Touseau?" said Susan. "I wish to go out before the rain comes." Would the woman boldly refuse?

But her dark eyes met Susan's and glowed. Then she smiled and said:

"But certainly, if one wishes." She turned and opened the door. "However – when the storm comes it will be bad."

Susan was conscious of Kinder's face turned inquiringly toward her; of Louis Malmin's presence there on the stairway behind her. But the door to the street stood open, and Susan walked past Madame and out upon the steps.

A string of shops ought to be found a street or two beyond, for Susan remembered vaguely a patch of radiance off toward her right as she and Mariette had walked from the church the night before. She turned in that direction.

Her easy victory was perplexing; it led Susan to doubt her own conclusions. For it was as if Madame had warned her merely to go no further but had scorned, smilingly, any notion that Susan was already in possession of a fact that might be dangerous.

It became clearer to Susan that the little episode had been merely a warning on Madame Touseau's part. Madame, then, was very sure of herself. But she did not know that Susan had seen the sketches. She did not know that one of her own wooden bobbins was at that moment in Susan's white handbag. She did not know that Susan had seen the woman on the church steps.

Yet perhaps the entire fabric of reasoning that Susan had built up was wrong. Perhaps she had missed some salient and pivotal fact.

Few corners are without drugstores and the corner upon which Susan emerged was no exception. It was small and crowded at the soda fountain where perspiring and frenzied clerks dealt out tall, iced glasses. Susan supplied herself with nickels and went to the little row of mahogany-stained telephone booths at the back.

The telephone number of the *Record* is famous in Chicago. Susan called it and waited. Jim had been out of town yesterday, of course; but that didn't mean that he was not in town today. If he had not returned, she didn't know exactly what to do next; it would be best, perhaps, simply to wait. But she wasn't sure that she dared wait.

It was terrifically hot in the little booth. A faraway voice said it was the *Record* and referred her to another voice which hesitated and then to Susan's immense relief, turned and called distantly: "Hey, Jim!"

"Hello – hello—" It was Jim Byrne.

"Jim," said Susan in a small voice, "oh, Jim, I'm so glad you are here."

"Oh, hello, Sue. What's the matter?"

"I don't know. I don't know, but I think it's murder—"

"My God!" said Jim. "In this heat!"

"And I think I know who did it."

"Where are you? Where's the body?"

"I'm at Sibley and Loomis—"

"What?" shouted Jim.

"At Sibley and Loomis," repeated Susan firmly. "In a drugstore in a booth."

Then Jim said: "You sound scared. Stay there where you are. I'll be there in – oh, ten minutes. 'Bye."

Susan sat down at a table. "Two tall lemonades," she said to the white-aproned boy who approached. "With lots of ice."

"Two?" he said, eyeing Susan as if measuring her capacity. Jim bettered his promise by three minutes.

"Angel," he said looking at the frosted glass, "is that for me?"

"Drink it," said Susan. "And don't ask me questions till I've finished. Jim, is there anyone who might be in hiding there at Madame Touseau's? That is a rooming house in the French quarter. Someone a great deal in the public eye; someone who would want to escape attention?"

He grinned.

"A lot of people, my Susan. The bird I've been trying to locate for one." He took a long swallow and added: "But everybody says he's got out of the country. Best for his health. You've read about the Anton Burgess disclosures. As long as he can stay out of sight a whole lot of fellows here in Chicago are that much better off. There's an embezzlement charge."

Susan frowned.

"Yes, I read that. Jim, can you come back there with me? You see, I've got some sketches that I want to show you. The main facts of the thing are simple. A man by the name of André Cavalliere, an artist, engaged to marry little Mariette Berne—"

"Berne," said Jim. "That little ballet dancer?"

"Yes. He – well, he just vanished. And I think he's murdered."

"Why?"

"Because," said Susan, "there's blood on the attic floor. And it's been washed."

Jim gave her a long look. Then he beckoned to the boy. "Two more drinks," he said. "Whose blood, Susan?"

"I want you to see the sketches," she said obliquely. "I want to know if you see in them what I see." She frowned again. "Burgess," she said thoughtfully. "Yes, that might be right."

Jim put down his glass.

"Look here, Susan," he said earnestly, "if you've stumbled over Anton Burgess, lead me there, Miss Santa Claus. Every paper in the United States has been trying to find him for nearly two years."

Susan shook her head. "Are you sure you would recognize him if you saw him?"

"Yes," he said soberly. "I believe so – you're keeping something back, Susan. What is it?" She shook her head again. "I want you to see it for yourself," she said. "I may be wrong."

He stared at her over the empty glasses. His blue eyes were thoughtful; his irregular but agreeable features were intent.

"All right," he said. "Are we apt to need reinforcements?"

"Police? No. It's a case for your Irish tongue, Jim. I think," said Susan slowly, "that we've got a lever that you can work."

He flipped the coins to the weary boy. They emerged upon a heat-stricken street. They turned toward Notre Dame.

"I'd forgotten there was a French quarter," said Jim. "What a place for anyone to hide! A forgotten section in the middle of a great city. Hedged in completely with little foreign worlds. Tell me all, Sue."

"Well," said Susan cautiously, "I've made a little plan. It's not much. But it may work. I sent Mariette for some movie magazines. And a small mirror."

"The mirror," said Jim, "suggests a periscope. But I'll be damned if I know what you want movie magazines for. And how are you going to get me in this place? Tell them you've picked up a boyfriend?"

"I don't know," said Susan, eyeing him doubtfully. "I don't think even money would persuade Madame to take another lodger just now. Especially a suspiciously well-tailored one arriving promptly upon my return. I believe the simplest way will be best – that is, for me to let you in while the others are at dinner."

It was quite simple. The house was very much darker than the street and though a light burned in the drawing room there was no one to see Jim cross the hall. With the knowledge that Jim was upstairs, Susan felt more certain of herself.

Susan was never to forget the dinner – her first and last dinner – in Madame Touseau's house. She was always to remember the narrow room with its brown walls, its mirrored built-in sideboard, and its heavy hanging center light. There was unexpectedly good linen and soup, and Madame, erect, with her black hair and eyes gleaming, presided quite as if they were in truth her guests. Louis Malmin was directly opposite Susan. John Kinder ate sparingly of what appeared to be a vegetable diet and said very little. As Susan appeared, Mariette uttered a little gasp of relief which she tried to cover by saying something about the storm.

A window had been opened, and now and then a hot breath of air swept the lace curtain inward and then sucked it back against the screen. Wasn't that an indication of a cyclonic area? thought Susan, accepting chicken gumbo and her first glimpse of the servant, Agnes, at the same time. Agnes was a plain, fat little woman, about as mysterious as a post, and she retired immediately to the kitchen.

Mariette lifted her dark eyes and looked straight at Madame Touseau.

"I think I'd better tell you," she said, "that I am going to call the police tomorrow morning." Madame's face darkened, and she shot a swift suspicious glance at Susan.

"You mean to investigate the departure of André?"

"Exactly," said Mariette with unaccustomed decision. Madame's broad hands fingered the silver beside her plate.

John Kinder paused with a forkful of lettuce in the air to look in a mildly reproving manner at Mariette, and Louis Malmin ate steadily.

"There are some sketches that André made," said Susan. "They are very interesting sketches. So interesting that we thought the police might be able to—" She stopped herself abruptly, as if she had said more than she had intended to say.

There was a little silence. Then Madame said:

"Sketches. What kind of sketches?"

"Oh, nothing much. Just little bits of – everyday things. Street scenes – people." Susan hoped she was making the right impression of flurried retraction.

"What people?" said Madame heavily.

Susan said nothing, and John Kinder let the lettuce travel to his mouth and said through it, mildly: "Me, for one. I used to pose for André often. But I don't quite see how this young lady expects the sketches he made to help solve the problem of his disappearance. And I do think police investigation is quite uncalled for."

Mariette repeated: "I'm going to call the police." And Louis Malmin rose suddenly, spoke briefly to Madame, and left the dining room.

After that, nothing more was said of police, though John Kinder kept up a mild barrage of conversation which covered Madame's glooming silence and the general air of discomfiture that silence induced.

Under cover of the little confusion of pushing back chairs Mariette whispered to Susan: "I found the woman that André sketched in one of the movie magazines," she said. "She is Sally Gowdy."

Sally Gowdy. One of the near-stars in the movie firmament. That was why the face was so familiar. "Go with the others," whispered Susan, and as Mariette disappeared, Agnes came to the table. "Agnes," said Susan directly, "for how many days have you been arranging extra trays?"

Agnes blinked, hesitated, and was lost.

"Since Monday," she said. "And I don't see where Mr. Malmin puts it all. Six meals a day that makes for him! Besides the extra work!"

Thoughtfully Susan returned to the living room. Madame had taken up her lace-making again. Mariette had waited for her, and she and Susan walked quietly toward the stairs. Over the banisters Susan saw that John Kinder was again mildly intent upon his card game. And as she paused at her own room, she caught a gleam of light from the transom above Louis Malmin's door.

"Go on to your room, Mariette," she said in a whisper. "Lock the door, and don't let anyone – anyone, mind you – in the room. Not on any pretext."

Mariette, her small face white and ghostly in the dusk, nodded and vanished.

Jim switched off a flashlight as Susan entered. She turned on the light. The sketches were again spread, but fanwise on the floor. And the movie magazines had been rummaged and tossed aside. He knew, then. And beside the door was an odd little contraption which consisted of a mirror fastened stoutly to the end of a light wood rod, obviously taken from the head of the window shade.

His eyes were black with excitement and jubilance.

"Susan," he said in a low voice, "you've got him. It's Burgess beyond all doubt. But it took an artist to penetrate the disguise. This fellow André Cavalliere was clever – too clever for his own good. Now then, what's the program? Your periscope is ready. Are the sketches the bait?"

"That," said Susan, calmly accepting Jim's immediate comprehension, "that and a threat of police in the morning. They'll do something tonight."

"They'll do something," said Jim, "right now. Better turn out your light."

Susan did so. Afterward she remembered that as they started their queer vigil, there was a sudden roll of thunder, close at hand and reverberating threateningly in the hushed, hot room.

Jim held the improvised periscope, which worked remarkably well, and Susan stood beside him, her eyes glued to the small reflection of the head of the stairs and a patch of intervening corridor.

"I think," said Jim in a whisper, "that I've got the main points. But there are some completely mysterious gaps. For instance, Sally Gowdy—"

"Sh-h—" breathed Susan. "You'll see, soon. There's Madame—"

It was queer to stand there in the darkness and watch Madame, a quickly moving figure with a white face, pause at the head of the stairs, look swiftly about her, and then glide directly toward them. Jim turned the mirror carefully so they could catch a glimpse of the back of the hall in time to see Madame disappear into the supposedly vacant room at its end.

There was another short wait. Very short. For the storm in all its pent-up fury swooped furiously upon the house with wind and rain and wild lightning that lit the small room eerily and then was gone.

And probably the tumult and frenzy of sound outside induced the murderer of André Cavalliere to do what must be done under cover of all that turmoil. A door along the hall opened. And a figure slipped quietly toward the attic stairway.

The mirror jerked to follow it, and Susan put her hand on Jim's arm. "Wait," she whispered. "Not yet. Wait—"

Jim would have remonstrated but she clutched his arm tighter, and he waited.

But, of course, Jim didn't know that she had no proof. That the figure that had slipped up those attic stairs must be trapped in another way.

Susan never knew how much longer they waited. The figure that had gone to the studio did not return. But finally the door at the end of the hall must have opened, for all at once there was a woman in the mirror – a woman who now crept silently along the corridor.

Susan's fingers were tight on the hard muscle of Jim's forearm.

"Now!" she said and the little mirrored picture vanished as Jim flung open the door.

The woman stopped and screamed and put her hands over her face. Then Madame Touseau was there, too.

Susan saw the glint of a revolver suddenly in Jim's hand, and the sight was inexpressibly comforting.

Madame cried: "What is the meaning of this? Who is the man? What—" She had grasped the meaning of it at once and was glaring at Susan. "You did this?" she panted.

And Jim's hand wavered suddenly on the revolver as the woman in the corridor lifted her head. "My God," he said, "it's Sally Gowdy herself!" He whirled toward Susan. "Where's Burgess?"

"Burgess," said Susan rapidly, "is upstairs in the attic, looking for the sketches. But I'm sure Madame Touseau would rather confess what she knows of the murder of André Cavalliere than have Miss Gowdy involved in a murder investigation. If you confess, Madame, merely to what you know, Miss Gowdy will be permitted to leave before the police come. You see," she said to Jim, "Miss Gowdy is Madame's niece. But, probably for publicity's sake, she does not want it known that this is her home. She arrived for a secret visit two days before the murder occurred. Madame tried to conceal the murder in order to keep Miss Gowdy out of it. It was most unfortunate that she was secretly in the house at the time. It would be still more unfortunate if the police investigation discovered her. So Madame undertook to keep them away. I am sure," said Susan, meaning the opposite, "that Madame would not have taken money from Anton Burgess for her silence."

"I don't know what you are talking about," said Madame. Her face and lips were ashen. Sally Gowdy looked up. Her beautifully regular face was stricken and terrified. Her voice that had thrilled thousands was trembling and harsh.

"Oh, tell them, tell them," she moaned. "You didn't help kill him. They can't do anything to you. And I've got to get away before the police come."

Madame's fixed dark eyes did not flicker. She said grimly: "Isn't there a thing called being an accessory after the fact?"

"There is," said Jim. "But we already know that you concealed the murder. You may as well tell it all."

"Murder—" Mariette was among them suddenly and stood swaying, her eyes wide and piteous.

"He's – dead, then—" Madame's lips were tight.

"He's dead, you little fool," she said. "But I know only that there was blood spilled. I didn't see him dead. And I didn't help remove the body—"

"The body," whispered Mariette.

"It's in the Chicago River, I suppose," said Madame. "Burgess got rid of it that night. Does it matter?"

A crash of thunder held them silent and transfixed for a queer moment or two. Mariette's white face was blurred, and Sally Gowdy's beauty was an empty mask, and the little black spots on Madame's eyelid worked and twitched, while thunder submerged them, shaking the house, and slowly rolled away. And on its heels came a violent, sharper sound from over their heads.

Jim sprang toward the stairway, and Louis Malmin's door opened, and quite suddenly they were all surging up those narrow steps and into the attic. John Kinder was slumped over a chair. There was a table beside him, and on the table a scrap of paper. He had died instantly.

The note was confused, yet clear enough.

"You've got me," he had scrawled. "I can't find the sketches. I've known it was coming. The artist fellow recognized me and told me. But I didn't know that he had made a sketch of me as I really looked. That is what the girl meant. After he told me, there was nothing else for me to do. I used the same revolver that is here beside me. I forced the Touseau woman to conceal the fact. She was ready to do it for many reasons. But she had nothing to do with the murder. I'm ready to go. I've been hunted. I'm tired. The notes on the embezzlement case are in my trunk."

It was signed Anton Burgess, with a broken line below Burgess.

Anton Burgess

"Look," Susan said, "at the line below. It's broken for the downward stroke of the 'g'. That's how I knew, you see, that Kinder wasn't his real name. That a man in the house was using a name not his own. He had the same kind of line under it, but that was no reason for it to be broken, for the 'd' below which the break appears has no downward stroke. And the line extended beyond the following two letters to about the space of another letter. Thus I supposed that his real name had had seven letters with a consonant in the middle of it that went downward. The flourish of a line below his name was too strong a habit for him to break – especially when there was nothing that seemed betraying about two short lines. It told me where to look." That was later, when she was showing Jim the register and comparing the mark below the signature of John Kinder with the mark below that of Anton Burgess.

It was still later, and the storm had died, when they left the Touseau house and walked slowly toward Notre Dame.

"The sketches were the betraying evidence," said Jim thoughtfully. "Without the beard, with light hair instead of dark hair, and a youthful figure – Burgess was very much younger than he appeared as John Kinder – he was immediately recognizable as Burgess. It must have been on the artist's part an idle bit of amusement. He couldn't have dreamed what it would cost him – unless, of course, he wanted money from Burgess to keep his secret. And Burgess knew where that would lead. How did you know about Sally Gowdy?"

"I didn't," said Susan, "until I realized that the woman of Notre Dame and the woman in the sketches were the same. Therefore, that she must be here now and must have been sometime connected with the place. Then Mariette said she thought Madame had a niece in California and, of course, I thought of the movies. She was so beautiful. And it was luck that her picture was in one of the magazines. And since Agnes had been taking trays upstairs for two days *before* the murder, I knew it couldn't be André who was concealed in that supposedly vacant room. Then I realized that the movie actress and Madame would do everything possible to escape becoming involved in a murder case. I don't know why she didn't leave at once – Sally Gowdy, I mean. But, of course, I knew she would leave at once after Mariette had said she would call the police."

Notre Dame loomed darkly above them into the clear, rain-washed night. The violence of the storm had left peace and clear, wet quiet in its wake.

"Do you realize," said Jim in a hushed voice, "what a furor this news is going to make? Anton Burgess found at last – I've got to hustle, Susan! This is one time when I've got a real scoop."

"I know." She looked up at the dim outline of a cross against the sky. "Poor little Mariette," she said. 'She was such a harmless little thing to be caught in such a big wheel. – All right, Jim. I'm coming."

The Deadly Sin of Sherlock Holmes

Tom English

HUNDREDS of years ago, around the time of Magna Carta, while England endured the growing pains of an empire in its infancy, and kings and kingdoms waged endless wars across Europe; and long before Prince Wilhelm von Ormstein's dalliance with the woman Irene Adler, the aftermath of which, were it not for the intervention of Sherlock Holmes, might have ended in a royal scandal in Bohemia, yet another chapter of history was being written in a Benedictine monastery in an obscure Bohemian village. Its consequences would span centuries, and dreadful would be its effects.

The architect of this singular item sat hunched behind a tiny, splintered table in a bare cell illuminated only by a thin shaft of moonlight from a high, narrow window. He was dying. His arms, legs, and face were lacerated with hundreds of self-inflicted cuts, his clothing scarlet with blood. When three robed men appeared at his door, he looked up weakly from his bloodstained fingers and smiled.

"Where is it, Brother?" asked one of the men.

"Of what do you speak, Abbot?"

"Brother Josef, Brother Ehren, bring the candles," the abbot said to the two monks behind him. "Search his cell – quickly!" He turned back to the man seated before him. "We know of the hellish instrument you have forged this night. God has revealed it to me in a dream."

"More a nightmare, I should think. For the power of the thing shall be hideous, its ministry implacable."

"How dare you use consecrated paper!" said Brother Josef.

"Where is it?" the abbot asked again.

"Gone out into the world," said the dying man, clinging to the edges of his blood-smeared desk.

"You have corrupted an instrument of God," cried Brother Josef. "Where is it?"

"As I have said, Josef, it is gone. Spirited away by the Prince of the Air."

"Satan!" Brother Ehren said with disgust.

"Certainly not your weakling god," he replied.

"You stand at death's door," said the abbot. "Have you no fear? Tell us now where the thing is hidden."

"Hidden?" laughed the man behind the table. "In this tiny room!" He coughed hard and struggled to regain his breath. "Nay," he said hoarsely, "though you search for it, you shall not find it. For I have sent it out into the world. To baptize all men into a new age of darkness set before them."

* * *

On a bone-chilling night in early May of 1891, a hooded figure crouched over the dead body of a young woman on Clements Lane in the district of Westminster, London. An icy rain spattered against the grey cobbles and ran away in grimy rivulets towards the Strand, only a short walk away, and the Thames River waiting just beyond. From the south the faint peal of Big Ben marked the midnight hour. While two other men watched from nearby, the veiled figure knelt before the corpse, a Bull's-eye lantern in one hand. His free hand moved quickly and expertly over the woman's body as he probed the bloodstained clothing. After several moments, he heard a voice above him ask, "Well?"

The man looked up from the corpse. Only the dripping beak of his tweed cap poked through his hood. "Well *what*, Lestrade?" he asked irritably. "This infernal rain has scrubbed the street clean. And despite what the good doctor may have written about my abilities, I cannot work without clues."

"She was obviously another drab who got more than she asked for," said Inspector Lestrade, pulling up the collar of his coat. "But her face, Mr. Holmes! Look at her face! Why would anyone do such a thing?"

"This was no streetwalker, Lestrade. Observe the clothing. It appears to be new and of the highest quality. This woman was dressed for an evening out. What brought her *here*, so far from the beaten path?"

Holmes tossed back the hood of his Ulster. The rain had died away to a fine mist that showed as a halo around the street lamp at the end of the lane. "This rain started a little after 3 p.m., but this woman is not dressed for inclement weather. As you can see, she has no cloak at all."

He motioned to the man in black coat and derby standing next to Lestrade. "Watson, notice the blood about the eyes and mouth – how thickly coagulated it is."

Watson knelt and winced at the mutilated features.

"Yet the body is face up," said Holmes. "The heavy rain would have washed away most of this blood – had it not been so thickly clotted. Now, since you put the time of death at only a couple of hours ago, and it has been raining since three…"

"Then the wounds were inflicted somewhere else," Watson said. "Someplace dry enough to allow the blood to harden."

"Come," said Holmes, "we can learn nothing more here. The scent has grown cold, and so have we. And what will Mrs. Watson have to say, should I detain you any longer?"

He turned to Lestrade, who quickly gestured to two uniformed policemen to remove the dead body. "If I can be of any further assistance…"

Lestrade watched the two men walk down the lane toward the Strand and disappear into the shadows. A few minutes later he heard two shrill blasts from a cab whistle – telling him that Holmes had hailed a hansom.

* * *

That same night, several streets away, a man sat alone in a dimly lit room and wept bitterly. He held something in his arms, something heavy and cool, which he was gently caressing. He laid the object on his lap, wiped the tears from his eyes, and then opened it with a trembling hand.

"It's gone!" he cried. "Gone!"

* * *

When Watson called on Holmes at his Baker Street lodgings the next morning, he found the detective sitting before the fire, absently scraping away at the violin that rested across his knees. Each screeching note from the Stradivarius sent a chill up the doctor's spine, making him cringe and grit his teeth. "Holmes! If you please!" he cried, tossing the morning newspaper on the table.

Holmes glanced at the headlines. "Miss Anne Skipton. Certainly not a streetwalker, and yet the *Times* is alluding to the Whitechapel murders of two and a half years ago."

"You must admit," said Watson, taking the other chair by the fire, "there has been no murder this gruesome since the days of Jack the Harlot Killer."

"And already the *Times* is capitalizing on it. Their coverage of the Ripper only served to sensationalize his crimes and feed his maniacal ego – encouraging his savagery and impeding my investigation. I am still bitterly disappointed at my inability to solve those crimes. You have heard me say the most difficult crime to track is the one which is purposeless – or at least appears to be so."

Holmes walked to the window with his violin. "Oh, I am well aware of the public opinion regarding the Ripper's motives, and the fanciful conclusions drawn by our friends at the Yard, but too many factors did not add up. To this day, the true motive for those horrible crimes remains a mystery."

"Thank goodness they ended when they did. No doubt the Ripper realized you were closing in on him and fled the country."

"Perhaps," said Holmes, placing the violin on his shoulder and raising the bow. "One thing I do know: *this* is absolutely the best fifty-five-shilling investment I ever made."

"Yes," said Watson, "and your second-best investment would be having it properly tuned!"

Holmes lowered the Stradivarius and was about to say something when he was interrupted by a knock at the door. Mrs. Hudson entered, followed by an elderly man wearing a battered black hat and faded cassock. A dull metallic cross hung from a chain about the man's neck.

"Ah! A client," said Holmes. "Thank you, Mrs. Hudson."

The man removed his hat and bowed, revealing a thick, unbroken tangle of gray hair. "I am Brother Eduardo. I have come on behalf of...well, you will not have heard of our order. It is a little-known offshoot of the Benedictines, whose mission is to safeguard certain antiquities."

Watson smiled. "A secret society?"

"Excuse me," Holmes interrupted, "this gentleman is my good friend and colleague, Dr. Watson. And I am Sherlock Holmes."

The old man nodded. "Not secret, Dr. Watson. The Church is well aware of our presence. Perhaps, though, our day-to-day activities may be somewhat obscure."

Holmes motioned for the man to be seated. "May I ask how you located me? No doubt my adventures have been rather sensationally chronicled by Dr. Watson, but my Boswell has always had the prudence to disguise the actual number of this Baker Street address."

"I was referred to you by a Mr. Lestrade. He feels my problem is not a matter for Scotland Yard."

"And what is your problem?"

"My brothers and I have hopes that you will be able to locate a missing book."

Holmes turned to Watson. "Our friend Lestrade has a habit of sending us his...more interesting cases."

"He told me of both your amazing abilities and your genuine goodness," the monk said anxiously. "And I pray you will be able to discern my deep sincerity when I say that this matter is of the utmost importance. I would not have come to you were it not so."

"I discern that you are indeed a man without guile," said Holmes reassuringly. "Surely you are also a humble man, to be so long in the service of your order as to attain a position of authority and yet choose to remain a novice."

At the surprise on Brother Eduardo's face, Watson used a finger to trace a circle about the crown of his own head: "The lack of a tonsure, quite elementary."

Holmes sighed heavily.

"In many ways, Mr. Holmes," said the monk, "we are all novices. Not one of us is ever fully capable of solving the great mysteries of this world."

"Really!" said Holmes. "You quite obviously have not come here to flatter me, Friar. So please, tell me about this missing book."

"It is a bound manuscript known as the *Codex Exsecrabilis*."

"*Cursed Book*," remarked Watson, taking notes.

"Watson," said Holmes, "be a good fellow and fetch my copy of *Librorum Prohibitorum*."

"You will not find it listed on the Church's index of banned books," said Brother Eduardo. "It is a singular work...composed in the early thirteenth century by an apostate monk in Podlažice, Bohemia. The manuscript pages mysteriously disappeared the night they were written, and were not recovered until 1477. By then the pages had been bound."

"Describe the physical appearance of the book," Holmes interrupted.

"It consists of vellum sheets gathered in wooden boards. The boards are covered in leather and ornamented with a metallic cross – an inverted cross. It is rather large and weighs over 32 pounds. The codex remained in Benedictine possession for over a hundred years...at a monastery in Broumov, until it was forcibly taken to Prague to become part of the collection of Rudolf II."

"Bohemian Kings," muttered Holmes, "I am besieged with the consequences of their mischief."

"Rudolf was a student of the occult," said the monk.

"An avocation that did nothing to help him prevent the Thirty Years' War."

"And when the Swedish army plundered the region, his entire collection was stolen and removed to Stockholm. A few years later the Swedish Royal Library allowed us to purchase the codex. Since then – except for three or four brief periods – the book has been in our safekeeping. Until three days ago. We are extremely anxious to locate it!"

"No doubt. Such a valuable and coveted book as—"

"Our desire to recover the codex does not stem from cupidity. The book has the power to corrupt the souls of decent men!"

"Your desire to protect us from this book is a noble one, Friar, but I believe each of us should be free to read and decide for ourselves what is moral and praiseworthy."

"But Mr. Holmes, the codex has been linked to numerous crimes! In fact, it is directly responsible for several ghastly murders."

"Is this book so poorly written," Holmes asked drily, "as to incite the reader to violence? Then why not simply fling the offending volume into the fireplace?"

The old monk nervously fingered the tiny cross hanging over his heart and stared mutely into the detective's piercing eyes.

"Friar, if I am to help you, I must have all the facts, and I must have them now."

"The facts will sound like fancy, I fear," the monk said at last.

"Allow me to be the judge of that."

"The codex is a compendium of evil acts, Mr. Holmes – all of them hideous, hellish. When anyone reads a passage from the book – and I stress, *anyone* – that person is compelled to enact what has been read, regardless how monstrous the deed. Later, after the evil has been enacted, the passage literally fades from the page, leaving absolutely no trace of the words."

"That is indeed a fanciful tale," said Holmes. "One worthy of Oscar Wilde, I might add."

"The book must be found," Brother Eduardo pleaded, "before it falls into the hands of another poor soul who will be powerless to resist its call."

"But, Friar," Holmes said soothingly, "a book composed by a thirteenth-century Benedictine scholar is undoubtedly written in Latin. How many people tramping the streets of London would be able to read such a book?"

"To be precise, the codex was written in the Vulgate. But that has never prevented anyone from reading it, regardless of a knowledge of Latin."

"And how do you explain this?"

"It is difficult to explain the unexplainable," the old man said slowly. "The author of the codex had been confined to his cell for breaking monastic vows. His abbot had ordered him to do penitence by transcribing several sacred documents. The manuscript *should* have been a common prayer book, but Brother Moriarty had long been under the sway of the Prince of Darkness."

"*Moriarty*," said Watson. "That does not sound Germanic."

"It is ancient Gaelic for 'greatly exalted'. In a perverse way, he lived up to his name: power accompanies exaltation – and his manuscript has become a source of relentless power. According to legend, he called upon Satan to anoint his writing, then repeatedly cut himself to supply the blood in which the codex is written. When it was finished, he was more dead than alive and the manuscript had mysteriously vanished."

Holmes withdrew a pipe from his pocket and examined its charred contents distractedly.

"Throughout the ages there have been many blasphemous books," continued Brother Eduardo. "Were this simply another such volume, we would not concern ourselves with it. But the parchment upon which it is written had been consecrated for sacred documents. Moriarty poured into that parchment everything that is evil. Somehow, on the night of its satanic creation, the codex took on a life of its own. And now, it is trying to revert to its original holy state."

"Fascinating," said Holmes, yawning.

"You must believe me! When an evil passage is read from the codex the reader is forced to enact that evil – and the passage is then wiped clean from the book! I assure you, Sir, many of its pages are now blank!"

"I believe only in those things which can be proven. You claim the book has special properties, but you have given me no proof."

The old monk stood and bowed. "You were our last hope, Mr. Holmes. Please forgive me for taking so much of your time."

"A moment, Friar. I may not believe the legend tied to the codex, but I *will* help you to recover it. Tell me the circumstances surrounding its disappearance. You said it was three days ago. Where?"

"In the library of All Hallows in Longbourn."

"I was not aware of a monastery in Longbourn."

"Our home is in Rome. We were in London on Church business and were extended hospitality by the priest at All Hallows."

"You brought the codex to London? Why?"

"It accompanies us wherever we go. I cannot give you the full reason for this – other than to say we are sworn to protect it."

"Very well," said Holmes. "We will accompany you back to Longbourn posthaste. Although I imagine by now the room and any clues it may once have held have been trampled by sandaled feet."

* * *

If judged by its dour façade, the Church of All Hallows was particularly uninviting: a squat and decrepit edifice of crumbling brick and stained-glass windows darkened by decades of soot. At one corner of the church, fronting the narrow street below, an imposing tower rose up against a gray sky; a much older structure, built of huge blocks of blackened stone, that stood out from the rest of All Hallows like a rook on the corner of a chessboard, thought Watson, stepping from the four-wheeler.

"How long have you been staying here?" Holmes asked, following Brother Eduardo inside the tower.

"We arrived six days ago," said the monk. "We would have been on our way the next morning but Brother Paolo became ill. Father Twitchell insisted we stay until he was well enough to travel. He said we would have the place to ourselves, for he was going up to Cambridge to attend to a Church matter and would be away for four days."

"When did he depart?"

"The morning after our arrival."

"And when was the last time you remember seeing the codex?"

Brother Eduardo opened a large oaken door and waited for Holmes and Watson to enter. "It was certainly here in his library the night after he left. It was gone the next morning."

The priest's study was large but austere and, like the tower rising above it, clearly much older than the rest of the church. Heavy beams crisscrossed the ceiling and extended down the walls, all of which were windowless. At one end of the room was a massive desk covered with curling documents and open books. Behind the desk a ceiling-high shelf held numerous volumes recording births, burials, and other church history, their leather bindings dry and brittle with age. All this was illuminated by a single great log burning in the massive fireplace.

Holmes circled the room, making a quick inspection of the bare floor. "Other than yourself," he asked the monk, "who else might have had access to this room?"

"Only my brothers. The study was kept locked to safeguard the codex."

"How can you be certain of this?"

"Upon his departure Father Twitchell entrusted me with the keys to the Church, including this room."

"Then I wish to speak to your brothers – but to each individually. Please go and ask one of them to step in."

Holmes walked to the fireplace. It was wide and deep, and almost a foot taller than the detective. He extended his hands before the blazing log. "I daresay, Watson, I could fit my entire bed upon this hearth. No more chilly nights!" he said longingly.

The library door opened slowly and the first of the two monks entered: a stout, balding man who went by the name of Brother Paolo. Holmes soon ascertained that the man had been seized with severe abdominal pains the night of his arrival and, until yesterday morning, had been far too ill to leave his bed. The detective thanked him and instructed the monk to show in his brother Eugenio.

When Eugenio entered, followed by Brother Eduardo, Holmes quickly realized the young man was a *true* novice, for he was hardly more than eighteen and demonstrated little of the qualities of meekness and humility that characterized the other monks. Holmes turned to the fireplace. "This is an inviting blaze. Certainly it is a temptation for someone in possession of an undesirable book. Tell me, Brother Eugenio, could the codex have found its way into the fire?"

"We do not burn books," the youth said petulantly.

"A book does not simply disappear from a locked room."

"We believe the codex has escaped," said Brother Eduardo, "just as it did the night of its creation."

"Escaped?" Holmes said peevishly. "Did it flap its pages and fly up the chimney? I should like to talk to the priest when he returns."

"He is due back tomorrow. But surely you cannot suspect Father Twitchell of taking the book!"

"At present, I suspect no one," said Holmes. "But I must question everyone. I shall call upon him tomorrow afternoon."

In the carriage, on the way back to Baker Street, Watson turned to Holmes and asked, "The murder last night – could it somehow be related?"

"Possibly," said Holmes, lighting a cigarette.

"*Could* the codex have some occult power?"

"We have dealt with many mysteries which at first appeared to have their explanation in the supernatural – like the case of that wretched hound upon the moors. In the end, all of them proved to have a logical explanation. No, Watson, when it comes to the art of detection, I give no credence to tales of the supernatural. Like the hound, these bothersome little things nip at our heels and send us hurrying down the wrong path of investigation. How unfortunate that our history is riddled with myths, ghost stories, rumors of witches. On the stage of life, they have provided unintentional moments of 'misdirection': for as long as our focus is upon such things the real and important matters of human existence will always elude our sight.

"Nevertheless," he continued, "I am excited to pit my skills against the bibliomane who stole this book."

"But if the book has indeed fallen into the hands of some as yet unknown collector, it is hardly likely he will part with it. The book therefore might be shelved in any one of a hundred private libraries."

"If this enigmatic gathering of paper and ink is indeed a nexus for crime, then its presence cannot remain a secret for very long. I assure you, it *will* come to light."

* * *

Hours later, in a boardinghouse in London's East End, a weary man slumped in the corner of a shabby room and opened the *Codex Exsecrabilis*. He ran his hand down the blank page and shook at the memory of what he had done to the retired seaman in the next room. He would have to be going soon, he thought, before the body was discovered; but then, that probably would not be until the next morning. He turned the page in the book and began to weep again. He wept at the prospect of killing once more, or perhaps doing things he felt were far worse; and because he knew he would go on reading – until he had reached the final page of the codex.

* * *

Holmes was mildly surprised when Father Twitchell arrived at Baker Street the next morning. "I knew you wished to speak to me about the missing codex," said the priest. "I returned from Cambridge early this morning and decided to save you a trip by coming here straightaway."

"What can you tell me of this strange book?" asked Holmes.

"Only what I have read of it in Brother Eduardo's monograph. Were you aware of the pamphlet?"

"I would be interested in reading it. Do you know of any book collectors in your parish?"

Before Father Twitchell could answer, there was a knock at the door: Watson entered the room and quickly introduced himself to the priest, who shook the doctor's hand vigorously.

"I confess to being one of your avid readers," said the priest. "Such marvelous adventures – quite exhilarating."

"Excuse me, Father, are there any book collectors among your flock?" asked Holmes.

"Not that I am aware." The priest turned to the shelves above Holmes' desk. "You have some interesting volumes here. Are you a collector of books?"

"A book is not unlike a soup tureen. Though some may covet it for its shape and pattern, it is only the broth inside that interests me. No, I keep books only to have easy access to the information they record. But I did notice a few rare volumes in your own library. Do *you* collect books?"

"Not unlike you; only for what they can tell me."

"Is there anyone in your parish in desperate need of money? Someone who might have chanced upon the codex, realized its rarity, and seized upon the opportunity to take it to a bookseller?"

"A few of my parishioners are indeed poor. But the codex was in my study, and my study is not open to the church. In fact, it is always kept locked."

"May I ask why?"

"Even priests need some small bit of privacy, Mr. Holmes. At any rate, I hope that you do not suspect anyone in my congregation."

"Not at present. But if I do not soon uncover a substantial lead in this investigation, I will need to start questioning the more needy members of your church."

"I am afraid I would not be able to assist you in such an endeavor. Most of what I know is told me in the privacy of the confessional – in the confidence that I will keep it secret. I cannot break my vow to protect this confidentiality."

"That is admirable, Father, but how far should such a vow extend? Should one protect the identity of a thief?

"No one in my congregation is guilty of stealing the codex, Mr. Holmes."

"The book did not simply vanish into thin air."

"You must not underestimate the supernatural power of this book."

"Now you are speaking nonsense, Father."

"Why is it so hard for you to believe in the supernatural? You have devoted your life and talents to the struggle between good and evil."

"The struggle between good and evil is your domain. I apply myself to the scientific study of crime and criminals."

"Then let us lay aside any theological bearing on the matter, and simply contemplate a metaphysical universe – a sphere beyond this existence."

"Can I see it, or touch it?" asked Holmes sardonically. "Where, pray tell, is this metaphysical world of yours?"

"It surrounds us. But as long as our focus remains fixed on the affairs of the physical world it remains invisible to our mortal eyes."

"Two worlds inhabiting the same space?"

"Even the materialist admits we simultaneously inhabit two planes of existence. We move about a three-dimensional world even as we are passing through a *fourth* dimension, that of time."

Holmes removed the watch from his vest pocket. "The passage of time I can measure. Show me your measurements of the so-called supernatural world, or do not waste my time."

The priest stood and took his hat. "The power of the codex is real, Mr. Holmes. I wish it were not." He strode to the door. "You would do well to read Brother Eduardo's monograph."

"Thank you, Father. And may I recommend Winwood Reade's *Martyrdom of Man* to you?"

When the priest was gone, Watson threw down his notebook and scowled. "You know, Holmes, at times you really are too much!"

* * *

Holmes spent the better part of the next day in the Reading Room of the British Museum. When Watson met him for lunch at Simpson's, Holmes laid a thick pamphlet on the doctor's charger.

Watson read the title aloud, "*A Most Uncommon Prayer Book, Being a History of the Codex Exsecrabilis and a Documentation of its Known Crimes*. It looks rather extensive."

"The sins of the book, Watson, documented by the friar in shocking detail. The man's willingness to believe in the absurd is unseemly, but his treatise bears all the hallmarks of serious scholarship."

"What a remarkable concept that one should commit a crime for no other reason than because one has read of it in a book."

"The idea has interest, for a crime committed in this manner would be without apparent motive, and therefore more difficult to solve."

Holmes lit his pipe. "Brother Eduardo links the codex to many of the most sensational crimes of the last several hundred years – all of them supposedly committed during those 'three or four brief periods' to which he alluded, when the codex was not in the brotherhood's possession." He blew out a tiny cloud of smoke. "Our humble friar attempts to cast a new light on the early eighteenth-century crimes of Jonathan Wild, and I must say, his monograph has me rethinking the poisonous career of Thomas Griffiths Wainewright."

"So what is our next move?"

"Lunch, dear fellow – we can do nothing until another crime is committed."

* * *

When Watson was awakened by his wife early the next morning, he learned that Holmes had sent a message urging the doctor to meet him at Scotland Yard. Although he had planned on devoting the day to his Kensington practice, Watson had long ago developed a craving for Holmes' little adventures and was soon in a cab racing toward Victoria Embankment. Upon his arrival, Holmes informed the doctor of an event he hoped would be the key to recovering the missing codex: sometime during the previous morning, a Longbourn bookseller had repeatedly stabbed his wife with a paper knife.

"Mr. Avery Felton," said Holmes as he and Watson entered the man's prison cell, "my name is Sherlock Holmes. I am a private consulting detective come to further investigate the circumstances that have brought you to this wretched place. Cooperate with me and I will do all I can to help you."

Felton stared at the floor. "I have read of you, Mr. Holmes. But you cannot help me. I killed my wife…stabbed her in the back…as she washed the breakfast dishes! But I loved her!" he sobbed. "Why did I do it?"

"Have you come across a leather-bound manuscript, adorned with an upside-down cross?"
He shook his head.

"Are you certain? It is a heavy book, very old, some of its leaves may have been blank."

"I would remember such a book. What does it have to do with me?"

"Where did you go yesterday?"

"Nowhere, I stayed home."

"Then why *did* you kill your wife, Mr. Felton? Did you have an argument with her?"

"My head is spinning."

"Think, man!"

"We were having breakfast. Everything was perfect. She left to clean up. I was lounging at table with the morning post."

"Was there anything unusual in the mail?"

"Just letters from other booksellers." Felton ran a hand across his face. "Except one which was absolute gibberish."

"In what way?"

"I am not a formally educated man, Mr. Holmes. I am well read, and I understand many things, but I do not speak any foreign languages."

"Where would this letter be now?"

He shrugged. "Still on the table, I suppose."

* * *

Holmes tossed several torn envelopes and creased sheets of paper upon the table of his sitting room. "These letters are unremarkable. As Felton said, they are simply correspondence from his associates about book-related nonsense."

"So we came up empty-handed," said Watson.

"Perhaps not."

Holmes pulled a magnifying lens from his desk drawer. "The only other scrap of paper in Felton's place was this blank piece I found upon his kitchen floor. That alone is significant." He briefly studied the item. "It is, as I first suspected, a very old piece of parchment...a fragment of a much larger leaf...torn off in some haste. The creases confirm that it was folded to fit inside an envelope. Also, there are several tiny water stains, which I believe are noteworthy. Beyond these salient points, it is nothing more than a thin sheet of sheep skin...soaked and stretched, then scraped smooth to remove the hair." He took a large beaker from the shelf. "—Unless I can prove that it was torn from our missing codex."

Holmes raised the parchment to the light. "Behold, Watson," he said, "an invention as important to the dissemination of knowledge in *its* day as Gutenberg's first printing press was in the fifteenth century! Proving what Plato wrote about the impetus of need: 'Necessity, who is the mother of invention'!"

"How so?" laughed Watson.

"Parchment was invented in the ancient Greek city of Pergamum," said Holmes, "where – according to The Book of Revelation – Satan was enthroned." He crumpled the fragment and dropped it into the beaker. "In the second century BC Pergamum established a great library rivaling even that of Alexandria." He added just enough water to cover the parchment and began stirring the mixture briskly. "Up until then, the collected knowledge of civilization had been transcribed on papyrus, which was produced only along the Nile delta in Alexandria; and which had been over-harvested towards local extinction. Whether due to an inability to supply the material, or a desire to shut down its rival library, Alexandria ceased exporting papyrus."

Holmes decanted the water into a test tube. "So Pergamum invented a more than adequate substitute – one much cheaper and easier to produce than papyrus. It remains an excellent example of adaptation under changing circumstances."

"Holmes, you amaze me!"

He waved away the compliment. "I am preparing a monograph on paper and papermaking. It will be an invaluable resource in criminal investigation, and I daresay, had it been available at the time, the Bank Holiday Blackmail Case would have been brought to a far more satisfactory conclusion!"

Holmes withdrew a vial of white crystals and tossed a few into the test tube. "Parchment allowed the great Library at Pergamum to continue operating – until Mark Antony emptied its shelves and made Cleopatra a wedding present of its 200,000 volumes. *She* was a conniving woman, Watson." He removed the stopper from a reagent bottle of clear liquid and inserted a glass pipette.

"Now, let us see what this torn leaf has to tell us," said Holmes. "Brother Eduardo insists the codex was written in blood. If at some time there was blood on this scrap of parchment, a sufficient amount of it has been dissolved into this solution. This reagent will precipitate that blood as a brownish sediment." He added several drops and swirled the test tube.

"Nothing!" snarled Holmes. "Perfectly clean. So much for legends!"

"What if the legend is true," asked Watson, "and all trace of the evil writing has vanished?"

"Blood does not simply vanish. Some trace would remain, and the Holmes Hemoglobin Test is capable of detecting blood at concentrations of barely one part in a million." He smoothed out the parchment and blotted it dry. "Either there was no blood on this parchment to begin with, or…"

Holmes walked to the fireplace and filled his pipe. "How does one prove or disprove the supernatural?" he murmured, dropping into his chair. He took off his shoes and sat cross-legged, smoking his pipe.

* * *

Watson awoke at the call of his name. He had dropped off to sleep with the *London Times* in his lap, while Holmes had been puffing at his pipe and, a while later, quietly puttering about his desk.

"Watson, would you mind taking care of something for me?" asked Holmes.

The doctor arose from his chair and stretched. "Run an errand? Yes, of course."

"I have written out some instructions for you," he said, extending a folded sheet. "Please read them and make certain everything is clear."

Watson unfolded the sheet, glanced at his friend's distinctive scrawl, and gasped. He looked down at Holmes sitting calmly at his desk. The detective's left hand was wrapped with a handkerchief, his jack-knife and a saucer of dark red liquid at his elbow. Upon the blotter lay a Latin dictionary and the doctor's old service revolver.

Watson dropped the note. His body abruptly stiffened as the most abhorrent idea went racing through his mind. "No!" he cried in genuine terror. A cold sweat broke out over his face, which had gone as white as a sheet. Within seconds he began to shake involuntarily – except for his hands, which he kept tightly clenched by his sides.

Holmes realized the doctor was struggling hard to control himself: his mouth had become a pale trembling line, his eyes two coals burning with hatred. Holmes glanced at the revolver upon the desk, then quickly returned his gaze to the seething volcano of emotion standing before him. His hand moved toward the gun but Watson sprung upon it like a Bengal tiger, snatching the revolver from the desk.

Watson pressed the barrel to Holmes' forehead and gazed into the detective's widening eyes. "God help me," he said, squeezing the trigger.

When the hammer fell Holmes flinched at its sharp *click*.

Watson dropped the gun upon the desk and crumpled to the floor where he lay sobbing uncontrollably. Holmes lifted him into a chair and handed him a glass of whiskey.

"Holmes! How could you?" he cried.

"My dear friend," said Holmes, deep concern written upon his features, "please forgive me, but I could turn to no other for such a test. You have a heart that is genuinely good. Fair weather or foul, you are constant in your friendship, and so you have become for me a barometer by which I am able to gauge all that is noble in men."

"I wanted to kill you! And I would have, had—"

"Had the revolver not been loaded. But I have far too much respect for your prowess with a gun to—"

"Did you stop to think I could have bashed in your bloody brains with the butt of it!"

"*That* idea," Holmes said resentfully, "was not written upon the parchment!" He took the empty glass from Watson's trembling hand and went to refill it. "Nevertheless," he said softly, "you are right. It *was* a dangerous experiment…which might well have proved deadly."

He extended another whiskey to the doctor. "And it was indeed a sin to try it on my dearest friend."

Watson wiped his sweat-soaked face and took the glass. "You might have warned me."

"That would have ruined the whole experiment. Besides, you would have refused to read it."

Holmes picked up the note where Watson had dropped it. "Astonishing!" he cried. "It is blank again!" He hurried to the microscope to examine the fragment. After a minute he looked up from the eyepiece. "Not a trace of what I wrote – not even an impression made by the pen!"

Holmes walked to the fireplace, the parchment gripped tightly in his clenched fist. "Now that I know the power of the codex is genuine," he said angrily, "I want to know why the accursed thing was not destroyed centuries ago? All those despicable crimes could have been prevented!"

After several minutes, Holmes coolly remarked, "The apostate monk who created the thing…this Brother Moriarty…in many ways, he was a napoleon of crime. Even now, hundreds of years after his death, he dispatches his orders on these parchment leaves."

Holmes gazed at the wrinkled page in his hand. "That miserable bookseller rotting away in jail is a pawn. Whoever mailed this page to him simply wanted to drag a red herring across the trail of my investigation. But whereas it was intended to lead me astray, it has only served to strengthen an earlier suspicion." He shoved the parchment into the drawer of his desk and locked it. "Watson, are you recovered enough to accompany me to Longbourn?"

* * *

"If the codex was *half* as dangerous as you claimed, you should have destroyed it when it first came into your possession," said Holmes.

"For hundreds of years we Benedictines have devoted ourselves to the preservation of books," said Brother Eduardo. "The codex is one of a kind. Destroying it would have been a crime."

"But by not destroying it," said Watson, "you and your brothers are indirectly responsible for far worse crimes."

"But we have worked hard to keep the book from being read."

"And yet it *has* been read," said Holmes.

"True, there have been two or three times when the codex was not in our possession."

"I believe there have been *many* times," said Holmes. "Your monograph was published over a decade ago. I believe it needs extensive updating. The Whitechapel murders, for instance. Who was reading your book in 1888?"

"The codex *did* escape that year…for several months," said the monk, unable to meet Holmes' gaze. "But we have tried so hard. We have cared for it for centuries."

"Cared for it?" asked Watson.

"The Brotherhood considers the codex to be a living thing," said Father Twitchell.

"At first," said Brother Eduardo, "our order saved the book from the fire because of its rarity. Years later, we made a startling discovery about the nature of the codex. It had developed a form of intelligence." He paused. "We believe it has a living soul."

"You are quite mad," said Holmes.

"It bore the sins which one man poured onto its pages. Now it seeks redemption from those sins."

"You may leave us now, Friar," said Holmes.

"Like any soul, it is deserving of redemption," said Brother Eduardo, walking to the door. "But unlike the man whose sins it now bears, the codex is not human…and therefore, not eligible for the same redemption offered to men."

"Astonishing," cried Watson, after the monk had left the room.

"That old man actually views the book as his brother," said Father Twitchell, "a member of his own order, in fact – which is why the codex accompanies the Brotherhood whenever they travel."

"This case has given me a headache," said Holmes, walking to the fireplace. "Father, may I trouble you for some water?"

"Allow me to make you a cup of tea."

"No, please, water is fine."

When the priest returned with a glass of water, Holmes thanked him and drained it of all but an inch of liquid. "I have been admiring your fireplace," he said. "I have never seen a hearth as large as this one. I imagine it is quite ancient."

"Like the rest of this tower," said Father Twitchell. "This hearth actually took up the better part of the wall. I had the opening made smaller by bricking up the front edges."

"And still it is a hearth of enormous dimensions," said Holmes. "—But returning to more important matters, someone in your parish is responsible for mailing a page of the codex to Mr. Avery Felton."

Holmes crossed over to the priest's desk and set down the glass. When he withdrew his hand he managed to spill the remainder of the water. "How clumsy of me. I have made a mess of your desk."

"That is quite alright," said Father Twitchell, with thinly disguised irritation.

"When I received news that a bookseller had murdered his wife," said Holmes, "I naturally assumed the codex had come into his possession."

Father Twitchell nodded, eyeing the spilled water. The desktop, weathered and slightly warped from years of similar abuse, was far from being level, and already the tiny puddle had begun to migrate toward a battered leather volume he had been reading. He glanced about for something to mop up the liquid and, when nothing presented itself, grew visibly agitated. When the water had crept to within half an inch of the book the priest hurriedly snatched it up before it got wet. "What is your point?" he snapped, carefully examining the edges of the volume.

"Father Twitchell," asked Holmes, "do you have a burden for books as well as for souls?"

"I beg your pardon," he said, recovering his composure. "It has been a long and trying day. What else did you wish to ask me?"

"Could someone in your parish have wished to divert my investigation?"

"I am not sure."

"Of course, there is another possible motive: sending that page could have been a plea for help. Tell me, Father, how does one track down a book which, according to Brother Eduardo, does not wish to be found?"

"Where would you go, if you were overburdened by the sins of your past?"

"I might seek a priest," said Holmes. "One who would hear my confession, or – if my sins were on paper – one who would *read* them. For I have lately learned that no matter what the consequences, a priest would never divulge my secrets."

Holmes held out his hand. "It is over, Father. Where is the codex?"

Father Twitchell sprang from behind his desk and charged across the room, shoving Watson on his way.

"Holmes!" the doctor cried. "He's running into the fire!"

"Quick, Watson! Follow me!" said Holmes, running to the hearth. He leapt over the great blazing log and then whirled about. To his left was a narrow opening in the blocks, barely more than a foot wide, and perfectly hidden from view by the newer bricks.

"Hurry," cried Watson, now at his friend's side, "this heat is unbearable!"

Holmes quickly squeezed sideways through the opening, followed by the doctor. They found themselves in a narrow passageway, with the sound of footsteps echoing in the blackness ahead of them.

Watson groped for a match as he and Holmes felt their way down the passage. "The footsteps are fading – he is getting away!"

"I doubt that."

The two men stumbled upon a wider chamber. They could feel a strong current of cool air blowing past them in the darkness. Watson struck a match, illuminating a large circular room. There were other passageways leading off the chamber, and narrow stone steps that wound up the center of the tower into the shadows above. "Which way did he—?"

"Quiet," whispered Holmes.

From the gloom above their heads several bits of crumbling mortar suddenly rained down, cascading on the lowest steps. Holmes raced up the steps with Watson close behind. When he reached the top of the tower, he found the priest standing at the edge of the parapet, clutching the codex and staring down at the street.

"Father Twitchell," Holmes called gently, "please come away from the edge."

The priest spun around to face him. "It is too late," he sobbed. "The things I have done... I can never forgive myself!" He took a step backward, the codex held tightly to his breast, and plummeted into the darkness below.

* * *

The sidewalk and cobbles of Baker Street were littered with shattered glass. Watson could hear it crunching beneath his feet when he stepped down from the carriage. He looked up at the open windows of Holmes' sitting room, briefly wondering what new eccentricity awaited him, and then hurried up to see his old friend.

Watson immediately felt the breeze upon his face when he opened the door. He strode across the room, past Holmes who was gazing sullenly into the fire, and stood before the two windows overlooking the street. There was no glass or mullions left in the frames. The doctor sighed deeply. "There is a decided draught in this room, Holmes. What on earth have you been up to?"

Mrs. Hudson tapped at the door and then ushered in three monks.

"The thing you seek is upon the table," Holmes said without rising.

Brother Eduardo hugged the book. "We are greatly indebted to you, Mr. Holmes."

"What a pity," said Brother Paolo, "that in offering absolution to a damned soul, Father Twitchell should lose his own."

"What do you mean?" asked Holmes.

"He committed suicide," said Brother Eduardo, "for which there is no forgiveness."

"And why is that?"

"Only God has authority in matters of life and death," said Brother Eugenio. "In taking his own life, Father Twitchell usurped that authority. He will burn in hell."

"I believe you are wrong," said Holmes. "Your faith is founded upon the belief that in a supreme act of benevolence, God sent His only son to take upon His shoulders the sins of the world. But after His son died for those sins, He was received back to His father.

"Gentlemen," Holmes continued, "how can you believe anything less in the case of a priest who, led by love, took upon his shoulders the sins of the book, and ultimately died for those sins? Father Twitchell's suicide was an act of sacrifice. *If* there is a heaven, I believe you will find him there...waiting for you."

Holmes motioned to the door. "But these are theological matters, of which I am out of my depth."

"Perhaps not, Mr. Holmes," said Brother Eduardo, departing.

"Holmes, is it wise to leave so much power in their hands?" Watson asked after the men had left.

"Most of the pages in the codex were blank once again, the parchment having long ago reverted to its original state: clean and blameless. What does it say in Isaiah? 'Though your sins be as scarlet, they shall be as white as snow.' I assure you, those leaves were as white as snow. Except for one last section of manuscript, which I sliced out of the binding while slightly averting my eyes, lest I should inadvertently read some of that hellish text. The pages I removed contained the last remaining words of malediction. I took the liberty of burning them shortly before you arrived. It is doubtful the Brotherhood will hazard too close an inspection of that volume; but if they should, they will not notice its thickness diminished by a mere few leaves."

Holmes turned back to the fireplace. "And I cannot imagine the codex will mind. For it is better to lose a few pages than to lose one's soul."

Watson took the chair next to Holmes. "For a man who has just solved an extremely unusual case, you seem rather down. You must not hold yourself responsible for the death of the priest."

"When Father Twitchell hurled himself from the tower, I plunged with him...into the depths of despair."

"But why, Holmes?"

"You were planning to ask me how the windows were shattered. No," Holmes smirked, "it was not one of my little experiments taken flight. When I burned that remaining evil signature an astonishing phenomenon occurred." He closed the collar of his dressing gown and hugged himself. "A black plume billowed from the fireplace. It was not smoke, but rather something more solid, something slick and oily in appearance. It behaved like a giant snake. I now wonder if it was not similar to the material referred to among spiritualists as *ectoplasm*."

"That's incredible!"

"Yes. But I have had the misfortune of seeing it."

Holmes walked to one of the shattered windows. Below him, Baker Street clattered and hummed with the activities of London life; a confusion of men and women, carriages and horses, all bustling to and fro across the soot-grey cobbles. "The damned thing bifurcated before exiting through these *closed* windows."

"You've grown pale," said Watson.

"I have a strong constitution, but I admit the sight of it has unnerved me."

"You have clearly had a shocking experience. Come and sit down. I will ask Mrs. Hudson to bring up some breakfast."

"Not just yet. There is something I wish to say first."

Holmes went back to the fireplace and dropped into his armchair. "A significant part of me plunged with that accursed tome...and was dashed against the pavement below: a bit of my philosophy, perhaps; certainly my spirits. Remember the horrible depression through which I suffered in the Spring of '87?"

"We came through it alright."

"I feel there are even blacker depths waiting to engulf me now. Which is why I am going away."

"Going away, Holmes?"

"These last few days I have witnessed many strange things – otherworldly phenomena which I cannot explain." He shuddered. "I have come to realize there is a significant tear in my logic. I must set myself to mending this tear before the entire fabric of my reason is rent asunder. To accomplish this I need time to think. And I need a change of scenery; as cozy and as safe as they are, I feel the need to temporarily escape the confines of these Baker Street rooms."

"But where will you go?"

"The Continent," said Holmes, gazing at the mezzotint hanging above the mantel: a reproduction of the Reichenbach Falls in Switzerland. He seemed to lapse into deep thought.

"Perhaps Tibet," he said at length, "to visit the Dalai Lama."

"But what of your work?"

"I have always felt it my duty to use my unusual talents for the public good, and in all the years you have known me, and before then, I have never forsaken that responsibility. But now..." He shrugged. "I am in need of a very long holiday."

"And what of all the people who have come to rely upon you? What will I tell them when they come calling and learn that their champion has disappeared, leaving them with no one to whom they can turn? That you are on holiday? Sightseeing? They will never understand."

"Tell them whatever you wish." Holmes grunted. "Tell them I am dead, for all I care."

"I am not very good at fabricating lies!"

"Come now, Watson!" laughed Holmes. "You underestimate your abilities as a fabulist. You have yet to chronicle a single case of mine where you have not played fast and loose with the facts."

"I believe you are quite serious."

"My dear fellow," Holmes said gently, "I may be asking too much of you, but…you *could* supply a cover story to disguise my hasty departure. And at any rate, I shall return…eventually."

"I will accompany you, then."

"Not necessary," said Holmes, smiling. "Remember, you have a wife to take care of now!"

* * *

The following day, after leaving Victoria Station where he had seen Holmes off to the Continent, Watson returned to Baker Street to contemplate those empty rooms. Later, while a glazier set about repairing the shattered windows, Watson sat at his friend's desk and started writing what he felt might very well be the last story in which he would ever record the singular gifts that had distinguished the best and wisest man he had ever known.

Gator Bait

T.Y. Euliano

"ALLIGATOR ATTACK at Kimball Botanical Gardens. Animal control and EMS are on their way."

I hit the lights and siren, and accelerated down Tower Road toward the park. My partner said nothing as the blood drained from his face, both of us hoping for a false alarm.

At the gardens we bumped through a minefield of rocks and axle-threatening holes disguised as an innocent field of coarse green grass. We stopped near a small group huddled around a figure on the ground.

The victim lay on his back, eyes closed, face glowing white in the early morning sunshine. A woman hovered, caressing his cheek. His right arm lay across his abdomen, his left at his side, wrapped in a red towel. No, not a red towel, a bloodied white towel. The arm was too short, much too short, with a belt cinched mid-biceps.

An ambulance siren cut through the thick morning air, still too far away. While my partner stood frozen, I knelt beside the victim, the metallic tang of blood nearly overpowering, and introduced myself while I felt for his pulse. Fast. "I'm Detective Yarborough. This is my partner, Detective Black." I opened the First Aid Kit, found the tourniquet, and apologized as I wrapped it tightly above the belt. The man barely winced.

"Tell me your name, sir."

His eyes remained closed, but his lips moved. Barely a whisper. I didn't catch it.

"Richard Simpson," one of the huddled men said. "He's our groundskeeper. Sheila's his wife." He put an arm around the woman's shaking shoulders.

In my peripheral vision, Matt took out his notebook and started writing.

Sheila let out a sob.

"Can you tell us what happened?" I asked.

"Rick was thinning out the swamp grass," the man continued. "Must have disturbed a nest. We heard thrashing and him hollering. He managed to twist away and get to shore."

The ambulance crew arrived at last, and moved everyone back, including us, for which we were grateful. Moments later, Mr. Simpson lay on a gurney, legs elevated, IV fluids pouring. The EMTs hoisted him into the ambulance, joined by his wife.

"You catch that gator and bring his arm," she said, to no one in particular, as the doors closed. My stomach churned a little at that image.

Matt and I collected names and contact information and were about to depart when the wildlife officer arrived.

"I don't want to see this," Matt said, quickening his pace toward the cruiser. "That gator was just doing what gators do – defending her home."

I didn't disagree, but once they attacked, they had to be destroyed. Getting a taste for human flesh or something. Made me shiver. As we drove away, I glanced in the rearview mirror, curious how one caught a man-eating alligator. But we had reports to file, and other cases, with actual criminals to pursue.

My phone rang. Gerald Baker…again. The man had lost his daughter, literally lost, like no idea where she was. His suffering struck close to home for me. Largely based on Mr. Baker's testimony, her boyfriend, Jeremy Hoyt, was tried for murder, but without a body, the jury found him not guilty. He was released yesterday, and her father wasn't handling it so well. Neither were we. It had been our case. Losing sucked.

"Mr. Baker," I said over the car's Bluetooth.

"He's packing up to leave."

"That would be within his rights," I said.

"So he can just move away? Start a new life? What about my Jillian?"

I said nothing. What could I say? I had told the D.A. to wait, that we didn't have enough evidence, but that whole constitutional 'speedy trial' thing got in the way, more so in an election year. Other than threats she'd communicated to her father and a friend, and Jeremy's lack of alibi, there was nothing. Her blood in his car and house were easily explained away by the defense. "They lived together. Everyone has cuts and scrapes." Beyond that we had no tangible evidence to show the jury. No smoking gun, no bloody knife, no body.

"What are you doing for my daughter?" Mr. Baker said through angry sobs.

"I'm sorry, sir. We hope new evidence will surface, but as we discussed, Jeremy Hoyt cannot be re-tried."

"What if we catch him with drugs, or stolen property?"

I exchanged a here-we-go-again look with Matt. "Sir, I must warn you against any contact with him, including his home and vehicle." Mr. Baker was on the edge, understandably, but nothing good could come from his current state of mind.

He disconnected.

I groaned. Matt's was even louder. "That man's got to let it go."

"Let it go?" Words came on reflex, in a harsh voice not my own. "His daughter's gone. You can't let that go."

Matt stared straight ahead, an uncomfortable silence between us. We'd been partners less than a year, but he knew about my family. He knew I visited the cemetery weekly. He knew I hadn't let it go.

But his comment wasn't directed at me. "Sorry," I said.

* * *

After several hours catching up on paperwork, Rachel called from dispatch. "The Medical Examiner wants you at the morgue asap."

I parked the cruiser along the access road behind the medical center. With no receptionist on duty at the morgue, we followed the increasing odor of formaldehyde, and knocked on the cold metal door. Dr. Karey opened it clad in his white coat, with matching hair color. As he ushered us inside, goose flesh erupted on my arms as it always did here. Disgust? Anxiety? Or maybe just the cold. He escorted us past several mercifully empty autopsy tables. On the last was a body…of sorts. Not a human body. An alligator, on its back, its light-colored underbelly splayed open, its tail hanging just off the end of the eight-foot table.

Dr. Karey said, "Since we were hoping to get the arm back in time to reattach it, we brought the gator here, and Professor Blair came over from the vet school." Dr. Karey nodded at another man returning from the sink. His green scrubs appeared clean, if wrinkled. He tossed a paper towel into a nearby trash can and offered his hand. I introduced myself and Matt.

"Any luck?" I asked.

"Depends on what you mean by luck. We did find a forearm." Dr. Karey pulled the sheet back from a nearby specimen table, revealing the lower part of an arm.

"That's great," Matt said, moving closer.

"But it's not his," Dr. Karey said.

Matt froze and met my eyes, his wide, mine too, probably. Dr. Karey chuckled, actually chuckled, in a morgue. "You should see your faces. Did I tell you, Blair?"

The vet nodded, a smile on his face as well. The whole scene was surreal.

An arm, but not our victim's? Another victim? What are the odds?

"How can you be sure it's not his?" Matt asked.

"It belongs to a woman," Dr. Karey said.

He was right, the arm, though discolored, was clearly a woman's. As I moved around the specimen table, I noticed a dark mark on the side of the wrist. "Can we turn it over?" I asked.

Dr. Karey slipped on a glove and turned the arm, revealing a butterfly tattoo on the inside of the wrist. Jillian Baker had a butterfly tattoo on the inside of her wrist.

Matt let out a low whistle.

"Fingerprints will be tricky," Dr. Karey said.

"It's Jillian Baker," I said.

Stunned silence. Blank looks. Except for Matt, his huge round eyes met mine.

"The young woman who disappeared a year ago," I said.

Matt snapped out of his fog. "But this arm can't be that old, right?"

"It hasn't been in this gator's belly for a year," Professor Blair said.

"And it shows up right after her killer is released from prison," Matt said.

"Thought he was found innocent," Dr. Karey said.

"No. Not guilty," I said. "Not the same thing."

After several moments of silence, Matt said, "So what happens now? Are they going to kill another gator?"

"Already did. It's on the way," Dr. Karey said. "Too late to reattach, but the victim's wife wants his wedding ring."

Matt recoiled.

We thanked them and walked through to the hospital to check on Mr. Simpson.

In the ICU, Mrs. Simpson sat at her husband's side, their hands clasped, his eyes closed. A nasal cannula crossed his face, multi-colored leads snaked from under his gown, and several lines traced across the monitor. The bandage on his arm was clean and white, and his face was somewhat less pale.

"Officers Yarborough and Black from this morning," I said, softly.

She nodded.

"How is he?"

"I'm awake," Mr. Simpson said, his eyes opening narrowly. "Did she get away?" He sounded hopeful.

I hedged. "We don't know yet."

"It wasn't her fault."

"Yes, sir," Matt said. "But that's not our call."

"How many alligators are in that area?" I asked.

"Varies. I thought they'd moved upstream." His lids fell closed. "I was wrong."

"Who has access, besides you?" I asked.

His eyes opened again, quizzical.

"Have you seen anyone near the swamp recently who didn't belong? Or strange vehicles?"

"Why? What's happened?"

"Just a routine question." Like that made any sense.

He shook his head. "No one goes near that swamp but me."

On the way out, we checked back at the morgue.

"Perfect timing," Dr. Karey said as he answered my knock, white coat replaced with a plastic green smock. We followed him to where a second enormous alligator lay beside the first. This one's tail nearly reached the floor.

Scalpel in hand, Professor Blair nodded to us, then made a long incision down the gator's front. I watched, mesmerized; there wasn't much blood. "Anyone taking bets on the stomach contents?" Dr. Karey said.

Under the harsh fluorescent lights, Matt's face glowed a pale yellow-green, sweat glistened on his cheeks, and his lips were no longer red. I was torn between watching the autopsy, and helping my partner.

When Dr. Karey reached his hand into the opening, the decision was made. I escorted Matt to the sink as he began to retch, which nearly did me in, until Dr. Karey said, "Here it is, wedding ring and all." A thud on metal, another retch from Matt, a splash in the sink, but my insides were distracted now.

"There's something else," Professor Blair said.

"Holy shit," Dr. Karey said.

"It eventually would have been," the professor said, and both men chuckled. Morgue humor.

I handed Matt several paper towels, then walked to the specimen table on surprisingly steady legs. Next to Jillian's arm, was Mr. Simpson's much larger and hairier one, and next to that was a lower leg. A woman's. Amputated below the knee. With a thin chain around the ankle, from which hung a charm, if that's the right term for something so hideous – a skull with a spider crawling from its mouth.

I recognized it immediately. It matched the one in Jeremy Hoyt's ear. His right ear lobe was expanded to more than an inch in diameter with a black plastic circle containing the same design. I'd stared at it during the trial, wondered how anyone could do that to his body, then wondered when I became so old.

"How could body parts be in two different gators?" Matt asked.

"A fight between hungry gators maybe," Dr. Blair said. "But these were cut, not torn."

"On that note," a still-pale Matt said, "I need some fresh air."

"Good call," I said, forcing the image from my mind.

We returned to the precinct, and updated Captain Marsh. "Holy shit," he said, apparently the response of the day.

"We have to tell her father," I said.

Captain Marsh rocked back in his chair. "When the M.E.s done."

"Can't take long enough," Matt said under his breath. Part of me agreed.

* * *

We were off on Sunday, but I couldn't stop thinking about the case. Had Jillian been alive all this time? Where was the rest of her? And the timing couldn't be a coincidence.

After Mass I headed to the cemetery, stopping for fresh flowers on the way. As I stood at the grave of my wife and daughter, my mind wandered to Gerald Baker. I understood his single-minded focus. There's nothing I wouldn't give to have my little girl back, and my wife, but at least their murderer was serving time. Two counts of DUI manslaughter got him fifteen years. Not nearly long enough. Never enough.

At last Mr. Baker finally had something of his daughter to bury.

On a whim, I drove by Jeremy Hoyt's house, where a large hand-written sign in the yard read, 'Moving Sale – Everything must go.' Which was a lot, much more than could have possibly fit in the tiny home we'd searched months ago. From clothing to electronics to appliances to furniture, he was truly starting over.

I pulled out my phone and snapped a picture through the car window as I drove slowly past. Jeremy was haggling and didn't look up, or he'd probably accuse me of harassment.

On my way home, Mr. Baker called again. I didn't answer. Would the news help or hurt? Before, there was still hope. He called again. I switched off my phone.

At home, I turned on the TV, for distraction more than entertainment. A knock at the door took me by surprise. I had few unexpected visitors, or even expected ones. Through the peep hole, I saw Gerald Baker. *Crap.*

"I know you're in there." His words were slurred. He needed to go home, but I couldn't let him drive.

"Mr. Baker, I'm calling you a taxi," I yelled through the closed door.

"I need to talk to you. He's leaving. He had a yard sale."

Against my better judgment, I opened the door. He swayed on his feet, and looked at me through glassy bloodshot eyes.

"He sold it all. Some of that stuff was Jillian's. He sold it." He held out a notebook. "I recorded everything he sold, and took video of the buyers." He held up his cellphone. "I'm gonna get her stuff back."

"You can't do that."

"I can't…" Mr. Baker began to sob, his voice coming out in fits and starts. "I can't let him… go live a life while my…baby lies somewhere…not even properly buried." He tumbled forward. I caught him in an awkward embrace. One grieving father to another.

"We found her," I said. I didn't mean to; it slipped out.

He pulled back, eyebrows drawn together, mouth open. His eyes shifted between mine, desperate for more.

"I'm sorry," I said. "We don't have all the information yet."

He collapsed to the stoop, head in his hands. "She's dead."

I sat beside him, hand on his quaking back. "Yes, I'm sorry."

"I knew," he said.

"Yeah."

"But…"

"Yeah," I said.

We sat there on the stoop for close to an hour. Both crying. Him more than me. I invited him in for sober-up coffee, resisting his efforts to extract details. He left around three a.m., after a cursory DUI exam, and a promise to go straight home.

Next morning, after report, I showed Matt my yard sale drive-by video on my laptop. He only half-watched as he listened to our phone messages. "Hey, there's one from the M.E.'s office," he said.

I put the call on speaker when he answered. "She was frozen."

"Jillian?" I said.

"Yes," Dr. Karey said. "Her skin had a different consistency than the other victim's, so I ran a test. Her body had been frozen."

"There's a test for that?" Matt asked.

"A SCHAD, the activity of short-chain—"

"We'll take your word for it," I said. "Can you tell how long?"

"No. But judging by the saw marks, I'd say she was frozen first, and then cut up."

I ended the call, sank into my chair and stared straight ahead, the video loop of the yard sale still playing. And then I saw it. I paused the video and pointed.

"A freezer," Matt said.

Toward the back of the array of appliances was a white deep freezer. "I don't remember it from our search," I said.

Matt typed on his computer. "Because it wasn't there. It's not on the inventory list. Any chance it's still on site?"

"No, but Mr. Baker might have video of the purchaser."

We ran to the cruiser and I called Mr. Baker. He was standing in the doorway when we arrived. Matt scanned the hand-written list of items while Mr. Baker opened a directory of the videos on his laptop.

"Four-fifteen," Matt said. "The freezer sold at four-fifteen."

Mr. Baker clicked on the video file from that time. A young man, his dark curls tucked under a backward ball cap, handed Jeremy a stack of bills, then he and several other young men used a dolly and a U-Haul with a drop gate to load the freezer. As the truck drove away, I reached over and froze the video on the license plate.

With a copy of the video file, we thanked him and promised to keep him informed. Except that was a lie. We hadn't told him about the frozen sawed-up body parts. Was it to protect him from the horrific truth? Or to protect ourselves from having to reveal it? Or to protect Jeremy from Mr. Baker's wrath? No, not that. Definitely not that.

Search warrant in hand, the rental company provided the name and address of the young man. It was outside of town, where land was plentiful, and grocery stores less so. A freezer would come in handy out here. We drove down a packed-dirt drive to a small wood home with a carport, empty of cars, but with a white freezer against the back wall.

When a woman answered the door, I held out the search warrant as I introduced myself and my partner. She was young, with a baby on her hip, and another child yelling from behind. "We need to take the freezer you purchased yesterday," I said.

In response to her confused expression, Matt said, "It may have been involved in a crime."

Her look of confusion rapidly morphed to revulsion. There weren't a lot of ways a freezer could be involved in a crime, and it appeared she'd guessed right.

"Take it," she said.

Matt excused himself to call for the evidence van waiting on the main street.

"I'll give you a receipt," I said.

"I don't want it back." Her body trembled as she turned to deal with a now screaming child, squeezing the one on her hip with motherly affection. I glanced into the home. It was clean, but messy. The home of small children. She and her husband had likely saved for months for that freezer, and we'd taken it from them.

I made an impulsive decision as we drove away. The best of the day. "Let's run by Herman's."

The appliance manager's a friend. We got it at cost, which we split, and had it delivered the next day. No name on the receipt, just 'thank you for your cooperation.'

* * *

Forensics found blood, and matched it to Jillian's. We couldn't arrest Jeremy, double-jeopardy and all, but I had a desperate need to confront the man, to tell him we knew, to warn him we'd be watching.

But he was gone. No forwarding address. His cell phone disconnected. His car showed up at a used car lot. Nothing on bus or airplane ticket purchases. He'd vanished, Mr. Baker's fears realized.

* * *

At Jillian's funeral, he thanked me. I knew I should say something comforting, something about finding peace, but that's crap.

Months later, the vet, Professor Blair, asked to see me. We met at a coffee shop, just the two of us. He'd been on an alligator hunt the weekend before, he said. They'd caught a twelve-footer. He took it to the school for his students to examine, before handing it over to the processors for meat. He swiped proudly through phone images, much less disturbing than a live dissection.

The last photo caused my breath to catch. On a specimen table was a ruler next to a black plastic circle that measured about an inch. Inside the circle, a spider crawled from the mouth of a skull. The professor's expression never wavered, though he may have winked.

Maybe Mr. Baker had found his peace after all.

Down We Go Together

Tracy Fahey

TONIGHT it feels like it might rain forever. I watch dirty water spatter the windows, sliding down the pane in thick rivulets. Outside the puddles are pocked with drops; streets liquorice-slick under the streetlights. Inside the diner it's muggy. A heavy warmth seeps from the Italian coffee machine that spits and gurgles behind the counter. The lighting is low, muted by outsize brown lampshades. I've been here for hours in the café I call my office, papers spread out on the table in front of me. Lou doesn't mind me sitting here, mainlining coffee long into the night. It's London. No-one cares, as long as I keep buying. The rain pours down faster and harder, streaming down the pane in thick rivulets. Just another rainy night in Soho.

The line tickles my memory…a song from long ago. It half-comes to me, so near I can almost but not quite hear the melody, and then it fades away into the darkness. I'm getting used to it now, the tantalising way that perception teases. The memories ebb and flow; from sharp-focus to dim. They feel like something on the tip of my tongue, on the cusp of my hearing, on the edge of my sight. Always elusive. Sometimes if I look sideways at these memories, try and recall the smell instead of the sound, the feel rather than the text, they'll come back to me. But not this time.

My phone rings; the unexpected noise makes me jump. The screen blazes with light. The caller ID reads 'Do Not Answer.' I press the red button. My hand is trembling. *Too much coffee*, I say to myself automatically, but I know differently.

I rub my eyes and focus again on the green files fanned out on the table in front of me. The café door opens, letting in a gust of rainy wind and a burst of noise from the street. I look out to see a mosaic of teenage boys, faces indistinct in the pouring rain, their voices roaring in shock and laughter as they splash by. I smile for a moment at their volume, their careless energy, and then select the thickest file. It's the one I always select. The cover is a dull green, faded almost to grey; edges soft and worn with age. *Simon*, it says. Inside is a thick mass of newspaper clippings and photographs. I bend my head over my case notes. The words buckle and blur under the dim light.

Everyone has a case they can't forget. And this is mine.

* * *

Simon's face smiles up at me. The photograph is bleached now, grown ghostly in the sunlight of other days. But I can still see that grin so clearly in my mind; those strong white teeth, those happy blue eyes, that blonde hair ruffled by the breeze. I see the ocean behind him, a grey-blue sheet. If I focus I can almost hear the rough *craw-craw* of the seagulls and smell the salt-stink of the Atlantic air. I pick up the photograph delicately, but my hand is shaking again, one long sustained tremor this time. The picture falls between my stiff fingers, face down on the handwritten notes. *Maybe that last coffee was a mistake*, I think, and breathe deeply. *Or maybe the one before it.*

"How ya doing, Dee?" I look up. It's Lou, one hand on her hip.

"Fine." I like Lou. She's somewhere in her forties, but fighting it with peroxide and heavy make-up. "'Nother coffee?" She's carrying the pot, already tilting it at an angle in anticipation.

"Better not right now." I hold my hand up, so she can see the tremble. It's usually something I hide, but Lou's sharp eyes spotted it a long time ago.

"That thing again, hon? Bloody nuisance, innit."

I smile at her. "Yes, Lou. Just have to wait for it to stop. Mind you, it doesn't matter. I can still read." I wave a hand at my files.

"Hard-working woman," says Lou. "Shout for me if you need anything. Good luck with the work."

"Sure," I say, but I'm already lifting the pages with my good hand.

Where are you? I sit back in the leather chair. He's nowhere, but he's everywhere I look. He always dreamed of living in London. Today alone I've seen him a couple of times; sitting opposite me on the Tube, standing waiting to cross the road in Westminster. I look out the crazy-paving glass buckled with rain, and sure enough, there he is too. I watch him pass by, indistinct but for his hair, bright and luminous under the street-light.

Is it you?

* * *

"Bloody rain!" It's the boys again. They come in, wet and shaking down their leather jackets with a high, animal energy. Drops spatter on the floor. "Hey, Ma, give us a cup of coffee." It's Lou's son Olly. His curly blond hair is frosted with rain, his teeth grin white in a brown face. He looks like eighteen summers of wholesomeness; sports teams and hot dinners and adulation.

Lou sighs and rolls her eyes, but her face creases in a begrudging smile. She hefts the coffee pot up. "One," she says. "And you'd all better pay. Quieten down now and I'll bring 'em over."

I bow my head and flip through the papers in front of me.

"Hey there." A blond young man is grinning at me.

I look down at my file, at the photograph attached.

"Is it you?" I ask.

He looks at me. "Yes," he says, puzzled. "It's me. Olly. You know. Lou's son." He looks at me carefully. "You OK, missus?"

I feel it wash over me again. That sluice of reality, cold as the sea.

"Sorry," I say. My face is hot.

"This fella bothering you?" It's Lou, jokey, coffee-pot in hand. I slide my mug over. I don't care about the shakes now. I need the comforting scald of black coffee on the back of my throat.

* * *

I lie awake in that tiny, cold flat. Outside the morning traffic has started up; a symphony of engines, bleeping horns, the occasional distant siren wailing. I want to sleep. I want to, but something won't close down. Images in my head run and rerun; transmogrifying into new and overwhelming waves.

It creeps. It starts with the bones. The aches in the muscles. That irritating tic at the corner of the eye. Deep shallow breaths; each one an effort. *It'll pass*, you say. *It was a late night. I'm just tired.* But morning after morning it's the same; shoulders like a rusty crane, creaking as they move. The heaviness, as if the very skin weighs down the scaffolding beneath. Your lower back forms a solid corset of knotted muscle. Even your face hurts; each plane of bone a separate ache.

And then it spreads. Your brain grows numb; heavy, slow. It's all too much. Inside you're a swollen lump of dense, corporeal agony. Outside… Outside it's like your skin is being wire-brushed away to reveal a glistening mass of nerves. You plummet; an anchor falling steadily into the deepness and the darkness. It's cold here. All the time.

Underneath the thick duvet, I shiver. Somewhere across the room, my phone is ringing.

* * *

The beginning is always different. The aftermath is always the same. I sit here in the coffee-scented café with its steamed-up windows, my good left hand holding my wretched, trembling right hand in a protective grip. I'm shivering although it's warm.

"You're back, love." It's Lou, her make-up slightly streaked in the harsh morning sunlight. Up close I can see the fissure on her skin; the hack of laughter-lines around her eyes and mouth. The café is deserted except for us.

"Mmmhmm." I smile up at her. "Coffee please."

She looks at me then. "You look like you could do with it," she says bluntly. "Bad night?"

"Yeah." I don't elaborate. Lou's seen me like this before. She knows.

She pours my coffee; aromatic steam rises from my cup. "I know all about it. Didn't get much sleep myself." She lingers. I wait.

"It's Olly." She sits down opposite me. The padded chair creaks under her. "You saw him last night, right?"

I nod.

"I don't like that crowd he runs with. He's coming home later and later. Got more money in his pocket than he should." She scowls briefly. "I know all mothers worry, but this stuff – it don't feel right."

There's more coming. I can sense it.

She sighs. "Dee. I know what you do. I've seen your files on the table. Willya do me a favour? Can you follow him around a bit? See what he's up to?"

I look at her. "You sure?" Sometimes people think they want to know the worst, but in their hearts they don't. Not really.

"Yeah. I've thought about it all night, and well…I was waiting for you to come in today to ask you."

I take a deep drink from my mug. "In that case, tell me all you know about his friends. Names, nicknames, hangouts, phone numbers. Give me as much information as you can."

She tilts the coffee-jug. "Thanks. I'll pay you of course, but as of now, all coffees're on the house."

* * *

I follow him. It's easy at first. He comes into the diner most days; I just wait for him to leave. Lou watches me go each day and says nothing.

It's hard to follow him. It shouldn't be, but it is. When he gets lost in the tidal surge of crowds I get confused. I find London confusing after my village in Ireland. No. I don't think about Ireland. I don't think about my old neighbours, their sad faces concealing a bright desire for gossip. I don't think about that beach; that sloping long spit of sand. I don't think about the scream of the seagulls, about those waves hissing on the shoreline, about that savage riptide that swirls everything out into the grey, foam-flecked ocean.

I think about Olly instead, and where he goes. I keep losing him in the streets; those endless rivers of people cleave together and hide him from view. My frustration grows. The first day goes by. Then the second. Then the third. Each time I go in to the café I feel the weight of Lou's gaze, her flat disappointment when I mouth "No."

She pours me coffee, I drink it. Our pact is sealed.

* * *

Of course I worry. I worry that I'm taking time off my own case. I tell myself I'm double-jobbing. I'm looking for them both. Two blond heads in a sea of drifting people. So I walk. I walk until my legs shiver with aches. At night I sit in that cramped little flat and soak my feet in a basin of gloriously hot water. I watch the brown stain on the wall that looks like a distorted face, revelling in the blossoming of muscles, the steady throb of pulsing blood.

From time to time the phone vibrates in my pocket, but it's always the same caller. It would be a relief to change my number, but it's the only one that Simon has for me.

I sleep, but only fitfully. My dreams are a kaleidoscope of waves and sand. Salt crusts my skin. I see myself running, screaming, wet sand hard under my feet. My throat tears with raw panic. *Simon.*

I wake to the sound of the gulls crying outside. It's no use. I give up trying to sleep and walk to the cosy fug of the diner.

Heat radiates from the mug between my palms. My face is reflected in the chrome of the coffee-machine. The lines are carved harsher now; crosshatching round the eyes, a cruel downturned slash slopes my mouth. Lou looks over at me, I shake my head.

I'll find him for you. I will the words at her.

And four days after I take on the job, I do.

* * *

He walks down the narrow pedestrian street. I focus on what he's wearing. Black leather jacket. Jeans. Motorcycle boots. I recite them to myself, setting the items in place in my head. It gets trickier when he turns onto Dean Street. It's a blur of colourful boutiques, bars, restaurants. I blink. People surge by, hiding him from view. I feel the old familiar rise of panic in my throat. He turns left, onto Old Compton Street.

As soon as I round the corner, the street buckles and swims. Shop signs blur, and then snap into focus. A babble of voices rises like a fog. The people in front of me start to intertwine; their bodies morphing, changing. A seagull descends, first one, then another, till the sky is thick with their wings.

"Simon?" It comes out louder than I intended. The street is full of blond boys, looking at me with identical, puzzled faces.

No. I can do this. When I shake my head the images resolve. There's only two blond boys now. They're locked in each other's arms, standing outside a bar.

For a wild moment I think *it's him*. But it isn't. It never is.

* * *

I sit down heavily at a table. It's coming for me now; that undertow. If I shut my eyes I can see the aftermath. Driftwood like dinosaur bones, wet sand crocheted with seaweed. Debris. Scoured bottles. Twisted cans. Plastic bags silted with dirt and bloated with water.

I'm a beach after the storm. I am what the sea has spat up.

"Dee." Someone is shaking my shoulder. I open my eyes. He is blond and blue-eyed. His face is wet. I reach out to him and touch his damp skin; that peach-firm cheek.

"Are you going to tell Ma?" Confused, I start to stutter. I look at him.

Olly. It's Olly. The beach recedes into memory, flat and sea-soaked.

I hold his hand. "Do you want me to?"

His blue eyes fill with tears.

* * *

"So there you go." The windows are covered in a thick layer of condensation. It's raining again.

Lou is silent, her fingers picking up the cutlery from the place-setting in front of her, then carefully putting it down again.

"So that's it," she says eventually. "No drugs?"

"No drugs," I affirm. Well maybe there is, but not in the way she means. I finger the shabby folder in front of me.

"It's just…it's just I wasn't expecting this." I'm not normally a tactile person, but I put my hand over hers. "I know," I say. "But it's just different. You haven't lost him."

"No," says Lou. There's a long silence, punctuated by the splatter of drops against the pane. That's when I start to hear it again; that slow boom of waves on sand. I sip coffee to distract myself, but it tastes faintly of salt.

"You think you see it all before you, you know." Lou is speaking almost to herself. "When they're little you try and imagine them growing up, getting older. You think about all that might happen."

The gulls are crying outside now, as they always do when the waves are high. For a second I smell the iodine-stink of seaweed, hear the flurry of wings overhead.

Lou's still talking. "Kids, eh? They never quite turn out the way you picture them."

I'm having difficulty focusing. My head throbs, a dull, pulsing beat at my temples. "Yeah," I say. "Sons."

"You have a kid? You're a dark horse, Dee." The condensation clears on the pane. A gull perches on the sill outside; huge, white, his beak a startling yellow.

"Yes. A son. Back in Ireland." The gull tilts his head. One eye fixes me with a clear, bright glare. It's coming faster than I can stop it now, that savage tide. I pick up the thick folder of my files but my fingers curl into useless fists. The thick folder falls, splits, collapses on the floor. My phone rings, a deep, abrupt shrill that makes the table vibrate.

Lou bends to pick up the scattered papers. She looks at me, startled. There's only one file in there. The rest are photographs. Newspaper photos of boys, young, blond, blue-eyed boys, their faces creased and faded with age. They smile up at me, endless missing versions of endless missing Simons.

"Which of these is him?"

My mouth opens and closes convulsively.

The last thing I remember is her face; her startled glance at me as I slip sideways in the chair. My body jerks, I slide into darkness to the sound of the phone's frantic, repeated buzz.

* * *

I'm in a hospital. I look down. Sterile white sheets, mint-green walls. One bandage, on my arm. Not too bad for a seizure. I lie here in the calm that descends afterwards. That deep, still calm rinsed in salt. Clarity. The beach re-emerges, broken and scattered, but whole once more. The ground recovered.

Lou sits beside me, bright make-up creased on her face.

"Hey," she says, her rough voice gentled. "You had a fit, they said. Don't worry. I'm here. And he's on his way over from Ireland. Peter. Your husband." She reaches out and strokes my forehead. "I answered the phone. He told me everything, Dee. He told me about Simon." I watch as tears ebb up and roll down her mascara-streaked face.

"That's why I'm here in London." My voice is rusty. "He always wanted to come here. If he's anywhere, he's here."

I turn my head on the pillow, so I don't have to look at her sad face.

* * *

They called us a few days afterwards to the mortuary. We went together, our last act of solidarity. Inside that cold building Peter tried to hold my hand. I let it lie in his.

The man draws back the curtain around the bed. There's a terribly familiarity under the sheet, under that stranger's grey skin.

It can't be. There's a fundamental impossibility of a whole life contained in that stiff body. I see Simon as he was. I see him laid out like a series of Russian dolls; a pink, screaming baby, a child with a mass of blond curls, an angry teenager, biting the inflamed skin around his nails. Somewhere outside myself I feel the tight clench of Peter's grip.

If it's him, he's gone. If he's gone, I'm gone.

"No," I say. "It's not him. It's not Simon."

* * *

I pretend to sleep. I need to think. I need to get out before Peter comes and finds me.

I'll keep looking, you know. I'll walk this world forever if I have to; my folder full of photographs. I never thought I had this softness in me, you know. This deep, unbelievable well of emotion. It just keeps rising in me, inexorable as a tide. Love and pain; a kind of black joy.

I'll look for him always. I see myself walking; mapping this multitudinous city, quarter by quarter, rainy street by rainy street. From time to time I'll open my folder and check it against the lost faces on the street.

I found Olly. I'll find the rest of the boys. I'll find them all. As many as I can.

And maybe someday, a face will turn and I'll see that blond hair, those blue eyes, that bright grin.

Someday that someone I find will be him.

The Echo of a Mutiny

R. Austin Freeman

Chapter I
Death on the Girdler

POPULAR BELIEF ascribes to infants and the lower animals certain occult powers of divining character denied to the reasoning faculties of the human adult; and is apt to accept their judgment as finally over-riding the pronouncements of mere experience.

Whether this belief rests upon any foundation other than the universal love of paradox it is unnecessary to inquire. It is very generally entertained, especially by ladies of a certain social status; and by Mrs. Thomas Solly it was loyally maintained as an article of faith.

"Yes," she moralised, "it's surprisin' how they know, the little children and the dumb animals. But they do. There's no deceivin' *them*. They can tell the gold from the dross in a moment, they can, and they reads the human heart like a book. Wonderful, I call it. I suppose it's instinct."

Having delivered herself of this priceless gem of philosophic thought, she thrust her arms elbow-deep into the foaming wash-tub and glanced admiringly at her lodger as he sat in the doorway, supporting on one knee an obese infant of eighteen months and on the other a fine tabby cat.

James Brown was an elderly sea-faring man, small and slight in build and in manner suave, insinuating and perhaps a trifle sly. But he had all the sailor's love of children and animals, and the sailor's knack of making himself acceptable to them, for, as he sat with an empty pipe wobbling in the grasp of his toothless gums, the baby beamed with humid smiles, and the cat, rolled into a fluffy ball and purring like a stocking-loom, worked its fingers ecstatically as if it were trying on a new pair of gloves.

"It must be mortal lonely out at the lighthouse," Mrs. Solly resumed. "Only three men and never a neighbour to speak to; and, Lord! what a muddle they must be in with no woman to look after them and keep 'em tidy. But you won't be overworked, Mr. Brown, in these long days; daylight till past nine o'clock. I don't know what you'll do to pass the time."

"Oh, I shall find plenty to do, I expect," said Brown, "what with cleanin' the lamps and glasses and paintin' up the ironwork. And that reminds me," he added, looking round at the clock, "that time's getting on. High water at half-past ten, and here it's gone eight o'clock."

Mrs. Solly, acting on the hint, began rapidly to fish out the washed garments and wring them out into the form of short ropes. Then, having dried her hands on her apron, she relieved Brown of the protesting baby.

"Your room will be ready for you, Mr. Brown," said she, "when your turn comes for a spell ashore; and main glad me and Tom will be to see you back."

"Thank you, Mrs. Solly, ma'am," answered Brown, tenderly placing the cat on the floor; "you won't be more glad than what I will." He shook hands warmly with his landlady, kissed the baby, chucked the cat under the chin, and, picking up his little chest by its becket, swung it on to his shoulder and strode out of the cottage.

His way lay across the marshes, and, like the ships in the offing, he shaped his course by the twin towers of Reculver that stood up grotesquely on the rim of the land; and as he trod the springy turf, Tom Solly's fleecy charges looked up at him with vacant stares and valedictory bleatings. Once, at a dyke-gate, he paused to look back at the fair Kentish landscape: at the grey tower of St. Nicholas-at-Wade peeping above the trees and the far-away mill at Sarre, whirling slowly in the summer breeze; and, above all, at the solitary cottage where, for a brief spell in his stormy life, he had known the homely joys of domesticity and peace. Well, that was over for the present, and the lighthouse loomed ahead. With a half-sigh he passed through the gate and walked on towards Reculver.

Outside the whitewashed cottages with their official black chimneys a petty-officer of the coast-guard was adjusting the halyards of the flagstaff. He looked round as Brown approached, and hailed him cheerily.

"Here you are, then," said he, "all figged out in your new togs, too. But we're in a bit of a difficulty, d'ye see. We've got to pull up to Whitstable this morning, so I can't send a man out with you and I can't spare a boat."

"Have I got to swim out, then?" asked Brown.

The coast-guard grinned. "Not in them new clothes, mate," he answered. "No, but there's old Willett's boat; he isn't using her today; he's going over to Minster to see his daughter, and he'll let us have the loan of the boat. But there's no one to go with you, and I'm responsible to Willett."

"Well, what about it?" asked Brown, with the deep-sea sailor's (usually misplaced) confidence in his power to handle a sailing-boat. "D'ye think I can't manage a tub of a boat? Me what's used the sea since I was a kid of ten?"

"Yes," said the coast-guard; "but who's to bring her back?"

"Why, the man that I'm going to relieve," answered Brown. "He don't want to swim no more than what I do."

The coast-guard reflected with his telescope pointed at a passing barge. "Well, I suppose it'll be all right," he concluded; "but it's a pity they couldn't send the tender round. However, if you undertake to send the boat back, we'll get her afloat. It's time you were off."

He strolled away to the back of the cottages, whence he presently returned with two of his mates, and the four men proceeded along the shore to where Willett's boat lay just above high-water mark.

The *Emily* was a beamy craft of the type locally known as a 'half-share skiff', solidly built of oak, with varnished planking and fitted with main and mizzen lugs. She was a good handful for four men, and, as she slid over the soft chalk rocks with a hollow rumble, the coast-guards debated the advisability of lifting out the bags of shingle with which she was ballasted. However, she was at length dragged down, ballast and all, to the water's edge, and then, while Brown stepped the mainmast, the petty-officer gave him his directions. "What you've got to do," said he, "is to make use of the flood-tide. Keep her nose nor'-east, and with this trickle of nor'-westerly breeze you ought to make the lighthouse in one board. Anyhow, don't let her get east of the lighthouse, or, when the ebb sets in, you'll be in a fix."

To these admonitions Brown listened with jaunty indifference as he hoisted the sails and watched the incoming tide creep over the level shore. Then the boat lifted on the gentle swell. Putting out an oar, he gave a vigorous shove off that sent the boat, with a final scrape, clear of the beach, and then, having dropped the rudder on to its pintles, he seated himself and calmly belayed the main-sheet.

"There he goes," growled the coast-guard; "makin' fast his sheet. They *will* do it" (he invariably did it himself), "and that's how accidents happen. I hope old Willett'll see his boat back all right."

He stood for some time watching the dwindling boat as it sidled across the smooth water; then he turned and followed his mates towards the station.

Out on the south-western edge of the Girdler Sand, just inside the two-fathom line, the spindle-shanked lighthouse stood a-straddle on its long screw-piles like some uncouth red-bodied wading-bird. It was now nearly half-flood tide. The highest shoals were long since covered, and the lighthouse rose above the smooth sea as solitary as a slaver becalmed in the 'middle passage'.

On the gallery outside the lantern were two men, the entire staff of the building, of whom one sat huddled in a chair with his left leg propped up with pillows on another, while his companion rested a telescope on the rail and peered at the faint grey line of the distant land and the two tiny points that marked the twin spires of Reculver.

"I don't see any signs of the boat, Harry," said he.

The other man groaned. "I shall lose the tide," he complained, "and then there's another day gone."

"They can pull you down to Birchington and put you in the train," said the first man.

"I don't want no trains," growled the invalid. "The boat'll be bad enough. I suppose there's nothing coming our way, Tom?"

Tom turned his face eastward and shaded his eyes. "There's a brig coming across the tide from the north," he said. "Looks like a collier." He pointed his telescope at the approaching vessel, and added: "She's got two new cloths in her upper fore top-sail, one on each leech."

The other man sat up eagerly. "What's her trysail like, Tom?" he asked.

"Can't see it," replied Tom. "Yes, I can, now: it's tanned. Why, that'll be the old *Utopia*, Harry; she's the only brig I know that's got a tanned trysail."

"Look here, Tom," exclaimed the other, "if that's the *Utopia*, she's going to my home and I'm going aboard of her. Captain Mockett'll give me a passage, I know."

"You oughtn't to go until you're relieved, you know, Barnett," said Tom doubtfully; "it's against regulations to leave your station."

"Regulations be blowed!" exclaimed Barnett. "My leg's more to me than the regulations. I don't want to be a cripple all my life. Besides, I'm no good here, and this new chap, Brown, will be coming out presently. You run up the signal, Tom, like a good comrade, and hail the brig."

"Well, it's your look-out," said Tom, "and I don't mind saying that if I was in your place I should cut off home and see a doctor, if I got the chance." He sauntered off to the flag-locker, and, selecting the two code-flags, deliberately toggled them on to the halyards. Then, as the brig swept up within range, he hoisted the little balls of bunting to the flagstaff-head and jerked the halyards, when the two flags blew out making the signal 'Need assistance'.

Promptly a coal-soiled answering pennant soared to the brig's main-truck; less promptly the collier went about, and, turning her nose downstream, slowly drifted stern-forwards towards the lighthouse. Then a boat slid out through her gangway, and a couple of men plied the oars vigorously.

"Lighthouse ahoy!" roared one of them, as the boat came within hail. "What's amiss?"

"Harry Barnett has broke his leg," shouted the lighthouse keeper, "and he wants to know if Captain Mockett will give him a passage to Whitstable."

The boat turned back to the brig, and after a brief and bellowed consultation, once more pulled towards the lighthouse.

"Skipper says yus," roared the sailor, when he was within earshot, "and he says look alive, 'cause he don't want to miss his tide."

The injured man heaved a sigh of relief. "That's good news," said he, "though, how the blazes I'm going to get down the ladder is more than I can tell. What do you say, Jeffreys?"

"I say you'd better let me lower you with the tackle," replied Jeffreys. "You can sit in the bight of a rope and I'll give you a line to steady yourself with."

"Ah, that'll do, Tom," said Barnett; "but, for the Lord's sake, pay out the fall-rope gently."

The arrangements were made so quickly that by the time the boat was fast alongside everything was in readiness, and a minute later the injured man, dangling like a gigantic spider from the end of the tackle, slowly descended, cursing volubly to the accompaniment of the creaking of the blocks. His chest and kit-bag followed, and, as soon as these were unhooked from the tackle, the boat pulled off to the brig, which was now slowly creeping stern-foremost past the lighthouse. The sick man was hoisted up the side, his chest handed up after him, and then the brig was put on her course due south across the Kentish Flats.

Jeffreys stood on the gallery watching the receding vessel and listening to the voices of her crew as they grew small and weak in the increasing distance. Now that his gruff companion was gone, a strange loneliness had fallen on the lighthouse. The last of the homeward-bound ships had long since passed up the Princes Channel and left the calm sea desolate and blank. The distant buoys, showing as tiny black dots on the glassy surface, and the spindly shapes of the beacons which stood up from invisible shoals, but emphasised the solitude of the empty sea, and the tolling of the bell buoy on the Shivering Sand, stealing faintly down the wind, sounded weird and mournful. The day's work was already done. The lenses were polished, the lamps had been trimmed, and the little motor that worked the fog-horn had been cleaned and oiled. There were several odd jobs, it is true, waiting to be done, as there always are in a lighthouse; but, just now, Jeffreys was not in a working humour. A new comrade was coming into his life today, a stranger with whom he was to be shut up alone, night and day, for a month on end, and whose temper and tastes and habits might mean for him pleasant companionship or jangling and discord without end. Who was this man Brown? What had he been? And what was he like? These were the questions that passed, naturally enough, through the lighthouse-keeper's mind and distracted him from his usual thoughts and occupations.

Presently a speck on the landward horizon caught his eye. He snatched up the telescope eagerly to inspect it. Yes, it was a boat; but not the coast-guard's cutter, for which he was looking. Evidently a fisherman's boat and with only one man in it. He laid down the telescope with a sigh of disappointment, and, filling his pipe, leaned on the rail with a dreamy eye bent on the faint grey line of the land.

Three long years had he spent in this dreary solitude, so repugnant to his active, restless nature: three blank, interminable years, with nothing to look back on but the endless succession of summer calms, stormy nights and the chilly fogs of winter, when the unseen steamers hooted from the void and the fog-horn bellowed its hoarse warning.

Why had he come to this God-forgotten spot? And why did he stay, when the wide world called to him? And then memory painted him a picture on which his mind's eye had often looked before and which once again arose before him, shutting out the vision of the calm sea and the distant land. It was a brightly-coloured picture. It showed a cloudless sky brooding over the deep blue tropic sea; and in the middle of the picture, see-sawing gently on the quiet swell, a white-painted barque.

Her sails were clewed up untidily, her swinging yards jerked at the slack braces and her untended wheel revolved to and fro to the oscillations of the rudder.

She was not a derelict, for more than a dozen men were on her deck; but the men were all drunk and mostly asleep, and there was never an officer among them.

Then he saw the interior of one of her cabins. The chart-rack, the tell-tale compass and the chronometers marked it as the captain's cabin. In it were four men, and two of them lay dead on the deck. Of the other two, one was a small, cunning-faced man, who was, at the moment, kneeling beside one of the corpses to wipe a knife upon its coat. The fourth man was himself.

Again, he saw the two murderers stealing off in a quarter-boat, as the barque with her drunken crew drifted towards the spouting surf of a river-bar. He saw the ship melt away in the surf like an icicle in the sunshine; and, later, two shipwrecked mariners, picked up in an open boat and set ashore at an American port.

That was why he was here. Because he was a murderer. The other scoundrel, Amos Todd, had turned Queen's Evidence and denounced him, and he had barely managed to escape. Since then he had hidden himself from the great world, and here he must continue to hide, not from the law – for his person was unknown now that his shipmates were dead – but from the partner of his crime. It was the fear of Todd that had changed him from Jeffrey Rorke to Tom Jeffreys and had sent him to the Girdler, a prisoner for life. Todd might die – might even now be dead – but he would never hear of it: would never hear the news of his release.

He roused himself and once more pointed his telescope at the distant boat. She was considerably nearer now and seemed to be heading out towards the lighthouse. Perhaps the man in her was bringing a message; at any rate, there was no sign of the coast-guard's cutter.

He went in, and, betaking himself to the kitchen, busied himself with a few simple preparations for dinner. But there was nothing to cook, for there remained the cold meat from yesterday's cooking, which he would make sufficient, with some biscuit in place of potatoes. He felt restless and unstrung; the solitude irked him, and the everlasting wash of the water among the piles jarred on his nerves.

When he went out again into the gallery the ebb-tide had set in strongly and the boat was little more than a mile distant; and now, through the glass, he could see that the man in her wore the uniform cap of the Trinity House. Then the man must be his future comrade, Brown; but this was very extraordinary. What were they to do with the boat? There was no one to take her back.

The breeze was dying away. As he watched the boat, he saw the man lower the sail and take to his oars; and something of hurry in the way the man pulled over the gathering tide, caused Jeffreys to look round the horizon. And then, for the first time, he noticed a bank of fog creeping up from the east and already so near that the beacon on the East Girdler had faded out of sight. He hastened in to start the little motor that compressed the air for the fog-horn and waited awhile to see that the mechanism was running properly. Then, as the deck vibrated to the roar of the horn, he went out once more into the gallery.

The fog was now all round the lighthouse and the boat was hidden from view. He listened intently. The enclosing wall of vapour seemed to have shut out sound as well as vision. At intervals the horn bellowed its note of warning, and then all was still save the murmur of the water among the piles below, and, infinitely faint and far away, the mournful tolling of the bell on the Shivering Sand.

At length there came to his ear the muffled sound of oars working in the tholes; then, at the very edge of the circle of grey water that was visible, the boat appeared through the fog, pale and spectral, with a shadowy figure pulling furiously. The horn emitted a hoarse growl; the man looked round, perceived the lighthouse and altered his course towards it.

Jeffreys descended the iron stairway, and, walking along the lower gallery, stood at the head of the ladder earnestly watching the approaching stranger. Already he was tired of being alone. The yearning for human companionship had been growing ever since Barnett left. But what sort of comrade was this stranger who was coming into his life? And coming to occupy so dominant a place in it. It was a momentous question.

The boat swept down swiftly athwart the hurrying tide. Nearer it came and yet nearer: and still Jeffreys could catch no glimpse of his new comrade's face. At length it came fairly alongside and bumped against the fender-posts; the stranger whisked in an oar and grabbed a rung of the ladder, and Jeffreys dropped a coil of rope into the boat. And still the man's face was hidden.

Jeffreys leaned out over the ladder and watched him anxiously, as he made fast the rope, unhooked the sail from the traveller and unstepped the mast. When he had set all in order, the stranger picked up a small chest, and, swinging it over his shoulder, stepped on to the ladder. Slowly, by reason of his encumbrance, he mounted, rung by rung, with never an upward glance, and Jeffreys gazed down at the top of his head with growing curiosity. At last he reached the top of the ladder and Jeffreys stooped to lend him a hand. Then, for the first time, he looked up, and Jeffreys started back with a blanched face.

"God Almighty!" he gasped; "It's Amos Todd!"

As the newcomer stepped on the gallery, the fog-horn emitted a roar like that of some hungry monster. Jeffreys turned abruptly without a word, and walked to the stairs, followed by Todd, and the two men ascended with never a sound but the hollow clank of their footsteps on the iron plates. Silently Jeffreys stalked into the living room and, as his companion followed, he turned and motioned to the latter to set down his chest.

"You ain't much of a talker, mate," said Todd, looking round the room in some surprise; "ain't you going to say 'good morning'? We're going to be good comrades, I hope. I'm Jim Brown, the new hand, I am; what might your name be?"

Jeffreys turned on him suddenly and led him to the window. "Look at me carefully, Amos Todd," he said sternly, "and then ask yourself what my name is."

At the sound of his voice Todd looked up with a start and turned pale as death. "It can't be," he whispered, "it can't be Jeff Rorke!"

The other man laughed harshly, and, leaning forward, said in a low voice: "Hast thou found me, O mine enemy!"

"Don't say that!" exclaimed Todd. "Don't call me your enemy, Jeff. Lord knows but I'm glad to see you, though I'd never have known you without your beard, and with that grey hair. I've been to blame, Jeff, and I know it; but it ain't no use raking up old grudges. Let bygones be bygones, Jeff, and let us be pals as we used to be." He wiped his face with his handkerchief and watched his companion apprehensively.

"Sit down," said Rorke, pointing to a shabby rep-covered armchair; "sit down and tell us what you've done with all that money. You've blued it all, I suppose, or you wouldn't be here."

"Robbed, Jeff," answered Todd; "robbed of every penny. Ah! That was an unfortunate affair, that job on board the old *Sea-flower*. But it's over and done with and we'd best forget it. They're all dead but us, Jeff, so we're safe enough so long as we keep our mouths shut; all at the bottom of the sea – and the best place for 'em, too."

"Yes," Rorke replied fiercely, "that's the best place for your shipmates when they know too much; at the bottom of the sea or swinging at the end of a rope." He paced up and down the little room with rapid strides, and each time that he approached Todd's chair the latter shrank back with an expression of alarm.

"Don't sit there staring at me," said Rorke. "Why don't you smoke or do something?"

Todd hastily produced a pipe from his pocket, and having filled it from a moleskin pouch, stuck it in his mouth while he searched for a match. Apparently he carried his matches loose in his pocket, for he presently brought one forth – a red-headed match, which, when he struck it on the wall, lighted with a pale-blue flame. He applied it to his pipe, sucking in his cheeks while he kept his eyes fixed on his companion. Rorke, meanwhile, halted in his walk to cut some shavings from a cake of hard tobacco with a large clasp-knife; and, as he stood, he gazed with frowning abstraction at Todd.

"This pipe's stopped," said the latter, sucking ineffectually at the mouth-piece. "Have you got such a thing as a piece of wire, Jeff?"

"No, I haven't," replied Rorke; "not up here. I'll get a bit from the store presently. Here, take this pipe till you can clean your own: I've got another in the rack there." The sailor's natural hospitality overcoming for the moment his animosity, he thrust the pipe that he had just filled towards Todd, who took it with a mumbled "Thank you" and an anxious eye on the open knife. On the wall beside the chair was a roughly-carved pipe-rack containing several pipes, one of which Rorke lifted out; and, as he leaned over the chair to reach it, Todd's face went several shades paler.

"Well, Jeff," he said, after a pause, while Rorke cut a fresh 'fill' of tobacco, "are we going to be pals same as what we used to be?"

Rorke's animosity lighted up afresh. "Am I going to be pals with the man that tried to swear away my life?" he said sternly; and after a pause he added: "That wants thinking about, that does; and meantime I must go and look at the engine."

When Rorke had gone the new hand sat, with the two pipes in his hands, reflecting deeply. Abstractedly he stuck the fresh pipe into his mouth, and, dropping the stopped one into the rack, felt for a match. Still with an air of abstraction he lit the pipe, and, having smoked for a minute or two, rose from the chair and began softly to creep across the room, looking about him and listening intently. At the door he paused to look out into the fog, and then, having again listened attentively, he stepped on tip-toe out on to the gallery and along towards the stairway. Of a sudden the voice of Rorke brought him up with a start.

"Hallo, Todd! Where are you off to?"

"I'm just going down to make the boat secure," was the reply.

"Never you mind about the boat," said Rorke. "I'll see to her."

"Right O, Jeff," said Todd, still edging towards the stairway. "But I say, mate, where's the other man – the man that I'm to relieve?"

"There ain't any other man," replied Rorke; "he went off aboard a collier."

Todd's face suddenly became grey and haggard. "Then, there's no one here but us two!" he gasped; and then, with an effort to conceal his fear, he asked: "But who's going to take the boat back?"

"We'll see about that presently," replied Rorke; "you get along in and unpack your chest."

He came out on the gallery as he spoke, with a lowering frown on his face. Todd cast a terrified glance at him, and then turned and ran for his life towards the stairway.

"Come back!" roared Rorke, springing forward along the gallery; but Todd's feet were already clattering down the iron steps. By the time Rorke reached the head of the stairs, the fugitive was near the bottom; but here, in his haste, he stumbled, barely saving himself by the handrail, and when he recovered his balance Rorke was upon him. Todd darted to the head of the ladder, but, as he grasped the stanchion, his pursuer seized him by the collar. In a moment he had turned with his hand under his coat. There was a quick blow, a loud curse from Rorke, an answering yell from Todd, and a knife fell spinning through the air and dropped into the fore-peak of the boat below.

"You murderous little devil!" said Rorke in an ominously quiet voice, with his bleeding hand gripping his captive by the throat. "Handy with your knife as ever, eh? So you were off to give information, were you?"

"No, I wasn't, Jeff," replied Todd in a choking voice; "I wasn't, s'elp me God. Let go, Jeff. I didn't mean no harm. I was only—" With a sudden wrench he freed one hand and struck out frantically at his captor's face. But Rorke warded off the blow, and, grasping the other wrist, gave a violent push and let go. Todd staggered backward a few paces along the staging, bringing up at the extreme edge; and here, for a sensible time, he stood with wide-open mouth and starting eyeballs, swaying and clutching wildly at the air. Then, with a shrill scream, he toppled backwards and fell, striking a pile in his descent and rebounding into the water.

In spite of the audible thump of his head on the pile, he was not stunned, for, when he rose to the surface, he struck out vigorously, uttering short, stifled cries for help. Rorke watched him with set teeth and quickened breath, but made no move. Smaller and still smaller grew the head with its little circle of ripples, swept away on the swift ebb-tide, and fainter the bubbling cries that came across the smooth water. At length as the small black spot began to fade in the fog, the drowning man, with a final effort, raised his head clear of the surface and sent a last, despairing shriek towards the lighthouse. The fog-horn sent back an answering bellow; the head sank below the surface and was seen no more; and in the dreadful stillness that settled down upon the sea there sounded faint and far away the muffled tolling of a bell.

Rorke stood for some minutes immovable, wrapped in thought. Presently the distant hoot of a steamer's whistle aroused him. The ebb-tide shipping was beginning to come down and the fog might lift at any moment; and there was the boat still alongside. She must be disposed of at once. No one had seen her arrive and no one must see her made fast to the lighthouse. Once get rid of the boat and all traces of Todd's visit would be destroyed.

He ran down the ladder and stepped into the boat. It was perfectly simple. She was heavily ballasted and would go down like a stone if she filled.

He shifted some of the bags of shingle, and, lifting the bottom boards, pulled out the plug. Instantly a large jet of water spouted up into the bottom. Rorke looked at it critically, and, deciding that it would fill her in a few minutes, replaced the bottom boards; and having secured the mast and sail with a few turns of the sheet round a thwart, to prevent them from floating away, he cast off the mooring-rope and stepped on the ladder.

As the released boat began to move away on the tide, he ran up and mounted to the upper gallery to watch her disappearance. Suddenly he remembered Todd's chest. It was still in the room below. With a hurried glance around into the fog, he ran down to the room, and snatching up the chest, carried it out on the lower gallery. After another nervous glance around to assure himself that no craft was in sight, he heaved the chest over the handrail, and, when it fell with a loud splash into the sea, he waited to watch it float away after its owner and the sunken boat. But it never rose; and presently he returned to the upper gallery.

The fog was thinning perceptibly now, and the boat remained plainly visible as she drifted away. But she sank more slowly than he had expected, and presently as she drifted farther away, he fetched the telescope and peered at her with growing anxiety. It would be unfortunate if anyone saw her; if she should be picked up here, with her plug out, it would be disastrous.

He was beginning to be really alarmed. Through the glass he could see that the boat was now rolling in a sluggish, water-logged fashion, but she still showed some inches of free-board, and the fog was thinning every moment.

Presently the blast of a steamer's whistle sounded close at hand. He looked round hurriedly and, seeing nothing, again pointed the telescope eagerly at the dwindling boat. Suddenly he gave a gasp of relief. The boat had rolled gunwale under; had staggered back for a moment and then rolled again, slowly, finally, with the water pouring in over the submerged gunwale.

In a few more seconds she had vanished. Rorke lowered the telescope and took a deep breath. Now he was safe. The boat had sunk unseen. But he was better than safe: he was free.

His evil spirit, the standing menace of his life, was gone, and the wide world, the world of life, of action, of pleasure, called to him.

In a few minutes the fog lifted. The sun shone brightly on the red-funnelled cattle-boat whose whistle had startled him just now, the summer blue came back to sky and sea, and the land peeped once more over the edge of the horizon.

He went in, whistling cheerfully, and stopped the motor; returned to coil away the rope that he had thrown to Todd; and, when he had hoisted a signal for assistance, he went in once more to eat his solitary meal in peace and gladness.

Chapter II
'The Singing Bone'
(Related by Christopher Jervis, M.D.)

TO EVERY KIND of scientific work a certain amount of manual labour naturally appertains, labour that cannot be performed by the scientist himself, since art is long but life is short. A chemical analysis involves a laborious 'clean up' of apparatus and laboratory, for which the chemist has no time; the preparation of a skeleton – the maceration, bleaching, 'assembling', and riveting together of bones – must be carried out by someone whose time is not too precious. And so with other scientific activities. Behind the man of science with his outfit of knowledge is the indispensable mechanic with his outfit of manual skill.

Thorndyke's laboratory assistant, Polton, was a fine example of the latter type; deft, resourceful, ingenious and untiring. He was somewhat of an inventive genius, too; and it was one of his inventions that connected us with the singular case that I am about to record.

Though by trade a watchmaker, Polton was, by choice, an optician. Optical apparatus was the passion of his life; and when, one day, he produced for our inspection an improved prism for increasing the efficiency of gas-buoys, Thorndyke at once brought the invention to the notice of a friend at the Trinity House.

As a consequence, we three – Thorndyke, Polton and I – found ourselves early on a fine July morning making our way down Middle Temple Lane bound for the Temple Pier. A small oil-launch lay alongside the pontoon, and, as we made our appearance, a red-faced, white-whiskered gentleman stood up in the cockpit.

"Here's a delightful morning, doctor," he sang out in a fine, brassy, resonant, sea-faring voice; "sort of day for a trip to the lower river, hey? Hallo, Polton! Coming down to take the bread out of our mouths, are you? Ha, ha!" The cheery laugh rang out over the river and mingled with the throb of the engine as the little launch moved off from the pier.

Captain Grumpass was one of the Elder Brethren of the Trinity House. Formerly a client of Thorndyke's, he had subsided, as Thorndyke's clients were apt to do, into the position of a personal friend, and his hearty regard included our invaluable assistant.

"Nice state of things," continued the captain, with a chuckle, "when a body of nautical experts have got to be taught their business by a parcel of lawyers or doctors, what? I suppose trade's slack and 'Satan findeth mischief still', hey, Polton?"

"There isn't much doing on the civil side, sir," replied Polton, with a quaint, crinkly smile, "but the criminals are still going strong."

"Ha! Mystery department still flourishing, what? And, by Jove! talking of mysteries, doctor, our people have got a queer problem to work out; something quite in your line – quite. Yes, and, by the Lord Moses, since I've got you here, why shouldn't I suck your brains?"

"Exactly," said Thorndyke. "Why shouldn't you?"

"Well, then, I will," said the captain, "so here goes, All hands to the pump!" He lit a cigar, and, after a few preliminary puffs, began: "The mystery, shortly stated, is this: one of our lighthousemen has disappeared – vanished off the face of the earth and left no trace. He may have bolted, he may have been drowned accidentally or he may have been murdered. But I'd better give you the particulars in order. At the end of last week a barge brought into Ramsgate a letter from the screw-pile lighthouse on the Girdler. There are only two men there, and it seems that one of them, a man named Barnett, had broken his leg, and he asked that the tender should be sent to bring him ashore. Well, it happened that the local tender, the *Warden*, was up on the slip in Ramsgate Harbour, having a scrape down, and wouldn't be available for a day or two, so, as the case was urgent the officer at Ramsgate sent a letter to the lighthouse by one of the pleasure steamers saying that the man should be relieved by boat on the following morning, which was Saturday. He also wrote to a new hand who had just been taken on, a man named James Brown, who was lodging near Reculver, waiting his turn, telling him to go out on Saturday morning in the coast-guard's boat; and he sent a third letter to the coast-guard at Reculver asking him to take Brown out to the lighthouse and bring Barnett ashore. Well, between them, they made a fine muddle of it. The coast-guard couldn't spare either a boat or a man, so they borrowed a fisherman's boat, and in this the man Brown started off alone, like an idiot, on the chance that Barnett would be able to sail the boat back in spite of his broken leg.

"Meanwhile Barnett, who is a Whitstable man, had signalled a collier bound for his native town, and got taken off; so that the other keeper, Thomas Jeffreys, was left alone until Brown should turn up.

"But Brown never did turn up. The coast-guard helped him to put off and saw him well out to sea, and the keeper, Jeffreys, saw a sailing-boat with one man in her, making for the lighthouse. Then a bank of fog came up and hid the boat, and when the fog cleared she was nowhere to be seen. Man and boat had vanished and left no sign."

"He may have been run down in the fog," Thorndyke suggested.

"He may," agreed the captain, "but no accident has been reported. The coast-guards think he may have capsized in a squall – they saw him make the sheet fast. But there weren't any squalls: the weather was quite calm."

"Was he all right and well when he put off?" inquired Thorndyke.

"Yes," replied the captain, "the coast-guards' report is highly circumstantial; in fact, it's full of silly details that have no bearing on anything. This is what they say." He pulled out an official letter and read: "'When last seen, the missing man was seated in the boat's stern to windward of the helm. He had belayed the sheet. He was holding a pipe and tobacco-pouch in his hands and steering with his elbow. He was filling the pipe from the tobacco-pouch.' There! 'He was holding the pipe in his hand,' mark you! not with his toes; and he was filling it from a tobacco-pouch, whereas you'd have expected him to fill it from a coal-scuttle or a feeding-bottle. Bah!" The captain rammed the letter back in his pocket and puffed scornfully at his cigar.

"You are hardly fair to the coast-guard," said Thorndyke, laughing at the captain's vehemence. "The duty of a witness is to give *all* the facts, not a judicious selection."

"But, my dear sir," said Captain Grumpass, "what the deuce can it matter what the poor devil filled his pipe from?"

"Who can say?" answered Thorndyke. "It may turn out to be a highly material fact. One never knows beforehand. The value of a particular fact depends on its relation to the rest of the evidence."

"I suppose it does," grunted the captain; and he continued to smoke in reflective silence until we opened Blackwall Point, when he suddenly stood up.

"There's a steam trawler alongside our wharf," he announced. "Now what the deuce can she be doing there?" He scanned the little steamer attentively, and continued: "They seem to be landing something, too. Just pass me those glasses, Polton. Why, hang me! It's a dead body! But why on earth are they landing it on our wharf? They must have known you were coming, doctor."

As the launch swept alongside the wharf, the captain sprang up lightly and approached the group gathered round the body. "What's this?" he asked. "Why have they brought this thing here?"

The master of the trawler, who had superintended the landing, proceeded to explain.

"It's one of your men, sir," said he. "We saw the body lying on the edge of the South Shingles Sand, close to the beacon, as we passed at low water, so we put off the boat and fetched it aboard. As there was nothing to identify the man by, I had a look in his pockets and found this letter." He handed the captain an official envelope addressed to "Mr. J. Brown, c/o Mr. Solly, Shepherd, Reculver, Kent."

"Why, this is the man we were speaking about, doctor," exclaimed Captain Grumpass. "What a very singular coincidence. But what are we to do with the body?"

"You will have to write to the coroner," replied Thorndyke. "By the way, did you turn out all the pockets?" he asked, turning to the skipper of the trawler.

"No, sir," was the reply. "I found the letter in the first pocket that I felt in, so I didn't examine any of the others. Is there anything more that you want to know, sir?"

"Nothing but your name and address, for the coroner," replied Thorndyke, and the skipper, having given this information and expressed the hope that the coroner would not keep him 'hanging about', returned to his vessel and pursued his way to Billingsgate.

"I wonder if you would mind having a look at the body of this poor devil, while Polton is showing us his contraptions," said Captain Grumpass.

"I can't do much without a coroner's order," replied Thorndyke; "but if it will give you any satisfaction, Jervis and I will make a preliminary inspection with pleasure."

"I should be glad if you would," said the captain. "We should like to know that the poor beggar met his end fairly."

The body was accordingly moved to a shed, and, as Polton was led away, carrying the black bag that contained his precious model, we entered the shed and commenced our investigation.

The deceased was a small, elderly man, decently dressed in a somewhat nautical fashion. He appeared to have been dead only two or three days, and the body, unlike the majority of seaborne corpses, was uninjured by fish or crabs. There were no fractured bones or other gross injuries, and no wounds, excepting a ragged tear in the scalp at the back of the head.

"The general appearance of the body," said Thorndyke, when he had noted these particulars, "suggests death by drowning, though, of course, we can't give a definite opinion until a *post mortem* has been made."

"You don't attach any significance to that scalp-wound, then?" I asked.

"As a cause of death? No. It was obviously inflicted during life, but it seems to have been an oblique blow that spent its force on the scalp, leaving the skull uninjured. But it is very significant in another way."

"In what way?" I asked.

Thorndyke took out his pocket-case and extracted a pair of forceps. "Consider the circumstances," said he. "This man put off from the shore to go to the lighthouse, but never arrived there. The question is, where did he arrive?" As he spoke he stooped over the corpse and turned back the hair round the wound with the beak of the forceps. "Look at those white objects among the hair, Jervis, and inside the wound. They tell us something, I think."

I examined, through my lens, the chalky fragments to which he pointed. "These seem to be bits of shells and the tubes of some marine worm," I said.

"Yes," he answered; "the broken shells are evidently those of the acorn barnacle, and the other fragments are mostly pieces of the tubes of the common serpula. The inference that these objects suggest is an important one. It is that this wound was produced by some body encrusted by acorn barnacles and serpulae; that is to say, by a body that is periodically submerged. Now, what can that body be, and how can the deceased have knocked his head against it?"

"It might be the stem of a ship that ran him down," I suggested.

"I don't think you would find many serpulae on the stem of a ship," said Thorndyke. "The combination rather suggests some stationary object between tide-marks, such as a beacon. But one doesn't see how a man could knock his head against a beacon, while, on the other hand, there are no other stationary objects out in the estuary to knock against except buoys, and a buoy presents a flat surface that could hardly have produced this wound. By the way, we may as well see what there is in his pockets, though it is not likely that robbery had anything to do with his death."

"No," I agreed, "and I see his watch is in his pocket; quite a good silver one," I added, taking it out. "It has stopped at 12:13."

"That may be important," said Thorndyke, making a note of the fact; "but we had better examine the pockets one at a time, and put the things back when we have looked at them."

The first pocket that we turned out was the left hip-pocket of the monkey jacket. This was apparently the one that the skipper had rifled, for we found in it two letters, both bearing the crest of the Trinity House. These, of course, we returned without reading, and then passed on to the right pocket. The contents of this were commonplace enough, consisting of a briar pipe, a moleskin pouch and a number of loose matches.

"Rather a casual proceeding, this," I remarked, "to carry matches loose in the pocket, and a pipe with them, too."

"Yes," agreed Thorndyke; "especially with these very inflammable matches. You notice that the sticks had been coated at the upper end with sulphur before the red phosphorus heads were put on. They would light with a touch, and would be very difficult to extinguish; which, no doubt, is the reason that this type of match is so popular among seamen, who have to light their pipes in all sorts of weather." As he spoke he picked up the pipe and looked at it reflectively, turning it over in his hand and peering into the bowl. Suddenly he glanced from the pipe to the dead man's face and then, with the forceps, turned back the lips to look into the mouth.

"Let us see what tobacco he smokes," said he.

I opened the sodden pouch and displayed a mass of dark, fine-cut tobacco. "It looks like shag," I said.

"Yes, it is shag," he replied; "and now we will see what is in the pipe. It has been only half smoked out." He dug out the 'dottle' with his pocket-knife on to a sheet of paper, and we both inspected it. Clearly it was not shag, for it consisted of coarsely-cut shreds and was nearly black.

"Shavings from a cake of 'hard'," was my verdict, and Thorndyke agreed as he shot the fragments back into the pipe.

The other pockets yielded nothing of interest, except a pocket-knife, which Thorndyke opened and examined closely. There was not much money, though as much as one would expect, and enough to exclude the idea of robbery.

"Is there a sheath-knife on that strap?" Thorndyke asked, pointing to a narrow leather belt. I turned back the jacket and looked.

"There is a sheath," I said, "but no knife. It must have dropped out."

"That is rather odd," said Thorndyke. "A sailor's sheath-knife takes a deal of shaking out as a rule. It is intended to be used in working on the rigging when the man is aloft, so that he can get it out with one hand while he is holding on with the other. It has to be and usually is very secure, for the sheath holds half the handle as well as the blade. What makes one notice the matter in this case is that the man, as you see, carried a pocket-knife; and, as this would serve all the ordinary purposes of a knife, it seems to suggest that the sheath-knife was carried for defensive purposes: as a weapon, in fact. However, we can't get much further in the case without a *post mortem*, and here comes the captain."

Captain Grumpass entered the shed and looked down commiseratingly at the dead seaman.

"Is there anything, doctor, that throws any light on the man's disappearance?" he asked.

"There are one or two curious features in the case," Thorndyke replied; "but, oddly enough, the only really important point arises out of that statement of the coast-guard's, concerning which you were so scornful."

"You don't say so!" exclaimed the captain.

"Yes," said Thorndyke; "the coast-guard states that when last seen deceased was filling his pipe from his tobacco-pouch. Now his pouch contains shag; but the pipe in his pocket contains hard cut."

"Is there no cake tobacco in any of the pockets?"

"Not a fragment. Of course, it is possible that he might have had a piece and used it up to fill the pipe; but there is no trace of any on the blade of his pocket-knife, and you know how this juicy black cake stains a knife-blade. His sheath-knife is missing, but he would hardly have used that to shred tobacco when he had a pocket-knife."

"No," assented the captain; "but are you sure he hadn't a second pipe?"

"There was only one pipe," replied Thorndyke, "and that was not his own."

"Not his own!" exclaimed the captain, halting by a huge, chequered buoy to stare at my colleague; "how do you know it was not his own?"

"By the appearance of the vulcanite mouth-piece," said Thorndyke. "It showed deep tooth-marks; in fact, it was nearly bitten through. Now a man who bites through his pipe usually presents certain definite physical peculiarities, among which is, necessarily, a fairly good set of teeth. But the dead man had not a tooth in his head."

The captain cogitated a while, and then remarked: "I don't quite see the bearing of this."

"Don't you?" said Thorndyke. "It seems to me highly suggestive. Here is a man who, when last seen, was filling his pipe with a particular kind of tobacco. He is picked up dead, and his pipe contains a totally different kind of tobacco. Where did that tobacco come from? The obvious suggestion is that he had met someone."

"Yes, it does look like it," agreed the captain.

"Then," continued Thorndyke, "there is the fact that his sheath-knife is missing. That may mean nothing, but we have to bear it in mind. And there is another curious circumstance: there is a wound on the back of the head caused by a heavy bump against some body that was covered with acorn barnacles and marine worms. Now there are no piers or stages out in the open estuary. The question is, what could he have struck?"

"Oh, there is nothing in that," said the captain. "When a body has been washing about in a tideway for close on three days—"

"But this is not a question of a body," Thorndyke interrupted. "The wound was made during life."

"The deuce it was!" exclaimed the captain. "Well, all I can suggest is that he must have fouled one of the beacons in the fog, stove in his boat and bumped his head, though, I must admit, that's rather a lame explanation." He stood for a minute gazing at his toes with a cogitative frown and then looked up at Thorndyke.

"I have an idea," he said. "From what you say, this matter wants looking into pretty carefully. Now, I am going down on the tender today to make inquiries on the spot. What do you say to coming with me as adviser – as a matter of business, of course – you and Dr. Jervis? I shall start about eleven; we shall be at the lighthouse by three o'clock, and you can get back to town tonight, if you want to. What do you say?"

"There's nothing to hinder us," I put in eagerly, for even at Bugsby's Hole the river looked very alluring on this summer morning.

"Very well," said Thorndyke, "we will come. Jervis is evidently hankering for a sea-trip, and so am I, for that matter."

"It's a business engagement, you know," the captain stipulated.

"Nothing of the kind," said Thorndyke; "it's unmitigated pleasure; the pleasure of the voyage and your high well-born society."

"I didn't mean that," grumbled the captain, "but, if you are coming as guests, send your man for your night-gear and let us bring you back tomorrow evening."

"We won't disturb Polton," said my colleague; "we can take the train from Blackwall and fetch our things ourselves. Eleven o'clock, you said?"

"Thereabouts," said Captain Grumpass; "but don't put yourselves out."

The means of communication in London have reached an almost undesirable state of perfection. With the aid of the snorting train and the tinkling, two-wheeled 'gondola', we crossed and re-crossed the town with such celerity that it was barely eleven when we reappeared on Trinity Wharf with a joint Gladstone and Thorndyke's little green case.

The tender had hauled out of Bow Creek, and now lay alongside the wharf with a great striped can buoy dangling from her derrick, and Captain Grumpass stood at the gangway, his jolly, red face beaming with pleasure. The buoy was safely stowed forward, the derrick hauled up to the mast, the loose shrouds rehooked to the screw-lanyards, and the steamer, with four jubilant hoots, swung round and shoved her sharp nose against the incoming tide.

For near upon four hours the ever-widening stream of the 'London River' unfolded its moving panorama. The smoke and smell of Woolwich Reach gave place to lucid air made soft by the summer haze; the grey huddle of factories fell away and green levels of cattle-spotted marsh stretched away to the high land bordering the river valley. Venerable training ships displayed their chequered hulls by the wooded shore, and whispered of the days of oak and hemp, when the tall three-decker, comely and majestic, with her soaring heights of canvas, like towers of ivory, had not yet given place to the mud-coloured saucepans that fly the white ensign nowadays and devour the substance of the British taxpayer: when a sailor was a sailor and not a mere sea-faring mechanic. Sturdily breasting the flood-tide, the tender threaded her way through the endless procession of shipping; barges, billy-boys, schooners, brigs; lumpish Black-seamen, blue-funnelled China tramps, rickety Baltic barques with twirling windmills, gigantic liners, staggering under a mountain of top-hamper. Erith, Purfleet, Greenhithe, Grays greeted us and passed astern. The chimneys of Northfleet, the clustering roofs of Gravesend, the populous anchorage and the lurking batteries, were left behind, and, as we swung out of the Lower Hope, the wide expanse of sea reach spread out before us like a great sheet of blue-shot satin.

About half-past twelve the ebb overtook us and helped us on our way, as we could see by the speed with which the distant land slid past, and the freshening of the air as we passed through it.

But sky and sea were hushed in a summer calm. Balls of fleecy cloud hung aloft, motionless in the soft blue; the barges drifted on the tide with drooping sails, and a big, striped bell buoy – surmounted by a staff and cage and labelled 'Shivering Sand' – sat dreaming in the sun above its motionless reflection, to rouse for a moment as it met our wash, nod its cage drowsily, utter a solemn ding-dong, and fall asleep again.

It was shortly after passing the buoy that the gaunt shape of a screw-pile lighthouse began to loom up ahead, its dull-red paint turned to vermilion by the early afternoon sun. As we drew nearer, the name *Girdler*, painted in huge, white letters, became visible, and two men could be seen in the gallery around the lantern, inspecting us through a telescope.

"Shall you be long at the lighthouse, sir?" the master of the tender inquired of Captain Grumpass; "because we're going down to the North-East Pan Sand to fix this new buoy and take up the old one."

"Then you'd better put us off at the lighthouse and come back for us when you've finished the job," was the reply. "I don't know how long we shall be."

The tender was brought to, a boat lowered, and a couple of hands pulled us across the intervening space of water.

"It will be a dirty climb for you in your shore-going clothes," the captain remarked – he was as spruce as a new pin himself – "but the stuff will all wipe off." We looked up at the skeleton shape. The falling tide had exposed some fifteen feet of the piles, and piles and ladder alike were swathed in sea-grass and encrusted with barnacles and worm-tubes. But we were not such town-sparrows as the captain seemed to think, for we both followed his lead without difficulty up the slippery ladder, Thorndyke clinging tenaciously to his little green case, from which he refused to be separated even for an instant.

"These gentlemen and I," said the captain, as we stepped on the stage at the head of the ladder, "have come to make inquiries about the missing man, James Brown. Which of you is Jeffreys?"

"I am, sir," replied a tall, powerful, square-jawed, beetle-browed man, whose left hand was tied up in a rough bandage.

"What have you been doing to your hand?" asked the captain.

"I cut it while I was peeling some potatoes," was the reply. "It isn't much of a cut, sir."

"Well, Jeffreys," said the captain, "Brown's body has been picked up and I want particulars for the inquest. You'll be summoned as a witness, I suppose, so come in and tell us all you know."

We entered the living room and seated ourselves at the table. The captain opened a massive pocket-book, while Thorndyke, in his attentive, inquisitive fashion, looked about the odd, cabin-like room as if making a mental inventory of its contents.

Jeffreys' statement added nothing to what we already knew. He had seen a boat with one man in it making for the lighthouse. Then the fog had drifted up and he had lost sight of the boat. He started the fog-horn and kept a bright look-out, but the boat never arrived. And that was all he knew. He supposed that the man must have missed the lighthouse and been carried away on the ebb-tide, which was running strongly at the time.

"What time was it when you last saw the boat?" Thorndyke asked.

"About half-past eleven," replied Jeffreys.

"What was the man like?" asked the captain.

"I don't know, sir: he was rowing, and his back was towards me."

"Had he any kit-bag or chest with him?" asked Thorndyke.

"He'd got his chest with him," said Jeffreys.

"What sort of chest was it?" inquired Thorndyke.

"A small chest, painted green, with rope beckets."

"Was it corded?"

"It had a single cord round, to hold the lid down."

"Where was it stowed?"

"In the stern-sheets, sir."

"How far off was the boat when you last saw it?"

"About half-a-mile."

"Half-a-mile!" exclaimed the captain. "Why, how the deuce could you see what the chest was like half-a-mile away?"

The man reddened and cast a look of angry suspicion at Thorndyke. "I was watching the boat through the glass, sir," he replied sulkily.

"I see," said Captain Grumpass. "Well, that will do, Jeffreys. We shall have to arrange for you to attend the inquest. Tell Smith I want to see him."

The examination concluded, Thorndyke and I moved our chairs to the window, which looked out over the sea to the east. But it was not the sea or the passing ships that engaged my colleague's attention. On the wall, beside the window, hung a rudely-carved pipe-rack containing five pipes. Thorndyke had noted it when we entered the room, and now, as we talked, I observed him regarding it from time to time with speculative interest.

"You men seem to be inveterate smokers," he remarked to the keeper, Smith, when the captain had concluded the arrangements for the 'shift'.

"Well, we do like our bit of 'baccy, sir, and that's a fact," answered Smith. "You see, sir," he continued, "it's a lonely life, and tobacco's cheap out here."

"How is that?" asked Thorndyke.

"Why, we get it given to us. The small craft from foreign, especially the Dutchmen, generally heave us a cake or two when they pass close. We're not ashore, you see, so there's no duty to pay."

"So you don't trouble the tobacconists much? Don't go in for cut tobacco?"

"No, sir; we'd have to buy it, and then the cut stuff wouldn't keep. No, it's hard tack to eat out here and hard tobacco to smoke."

"I see you've got a pipe-rack, too, quite a stylish affair."

"Yes," said Smith, "I made it in my off-time. Keeps the place tidy and looks more ship-shape than letting the pipes lay about anywhere."

"Someone seems to have neglected his pipe," said Thorndyke, pointing to one at the end of the rack which was coated with green mildew.

"Yes; that's Parsons, my mate. He must have left it when we went off near a month ago. Pipes do go mouldy in the damp air out here."

"How soon does a pipe go mouldy if it is left untouched?" Thorndyke asked.

"It's according to the weather," said Smith. "When it's warm and damp they'll begin to go in about a week. Now here's Barnett's pipe that he's left behind – the man that broke his leg, you know, sir – it's just beginning to spot a little. He couldn't have used it for a day or two before he went."

"And are all these other pipes yours?"

"No, sir. This here one is mine. The end one is Jeffreys', and I suppose the middle one is his too, but I don't know it."

"You're a demon for pipes, doctor," said the captain, strolling up at this moment; "you seem to make a special study of them."

"'The proper study of mankind is man,'" replied Thorndyke, as the keeper retired, "and 'man' includes those objects on which his personality is impressed. Now a pipe is a very personal thing. Look at that row in the rack. Each has its own physiognomy which, in a measure, reflects the peculiarities of the owner. There is Jeffreys' pipe at the end, for instance. The mouth-piece is nearly bitten through, the bowl scraped to a shell and scored inside and the brim battered and chipped. The whole thing speaks of rude strength and rough handling. He chews the stem as he smokes, he scrapes the bowl violently, and he bangs the ashes out with unnecessary force. And the man fits the pipe exactly: powerful, square-jawed and, I should say, violent on occasion."

"Yes, he looks a tough customer, does Jeffreys," agreed the captain.

"Then," continued Thorndyke, "there is Smith's pipe, next to it; 'coked' up until the cavity is nearly filled and burnt all round the edge; a talker's pipe, constantly going out and being relit. But the one that interests me most is the middle one."

"Didn't Smith say that that was Jeffreys' too?" I said.

"Yes," replied Thorndyke, "but he must be mistaken. It is the very opposite of Jeffreys' pipe in every respect. To begin with, although it is an old pipe, there is not a sign of any toothmark on the mouth-piece. It is the only one in the rack that is quite unmarked. Then the brim is quite uninjured: it has been handled gently, and the silver band is jet-black, whereas the band on Jeffreys' pipe is quite bright."

"I hadn't noticed that it had a band," said the captain. "What has made it so black?"

Thorndyke lifted the pipe out of the rack and looked at it closely. "Silver sulphide," said he, "the sulphur no doubt derived from something carried in the pocket."

"I see," said Captain Grumpass, smothering a yawn and gazing out of the window at the distant tender. "Incidentally it's full of tobacco. What moral do you draw from that?"

Thorndyke turned the pipe over and looked closely at the mouth-piece. "The moral is," he replied, "that you should see that your pipe is clear before you fill it." He pointed to the mouth-piece, the bore of which was completely stopped up with fine fluff.

"An excellent moral too," said the captain, rising with another yawn. "If you'll excuse me a minute I'll just go and see what the tender is up to. She seems to be crossing to the East Girdler." He reached the telescope down from its brackets and went out on to the gallery.

As the captain retreated, Thorndyke opened his pocket-knife, and, sticking the blade into the bowl of the pipe, turned the tobacco out into his hand.

"Shag, by Jove!" I exclaimed.

"Yes," he answered, poking it back into the bowl. "Didn't you expect it to be shag?"

"I don't know that I expected anything," I admitted. "The silver band was occupying my attention."

"Yes, that is an interesting point," said Thorndyke, "but let us see what the obstruction consists of." He opened the green case, and, taking out a dissecting needle, neatly extracted a little ball of fluff from the bore of the pipe. Laying this on a glass slide, he teased it out in a drop of glycerine and put on a cover-glass while I set up the microscope.

"Better put the pipe back in the rack," he said, as he laid the slide on the stage of the instrument. I did so and then turned, with no little excitement, to watch him as he examined the specimen. After a brief inspection he rose and waved his hand towards the microscope.

"Take a look at it, Jervis," he said, "and let us have your learned opinion."

I applied my eye to the instrument, and, moving the slide about, identified the constituents of the little mass of fluff. The ubiquitous cotton fibre was, of course, in evidence, and a few fibres of wool, but the most remarkable objects were two or three hairs – very minute hairs of a definite zigzag shape and having a flat expansion near the free end like the blade of a paddle.

"These are the hairs of some small animal," I said; "not a mouse or rat or any rodent, I should say. Some small insectivorous animal, I fancy. Yes! Of course! They are the hairs of a mole." I stood up, and, as the importance of the discovery flashed on me, I looked at my colleague in silence.

"Yes," he said, "they are unmistakable; and they furnish the keystone of the argument."

"You think that this is really the dead man's pipe, then?" I said.

"According to the law of multiple evidence," he replied, "it is practically a certainty. Consider the facts in sequence. Since there is no sign of mildew on it, this pipe can have been here only a short time, and must belong either to Barnett, Smith, Jeffreys or Brown. It is an old pipe, but it has no tooth-marks on it. Therefore it has been used by a man who has no teeth. But Barnett, Smith and Jeffreys all have teeth and mark their pipes, whereas Brown had no teeth. The tobacco in it is shag. But these three men do not smoke shag, whereas Brown had shag in his pouch. The silver band is encrusted with sulphide; and Brown carried sulphur-tipped matches loose in his pocket with his pipe. We find hairs of a mole in the bore of the pipe; and Brown carried a moleskin pouch in the pocket in which he appears to have carried his pipe. Finally, Brown's pocket contained a pipe which was obviously not his and which closely resembled that of Jeffreys; it contained tobacco similar to that which Jeffreys smokes and different from that in Brown's pouch. It appears to me quite conclusive, especially when we add to this evidence the other items that are in our possession."

"What items are they?" I asked.

"First there is the fact that the dead man had knocked his head heavily against some periodically submerged body covered with acorn barnacles and serpulae. Now the piles of this lighthouse answer to the description exactly, and there are no other bodies in the neighbourhood that do: for even the beacons are too large to have produced that kind of wound. Then the dead man's sheath-knife is missing, and Jeffreys has a knife-wound on his hand. You must admit that the circumstantial evidence is overwhelming."

At this moment the captain bustled into the room with the telescope in his hand. "The tender is coming up towing a strange boat," he said. "I expect it's the missing one, and, if it is, we may learn something. You'd better pack up your traps and get ready to go on board."

We packed the green case and went out into the gallery, where the two keepers were watching the approaching tender; Smith frankly curious and interested, Jeffreys restless, fidgety and noticeably pale. As the steamer came opposite the lighthouse, three men dropped into the boat and pulled across, and one of them – the mate of the tender – came climbing up the ladder.

"Is that the missing boat?" the captain sang out.

"Yes, sir," answered the officer, stepping on to the staging and wiping his hands on the reverse aspect of his trousers, "we saw her lying on the dry patch of the East Girdler. There's been some hanky-panky in this job, sir."

"Foul play, you think, hey?"

"Not a doubt of it, sir. The plug was out and lying loose in the bottom, and we found a sheath-knife sticking into the kelson forward among the coils of the painter. It was stuck in hard as if it had dropped from a height."

"That's odd," said the captain. "As to the plug, it might have got out by accident."

"But it hadn't, sir," said the mate. "The ballast-bags had been shifted along to get the bottom boards up. Besides, sir, a seaman wouldn't let the boat fill; he'd have put the plug back and baled out."

"That's true," replied Captain Grumpass; "and certainly the presence of the knife looks fishy. But where the deuce could it have dropped from, out in the open sea? Knives don't drop from the clouds – fortunately. What do you say, doctor?"

"I should say that it is Brown's own knife, and that it probably fell from this staging."

Jeffreys turned swiftly, crimson with wrath. "What d'ye mean?" he demanded. "Haven't I said that the boat never came here?"

"You have," replied Thorndyke; "but if that is so how do you explain the fact that your pipe was found in the dead man's pocket and that the dead man's pipe is at this moment in your pipe-rack?"

The crimson flush on Jeffreys' face faded as quickly as it had come. "I don't know what you're talking about," he faltered.

"I'll tell you," said Thorndyke. "I will relate what happened and you shall check my statements. Brown brought his boat alongside and came up into the living room, bringing his chest with him. He filled his pipe and tried to light it, but it was stopped and wouldn't draw. Then you lent him a pipe of yours and filled it for him. Soon afterwards you came out on this staging and quarrelled. Brown defended himself with his knife, which dropped from his hand into the boat. You pushed him off the staging and he fell, knocking his head on one of the piles. Then you took the plug out of the boat and sent her adrift to sink, and you flung the chest into the sea. This happened about ten minutes past twelve. Am I right?"

Jeffreys stood staring at Thorndyke, the picture of amazement and consternation; but he uttered no word in reply.

"Am I right?" Thorndyke repeated.

"Strike me blind!" muttered Jeffreys. "Was you here, then? You talk as if you had been. Anyhow," he continued, recovering somewhat, "you seem to know all about it. But you're wrong about one thing. There was no quarrel. This chap, Brown, didn't take to me and he didn't mean to stay out here. He was going to put off and go ashore again and I wouldn't let him. Then he hit out at me with his knife and I knocked it out of his hand and he staggered backwards and went overboard."

"And did you try to pick him up?" asked the captain.

"How could I," demanded Jeffreys, "with the tide racing down and me alone on the station? I'd never have got back."

"But what about the boat, Jeffreys? Why did you scuttle her?"

"The fact is," replied Jeffreys, "I got in a funk, and I thought the simplest plan was to send her to the cellar and know nothing about it. But I never shoved him over. It was an accident, sir; I swear it!"

"Well, that sounds a reasonable explanation," said the captain. "What do you say, doctor?"

"Perfectly reasonable," replied Thorndyke, "and, as to its truth, that is no affair of ours."

"No. But I shall have to take you off, Jeffreys, and hand you over to the police. You understand that?"

"Yes, sir, I understand," answered Jeffreys.

* * *

"That was a queer case, that affair on the Girdler," remarked Captain Grumpass, when he was spending an evening with us some six months later. "A pretty easy let-off for Jeffreys, too – eighteen months, wasn't it?"

"Yes, it was a very queer case indeed," said Thorndyke. "There was something behind that 'accident', I should say. Those men had probably met before."

"So I thought," agreed the captain. "But the queerest part of it to me was the way you nosed it all out. I've had a deep respect for briar pipes since then. It was a remarkable case," he continued. "The way in which you made that pipe tell the story of the murder seems to me like sheer enchantment."

"Yes," said I; "it spoke like the magic pipe – only that wasn't a tobacco-pipe – in the German folk-story of the 'Singing Bone'. Do you remember it? A peasant found the bone of a murdered man and fashioned it into a pipe. But when he tried to play on it, it burst into a song of its own –

> *'My brother slew me and buried my bones*
> *Beneath the sand and under the stones.'"*

"A pretty story," said Thorndyke, "and one with an excellent moral. The inanimate things around us have each of them a song to sing to us if we are but ready with attentive ears."

The Grotto Spectre

Anna Katharine Green

MISS STRANGE was not often pensive – at least not at large functions or when under the public eye. But she certainly forgot herself at Mrs. Provost's musicale and that, too, without apparent reason. Had the music been of a high order one might have understood her abstraction; but it was of a decidedly mediocre quality, and Violet's ear was much too fine and her musical sense too cultivated for her to be beguiled by anything less than the very best.

Nor had she the excuse of a dull companion. Her escort for the evening was a man of unusual conversational powers; but she seemed to be almost oblivious of his presence; and when, through some passing courteous impulse, she did turn her ear his way, it was with just that tinge of preoccupation which betrays the divided mind.

Were her thoughts with some secret problem yet unsolved? It would scarcely seem so from the gay remark with which she had left home. She was speaking to her brother and her words were: "I am going out to enjoy myself. I've not a care in the world. The slate is quite clean." Yet she had never seemed more out of tune with her surroundings nor shown a mood further removed from trivial entertainment. What had happened to becloud her gaiety in the short time which had since elapsed?

We can answer in a sentence.

She had seen, among a group of young men in a distant doorway, one with a face so individual and of an expression so extraordinary that all interest in the people about her had stopped as a clock stops when the pendulum is held back. She could see nothing else, think of nothing else. Not that it was so very handsome – though no other had ever approached it in its power over her imagination – but because of its expression of haunting melancholy – a melancholy so settled and so evidently the result of long-continued sorrow that her interest had been reached and her heartstrings shaken as never before in her whole life.

She would never be the same Violet again.

Yet moved as she undoubtedly was, she was not conscious of the least desire to know who the young man was, or even to be made acquainted with his story. She simply wanted to dream her dream undisturbed.

It was therefore with a sense of unwelcome shock that, in the course of the reception following the programme, she perceived this fine young man approaching herself, with his right hand touching his left shoulder in the peculiar way which committed her to an interview with or without a formal introduction.

Should she fly the ordeal? Be blind and deaf to whatever was significant in his action, and go her way before he reached her; thus keeping her dream intact? Impossible. His eye prevented that. His glance had caught hers and she felt forced to await his advance and give him her first spare moment.

It came soon, and when it came she greeted him with a smile. It was the first she had ever bestowed in welcome of a confidence of whose tenor she was entirely ignorant.

To her relief he showed his appreciation of the dazzling gift though he made no effort to return it. Scorning all preliminaries in his eagerness to discharge himself of a burden which was fast becoming intolerable, he addressed her at once in these words:

"You are very good, Miss Strange, to receive me in this unconventional fashion. I am in that desperate state of mind which precludes etiquette. Will you listen to my petition? I am told – you know by whom—" (and he again touched his shoulder) "that you have resources of intelligence which especially fit you to meet the extraordinary difficulties of my position. May I beg you to exercise them in my behalf? No man would be more grateful if—. But I see that you do not recognize me. I am Roger Upjohn. That I am admitted to this gathering is owing to the fact that our hostess knew and loved my mother. In my anxiety to meet you and proffer my plea, I was willing to brave the cold looks you have probably noticed on the faces of the people about us. But I have no right to subject you to criticism. I—"

"Remain." Violet's voice was troubled, her self-possession disturbed; but there was a command in her tone which he was only too glad to obey. "I know the name" (who did not!) "and possibly my duty to myself should make me shun a confidence which may burden me without relieving you. But you have been sent to me by one whose behests I feel bound to respect and—"

Mistrusting her voice, she stopped. The suffering which made itself apparent in the face before her appealed to her heart in a way to rob her of her judgment. She did not wish this to be seen, and so fell silent.

He was quick to take advantage of her obvious embarrassment. "Should I have been sent to you if I had not first secured the confidence of the sender? You know the scandal attached to my name, some of it just, some of it very unjust. If you will grant me an interview tomorrow, I will make an endeavor to refute certain charges which I have hitherto let go unchallenged. Will you do me this favor? Will you listen in your own house to what I have to say?"

Instinct cried out against any such concession on her part, bidding her beware of one who charmed without excellence and convinced without reason. But compassion urged compliance and compassion won the day. Though conscious of weakness – she, Violet Strange on whom strong men had come to rely in critical hours calling for well-balanced judgment – she did not let this concern her, or allow herself to indulge in useless regrets even after the first effect of his presence had passed and she had succeeded in recalling the facts which had cast a cloud about his name.

Roger Upjohn was a widower, and the scandal affecting him was connected with his wife's death.

Though a degenerate in some respects, lacking the domineering presence, the strong mental qualities, and inflexible character of his progenitors, the wealthy Massachusetts Upjohns whose great place on the coast had a history as old as the State itself, he yet had gifts and attractions of his own which would have made him a worthy representative of his race, if only he had not fixed his affections on a woman so cold and heedless that she would have inspired universal aversion instead of love, had she not been dowered with the beauty and physical fascination which sometimes accompany a hard heart and a scheming brain. It was this beauty which had caught the lad; and one day, just as the careful father had mapped out a course of study calculated to make a man of his son, that son drove up to the gates with this lady whom he introduced as his wife.

The shock, not of her beauty, though that was of the dazzling quality which catches a man in the throat and makes a slave of him while the first surprise lasts, but of the overthrow of all his hopes and plans, nearly prostrated Homer Upjohn. He saw, as most men did the moment judgment returned, that for all her satin skin and rosy flush, the wonder of her hair and the smile which pierced like arrows and warmed like wine, she was more likely to bring a curse into the house than a blessing.

And so it proved. In less than a year the young husband had lost all his ambitions and many of his best impulses. No longer inclined to study, he spent his days in satisfying his wife's whims and his evenings in carousing with the friends with which she had provided him. This in Boston whither they had fled from the old gentleman's displeasure; but after their little son came the father insisted upon their returning home, which led to great deceptions, and precipitated a tragedy no one ever understood. They were natural gamblers – this couple – as all Boston society knew; and as Homer Upjohn loathed cards, they found life slow in the great house and grew correspondingly restless till they made a discovery – or shall I say a rediscovery – of the once famous grotto hidden in the rocks lining their portion of the coast. Here they found a retreat where they could hide themselves (often when they were thought to be abed and asleep) and play together for money or for a supper in the city or for anything else that foolish fancy suggested. This was while their little son remained an infant; later, they were less easily satisfied. Both craved company, excitement, and gambling on a large scale; so they took to inviting friends to meet them in this grotto which, through the agency of one old servant devoted to Roger to the point of folly, had been fitted up and lighted in a manner not only comfortable but luxurious. A small but sheltered haven hidden in the curve of the rocks made an approach by boat feasible at high tide; and at low the connection could be made by means of a path over the promontory in which this grotto lay concealed. The fortune which Roger had inherited from his mother made these excesses possible, but many thousands, let alone the few he could call his, soon disappeared under the witchery of an irresponsible woman, and the half-dozen friends who knew his secret had to stand by and see his ruin, without daring to utter a word to the one who alone could stay it. For Homer Upjohn was not a man to be approached lightly, nor was he one to listen to charges without ocular proof to support them; and this called for courage, more courage than was possessed by anyone who knew them both.

He was a hard man was Homer Upjohn, but with a heart of gold for those he loved. This, even his wary daughter-in-law was wise enough to detect, and for a long while after the birth of her child she besieged him with her coaxing ways and bewitching graces. But he never changed his first opinion of her, and once she became fully convinced of the folly of her efforts, she gave up all attempt to please him and showed an open indifference. This in time gradually extended till it embraced not only her child but her husband as well. Yes, it had come to that. His love no longer contented her. Her vanity had grown by what it daily fed on, and now called for the admiration of the fast men who sometimes came up from Boston to play with them in their unholy retreat. To win this, she dressed like some demon queen or witch, though it drove her husband into deeper play and threatened an exposure which would mean disaster not only to herself but to the whole family.

In all this, as anyone could see, Roger had been her slave and the willing victim of all her caprices. What was it, then, which so completely changed him that a separation began to be talked of and even its terms discussed? One rumor had it that the father had discovered the secret of the grotto and exacted this as a penalty from the son who had dishonored him. Another, that Roger himself was the one to take the initiative in this matter: That, on returning unexpectedly from New York one evening and finding her missing from the house, he had traced her to the grotto where he came upon her playing a desperate game with the one man he had the greatest reason to distrust.

But whatever the explanation of this sudden change in their relations, there is but little doubt that a legal separation between this ill-assorted couple was pending, when one bleak autumn morning she was discovered dead in her bed under circumstances peculiarly open to comment.

The physicians who made out the certificate ascribed her death to heart disease, symptoms of which had lately much alarmed the family doctor; but that a personal struggle of some kind had preceded the fatal attack was evident from the bruises which blackened her wrists. Had there been the like upon her throat it might have gone hard with the young husband who was known to be contemplating her dismissal from the house. But the discoloration of her wrists was all, and as bruised wrists do not kill and there was besides no evidence forthcoming of the two having spent one moment together for at least ten hours preceding the tragedy but rather full and satisfactory testimony to the contrary, the matter lapsed and all criminal proceedings were avoided.

But not the scandal which always follows the unexplained. As time passed and the peculiar look which betrays the haunted soul gradually became visible in the young widower's eyes, doubts arose and reports circulated which cast strange reflections upon the tragic end of his mistaken marriage. Stories of the disreputable use to which the old grotto had been put were mingled with vague hints of conjugal violence never properly investigated. The result was his general avoidance not only by the social set dominated by his high-minded father, but by his own less reputable coterie, which, however lax in its moral code, had very little use for a coward.

Such was the gossip which had reached Violet's ears in connection with this new client, prejudicing her altogether against him till she caught that beam of deep and concentrated suffering in his eye and recognized an innocence which ensured her sympathy and led her to grant him the interview for which he so earnestly entreated.

He came prompt to the hour, and when she saw him again with the marks of a sleepless night upon him and all the signs of suffering intensified in his unusual countenance, she felt her heart sink within her in a way she failed to understand. A dread of what she was about to hear robbed her of all semblance of self-possession, and she stood like one in a dream as he uttered his first greetings and then paused to gather up his own moral strength before he began his story. When he did speak it was to say:

"I find myself obliged to break a vow I have made to myself. You cannot understand my need unless I show you my heart. My trouble is not the one with which men have credited me. It has another source and is infinitely harder to bear. Personal dishonor I have deserved in a greater or less degree, but the trial which has come to me now involves a person more dear to me than myself, and is totally without alleviation unless you—" He paused, choked, then recommenced abruptly: "My wife" – Violet held her breath—"was supposed to have died from heart disease or – or some strange species of suicide. There were reasons for this conclusion – reasons which I accepted without serious question till some five weeks ago when I made a discovery which led me to fear—"

The broken sentence hung suspended. Violet, notwithstanding his hurried gesture, could not restrain herself from stealing a look at his face. It was set in horror and, though partially turned aside, made an appeal to her compassion to fill the void made by his silence, without further suggestion from him.

She did this by saying tentatively and with as little show of emotion as possible:

"You feared that the event called for vengeance and that vengeance would mean increased suffering to yourself as well as to another?"

"Yes; great suffering. But I may be under a most lamentable mistake. I am not sure of my conclusions. If my doubts have no real foundation – if they are simply the offspring of my own diseased imagination, what an insult to one I revere! What a horror of ingratitude and misunderstanding—"

"Relate the facts," came in startled tones from Violet. "They may enlighten us."

He gave one quick shudder, buried his face for one moment in his hands, then lifted it and spoke up quickly and with unexpected firmness:

"I came here to do so and do so I will. But where begin? Miss Strange, you cannot be ignorant of the circumstances, open and avowed, which attended my wife's death. But there were other and secret events in its connection which happily have been kept from the world, but which I must now disclose to you at any cost to my pride and so-called honor. This is the first one: On the morning preceding the day of Mrs. Upjohn's death, an interview took place between us at which my father was present. You do not know my father, Miss Strange. A strong man and a stern one, with a hold upon old traditions which nothing can shake. If he has a weakness it is for my little boy Roger in whose promising traits he sees the one hope which has survived the shipwreck of all for which our name has stood. Knowing this, and realizing what the child's presence in the house meant to his old age, I felt my heart turn sick with apprehension, when in the midst of the discussion as to the terms on which my wife would consent to a permanent separation, the little fellow came dancing into the room, his curls atoss and his whole face beaming with life and joy.

"She had not mentioned the child, but I knew her well enough to be sure that at the first show of preference on his part for either his grandfather or myself, she would raise a claim to him which she would never relinquish. I dared not speak, but I met his eager looks with my most forbidding frown and hoped by this show of severity to hold him back. But his little heart was full and, ignoring her outstretched arms, he bounded towards mine with his most affectionate cry. She saw and uttered her ultimatum. The child should go with her or she would not consent to a separation. It was useless for us to talk; she had said her last word. The blow struck me hard, or so I thought, till I looked at my father. Never had I beheld such a change as that one moment had made in him. He stood as before; he faced us with the same silent reprobation; but his heart had run from him like water.

"It was a sight to call up all my resources. To allow her to remain now, with my feelings towards her all changed and my father's eyes fully opened to her stony nature, was impossible. Nor could I appeal to law. An open scandal was my father's greatest dread and divorce proceedings his horror. The child would have to go unless I could find a way to influence her through her own nature. I knew of but one – do not look at me, Miss Strange. It was dishonoring to us both, and I'm horrified now when I think of it. But to me at that time it was natural enough as a last resort. There was but one debt which my wife ever paid, but one promise she ever kept. It was that made at the gaming-table. I offered, as soon as my father, realizing the hopelessness of the situation, had gone tottering from the room, to gamble with her for the child."

"And she accepted."

The shame and humiliation expressed in this final whisper; the sudden darkness – for a storm was coming up – shook Violet to the soul. With strained gaze fixed on the man before her, now little more than a shadow in the prevailing gloom, she waited for him to resume, and waited in vain. The minutes passed, the darkness became intolerable, and instinctively her hand crept towards the electric button beneath which she was sitting. But she failed to press it. A tale so dark called for an atmosphere of its own kind. She would cast no light upon it. Yet she shivered as the silence continued, and started in uncontrollable dismay when at length her strange visitor rose, and still, without speaking, walked away from her to the other end of the room. Only so could he go on with the shameful tale; and presently she heard his voice once more in these words:

"Our house is large and its rooms many; but for such work as we two contemplated there was but one spot where we could command absolute seclusion. You may have heard of it, a famous natural grotto hidden in our own portion of the coast and so fitted up as to form a retreat for our miserable selves when escape from my father's eye seemed desirable. It was not easy of access, and no one, so far as we knew, had ever followed us there.

"But to ensure ourselves against any possible interruption, we waited till the whole house was abed before we left it for the grotto. We went by boat and oh! the dip of those oars! I hear them yet. And the witchery of her face in the moonlight; and the mockery of her low fitful laugh! As I caught the sinister note in its silvery rise and fall, I knew what was before me if I failed to retain my composure. And I strove to hold it and to meet her calmness with stoicism and the taunt of her expression with a mask of immobility. But the effort was hopeless, and when the time came for dealing out the cards, my eyes were burning in their sockets and my hands shivering like leaves in a rising gale.

"We played one game – and my wife lost. We played another – and my wife won. We played the third – and the fate I had foreseen from the first became mine. The luck was with her, and I had lost my boy!"

A gasp – a pause, during which the thunder spoke and the lightning flashed – then a hurried catching of his breath and the tale went on.

"A burst of laughter, rising gaily above the boom of the sea, announced her victory – her laugh and the taunting words: 'You play badly, Roger. The child is mine. Never fear that I shall fail to teach him to revere his father.' Had I a word to throw back? No. When I realized anything but my dishonored manhood, I found myself in the grotto's mouth staring helplessly out upon the sea. The boat which had floated us in at high tide lay stranded but a few feet away, but I did not reach for it. Escape was quicker over the rocks, and I made for the rocks.

"That it was a cowardly act to leave her there to find her way back alone at midnight by the same rough road I was taking, did not strike my mind for an instant. I was in flight from my own past; in flight from myself and the haunting dread of madness. When I awoke to reality again it was to find the small door, by which we had left the house, standing slightly ajar. I was troubled by this, for I was sure of having closed it. But the impression was brief, and entering, I went stumbling up to my room, leaving the way open behind me more from sheer inability to exercise my will than from any thought of her.

"Miss Strange" (he had come out of the shadows and was standing now directly before her), "I must ask you to trust implicitly in what I tell you of my further experiences that fatal night. It was not necessary for me to pass my little son's door in order to reach the room I was making for; but anguish took me there and held me glued to the panels for what seemed a long, long time. When I finally crept away it was to go to the room I had chosen in the top of the house, where I had my hour of hell and faced my desolated future. Did I hear anything meantime in the halls below? No. Did I even listen for the sound of her return? No. I was callous to everything, dead to everything but my own misery. I did not even heed the approach of morning, till suddenly, with a shrillness no ear could ignore, there rose, tearing through the silence of the house, that great scream from my wife's room which announced the discovery of her body lying stark and cold in her bed.

"They said I showed little feeling." He had moved off again and spoke from somewhere in the shadows. "Do you wonder at this after such a manifest stroke by a benevolent Providence?

My wife being dead, Roger was saved to us! It was the one song of my still undisciplined soul, and I had to assume coldness lest they should see the greatness of my joy. A wicked and guilty rejoicing you will say, and you are right. But I had no memory then of the part I had played in this fatality. I had forgotten my reckless flight from the grotto, which left her with no aid but that of her own triumphant spirit to help her over those treacherous rocks. The necessity for keeping secret this part of our disgraceful story led me to exert myself to keep it out of my own mind. It has only come back to me in all its force since a new horror, a new suspicion, has driven me to review carefully every incident of that awful night.

"I was never a man of much logic, and when they came to me on that morning of which I have just spoken and took me in where she lay and pointed to her beautiful cold body stretched out in seeming peace under the satin coverlet, and then to the pile of dainty clothes lying neatly folded on a chair with just one fairy slipper on top, I shuddered at her fate but asked no questions, not even when one of the women of the house mentioned the circumstance of the single slipper and said that a search should be made for its mate. Nor was I as much impressed as one would naturally expect by the whisper dropped in my ear that something was the matter with her wrists. It is true that I lifted the lace they had carefully spread over them and examined the discoloration which extended like a ring about each pearly arm; but having no memories of any violence offered her (I had not so much as laid hand upon her in the grotto), these marks failed to rouse my interest. But – and now I must leap a year in my story – there came a time when both of these facts recurred to my mind with startling distinctness and clamored for explanation.

"I had risen above the shock which such a death following such events would naturally occasion even in one of my blunted sensibilities, and was striving to live a new life under the encouragement of my now fully reconciled father, when accident forced me to re-enter the grotto where I had never stepped foot since that night. A favorite dog in chase of some innocent prey had escaped the leash and run into its dim recesses and would not come out at my call. As I needed him immediately for the hunt, I followed him over the promontory and, swallowing my repugnance, slid into the grotto to get him. Better a plunge to my death from the height of the rocks towering above it. For there in a remote corner, lighted up by a reflection from the sea, I beheld my setter crouched above an object which in another moment I recognized as my dead wife's missing slipper. Here! Not in the waters of the sea or in the intersticcs of the rocks outside, but here! Proof that she had never walked back to the house where she was found lying quietly in her bed; proof positive; for I knew the path too well and the more than usual tenderness of her feet.

"How then, did she get there; and by whose agency? Was she living when she went, or was she already dead? A year had passed since that delicate shoe had borne her from the boat into these dim recesses; but it might have been only a day, so vividly did I live over in this moment of awful enlightenment all the events of the hour in which we sat there playing for the possession of our child. Again I saw her gleaming eyes, her rosy, working mouth, her slim, white hand, loaded with diamonds, clutching the cards. Again I heard the lap of the sea on the pebbles outside and smelt the odor of the wine she had poured out for us both. The bottle which had held it; the glass from which she had drunk lay now in pieces on the rocky floor. The whole scene was mine again and as I followed the event to its despairing close, I seemed to see my own wild figure springing away from her to the grotto's mouth and so over the rocks. But here fancy faltered, caught by a quick recollection to which I had never given a thought till now. As I made my way along those rocks, a sound had struck my ear from where some stunted bushes made a shadow in the moonlight. The wind might have caused it or some small night creature hustling away at my approach; and to some such cause I must at the time have attributed it. But now, with brain fired by suspicion, it seemed more like the quick intake of a human breath. Someone had been lying there in wait, listening at the one loophole in the rocks where it was possible to hear what was said and done in the heart of the grotto. But who? Who? And for what purpose this listening; and to what end did it lead?

"Though I no longer loved even the memory of my wife, I felt my hair lift, as I asked myself these questions. There seemed to be but one logical answer to the last, and it was this: A struggle followed by death. The shoe fallen from her foot, the clothes found folded in her room (my wife was never orderly), and the dimly blackened wrists which were snow-white when she dealt the cards – all seemed to point to such a conclusion. She may have died from heart failure, but a struggle had preceded her death, during which some man's strong fingers had been locked about her wrists. And again the question rose: Whose?

"If any place was ever hated by mortal man that grotto was hated by me. I loathed its walls, its floor, its every visible and invisible corner. To linger there – to look – almost tore my soul from my body; yet I did linger and did look and this is what I found by way of reward.

"Behind a projecting ledge of stone from which a tattered rug still hung, I came upon two nails driven a few feet apart into a fissure of the rock. I had driven those nails myself long before for a certain gymnastic attachment much in vogue at the time, and on looking closer, I discovered hanging from them the rope-ends by which I was wont to pull myself about. So far there was nothing to rouse any but innocent reminiscences. But when I heard the dog's low moan and saw him leap at the curled-up ends, and nose them with an eager look my way, I remembered the dark marks circling the wrists about which I had so often clasped my mother's bracelets, and the world went black before me.

"When consciousness returned – when I could once more move and see and think, I noted another fact. Cards were strewn about the floor, face up and in a fixed order as if laid in a mocking mood to be looked upon by reluctant eyes; and near the ominous half-circle they made, a cushion from the lounge, stained horribly with what I then thought to be blood, but which I afterwards found to be wine. Vengeance spoke in those ropes and in the carefully spread-out cards, and murder in the smothering pillow. The vengeance of one who had watched her corroding influence eat the life out of my honor and whose love for our little Roger was such that any deed which ensured his continued presence in the home appeared not only warrantable but obligatory. Alas! I knew of but one person in the whole world who could cherish feeling to this extent or possess sufficient willpower to carry her lifeless body back to the house and lay it in her bed and give no sign of the abominable act from that day on to this.

"Miss Strange, there are men who have a peculiar conception of duty. My father—"

"You need not go on." How gently, how tenderly our Violet spoke. "I understand your trouble—"

Did she? She paused to ask herself if this were so, and he, deaf perhaps to her words, caught up his broken sentence and went on:

"My father was in the hall the day I came staggering in from my visit to the grotto. No words passed, but our eyes met and from that hour I have seen death in his countenance and he has seen it in mine, like two opponents, each struck to the heart, who stand facing each other with simulated smiles till they fall. My father will drop first. He is old – very old since that day five weeks ago; and to see him die and not be sure – to see the grave close over a possible innocence, and I left here in ignorance of the blissful fact till my own eyes close forever, is more than I can hold up under; more than any son could. Cannot you help me then to a positive knowledge? Think! Think! A woman's mind is strangely penetrating, and yours, I am told, has an intuitive faculty more to be relied upon than the reasoning of men. It must suggest some means of confirming my doubts or of definitely ending them."

Then Violet stirred and looked about at him and finally found voice.

"Tell me something about your father's ways. What are his habits? Does he sleep well or is he wakeful at night?"

"He has poor nights. I do not know how poor because I am not often with him. His valet, who has always been in our family, shares his room and acts as his constant nurse. He can watch over him better than I can; he has no distracting trouble on his mind."

"And little Roger? Does your father see much of little Roger? Does he fondle him and seem happy in his presence?"

"Yes; yes. I have often wondered at it, but he does. They are great chums. It is a pleasure to see them together."

"And the child clings to him – shows no fear – sits on his lap or on the bed and plays as children do play with his beard or with his watch-chain?"

"Yes. Only once have I seen my little chap shrink, and that was when my father gave him a look of unusual intensity – looking for his mother in him perhaps."

"Mr. Upjohn, forgive me the question; it seems necessary. Does your father – or rather did your father before he fell ill – ever walk in the direction of the grotto or haunt in any way the rocks which surround it?"

"I cannot say. The sea is there; he naturally loves the sea. But I have never seen him standing on the promontory."

"Which way do his windows look?"

"Towards the sea."

"Therefore towards the promontory?"

"Yes."

"Can he see it from his bed?"

"No. Perhaps that is the cause of a peculiar habit he has."

"What habit?"

"Every night before he retires (he is not yet confined to his bed) he stands for a few minutes in his front window looking out. He says it's his goodnight to the ocean. When he no longer does this, we shall know that his end is very near."

The face of Violet began to clear. Rising, she turned on the electric light, and then, reseating herself, remarked with an aspect of quiet cheer:

"I have two ideas; but they necessitate my presence at your place. You will not mind a visit? My brother will accompany me."

Roger Upjohn did not need to speak, hardly to make a gesture; his expression was so eloquent.

She thanked him as if he had answered in words, adding with an air of gentle reserve: "Providence assists us in this matter. I am invited to Beverly next week to attend a wedding. I was intending to stay two days, but I will make it three and spend the extra one with you."

"What are your requirements, Miss Strange? I presume you have some."

Violet turned from the imposing portrait of Mr. Upjohn which she had been gravely contemplating, and met the troubled eye of her young host with an enigmatical flash of her own. But she made no answer in words. Instead, she lifted her right hand and ran one slender finger thoughtfully up the casing of the door near which they stood till it struck a nick in the old mahogany almost on a level with her head.

"Is your son Roger old enough to reach so far?" she asked with another short look at him as she let her finger rest where it had struck the roughened wood. "I thought he was a little fellow."

"He is. That cut was made by – by my wife; a sample of her capricious willfulness. She wished to leave a record of herself in the substance of our house as well as in our lives. That nick marks her height. She laughed when she made it. 'Till the walls cave in or burn,' is what she said. And I thought her laugh and smile captivating."

Cutting short his own laugh which was much too sardonic for a lady's ears, he made a move as if to lead the way into another portion of the room. But Violet failed to notice this, and lingering in quiet contemplation of this suggestive little nick – the only blemish in a room of ancient colonial magnificence – she thoughtfully remarked:

"Then she was a small woman?" adding with seeming irrelevance – "like myself."

Roger winced. Something in the suggestion hurt him, and in the nod he gave there was an air of coldness which under ordinary circumstances would have deterred her from pursuing this subject further. But the circumstances were not ordinary, and she allowed herself to say:

"Was she so very different from me – in figure, I mean?"

"No. Why do you ask? Shall we not join your brother on the terrace?"

"Not till I have answered the question you put me a moment ago. You wished to know my requirements. One of the most important you have already fulfilled. You have given your servants a half-holiday and by so doing ensured to us full liberty of action. What else I need in the attempt I propose to make, you will find listed in this memorandum." And taking a slip of paper from her bag, she offered it to him with a hand, the trembling of which he would have noted had he been freer in mind.

As he read, she watched him, her fingers nervously clutching her throat.

"Can you supply what I ask?" she faltered, as he failed to raise his eyes or make any move or even to utter the groan she saw surging up to his lips. "Will you?" she impetuously urged, as his fingers closed spasmodically on the paper, in evidence that he understood at last the trend of her daring purpose.

The answer came slowly, but it came. "I will. But what—"

Her hand rose in a pleading gesture.

"Do not ask me, but take Arthur and myself into the garden and show us the flowers. Afterwards, I should like a glimpse of the sea."

He bowed and they joined Arthur who had already begun to stroll through the grounds.

Violet was seldom at a loss for talk even at the most critical moments. But she was strangely tongue-tied on this occasion, as was Roger himself. Save for a few observations casually thrown out by Arthur, the three passed in a disquieting silence through pergola after pergola, and around beds gorgeous with every variety of fall flowers, till they turned a sharp corner and came in full view of the sea.

"Ah!" fell in an admiring murmur from Violet's lips as her eyes swept the horizon. Then as they settled on a mass of rock jutting out from the shore in a great curve, she leaned towards her host and softly whispered:

"The promontory?"

He nodded, and Violet ventured no farther, but stood for a little while gazing at the tumbled rocks. Then, with a quick look back at the house, she asked him to point out his father's window.

He did so, and as she noted how openly it faced the sea, her expression relaxed and her manner lost some of its constraint. As they turned to re-enter the house, she noticed an old man picking flowers from a vine clambering over one end of the piazza.

"Who is that?" she asked.

"Our oldest servant, and my father's own man," was Roger's reply. "He is picking my father's favorite flowers, a few late honeysuckles."

"How fortunate! Speak to him, Mr. Upjohn. Ask him how your father is this evening."

"Accompany me and I will; and do not be afraid to enter into conversation with him. He is the mildest of creatures and devoted to his patient. He likes nothing better than to talk about him."

Violet, with a meaning look at her brother, ran up the steps at Roger's side. As she did so, the old man turned and Violet was astonished at the wistfulness with which he viewed her.

"What a dear old creature!" she murmured. "See how he stares this way. You would think he knew me."

"He is glad to see a woman about the place. He has felt our isolation – Good evening, Abram. Let this young lady have a spray of your sweetest honeysuckle. And, Abram, before you go, how is Father tonight? Still sitting up?"

"Yes, sir. He is very regular in his ways. Nine is his hour; not a minute before and not a minute later. I don't have to look at the clock when he says: 'There, Abram, I've sat up long enough.'"

"When my father retires before his time or goes to bed without a final look at the sea, he will be a very sick man, Abram."

"That he will, Mr. Roger; that he will. But he's very feeble tonight, very feeble. I noticed that he gave the boy fewer kisses than usual. Perhaps he was put out because the child was brought in a half-hour earlier than the stated time. He don't like changes; you know that, Mr. Roger; he don't like changes. I hardly dared to tell him that the servants were all going out in a bunch tonight."

"I'm sorry," muttered Roger. "But he'll forget it by tomorrow. I couldn't bear to keep a single one from the concert. They'll be back in good season and meantime we have you. Abram is worth half a dozen of them, Miss Strange. We shall miss nothing."

"Thank you, Mr. Roger, thank you," faltered the old man. "I try to do my duty." And with another wistful glance at Violet, who looked very sweet and youthful in the half-light, he pottered away.

The silence which followed his departure was as painful to her as to Roger Upjohn. When she broke it it was with this decisive remark:

"That man must not speak of me to your father. He must not even mention that you have a guest tonight. Run after him and tell him so. It is necessary that your father's mind should not be taken up with present happenings. Run."

Roger made haste to obey her. When he came back she was on the point of joining her brother but stopped to utter a final injunction:

"I shall leave the library, or wherever we may be sitting, just as the clock strikes half-past eight. Arthur will do the same, as by that time he will feel like smoking on the terrace. Do not follow either him or myself, but take your stand here on the piazza where you can get a full view of the right-hand wing without attracting any attention to yourself. When you hear the big clock in the hall strike nine, look up quickly at your father's window. What you see may determine – oh, Arthur! still admiring the prospect? I do not wonder. But I find it chilly. Let us go in."

Roger Upjohn, sitting by himself in the library, was watching the hands of the mantel clock slowly approaching the hour of nine.

Never had silence seemed more oppressive nor his sense of loneliness greater. Yet the boom of the ocean was distinct to the ear, and human presence no farther away than the terrace where Arthur Strange could be seen smoking out his cigar in solitude. The silence and the loneliness were in Roger's own soul; and, in face of the expected revelation which would make or unmake his future, the desolation they wrought was measureless.

To cut his suspense short, he rose at length and hurried out to the spot designated by Miss Strange as the best point from which to keep watch upon his father's window. It was at the end of the piazza where the honeysuckle hung, and the odor of the blossoms, so pleasing to his father, well-nigh overpowered him not only by its sweetness but by the many memories it called up. Visions of that father as he looked at all stages of their relationship passed in a bewildering maze before him. He saw him as he appeared to his childish eyes in those early days of confidence when the loss of the mother cast them in mutual dependence upon each other. Then a sterner picture of the relentless parent who sees but one straight course to success in this world and the next. Then the teacher and the matured adviser; and then – oh, bitter change! The man whose hopes he had crossed – whose life he had undone, and all for her who now came stealing upon the scene with her slim, white, jewelled hand forever lifted up between them. And she! Had he ever seen her more clearly? Once more the dainty figure stepped from fairyland, beauteous with every grace that can allure and finally destroy a man. And as he saw, he trembled and wished that these moments of awful waiting might pass and the test be over which would lay bare his father's heart and justify his fears or dispel them forever.

But the crisis, if crisis it was, was one of his own making and not to be hastened or evaded. With one quick glance at his father's window, he turned in his impatience towards the sea whose restless and continuous moaning had at length struck his ear. What was in its call tonight that he should thus sway towards it as though drawn by some dread magnetic force? He had been born to the dashing of its waves and knew its every mood and all the passion of its song from frolicsome ripple to melancholy dirge. But there was something odd and inexplicable in its effect upon his spirit as he faced it at this hour. Grim and implacable – a sound rather than a sight – it seemed to hold within its invisible distances the image of his future fate. What this image was and why he should seek for it in this impenetrable void, he did not know. He felt himself held and was struggling with this influence as with an unknown enemy when there rang out, from the hall within, the preparatory chimes for which his ear was waiting, and then the nine slow strokes which signalized the moment when he was to look for his father's presence at the window.

Had he wished, he could not have forborne that look. Had his eyes been closing in death, or so he felt, the trembling lids would have burst apart at this call and the revelations it promised.

And what did he see? What did that window hold for him?

Nothing that he might not have seen there any night at this hour. His father's figure drawn up behind the panes in wistful contemplation of the night. No visible change in his attitude, nothing forced or unusual in his manner. Even the hand, lifted to pull down the shade, moves with its familiar hesitation. In a moment more that shade will be down and – But no! the lifted hand falls back; the easy attitude becomes strained, fixed. He is staring now – not merely gazing out upon the wastes of sky and sea; and Roger, following the direction of his glance, stares also in breathless emotion at what those distances, but now so impenetrable, are giving to the eye.

A spectre floating in the air above the promontory! The spectre of a woman – of his wife, clad, as she had been clad that fatal night! Outlined in supernatural light, it faces them with lifted arms showing the ends of rope dangling from either wrist. A sight awful to any eye, but to the man of guilty heart—

Ah! it comes – the cry for which the agonized son had been listening! An old man's shriek, hoarse with the remorse of sleepless nights and days of unimaginable regret and foreboding! It cuts the night. It cuts its way into his heart. He feels his senses failing him, yet he must glance once more at the window and see with his last conscious look—. But what is this! A change has taken place in the picture and he beholds, not the distorted form of his father sinking back in shame and terror before this visible image of his secret sin, but that of another weak, old man falling to the floor behind his back! Abram! The attentive, seemingly harmless, guardian of the household! Abram! Who had never spoken a word or given a look in any way suggestive of his having played any other part in the hideous drama of their lives than that of the humble and sympathetic servant!

The shock was too great, the relief too absolute for credence. He, the listener at the grotto? He, the avenger of the family's honor? He, the insurer of little Roger's continuance with the family at a cost the one who loved him best would rather have died himself than pay? Yes! There is no misdoubting this old servitor's attitude of abject appeal, or the meaning of Homer Upjohn's joyfully uplifted countenance and outspreading arms. The servant begs for mercy from man, and the master is giving thanks to Heaven. Why giving thanks? Has he been the prey of cankering doubts also? Has the father dreaded to discover that in the son which the son has dreaded to discover in the father?

It might easily be; and as Roger recognizes this truth and the full tragedy of their mutual lives, he drops to his knees amid the honeysuckles.

* * *

"Violet, you are a wonder. But how did you dare?"

This from Arthur as the two rode to the train in the early morning.

The answer came a bit waveringly.

"I do not know. I am astonished yet, at my own daring. Look at my hands. They have not ceased trembling since the moment you threw the light upon me on the rocks. The figure of old Mr. Upjohn in the window looked so august."

Arthur, with a short glance at the little hands she held out, shrugged his shoulders imperceptibly. It struck him that the tremulousness she complained of was due more to some parting word from their young host, than from prolonged awe at her own daring. But he made no remark to this effect, only observed:

"Abram has confessed his guilt, I hear."

"Yes, and will die of it. The master will bury the man, and not the man the master."

"And Roger? Not the little fellow, but the father?"

"We will not talk of him," said she, her eyes seeking the sea where the sun in its rising was battling with a troop of lowering clouds and slowly gaining the victory.

The Case of the Golden Bullet

Auguste Groner, translated by Grace Isabel Colbron

"PLEASE, SIR, there is a man outside who asks to see you."

"What does he want?" asked Commissioner Horn, looking up.

"He says he has something to report, sir."

"Send him in, then."

The attendant disappeared, and the commissioner looked up at the clock. It was just striking eleven, but the fellow official who was to relieve him at that hour had not yet appeared. And if this should chance to be a new case, he would probably be obliged to take it himself. The commissioner was not in a very good humour as he sat back to receive the young man who entered the room in the wake of the attendant. The stranger was a sturdy youth, with an unintelligent, good-natured face. He twisted his soft hat in his hands in evident embarrassment, and his eyes wandered helplessly about the great bare room.

"Who are you?" demanded the commissioner.

"My name is Dummel, sir, Johann Dummel."

"And your occupation?"

"My occupation? Oh, yes, I – I am a valet, valet to Professor Fellner."

The commissioner sat up and looked interested. He knew Fellner personally and liked him. "What have you to report to me?" he asked eagerly.

"I – I don't know whether I ought to have come here, but at home—"

"Well, is anything the matter?" insisted Horn.

"Why, sir, I don't know; but the Professor – he is so still – he doesn't answer."

Horn sprang from his chair. "Is he ill?" he asked.

"I don't know, sir. His room is locked – he never locked it before."

"And you are certain he is at home?"

"Yes, sir. I saw him during the night – and the key is in the lock on the inside."

The commissioner had his hat in his hand when the colleague who was to relieve him appeared. "Good and cold out today!" was the latter's greeting. Horn answered with an ironical: "Then I suppose you'll be glad if I relieve you of this case. But I assure you I wouldn't do it if it wasn't Fellner. Goodbye. Oh, and one thing more. Please send a physician at once to Fellner's house, No. 7 Field Street."

Horn opened the door and passed on into the adjoining room, accompanied by Johann. The commissioner halted a moment as his eyes fell upon a little man who sat in the corner reading a newspaper. "Hello, Muller; you there? Suppose I take you with me? You aren't doing anything now, are you?"

"No, sir.

"Well, come with me, then. If this should turn out to be anything serious, we may need you."

The three men entered one of the cabs waiting outside the police station. As they rattled through the streets, Commissioner Horn continued his examination of the valet.

"When did you see your master last?"

"About eleven o'clock last evening."

"Did you speak with him then?

"No, I looked through the keyhole."

"Oh, indeed; is that a habit of yours?"

Dummel blushed deeply, but his eyes flashed, and he looked angry.

"No, it is not, sir," he growled. "I only did it this time because I was anxious about the master. He's been so worked up and nervous the last few days. Last night I went to the theatre, as I always do Saturday evenings. When I returned, about half-past ten it was, I knocked at the door of his bedroom. He didn't answer, and I walked away softly, so as not to disturb him in case he'd gone to sleep already. The hall was dark, and as I went through it I saw a ray of light coming from the keyhole of the Professor's study. That surprised me, because he never worked as late as that before. I thought it over a moment, then I crept up and looked through the keyhole."

"And what did you see?"

"He sat at his desk, quite quiet. So I felt easy again, and went off to bed."

"Why didn't you go into the room?"

"I didn't dare, sir. The Professor never wanted to be disturbed when he was writing."

"Well, and this morning?"

"I got up at the usual time this morning, set the breakfast table, and then knocked at the Professor's bedroom door to waken him. He didn't answer, and I thought he might want to sleep, seeing as it was Sunday, and he was up late last night. So I waited until ten o'clock. Then I knocked again and tried the door, but it was locked. That made me uneasy, because he never locked his bedroom door before. I banged at the door and called out, but there wasn't a sound. Then I ran to the police station."

Horn was evidently as alarmed as was the young valet. But Muller's cheeks were flushed and a flash of secret joy, of pleasurable expectation, brightened his deep-set, grey eyes. He sat quite motionless, but every nerve in his body was alive and tingling. The humble-looking little man had become quite another and a decidedly interesting person. He laid his thin, nervous hand on the carriage door.

"We are not there yet," said the commissioner.

"No, but it's the third house from here," replied Muller.

"You know where everybody lives, don't you?" smiled Horn.

"Nearly everybody," answered Muller gently, as the cab stopped before an attractive little villa surrounded by its own garden, as were most of the houses in this quiet, aristocratic part of the town.

The house was two stories high, but the upper windows were closed and tightly curtained. This upper story was the apartment occupied by the owner of the house, who was now in Italy with his invalid wife. Otherwise the dainty little villa, built in the fashionable Nuremberg style, with heavy wooden doors and lozenged-paned windows, had no occupants except Professor Fellner and his servant. With its graceful outlines and well-planned garden, the dwelling had a most attractive appearance. Opposite it was the broad avenue known as the Promenade, and beyond this were open fields. To the right and to the left were similar villas in their gardens.

Dummel opened the door and the three men entered the house. The commissioner and the valet went in first, Muller following them more slowly. His sharp eyes glanced quickly over the coloured tiles of the flooring, over the white steps and the carpeted hallway beyond. Once he bent quickly and picked up something, then he walked on with his usual quiet manner, out of which every trace of excitement had now vanished.

The dull winter sun seemed only to make the gloom of the dark vestibule more visible. Johann turned up the light, and Horn, who had visited the Professor several times and knew the situation of the rooms, went at once to the heavy, carved and iron trimmed door of the study. He attempted to open the door, but it resisted all pressure. The heavy key was in the inner side of the big lock with its medieval iron ornamentation. But the key was turned so that the lower part of the lock was free, a round opening of unusual size. Horn made sure of this by holding a lighted match to the door.

"You are right," he said to the valet, "the door is locked from the inside. We'll have to go through the bedroom. Johann, bring me a chisel or a hatchet. Muller, you stay here and open the door when the doctor comes."

Muller nodded. Johann disappeared, returning in a few moments with a small hatchet, and followed the commissioner through the dining room. It was an attractive apartment with its high wooden panelling and its dainty breakfast table. But a slight shiver ran through the commissioner's frame as he realised that some misfortune, some crime even might be waiting for them on the other side of the closed door. The bedroom door also was locked on the inside, and after some moments of knocking and calling, Horn set the hatchet to the framework just as the bell of the house-door pealed out.

With a cracking and tearing of wood the bedroom door fell open, and in the same moment Muller and the physician passed through the dining room. Johann hurried into the bedroom to open the window shutters, and the others gathered in the doorway. A single look showed each of the men that the bed was untouched, and they passed on through the room. The door from the bedroom to the study stood open. In the latter room the shutters were tightly closed, and the lamp had long since gone out. But sufficient light fell through the open bedroom door for the men to see the figure of the Professor seated at his desk, and when Johann had opened the shutters, it was plain to all that the silent figure before them was that of a corpse.

"Heart disease, probably," murmured the physician, as he touched the icy forehead. Then he felt the pulse of the stiffened hand from which the pen had fallen in the moment of death, raised the drooping head and lifted up the half-closed eyelids. The eyes were glazed.

The others looked on in silence. Horn was very pale, and his usually calm face showed great emotion. Johann seemed quite beside himself, the tears rolled down his cheeks unhindered. Muller stood without a sign of life, his sallow face seemed made of bronze; he was watching and listening. He seemed to hear and see what no one else could see or hear. He smiled slightly when the doctor spoke of 'heart disease', and his eyes fell on the revolver that lay near the dead man's hand on the desk. Then he shook his head, and then he started suddenly. Horn noticed the movement; it was in the moment when the physician raised up the sunken figure that had fallen half over the desk.

"He was killed by a bullet," said Muller.

"Yes, that was it," replied the doctor. With the raising of the body the dead man's waistcoat fell back into its usual position, and they could see a little round hole in his shirt. The doctor opened the shirt bosom and pointed to a little wound in the Professor's left breast. There were scarcely three or four drops of blood visible. The hemorrhage had been internal.

"He must have died at once, without suffering," said the physician.

"He killed himself – he killed himself," murmured Johann, as if bewildered.

"It's strange that he should have found time to lay down the revolver before he died," remarked Horn. Johann put out his hand and raised the weapon before Horn could prevent him. "Leave that pistol where it was," commanded the commissioner. "We have to look into this matter more closely."

The doctor turned quickly. "You think it was a murder?" he exclaimed. "The doors were both locked on the inside – where could the murderer be?"

"I don't pretend to see him myself yet. But our rule is to leave things as they are discovered, until the official examination. Muller, did you shut the outer door?"

"Yes, sir; here is the key."

"Johann, are there any more keys for the outer door?"

"Yes, sir. One more, that is, for the third was lost some months ago. The Professor's own key ought to be in the drawer of the little table beside the bed."

"Will you please look for it, Muller?"

Muller went into the bedroom and soon returned with the key, which he handed to the commissioner. The detective had found something else in the little table drawer – a tortoise-shell hairpin, which he had carefully hidden in his own pocket before rejoining the others.

Horn turned to the servant again. "How many times have you been out of the apartment since last night?"

"Once only, sir, to go to the police station to fetch you."

"And you locked the door behind you?"

"Why, yes, sir. You saw that I had to turn the key twice to let you in."

Horn and Muller both looked the young man over very carefully. He seemed perfectly innocent, and their suspicion that he might have turned the key in pretence only, soon vanished. It would have been a foolish suspicion anyway. If he were in league with the murderer, he could have let the latter escape with much more safety during the night. Horn let his eyes wander about the rooms again, and said slowly: "Then the murderer is still here – or else—"

"Or else?" asked the doctor.

"Or else we have a strange riddle to solve."

Johann had laid the pistol down again. Muller stretched forth his hand and took it up. He looked at it a moment, then handed it to the commissioner. "We have to do with a murder here. There was not a shot fired from this revolver, for every chamber is still loaded. And there is no other weapon in sight," said the detective quietly.

"Yes, he was murdered. This revolver is fully loaded. Let us begin the search at once." Horn was more excited than he cared to show.

Johann looked about in alarm, but when he saw the others beginning to peer into every corner and every cupboard, he himself joined in the man-hunt. A quarter of an hour later, the four men relinquished their fruitless efforts and gathered beside the corpse again.

"Doctor, will you have the kindness to report to the head Commissioner of Police, and to order the taking away of the body? We will look about for some motive for this murder in the meantime," said Horn, as he held out his hand to the physician.

Muller walked out to the door of the house with the doctor.

"Do you think this valet did it?" asked the physician softly.

"He? Oh, dear, no," replied the detective scornfully.

"You think he's too stupid? But this stupidity might be feigned."

"It's real enough, doctor."

"But what do you think about it – you, who have the gift of seeing more than other people see, even if it does bring you into disfavour with the Powers that Be?"

"Then you don't believe me yet?"

"You mean about the beautiful Mrs. Kniepp?

"And yet I tell you I am right. It was an intentional suicide."

"Muller, Muller, you must keep better watch over your imagination and your tongue! It is a dangerous thing to spread rumours about persons high in favour with the Arch-duke. But you had better tell me what you think about this affair," continued the doctor, pointing back towards the room they had just left.

"There's a woman in the case."

"Aha! You are romancing again. Well, they won't be so sensitive about this matter, but take care that you don't make a mistake again, my dear Muller. It would be likely to cost you your position, don't forget that."

The doctor left the house. Muller smiled bitterly as he closed the door behind him, and murmured to himself: "Indeed, I do not forget it, and that is why I shall take this matter into my own hands. But the Kniepp case is not closed yet, by any means."

When he returned to the study he saw Johann sitting quietly in a corner, shaking his head, as if trying to understand it all. Horn was bending over a sheet of writing paper which lay before the dead man. Fellner must have been busy at his desk when the bullet penetrated his heart. His hand in dying had let fall the pen, which had drawn a long black mark across the bottom of the sheet. One page of the paper was covered with a small, delicate handwriting.

Horn called up the detective, and together they read the following words:

> *Dear Friend: –*
> *He challenged me – pistols – it means life or death. My enemy is very bitter. But I am not ready to die yet. And as I know that I would be the one to fall, I have refused the duel. That will help me little, for his revenge will know how to find me. I dare not be a moment without a weapon now – his threats on my refusal let me fear the worst. I have an uncanny presentiment of evil. I shall leave here tomorrow. With the excuse of having some pressing family affair to attend to, I have secured several days' leave. Of course I do not intend to return. I am hoping that you will come here and break up my establishment in my stead. I will tell you everything else when I see you. I am in a hurry now, for there is a good deal of packing to do. If anything should happen to me, you will know who it is who is responsible for my death. His name is—*

Here the letter came to an abrupt close.

Muller and Horn looked at each other in silence, then they turned their eyes again toward the dead man.

"He was a coward," said the detective coldly, and turned away. Horn repeated mechanically, "A coward!" and his eyes also looked down with a changed expression upon the handsome, soft-featured face, framed in curly blond hair, that lay so silent against the chair-back. Many women had loved this dead man, and many men had been fond of him, for they had believed him capable and manly.

The commissioner and Muller continued their researches in silence and with less interest than before. They found a heap of loose ashes in the bedroom stove. Letters and other trifles had been burned there. Muller raked out the heap very carefully, but the writing on the few pieces of paper still left whole was quite illegible. There were several envelopes in the waste-basket, but all of them were dated several months back. There was nothing that could give the slightest clue.

The letter written by the murdered man was sufficient proof that his death had been an act of vengeance. But who was it who had carried out this secret, terrible deed? The victim had not been allowed the time to write down the name of his murderer.

Horn took the letter into his keeping. Then he left the room, followed by Muller and the valet, to look about the rest of the house as far as possible. This was not very far, for the second storey was closed off by a tall iron grating.

"Is the house door locked during the daytime?" asked Horn of the servant.

"The front door is, but the side door into the garden is usually open."

"Has it ever happened that anyone got into the house from this side door without your knowing it?"

"No, sir. The garden has a high wall around it. And there is extra protection on the side toward the Promenade."

"But there's a little gate there?"

"Yes, sir."

"Is that usually closed?"

"We never use the key for that, sir. It has a trick lock that you can't open unless you know how."

"You said you went to the theatre yesterday evening. Did your master give you permission to go?"

"Yes, sir. It's about a year now that he gave me money for a theatre ticket every Saturday evening. He was very kind."

"Did you come into the house last night by the front door, or through the garden?"

"Through the garden, sir. I walked down the Promenade from the theatre."

"And you didn't notice anything – you saw no traces of footsteps?"

"No, sir. I didn't notice anything unusual. We shut the side door, the garden door, every evening, also. It was closed yesterday and I found the key – we've only got one key to the garden door – in the same place where I was told to hide it when I went out in the evening."

"What place was that?"

"In one of the pails by the well."

"You say you were told to hide it there?"

"Yes, sir; the Professor told me. He'd go out in the evening sometimes, too, I suppose, and he wanted to be able to come in that way if necessary."

"And no one else knew where the key was hidden?"

"No one else, sir. It's nearly a year now that we've been alone in the house. Who else should know of it?"

"When you looked through the keyhole last night, are you sure that the Professor was still alive?"

"Why, yes, sir; of course I couldn't say so surely. I thought he was reading or writing, but oh, dear Lord! there he was this morning, nearly twelve hours later, in just the same position." Johann shivered at the thought that he might have seen his master sitting at his desk, already a corpse.

"He must have been dead when you came home. Don't you think the sound of that shot would have wakened you?"

"Yes, sir, I think likely, sir," murmured Johann. "But if the murderer could get into the house, how could he get into the apartment?"

"There must have been a third key of which you knew nothing," answered Horn, turning to Muller again. "It's stranger still how Fellner could have been shot, for the window shutters were fastened and quite uninjured, and both doors were locked on the inside."

As he said these words, Horn looked sharply at his subordinate; but Muller's calm face did not give the slightest clue to his thoughts. The experienced police commissioner was pleased and yet slightly angered at this behaviour on the part of the detective. He knew that it was quite possible that Muller had already formed a clear opinion about the case, and that he was merely keeping it to himself. And yet he was glad to see that the little detective had apparently learned a lesson from his recent mistake concerning the death of Mrs. Kniepp – that he had somewhat lost confidence in his hitherto unerring instinct, and did not care to express any opinion until he had studied the matter a little closer. The commissioner was just a little bit vain, and just a little bit jealous of this humble detective's fame.

Muller shrugged his shoulders at the remark of his superior, and the two men stood silent, thinking over the case, as the Chief of Police appeared, accompanied by the doctor, a clerk, and two hospital attendants. The chief commissioner received the report of what had been discovered, while the corpse was laid on a bier to be taken to the hospital.

Muller handed the commissioner his hat and cane and helped him into his overcoat. Horn noticed that the detective himself was making no preparations to go out. "Aren't you coming with us?" he asked, astonished.

"I hope the gentlemen will allow me to remain here for a little while," answered Muller modestly.

"But you know that we will have to close the apartment officially," said Horn, his voice sharpening in his surprise and displeasure.

"I do not need to be in these rooms any longer."

"Don't let them disturb you, my dear Muller; we will allow your keenness all possible leeway here." The Head of Police spoke with calm politeness, but Muller started and shivered. The emphasis on the 'here' showed him that even the head of the department had been incensed at his suggestion that the beautiful Mrs. Kniepp had died of her own free will. It had been his assertion of this which, coming to the ears of the bereaved husband, had enraged and embittered him, and had turned the power of his influence with the high authorities against the detective. Muller knew how greatly he had fallen from favour in the Police Department, and the words of his respected superior showed him that he was still in disgrace.

But the strange, quiet smile was still on his lips as, with his usual humble deference, he accompanied the others to the sidewalk. Before the commissioners left the house, the Chief commanded Johann to answer carefully any questions Muller might put to him.

"He'll find something, you may be sure," said Horn, as they drove off in the cab.

"Let him – that's his business. He is officially bound to see more than the rest of us," smiled the older official good-naturedly. "But in spite of it, he'll never get any further than the vestibule; he'll be making bows to us to the end of his days."

"You think so? I've wondered at the man. I know his fame in the capital, indeed, in police circles all over Austria and Germany. It seems hard on him to be transferred to this small town, now that he is growing old. I've wondered why he hasn't done more for himself, with his gifts."

"He never will," replied the Chief. "He may win more fame – he may still go on winning triumphs, but he will go on in a circle; he'll never forge ahead as his capabilities deserve. Muller's peculiarity is that his genius – for the man has undeniable genius – will always make concessions to his heart just at the moment when he is about to do something great – and his triumph is lost."

Horn looked up at his superior, whom, in spite of his good nature, he knew to be a sharp, keen, capable police official. "I forgot you have known Muller longer than the rest of us," he said. "What was that you said about his heart?"

"I said that it is one of those inconvenient hearts that will always make itself noticeable at the wrong time. Muller's heart has played several tricks on the police department, which has, at other times, profited so well by his genius. He is a strange mixture. While he is on the trail of the criminal he is like the bloodhound. He does not seem to know fatigue nor hunger; his whole being is absorbed by the excitement of the chase. He has done many a brilliant service to the cause of justice, he has discovered the guilt, or the innocence, of many in cases where the official department was as blind as Justice is proverbially supposed to be. Joseph Muller has become the idol of all who are engaged in this weary business of hunting down wrong and punishing crime. He is without a peer in his profession. But he has also become the idol of some of the criminals. For if he discovers (as sometimes happens) that the criminal is a good sort after all, he is just as likely to warn his prey, once he has all proofs of the guilt and a conviction is certain. Possibly this is his way of taking the sting from his irresistible impulse to ferret out hidden mysteries. But it is rather inconvenient, and he has hurt himself by it – hurt himself badly. They were tired of his peculiarities at the capital, and wanted to make his years an excuse to discharge him. I happened to get wind of it, and it was my weakness for him that saved him."

"Yes, you brought him here when they transferred you to this town, I remember now."

"I'm afraid it wasn't such a good thing for him, after all. Nothing ever happens here, and a gift like Muller's needs occupation to keep it fresh. I'm afraid his talents will dull and wither here. The man has grown perceptibly older in this inaction. His mind is like a high-bred horse that needs exercise to keep it in good condition."

"He hasn't grown rich at his work, either," said Horn.

"No, there's not much chance for a police detective to get rich. I've often wondered why Muller never had the energy to set up in business for himself. He might have won fame and fortune as a private detective. But he's gone on plodding along as a police subordinate, and letting the department get all the credit for his most brilliant achievements. It's a sort of incorrigible humbleness of nature – and then, you know, he had the misfortune to be unjustly sentenced to a term in prison in his early youth."

"No, I did not know that."

"The stigma stuck to his name, and finally drove him to take up this work. I don't think Muller realised, when he began, just how greatly he is gifted. I don't know that he really knows now. He seems to do it because he likes it – he's a queer sort of man."

While the commissioners drove through the streets to the police station the man of whom they were speaking sat in Johann's little room in close consultation with the valet.

"How long is it since the Professor began to give you money to go to the theatre on Saturday evenings?"

"The first time it happened was on my name day."

"What's the rest of your name? There are so many Johanns on the calendar."

"I am Johann Nepomuk."

Muller took a little calendar from his pocket and turned its pages. "It was May sixteenth," volunteered the valet.

"Quite right. May sixteenth was a Saturday. And since then you have gone to the theatre every Saturday evening?"

"Yes, sir."

"When did the owner of the house go away?"

"Last April. His wife was ill and he had to take her away. They went to Italy."

"And you two have been alone in the house since April?"

"Yes, sir, we two."

"Was there no janitor?"

"No, sir. The garden was taken care of by a man who came in for the day."

"And you had no dog? I haven't seen any around the place."

"No, sir; the Professor did not like animals. But he must have been thinking about buying a dog, because I found a new dog-whip in his room one day."

"Somebody might have left it there. One usually buys the dog first and then the whip."

"Yes, sir. But there wasn't anybody here to forget it. The Professor did not receive any visits at that time."

"Why are you so sure of that?"

"Because it was the middle of summer, and everybody was away."

"Oh, then, we won't bother about the whip. Can you tell me of any ladies with whom the Professor was acquainted?"

"Ladies? I don't know of any. Of course, the Professor was invited out a good deal, and most of the other gentlemen from the college were married."

"Did he ever receive letters from ladies?" continued Muller.

Johann thought the matter over, then confessed that he knew very little about writing and couldn't read handwriting very well anyway. But he remembered to have seen a letter now and then, a little letter with a fine and delicate handwriting.

"Have you any of these envelopes?" asked Muller. But Johann told him that in spite of his usual carelessness in such matters, Professor Fellner never allowed these letters to lie about his room.

Finally the detective came out with the question to which he had been leading up. "Did your master ever receive visits from ladies?"

Johann looked extremely stupid at this moment. His lack of intelligence and a certain crude sensitiveness in his nature made him take umbrage at what appeared to him a very unnecessary question. He answered it with a shake of the head only. Muller smiled at the young man's ill-concealed indignation and paid no attention to it.

"Your master has been here for about a year. Where was he before that?"

"In the capital."

"You were in his service then?"

"I have been with him for three years."

"Did he know any ladies in his former home?"

"There was one – I think he was engaged to her."

"Why didn't he marry her?"

"I don't know."

"What was her name?"

"Marie. That's all I know about it."

"Was she beautiful?"

"I never saw her. The only way I knew about her was when the Professor's friends spoke of her."

"Did he have many friends?"

"There were ever so many gentlemen whom he called his friends."

"Take me into the garden now."

"Yes, sir." Muller took his hat and coat and followed the valet into the garden. It was of considerable size, carefully and attractively planned, and pleasing even now when the bare twigs bent under their load of snow.

"Now think carefully, Johann. We had a full moon last night. Don't you remember seeing any footsteps in the garden, leading away from the house?" asked Muller, as they stood on the snow-covered paths.

Johann thought it over carefully, then said decidedly, "No. At least I don't remember anything of the kind. There was a strong wind yesterday anyway, and the snow drifts easily out here. No tracks could remain clear for long."

The men walked down the straight path which led to the little gate in the high wall. This gate had a secret lock, which, however, was neither hard to find nor hard to open. Muller managed it with ease, and looked out through the gate on the street beyond. The broad promenade, deserted now in its winter snowiness, led away in one direction to the heart of the city. In the other it ended in the main county high-road. This was a broad, well-made turnpike, with footpath and rows of trees. A half-hour's walk along it would bring one to the little village clustering about the Archduke's favourite hunting castle. There was a little railway station near the castle, but it was used only by suburban trains or for the royal private car.

Muller did not intend to burden his brain with unnecessary facts, so with his usual thoroughness he left the further investigation of what lay beyond the gate, until he had searched the garden thoroughly. But even for his sharp eyes there was no trace to be found that would tell of the night visit of the murderer.

"In which of the pails did you put the key to the side door?" he asked.

"In the first pail on the right hand side. But be careful, sir; there's a nail sticking out of the post there. The wind tore off a piece of wood yesterday."

The warning came too late. Muller's sleeve tore apart with a sharp sound just as Johann spoke, for the detective had already plunged his hand into the pail. The bottom of the bucket was easy to reach, as this one hung much lower than the others. Looking regretfully at the rent in his coat, Muller asked for needle and thread that he might repair it sufficiently to get home.

"Oh, don't bother about sewing it; I'll lend you one of mine," exclaimed Johann. "I'll carry this one home for you, for I'm not going to stay here alone – I'd be afraid. I'm going to a friend's house. You can find me there any time you need me. You'd better take the key of the apartment and give it to the police."

The detective had no particular fondness for the task of sewing, and he was glad to accept the valet's friendly offering. He was rather astonished at the evident costliness of the garment the young man handed him, and when he spoke of it, the valet could not say enough in praise of the kindness of his late master. He pulled out several other articles of clothing, which, like the overcoat, had been given to him by Fellner. Then he packed up a few necessities and announced himself as ready to start. He insisted on carrying the torn coat, and Muller permitted it after some protest. They carefully closed the apartment and the house, and walked toward the centre of the city to the police station, where Muller lived.

As they crossed the square, it suddenly occurred to Johann that he had no tobacco. He was a great smoker, and as he had many days of enforced idleness ahead of him, he ran into a tobacco shop to purchase a sufficiency of this necessity of life.

Muller waited outside, and his attention was attracted by a large grey Ulmer hound which was evidently waiting for someone within the shop. The dog came up to him in a most friendly manner, allowed him to pat its head, rubbed up against him with every sign of pleasure, and would not leave him even when he turned to go after Johann came out of the shop. Still accompanied by the dog, the two men walked on quite a distance, when a sharp whistle was heard behind them, and the dog became uneasy. He would not leave them, however, until a powerful voice called "Tristan!" several times. Muller turned and saw that Tristan's master was a tall, stately man wearing a handsome fur overcoat.

It was impossible to recognise his face at this distance, for the snowflakes were whirling thickly in the air. But Muller was not particularly anxious to recognise the stranger, as he had his head full of more important thoughts.

When Johann had given his new address and remarked that he would call for his coat soon, the men parted, and Muller returned to the police station.

DETECTIVE THRILLERS SHORT STORIES

The next day the principal newspaper of the town printed the following notice:

THE GOLDEN BULLET

It is but a few days since we announced to our readers the sad news of the death of a beautiful woman, whose leap from her window, while suffering from the agonies of fever, destroyed the happiness of an unusually harmonious marriage. And now we are compelled to print the news of another equally sad as well as mysterious occurrence. This time, Fate has demanded the sacrifice of the life of a capable and promising young man. Professor Paul Fellner, a member of the faculty of our college, was found dead at his desk yesterday morning. It was thought at first that it was a case of suicide, for doors and windows were carefully closed from within and those who discovered the corpse were obliged to break open one of the doors to get to it. And a revolver was found lying close at hand, upon the desk. But this revolver was loaded in every chamber and there was no other weapon to be seen in the room. There was a bullet wound in the left breast of the corpse, and the bullet had penetrated the heart. Death must have been instantaneous.

The most mysterious thing about this strange affair was discovered during the autopsy. It is incredible, but it is absolutely true, as it is vouched for under oath by the authorities who were present, that the bullet which was found in the heart of the dead man was made of solid gold. And yet, strange as is this circumstance, it is still more a riddle how the murderer could have escaped from the room where he had shot down his victim, for the keys in both doors were in the locks from the inside. We have evidently to do here with a criminal of very unusual cleverness and it is therefore not surprising that there has been no clue discovered thus far. The only thing that is known is that this murder was an act of revenge.

The entire city was in excitement over the mystery, even the police station was shaken out of its usual business-like indifference. There was no other topic of conversation in any of the rooms but the mystery of the golden bullet and the doors closed from the inside. The attendants and the policeman gathered whispering in the corners, and strangers who came in on their own business forgot it in their excitement over this new and fascinating mystery.

That afternoon Muller passed through Horn's office with a bundle of papers, on his way to the inner office occupied by his patron, Chief of Police Bauer. Horn, who had avoided Muller since yesterday although he was conscious of a freshened interest in the man, raised his head and watched the little detective as he walked across the room with his usual quiet tread. The commissioner saw nothing but the usual humble business-like manner to which he was accustomed – then suddenly something happened that came to him like a distinct shock. Muller stopped in his walk so suddenly that one foot was poised in the air. His bowed head was thrown back, his face flushed to his forehead, and the papers trembled in his hands. He ran the fingers of his unoccupied hand through his hair and murmured audibly, "That dog! That dog!" It was evident that some thought had struck him with such insistence as to render him oblivious of his surroundings. Then he finally realised where he was, and walked on quickly to Bauer's room, his face still flushed, his hands trembling. When he came out from the office again, he was his usual quiet, humble self.

But the commissioner, with his now greater knowledge of the little man's gifts and past, could not forget the incident. During the afternoon he found himself repeating mechanically,

"That dog – that dog." But the words meant nothing to him, hard as he might try to find the connection.

When the commissioner left for his home late that afternoon, Muller re-entered the office to lay some papers on the desk. His duties over, he was about to turn out the gas, when his eye fell on the blotter on Horn's desk. He looked at it more closely, then burst into a loud laugh. The same two words were scribbled again and again over the white surface, but it was not the name of any fair maiden, or even the title of a love poem; it was only the words, "That dog—"

Several days had passed since the discovery of the murder. Fellner had been buried and his possessions taken into custody by the authorities until his heirs should appear. The dead man's papers and affairs were in excellent condition and the arranging of the inheritance had been quickly done. Until the heirs should take possession, the apartment was sealed by the police. There was nothing else to do in the matter, and the commission appointed to make researches had discovered nothing of value. The murderer might easily feel that he was absolutely safe by this time.

The day after the publication of the article we have quoted, Muller appeared in Bauer's office and asked for a few days' leave.

"In the Fellner case?" asked the Chief with his usual calm, and Muller replied in the affirmative. Two days later he returned, bringing with him nothing but a single little notice.

"Marie Dorn, now Mrs. Kniepp," was one line in his notebook, and beside it some dates. The latter showed that Marie Dorn had for two years past been the wife of the Archducal Forest-Councillor, Leo Kniepp.

And for one year now Professor Paul Fellner had been in the town, after having applied for his transference from the university in the capital to this place, which was scarce half an hour's walk distant from the home of the beautiful young woman who had been the love of his youth.

And Fellner had made his home in the quietest quarter of the city, in that quarter which was nearest the Archducal hunting castle. He had lived very quietly, had not cultivated the acquaintance of the ladies of the town, but was a great walker and bicycle rider; and every Saturday evening since he had been alone in the house, he had sent his servant to the theatre. And it was on Saturday evenings that Forest-Councillor Kniepp went to his Bowling Club at the other end of the city, and did not return until the last train at midnight.

And during these evening hours Fellner's apartment was a convenient place for pleasant meetings; and nothing prevented the Professor from accompanying his beautiful friend home through the quiet Promenade, along the turnpike to the hunting castle. And Johann had once found a dog-whip in his master's room – and Councillor Leo Kniepp, head of the Forestry Department, was the possessor of a beautiful Ulmer hound which took an active interest in people who wore clothes belonging to Fellner.

Furthermore, in the little drawer of the bedside table in the murdered man's room, there had been found a tortoise-shell hairpin; and in the corner of the vestibule of his house, a little mother-of-pearl glove button, of the kind much in fashion that winter, because of a desire on the part of the ladies of the town to help the home industry of the neighbourhood. Mrs. Marie Kniepp was one of the fashionable women of the town, and several days before the Professor was murdered, this woman had thrown herself from the second-storey window of her home, and her husband, whose passionate eccentric nature was well known, had been a changed man from that hour.

It was his deep grief at the loss of his beloved wife that had turned his hair grey and had drawn lines of terrible sorrow in his face – said gossip. But Muller, who did not know Kniepp personally although he had been taking a great interest in his affairs for the last few days, had his own ideas on the subject, and he decided to make the acquaintance of the Forest Councillor as soon as possible – that is, after he had found out all there was to be found out about his affairs and his habits.

Just a week after the murder, on Saturday evening therefore, the snow was whirling merrily about the gables and cupolas of the Archducal hunting castle. The weather-vanes groaned and the old trees in the park bent their tall tops under the mad wind which swept across the earth and tore the protecting snow covering from their branches. It was a stormy evening, not one to be out in if a man had a warm corner in which to hide.

An old peddler was trying to find shelter from the rapidly increasing storm under the lea of the castle wall. He crouched so close to the stones that he could scarcely be seen at all, in spite of the light from the snow. Finally he disappeared altogether behind one of the heavy columns which sprang out at intervals from the magnificent wall. Only his head peeped out occasionally as if looking for something. His dark, thoughtful eyes glanced over the little village spread out on one side of the castle, and over the railway station, its most imposing building. Then they would turn back again to the entrance gate in the wall near where he stood. It was a heavy iron-barred gate, its handsome ornamentation outlined in snow, and behind it the body of a large dog could be occasionally seen. This dog was an enormous grey Ulmer hound.

The peddler stood for a long time motionless behind the pillar, then he looked at his watch. "It's nearly time," he murmured, and looked over towards the station again, where lights and figures were gathering.

At the same time the noise of an opening door was heard, and steps creaked over the snow. A man, evidently a servant, opened the little door beside the great gate and held it for another man to pass out. "You'll come back by the night train as usual, sir?" he asked respectfully.

"Yes," replied the other, pushing back the dog, which fawned upon him.

"Come back here, Tristan," called the servant, pulling the dog in by his collar, as he closed the door and re-entered the house.

The Councillor took the path to the station. He walked slowly, with bowed head and uneven step. He did not look like a man who was in the mood to join a merry crowd, and yet he was evidently going to his Club. "He wants to show himself; he doesn't want to let people think that he has anything to be afraid of," murmured the peddler, looking after him sharply. Then his eyes suddenly dimmed and a light sigh was heard, with another murmur, "Poor man." The Councillor reached the station and disappeared within its door. The train arrived and departed a few moments later. Kniepp must have really gone to the city, for although the man behind the pillar waited for some little time, the Councillor did not return – a contingency that the peddler had not deemed improbable.

About half an hour after the departure of the train the watcher came out of his hiding place and walked noisily past the gate. What he expected, happened. The dog rushed up to the bars, barking loudly, but when the peddler had taken a silk muffler from the pack on his back and held it out to the animal, the noise ceased and the dog's anger turned to friendliness. Tristan was quite gentle, put his huge head up to the bars to let the stranger pat it, and seemed not at all alarmed when the latter rang the bell.

The young man who had opened the door for the Councillor came out from a wing of the castle. The peddler looked so frozen and yet so venerable that the youth had not the heart to turn him away. Possibly he was glad of a little diversion for his own sake.

"Who do you want to see?" he asked.

"I want to speak to the maid, the one who attended your dead mistress."

"Oh, then you know—?"

"I know of the misfortune that has happened here."

"And you think that Nanette might have something to sell to you?"

"Yes, that's it; that's why I came. For I don't suppose there's much chance for any business with my cigar holders and other trifles here so near the city."

"Cigar holders? Why, I don't know; perhaps we can make a trade. Come in with me. Why, just see how gentle the dog is with you!"

"Isn't he that way with everybody? I supposed he was no watchdog."

"Oh, indeed he is. He usually won't allow anybody to touch him, except those whom he knows well. I'm astonished that he lets you come to the house at all."

They had reached the door by this time. The peddler laid his hand on the servant's arm and halted a moment. "Where was it that she threw herself out?"

"From the last window upstairs there."

"And did it kill her at once?"

"Yes. Anyway she was unconscious when we came down."

"Was the master at home?"

"Why, yes, it happened in the middle of the night."

"She had a fever, didn't she? Had she been ill long?"

"No. She was in bed that day, but we thought it was nothing of importance."

"These fevers come on quickly sometimes," remarked the old man wisely, and added: "This case interests the entire neighbourhood and I will show you that I can be grateful for anything you may tell me – of course, only what a faithful servant could tell. It will interest my customers very much."

"You know all there is to know," said the valet, evidently disappointed that he had nothing to tell which could win the peddler's gratitude. "There are no secrets about it. Everybody knows that they were a very happy couple, and even if there was a little talk between them on that day, why it was pure accident and had nothing to do with the mistress' excitement."

"Then there was a quarrel between them?"

"Are people talking about it?"

"I've heard some things said. They even say that this quarrel was the reason for – her death."

"It's stupid nonsense!" exclaimed the servant. The old peddler seemed to like the young man's honest indignation.

While they were talking, they had passed through a long corridor and the young man laid his hand on one of the doors as the peddler asked, "Can I see Miss Nanette alone?"

"Alone? Oho, she's engaged to me!"

"I know that," said the stranger, who seemed to be initiated into all the doings of this household. "And I am an old man – all I meant was that I would rather not have any of the other servants about."

"I'll keep the cook out of the way if you want me to."

"That would be a good idea. It isn't easy to talk business before others," remarked the old man as they entered the room. It was a comfortably furnished and cozily warm apartment. Only two people were there, an old woman and a pretty young girl, who both looked up in astonishment as the men came in.

"Who's this you're bringing in, George?" asked Nanette.

"He's a peddler and he's got some trifles here you might like to look at."

"Why, yes, you wanted a thimble, didn't you, Lena?" asked Nanette, and the cook beckoned to the peddler. "Let's see what you've got there," she said in a friendly tone. The old man pulled out his wares from his pack; thimbles and scissors, coloured ribbons, silks, brushes and combs, and many other trifles. When the women had made their several selections they noticed that the old man was shivering with the cold, as he leaned against the stove. Their sympathies were aroused in a moment. "Why don't you sit down?" asked Nanette, pushing a chair towards him, and Lena rose to get him something warm from the kitchen.

The peddler threw a look at George, who nodded in answer. "He said he'd like to see the things they gave you after Mrs. Kniepp's death," the young man remarked.

"Do you buy things like that?" Nanette turned to the peddler.

"I'd just like to look at them first, if you'll let me."

"I'd be glad to get rid of them. But I won't go upstairs, I'm afraid there."

"Well, I'll get the things for you if you want me to," offered George and turned to leave the room. The door had scarcely closed behind him when a change came over the peddler. His old head rose from its drooping position, his bowed figure started up with youthful elasticity.

"Are you really fond of him?" he asked of the astonished Nanette, who stepped back a pace, stammering in answer: "Yes. Why do you ask? And who are you?"

"Never mind that, my dear child, but just answer the questions I have to ask, and answer truthfully, or it might occur to me to let your George know that he is not the first man you have loved."

"What do you know?" she breathed in alarm.

The peddler laughed. "Oho, then he's jealous! All the better for me – the Councillor was jealous too, wasn't he?" Nanette looked at him in horror.

"The truth, therefore, you must tell me the truth, and get the others away, so I can speak to you alone. You must do this – or else I'll tell George about the handsome carpenter in Church street, or about Franz Schmid, or—"

"For God's sake, stop – stop – I'll do anything you say."

The girl sank back on her chair pale and trembling, while the peddler resumed his pose of a tired old man leaning against the stove. When George returned with a large basket, Nanette had calmed herself sufficiently to go about the unpacking of the articles in the hamper.

"George, won't you please keep Lena out in the kitchen. Ask her to make some tea for us," asked Nanette with well-feigned assurance. George smiled a meaning smile and disappeared.

"I am particularly interested in the dead lady's gloves," said the peddler when they were alone again.

Nanette looked at him in surprise but was still too frightened to offer any remarks. She opened several boxes and packages and laid a number of pairs of gloves on the table. The old man looked through them, turning them over carefully. Then he shook his head: "There must be some more somewhere," he said. Nanette was no longer astonished at anything he might say or do, so she obediently went through the basket again and found a little box in which were several pair of grey suede gloves, fastened by bluish mother-of-pearl buttons. One of the pairs had been worn, and a button was missing.

"These are the ones I was looking for," said the peddler, putting the gloves in his pocket. Then he continued: "Your mistress was rather fond of taking long walks by herself, wasn't she?"

The girl's pale face flushed hotly and she stammered: "You know – about it?"

"You know about it also, I see. And did you know everything?"

"Yes, everything," murmured Nanette.

"Then it was you and Tristan who accompanied the lady on her walks?"

"Yes."

"I supposed she must have taken someone into her confidence. Well, and what do you think about the murder?"

"The Professor?" replied Nanette hastily. "Why, what should I know about it?"

"The Councillor was greatly excited and very unhappy when he discovered this affair, I suppose?"

"He is still."

"And how did he act after the – let us call it the accident?"

"He was like a crazy man."

"They tell me that he went about his duties just the same – that he went away on business."

"It wasn't business this time, at least not professional business. But before that he did have to go away frequently for weeks at a time."

"And it was then that your mistress was most interested in her lonely walks, eh?"

"Yes." Nanette's voice was so low as to be scarcely heard.

"Well, and this time?" continued the peddler. "Why did he go away this time?"

"He went to the capital on private business of his own."

"Are you sure of that?"

"Quite sure. He went two different times. I thought it was because he couldn't stand it here and wanted to see something different. He went to his club this evening, too."

"And when did he go away?"

"The first time was the day after his wife was buried."

"And the second time?"

"Two or three days after his return."

"How long did he stay away the first time?"

"Only one day."

"Good! Pull yourself together now. I'll send your George in to you and tell him you haven't been feeling well. Don't tell anyone about our conversation. Where is the kitchen?"

"The last door to the right down the hall."

The peddler left the room and Nanette sank down dazed and trembling on the nearest chair. George found her still pale, but he seemed to think it quite natural that she should have been overcome by the recollection of the terrible death of her mistress. He gave the old man a most cordial invitation to return during the next few days. The cook brought the peddler a cup of steaming tea, and purchased several trifles from him, before he left the house.

When the old man had reached a lonely spot on the road, about halfway between the hunting castle and the city, he halted, set down his pack, divested himself of his beard and his wig and washed the wrinkles from his face with a handful of snow from the wayside. A quarter of an hour later, Detective Muller entered the railway station of the city, burdened with a large grip. He took a seat in the night express which rolled out from the station a few moments later.

As he was alone in his compartment, Muller gave way to his excitement, sometimes even murmuring half-aloud the thoughts that rushed through his brain. "Yes, I am convinced of it, but can I find the proofs?" the words came again and again, and in spite of the comfortable warmth in the compartment, in spite of his tired and half-frozen condition, he could not sleep.

He reached the capital at midnight and took a room in a small hotel in a quiet street. When he went out next morning, the servants looked after him with suspicion, as in their opinion a man who spent most of the night pacing up and down his room must surely have a guilty conscience.

Muller went to police headquarters and looked through the arrivals at the hotels on the 21st of November. The burial of Mrs. Kniepp had taken place on the 20th. Muller soon found the name he was looking for, 'Forest Councillor Leo Kniepp', in the list of guests at the Hotel

Imperial. The detective went at once to the Hotel Imperial, where he was already well known. It cost him little time and trouble to discover what he wished to know, the reason for the Councillor's visit to the capital.

Kniepp had asked for the address of a goldsmith, and had been directed to one of the shops which had the best reputation in the city. He had been in the capital altogether for about twenty-four hours. He had the manner and appearance of a man suffering under some terrible blow.

Muller himself was deep in thought as he entered the train to return to his home, after a visit to the goldsmith in question. He had a short interview with Chief of Police Bauer, who finally gave him the golden bullet and the keys to the apartment of the murdered man. Then the two went out together.

An hour later, the chief of police and Muller stood in the garden of the house in which the murder had occurred. Bauer had entered from the Promenade after Muller had shown him how to work the lock of the little gate. Together they went up into the apartment, which was icy cold and uncanny in its loneliness. But the two men did not appear to notice this, so greatly were they interested in the task that had brought them there. First of all, they made a most minute examination of the two doors which had been locked. The keys were still in both locks on the inside. They were big heavy keys, suitable for the tall massive heavily-panelled and iron-ornamented doors. The entire villa was built in this heavy old German style, the favourite fashion of the last few years.

When they had looked the locks over carefully, Muller lit the lamp that hung over the desk in the study and closed the window shutters tight. Bauer had smiled at first as he watched his protégé's actions, but his smile changed to a look of keen interest as he suddenly understood. Muller took his place in the chair before the desk and looked over at the door of the vestibule, which was directly opposite him. "Yes, that's all right," he said with a deep breath.

Bauer had sat down on the sofa to watch the proceedings, now he sprang up with an exclamation: "Through the keyhole?"

"Through the keyhole," answered Muller.

"It is scarcely possible."

"Shall we try it?"

"Yes, yes, you do it." Even the usually indifferent old chief of police was breathing more hastily now. Muller took a roll of paper and a small pistol out of his pocket. He unrolled the paper, which represented the figure of a French soldier with a marked target on the breast. The detective pinned the paper on the back of the chair in which Professor Fellner had been seated when he met his death.

"But the key was in the hole," objected Bauer suddenly.

"Yes, but it was turned so that the lower part of the hole was free. Johann saw the light streaming through and could look into the room. If the murderer put the barrel of his pistol to this open part of the keyhole, the bullet would have to strike exactly where the dead man sat. There would be no need to take any particular aim." Muller gazed into space like a seer before whose mental eye a vision has arisen, and continued in level tones: "Fellner had refused the duel and the murderer was crazed by his desire for revenge. He came here to the house, he must have known just how to enter the place, how to reach the rooms, and he must have known also, that the Professor, coward as he was—"

"Coward? Is a man a coward when he refuses to stand up to a maniac?" interrupted Bauer.

Muller came back to the present with a start and said calmly, "Fellner was a coward."

"Then you know more than you are telling me now?"

Muller nodded. "Yes, I do," he answered with a smile. "But I will tell you more only when I have all the proofs in my own hand."

"And the criminal will escape us in the meantime."

"He has no idea that he is suspected."

"But – you'll promise to be sensible this time, Muller?"

"Yes. But you will pardon me my present reticence, even towards you? I – I don't want to be thought a dreamer again."

"As in the Kniepp case?"

"As in the Kniepp case," repeated the little man with a strange smile. "So please allow me to go about it in my own way. I will tell you all you want to know tomorrow."

"Tomorrow, then."

"May I now continue to unfold my theories?" Bauer nodded and Muller continued: "The criminal wanted Fellner's blood, no matter how."

"Even if it meant murder," said Bauer.

Muller nodded calmly. "It would have been nobler, perhaps, to have warned his victim of his approach, but it might have all come to nothing then. The other could have called for help, could have barricaded himself in his room, one crime might have been prevented, and another, more shameful one, would have gone unavenged."

"Another crime? Fellner a criminal?"

"Tomorrow you shall know everything, my kind friend. And now, let us make the trial. Please lock the door behind me as it was locked then."

Muller left the room, taking the pistol with him. Bauer locked the door. "Is this right?" he asked.

"Yes, I can see a wide curve of the room, taking in the entire desk. Please stand to one side now."

There was deep silence for a moment, then a slight sound as of metal on metal, then a report, and Muller re-entered the study through the bedroom. He found Bauer stooping over the picture of the French soldier. There was a hole in the left breast, where the bullet, passing through, had buried itself in the back of the chair.

"Yes, it was all just as you said," began the chief of police, holding out his hand to Muller. "But – why the golden bullet?"

"Tomorrow, tomorrow," replied the detective, looking up at his superior with a glance of pleading.

They left the house together and in less than an hour's time Muller was again in the train rolling towards the capital.

He went to the goldsmith's shop as soon as he arrived. The proprietor received him with eager interest and Muller handed him the golden bullet. "Here is the golden object of which I spoke," said the detective, paying no heed to the other's astonishment. The goldsmith opened a small locked drawer, took a ring from it and set about an examination of the two little objects. When he turned to his visitor again, he was evidently satisfied with what he had discovered. "These two objects are made of exactly the same sort of gold, of a peculiar old French composition, which can no longer be produced in the same richness. The weight of the gold in the bullet is exactly the same as in the ring."

"Would you be willing to take an oath on that if you were called in as an expert?"

"I am willing to stand up for my judgment."

"Good. And now will you read this over please, it contains the substance of what you told me yesterday. Should I have made any mistakes, please correct them, for I will ask you to set your signature to it."

Muller handed several sheets of close writing to the goldsmith and the latter read aloud as follows:

"On the 22nd of November, a gentleman came into my shop and handed me a wedding ring with the request that I should make another one exactly like it. He was particularly anxious that the work should be done in two days at the very latest, and also that the new ring, in form, colour, and in the engraving on the inside, should be a perfect counterpart of the first. He explained his order by saying that his wife was ill, and that she was grieving over the loss of her wedding ring which had somehow disappeared. The new ring could be found somewhere as if by chance and the sick woman's anxiety would be over. Two days later, as arranged, the same gentleman appeared again and I handed him the two rings.

"He left the shop, greatly satisfied with my work and apparently much relieved in his mind. But he left me uneasy in spirit because I had deceived him. It had not been possible for me to reproduce exactly the composition of the original ring, and as I believed that the work was to be done in order to comfort an invalid, and I was getting no profit, but on the contrary a little extra work out of it, I made two new rings, lettered them according to the original and gave them to my customer. The original ring I am now, on this seventh day of December, giving to Mr. Joseph Muller, who has shown me his legitimation as a member of the Secret Police. I am willing to put myself at the service of the authorities if I am called for."

"You are willing to do this, aren't you?" asked Muller when the goldsmith had arrived at the end of the notice.

"Of course."

"Have you anything to add to this?"

"No, it is quite complete. I will sign it at once."

Several hours later, Muller re-entered the police station in his hometown and saw the windows of the chief's apartment brilliantly lighted. "What's going on," he asked of Bauer's servant who was just hurrying up the stairs.

"The mistress' birthday, we've got company."

Muller grumbled something and went on up to his own room. He knew it would not be pleasant for his patron to be disturbed in the midst of entertaining his guests, but the matter was important and could not wait.

The detective laid off his outer garments, made a few changes in his toilet and putting the goldsmith's declaration, with the ring and the bullet in his pocketbook, he went down to the first floor of the building, in one wing of which was the apartment occupied by the Chief. He sent in his name and was told to wait in the little study. He sat down quietly in a corner of the comfortable little room beyond which, in a handsomely furnished smoking room, a number of guests sat playing cards. From the drawing rooms beyond, there was the sound of music and many voices.

It was all very attractive and comfortable, and the solitary man sat there enjoying once more the pleasant sensation of triumph, of joy at the victory that was his alone and that would win him back all his old friends and prestige. He was looking forward in agreeable anticipation to the explanations he had to give, when he suddenly started and grew pale. His eyes dimmed a moment, then he pulled himself together and murmured: "No, no, not this time. I will not be weak this time."

Just then the Chief entered the room, accompanied by Councillor Kniepp.

"Won't you sit down here a little?" asked the friendly host. "You will find it much quieter in this room." He pulled up a little table laden with cigars and wine, close to a comfortable armchair. Then, noticing Muller, he continued with a friendly nod: "I'm glad they told you to wait in here. You must be frozen after your long ride. If you will wait just a moment more, I will return at once and we can go into my office. And if you will make yourself comfortable here, my dear Kniepp, I will send our friend Horn in to talk with you. He is bright and jovial and will keep you amused."

The chief chattered on, making a strenuous endeavour to appear quite harmless. But Kniepp, more apt than ever just now to notice the actions of others, saw plainly that his genial host was concealing some excitement. When the latter had gone out the Councillor looked after him, shaking his head. Then his glance fell by chance on the quiet-looking man who had risen at his entrance and had not sat down again.

"Please sit down," he said in a friendly tone, but the other did not move. His grey eyes gazed intently at the man whose fate he was to change so horribly.

Kniepp grew uneasy under the stare. "What is there that interests you so about me?" he asked in a tone that was an attempt at a joke.

"The ring, the ring on your watch chain," murmured Muller.

"It belonged to my dead wife. I have worn it since she left me," answered the unhappy man with the same iron calm with which he had, all these past days, been emphasizing his love for the woman he had lost. Yet the question touched him unpleasantly and he looked more sharply at the strange man over in the corner. He saw the latter's face turn pale and a shiver run through his form. A feeling of sympathy came over Kniepp and he asked warmly: "Won't you take a glass of this wine? If you have been out in the cold it will be good for you." His tone was gentle, almost cordial, but the man to whom he offered the refreshment turned from him with a gesture that was almost one of terror.

The Councillor rose suddenly from his chair. "Who are you? What news is it you bring?" he asked with a voice that began to tremble.

Muller raised his head sharply as if his decision had been made, and his kind intelligent eyes grew soft as they rested on the pale face of the stately man before him. "I belong to the Secret Police and I am compelled to find out the secrets of others – not because of my profession – no, because my own nature compels me – I must do it. I have just come from Vienna and I bring the last of the proofs necessary to turn you over to the courts. And yet you are a thousand times better than the coward who stole the honour of your wife and who hid behind the shelter of the law – and therefore, therefore, therefore—" Muller's voice grew hoarse, then died away altogether.

Kniepp listened with pallid cheeks but without a quiver. Now he spoke, completing the other's words: "And therefore you wish to save me from the prison or from the gallows? I thank you. What is your name?" The unhappy man spoke as calmly as if the matter scarcely concerned him at all.

The detective told him his name.

"Muller, Muller," repeated the Councillor, as if he were particularly anxious to remember the name. He held out his hand to the detective. "I thank you, indeed, thank you," he said with the first sign of emotion he had shown, and then added low: "Do not fear that you will have trouble on my account. They can find me in my home." With these words he turned away and sat down in his chair again. When Bauer entered the room a few moments later, Kniepp was smoking calmly.

"Now, Muller, I'm ready. Horn will be in in a moment, friend Kniepp; I know you will enjoy his chatter." The chief led the way out of the room through another door. He could not see the ghastly pale face of the guest he left behind him, for it was almost hidden in a cloud of thick smoke, but Muller turned back once more at the threshold and caught a last grateful glance from eyes shadowed by deep sadness, as the Councillor raised his hand in a friendly gesture.

"Dear Muller, you take so long to get at the point of the story! Don't you see you are torturing me?" This outburst came from the Chief about an hour later. But the detective would not permit himself to be interrupted in spinning out his story in his own way, and it was nearly another hour before Bauer knew that the man for whose name he had been waiting so long was Leo Kniepp.

The knowledge came as a terrible surprise to him. He was dazed almost. "And I – I've got to arrest him in my own house?" he exclaimed as if horrified. And Muller answered calmly: "I doubt if you will have the opportunity, sir."

"Muller! Did you, again—"

"Yes, I did! I have again warned an unfortunate. It's my nature, I can't seem to help it. But you will find the Councillor in his house. He promised me that."

"And you believe it?"

"That man will keep his promise," said Muller quietly.

Councillor Kniepp did keep his promise. When the police arrived at the hunting castle shortly after midnight, they found the terrified servants standing by the body of their master.

"Well, Muller, you had better luck than you deserved this time," Bauer said a few days later. "This last trick has made you quite impossible for the service. But you needn't worry about that, because the legacy Kniepp left you will put you out of reach of want."

The detective was as much surprised as anybody. He was as if dazed by his unexpected good fortune. The day before he was a poor man bowed under the weight of sordid cares, and now he was the possessor of twenty thousand gulden. And it was not his clever brain but his warm heart that had won this fortune for him. His breast swelled with gratitude as he thought of the unhappy man whose life had been ruined by the careless cruelty of others and his own passions. Again and again he read the letter which had been found on Kniepp's desk, addressed to him and which had been handed out to him after the inquest.

> My friend: –
> You have saved me from the shame of an open trial. I thank you for this from the very depth of my heart. I have left you a part of my own private fortune, that you may be a free man, free as a poor man never can be. You can accept this present for it comes from the hand of an honest man in spite of all. Yes, I compelled my wife to go to her death after I had compelled her to confess her shame to me, and I entered her lover's house with the knowledge I had forced from her. When I looked through the keyhole and saw his false face before me, I murdered him in cold blood. Then, that the truth might not be suspected, I continued to play the sorrowing husband. I wore on my watch chain the ring I had had made in imitation of the one my wife had worn. This original ring of hers, her wedding ring which she had defiled, I sent in the form of a bullet straight to her lover's heart. Yes, I have committed a crime, but I feel that I am less criminal than those two whom I judged and condemned, and whose sentence I carried out as I now shall carry out my own sentence with a hand

which will not tremble. That I can do this myself, I have you to thank for, you who can look into the souls of men and recognise the most hidden motives, you who have not only a wonderful brain but a heart that can feel. You, I hope, will sometimes think kindly of your grateful
LEO KNIEPP.

Muller kept this letter as one of his most sacred treasures.

The 'Kniepp Case' was really, as Bauer had predicted, the last in Muller's public career. Even the friendliness of the kind old chief could not keep him in his position after this new display of the unreliability of his heart. But his quiet tastes allowed him to live in humble comfort from the income of his little fortune.

Every now and then letters or telegrams will come for him and he will disappear for several days. His few friends believe that the police authorities, who refused to employ him publicly owing to his strange weakness, cannot resist a private appeal to his talent whenever a particularly difficult case arises.

A Case of Purloined Lager

Tina L. Jens

PAT THE CAT uncurled herself from a ball, stretched, and yawned. Her sleek gray fur didn't shine the way it once did, and perhaps she spent more time napping now than she had as a kitten. Truth be told, she wanted nothing more than to turn around and catch another forty winks atop the warm cable box behind the bar counter...but the Old Man and the dogs had just entered the pub, and the mutts, as usual, were being rowdy.

Normally, the Red Lion Pub was a quiet, respectable establishment, where you could dine, drink and engage in a bit of conversation with your neighbor, or perhaps watch *Patton* on the TV at the end of the bar. Only small quantities of rowdiness were tolerated. (Once the doors were closed and the Late-Nite Regulars had settled in under the 'private party' ordinance, larger quantities of rowdiness were tolerated.) For now, though, decorum should be maintained.

But how much decorum could you have with two yapping pooches in the place?

The Old Man was the senior proprietor of the pub. He was a good sort, with a fondness for all four-legged creatures. That was no reason to allow dogs in the pub, as far as Pat was concerned, but he did insist, and old men had to be indulged. As did their dogs. He usually brought a can of tuna and spent a good half hour petting Pat, too. But that wasn't enough of a bribe to convince Pat to tolerate two fluffy, yipping dogs with good grace.

The Old Man let go of the dogs' leashes and shuffled to the bar, easing himself onto a stool as the mutts yipped and jumped around his feet. He had named the pair of Shih Tzus Bonnie and Clyde – 'cause Chicago was a gangster town – though the bank-robbing duo never made it to Chicago. Pat wished the pooches hadn't either.

The Old Man motioned to Bill the waiter, who gently picked the dogs up and sat them each onto their own barstool. But Pat knew they wouldn't stay there. The next moment the dogs had climbed onto the bar and were running the length of it, like it was the straightaway at a racetrack and they were greyhounds. In their dreams!

The Joe-human called them 'furry bedroom slippers', though Pat wasn't certain he meant it as an insult. She'd certainly take it that way! But dogs were funny, no sense of pride; they'd do anything for a little praise from any human who happened to be passing by.

These mutts proved it. A crowd had gathered around the bar, like it always did when the mongrels came in. All it took was a *Yip!* and one little backflip and the people left their dinners to get cold and their drinks to get warm, just so they could watch the show.

They'd been a pair of circus dogs. The Old Man had rescued the pooches from the pound when the traveling show had shut down. They'd been part of a clown review; dressed in little pink tutus, they'd wear big red balls on their noses, do backflips and frontflips, and play dead when they were shot with a toy gun.

What a disgusting, demeaning life, Pat thought. But the pooches reveled in the memory of their glory days, and never missed an opportunity to show off their old tricks.

On his third flip, Clyde made a bad landing and tipped over the shallow tin that held Pat's cat food. That pushed things too far.

Pat arched her back to crack the stiffness out of her spine, huffed, then jumped down from the cable box to the floor below. Regally she marched out to mingle with the customers.

"Go get 'em, Pattie!" Joe, the bartender, her most doting human, chuckled.

She rubbed herself against his leg and purred loudly, to let him know that while she was annoyed at the dogs, she didn't hold it against her human.

She wove through the maze of tables, chair legs, and reaching hands. The hands tried to lure her into familiar laps for a cuddle. These were the more discriminating patrons, not fooled by a couple of scheming show-dogs. But she wasn't in the mood for company just now. The dogs could play, but she had work to do.

Somebody was stealing from the bar, pilfering small quantities of ale from the storage room every Friday night. Pat kept track of the way the stock was stacked when she did her nightly patrols for mice. Just one six-pack went missing each week. Only a cat as devoted as her would ever notice.

Pat was investigating the burglaries, but so far, she hadn't been able to catch the criminal. Usually, her duties didn't allow her to stake out the storeroom for the entire night. She had to make the rounds, greet the patrons, and keep the waiters on their toes. Not to mention, the storeroom wasn't heated, and her old bones didn't tolerate the cold so well anymore – not that she'd let the humans notice that! But tonight, she would do whatever it took to catch the criminal.

She didn't think the Joe-human had noticed the thefts yet – though he surely would when he did inventory next week. She was determined to solve the problem before then. There was no sense in him worrying about such things. He had enough to do with bartending and paperwork. After all, she was responsible.

Rumor among the humans said the bar was in Pat's name. The rumor was true. That's politics and real estate, Chicago-style. But Pat the Cat took her management responsibilities seriously.

The hallway that led to the storage area was closed to patrons, but the waiters and many of the Regulars used it as a short-cut or when they were lending a helping hand. Pat didn't like suspecting the Regulars or the staff, but a good detective considered all suspects. To complicate matters, many of the waiters were college students; with the new semester came the inevitable turnover in staff. Pat didn't have all the new people-smells straight in her nose yet.

Speaking of noses, it was time to do some sniffing around. The place to start was the storage room. She padded down the hall and peeked into the room. The oversized closet was packed nearly to the ceiling with cases of lagers and ales and wine, with the occasional crate of whiskey to sweeten the smell. It was a heady aroma – soured only by the stench of a dirty throw-rug, covered with the fur of the evil pair of carny-dogs.

The smelly pair liked to cool off in the storage room after their daily walk to the pub. They'd lie there panting, out of breath from the short walk, because they were over-fed and under-exercised, purely by their own choice. Half the time they made the Old Man carry them, as if their eight legs didn't work far better than his two!

Though Pat poked her little pink nose into every nook and cranny of the storage room, there were too many conflicting scents; she couldn't detect the criminal's identity there.

She wandered further down the hallway, letting her mind meander over the problem.

Out of the corner of her eye, she saw a shadow flicker at the top of the basement steps. She pounced toward it, certain it was an uppity rat encroaching on restricted territory. She bounded down the stairs after the shadow, only to discover at the bottom she'd been chasing the shadow of a suspended light bulb, gently blowing in the breeze of an open window.

She'd turned to climb back up the steps when she spied a glint of light. Investigating, she found a large shard of glass in the shadows under the stairs.

Now, broken glass in a bar is hardly a novelty, but the basement was used to store old furniture, floor-sanders, and large, discarded equipment. No food or beverages were kept down here, and no one came here to drink...or did they?

She sniffed the floor around the glass and detected the faint trace of a cheap lager. With four cozy rooms above for a patron's imbibing pleasure, no one would come to the dank basement to drink, unless they were doing it on the sly. And no one would drink on the sly in a bar unless they were stealing the spirits. She'd found the crime scene! Now if she could just catch the criminal in the act.

When she was certain she'd sniffed out all the clues she could find in the basement, Pat climbed the stairs and strolled through the dining area stopping to collect pats on the head and admiring comments from the customers. She might be on the case, but she had to act natural. If she didn't follow her nightly routine, the burglar might realize she was onto them.

She made it to the end of the bar, collected herself, then leaped into an empty bar stool. She curled her tail around her legs and sat primly in the chair waiting for Joe to join her before she meowed her drink order to him.

"Done the rounds then, Pattie?" Joe asked, wiping a glass ashtray clean with his bar towel. He opened three plastic containers of cream and dumped them into the ashtray then placed it before her on the bar. She raised herself up until she could rest her front paws on the counter and daintily lapped the drink up, careful not to spill a drop. When she had finished, she sat back down and set about the task of licking her whiskers clean.

* * *

Pat had kept her eye on the back hall and patrolled every half-hour. But she'd indulged in her regular bit of Monday night fun. There were several literary and theater groups that met upstairs on weeknights to put on shows; comedy improv, women's theater alliance, some group called TallGrass – whose members never wrote about grass, which confused Pat mightily – but her favorite was the Monday night Twilight Tales group; they did horror, fantasy, science fiction, mystery – they'd even devoted an entire night to cats stories and made Pat the guest of honor. But most often, they turned the lights down low and read ghost stories aloud. Which meant, if Pat sneaked up the backstairs and waited for an appropriately dramatic moment, she could dash through the shadowy room and scare them. She did it weekly, and still, it never failed to get a gasp and sometimes even a shriek out of one of the newer members of the crowd. The horror writers were easy to scare. The comedians just made jokes, and the Grass people would declare how cute she was and start reading poems about their own cats. Pat wasn't much of a poetry fan.

Pat came down the stairs grinning. It'd been a horror night, and she'd scared one guy so badly he nearly fell out of his chair.

After that bit of fun, she got back to her detecting, patrolling diligently and sniffing suspicious patrons. She'd even foregone her pre-midnight nap on the warm cable box, settling instead for a fitful doze on the top of a stack of beer boxes in the cold storage room, hoping the thief might come in.

While it was warmer up near the ceiling, she still woke with stiff joints and a creaky spine. But it was a good vantage point for surveillance.

She took the long route down, opting for short hops from box to box to favor her stiff legs, rather than one quick leap to the ground. She needed a slow stroll through the bar to warm her joints up.

Ducking through a waitress's legs, she slipped behind the bar and rubbed against Joe's ankle. He popped a beer-tap off, delivered a not-quite-full pint to the customer before him and bent down to pick her up. The ankle rub was their secret code when she needed a lift. He cuddled her in the crook of his arm and scratched her ears.

"That old arthritis bothering you tonight, Pattie? Best take a nap on the cable box. Works better than a heating pad."

She purred a warning not to talk so loud. She was self-conscious about her age and ailments and didn't want the customers to know.

"How 'bout a bit of supper first, eh?" Joe said.

He set her down on the cooler and she pranced along its edge, following him to the cookie tin where her morsels were kept. He uncapped the tin then chucked her under the chin. "Be right back with an extra treat," he promised. At the other end of the bar he lifted the British flag that hid the serving window to the kitchen. "Jorge, open a can of tuna for me, Pattie's feeling a bit peckish."

Pat hated to eat and run, still, after a quick supper she returned to her stakeout, high atop the beer cases in the storage room.

* * *

Pat lifted one eyelid sleepily. It was well past two a.m. The casual patrons had all been bid 'cheerio', and the Late-Nite Regulars were tipping mugs and telling tales in the front room. The kitchen had closed hours ago; the waiters had all counted out and gone home or joined the Regulars on the other side of the bar. And yet, Pat had heard a noise in the hallway. No reason for anyone to be back here now, unless they had a nefarious purpose. Pat crept to the edge of the box and peeked over.

With a jingle and a flounce, the two white Shih Tzus waltzed into the storeroom, the bells on their collars ringing with each prance of their paws. Pat hissed quietly. She had no respect for a couple of mutts that wore jingle-bells around their necks. But the mutts weren't alone. They yapped excitedly at a human walking behind them. He didn't have the unsteady tread of their Old Man – he would be drinking at one end of the bar, holding court at the ritual gathering.

It was another young pup, of the two-legged variety – Jorge, from the kitchen. Pat's heart sank. She liked Jorge. They'd quickly reached an understanding: she didn't step foot in the kitchen, and he saved her tasty morsels from the food he prepared. After sampling some of his dishes, she'd had high hopes he'd soon graduate to position of Top Cook.

Dejected, Pat crossed her paws in front of her and rested her chin on them, prepared to witness the beer-pilfering.

Jorge picked out a six-pack of cheap ale, but instead of carrying it away himself, he set it on the dirty throw-rug, stepped back and said, "*Andale*, little doggies, if you're thirsty."

The dogs yipped. One even leapt into the air to do a backward somersault. Then the little scamps grabbed the knotted fringes of the rug and dragged it into the hall, growling all the way. Jorge followed along slowly behind them, uttering soft sounds of laughter and encouragement. Pat sneaked down and peeked her head around the doorway. She slipped across the hall into the shadows on the far wall, following the procession. The parade stopped at the foot of the basement stairs.

"Now whatcha gonna do?" Jorge asked, as Clyde nosed through the slats of the railing and yipped.

The stairs turned a corner at the top, and the opening in the railing was just big enough for a dog to fit through. Pat wanted to pounce and send the mutt plummeting to his death on the cold floor below, but she was outnumbered. She waited.

While her partner was yipping at the empty basement below, Bonnie lowered her head and butted up against the beer carton. After much head-shaking, the dog repeated the action and the six-pack tipped over, much to Pat's amazement. A quick yip brought Clyde running. Grabbing a bottle top in his teeth, he wrestled the bottle out of the carton and rolled it to the railing with the tip of his nose. With a final nudge, the bottle went through and shattered on the floor below.

Pat jumped. Surely a noise like that would bring Joe running. Then she realized the revelries of the Late-Nite Regulars would cover up the sound of the bottle breaking.

The dogs yipped, Jorge laughed, and the mutts went bounding down the stairs to lap happily at the spilled beer. Pat crept closer to watch the debauchery.

When the beer was all gone, either in the tummies of the dogs or run off in tiny rivulets to the dark corners of the basement, the dogs pranced up the stairs and eagerly began the procedure again.

"Silly dogs, why don't you tip them all over at once, and save yourself the exercise?" Jorge asked.

Pat watched the next bottle go over the edge and the dogs go careening down the steps after it. Obviously, this was a routine they'd practiced for many weeks.

By the fourth bottle, the mutts were as yippy and eager as ever, but they were stumbling on the stairs. After the fifth, they made it only halfway up before passing out to sleep off their drunken bender.

Boldly, Pat strode up to Jorge where he sat on the top landing watching the dogs sleep. He was an accessory to the crime, but the odds were better now, and Pat didn't think Jorge was capable of cat-assault.

"Hello, Pattie," Jorge said. He reached toward her, but instead of petting her head, he snagged the last bottle out of the six-pack and twisted the cap off. "Come to share the beer?" He held the open bottle out for her to sniff, then poured some on the floor and waited to see if she'd drink it.

Pat turned her nose up.

"No taste for hops, eh? Leaves more for me." He upended the bottle in a long swig.

Pat meowed sadly. Now he wasn't just an accessory, he was an accomplice.

A second draw emptied the bottle, and Jorge sighed contentedly. "Time to clean up after the little ones," he said. He stood and headed for the broom closet.

Pat realized she had only minutes to get help before the evidence was swept away and the thieving dogs succeeded again.

She raced toward the bar.

She slid on the linoleum, fighting for her balance. She meowed frantically at Joe, but he couldn't hear her over the TV. The volume had been turned up with the start of a Three Stooges feature. She rubbed against Joe's leg but danced out of reach as he bent to pick her up.

"Silly Pattie, can't decide what you want?" Joe said, returning to his perch on the beer cooler.

Jorge must be nearly done disposing of the evidence! In desperation she extended her claws and swiped at his leg, careful not to gouge too deep.

"Ouch! Pattie!" Joe yelled.

"What's the matter?" the Old Man called from his chair.

"Pattie just scratched me!"

A nearby conversation stopped – everyone knew Pat could be temperamental, but never with Joe.

"Cats are grand, but moody. That's why the dog is man's best friend," the Old Man said knowingly.

Pattie yowled pitifully, then limped away in her most dramatic manner. Scratch or no, she knew Joe wouldn't turn his back on her in the face of injury.

"She's hurt! C'mere Pattie, let me see, " he crooned, following her around the bar.

She hated deceiving her human so, but she knew no other way to lure him to the crime scene. She darted under a table to stay out of reach, then made a show of limping away on the other side. Joe followed, calling to her in soft tones that nearly broke her heart.

Once into the hallway, she gave up the act and dashed toward the stairs, mewling over her shoulder for Joe to follow. When he heard the clinking of broken glass, he needed no further encouragement.

Pat sat triumphant at the top of the stairs as Joe stood and stared. Below, the villains were caught in the act; the drunken dogs still passed out and snoring on the stairs, Jorge sweeping up the broken glass.

"What's going on here?" Joe demanded.

"Senor Joe," Jorge stammered. "The dogs...they tipped over a pack of beer. I was just sweeping up so they do not cut themself."

"Oh, Okay."

Joe started to turn away, but Pat meowed impatiently. Surely he wasn't going to fall for so obvious a lie.

Joe turned back and asked, "What's wrong with the dogs?"

Pat hissed at him. He was asking the wrong questions. It was obvious the dogs were drunk.

"Oh, they beat me to the mess and drank too much, I think. They got a little sleepy."

"You don't think they got hold of any glass, do you?"

Pat fumed. The mutts weren't worth the worry. Joe turned away again.

There was one last chance; Pat spied the sixth beer bottle, now empty, sitting near the railing. With a single swipe, she sent it toppling over the edge, to shatter at Jorge's feet below.

Joe jumped, the dogs yelped in their sleep, and a look of deep guilt spread across Jorge's face.

The pieces fell into place. Joe lowered his voice, and it took on a menacing tone, "Finish sweeping up, then get out. You can pick up your final paycheck on Friday." He turned and strode back to the bar, Pat matching him step for step.

* * *

The Late-Nite Regulars had been shooed out, and the Old Man had collected his drunken dogs, tucked one under each arm, and gone home. It was just Joe and Pat enjoying a final drink in the glow of a neon beer-sign. Pat enjoyed a triple cream-cocktail out of a spotless glass ashtray. Joe sipped a cup of decaf.

"Imagine that, Pattie. Contributing to the delinquency of those mutts...with a watered-down domestic lager, to boot. His taste in beer matched his taste in pets. I'll take coffee and a cat any day, how 'bout you?"

She climbed on the bar and bumped her head under his hand, stating her name and making a request...Pat, the cat.

The Woman with a Blemish

William Le Queux

THE WEIRD PROLOGUE of the drama was enacted some years ago, yet time, alas! does not obliterate it from my memory.

To the hail of bullets, the whistling of shells, the fitful flash of powder, and the thunder of guns I had grown callous. During the months I had been in Servia and Bulgaria watching and describing the terrible struggle between Turkey and Russia, I had grown world-weary, careless of everything, even of life. I had been present at the relief of Kars, had witnessed the wholesale slaughter in various parts of the Ottoman Empire, and was now attached to the Russian forces bombarding Plevna.

Those who have never experienced actual warfare cannot imagine how terrible are the horrors of life at the front.

Picture for a moment a great multitude of men whose sole occupation is slaughter – some with smoke-blackened faces toiling in the earthworks, discharging their heavy field-pieces which day and night dispatch their death-dealing missiles into the shattered town yonder, while hordes of Cossacks and Russian grenadiers engage the enemy at every point; the rattle of musketry and artillery is deafening, the rain of bullets incessant, and on every side is suffering and death. And you are a war-correspondent, a spectator, a non-combatant! You have travelled across Europe to witness this frightful carnage, and paint word-pictures of it for the folk at home. At any moment a stray bullet might end your existence; nevertheless, you must not be fatigued, for after the toil of the day your work commences, and you must find a quiet corner where you can write a column of description for transmission to Fleet Street.

Such were the circumstances in which I was placed when, after a six months' absence from England, I found myself before Plevna. The brief December day was drawing to a close as I stood, revolver in hand, near one of the great guns that at regular intervals thundered forth in chorus with the others. I was in conversation with Captain Alexandrovitch, a smart young officer with whom I was on very friendly terms, and we were watching through our field-glasses the effect of our fire upon the town.

"Now my lads," the captain shouted in Russian, to the men working the gun. "Let us test our accuracy. See! One of Osman's officers has just appeared on the small redoubt yonder to encourage his men. There is a good target. See!"

Scarcely had he spoken when the men sprang back, the great gun belched forth flame, and the shell, striking the enemy's fortification, took part of it away, blowing the unfortunate Turkish officer into fragments.

Such are the fortunes of war!

"Good!" exclaimed Alexandrovitch, laughing; as, turning to me, he added, "If we continue like this, we shall silence the redoubts before tomorrow. How suicidal of Osman Pasha to imagine his handful of lean, hungry dogs capable of defence against the army of the Great White Tzar. Bah! We shall—"

The sentence was left unfinished, for a bullet whistled close to me, and a second later he threw up his hands, and, uttering a loud cry of pain, staggered and fell, severely wounded in the side.

Our ambulance and medical staff was on that day very disorganised, so, instead of conveying him to the field hospital, they carried him into my tent, close by.

Night fell, and for hours I knelt beside him, trying to alleviate his agony. The surgeon had dressed the wound, and the officer lay writhing and groaning, while by the meagre light of an evil-smelling oil-lamp I scribbled my dispatch. At last the wounded man became quieter, and presently slept; while I, jaded and worn, wrapped my blanket about me, placed my revolver under my saddle, and lay down to snatch an hour's repose.

How long I slept I scarcely know; but I was awakened by a strange rustling.

The flap of the tent was open, and I saw against the faint grey glimmering of the wintry morning's struggling dawn a figure stealthily bending over the wounded man who lay asleep at my side.

The intruder wore the heavy greatcoat and round cap of a Cossack officer, and was evidently searching my comrade's pockets.

"Who are you? What do you want?" I cried in Russian, clutching my revolver.

The man started, withdrew his hand, and stood upright, looking down upon me. For a moment I fixed my eyes upon the statuesque figure, and gazed at him amazed. I am not by any means a nervous man, but there was something weird about the fellow's appearance.

Whether it was due to the suddenness with which I had discovered him, or whether some peculiar phenomenon was caused by his presence, I was unable to determine.

I remember asking myself if I were really awake, and becoming convinced that I was in possession of all my faculties.

"Speak!" I said sternly. "Speak – or I'll fire!"

Raising the weapon, I waited for a moment.

The figure remained motionless, facing the muzzle of the pistol unflinchingly.

Again I repeated my challenge. There was, however, no reply.

I pulled the trigger.

In the momentary flash that followed I caught a glimpse of the face of the intruder. It was that of a woman!

She was young and beautiful. Her parted lips revealed an even row of tightly-clenched teeth, her dark eyes had a look of unutterable horror in them, and her cheeks were deathly pale.

It was the most lovely face I had ever gazed upon.

Its beauty was perfect, yet there was something about the forehead that struck me as peculiar.

The thick dark hair was brushed back severely, and high up, almost in the centre of the white brow, was a curious mark, which, in the rapid flash of light, appeared to be a small but *perfectly-defined bluish-grey ring*!

As I fired, the arm of the mysterious visitor was raised as if to ward off a blow, and in the hand I saw the gleam of steel.

The slender fingers were grasping a murderous weapon – a long, keen surgeon's knife, the blade of which was besmeared with blood.

Was I dreaming? I again asked myself. No, it was not a visionary illusion, for I saw it plainly with my eyes wide-open.

So great a fascination did this strange visitant possess over me, that I had been suddenly overcome by a terrible dread that had deprived me of the power of speech. My tongue clave to the roof of my mouth.

I felt more than ever convinced that there must be something supernatural about the silent masquerader.

In the dim light the puff of grey smoke from the revolver slowly curled before my eyes, hiding for a few seconds the singularly-beautiful countenance.

When, however, a moment later, the veil had cleared, I was amazed to discover that the figure had vanished.

My hand had been unsteady.

Grasping my revolver firmly, I sprang to my feet and rushed out of the tent. While gazing quickly around, a Cossack sentry, whose attention had been attracted by the shot, ran towards me.

"Has a woman passed you?" I asked excitedly, in the best Russian I could muster.

"A woman! No, sir. I was speaking with Ivan, my comrade on duty, when I heard a pistol-shot; but I have seen no one except yourself."

"Didn't you see an officer?"

"No, sir," the man replied, leaning on his Berdan rifle and regarding me with astonishment.

"Are you positive?"

"I could swear before the holy *ikon*," answered the soldier. "You could not have seen a woman, sir. There's not one in the camp, and one could not enter, for we are exercising the greatest vigilance to exclude spies."

"Yes, yes, I understand," I said, endeavouring to laugh. "I suppose, after all, I've been dreaming"; and then, wishing the man good morning, I returned to the tent.

It was, I tried to persuade myself, merely a chimera of a disordered imagination and a nervous system that had been highly strained by constant fatigue and excitement. I had of late, I remembered, experienced curious delusions, and often in the midst of most exciting scenes I could see vividly how peaceful and happy was my home in London, and how anxiously yet patiently my friends and relatives were awaiting my return from the dreaded seat of war.

On entering the tent, I was about to fling myself down to resume my rest, when it occurred to me that my wounded comrade might require something. Apparently he was asleep, and it seemed a pity to rouse him to administer the cooling draught the surgeon had left.

Bending down, I looked into his face, but could not see it distinctly, for the light was still faint and uncertain. His breathing was very slight, I thought; indeed, as I listened, I could not detect any sound of respiration. I placed my hand upon his breast, but withdrew it quickly.

My fingers were covered with blood.

Striking a match and holding it close to his recumbent figure, my eyes fell upon a sight which caused me to start back in horror. The face was bloodless, the jaw had dropped; he was dead!

There was a great ugly knife wound. Captain Alexandrovitch had been stabbed to the heart!

At that moment the loud rumble of cannon broke the stillness, and a second later there was a vivid flash of light, followed by a terrific explosion. The redoubts of Plevna had opened fire upon us again, and a shell had burst in unpleasant proximity to my tent. The sullen roar of the big guns, and the sharp rattle from the rifle-pits, quickly placed us on the defence.

Bugles sounded everywhere, words of command were shouted, there was bustle and confusion for a few minutes, then everyone sprang to his post, and our guns recommenced pouring their deadly fire into the picturesque little town, with its two white minarets, its domed church, and its flat-roofed houses, nestling in the wooded hollow.

With a final glance at my murdered comrade, I hastily buckled on my traps, reloaded my revolver, and, taking a photograph from my pocket, kissed it. Need I say that it was a woman's? A moment later, I was outside amid the deafening roar of the death-dealing guns. Our situation was more critical than we had imagined, for Osman, believing that he had discovered a weak point in the girdle of Muscovite steel, was advancing, notwithstanding our fire. A terrible conflict ensued; but our victory is now historical.

We fought the Turks hand to hand, bayonet to bayonet, with terrible desperation, knowing well that the battle must be decisive. The carnage was fearful, yet to me there was one thing still more horrible, for throughout that well-remembered day the recollection of the mysterious murder of my friend was ever present in my mind. Amid the cannon smoke I saw distinctly the features of the strange visitant. They were, however, not so beautiful as I had imagined. The countenance was hideous. Indeed, never in my life have I seen such a sinister female face, or flashing eyes starting from their sockets in so horrible a manner.

But the most vivid characteristic of all was the curious circular mark on the forehead, that seemed to stand out black as jet.

* * *

Three months afterwards, on a rainy, cheerless March afternoon, I arrived at Charing Cross, and with considerable satisfaction set foot once again upon the muddy pavement of the Strand. It is indeed pleasant to be surrounded by English faces, and hear English voices, after a long period of enforced exile, wearying work, and constant uncertainty as to whether one will live to return to old associations and acquaintances. Leaving my luggage at the station, I walked down to the office in Fleet Street to report myself, and having received the welcome of such of the staff as were about the premises at that hour, afterwards took a cab to my rather dreary bachelor rooms in Russell Square.

My life in London during the next few months was uneventful, save for two exceptions. The first was when the Russian Ambassador conferred upon me, in the name of his Imperial master the Tzar, a little piece of orange and purple ribbon, in recognition of a trifling accident whereby I was enabled to save the lives of several of his brave Sibirsky soldiers. The second and more important was that I renounced the Bohemian ease of bachelorhood, and married Mabel Travers, the girl to whom for five years I had been engaged, and whose portrait I had carried in my pocket through so many scenes of desolation and hours of peril.

We took up our residence in a pretty bijou flat in Kensington Court, and our married life was one of unalloyed happiness. I found my wife amiable and good as she was young and handsome, and although she moved in a rather smart set, there was nothing of the butterfly of fashion about her. Her father was a wealthy Manchester cotton-spinner, who had a town house at Gloucester Gate, and her dowry, being very considerable, enabled us to enter society.

On a winter's afternoon, six months after our marriage, I arrived home about four o'clock, having been at the office the greater part of the day, writing an important article for the next morning's issue. Mabel was not at home, therefore, after a while, I entered the dining room to await her. The hours dragged on, and though the marble clock on the mantelshelf chimed six, seven, and even eight o'clock, still she did not return. Although puzzled at her protracted absence, I was also hungry, so, ringing for dinner to be served, I sat down to a lonely meal.

Soon afterwards Mabel returned. She dashed into the room, gazed at me with a strange, half-frightened glance, then, rushing across, kissed me passionately, flinging her arms about my neck, and pleading to be forgiven for being absent so long, explaining that a lady, to whose 'At Home' she had been, was very unwell, and she had remained a couple of hours longer with her. Of course I concealed my annoyance, and we spent the remainder of the evening very happily; for, seated before the blazing fire in full enjoyment of a good cigar and liqueur, I related how

I had spent the day, while she gave me a full description of what she had been doing, and the people she had met.

Shortly before eleven o'clock the maid entered with a telegram addressed to Mabel. A message at that hour was so extraordinary, that I took it and eagerly broke open the envelope.

It was an urgent request that my wife should proceed at once to the house of her brother George at Chiswick, as something unusual had happened. We had a brief consultation over the extraordinary message, and as it was late, and raining heavily, I decided to go in her stead.

An hour's drive in a cab brought me to a large red-brick, ivy-covered house, standing back from the road, and facing the Thames near Chiswick Mall. It was one of those residences built in the Georgian era, at a time when the *fêtes champêtres* at Devonshire House were attended by the King, and when Chiswick was a fashionable country retreat. It stood in the centre of spacious grounds, with pretty serpentine walks, where long ago dainty dames in wigs and patches strolled arm-in-arm with splendid silk-coated beaux. The house was one of those time-mellowed relics of an age bygone, that one rarely comes across in London suburbs nowadays.

Mabel's brother had resided here with his wife and their two children for four years, and being an Oriental scholar and enthusiast, he spent a good deal of his time in his study.

It was midnight when the old man-servant opened the door to me.

"Ah, Mr. Harold!" he cried, on recognising me. "I'm glad you've come, sir. It's a terrible night's work that's been done here."

"What do you mean?" I gasped; then, as I noticed old Mr. Travers standing pale and haggard in the hall, I rushed towards him, requesting an explanation.

"It's horrible," he replied. "I – I found poor George dead – *murdered*!"

"Murdered?" I echoed.

"Yes, it is all enshrouded in mystery," he said. "The detectives are now making their examination."

As I followed him into the study, I felt I must collect myself and show some reserve of mental strength and energy, but on entering, I was horror-stricken at the sight.

This room, in which George Travers spent most of his time, was of medium size, with French windows opening upon the lawn, and lined from floor to ceiling with books, while the centre was occupied by a large writing-table, littered with papers.

Beside the table, with blanched face upturned to the green-tinted light of the reading lamp, lay the corpse of my brother-in-law, while from a wound in his neck the blood had oozed, forming a great dark pool upon the carpet.

It was evident that he had fallen in a sitting posture in the chair when the fatal blow had been dealt; then the body had rolled over on to the floor, for in the position it had been discovered it still remained.

The crime was a most remarkable one. George Travers had retired to do some writing shortly before eight o'clock, leaving his father and his wife together in the drawing room, and expressing a wish not to be disturbed.

At ten, old Mr. Travers, who was about to return home, entered the room for the purpose of bidding his son goodnight, when, to his dismay, he found him stabbed to the heart, the body rigid and cold. The window communicating with the garden stood open, the small safe had been ransacked, the drawers in the writing table searched, and there was every evidence that the crime was the deliberate work of an assassin who had been undisturbed.

No sound had been heard by the servants, for the murderer must have struck down the defenceless man at one blow.

Entrance had been gained from the lawn, as the detectives found muddy footprints upon the grass and on the carpet, prints which they carefully sketched and measured, at length arriving at the conclusion that they were those of a woman.

They appeared to be the marks of thin-soled French shoes, with high heels slightly worn over.

Beyond this there was an entire absence of anything that could lead to the identification of the murderer, and though they searched long and diligently over the lawn and shrubbery beyond, their efforts were unrewarded.

It was dawn when I returned home, and having occasion to enter the kitchen, I noticed that on a chair a pair of woman's shoes had been placed.

They were Mabel's. Scarcely knowing why I did so, I took them up and glanced at them. They were very muddy, and, strangely enough, some blades of grass were embedded in the mud. Then terrible thoughts occurred to me.

I recollected Mabel's long absence, and remembered that one does not get grass on one's shoes in Kensington.

The shoes were of French make, stamped with the name of 'Pinet'. They were thin-soled, and the high Louis XV heels were slightly worn on one side.

Breathlessly I took them to the window, and, in the grey light, examined them scrupulously. They coincided exactly with the pair the detectives were searching for, the wearer of which they declared was the person who stabbed George Travers to the heart!

The dried clay and the blades of grass were positive proof that Mabel had walked somewhere besides on London pavements.

Could she really have murdered her brother? A terrible suspicion entered my soul, although I strove to resist it, endeavouring to bring myself to believe that such a thought was absolutely absurd; but at length, fearing detection, I found a brush and removed the mud with my own hands.

Then I walked through the flat and entered the room where Mabel was soundly sleeping. At the foot of the bed something white had fallen. Picking it up, I discovered it was a handkerchief.

A second later it fell from my nerveless grasp. It had dark, stiff patches upon it – the ugly stains of blood!

* * *

The one thought that took possession of me was of Mabel's guilt. Yet she gave me no cause for further suspicion, except, indeed, that she eagerly read all the details as 'written up' in those evening papers that revel in sensation.

George was buried, his house was sold, and his widow went with her children to live at Alversthorpe Hall, old Mr. Travers' place in Cumberland.

Mabel appeared quite as inconsolable as the bereaved wife.

"Do you believe the police will ever find the murderer?" she asked me one evening, when we were sitting alone.

"I really can't tell, dear," I replied, noticing how haggard and serious was her face as she gazed fixedly into the fire.

"Have – have they discovered anything?" she inquired hesitatingly.

"Yes," I answered. "They found the marks of a woman's shoes upon the lawn."

She started visibly and held her breath.

"Ah!" she gasped; "I – I thought they would. I knew it – I knew—"

Then, sighing, she drew her hand quickly across her brow, and, rising, left me abruptly.

* * *

About two months afterwards, Mabel and I went down to Alversthorpe on a visit, and as we sat at dinner on the evening of our arrival, Fraulein Steinbock, the new German governess, entered to speak with her mistress.

For a moment she stood behind the widow's chair, glancing furtively at me. It was very remarkable. Although her features bore not the slightest resemblance to any I had ever seen before, they seemed somehow familiar. It was not the expression of tenderness and purity of soul that entranced me, but there was something strange about the forehead. The dark hair in front had accidentally been parted, disclosing what appeared to be *a portion of a dark ugly scar*!

Chancing to glance at Mabel, I was amazed to notice that she had dropped her knife and fork, and was sitting pale and haggard, with her eyes fixed upon the wall opposite.

Her lips were moving slightly, but no sound came from them.

When, on the following morning, I was chatting with the widow alone, I carelessly inquired about the new governess.

"She was called away suddenly last night. Her brother is dying," she said.

"Called away!" I echoed. "Where has she gone?"

"To London. I do hope she won't be long away, for I really can't do without her. She is so kind and attentive to the children."

"Do you know her brother's address?"

She shook her head. Then I asked for some particulars about her, but discovered that nothing was known of her past. She was an excellent governess – that was all.

* * *

Twelve months later. One evening I had been busy writing in my own little den, and had left Mabel in the drawing room reading a novel. It was almost ten o'clock when I rose from my table, and, having turned out my lamp, I went along the passage to join my wife.

Pushing open the door, I saw she had fallen asleep in her little wicker chair.

But she was not alone.

The tall, statuesque form of a woman in a light dress stood over her. The profile of the mysterious visitor was turned towards me. The face wore the same demoniacal expression, it had the same dark, flashing eyes, the same white teeth, that I had seen on that terrible day before Plevna!

As she bent over my sleeping wife, one hand rested on the chair, while the other grasped a gleaming knife, which she held uplifted, ready to strike.

For a moment I stood rooted to the spot; then, next second, I dashed towards her, just in time to arrest a blow that must otherwise have proved fatal.

She turned on me ferociously, and fought like a wild animal, scratching and biting me viciously. Our struggle for the weapon was desperate, for she seemed possessed of superhuman strength. At last, however, I proved victor, and, wrenching the knife from her bony fingers, flung it across the room.

Meanwhile Mabel awoke, and, springing to her feet, recognised the unwelcome guest.

"See!" she cried, terrified. "Her face! It is the face of the man I met on the night George was murdered!"

So distorted were the woman's features by passion and hatred, that it was very difficult to recognise her as Fraulein Steinbock, the governess.

In a frenzy of madness she flew across to Mabel, but I rushed between them, and by sheer brute force threw her back upon an ottoman, where I held her until assistance arrived. I was compelled to clutch her by the throat, and as I forced her head back, the thick hair fell aside from her brow, disclosing a deep, distinct mark upon the white flesh – a bluish-grey ring in the centre of her forehead.

Screaming hysterically, she shouted terrible imprecations in some language I was unable to understand; and eventually, after a doctor had seen her, I allowed the police to take her to the station, where she was charged as a lunatic.

It was many months before I succeeded in gleaning the remarkable facts relating to her past. It appears that her real name was Dàrya Goltsef, and she was the daughter of a Cossack soldier, born at Darbend, on the Caspian Sea. With her family she led a nomadic life, wandering through Georgia and Armenia, and often accompanying the Cossacks on their incursions and depredations over the frontier into Persia.

It was while on one of these expeditions that she was guilty of a terrible crime. One night, wandering alone in one of the wild mountain passes near Tabreez, she discovered a lonely hut, and, entering, found three children belonging to the Iraks, a wandering tribe of robbers that infest that region.

She was seized with a terrible mania, and in a semi-unconscious state, and without premeditation, she took up a knife and stabbed all three. Some men belonging to the tribe, however, detected her, and at first it was resolved to torture her and end her life; but on account of her youth – for she was then only fifteen – it was decided to place on her forehead an indelible mark, to brand her as a murderess.

It is the custom of the Iraks to brand those guilty of murder; therefore, an iron ring was made red hot, and its impression burned deeply into the flesh.

During the three years that followed, Dàrya was perfectly sane, but it appeared that my friend, Captain Alexandrovitch, while quartered at Deli Musa, in Transcaucasia, killed, in a duel, a man named Peschkoff, who was her lover. The sudden grief at losing the man she loved caused a second calenture of the brain, and, war being declared against Turkey just at that time, she joined the Red Cross Sisters, and went to the front to aid the wounded. I have since remembered that one evening, while before Plevna, I was passing through the camp hospital with Alexandrovitch, when he related to me his little escapade, explaining with happy, careless jest how recklessly he had flirted, and how foolishly jealous Peschkoff had been.

He told me that it was an Englishman who had been travelling for pleasure to Teheran, but whose name he did not remember, that had really been the cause of the quarrel, and laughed heartily, with a Russian's pride of swordsmanship, as he narrated how evenly matched Peschkoff and he had been.

That just cost my friend his life, for Dàrya must have overheard.

Then the desire for revenge, the mad, insatiable craving for blood that had remained dormant, was again aroused; and, under the weird circumstances already described, she disguised herself as a man, and, entering our tent, murdered Alexandrovitch.

On further investigation, I discovered that the unknown English traveller was none other than George Travers, for in one of the sketchbooks he had carried during his tour in the East, I found a well-executed pencil portrait of the Cossack maiden.

Dàrya's motive in coming to England was, without doubt, one of revenge, prompted by the terrible aberration from which she was suffering.

Mabel, who had refrained from saying anything regarding the murder of her brother, fearing lest her story should appear absurd, now made an explanation. On the night of the tragedy, she was on her way to the house at Chiswick, and, when near the gates, a well-dressed young man had accosted her, explaining that he was an old friend of George's recently returned from abroad, and wished to speak with him privately without his wife's knowledge. He concluded by asking her whether, as a favour, she would show him the way to enter her brother's room without going in at the front door. The story told by the young man seemed quite plausible, and she led him up to the French windows of the study.

Then she left the stranger, and crossed the lawn to go round to the front door, but at that moment the clock of Chiswick church chimed, and, finding the hour so late, she suddenly resolved to return home.

Later, when she heard of the tragedy, she was horrified to discover that she had actually aided the assassin, but resolved to preserve silence lest suspicion might attach itself to her.

She now identified the distorted features of the madwoman as those of the young man, and when I questioned her with regard to the bloodstained handkerchief, she explained how, in groping about the shrubbery in the dark, she had torn her hand severely on some thorns.

* * *

The cloud of suspicion that had rested so long upon Mabel is now removed, and we are again happy.

The carefully-devised plots and the devilish cunning that characterised all the murderess's movements appeared most extraordinary; nevertheless, in cases such as hers, they are not unheard of. Dàrya is now in Brookwood Asylum, hopelessly insane, for she is still suffering from that most terrible form of madness – acute homicidal mania – and is known to the attendants as 'The Woman with a Blemish'.

Murderer's Encore

Murray Leinster

DOREN'S dying was over too soon. Much too soon. When the tree branch crashed down on his shoulder, Doren jerked his fat face around in incredulous astonishment. He took the second blow slantingly on his head and then his face went terrified. At the third blow he went down, squealing feebly, and saw Thad Hunt for the first time. His expression took on a look of ultimate horror. He knew he was going to be murdered and that there was nothing that could save him from it.

There were trees all about and the rustling of wind in the foliage overhead. Somewhere a little brook made small, tranquil, liquid sounds and somewhere the flute-like call of a bob-white quail floated over the hills. No other noises sounded but for impacts of the maniacal blows Thad Hunt dealt his enemy.

The frenzied satisfaction he felt almost paid him for his seven years of waiting for that moment. It was the realization of dreams that had haunted him in the penitentiary and filled even his waking moments since. He battered his corpulent, twitching victim in an ecstasy of hatred, panting with the satisfaction of his lust to destroy. He wanted to smash the fat man until he was no longer human, until he was not even vaguely recognizable as that Charles Doren who had sent him to the penitentiary for a crime Doren himself had committed. As a lawyer, Doren had known of tricks Thad Hunt could not combat – and now had a document on file in the County Prosecutor's office naming him the man responsible if he should ever be found murdered.

He'd be found murdered now! Thad Hunt panted and struck and panted and struck, sobbing curses and revilings at the thing he battered, until no blow, however furious, made the battered object even twitch. It was a most complete, most satisfying vengeance.

Reluctantly, Thad Hunt stopped. He could find no zest in further outrage against his victim. Panting from his exertions he turned and stalked away.

All was peace about him. Branches rustled. Something small and gray and furtive scurried through fallen leaves, leaped to a tree trunk, and whisked out of sight. A squirrel. A cat-bird squawked raucously in the distance. Crows cawed. Thad Hunt tramped heavily through underbrush, careless of leaving a trail. Presently he stood at the edge of an abandoned and flooded quarry, unused these twenty years and more. He sat deliberately on its edge and removed the oversized boots he wore and replaced them with others neatly placed in readiness for this transfer. He put stones in the discarded boots and re-laced them. He heaved them out to where he knew the water in the quarry was deepest. They splashed and were gone forever.

These boots were not his own. He'd bought them in a second-hand store two hundred miles away and had them heavily wrapped by the salesman he'd bought them from: had not touched them until he put them on today with gloved hands and over a double pair of brand new socks. They'd have human scent on them, to be sure, but it wouldn't be Thad Hunt's. In the remote event that bloodhounds were brought to hunt down Doren's killer, those bloodhounds were brought to hunt down Doren's killer, those bloodhounds would trail the killer to the brink of the quarry…and halt. There'd be no trail beyond that. Even if a diver found the boots, it would be impossible to link them to Thad Hunt; and besides, nobody would suspect him!

Wearing his own boots he picked his way around the quarry's edge to the other side and followed a dim trail a quarter-mile to a tiny stream that ran down toward the valley. He waded into the stream and walked up it. Now he was utterly safe.

* * *

A good two miles from the scene of the murder he left the stream, and went over a rise to the home in which he had lived before he went to the penitentiary. The house had been left tenantless for seven years. Doors sagged open, shingles were missing, and the windows were lackluster, though unbroken. No small boys came by here to break the windows of empty houses. Even when he'd lived here, he'd had no more than one visitor a month, outside of those in the business he'd done for Doren, and for which Doren had let him go to prison. Now that the place was known to be empty, nobody would come by at all.

He sat down on a rotting chopping log, his eyes like glowing coals. The house and few outbuildings were desolation. The inside of the house was only dust and cobwebs. Doren owned it now…had owned it. He'd bought it in at a tax sale while Thad Hunt was in the penitentiary, to take away his last excuse or reason for coming back to his home country. But the loss of his house hadn't kept him away. He was here now. He'd come back, and Doren was a mass of pulp, corpulent flesh two miles away, which was exactly what Doren had feared most in all the world…what he'd tried to prevent by filing an accusation against Thad Hunt in advance should he ever be found murdered. And Thad, sitting on the chopping log, laughed softly to himself. It was a low-pitched, not-loud, satisfied laughter sound.

Presently he smoked, in flamboyant ease. He didn't have to run away. He'd arranged to be found here. And when he was discovered, he'd have an absolutely perfect alibi. Nobody in the world would ever suspect that he'd been the one to murder Doren. Doren's filed accusation would be absurd. His innocence would be so unquestionable that actually he'd be a hero, and public opinion would turn against the dead Doren and make him out the most villainous of scoundrels, whose murder was an act of justice no matter who'd done it or why.

Thad Hunt relaxed, reveling in his memory. He could eat now, if he chose. He looked at the food he'd brought wrapped up in butcher's paper; bread and cheese only. It was the sort of lunch a man might take with him when he had to count pennies and couldn't afford even the cheapest of public eating places while traveling. But he wouldn't eat now. His revenge had satisfied his every craving. He sat and smoked leisurely, filled with the triumph of this beautifully, perfectly contrived act of retribution.

Not the least of its perfection was that he had been able to destroy Doren in maniacal, insensate fury. It was no cunning destruction he'd had to content himself with. He'd killed Doren by brute strength and Doren knew who was doing it. He'd had leisure to exhaust himself in the fulfilment of every atom of his hate. It had been just as he had pictured it a million times.

Time passed as he sat and remembered. He was waiting now to be found. It wasn't likely that anybody would come today, of course. He'd turned one of Doren's own tricks against him. A letter to the County Prosecutor, in the little town down the valley, had said that he'd heard from Doren, asking that he meet Doren up at this place, and he was afraid. If he didn't report to the County Prosecutor within two days, he should be looked for. Doren most probably would have murdered him. Doren believed he had evidence of a crime that Doren had done and had offered to make amends for past injuries if Thad Hunt would surrender it. The letter was very bitter indeed, coming from an ex-convict and accusing a prominent citizen of intent to murder him. No attention would be paid to it normally, but when Doren was missed…

The long afternoon wore on as Thad Hunt lived and relived, with infinite relish, the murder of his enemy. There was sunshine upon the hills and in the valleys between them. There were birdcalls and chirping insects and the drowsy, somnolent humming bees. All of nature was very quiet and very peaceful. Here Thad Hunt sat, with a queer twisted grin on his face, and remembered.

* * *

Night fell. Fireflies appeared and their lamps made little streaks of greenish light against the darkness. He sat grinning beneath the stars. Seven years of hate, and now this vast contentment. He did not even care to worry about his own safety.

That letter was in the town, saying he was to meet Doren here and was afraid that he would be murdered. The letter would have been delivered to the County Prosecutor today. He'd take no action at once, of course. He'd want to ask Doren about it, Doren being a prominent citizen. But Doren wouldn't be going back to answer questions. The County Prosecutor might wait through tomorrow, or maybe not. Sooner or later, though, with Doren missing, he'd send someone up to this house to see what had happened. And they'd find Thad Hunt, and he'd tell a tale of threats and near-murder which would be infinitely convincing. He'd be practically a hero thereafter and the finding of Doren's battered body would make no difference whatever, because nobody could possibly suspect Thad Hunt of killing him.

When he grew drowsy as hours passed, he almost begrudged the need of sleep because it meant he would not be reveling in his monstrous pleasure. But he did doze, and in his dreams he killed Doren all over again in such an ecstasy of satisfaction that it woke him once. When he dozed off again, his mind absurdly framed a dream of doom, of arrest for the murder he'd planned so long.

When day broke, he woke with contentment. Undoubtedly someone would come up here to find him today. The County Prosecutor would have gotten his letter yesterday, expressing fear that he'd be murdered by Doren. There was another letter on file in the County Prosecutor's office, too, from Doren, accusing Thad Hunt in advance if he should be found dead. And two such letters from two men each fearing the other would surely produce action when Doren was missing overnight.

This morning brought no doubts and no regrets – except that Doren had not taken longer to die under his rain of blows. Thad Hunt had hardly stirred from his seat all night, absorbed in his obsessed reenactments of the killing. Now he looked out over the hills, fresh and clean in the dawn light, and laughed softly to himself. This was his home country. Five years in the penitentiary had kept him away from it, and during the two years since his release he hadn't come back because he knew the local attitude toward ex-convicts. From now on though, as soon as he was found, that attitude would be changed for him. Doren would be blamed for everything. Thad Hunt would be almost a hero, and certainly he'd be a respected citizen immediately, ultimately because he'd murdered Doren! But they'd never dream of that!

He got up and moved about. If he'd been quite sure that he'd be found today he'd have left his sandwiches intact as a pathetic indication of his presence. But he wasn't absolutely certain, and he was a little bit hungry. He ate, carefully putting the fresh wrapping paper where it would catch the eye of anyone who came. And then he was thirsty; and as it was too early for any searchers, he went out to the spring a half mile or more away. There was a well by the house – a deep well – but he did not try to get water from it. He had another use for the well.

He came back and expansively surveyed the hills and sky and all the earth. Everything was perfect. Four days before he'd called Doren by long-distance telephone. In a disguised voice, he'd identified himself as a sportsman looking for a hunting camp in this neighborhood. He said he'd heard of this place and would buy it if the price were right. He'd made an appointment to meet Doren here.

He hadn't kept the appointment. From hiding, he'd watched Doren climb up to the house that once had been Thad Hunt's home. He'd waited downhill, hugging his anticipation to himself, while Doren waited for the mythical sportsman, until Doren gave him up; until Doren came down…to his death.

His plan was perfection! He'd done enough, but not one atom too much. He'd written one letter which he'd duly signed with his own name. He'd made one long-distance phone call which could never be traced to him. And he'd killed Doren going away from this house – not at it, or going to to it – and he'd be found here with the most perfect alibi any man ever had. There was nothing to go wrong! He hadn't even gone into the house. Since the murder, he'd stayed almost motionless leaving no sign of a long wait here. There wasn't anything to go wrong!

The morning passed. By nine o'clock, the County Prosecutor would be thinking about Thad Hunt's letter and asking for Doren, whom he hadn't been able to locate the day before. By ten, he'd know Doren hadn't come home all night. By eleven, he'd have sent someone up to see if anything had happened.

* * *

It was a beautiful morning and Thad Hunt loafed, zestfully grinning to himself and enjoying every second of it. It was warm, almost, but not quite hot, and the smell of green things on the hillside and in the thicket was good. The sound of bob-whites' calling was soothing and homelike. An occasional butterfly, a homing bee or two, now and then a discordantly cawing crow; these things spoke of vast tranquility. Now that he had sated his craving for vengeance, Thad Hunt looked forward to years and years of happy remembering, while his neighbors were extra cordial to him because of the monstrous crime they would believe that Doren had perpetrated against him.

It was almost noon when he heard a car on the dirt road far away. He went to the yard in front of the house to watch. He was careful not to show himself. He watched from behind a thicket of tall weeds.

He saw four men. They were headed in his direction. They couldn't be headed anywhere else. They must have been sent by the County Prosecutor to hunt over this place for signs that Thad Hunt had been murdered here. They had two dogs with them.

He watched them until they were less than half a mile away, downhill. He didn't recognize them, but an enormous satisfaction made him grin wildly and rather unpleasantly. He turned to go to the spot where he was to be found.

For the first time in seven years he faced the front door of the house that had been his home. There was a folded sheet of paper stuck to it with a pin. A scrawled, penciled name was written across the folded outer surface. It was fresh. It hadn't been there long. For an instant, he was shocked. Then he realized Doren had expected to meet a mythical sportsman here. Thad Hunt had murdered him as he descended after a vain wait. He'd…

Yes. Thad plucked it away from the door, grinning. The writing on the outside was simply the name of that non-existent, would-be purchaser of this house and land. Doren, after fruitless waiting, had left a note for the man he'd failed to meet.

Chuckling, Thad Hunt went across the weed-grown yard, carrying a length of rope. He heaved up a rotten board from the cover of the deep, dark well. He threw it to one side. It would be very obviously a new happening. And since they'd be looking for a murdered man...

He passed the rope around a four-inch tree some two yards from the hole. With the doubled rope in his hands, he went to the opening in the well cover. He let himself down carefully.

It was thirty feet to the bottom. There was a foot and a half of water there and under it, all manner of foulness and mud. He stood in the mud and pulled on one strand of the rope. The other end went up toward the rectangular patch of blue sky directly overhead. It vanished, and only one strand remained. He continued to pull. Suddenly, the rope tumbled down upon him. There was no possible way for him to climb out.

He trampled the rope underfoot, thrusting it into the mud beneath the water. It made a firmer foundation for him to stand on. He stood looking up at the long narrow, rectangular patch of sky. The men the County Prosecutor had sent to hunt over the place for a murder victim, of course, would find the broken well-top. They'd look in the well, in any case, as a place for the disposal of a body. But, besides, he'd shout hoarsely as if he'd been calling despairingly for hours. Presently, astonished faces would stare down at him, cutting off part of the sky. He'd cry out. They'd have trouble getting him up. And by the time he was on top of the ground they'd have accepted as gospel his hysterical story that Doren had left him there. Doren had demanded that he surrender evidence of some one of Doren's crimes. When he protested that he couldn't, Doren had driven him down into the well at pistol point and said he'd come back to see if Thad Hunt changed his mind when he got hungry.

Everything fitted together perfectly, too. The County Prosecutor had sent to look for him because of the letter which was the perfect preparation for this tale. The tale was a perfect alibi for when Doren's body was found. Nobody would imagine that a man who had been fearful of murder would commit the insensately violent battering of Doren. Nobody could imagine that a man who'd murder Doren would put himself in the most hopelessly inescapable of traps. Nobody could doubt, from now on, Thad Hunt's story that he had gone to prison for Doren's crime. It was utterly, absolutely perfect, and he had the memory of having killed Doren to relive and gloat over all the rest of his life.

The four men and the dogs would be arriving here soon. Thad Hunt sent a wailing call for help up the resonant shaft of the well. They wouldn't hear it yet, but he wanted them to hear faint cries as they neared the house. He'd better begin now.

The sound of his voice was ghostly. It rang and echoed hollowly against the smooth, concrete walls of the well. Thad Hunt chuckled. He stirred, and there was a rustling of paper – the note Doren had left for the mythical man he'd thought to meet here. It had to be gotten rid of, but trampling it into the mud would be enough. It would be amusing, though, to read Doren's trustful message to a figment of Thad Hunt's imagination.

He unfolded the sheet and read it. It was addressed to the man Doren had thought talked to him by long-distance. It said that Doren had been there, and waited, and nobody had turned up. And it said that if the would-be purchaser came to his office in town they could discuss the sale of the property. Doren added that he was the County Prosecutor and his office was just opposite the court house so it would be easy to find.

Thad Hunt started to trample the note underfoot. Then he checked. His breath stopped. Doren was the County Prosecutor... Then the letter addressed to the County Prosecutor would have been delivered to his office after he left…to be murdered! Nobody'd been sent to look for Thad Hunt at his homeplace! His letter hadn't been opened! It wouldn't be opened until Doren was missed and his disappearance was accepted as final or his body found! Even after that it wouldn't be opened until somebody else was elected or appointed as his successor and leisurely got around to cleaning up the accumulated mail. The four men and two dogs weren't coming to this house. The men might be training the dogs for hunting, or trying them out with a view to purchase! They might…

Thad Hunt couldn't get out. He knew that his only chance of living was to make those men hear him. He screamed. He shrieked. He raised a hellish clamor at the bottom of the hole into which he had lowered himself. He screamed so shrilly and so long that he could not believe that he could go unheard.

But nobody came. When it grew dark, his voice was a croak, and he knew that nobody would come. By that time, too, his hands were raw and bleeding from desperate attempts to climb the smooth, concrete wall. When night fell and the thin, rectangular bit of sky above him grew dark and cold, incurious stars looked down into the well upon him, he wept in utter despair.

He could think about the vast satisfaction he'd had in killing Doren, to be sure, but it was no comfort. He even knew that some time, maybe one month, maybe two, or even three months hence, his letter would bring somebody here to look for him. But that was no comfort either. From this instant, until starvation ended it, he would be dying…slowly. In murdering Doren and arranging so cleverly to escape all suspicion, he'd been remarkably successful. No one would ever dream that he'd killed Doren. But he'd planned a single murder and it had turned out a double one…

There was one difference between the two murders, though. Thad Hunt's own dying wasn't over so soon. In fact, it wasn't completely over until far into the third week.

Heatwave

Tom Mead

THE SUMMER of 1954, we were pushing 110 degrees in Los Angeles. Windows and doors gaped wide; you could have mistaken Downtown LA for the most welcoming place on Earth. The papers screamed about the increasing death rate: the old and the weak sizzling away in their armchairs and hospital beds. But heat like that brings with it the threat of violence. The air in those empty streets gets so thick that it eats at your mind. Some people get desperate.

The papers were promising the heat would break within a day or two; they'd been making similar promises for about two weeks. Skipping through pages of this kind of stuff, I dived straight into the police beat on page fourteen. There I found, among others, the story of a dead girl on La Cienega. A cashier at Thrifty's All-Night Drug Store. She'd been shot to death in a messy, heat-crazed robbery. The perpetrators made off with six thousand dollars from the safe and a drizzling of the young girl's blood on their clothes.

Elsewhere a family man had bludgeoned his eight-year-old daughter into a coma with a teakettle, a delirious teenager had set himself afire in Inglewood, and an elderly couple were missing (presumed dead) after their neatly-piled clothes and an elegantly calligraphed suicide note were found under a rock on Venice Beach. I was reading that story when the phone rang.

* * *

I pulled up at the roadside on Washington Boulevard, letting the Pontiac amble to a halt in the shade of a camphor tree. I'd picked out the house straightaway: it was the only one on the street with all its doors bolted shut. I waited for a moment, watching for movement in either of the twin front windows. I saw none.

Loosening my tie, undoing a second button on my shirt and tilting the brim of my lead-grey trilby to dab the sweat against my forehead, I looked bad and knew it. My face was an unshaven brick and my suit didn't fit anymore. I couldn't tell if the sweats were from the heatwave or the DTs.

I approached at a slow, lumbering pace, taking in the faded pink stucco and terracotta roof tiles lined up like row upon row of crooked, off-white teeth. When I reached the door, my knock was loud and businesslike. I wanted her to think that God himself might be on the other end of that knock.

She opened the door slowly and a wave of fetid warmth seeped out. "Yes?"

I didn't smile. "Mrs. Lukather?"

"Yes?"

"My name is Max Ehrlich. You called me this morning."

"Have you any identification Mr. Ehrlich?" her tone was not unfriendly. I showed her the photostat of my license I carried everywhere, though the thin-faced thirty-something in the photo no longer looked like me.

Mrs. Lukather threw open the door to let me in and it was as if the whole house sighed, as if it had been holding its breath in anticipation. She led me through to the living room, babbling the whole time. "To be frank, Mr. Ehrlich, I'm afraid I may be bothering you unnecessarily. My phone call this morning was made while I was under extreme mental anguish – I have a tendency toward irrational emotional responses – and now that I'm in my right mind I can see that all this bother might very well be over nothing...' She wore a natty, cinnamon-colored gabardine suit, her hands fluttering like a couple of calloused butterflies as she spoke. When my eyes were on her, she grinned, but as my gaze wandered around the room, her face sagged.

"You mentioned your son. You said he was missing."

"Uh yes, uh, well, that's right, I haven't heard from my son Arnold in a little while, but perhaps I'm worrying too much, he always tells me I worry too much, that I should lay off once in a while and..."

"Mrs. Lukather, why did you call me and not the police?"

Suddenly, her face crumpled and she let out a long sob. I waited for her to catch her breath. "I'm sorry. I'm so sorry, it's just..."

She reached behind the couch and produced an object wrapped in a yellow dishrag. She proffered it like a holy relic and I took it from her – its dead weight was fearfully familiar. I unwrapped a snub-nosed .38.

"I found that under his mattress. He didn't come home last night, Mr. Ehrlich, and now I'm completely terrified."

I leaned back and felt the easy-chair groan under my weight.

"My rates are thirty dollars *per diem*."

"That's not a problem, Mr. Ehrlich. I have a little rainy-day fund put aside. And, though the sun may be shining out there, this looks like quite a rainy day to me. In fact, let's say I'll give you an additional seventy-five dollars if you can get Arnie back here today."

I nodded. "How old is your son?"

"Seventeen. It was his birthday two weeks ago. We had a little get-together at home, just me and him."

"When's the last time you heard from him?"

"Yesterday. Around eight. A friend of his came by to pick him up. They were going somewhere, movies I think."

"Who's the friend?"

"Just a kid, I don't know, I don't keep track of Arnie's friends, he hates it when I do that."

"Male, female?"

"Arnie's not the type to run around with girls. It was one of his high school buddies – Roy, I think the name is." She rubbed her forehead then struggled to her feet. "Hold on a second."

I waited while she shuffled out of the room, then came back bearing a small square photograph, a polaroid. It showed two adolescent males in baseball uniforms, both grinning widely and stupidly. The uniforms were nondescript: plain white, with bold vertical stripes. Each had numbers stitched to their breast pockets, like a pair of jailbirds.

"That's my Arnie," she said, pointing to the kid on the left, number nine. He was wiry, smooth-chinned, with dark eyes and wild black hair. He looked like he would make a good baseball player. "And that—" she indicated the kid next to him, number fifteen, "is Roy. Roy Moretz, I remember the name now." Roy was wider, with a belly like a beer cask. Skin and hair shimmeringly pale.

"Can I borrow this photo?"

"All yours, Mr. Ehrlich. I took it last summer."

"Uh-huh. So this Roy kid picked up Arnie last night. Do you know where Roy lives?"

"I'm afraid not."

"Did they leave in a car?"

"Oh yes. Roy owns a dreadful old Ford De Luxe, such a noisy machine, churning out black smoke. I don't know how he keeps it running. Anyway, he came for Arnie in that."

"Color?"

"Rust."

"I see."

As soon as she mentioned it, I knew the car would be the key. Who would forget a car like that?

"Does Arnie have a father, Mrs. Lukather?"

She didn't answer. She aimed her grey eyes at the window and pretended not to hear.

"Could I take a look at Arnie's room, Mrs. Lukather?"

"Well of course, right this way."

The only conclusion I drew from that little bedroom was that it did not belong to a would-be gangster. Various trophies for sporting achievement served as bookends, sealing in row upon row of trashy adventure novels: *Tarzan*, *Sinbad*, *Conan the Barbarian*, *King Solomon's Mines*. The walls were lined with posters of famous athletes. The bed was narrow, more fit for a child than an adolescent on the cusp of manhood. There was nothing of use here.

"Do you have a phone I could use?"

"In the hall."

She let me find my own way, but I could hear her bustling conspicuously in the kitchen as I gave the operator a number. I pictured her leaning toward the wall, aching to hear what I had to say about her boy. My first call was to a friend in police dispatch, who was able to give me the lowdown on Roy Moretz.

Roy, it seemed, was a problem child. Mother dead, father jailed for embezzling funds from the venetian-blind manufacturer where he worked. Roy was legally emancipated at age seventeen, only to be subsequently arrested for marijuana possession, drunkenness and disorderly conduct, all within a six-month period. His last known address was a bungalow a couple of blocks away from the Lukather residence.

As for Arnie, he had no record of any kind. His mother must have been proud.

My second call was to ambulance dispatch. The girl I spoke to was bright and keen, her voice like sunshine over the telephone wires. I had never met her, but she knew me by reputation. I gave her a description of Roy's infamous automobile and she swiftly responded that a car matching that description had been involved in a collision at around three a.m. that very morning, somewhere up in the Hollywood Hills. Just a drunken accident which resulted in said vehicle getting wrapped around a palm tree. I waited on the line while she tried to identify the ambulance men who took the callout.

She gave me the name Jasper Monroe, and provided a direct line to the ambulance-drivers' break room in the Santa Monica depot. While I waited for Monroe to come on the line, I developed a pretty firm idea of what had happened: two drunken kids had gone on a wild bender, culminating in an ugly smash. Roy and Arnie were probably being patched up in hospital rooms at that very moment.

"Hello?" said a voice on the other end of the line.

"Yes, am I speaking to Jasper Monroe?"

"That's me."

"My name is Max Ehrlich, Jasper. I understand you drove the ambulance from the scene of a crash in the Hollywood Hills this morning."

"Uh-huh." He was impatient. That was fine, my questions were easy enough.

"I just have a couple of things I need to ask, Jasper. The guys in the car, were they a pair of teenagers, one skinny and dark, the other fair and fat?"

There was a pause. "Well, you got it half right. There was only one kid in the car, though. He was skinny, like you say."

"Huh." So Arnie had ditched Roy somewhere along the way and ridden off in his car. Naughty boy. "Dark-haired boy?"

"Yeah, dark curly hair. He was unconscious when we pulled him out of the wreck."

"I.D.?"

"He had a driver's license on him, but I forget the name."

"Could it have been Arnold Lukather?"

A pause. "Yeah. Hey, yeah, I think that's it."

"Where did you take him, Jasper?"

"We had to drive around for a while, all the emergency rooms were so busy. In the end we wound up at Linda Vista Community."

"What time was that?"

"That would have been around four a.m."

"Wonderful. Thanks Jasper, I owe you a beer."

As I hung up the phone, Mrs. Lukather came out from the kitchen to check on me. "Success?" she inquired.

"Just putting a few feelers out there. Thanks for the use of your phone. Now if you'll excuse me, I'd better get to work."

* * *

The drive to the emergency room was strangely relaxed, in spite of the humidity. I had just made an easy thirty dollars and was well on track for an easy seventy-five. Of course, I did not know what had gone on between the two boys, Arnold and Roy, or how Arnold had come to wrap Roy's car around a tree in the early hours of the morning, but those unanswered questions were not a part of this particular job description.

I found the parking lot packed to the gills, eventually giving up and abandoning the Pontiac with two wheels bumped up on the sidewalk. No one was around to stop me. I straightened my tie and marched toward the double doors of the vast, white building.

"I'm looking for a patient named Arnold Lukather. You got a man by that name?"

The desk nurse looked up at me, unimpressed. She didn't reply, and went back to her paperwork.

"Vehicular smash. He was brought in this morning."

Still, no answer. Rolling my eyes, I removed a loose cigarette from my pocket and slipped it between my lips.

"Don't you dare," the nurse said.

"Maybe you didn't hear me…"

"I heard you, mister, I'm not deaf. But look here, this is a heatwave. We've been getting tens of thousands of new patients every day for the past two weeks. Every hour, it feels like. I'm just one woman here!"

"Remind me to write a letter to *Queen for a Day*. I'm sure your work is sterling, but how is that going to help me find my friend?"

The nurse exhaled slowly, and it was the most desolate sound I had heard. "Try Ward 6. Most of the new arrivals this morning ended up there."

"God bless you," I said with an antiseptic smile. I turned on my heel and marched off, dropping the cigarette to the floor unlit.

After a few minutes' bemused wandering, I found Ward 6 halfway down a long, bone-colored corridor on the first floor. I took a deep breath at the door. I removed the photo from my pocket. Then I plunged in.

Molten sunlight streaked in on row upon row of deathly pallid men. The whole ward screamed and broiled to the beat of nurses' skittering footsteps. Gurneys shrieked past. I strode up and down a few times like a commander inspecting troops. I took about ten minutes making sure none of these men was Arnold Lukather. When I'd been there so long that my presence could no longer be reasonably ignored, a stout matron (is there any other kind?) approached.

"Can I do something for you?" she said.

"I hope so. My name is Max Lukather, I'm looking for a relative of mine named Arnold."

The name meant something to her; her eyes flashed. "Oh, Mr. Lukather. Please come with me." She led me to a row of sleeping old men, which was obviously the closest this place had to a sanctuary. There, she lowered her voice. "I'm afraid I have some terrible news, Mr. Lukather. Arnold Lukather passed away an hour ago."

I breathed in the thin, disinfected air. "I see. That is most upsetting."

"My condolences. It was quite peaceful, I assure you," said the matron. The suffering in this place was so pointedly vocal that I found her second statement difficult to credit. "And anyway, he's with God now. Were you close?"

"Cousins. Yes, very close."

"Would you like to see him? Perhaps say a final goodbye?"

"That would be nice."

I found my way down to the morgue in spite of the matron's directions. Morgues are never hard to find. They are always below, isolated and sealed off by steel doors. Death is a dirty secret. When I got there, just saying 'Arnold Lukather' in somber tones was all the soft-spoken mortician required. A steel body-drawer was swiftly pulled out, a toe-tag checked.

"You might want to…" the mortician demonstrated covering his mouth and nose. I didn't argue, I removed my handkerchief and put it to use. When the shroud was folded back, I surveyed the corpse's face dispassionately. I had seen all shapes and sizes in my time, but none quite so…tumescent. This one looked like an effigy in melting candlewax. I was seized by the irrational urge to reach out and poke it, to see if my fingers would sink right into the soft, yellow flesh.

In death, a body loses its shape. The muscles holding the facial features in place go slack, so the skin flaps like a pancake. Even so, and with the eyes riveted shut and the mouth gaping open, there was no mistaking: this body was not Arnie Lukather.

"This is him?" I said. "You sure?"

"I know he looks a little different. That's perfectly natural, honestly. There's no mistake. I'm very sorry."

The body was at least seventy years old – bald, liver-spotted and toothless. Another martyr to the crippling heat, no doubt.

"Do you mind if I take a look at his records?"

The mortician was briefly flummoxed. "Sure. If you want." He covered up the body and ushered me into a tiny, crypt-like office. There, he handed me a brown manila folder. I flicked through, and realized two things. The first was that this mortician, for all his professional merits, was not an avid reader of records. The second was that by now Arnie Lukather could be, quite literally, anywhere.

The kid had switched records with this dead old man. Perhaps he had been in the same ward and watched the geezer check out. Now he, Arnie, was officially dead, with all the freedom that brought.

"Thanks for your time," I said.

* * *

After a couple of minutes' contemplation at the wheel of my car, I decided to head for Roy Moretz's bungalow. Of course it was a long shot, but by now it had dawned on me that I was lucky to have any shot at all. The place was identical to the Lukather house in design, but the stucco which was so carefully tended there had all but entirely peeled away here. Most of the terracotta roof tiles were chipped away to nothing. The patch of garden out front was a knot of weeds. Amongst this mess of yellowish-green vines and leaves, I glimpsed a pair of rusted lawn chairs, most likely irretrievable.

I rang the bell a few times, to be met only by angry silence within the house. I tried the door handle and, to my dismay, the front door was unlocked and fell obligingly open. I stepped through into the hallway. It was dingy and under-decorated, with patches of mold spreading outward from the corners of the room like wandering shadows. The distant sound of flies buzzing drew me toward the closed kitchen door, and I became conscious of an insidious odor seeping out from under it.

"I wouldn't do that," said a man's voice from behind me.

I spun round, heart thundering, and found myself confronted by two men.

The man who had spoken was unimpressive. His suit, like his slick-back hair, was grey before its time. The sole distinguishing feature of his smooth, insufferably oval face was a pair of small, circular and very dark sunglasses shielding his eyes. He grinned fleetingly, flashing a set of angry little teeth.

At his side was another officious-looking nobody, this one dressed like an undertaker. He watched me through passive, half-lidded eyes.

"I don't think you'd like what you found in there," the first man went on. "Now let me see. Would you happen to be Mr. Max Ehrlich by any chance? We've been waiting for you. It took you longer to get here than we expected. Mind you, my friend tells me I'm looking at the most out-of-shape piece of shit he's ever laid eyes on. He says he's seen gentlemen who've been in the river for fourteen days and bobbed up in better shape than you."

"He's got a lot to say for a man who never opens his mouth."

The sidekick took a step closer, but the man with sunglasses placed a gentle hand on his forearm. "Careful," Sunglasses said, "he's got ears, you know. Perhaps I should make it plain to you, Mr. Ehrlich, just how much trouble you are in. Do you know who I am?"

"Tell me."

"My name is Frank Mellish."

I halted mid-breath. "Bullshit."

"I'd tell you to check my driver's license, but they don't let me out on the roads these days."

"So is it really true that you're…?"

Mellish removed the sunglasses with a practiced flourish. The eyelids beneath gaped wide and unblinking, encircled with tender, pinkish red. The eyeballs themselves were off-white globes, like twin cue balls, unmarred by pupils or irises. Everybody knew Mellish's name. When it came to contract killers, he had been top of the heap for a long, long time; a real wizard with a knife. He had style and the psychosis to back it up. But he'd dropped out of the game a couple of years ago when a punk threw corrosive acid in his face.

"Oh, it's true all right. But you should see the other guy."

I resisted the urge to swallow the lump of fear which had bubbled up in my throat.

Mellish went on, nodding in the undertaker's direction: "Meet my new eyes. His name is Ormerod, but don't bother speaking to him. He's been a mute ever since he was a little kid. Isn't that funny, the two of us ending up together? Suits me fine of course, I have plenty to say. But some people might find it funny, a blind man and a mute."

"Look Mr. Mellish, I don't know how you found me, but there's really nothing I can do for you. Honestly."

"Let's see about that, shall we. I'm told you were hired by a woman named Lukather to retrieve her errant son, Arnold."

"That's right. He's just a kid on a bender, probably drunk in an alley somewhere, no use to you at all."

Mellish smiled faintly. "Well, you seem to know an awful lot about a lot of things. You hear about a robbery last night? Old-fashioned stick-up?"

I made a show of thinking about it, then shook my head.

"Out on La Cienega. Things turned messy. A checkout girl took a bullet in the throat and the two perpetrators made off with six thousand and change. Is that ringing any bells?"

I didn't reply, so Mellish continued: "Your guy, Arnie, was one of the perps." He waited a moment for that to sink in. "It was Arnie and his good buddy Roy, who you'll find in the kitchen. They were just stupid kids trying to pull off a big score, make themselves look like big men. Ordinarily this kind of operation wouldn't fall within the remit of Mr. Ormerod and myself, but that particular drug store just happened to be, shall we say, *protected*. The girl who died was the store-owner's daughter, who just happens to be a personal friend of my employer. Do you see now?"

Bewildered, I nodded.

"We already caught up with Roy but, credit where it's due, he never opened his mouth. Except to scream, that is, when we turned his insides into outsides. They were kind of warm and juicy to the touch, like hamburger meat. But the smell isn't quite so appetizing, of course. Although," he added parenthetically, "I wouldn't put anything past Ormerod. Between you and me, he's crazy."

On cue, Ormerod offered the first flicker of a smile. It was not an expression so much as an absence. Just a muscle spasm.

"So now we have something of a problem," Mellish went on, mock-casual. "No Arnie. And no cash."

"That is a problem."

"Yes indeed. And now it's your problem. We know you're looking for Arnie, and we know you're being paid to do it. That's fine. A man's got to make a living. But I want you to know that we'll be keeping an eye on you, so to speak. You find Arnie and collect your payoff, and then get the hell out, because Ormerod and I want to have a few words with young Arnold Lukather. Any objections?"

I cleared my throat. "None at all. May I leave now?"

"It's a free country," Mellish said.

* * *

My hands shook as I turned the key in the ignition. I drove away from the late Roy Moretz's home with my heart still racing and my chest heaving with frantic breaths. It was true that, since his injury, Frank Mellish's name was no longer synonymous with underworld supremacy. However, with Ormerod at his side he still presented a degree of danger which I'd not foreseen. No doubt Arnie and Roy had not foreseen it either.

Although, thinking it through as I drove, Arnie's behavior started to make more sense. After the robbery, he had ditched Roy, taking both the car and the money. Roy, for whatever foolish reason, had returned home to find Mellish and Ormerod waiting for him. While this was going on, Arnie had taken an ill-fated trip to the Hollywood Hills and promptly wrecked Roy's automobile.

Odd, I thought, that Arnie had chosen for his getaway those narrow, circuitous country roads. Surely LAX, the bus terminal or even the freeway would have seemed like more agreeable options to a seventeen-year-old on the run with a sack full of cash. But the Hills? There was nothing for him there.

With this fleeting notion snagging on my brain like a thin strand of gossamer, I pulled over at the corner, next to a payphone. I got out and dialed. Eventually I got through to the ambulance-driver once again.

"Jasper? It's Max Ehrlich."

"You again? I'm trying to work here! Don't you know there's a heatwave going on out there?"

"Yeah, somebody mentioned that. I'll buy you sun tan lotion for your trouble. I only need to ask you one quick question and then I'll be out of your hair for good."

Jasper sighed breathily like the drama queen he was. "Go ahead."

"Where exactly did you pick Arnold Lukather up from? Where *exactly* did he have his smash?"

"Southbound on Canyon Lake Drive."

"Southbound? You mean he was headed back into Los Angeles?"

"That's what I mean."

"Did he say anything to you?"

"He was unconscious, Max. Use your noodle."

"Did you find anything in the car, Jasper? Anything unusual?"

"Such as?"

Such as a bag of blood money. "Such as anything unusual. I don't know."

"Nothing. The car was empty."

I thanked him and hung up. Supposing this ambulance man was telling the truth, the cash had already been stashed somewhere when they pulled Arnie out of his wrecked car. Roy hadn't had it, and Arnie hadn't had it. There was only a small window of time in which Arnie could have disposed of it. That would also explain his mysterious trip into the Hollywood Hills. I thought back to those old adventure stories which had lined the boy's shelves, and the whole thing made sense. Arnie had driven up there to bury his treasure.

* * *

I found the crash site with minimal effort. There is a devilish hairpin bend a mile along Canyon Lake Drive, and it was there that the asphalt was scattered with broken glass and errant slivers of rusty metal. I pictured Arnie, delirious with adrenaline in the early hours of the morning, losing control and spinning himself off into a tree.

From there, tracing Arnie's steps back into the Hollywood Hills was surprisingly easy. The old Ford De Luxe had had uncharacteristically narrow tire treads, probably the cheapest Roy could find. The speed Arnie travelled had left frequent, serpentine black markings on the road itself. Max followed these uphill for almost a quarter-mile, until they unceremoniously stopped. So this was as far as Arnie had come. I pulled up at the roadside. It was reasonable to assume, therefore, that the money was stashed within walking distance of this very spot.

It was an isolated area, and easy to understand why Arnie had chosen it. If he had covered his tracks a little better, it would have been damn near untraceable. Just an anonymous stretch of road, shielded from the sun by dense clusters of trees. Above me was the Hollywood sign, beaming down on all like the smile of a benevolent God. Below me lay the city.

I climbed out of the car and wandered slowly up the road for another hundred yards. Then I wandered back down the road a similar distance. It was only on my third or fourth circuit, with my eyes fixed firmly on the ground, that I spotted familiar narrow tire treads in the dust, veering off the road to the right-hand side. I followed them through a patch of greenery into a small clearing, where they halted once more. Perfect.

The heat had dried out the terrain, giving it the texture and hue of scorched concrete. I dared not imagine how difficult it had been for Arnie digging a moneybag-sized hole in that unforgiving earth.

At the foot of a nearby palm, I found shovel marks in the smooth, dusty ground. When it's as dry as this, it's virtually impossible to smooth over. The ground does not decimate into powder; it splinters into messy chunks. There is no way to hide the fact that you have been digging. Arnie, after concealing the cash, had done what he could to rearrange the chunks over the hollow. But, inevitably, they had not quite fit. Just his luck. So, he had left the job half-finished; the money stowed in the ground with the sun-dried earth messily rearranged on top of it. Now, I did not even need a shovel. I merely kicked the dirt aside with my shoe, revealing a small black travelling case in a little cavity about eight inches deep.

I seized the bag and unzippered it a little to check that the cash was still there. It was. So Arnie had not yet returned to retrieve it. This was perfect. It meant the clearing was the one spot in the whole of Los Angeles where Arnie was guaranteed to show up. And I would be there waiting for him.

By nightfall, however, I had almost given up hope. I'd parked my Pontiac on the far side of the clearing and now sat behind the wheel, watching for the vaguest hint of movement in the seeping darkness. It was only the tangible presence of the moneybag at my side, like a loyal pet curled up in a shadow, which kept me from drifting off into a well-earned sleep. As I was breaking the seal on my third pack of Camels, I heard the chug of a car engine struggling uphill. I hastily lit the cigarette as a pair of headlamps swung into view.

It was a dirt-crusted Dodge pickup, and God knows where Arnie got it from. It rattled to a halt in the center of the clearing, the lights aimed straight at the burial site. A spindly figure that could only be Arnie clambered out, leaving the engine running. I watched as Arnie retrieved a shovel from the truck bed, then started to dig.

After about five minutes had passed and he had still not unearthed the case, Arnie gave in. In silhouette, I saw him drop the shovel and cover his eyes with his hands. Was he crying?

I gripped the handle of the Webley revolver I kept at my shoulder, and slithered out of the Pontiac's driving seat. "Don't move!" I called, my voice wet with smoke and rattling in the darkness. Arnie, who had dropped to his knees in despair, sprang upright.

I cocked the hammer. "Don't you goddamn move Arnie. I'm not kidding."

Arnie was obviously itching to make a run for it, and probably could have pulled it off; it was, after all, dark and the shadows were untrustworthy. But his greed won out. He wanted his money more. "Who are you?" the kid called out, his voice cracking. Both of his eyes were blackened and he had a long, messy wound over his right brow, held together by a tangle of stitches.

I approached, the Webley still trained firmly on Arnie's bony carcass. "Don't talk. We need to get out of here." I saw that Arnie's limbs were quivering, like a half-drowned river rat.

"I ain't going anywhere with you."

I swung the butt of the pistol, catching Arnie a vicious blow across the jaw. Arnie dropped, spitting teeth. He struggled to his knees and hawked a chunk of bloody phlegm.

I knelt down beside him and seized a handful of his fulsome, oil-black hair. With my other hand I patted the kid down, removing a .45 which was stuffed down the back of Arnie's Levis. "Quite a collector, aren't you?" I said as I pulled him to his feet.

Bundling the sack full of dollars into the rear of the Pontiac, I installed Arnie in the passenger seat and calmly fired up the engine. We left the pickup with its headlights trained on the shallow ditch, and slowly snaked our way down from the Hollywood Hills. Along the way, Arnie began to snivel. "What…what happened to Roy?" he wanted to know. "I tried to get in touch, to say I was sorry, but he didn't pick up the phone. Did you hurt him?"

"Me? No. This whole mess is nothing to do with me. But I wouldn't make any plans on seeing Roy again any time soon."

Arnie fell silent.

"So," I said, as if making conversation, "which one of you was it that shot the checkout girl?"

"Roy," said Arnie without hesitation, "it was Roy I swear."

I laughed. "Whatever you say."

"It was all Roy's big idea. He wanted the money so he could leave home."

"And what about you? What about your mother?"

Arnie's gaze snapped toward me. "What *about* my mother?"

"Easy now. I'm only asking."

Arnie's shoulders slumped; he deflated like a corpse. "Yeah, I guess I wanted to get away too. Things were getting a little…*close,* at home."

"Well, it sounds like you boys came up with the perfect crime," I said, smirking at myself in the rearview mirror.

We picked up the tail on Homebrook Street. It was a burgundy Oldsmobile, with two shadowed passengers. I made no effort to lose them. "See that car?" I said to Arnie.

Arnie looked and nodded.

"In there are the two men who killed Roy."

Arnie gasped. "You mean Roy's really dead?"

"As dead as that cashier girl. And now they're coming for you."

"No!" Arnie shrieked, making a desperate grab for the steering wheel. I put a stop to that with a swift punch to the nose. I felt the bone crunch beneath my fist, and saw the gout of blood shimmer beneath the streetlamps. Arnie was quiet after that, his hands clamped to his face as fresh blood spilled out between his fingers.

We reached Mrs. Lukather's house at around eleven p.m. She came out onto the veranda to meet us, sobbing with joy and relief. When she saw the mess Arnie was in, she stopped. "Hey, what have you done to my boy, you animal?"

"Let's go inside, Mrs. Lukather. I believe you owe me seventy-five dollars."

Grudgingly, she ushered me in. Before I stepped across the threshold, I glanced along the street, where the Oldsmobile sat idling by the curb.

Mrs. Lukather positioned Arnie at the kitchen table and handed him a wet washcloth for his bloody face. "Thanks Mom," he said softly and nasally. Then she turned on me.

"Well, you found my son. I don't know how you did it, and I don't want to know, but I guess you did your job. I have your money in the other room." Not waiting for me to reply, she marched out to fetch it. I seated myself at the table opposite Arnie, who did not look up.

It was then, in the heavy silence of the kitchen, that I heard the front door quietly unlatch from outside. Arnie heard it too, and his whole body snapped upright. The boy flung the washcloth aside and sprang to his feet.

I, however, remained seated. I did not even turn around when Mellish and Ormerod entered the room. Arnie whimpered as the two men approached him. Nobody spoke.

The two assassins quickly cornered Arnie. The blind man produced a flick-knife and sliced the air with a venomous swing. Ormerod reached out and gripped Arnie around the waist. Arnie shrieked, and it was only then that I got up to leave.

From nowhere, Mrs. Lukather exploded into the room. Under ordinary circumstances, the two hitmen would have made short work of her as well, but she had caught them off-guard. They were stealthy operators and had not expected a frontal assault. She was waving a baseball bat over her head – I recognized it as the same one Arnie had clutched in the photograph. In the split second Ormerod's attention faltered, Arnie flung his leg back and kicked him square in the groin. Ormerod crumpled, his face frozen in open-mouthed, silent agony. Arnie broke free of the two killers and darted over to his mother.

Before Ormerod could struggle to his feet, Mrs. Lukather swung the bat in his direction. The wet crunch as it connected with the side of his head made me cringe. Ormerod keeled over sideways, blood spilling from the side of his head onto the bare floorboards.

Mellish, meanwhile, still had the knife. Fortunately for mother and son, without his guide dog he was powerless to use it. He swung it out in wild, desperate arcs, grunting like an animal.

Arnie, finally finding his courage, leapt on the blind man, gripping his wrist and battering it against the kitchen counter until Mellish let go of the blade. Then Arnie punched him in the stomach and watched him double up, panting helplessly. His dark glasses dropped to the ground and cracked.

Silence. Arnie and Mrs. Lukather looked at one another questioningly, then they turned to me. "What now?" Mrs. Lukather spat.

"Well, I guess that depends," I said. "You love your son, ma'am?"

"Don't play games."

I laughed. "Of course not," I nodded toward the bat. "Besides, you don't follow the rules. Now let me ask you again: do you love your son?"

She nodded.

I sauntered over to the counter, where the .38 Arnie had stuffed under his mattress now lay. I picked it up – it was cool and sturdy in my palm. Then I turned and placed it in the center of the kitchen table, with the barrel facing pointedly toward Mellish. The blind man still lay jack-knifed on the floor, too winded to speak.

"Maybe you need to decide just how much you love him, Mrs. Lukather."

* * *

I counted out seventy-five dollars in cash from the woman's purse, and stepped out of the house before I saw anything I shouldn't. I waited on the porch for a moment, in case there came from within the startling whipcrack of a gunshot. In that moment I thought about the nameless checkout girl from Thrifty's Drug Store. I also thought about Roy Moretz. I listened, but there was no sound at all.

Then I walked shakily back toward my car. I spotted the suitcase on the back seat and, without thinking, pulled it out and left it on the sidewalk. Gripping the steering wheel, I paused and counted to ten slowly until my heartrate steadied. A fresh summer rain speckled the Pontiac's windshield as I gunned the engine and pulled away from the curb.

The Mystery of the Circular Chamber

L.T. Meade and Robert Eustace

ONE DAY in late September I received the following letter from my lawyer:

> *My Dear Bell,*
> *I shall esteem it a favour if you can make it convenient to call upon me at ten o'clock tomorrow morning on a matter of extreme privacy.*

At the appointed hour I was shown into Mr. Edgcombe's private room. I had known him for years – we were, in fact, old friends – and I was startled now by the look of worry, not to say anxiety, on his usually serene features.

"You are the very man I want, Bell," he cried. "Sit down; I have a great deal to say to you. There is a mystery of a very grave nature which I hope you may solve for me. It is in connection with a house said to be haunted."

He fixed his bright eyes on my face as he spoke. I sat perfectly silent, waiting for him to continue.

"In the first place," he resumed, "I must ask you to regard the matter as confidential."

"Certainly," I answered.

"You know," he went on, "that I have often laughed at your special hobby, but it occurred to me yesterday that the experiences you have lived through may enable you to give me valuable assistance in this difficulty."

"I will do my best for you, Edgcombe," I replied.

He lay back in his chair, folding his hands.

"The case is briefly as follows," he began. "It is connected with the family of the Wentworths. The only son, Archibald, the artist, has just died under most extraordinary circumstances. He was, as you probably know, one of the most promising watercolour painters of the younger school, and his pictures in this year's Academy met with universal praise. He was the heir to the Wentworth estates, and his death has caused a complication of claims from a member of a collateral branch of the family, who, when the present squire dies, is entitled to the money. This man has spent the greater part of his life in Australia, is badly off, and evidently belongs to a rowdy set. He has been to see me two or three times, and I must say frankly that I am not taken with his appearance."

"Had he anything to do with the death?" I interrupted.

"Nothing whatever, as you will quickly perceive. Wentworth has been accustomed from time to time to go alone on sketching tours to different parts of the country. He has tramped about on foot, and visited odd, out-of-the-way nooks searching for subjects. He never took much money with him, and always travelled as an apparently poor man. A month ago he started off alone on one of these tours. He had a handsome commission from Barlow & Co., picture-dealers in the

Strand. He was to paint certain parts of the river Merran; and although he certainly did not need money, he seemed glad of an object for a good ramble. He parted with his family in the best of health and spirits, and wrote to them from time to time; but a week ago they heard the news that he had died suddenly at an inn on the Merran. There was, of course, an inquest and an autopsy. Dr. Miles Gordon, the Wentworths' consulting physician, was telegraphed for, and was present at the post-mortem examination. He is absolutely puzzled to account for the death. The medical examination showed Wentworth to be in apparently perfect health at the time. There was no lesion to be discovered upon which to base a different opinion, all the organs being healthy. Neither was there any trace of poison, nor marks of violence. The coroner's verdict was that Wentworth died of syncope, which, as you know perhaps, is a synonym for an unknown cause. The inn where he died is a very lonely one, and has the reputation of being haunted. The landlord seems to bear a bad character, although nothing has ever been proved against him. But a young girl who lives at the inn gave evidence which at first startled everyone. She said at the inquest that she had earnestly warned Wentworth not to sleep in the haunted room. She had scarcely told the coroner so before she fell to the floor in an epileptic fit. When she came to herself she was sullen and silent, and nothing more could be extracted from her. The old man, the innkeeper, explained that the girl was half-witted, but he did not attempt to deny that the house had the reputation of being haunted, and said that he had himself begged Wentworth not to put up there. Well, that is about the whole of the story. The coroner's inquest seems to deny the evidence of foul play, but I have my very strong suspicions. What I want you to do is to ascertain if they are correct. Will you undertake the case?"

"I will certainly do so," I replied. "Please let me have any further particulars, and a written document to show, in case of need, that I am acting under your directions."

Edgcombe agreed to this, and I soon afterwards took my leave. The case had the features of an interesting problem, and I hoped that I should prove successful in solving it.

That evening I made my plans carefully. I would go into ——shire early on the following morning, assuming for my purpose the character of an amateur photographer. Having got all necessary particulars from Edgcombe, I made a careful mental map of my operations. First of all I would visit a little village of the name of Harkhurst, and put up at the inn, the Crown and Thistle. Here Wentworth spent a fortnight when he first started on his commission to make drawings of the river Merran. I thought it likely that I should obtain some information there. Circumstances must guide me as to my further steps, but my intention was to proceed from Harkhurst to the Castle Inn, which was situated about six miles further up the river. This was the inn where the tragedy had occurred.

Towards evening on the following day I arrived at Harkhurst. When my carriage drew up at the Crown and Thistle, the landlady was standing in the doorway. She was a buxom-looking dame, with a kindly face. I asked for a bed.

"Certainly, sir," she answered. She turned with me into the little inn, and taking me upstairs, showed me a small room, quite clean and comfortable, looking out on the yard. I said it would do capitally, and she hurried downstairs to prepare my supper. After this meal, which proved to be excellent, I determined to visit the landlord in the bar. I found him chatty and communicative.

"This is a lonely place," he said; "we don't often have a soul staying with us for a month at a time." As he spoke he walked to the door, and I followed him. The shades of night were beginning to fall, but the picturesqueness of the little hamlet could not but commend itself to me.

"And yet it is a lovely spot," I said. "I should have thought tourists would have thronged to it. It is at least an ideal place for photographers."

"You are right there, sir," replied the man; "and although we don't often have company to stay in the inn, now and then we have a stray artist. It's not three weeks back," he continued, "that we had a gentleman like you, sir, only a bit younger, to stay with us for a week or two. He was an artist, and drew from morning till night – ah, poor fellow!"

"Why do you say that?" I asked.

"I have good cause, sir. Here, wife," continued the landlord, looking over his shoulder at Mrs. Johnson, the landlady, who now appeared on the scene, "this gentleman has been asking me questions about our visitor, Mr. Wentworth, but perhaps we ought not to inflict such a dismal story upon him tonight."

"Pray do," I said; "what you have already hinted at arouses my curiosity. Why should you pity Mr. Wentworth?"

"He is dead, sir," said the landlady, in a solemn voice. I gave a pretended start, and she continued—

"And it was all his own fault. Ah, dear! It makes me almost cry to think of it. He was as nice a gentleman as I ever set eyes on, and so strong, hearty, and pleasant. Well, sir, everything went well until one day he said to me, 'I am about to leave you, Mrs. Johnson. I am going to a little place called the Castle Inn, further up the Merran.'

"'The Castle Inn!' I cried. 'No, Mr. Wentworth, that you won't, not if you value your life.'

"'And why not?' he said, looking at me with as merry blue eyes as you ever saw in anybody's head. 'Why should I not visit the Castle Inn? I have a commission to make some drawings of that special bend of the river.'

"'Well, then, sir,' I answered, 'if that is the case, you'll just have a horse and trap from here and drive over as often as you want to. For the Castle Inn ain't a fit place for a Christian to put up at.'

"'What do you mean?' he asked of me.

"'It is said to be haunted, sir, and what does happen in that house the Lord only knows, but there's not been a visitor at the inn for some years, not since Bailiff Holt came by his death.'

"'Came by his death?' he asked. 'And how was that?'

"'God knows, but I don't,' I answered. 'At the coroner's inquest it was said that he died from syncope, whatever that means, but the folks round here said it was fright.' Mr. Wentworth just laughed at me. He didn't mind a word I said, and the next day, sir, he was off, carrying his belongings with him."

"Well, and what happened?" I asked, seeing that she paused.

"What happened, sir? Just what I expected. Two days afterwards came the news of his death. Poor young gentleman! He died in the very room where Holt had breathed his last; and, oh, if there wasn't a fuss and to-do, for it turned out that, although he seemed quite poor to us, with little or no money, he was no end of a swell, and had rich relations, and big estates coming to him; and, of course, there was a coroner's inquest and all the rest, and great doctors came down from London, and our Dr. Stanmore, who lives down the street, was sent for, and though they did all they could, and examined him, as it were, with a microscope, they could find no cause for death, and so they give it out that it was syncope, just as they did in the case of poor Holt. But, sir, it wasn't; it was fright, sheer fright. The place is haunted. It's a mysterious, dreadful house, and I only hope you won't have nothing to do with it."

She added a few more words and presently left us.

"That's a strange story," I said, turning to Johnson; "your wife has excited my curiosity. I should much like to get further particulars."

"There don't seem to be anything more to tell, sir," replied Johnson. "It's true what the wife says, that the Castle Inn has a bad name. It's not the first, no, nor the second, death that has occurred there."

"You mentioned your village doctor; do you think he could enlighten me on the subject?"

"I am sure he would do his best, sir. He lives only six doors away, in a red house. Maybe you wouldn't mind stepping down the street and speaking to him?"

"You are sure he would not think it a liberty?"

"Not he, sir; he'll be only too pleased to exchange a word with someone outside this sleepy little place."

"Then I'll call on him," I answered, and taking up my hat I strolled down the street. I was lucky in finding Dr. Stanmore at home, and the moment I saw his face I determined to take him into my confidence.

"The fact is this," I said, when he had shaken hands with me, "I should not dream of taking this liberty did I not feel certain that you could help me."

"And in what way?" he asked, not stiffly, but with a keen, inquiring, interested glance.

"I have been sent down from London to inquire into the Wentworth mystery," I said.

"Is that so?" he said, with a start. Then he continued gravely: "I fear you have come on a wild goose chase. There was nothing discovered at the autopsy to account for the death. There were no marks on the body, and all the organs were healthy. I met Wentworth often while he was staying here, and he was as hearty and strong-looking a young man as I have ever come across."

"But the Castle Inn has a bad reputation," I said.

"That is true; the people here are afraid of it. It is said to be haunted. But really, sir, you and I need not trouble ourselves about stupid reports of that sort. Old Bindloss, the landlord, has lived there for years, and there has never been anything proved against him."

"Is he alone?"

"No; his wife and a grandchild live there also."

"A grandchild?" I said. "Did not this girl give some startling evidence at the inquest?"

"Nothing of any consequence," replied Dr. Stanmore; "she only repeated what Bindloss had already said himself – that the house was haunted, and that she had asked Wentworth not to sleep in the room."

"Has anything ever been done to explain the reason why this room is said to be haunted?" I continued.

"Not that I know of. Rats are probably at the bottom of it."

"But have not there been other deaths in the house?"

"That is true."

"How many?"

"Well, I have myself attended no less than three similar inquests."

"And what was the verdict of the jury?"

"In each case the verdict was death from syncope."

"Which means, cause unknown," I said, jumping impatiently to my feet. "I wonder, Dr. Stanmore, that you are satisfied to leave the matter in such a state."

"And, pray, what can I do?" he inquired. "I am asked to examine a body. I find all the organs in perfect health; I cannot trace the least appearance of violence, nor can I detect poison. What other evidence can I honestly give?"

"I can only say that I should not be satisfied," I replied. "I now wish to add that I have come down from London determined to solve this mystery. I shall myself put up at the Castle Inn."

"Well?" said Dr. Stanmore.

"And sleep in the haunted room."

"Of course you don't believe in the ghost."

"No; but I believe in foul play. Now, Dr. Stanmore, will you help me?"

"Most certainly, if I can. What do you wish me to do?"

"This – I shall go to the Castle Inn tomorrow. If at the end of three days I do not return here, will you go in search of me, and at the same time post this letter to Mr. Edgcombe, my London lawyer?"

"If you do not appear in three days I'll kick up no end of a row," said Dr. Stanmore, "and, of course, post your letter."

Soon afterwards I shook hands with the doctor and left him.

After an early dinner on the following day, I parted with my good-natured landlord and his wife, and with my knapsack and kodak strapped over my shoulders, started on my way. I took care to tell no one that I was going to the Castle Inn, and for this purpose doubled back through a wood, and so found the right road. The sun was nearly setting when at last I approached a broken-down signpost, on which, in half-obliterated characters, I could read the words, 'To the Castle Inn'. I found myself now at the entrance of a small lane, which was evidently little frequented, as it was considerably grass-grown. From where I stood I could catch no sight of any habitation, but just at that moment a low, somewhat inconsequent laugh fell upon my ears. I turned quickly and saw a pretty girl, with bright eyes and a childish face, gazing at me with interest. I had little doubt that she was old Bindloss's grand-daughter.

"Will you kindly tell me," I asked, "if this is the way to the Castle Inn?"

My remark evidently startled her. She made a bound forward, seized me by my hand, and tried to push me away from the entrance to the lane into the high road.

"Go away!" she cried; "We have no beds fit for gentlemen at the Castle Inn. Go! Go!" she continued, and she pointed up the winding road. Her eyes were now blazing in her head, but I noticed that her lips trembled, and that very little would cause her to burst into tears.

"But I am tired and footsore," I answered. "I should like to put up at the inn for the night."

"Don't!" she repeated; "They'll put you into a room with a ghost. Don't go; 'tain't a place for gentlemen." Here she burst not into tears, but into a fit of high, shrill, almost idiotic laughter. She suddenly clapped one of her hands to her forehead, and, turning, flew almost as fast as the wind down the narrow lane and out of sight.

I followed her quickly. I did not believe that the girl was quite as mad as she seemed, but I had little doubt that she had something extraordinary weighing on her mind.

At the next turn I came in view of the inn. It was a queer-looking old place, and I stopped for a moment to look at it.

The house was entirely built of stone. There were two storeys to the centre part, which was square, and at the four corners stood four round towers. The house was built right on the river, just below a large mill-pond. I walked up to the door and pounded on it with my stick. It was shut, and looked as inhospitable as the rest of the place. After a moment's delay it was opened two or three inches, and the surly face of an old woman peeped out.

"And what may you be wanting?" she asked.

"A bed for the night," I replied; "can you accommodate me?"

She glanced suspiciously first at me and then at my camera.

"You are an artist, I make no doubt," she said, "and we don't want no more of them here."

She was about to slam the door in my face, but I pushed my foot between it and the lintel.

"I am easily pleased," I said; "can you not give me some sort of bed for the night?"

"You had best have nothing to do with us," she answered. "You go off to Harkhurst; they can put you up at the Crown and Thistle."

"I have just come from there," I answered. "As a matter of fact, I could not walk another mile."

"We don't want visitors at the Castle Inn," she continued. Here she peered forward and looked into my face. "You had best be off," she repeated; "they say the place is haunted."

I uttered a laugh.

"You don't expect me to believe that?" I said. She glanced at me from head to foot. Her face was ominously grave.

"You had best know all, sir," she said, after a pause. "Something happens in this house, and no living soul knows what it is, for they who have seen it have never yet survived to tell the tale. It's not more than a week back that a young gentleman came here. He was like you, bold as brass, and he too wanted a bed, and would take no denial. I told him plain, and so did my man, that the place was haunted. He didn't mind no more than you mind. Well, he slept in the only room we have got for guests, and he – he *died there*."

"What did he die of?" I asked.

"Fright," was the answer, brief and laconic. "Now do you want to come or not?"

"Yes; I don't believe in ghosts. I want the bed, and I am determined to have it."

The woman flung the door wide open.

"Don't say as I ain't warned you," she cried. "Come in, if you must." She led me into the kitchen, where a fire burned sullenly on the hearth.

"Sit you down, and I'll send for Bindloss," she said. "I can only promise to give you a bed if Bindloss agrees. Liz, come along here this minute."

A quick young step was heard in the passage, and the pretty girl whom I had seen at the top of the lane entered. Her eyes sought my face, her lips moved as if to say something, but no sound issued from them.

"Go and find your grandad," said the old woman. "Tell him there is a gentleman here that wants a bed. Ask him what's to be done."

The girl favoured me with a long and peculiar glance, then turning on her heel she left the room. As soon as she did so the old woman peered forward and looked curiously at me.

"I'm sorry you are staying," she said; "don't forget as I warned you. Remember, this ain't a proper inn at all. Once it was a mill, but that was afore Bindloss's day and mine. Gents would come in the summer and put up for the fishing, but then the story of the ghost got abroad, and lately we have no visitors to speak of, only an odd one now and then who ain't wanted – no, he ain't wanted. You see, there was three deaths here. Yes" – she held up one of her skinny hands and began to count on her fingers – "yes, three up to the present; three, that's it. Ah, here comes Bindloss."

A shuffling step was heard in the passage, and an old man, bent with age, and wearing a long white beard, entered the room.

"We has no beds for strangers," he said, speaking in an aggressive and loud tone. "Hasn't the wife said so? We don't let out beds here."

"As that is the case, you have no right to have that signpost at the end of the lane," I retorted. "I am not in a mood to walk eight miles for a shelter in a country I know nothing about. Cannot you put me up somehow?"

"I have told the gentleman everything, Sam," said the wife. "He is just for all the world like young Mr. Wentworth, and not a bit frightened."

The old landlord came up and faced me.

"Look you here," he said, "you stay on at your peril. I don't want you, nor do the wife. Now is it 'yes' or 'no'?"

"It is 'yes'," I said.

"There's only one room you can sleep in."

"One room is sufficient."

"It's the one Mr. Wentworth died in. Hadn't you best take up your traps and be off?"

"No, I shall stay."

"Then there's no more to be said."

"Run, Liz," said the woman, "and light the fire in the parlour."

The girl left the room, and the woman, taking up a candle, said she would take me to the chamber where I was to sleep. She led me down a long and narrow passage, and then, opening a door, down two steps into the most extraordinary-looking room I had ever seen. The walls were completely circular, covered with a paper of a staring grotesque pattern. A small iron bedstead projected into the middle of the floor, which was uncarpeted except for a slip of matting beside it. A cheap deal wash-hand stand, a couple of chairs, and a small table with a blurred looking-glass stood against the wall beneath a deep embrasure, in which there was a window. This was evidently a room in one of the circular towers. I had never seen less inviting quarters.

"Your supper will be ready directly, sir," said the woman, and placing the candle on the little table, she left me.

The place felt damp and draughty, and the flame of the candle flickered about, causing the tallow to gutter to one side. There was no fireplace in the room, and above, the walls converged to a point, giving the whole place the appearance of an enormous extinguisher. I made a hurried and necessarily limited toilet, and went into the parlour. I was standing by the fire, which was burning badly, when the door opened, and the girl Liz came in, bearing a tray in her hand. She laid the tray on the table and came up softly to me.

"Fools come to this house," she said, "and you are one."

"Pray let me have my supper, and don't talk," I replied. "I am tired and hungry, and want to go to bed."

Liz stood perfectly still for a moment.

"'Tain't worth it," she said; then, in a meditative voice, "no, 'tain't worth it. But I'll say no more. Folks will never be warned!"

Her grandmother's voice calling her caused her to bound from the room.

My supper proved better than I had expected, and, having finished it, I strolled into the kitchen, anxious to have a further talk with the old man. He was seated alone by the fire, a great mastiff lying at his feet.

"Can you tell me why the house is supposed to be haunted?" I asked suddenly, stooping down to speak to him.

"How should I know?" he cried hoarsely. "The wife and me have been here twenty years, and never seen nor heard anything, but for certain folks *do* die in the house. It's mortal unpleasant for me, for the doctors come along, and the coroner, and there's an inquest and no end of fuss. The folks die, although no one has ever laid a finger on 'em; the doctors can't prove why they are dead, but dead they be. Well, there ain't no use saying more. You are here, and maybe you'll pass the one night all right."

"I shall go to bed at once," I said, "but I should like some candles. Can you supply me?"

The man turned and looked at his wife, who at that moment entered the kitchen. She went to the dresser, opened a wooden box, and taking out three or four tallow candles, put them into my hand.

I rose, simulating a yawn.

"Goodnight, sir," said the old man; "goodnight; I wish you well."

A moment later I had entered my bedroom, and having shut the door, proceeded to give it a careful examination. As far as I could make out, there was no entrance to the room except by the door, which was shaped to fit the circular walls. I noticed, however, that there was an unaccountable draught, and this I at last discovered came from below the oak wainscoting of the wall. I could not in any way account for the draught, but it existed to an unpleasant extent. The bed, I further saw, was somewhat peculiar; it had no castors on the four legs, which were let down about half an inch into sockets provided for them in the wooden floor. This discovery excited my suspicions still further. It was evident that the bed was intended to remain in a particular position. I saw that it directly faced the little window sunk deep into the thick wall, so that anyone in bed would look directly at the window. I examined my watch, found that it was past eleven, and placing both the candles on a tiny table near the bed, I lay down without undressing. I was on the alert to catch the slightest noise, but the hours dragged on and nothing occurred. In the house all was silence, and outside the splashing and churning of the water falling over the wheel came distinctly to my ears.

I lay awake all night, but as morning dawned fell into an uneasy sleep. I awoke to see the broad daylight streaming in at the small window.

Making a hasty toilet, I went out for a walk, and presently came in to breakfast. It had been laid for me in the big kitchen, and the old man was seated by the hearth.

"Well," said the woman, "I hope you slept comfortable, sir."

I answered in the affirmative, and now perceived that old Bindloss and his wife were in the humour to be agreeable. They said that if I was satisfied with the room I might spend another night at the inn. I told them that I had a great many photographs to take, and would be much obliged for the permission. As I spoke I looked round for the girl, Liz. She was nowhere to be seen.

"Where is your grand-daughter?" I asked of the old woman.

"She has gone away for the day," was the reply. "It's too much for Liz to see strangers. She gets excited, and then the fits come on."

"What sort of fits?"

"I can't tell what they are called, but they're bad, and weaken her, poor thing! Liz ought never to be excited." Here Bindloss gave his wife a warning glance; she lowered her eyes, and going across to the range, began to stir the contents of something in a saucepan.

That afternoon I borrowed some lines from Bindloss, and, taking an old boat which was moored to the bank of the mill-pond, set off under the pretence of fishing for pike. The weather was perfect for the time of year.

Waiting my opportunity, I brought the boat up to land on the bank that dammed up the stream, and getting out walked along it in the direction of the mill wheel, over which the water was now rushing.

As I observed it from this side of the bank, I saw that the tower in which my room was placed must at one time have been part of the mill itself, and I further noticed that the masonry was comparatively new, showing that alterations must have taken place when the house was abandoned as a mill and was turned into an inn. I clambered down the side of the wheel, holding on to the beams, which were green and slippery, and peered through the paddles.

As I was making my examination, a voice suddenly startled me.

"What are you doing down there?"

I looked up; old Bindloss was standing on the bank looking down at me. He was alone, and his face was contorted with a queer mixture of fear and passion. I hastily hoisted myself up, and stood beside him.

"What are you poking about down there for?" he said, pushing his ugly old face into mine as he spoke. "You fool! If you had fallen you would have been drowned. No one could swim a stroke in that mill-race. And then there would have been another death, and all the old fuss over again! Look here, sir, will you have the goodness to get out of the place? I don't want you here anymore."

"I intend to leave tomorrow morning," I answered in a pacifying voice, "and I am really very much obliged to you for warning me about the mill."

"You had best not go near it again," he said in a menacing voice, and then he turned hastily away. I watched him as he climbed up a steep bank and disappeared from view. He was going in the opposite direction from the house. Seizing the opportunity of his absence, I once more approached the mill. Was it possible that Wentworth had been hurled into it? But had this been the case there would have been signs and marks on the body. Having reached the wheel, I clambered boldly down. It was now getting dusk, but I could see that a prolongation of the axle entered the wall of the tower. The fittings were also in wonderfully good order, and the bolt that held the great wheel only required to be drawn out to set it in motion.

That evening during supper I thought very hard. I perceived that Bindloss was angry, also that he was suspicious and alarmed. I saw plainly that the only way to really discover what had been done to Wentworth was to cause the old ruffian to try similar means to get rid of me. This was a dangerous expedient, but I felt desperate, and my curiosity as well as interest were keenly aroused. Having finished my supper, I went into the passage preparatory to going into the kitchen. I had on felt slippers, and my footfall made no noise. As I approached the door I heard Bindloss saying to his wife –

"He's been poking about the mill wheel; I wish he would make himself scarce."

"Oh, he can't find out anything," was the reply. "You keep quiet, Bindloss; he'll be off in the morning."

"That's as maybe," was the answer, and then there came a harsh and very disagreeable laugh. I waited for a moment, and then entered the kitchen. Bindloss was alone now; he was bending over the fire, smoking.

"I shall leave early in the morning," I said, "so please have my bill ready for me." I then seated myself near him, drawing up my chair close to the blaze. He looked as if he resented this, but said nothing.

"I am very curious about the deaths which occur in this house," I said, after a pause. "How many did you say there were?"

"That is nothing to you," he answered. "We never wanted you here; you can go when you please."

"I shall go tomorrow morning, but I wish to say something now."

"And what may that be?"

"I don't believe in that story about the place being haunted."

"Oh, you don't, don't you?" He dropped his pipe, and his glittering eyes gazed at me with a mixture of anger and ill-concealed alarm.

"No," I paused, then I said slowly and emphatically, "I went back to the mill even after your warning, and—"

"What?" he cried, starting to his feet.

"Nothing," I answered; "only I don't believe in the ghost."

His face turned not only white but livid. I left him without another word. I saw that his suspicions had been much strengthened by my words. This I intended. To induce the ruffian to do his worst was the only way to wring his secret from him.

My hideous room looked exactly as it had done on the previous evening. The grotesque pattern on the walls seemed to start out in bold relief. Some of the ugly lines seemed at that moment, to my imagination, almost to take human shape, to convert themselves into ogre-like faces, and to grin at me. Was I too daring? Was it wrong of me to risk my life in this manner? I was terribly tired, and, curious as it may seem, my greatest fear at that crucial moment was the dread that I might fall asleep. I had spent two nights with scarcely any repose, and felt that at any moment, notwithstanding all my efforts, slumber might visit me. In order to give Bindloss full opportunity for carrying out his scheme, it was necessary for me to get into bed, and even to feign sleep. In my present exhausted condition the pretence of slumber would easily lapse into the reality. This risk, however, which really was a very grave one, must be run. Without undressing I got into bed, pulling the bed-clothes well over me. In my hand I held my revolver. I deliberately put out the candles, and then lay motionless, waiting for events. The house was quiet as the grave – there was not a stir, and gradually my nerves, excited as they were, began to calm down. As I had fully expected, overpowering sleepiness seized me, and, notwithstanding every effort, I found myself drifting away into the land of dreams. I began to wish that whatever apparition was to appear would do so at once and get it over. Gradually but surely I seemed to pass from all memory of my present world, and to live in a strange and terrible phantasmagoria. In that state I slept, in that state also I dreamt, and dreamt horribly.

I thought that I was dancing a waltz with an enormously tall woman. She towered above me, clasping me in her arms, and began to whirl me round and round at a giddy speed. I could hear the crashing music of a distant band. Faster and faster, round and round some great empty hall was I whirled. I knew that I was losing my senses, and screamed to her to stop and let me go. Suddenly there was a terrible crash close to me. Good God! I found myself awake, but – I was still moving. Where was I? Where was I going? I leapt up on the bed, only to reel and fall heavily backwards upon the floor. What was the matter? Why was I sliding, sliding? Had I suddenly gone mad, or was I still suffering from some hideous nightmare? I tried to move, to stagger to my feet. Then by slow degrees my senses began to return, and I knew where I was. I was in the circular room, the room where Wentworth had died; but what was happening to me I could not divine. I only knew that I was being whirled round and round at a velocity that was every moment increasing. By the moonlight that struggled in through the window I saw that the floor and the bed upon it was revolving, but the table was lying on its side, and its fall must have awakened me.

I could not see any other furniture in the room. By what mysterious manner had it been removed? Making a great effort, I crawled to the centre of this awful chamber, and, seizing the foot of the bed, struggled to my feet. Here I knew there would be less motion, and I could just manage to see the outline of the door. I had taken the precaution to slip the revolver into my pocket, and I still felt that if human agency appeared, I had a chance of selling my life dearly; but surely the horror I was passing through was invented by no living man! As the floor of the room revolved in the direction of the door I made a dash for it, but was carried swiftly past, and again fell heavily. When I came round again I made a frantic effort to cling to one of the steps, but in vain; the head of the bedstead caught me as it flew round, and tore my arms away. In another moment I believe I should have gone raving mad with terror. My head felt as if it would burst; I found it impossible to think consecutively. The only idea which really possessed me was a mad wish to escape from this hideous place. I struggled to the bedstead, and dragging the legs from their sockets, pulled it into the middle of the room away from the wall. With this out of the way, I managed at last to reach the door in safety.

The moment my hand grasped the handle I leapt upon the little step and tried to wrench the door open. It was locked, locked from without; it defied my every effort. I had only just standing room for my feet. Below me the floor of the room was still racing round with terrible speed. I dared scarcely look at it, for the giddiness in my head increased each moment. The next instant a soft footstep was distinctly audible, and I saw a gleam of light through a chink of the door. I heard a hand fumbling at the lock, the door was slowly opened outwards, and I saw the face of Bindloss.

For a moment he did not perceive me, for I was crouching down on the step, and the next instant with all my force I flung myself upon him. He uttered a yell of terror. The lantern he carried dropped and went out, but I had gripped him round the neck with my fingers, driving them deep down into his lean, sinewy throat. With frantic speed I pulled him along the passage up to a window, through which the moonlight was shining. Here I released my hold of his throat, but immediately covered him with my revolver.

"Down on your knees, or you are a dead man!" I cried. "Confess everything, or I shoot you through the heart."

His courage had evidently forsaken him; he began to whimper and cry bitterly.

"Spare my life," he screamed. "I will tell everything, only spare my life."

"Be quick about it," I said; "I am in no humour to be merciful. Out with the truth."

I was listening anxiously for the wife's step, but except for the low hum of machinery and the splashing of the water I heard nothing.

"Speak," I said, giving the old man a shake. His lips trembled, his words came out falteringly.

"It was Wentworth's doing," he panted.

"Wentworth? Not the murdered man?" I cried.

"No, no, his cousin. The ruffian who has been the curse of my life. Owing to that last death he inherits the property. He is the real owner of the mill, and he invented the revolving floor. There were deaths – oh yes, oh yes. It was so easy, and I wanted the money. The police never suspected, nor did the doctors. Wentworth was bitter hard on me, and I got into his power." Here he choked and sobbed. "I am a miserable old man, sir," he gasped.

"So you killed your victims for the sake of money?" I said, grasping him by the shoulder.

"Yes," he said, "yes. The bailiff had twenty pounds all in gold; no one ever knew. I took it and was able to satisfy Wentworth for a bit."

"And what about Archibald Wentworth?"

"That was *his* doing, and I was to be paid."

"And now finally you wanted to get rid of me?"

"Yes; for you suspected."

As I spoke I perceived by the ghastly light of the moon another door near. I opened it and saw that it was the entrance to a small dark lumber room. I pushed the old man in, turned the key in the lock, and ran downstairs. The wife was still unaccountably absent. I opened the front door, and trembling, exhausted, drenched in perspiration, found myself in the open air. Every nerve was shaken. At that terrible moment I was not in the least master of myself. My one desire was to fly from the hideous place. I had just reached the little gate when a hand, light as a feather, touched my arm. I looked up; the girl Liz stood before me.

"You are saved," she said; "thank God! I tried all I could to stop the wheel. See, I am drenched to the skin; I could not manage it. But at least I locked Grannie up. She's in the kitchen, sound asleep. She drank a lot of gin."

"Where were you all day yesterday?" I asked.

"Locked up in a room in the further tower, but I managed to squeeze through the window, although it half killed me. I knew if you stayed that they would try it on tonight. Thank God you are saved."

"Well, don't keep me now," I said; "I have been saved as by a miracle. You are a good girl; I am much obliged to you. You must tell me another time how you manage to live through all these horrors."

"Ain't I all but mad?" was her pathetic reply. "Oh, my God, what I suffer!" She pressed her hand to her face; the look in her eyes was terrible. But I could not wait now to talk to her further. I hastily left the place.

How I reached Harkhurst I can never tell, but early in the morning I found myself there. I went straight to Dr. Stanmore's house, and having got him up, I communicated my story. He and I together immediately visited the superintendent of police. Having told my exciting tale, we took a trap and all three returned to the Castle Inn. We were back there before eight o'clock on the following morning. But as the police officer expected, the place was empty. Bindloss had been rescued from the dark closet, and he and his wife and the girl Liz had all flown. The doctor, the police officer, and I, all went up to the circular room. We then descended to the basement, and after a careful examination we discovered a low door, through which we crept; we then found ourselves in a dark vault, which was full of machinery. By the light of a lantern we examined it. Here we saw an explanation of the whole trick. The shaft of the mill wheel which was let through the wall of the tower was *continuous as the axle of a vertical cogged wheel*, and by a multiplication action turned a large horizontal wheel into which a vertical shaft descended. This shaft was let into the centre of four crossbeams, supporting the floor of the room in which I had slept. All round the circular edge of the floor was a steel rim which turned in a circular socket. It needed but a touch to set this hideous apparatus in motion.

The police immediately started in pursuit of Bindloss, and I returned to London. That evening Edgcombe and I visited Dr. Miles Gordon. Hard-headed old physician that he was, he was literally aghast when I told him my story. He explained to me that a man placed in the position in which I was when the floor began to move would by means of centrifugal force suffer from enormous congestion of the brain. In fact, the revolving floor would induce an artificial condition of apoplexy. If the victim were drugged or even only sleeping heavily, and the floor began to move slowly, insensibility would almost immediately be induced, which would soon pass into coma and death, and a post-mortem examination some hours afterwards would show no cause for death, as the brain would appear perfectly healthy, the blood having again left it.

From the presence of Dr. Miles Gordon, Edgcombe and I went to Scotland Yard, and the whole affair was put into the hands of the London detective force. With the clue which I had almost sacrificed my life to furnish, they quickly did the rest. Wentworth was arrested, and under pressure was induced to make a full confession, but old Bindloss had already told me the gist of the story. Wentworth's father had owned the mill, had got into trouble with the law, and changed his name. In fact, he had spent five years in penal servitude. He then went to Australia and made money. He died when his son was a young man. This youth inherited all the father's vices. He came home, visited the mill, and, being of a mechanical turn of mind, invented the revolving floor. He changed the mill into an inn, put Bindloss, one of his 'pals', into possession with the full intention of murdering unwary travellers from time to time for their money.

The police, however, wanted him for a forged bill, and he thought it best to fly. Bindloss was left in full possession. Worried by Wentworth, who had him in his power for a grave crime committed years ago, he himself on two occasions murdered a victim in the circular room. Meanwhile several unexpected deaths had taken place in the older branch of the Wentworth family, and Archibald Wentworth alone stood between his cousin and the great estates. Wentworth came home, and with the aid of Bindloss got Archibald into his power. The young artist slept in the fatal room, and his death was the result. At this moment Wentworth and Bindloss are committed for trial at the Old Bailey, and there is no doubt what the result will be.

The ghost mystery in connection with the Castle Inn has, of course, been explained away for ever.

Madame Sara

L.T. Meade and Robert Eustace

EVERYONE in trade and a good many who are not have heard of Werner's Agency, the Solvency Inquiry Agency for all British trade. Its business is to know the financial condition of all wholesale and retail firms, from Rothschild's to the smallest sweetstuff shop in Whitechapel. I do not say that every firm figures on its books, but by methods of secret inquiry it can discover the status of any firm or individual. It is the great safeguard to British trade and prevents much fraudulent dealing.

Of this agency I, Dixon Druce, was appointed manager in 1890. Since then I have met queer people and seen strange sights, for men do curious things for money in this world.

It so happened that in June, 1899, my business took me to Madeira on an inquiry of some importance. I left the island on the 14th of the month by the *Norham Castle* for Southampton. I embarked after dinner. It was a lovely night, and the strains of the band in the public gardens of Funchal came floating across the star-powdered bay through the warm, balmy air. Then the engine bells rang to 'Full speed ahead', and, flinging a farewell to the fairest island on earth, I turned to the smoking-room in order to light my cheroot.

"Do you want a match, sir?"

The voice came from a slender, young-looking man who stood near the taffrail. Before I could reply he had struck one and held it out to me.

"Excuse me," he said, as he tossed it overboard, "but surely I am addressing Mr. Dixon Druce?"

"You are, sir," I said, glancing keenly back at him, "but you have the advantage of me."

"Don't you know me?" he responded, "Jack Selby, Hayward's House, Harrow, 1879."

"By Jove! So it is," I cried.

Our hands met in a warm clasp, and a moment later I found myself sitting close to my old friend, who had fagged for me in the bygone days, and whom I had not seen from the moment when I said goodbye to the 'Hill' in the grey mist of a December morning twenty years ago. He was a boy of fourteen then, but nevertheless I recognised him. His face was bronzed and good-looking, his features refined. As a boy Selby had been noted for his grace, his well-shaped head, his clean-cut features; these characteristics still were his, and although he was now slightly past his first youth he was decidedly handsome. He gave me a quick sketch of his history.

"My father left me plenty of money," he said, "and The Meadows, our old family place, is now mine. I have a taste for natural history; that taste took me two years ago to South America. I have had my share of strange adventures, and have collected valuable specimens and trophies. I am now on my way home from Para, on the Amazon, having come by a Booth boat to Madeira and changed there to the Castle Line. But why all this talk about myself?" he added, bringing his deck chair a little nearer to mine. "What about your history, old chap? Are you settled down with a wife and kiddies of your own, or is that dream of your school days fulfilled, and are you the owner of the best private laboratory in London?"

"As to the laboratory," I said, with a smile, "you must come and see it. For the rest I am unmarried. Are you?"

"I was married the day before I left Para, and my wife is on board with me."

"Capital," I answered. "Let me hear all about it."

"You shall. Her maiden name was Dallas; Beatrice Dallas. She is just twenty now. Her father was an Englishman and her mother a Spaniard; neither parent is living. She has an elder sister, Edith, nearly thirty years of age, unmarried, who is on board with us. There is also a step-brother, considerably older than either Edith or Beatrice. I met my wife last year in Para, and at once fell in love. I am the happiest man on earth. It goes without saying that I think her beautiful, and she is also very well off. The story of her wealth is a curious one. Her uncle on the mother's side was an extremely wealthy Spaniard, who made an enormous fortune in Brazil out of diamonds and minerals; he owned several mines. But it is supposed that his wealth turned his brain. At any rate, it seems to have done so as far as the disposal of his money went. He divided the yearly profits and interest between his nephew and his two nieces, but declared that the property itself should never be split up. He has left the whole of it to that one of the three who should survive the others. A perfectly insane arrangement, but not, I believe, unprecedented in Brazil."

"Very insane," I echoed. "What was he worth?"

"Over two million sterling."

"By Jove!" I cried, "What a sum! But what about the half-brother?"

"He must be over forty years of age, and is evidently a bad lot. I have never seen him. His sisters won't speak to him or have anything to do with him. I understand that he is a great gambler; I am further told that he is at present in England, and, as there are certain technicalities to be gone through before the girls can fully enjoy their incomes, one of the first things I must do when I get home is to find him out. He has to sign certain papers, for we shan't be able to put things straight until we get his whereabouts. Some time ago my wife and Edith heard that he was ill, but dead or alive we must know all about him, and as quickly as possible."

I made no answer, and he continued:

"I'll introduce you to my wife and sister-in-law tomorrow. Beatrice is quite a child compared to Edith, who acts towards her almost like a mother. Bee is a little beauty, so fresh and round and young-looking. But Edith is handsome, too, although I sometimes think she is as vain as a peacock. By the way, Druce, this brings me to another part of my story. The sisters have an acquaintance on board, one of the most remarkable women I have ever met. She goes by the name of Madame Sara, and knows London well. In fact, she confesses to having a shop in the Strand. What she has been doing in Brazil I do not know, for she keeps all her affairs strictly private. But you will be amazed when I tell you what her calling is."

"What?" I asked.

"A professional beautifier. She claims the privilege of restoring youth to those who consult her. She also declares that she can make quite ugly people handsome. There is no doubt that she is very clever. She knows a little bit of everything, and has wonderful recipes with regard to medicines, surgery, and dentistry. She is a most lovely woman herself, very fair, with blue eyes, an innocent, childlike manner, and quantities of rippling gold hair. She openly confesses that she is very much older than she appears. She looks about five-and-twenty. She seems to have travelled all over the world, and says that by birth she is a mixture of Indian and Italian, her father having been Italian and her mother Indian. Accompanying her is an Arab, a handsome, picturesque sort of fellow, who gives her the most absolute devotion, and she is also bringing back to England two Brazilians from Para. This woman deals in all sorts of curious secrets, but principally in cosmetics. Her shop in the Strand could, I fancy, tell many a strange history. Her clients go to her there, and she does what is necessary for them. It is a fact that she occasionally performs small surgical operations, and there is not a dentist in London who can vie with her. She confesses quite naively that she holds some secrets for making false teeth cling to the palate that no one knows of. Edith Dallas is devoted to her – in fact, her adoration amounts to idolatry."

"You give a very brilliant account of this woman," I said. "You must introduce me tomorrow."

"I will," answered Jack, with a smile. "I should like your opinion of her. I am right glad I have met you, Druce, it is like old times. When we get to London I mean to put up at my town house in Eaton Square for the remainder of the season. The Meadows shall be re-furnished, and Bee and I will take up our quarters sometime in August; then you must come and see us. But I am afraid before I give myself up to mere pleasure I must find that precious brother-in-law, Henry Joachim Silva."

"If you have any difficulty apply to me," I said. "I can put at your disposal, in an unofficial way, of course, agents who would find almost any man in England, dead or alive." I then proceeded to give Selby a short account of my own business.

"Thanks," he said presently, 'that is capital. You are the very man we want."

The next morning after breakfast Jack introduced me to his wife and sister-in-law. They were both foreign-looking, but very handsome, and the wife in particular had a graceful and uncommon appearance. We had been chatting about five minutes when I saw coming down the deck a slight, rather small woman, wearing a big sun hat.

"Ah, Madame," cried Selby, "here you are. I had the luck to meet an old friend on board – Mr. Dixon Druce – and I have been telling him all about you. I should like you to know each other. Druce, this lady is Madame Sara, of whom I have spoken to you. Mr. Dixon Druce – Madame Sara."

She bowed gracefully and then looked at me earnestly. I had seldom seen a more lovely woman. By her side both Mrs. Selby and her sister seemed to fade into insignificance. Her complexion was almost dazzlingly fair, her face refined in expression, her eyes penetrating, clever, and yet with the innocent, frank gaze of a child. Her dress was very simple; she looked altogether like a young, fresh, and natural girl.

As we sat chatting lightly and about commonplace topics, I instinctively felt that she took an interest in me even greater than might be expected upon an ordinary introduction. By slow degrees she so turned the conversation as to leave Selby and his wife and sister out, and then as they moved away she came a little nearer, and said in a low voice:

"I am very glad we have met, and yet how odd this meeting is! Was it really accidental?"

"I do not understand you," I answered.

"I know who you are," she said, lightly. "You are the manager of Werner's Agency; its business is to know the private affairs of those people who would rather keep their own secrets. Now, Mr. Druce, I am going to be absolutely frank with you. I own a small shop in the Strand – a perfumery shop – and behind those innocent-looking doors I conduct the business which brings me in gold of the realm. Have you, Mr. Druce, any objection to my continuing to make a livelihood in perfectly innocent ways?"

"None whatever," I answered." You puzzle me by alluding to the subject."

"I want you to pay my shop a visit when you come to London. I have been away for three or four months. I do wonders for my clients, and they pay me largely for my services. I hold some perfectly innocent secrets which I cannot confide to anybody. I have obtained them partly from the Indians and partly from the natives of Brazil. I have lately been in Para to inquire into certain methods by which my trade can be improved."

"And your trade is—?" I said, looking at her with amusement and some surprise.

"I am a beautifier," she said, lightly. She looked at me with a smile. "You don't want me yet, Mr. Druce, but the time may come when even you will wish to keep back the infirmities of years. In the meantime can you guess my age?"

"I will not hazard a guess," I answered.

"And I will not tell you. Let it remain a secret. Meanwhile, understand that my calling is quite an open one, and I do hold secrets. I should advise you, Mr. Druce, even in your professional capacity, not to interfere with them."

The childlike expression faded from her face as she uttered the last words. There seemed to ring a sort of challenge in her tone. She turned away after a few moments and I rejoined my friends.

"You have been making acquaintance with Madame Sara, Mr. Druce," said Mrs. Selby. "Don't you think she is lovely?"

"She is one of the most beautiful women I have ever seen," I answered, "but there seems to be a mystery about her."

"Oh, indeed there is," said Edith Dallas, gravely.

"She asked me if I could guess her age," I continued. "I did not try, but surely she cannot be more than five-and-twenty."

"No one knows her age," said Mrs. Selby, "but I will tell you a curious fact, which, perhaps, you will not believe. She was bridesmaid at my mother's wedding thirty years ago. She declares that she never changes, and has no fear of old age."

"You mean that seriously?" I cried. "But surely it is impossible?"

"Her name is on the register, and my mother knew her well. She was mysterious then, and I think my mother got into her power, but of that I am not certain. Anyhow, Edith and I adore her, don't we, Edie?"

She laid her hand affectionately on her sister's arm. Edith Dallas did not speak, but her face was careworn. After a time she said slowly: "Madame Sara is uncanny and terrible."

There is, perhaps, no business imaginable – not even a lawyer's – that engenders suspicions more than mine. I hate all mysteries – both in persons and things. Mysteries are my natural enemies; I felt now that this woman was a distinct mystery. That she was interested in me I did not doubt, perhaps because she was afraid of me.

The rest of the voyage passed pleasantly enough. The more I saw of Mrs. Selby and her sister the more I liked them. They were quiet, simple, and straightforward. I felt sure that they were both as good as gold.

We parted at Waterloo, Jack and his wife and her sister going to Jack's house in Eaton Square, and I returning to my quarters in St. John's Wood. I had a house there, with a long garden, at the bottom of which was my laboratory, the laboratory that was the pride of my life, it being, I fondly considered, the best private laboratory in London. There I spent all my spare time making experiments and trying this chemical combination and the other, living in hopes of doing great things some day, for Werner's Agency was not to be the end of my career. Nevertheless, it interested me thoroughly, and I was not sorry to get back to my commercial conundrums.

The next day, just before I started to go to my place of business, Jack Selby was announced.

"I want you to help me," he said. "I have been already trying in a sort of general way to get information about my brother-in-law, but all in vain. There is no such person in any of the directories. Can you put me on the road to discovery?"

I said I could and would if he would leave the matter in my hands.

"With pleasure," he replied. "You see how we are fixed up. Neither Edith nor Bee can get money with any regularity until the man is found. I cannot imagine why he hides himself."

"I will insert advertisements in the personal columns of the newspapers," I said, "and request anyone who can give information to communicate with me at my office. I will also give instructions to all the branches of my firm, as well as to my head assistants in London, to keep their eyes open for any news. You may be quite certain that in a week or two we shall know all about him."

Selby appeared cheered at this proposal, and, having begged of me to call upon his wife and her sister as soon as possible, took his leave.

On that very day advertisements were drawn up and sent to several newspapers and inquiry agents; but week after week passed without the slightest result. Selby got very fidgety at the delay. He was never happy except in my presence, and insisted on my coming, whenever I had time, to his house. I was glad to do so, for I took an interest both in him and his belongings, and as to Madame Sara I could not get her out of my head. One day Mrs. Selby said to me:

"Have you ever been to see Madame? I know she would like to show you her shop and general surroundings."

"I did promise to call upon her," I answered, "but have not had time to do so yet."

"Will you come with me tomorrow morning?" asked Edith Dallas, suddenly.

She turned red as she spoke, and the worried, uneasy expression became more marked on her face. I had noticed for some time that she had been looking both nervous and depressed. I had first observed this peculiarity about her on board the *Norham Castle*, but, as time went on, instead of lessening it grew worse. Her face for so young a woman was haggard; she started at each sound, and Madame Sara's name was never spoken in her presence without her evincing almost undue emotion.

"Will you come with me?" she said, with great eagerness.

I immediately promised, and the next day, about eleven o'clock, Edith Dallas and I found ourselves in a hansom driving to Madame Sara's shop. We reached it in a few minutes, and found an unpretentious little place wedged in between a hosier's on one side and a cheap print-seller's on the other. In the windows of the shop were pyramids of perfume bottles, with scintillating facet stoppers tied with coloured ribbons. We stepped out of the hansom and went indoors. Inside the shop were a couple of steps, which led to a door of solid mahogany.

"This is the entrance to her private house," said Edith, and she pointed to a small brass plate, on which was engraved the name – 'Madame Sara, Parfumeuse'. Edith touched an electric bell and the door was immediately opened by a smartly-dressed page-boy. He looked at Miss Dallas as if he knew her very well, and said:

"Madame is within, and is expecting you, miss."

He ushered us both into a quiet-looking room, soberly but handsomely furnished. He left us, closing the door. Edith turned to me.

"Do you know where we are?" she asked.

"We are standing at present in a small room just behind Madame Sara's shop," I answered. "Why are you so excited, Miss Dallas? What is the matter with you?"

"We are on the threshold of a magician's cave," she replied. "We shall soon be face to face with the most marvellous woman in the whole of London. There is no one like her."

"And you – fear her?" I said, dropping my voice to a whisper.

She started, stepped back, and with great difficulty recovered her composure. At that moment the page-boy returned to conduct us through a series of small waiting rooms, and we soon found ourselves in the presence of Madame herself.

"Ah!" she said, with a smile. "This is delightful. You have kept your word, Edith, and I am greatly obliged to you. I will now show Mr. Druce some of the mysteries of my trade. But understand, sir," she added, 'that I shall not tell you any of my real secrets, only as you would like to know something about me you shall."

"How can you tell I should like to know about you?" I asked.

She gave me an earnest glance which somewhat astonished me, and then she said: "Knowledge is power; don't refuse what I am willing to give. Edith, you will not object to waiting here while I show Mr. Druce through the rooms. First observe this room, Mr. Druce. It is lighted only from the roof. When the door shuts it automatically locks itself, so that any intrusion from without is impossible. This is my *sanctum sanctorum* – a faint odour of perfume pervades the room. This is a hot day, but the room itself is cool. What do you think of it all?"

I made no answer. She walked to the other end and motioned to me to accompany her. There stood a polished oak square table, on which lay an array of extraordinary-looking articles and implements – stoppered bottles full of strange medicaments, mirrors, plane and concave, brushes, sprays, sponges, delicate needle-pointed instruments of bright steel, tiny lancets, and forceps. Facing this table was a chair, like those used by dentists. Above the chair hung electric lights in powerful reflectors, and lenses like bull's-eye lanterns. Another chair, supported on a glass pedestal, was kept there, Madame Sara informed me, for administering static electricity. There were dry-cell batteries for the continuous currents and induction coils for Faradic currents. There were also platinum needles for burning out the roots of hairs.

Madame took me from this room into another, where a still more formidable array of instruments was to be found. Here were a wooden operating table and chloroform and ether apparatus. When I had looked at everything, she turned to me.

"Now you know," she said. "I am a doctor – perhaps a quack. These are my secrets. By means of these I live and flourish."

She turned her back on me and walked into the other room with the light, springy step of youth. Edith Dallas, white as a ghost, was waiting for us.

"You have done your duty, my child," said Madame. "Mr. Druce has seen just what I want him to see. I am very much obliged to you both. We shall meet tonight at Lady Farringdon's 'At Home'. Until then, farewell."

When we got into the street and were driving back again to Eaton Square, I turned to Edith.

"Many things puzzle me about your friend," I said, "but perhaps none more than this. By what possible means can a woman who owns to being the possessor of a shop obtain the entrée to some of the best houses in London? Why does Society open her doors to this woman, Miss Dallas?"

"I cannot quite tell you," was her reply. "I only know the fact that wherever she goes she is welcomed and treated with consideration, and wherever she fails to appear there is a universally expressed feeling of regret."

I had also been invited to Lady Farringdon's reception that evening, and I went there in a state of great curiosity. There was no doubt that Madame interested me. I was not sure of her. Beyond doubt there was a mystery attached to her, and also, for some unaccountable reason, she wished both to propitiate and defy me. Why was this?

I arrived early, and was standing in the crush near the head of the staircase when Madame was announced. She wore the richest white satin and quantities of diamonds. I saw her hostess bend towards her and talk eagerly. I noticed Madame's reply and the pleased expression that crossed Lady Farringdon's face. A few minutes later a man with a foreign-looking face and long beard sat down before the grand piano. He played a light prelude and Madame Sara began to sing. Her voice was sweet and low, with an extraordinary pathos in it. It was the sort of voice that penetrates to the heart. There was an instant pause in the gay chatter. She sang amidst perfect silence, and when the song had come to an end there followed a furore of applause. I was just turning to say something to my nearest neighbour when I observed Edith Dallas, who was standing close by. Her eyes met mine; she laid her hand on my sleeve.

"The room is hot," she said, half panting as she spoke. "Take me out on the balcony."

I did so. The atmosphere of the reception rooms was almost intolerable, but it was comparatively cool in the open air.

"I must not lose sight of her," she said, suddenly.

"Of whom?" I asked, somewhat astonished at her words.

"Of Sara."

"She is there," I said. "You can see her from where you stand."

We happened to be alone. I came a little closer.

"Why are you afraid of her?" I asked.

"Are you sure that we shall not be heard?" was her answer. "She terrifies me," were her next words.

"I will not betray your confidence, Miss Dallas. Will you not trust me? You ought to give me a reason for your fears."

"I cannot – I dare not; I have said far too much already. Don't keep me, Mr. Druce. She must not find us together." As she spoke she pushed her way through the crowd, and before I could stop her was standing by Madame Sara's side.

The reception in Portland Place was, I remember, on the 26th of July. Two days later the Selbys were to give their final 'At Home' before leaving for the country. I was, of course, invited to be present, and Madame was also there. She had never been dressed more splendidly, nor had she ever before looked younger or more beautiful. Wherever she went all eyes followed her. As a rule her dress was simple, almost like what a girl would wear, but tonight she chose rich Oriental stuffs made of many colours, and absolutely glittering with gems. Her golden hair was studded with diamonds. Round her neck she wore turquoise and diamonds mixed. There were many younger women in the room, but not the youngest nor the fairest had a chance beside Madame. It was not mere beauty of appearance, it was charm – charm which carries all before it.

I saw Miss Dallas, looking slim and tall and pale, standing at a little distance. I made my way to her side. Before I had time to speak she bent towards me.

"Is she not divine?" she whispered. "She bewilders and delights everyone. She is taking London by storm."

"Then you are not afraid of her tonight?" I said.

"I fear her more than ever. She has cast a spell over me. But listen, she is going to sing again."

I had not forgotten the song that Madame had given us at the Farringdons', and stood still to listen. There was a complete hush in the room. Her voice floated over the heads of the assembled guests in a dreamy Spanish song. Edith told me that it was a slumber song, and that Madame boasted of her power of putting almost anyone to sleep who listened to her rendering of it.

"She has many patients who suffer from insomnia," whispered the girl, "and she generally cures them with that song, and that alone. Ah! We must not talk; she will hear us."

Before I could reply Selby came hurrying up. He had not noticed Edith. He caught me by the arm.

"Come just for a minute into this window, Dixon," he said. "I must speak to you. I suppose you have no news with regard to my brother-in-law?"

"Not a word," I answered.

"To tell you the truth, I am getting terribly put out over the matter. We cannot settle any of our money affairs just because this man chooses to lose himself. My wife's lawyers wired to Brazil yesterday, but even his bankers do not know anything about him."

"The whole thing is a question of time," was my answer. "When are you off to Hampshire?"

"On Saturday."

As Selby said the last words he looked around him, then he dropped his voice.

"I want to say something else. The more I see—" he nodded towards Madame Sara – "the less I like her. Edith is getting into a very strange state. Have you not noticed it? And the worst of it is my wife is also infected. I suppose it is that dodge of the woman's for patching people up and making them beautiful. Doubtless the temptation is overpowering in the case of a plain woman, but Beatrice is beautiful herself and young. What can she have to do with cosmetics and complexion pills?"

"You don't mean to tell me that your wife has consulted Madame Sara as a doctor?"

"Not exactly, but she has gone to her about her teeth. She complained of toothache lately, and Madame's dentistry is renowned. Edith is constantly going to her for one thing or another, but then Edith is infatuated."

As Jack said the last words he went over to speak to someone else, and before I could leave the seclusion of the window I perceived Edith Dallas and Madame Sara in earnest conversation together. I could not help overhearing the following words:

"Don't come to me tomorrow. Get into the country as soon as you can. It is far and away the best thing to do."

As Madame spoke she turned swiftly and caught my eye. She bowed, and the peculiar look, the sort of challenge, she had given me before flashed over her face. It made me uncomfortable, and during the night that followed I could not get it out of my head. I remembered what Selby had said with regard to his wife and her money affairs. Beyond doubt he had married into a mystery – a mystery that Madame knew all about. There was a very big money interest, and strange things happen when millions are concerned.

The next morning I had just risen and was sitting at breakfast when a note was handed to me. It came by special messenger, and was marked 'Urgent'. I tore it open. These were its contents:

> *My dear Druce, A terrible blow has fallen on us. My sister-in-law, Edith, was taken suddenly ill this morning at breakfast. The nearest doctor was sent for, but he could do nothing, as she died half an hour ago. Do come and see me, and if you know any very clever specialist bring him with you. My wife is utterly stunned by the shock. Yours, Jack Selby.*

I read the note twice before I could realize what it meant. Then I rushed out and, hailing the first hansom I met, said to the man: "Drive to No. 192, Victoria Street, as quickly as you can."

Here lived a certain Mr. Eric Vandeleur, an old friend of mine and the police surgeon for the Westminster district, which included Eaton Square. No shrewder or sharper fellow existed than

Vandeleur, and the present case was essentially in his province, both legally and professionally. He was not at his flat when I arrived, having already gone down to the court. Here I accordingly hurried, and was informed that he was in the mortuary.

For a man who, as it seemed to me, lived in a perpetual atmosphere of crime and violence, of death and coroners' courts, his habitual cheerfulness and brightness of manner were remarkable. Perhaps it was only the reaction from his work, for he had the reputation of being one of the most astute experts of the day in medical jurisprudence, and the most skilled analyst in toxicological cases on the Metropolitan Police staff. Before I could send him word that I wanted to see him I heard a door bang, and Vandeleur came hurrying down the passage, putting on his coat as he rushed along.

"Halloa!" he cried. "I haven't seen you for ages. Do you want me?"

"Yes, very urgently," I answered. "Are you busy?"

"Head over ears, my dear chap. I cannot give you a moment now, but perhaps later on."

"What is it? You look excited."

"I have got to go to Eaton Square like the wind, but come along, if you like, and tell me on the way."

"Capital," I cried. "The thing has been reported then? You are going to Mr. Selby's, No. 34a; then I am going with you."

He looked at me in amazement.

"But the case has only just been reported. What can you possibly know about it?"

"Everything. Let us take this hansom, and I will tell you as we go along."

As we drove to Eaton Square I quickly explained the situation, glancing now and then at Vandeleur's bright, clean-shaven face. He was no longer Eric Vandeleur, the man with the latest club story and the merry twinkle in his blue eyes: he was Vandeleur the medical jurist, with a face like a mask, his lower jaw slightly protruding and features very fixed.

"The thing promises to be serious," he replied, as I finished, "but I can do nothing until after the autopsy. Here we are, and there is my man waiting for me; he has been smart."

On the steps stood an official-looking man in uniform, who saluted.

"Coroner's officer," explained Vandeleur.

We entered the silent, darkened house. Selby was standing in the hall. He came to meet us. I introduced him to Vandeleur, and he at once led us into the dining room, where we found Dr. Osborne, whom Selby had called in when the alarm of Edith's illness had been first given. Dr. Osborne was a pale, under-sized, very young man. His face expressed considerable alarm. Vandeleur, however, managed to put him completely at his ease.

"I will have a chat with you in a few minutes, Dr. Osborne, he said; "but first I must get Mr. Selby's report. Will you please tell me, sir, exactly what occurred?"

"Certainly," he answered. "We had a reception here last night, and my sister-in-law did not go to bed until early morning; she was in bad spirits, but otherwise in her usual health. My wife went into her room after she was in bed, and told me later on that she had found Edith in hysterics, and could not get her to explain anything. We both talked about taking her to the country without delay. Indeed, our intention was to get off this afternoon."

"Well?" said Vandeleur.

"We had breakfast about half-past nine, and Miss Dallas came down, looking quite in her usual health, and in apparently good spirits. She ate with appetite, and, as it happened, she and my wife were both helped from the same dish. The meal had nearly come to an end when she jumped up from the table, uttered a sharp cry, turned very pale, pressed her hand to her side, and ran out of the room. My wife immediately followed her. She came back again in a minute or two, and said that Edith was in violent pain, and begged of me to send for a doctor. Dr. Osborne lives just round the corner. He came at once, but she died almost immediately after his arrival."

"You were in the room?" asked Vandeleur, turning to Osborne.

"Yes," he replied. "She was conscious to the last moment, and died suddenly."

"Did she tell you anything?"

"No, except to assure me that she had not eaten any food that day until she had come down to breakfast. After the death occurred I sent immediately to report the case, locked the door of the room where the poor girl's body is, and saw also that nobody touched anything on this table."

Vandeleur rang the bell and a servant appeared. He gave quick orders. The entire remains of the meal were collected and taken charge of, and then he and the coroner's officer went upstairs.

When we were alone Selby sank into a chair. His face was quite drawn and haggard.

"It is the horrible suddenness of the thing which is so appalling," he cried. "As to Beatrice, I don't believe she will ever be the same again. She was deeply attached to Edith. Edith was nearly ten years her senior, and always acted the part of mother to her. This is a sad beginning to our life. I can scarcely think collectedly."

I remained with him a little longer, and then, as Vandeleur did not return, went back to my own house. There I could settle to nothing, and when Vandeleur rang me up on the telephone about six o'clock I hurried off to his rooms. As soon as I arrived I saw that Selby was with him, and the expression on both their faces told me the truth.

"This is a bad business," said Vandeleur. "Miss Dallas has died from swallowing poison. An exhaustive analysis and examination have been made, and a powerful poison, unknown to European toxicologists, has been found. This is strange enough, but how it has been administered is a puzzle. I confess, at the present moment, we are all nonplussed. It certainly was not in the remains of the breakfast, and we have her dying evidence that she took nothing else. Now, a poison with such appalling potency would take effect quickly. It is evident that she was quite well when she came to breakfast, and that the poison began to work towards the close of the meal. But how did she get it? This question, however, I shall deal with later on. The more immediate point is this. The situation is a serious one in view of the monetary issues and the value of the lady's life. From the aspects of the case, her undoubted sanity and her affection for her sister, we may almost exclude the idea of suicide. We must, therefore, call it murder. This harmless, innocent lady is struck down by the hand of an assassin, and with such devilish cunning that no trace or clue is left behind. For such an act there must have been some very powerful motive, and the person who designed and executed it must be a criminal of the highest order of scientific ability. Mr. Selby has been telling me the exact financial position of the poor lady, and also of his own young wife. The absolute disappearance of the step-brother, in view of his previous character, is in the highest degree strange. Knowing, as we do, that between him and two million sterling there stood two lives – *one is taken!*"

A deadly sensation of cold seized me as Vandeleur uttered these last words. I glanced at Selby. His face was colourless and the pupils of his eyes were contracted, as though he saw something which terrified him.

"What happened once may happen again," continued Vandeleur. "We are in the presence of a great mystery, and I counsel you, Mr. Selby, to guard your wife with the utmost care."

These words, falling from a man of Vandeleur's position and authority on such matters, were sufficiently shocking for me to hear, but for Selby to be given such a solemn warning about his young and beautiful and newly-married wife, who was all the world to him, was terrible indeed. He leant his head on his hands.

"Mercy on us!" he muttered. "Is this a civilized country when death can walk abroad like this, invisible, not to be avoided? Tell me, Mr. Vandeleur, what I must do."

"You must be guided by me," said Vandeleur, "and, believe me, there is no witchcraft in the world. I shall place a detective in your household immediately. Don't be alarmed; he will come to you in plain clothes and will simply act as a servant. Nevertheless, nothing can be done to your wife without his knowledge. As to you, Druce," he continued, turning to me, "The police are doing all they can to find this man Silva, and I ask you to help them with your big agency, and to begin at once. Leave your friend to me. Wire instantly if you hear news."

"You may rely on me," I said, and a moment later I had left the room. As I walked rapidly down the street the thought of Madame Sara, her shop and its mysterious background, its surgical instruments, its operating table, its induction coils, came back to me. And yet what could Madame Sara have to do with the present strange, inexplicable mystery?

The thought had scarcely crossed my mind before I heard a clatter alongside the kerb, and turning round I saw a smart open carriage, drawn by a pair of horses, standing there. I also heard my own name. I turned. Bending out of the carriage was Madame Sara.

"I saw you going by, Mr. Druce. I have only just heard the news about poor Edith Dallas. I am terribly shocked and upset. I have been to the house, but they would not admit me. Have you heard what was the cause of her death?"

Madame's blue eyes filled with tears as she spoke.

"I am not at liberty to disclose what I have heard, Madame," I answered, "Since I am officially connected with the affair."

Her eyes narrowed. The brimming tears dried as though by magic. Her glance became scornful.

"Thank you," she answered, "your reply tells me that she did not die naturally. How very appalling! But I must not keep you. Can I drive you anywhere?"

"No, thank you."

"Goodbye, then."

She made a sign to the coachman, and as the carriage rolled away turned to look at me. Her face wore the defiant expression I had seen there more than once. Could she be connected with the affair? The thought came upon me with a violence that seemed almost conviction. Yet I had no reason for it – none.

To find Henry Joachim Silva was now my principal thought. My staff had instructions to make every possible inquiry, with large money rewards as incitements. The collateral branches of other agencies throughout Brazil were communicated with by cable, and all the Scotland Yard channels were used. Still there was no result. The newspapers took up the case; there were paragraphs in most of them with regard to the missing step-brother and the mysterious death of Edith Dallas. Then someone got hold of the story of the will, and this was retailed with many additions for the benefit of the public. At the inquest the jury returned the following verdict:

"We find that Miss Edith Dallas died from taking poison of unknown name, but by whom or how administered there is no evidence to say."

This unsatisfactory state of things was destined to change quite suddenly. On the 6th of August, as I was seated in my office, a note was brought me by a private messenger. It was as follows:

Norfolk Hotel, Strand.

Dear Sir – I have just arrived in London from Brazil, and have seen your advertisements. I was about to insert one myself in order to find the whereabouts of my sisters. I am a great invalid and unable to leave my room. Can you come to see me at the earliest possible moment? Yours, Henry Joachim Silva.

In uncontrollable excitement I hastily dispatched two telegrams, one to Selby and the other to Vandeleur, begging of them to be with me, without fail, as soon as possible. So the man had never been in England at all. The situation was more bewildering than ever. One thing, at least, was probable – Edith Dallas's death was not due to her step-brother. Soon after half-past six Selby arrived, and Vandeleur walked in ten minutes later. I told them what had occurred and showed them the letter. In half an hour's time we reached the hotel, and on stating who I was we were shown into a room on the first floor by Silva's private servant. Resting in an armchair, as we entered, sat a man; his face was terribly thin. The eyes and cheeks were so sunken that the face had almost the appearance of a skull. He made no effort to rise when we entered, and glanced from one of us to the other with the utmost astonishment. I at once introduced myself and explained who we were. He then waved his hand for his man to retire.

"You have heard the news, of course, Mr. Silva?" I said.

"News! What?" He glanced up to me and seemed to read something in my face. He started back in his chair.

"Good heavens," he replied. "Do you allude to my sisters? Tell me, quickly, are they alive?"

"Your elder sister died on the 29th of July, and there is every reason to believe that her death was caused by foul play."

As I uttered these words the change that passed over his face was fearful to witness. He did not speak, but remained motionless. His claw-like hands clutched the arms of the chair, his eyes were fixed and staring, as though they would start from their hollow sockets, the colour of his skin was like clay. I heard Selby breathe quickly behind me, and Vandeleur stepped towards the man and laid his hand on his shoulder.

"Tell us what you know of this matter," he said sharply.

Recovering himself with an effort, the invalid began in a tremulous voice: "Listen closely, for you must act quickly. I am indirectly responsible for this fearful thing. My life has been a wild and wasted one, and now I am dying. The doctors tell me I cannot live a month, for I have a large aneurism of the heart. Eighteen months ago I was in Rio. I was living fast and gambled heavily. Among my fellow-gamblers was a man much older than myself. His name was José Aranjo. He was, if anything, a greater gambler than I. One night we played alone. The stakes ran high until they reached a big figure. By daylight I had lost to him nearly £200,000. Though I am a rich man in point of income under my uncle's will, I could not pay a twentieth part of that sum. This man knew my financial position, and, in addition to a sum of £5,000 paid down, I gave him a document. I must have been mad to do so. The document was this – it was duly witnessed and attested by a lawyer – that, in the event of my surviving my two sisters and thus inheriting the whole of my uncle's vast wealth, half a million should go to José Aranjo. I felt I was breaking up at the time, and the chances of my inheriting the money were small. Immediately after the completion of the document this man left Rio, and I then heard a great deal about him that I had not previously known. He was a man of the queerest antecedents, partly Indian, partly Italian. He had spent many years of his life amongst the Indians. I heard also that he was as cruel as he was clever, and possessed some wonderful secrets of poisoning unknown to the West. I thought a great deal about this, for I knew that by signing that document I had placed the lives of my two sisters between him and a fortune. I came to Para six weeks ago, only to learn that one of my sisters was married and that both had gone to England. Ill as I was, I determined to follow them in order to warn them. I also wanted to arrange matters with you, Mr. Selby."

"One moment, sir," I broke in, suddenly. "Do you happen to be aware if this man, José Aranjo, knew a woman calling herself Madame Sara?"

"Knew her?" cried Silva. "Very well indeed, and so, for that matter, did I. Aranjo and Madame Sara were the best friends, and constantly met. She called herself a professional beautifier – was very handsome, and had secrets for the pursuing of her trade unknown even to Aranjo."

"Good heavens!" I cried, "And the woman is now in London. She returned here with Mrs. Selby and Miss Dallas. Edith was very much influenced by her, and was constantly with her. There is no doubt in my mind that she is guilty. I have suspected her for some time, but I could not find a motive. Now the motive appears. You surely can have her arrested?"

Vandeleur made no reply. He gave me a strange look, then he turned to Selby.

"Has your wife also consulted Madame Sara?" he asked, sharply.

"Yes, she went to her once about her teeth, but has not been to the shop since Edith's death. I begged of her not to see the woman, and she promised me faithfully she would not do so."

"Has she any medicines or lotions given to her by Madame Sara – does she follow any line of treatment advised by her?"

"No, I am certain on that point."

"Very well. I will see your wife tonight in order to ask her some questions. You must both leave town at once. Go to your country house and settle there. I am quite serious when I say that Mrs. Selby is in the utmost possible danger until after the death of her brother. We must leave you now, Mr. Silva. All business affairs must wait for the present. It is absolutely necessary that Mrs. Selby should leave London at once. Goodnight, sir. I shall give myself the pleasure of calling on you tomorrow morning."

We took leave of the sick man. As soon as we got into the street Vandeleur stopped.

"I must leave it to you, Selby," he said, 'to judge how much of this matter you tell to your wife. Were I you I would explain everything. The time for immediate action has arrived, and she is a brave and sensible woman. From this moment you must watch all the foods and liquids that she takes. She must never be out of your sight or out of the sight of some other trustworthy companion."

"I shall, of course, watch my wife myself," said Selby. "But the thing is enough to drive one mad."

"I will go with you to the country, Selby," I said, suddenly.

"Ah!" cried Vandeleur, "That is the best thing possible, and what I wanted to propose. Go, all of you, by an early train tomorrow."

"Then I will be off home at once, to make arrangements," I said. "I will meet you, Selby, at Waterloo for the first train to Cronsmoor tomorrow."

As I was turning away Vandeleur caught my arm.

"I am glad you are going with them," he said. "I shall write to you tonight re instructions. Never be without a loaded revolver. Goodnight." By 6:15 the next morning Selby, his wife, and I were in a reserved, locked, first-class compartment, speeding rapidly west. The servants and Mrs. Selby's own special maid were in a separate carriage. Selby's face showed signs of a sleepless night, and presented a striking contrast to the fair, fresh face of the girl round whom this strange battle raged. Her husband had told her everything, and, though still suffering terribly from the shock and grief of her sister's death, her face was calm and full of repose. A carriage was waiting for us at Cronsmoor, and by half-past nine we arrived at the old home of the Selbys, nestling amid its oaks and elms. Everything was done to make the home-coming of the bride as cheerful as circumstances would permit, but a gloom, impossible to lift, overshadowed Selby himself. He could scarcely rouse himself to take the slightest interest in anything.

The following morning I received a letter from Vandeleur. It was very short, and once more impressed on me the necessity of caution. He said that two eminent physicians had examined Silva, and the verdict was that he could not live a month. Until his death precautions must be strictly observed.

The day was cloudless, and after breakfast I was just starting out for a stroll when the butler brought me a telegram. I tore it open; it was from Vandeleur:

"Prohibit all food until I arrive. Am coming down," were the words. I hurried into the study and gave it to Selby. He read it and looked up at me.

"Find out the first train and go and meet him, old chap," he said. "Let us hope that this means an end of the hideous affair."

I went into the hall and looked up the trains. The next arrived at Cronsmoor at 10:45. I then strolled round to the stables and ordered a carriage, after which I walked up and down on the drive. There was no doubt that something strange had happened. Vandeleur coming down so suddenly must mean a final clearing up of the mystery. I had just turned round at the lodge gates to wait for the carriage when the sound of wheels and of horses galloping struck on my ears. The gates were swung open, and Vandeleur in an open fly dashed through them. Before I could recover from my surprise he was out of the vehicle and at my side. He carried a small black bag in his hand.

"I came down by special train," he said, speaking quickly. "There is not a moment to lose. Come at once. Is Mrs. Selby all right?"

"What do you mean?" I replied. "Of course she is. Do you suppose that she is in danger?"

"Deadly," was his answer. "Come."

We dashed up to the house together. Selby, who had heard our steps, came to meet us.

"Mr. Vandeleur," he cried. "What is it? How did you come?"

"By special train, Mr. Selby. And I want to see your wife at once. It will be necessary to perform a very trifling operation."

"Operation!" he exclaimed. "Yes; at once."

We made our way through the hall and into the morning-room, where Mrs. Selby was busily engaged reading and answering letters. She started up when she saw Vandeleur and uttered an exclamation of surprise.

"What has happened?" she asked. Vandeleur went up to her and took her hand.

"Do not be alarmed," he said, "for I have come to put all your fears to rest. Now, please, listen to me. When you visited Madame Sara with your sister, did you go for medical advice?"

The colour rushed into her face.

"One of my teeth ached," she answered. "I went to her about that. She is, as I suppose you know, a most wonderful dentist. She examined the tooth, found that it required stopping, and got an assistant, a Brazilian, I think, to do it."

"And your tooth has been comfortable ever since?"

"Yes, quite. She had one of Edith's stopped at the same time."

"Will you kindly sit down and show me which was the tooth into which the stopping was put?"

She did so.

"This was the one," she said, pointing with her finger to one in the lower jaw. "What do you mean? Is there anything wrong?"

Vandeleur examined the tooth long and carefully. There was a sudden rapid movement of his hand, and a sharp cry from Mrs. Selby. With the deftness of long practice, and a powerful wrist, he had extracted the tooth with one wrench. The suddenness of the whole thing, startling as it was, was not so strange as his next movement.

"Send Mrs. Selby's maid to her," he said, turning to her husband; "Then come, both of you, into the next room."

The maid was summoned. Poor Mrs. Selby had sunk back in her chair, terrified and half fainting. A moment later Selby joined us in the dining room.

"That's right," said Vandeleur; "close the door, will you?"

He opened his black bag and brought out several instruments. With one he removed the stopping from the tooth. It was quite soft and came away easily. Then from the bag he produced a small guinea-pig, which he requested me to hold. He pressed the sharp instrument into the tooth, and opening the mouth of the little animal placed the point on the tongue. The effect was instantaneous. The little head fell on to one of my hands – the guinea-pig was dead. Vandeleur was white as a sheet. He hurried up to Selby and wrung his hand.

"Thank heaven!" he said, "I've been in time, but only just. Your wife is safe. This stopping would hardly have held another hour. I have been thinking all night over the mystery of your sister-in-law's death, and over every minute detail of evidence as to how the poison could have been administered. Suddenly the coincidence of both sisters having had their teeth stopped struck me as remarkable. Like a flash the solution came to me. The more I considered it the more I felt that I was right; but by what fiendish cunning such a scheme could have been conceived and executed is still beyond my power to explain. The poison is very like hyoscine, one of the worst toxic-alkaloids known, so violent in its deadly proportions that the amount that would go into a tooth would cause almost instant death. It has been kept in by a gutta-percha stopping, certain to come out within a month, probably earlier, and most probably during mastication of food. The person would die either immediately or after a very few minutes, and no one would connect a visit to the dentist with a death a month afterwards."

What followed can be told in a very few words. Madame Sara was arrested on suspicion. She appeared before the magistrate, looking innocent and beautiful, and managed during her evidence completely to baffle that acute individual. She denied nothing, but declared that the poison must have been put into the tooth by one of the two Brazilians whom she had lately engaged to help her with her dentistry. She had her suspicions with regard to these men soon afterwards, and had dismissed them. She believed that they were in the pay of José Aranjo, but she could not tell anything for certain. Thus Madame escaped conviction. I was certain that she was guilty, but there was not a shadow of real proof. A month later Silva died, and Selby is now a double millionaire.

The Narrative of Mr. James Rigby

Arthur Morrison

I SHALL HERE set down in language as simple and straightforward as I can command, the events which followed my recent return to England; and I shall leave it to others to judge whether or not my conduct has been characterised by foolish fear and ill-considered credulity. At the same time I have my own opinion as to what would have been the behaviour of any other man of average intelligence and courage in the same circumstances; more especially a man of my exceptional upbringing and retired habits.

I was born in Australia, and I have lived there all my life till quite recently, save for a single trip to Europe as a boy, in company with my father and mother. It was then that I lost my father. I was less than nine years old at the time, but my memory of the events of that European trip is singularly vivid.

My father had emigrated to Australia at the time of his marriage, and had become a rich man by singularly fortunate speculations in land in and about Sydney. As a family we were most uncommonly self-centred and isolated. From my parents I never heard a word as to their relatives in England; indeed to this day I do not as much as know what was the Christian name of my grandfather. I have often supposed that some serious family quarrel or great misfortune must have preceded or accompanied my father's marriage. Be that as it may, I was never able to learn anything of my relatives, either on my mother's or my father's side. Both parents, however, were educated people, and indeed I fancy that their habit of seclusion must first have arisen from this circumstance, since the colonists about them in the early days, excellent people as they were, were not as a class distinguished for extreme intellectual culture. My father had his library stocked from England, and added to by fresh arrivals from time to time; and among his books he would pass most of his days, taking, however, now and again an excursion with a gun in search of some new specimen to add to his museum of natural history, which occupied three long rooms in our house by the Lane Cove river.

I was, as I have said, eight years of age when I started with my parents on a European tour, and it was in the year 1873. We stayed but a short while in England at first arrival, intending to make a longer stay on our return from the Continent. We made our tour, taking Italy last, and it was here that my father encountered a dangerous adventure.

We were at Naples, and my father had taken an odd fancy for a picturesque-looking ruffian who had attracted his attention by a complexion unusually fair for an Italian, and in whom he professed to recognise a likeness to Tasso the poet. This man became his guide in excursions about the neighbourhood of Naples, though he was not one of the regular corps of guides, and indeed seemed to have no regular occupation of a definite sort. 'Tasso', as my father always called him, seemed a civil fellow enough, and was fairly intelligent; but my mother disliked him extremely from the first, without being able to offer any very distinct reason for her aversion. In the event her instinct was proved true.

'Tasso' – his correct name, by the way, was Tommaso Marino – persuaded my father that something interesting was to be seen at the Astroni crater, four miles west of the city, or thereabout; persuaded him, moreover, to make the journey on foot; and the two accordingly set out. All went well enough till the crater was reached, and then, in a lonely and broken part of the hill, the guide suddenly turned and attacked my father with a knife, his intention, without a doubt, being murder and the acquisition of the Englishman's valuables. Fortunately my father had a hip-pocket with a revolver in it, for he had been warned of the danger a stranger might at that time run wandering in the country about Naples. He received a wound in the flesh of his left arm in an attempt to ward off a stab, and fired, at wrestling distance, with the result that his assailant fell dead on the spot. He left the place with all speed, tying up his arm as he went, sought the British consul at Naples, and informed him of the whole circumstances. From the authorities there was no great difficulty. An examination or two, a few signatures, some particular exertions on the part of the consul, and my father was free, so far as the officers of the law were concerned. But while these formalities were in progress no less than three attempts were made on his life – two by the knife and one by shooting – and in each his escape was little short of miraculous. For the dead ruffian, Marino, had been a member of the dreaded Camorra, and the Camorristi were eager to avenge his death. To anybody acquainted with the internal history of Italy – more particularly the history of the old kingdom of Naples – the name of the Camorra will be familiar enough. It was one of the worst and most powerful of the many powerful and evil secret societies of Italy, and had none of the excuses for existence which have been from time to time put forward on behalf of the others. It was a gigantic club for the commission of crime and the extortion of money. So powerful was it that it actually imposed a regular tax on all food material entering Naples – a tax collected and paid with far more regularity than were any of the taxes due to the lawful Government of the country. The carrying of smuggled goods was a monopoly of the Camorra, a perfect organisation existing for the purpose throughout the kingdom. The whole population was terrorised by this detestable society, which had no less than twelve centres in the city of Naples alone. It contracted for the commission of crime just as systematically and calmly as a railway company contracts for the carriage of merchandise. A murder was so much, according to circumstances, with extras for disposing of the body; arson was dealt in profitably; maimings and kidnappings were carried out with promptitude and despatch; and any diabolical outrage imaginable was a mere matter of price. One of the staple vocations of the concern was of course brigandage. After the coming of Victor Emanuel and the fusion of Italy into one kingdom the Camorra lost some of its power, but for a long time gave considerable trouble. I have heard that in the year after the matters I am describing two hundred Camorristi were banished from Italy.

As soon as the legal forms were complied with, my father received the broadest possible official hint that the sooner and the more secretly he left the country the better it would be for himself and his family. The British consul, too, impressed it upon him that the law would be entirely unable to protect him against the machinations of the Camorra; and indeed it needed but little persuasion to induce us to leave, for my poor mother was in a state of constant terror lest we were murdered together in our hotel; so that we lost no time in returning to England and bringing our European trip to a close.

In London we stayed at a well-known private hotel near Bond Street. We had been but three days here when my father came in one evening with a firm conviction that he had been followed for something like two hours, and followed very skilfully too. More than once he had doubled suddenly with a view to confront the pursuers, who he felt were at his heels, but he had met nobody of a suspicious appearance. The next afternoon I heard my mother telling my governess (who was travelling with us) of an unpleasant-looking man, who had been hanging about opposite the hotel door, and who, she felt sure, had afterwards been following her and my father as they were walking. My mother grew nervous, and communicated her fears to my father. He, however, pooh-poohed the thing, and took little thought of its meaning. Nevertheless the dogging continued, and my father, who was never able to fix upon the persons who caused the annoyance – indeed he rather felt their presence by instinct, as one does in such cases, than otherwise – grew extremely angry, and had some idea of consulting the police. Then one morning my mother discovered a little paper label stuck on the outside of the door of the bedroom occupied by herself and my father. It was a small thing, circular, and about the size of a sixpenny-piece, or even smaller, but my mother was quite certain that it had not been there when she last entered the door the night before, and she was much terrified. For the label carried a tiny device, drawn awkwardly in ink – a pair of knives of curious shape, crossed: the sign of the Camorra.

Nobody knew anything of this label, or how it came where it had been found. My mother urged my father to place himself under the protection of the police at once, but he delayed. Indeed, I fancy he had a suspicion that the label might be the production of some practical joker staying at the hotel who had heard of his Neapolitan adventure (it was reported in many newspapers) and designed to give him a fright. But that very evening my poor father was found dead, stabbed in a dozen places, in a short, quiet street not forty yards from the hotel. He had merely gone out to buy a few cigars of a particular brand which he fancied, at a shop two streets away, and in less than half an hour of his departure the police were at the hotel door with the news of his death, having got his address from letters in his pockets.

It is no part of my present design to enlarge on my mother's grief, or to describe in detail the incidents that followed my father's death, for I am going back to this early period of my life merely to make more clear the bearings of what has recently happened to myself. It will be sufficient therefore to say that at the inquest the jury returned a verdict of wilful murder against some person or persons unknown; that it was several times reported that the police had obtained a most important clue, and that being so, very naturally there was never any arrest. We returned to Sydney, and there I grew up.

I should perhaps have mentioned ere this that my profession – or I should rather say my hobby – is that of an artist. Fortunately or unfortunately, as you may please to consider it, I have no need to follow any profession as a means of livelihood, but since I was sixteen years of age my whole time has been engrossed in drawing and painting. Were it not for my mother's invincible objection to parting with me, even for the shortest space of time, I should long ago have come to Europe to work and to study in the regular schools. As it was I made shift to do my best in Australia, and wandered about pretty freely, struggling with the difficulties of moulding into artistic form the curious Australian landscape. There is an odd, desolate, uncanny note in characteristic Australian scenery, which most people are apt to regard as of little value for the purposes of the landscape painter, but with which I have always been convinced that an able painter could do great things. So I did my feeble best.

Two years ago my mother died. My age was then twenty-eight, and I was left without a friend in the world, and, so far as I know, without a relative. I soon found it impossible any longer to inhabit the large house by the Lane Cove river. It was beyond my simple needs, and the whole thing was an embarrassment, to say nothing of the associations of the house with my dead mother, which exercised a painful and depressing effect on me. So I sold the house, and cut myself adrift. For a year or more I pursued the life of a lonely vagabond in New South Wales, painting as well as I could its scattered forests of magnificent trees, with their curious upturned foliage. Then, miserably dissatisfied with my performance, and altogether filled with a restless spirit, I determined to quit the colony and live in England, or at any rate somewhere in Europe.

I would paint at the Paris schools, I promised myself, and acquire that technical mastery of my material that I now felt the lack of.

The thing was no sooner resolved on than begun. I instructed my solicitors in Sydney to wind up my affairs and to communicate with their London correspondents in order that, on my arrival in England, I might deal with business matters through them. I had more than half resolved to transfer all my property to England, and to make the old country my permanent headquarters; and in three weeks from the date of my resolve I had started. I carried with me the necessary letters of introduction to the London solicitors, and the deeds appertaining to certain land in South Australia, which my father had bought just before his departure on the fatal European trip. There was workable copper in this land, it had since been ascertained, and I believed I might profitably dispose of the property to a company in London.

I found myself to some extent out of my element on board a great passenger steamer. It seemed no longer possible for me in the constant association of shipboard to maintain that reserve which had become with me a second nature. But so much had it become my nature that I shrank ridiculously from breaking it, for, grown man as I was, it must be confessed that I was absurdly shy, and indeed I fear little better than an overgrown schoolboy in my manner. But somehow I was scarce a day at sea before falling into a most pleasant acquaintanceship with another passenger, a man of thirty-eight or forty, whose name was Dorrington. He was a tall, well-built fellow, rather handsome, perhaps, except for a certain extreme roundness of face and fulness of feature; he had a dark military moustache, and carried himself erect, with a swing as of a cavalryman, and his eyes had, I think, the most penetrating quality I ever saw. His manners were extremely engaging, and he was the only good talker I had ever met. He knew everybody, and had been everywhere. His fund of illustration and anecdote was inexhaustible, and during all my acquaintance with him I never heard him tell the same story twice. Nothing could happen – not a bird could fly by the ship, not a dish could be put on the table, but Dorrington was ready with a pungent remark and the appropriate anecdote. And he never bored nor wearied one. With all his ready talk he never appeared unduly obtrusive nor in the least egotistic. Mr. Horace Dorrington was altogether the most charming person I had ever met. Moreover we discovered a community of taste in cigars.

"By the way," said Dorrington to me one magnificent evening as we leaned on the rail and smoked, "Rigby isn't a very common name in Australia, is it? I seem to remember a case, twenty years ago or more, of an Australian gentleman of that name being very badly treated in London – indeed, now I think of it, I'm not sure that he wasn't murdered. Ever hear anything of it?"

"Yes," I said, "I heard a great deal, unfortunately. He was my father, and he *was* murdered."

"Your father? There – I'm awfully sorry. Perhaps I shouldn't have mentioned it; but of course I didn't know."

"Oh," I replied, "that's all right. It's so far back now that I don't mind speaking about it. It was a very extraordinary thing altogether." And then, feeling that I owed Dorrington a story of some sort, after listening to the many he had been telling me, I described to him the whole circumstances of my father's death.

"Ah," said Dorrington when I had finished, "I have heard of the Camorra before this – I know a thing or two about it, indeed. As a matter of fact it still exists; not quite the widespread and open thing it once was, of course, and much smaller; but pretty active in a quiet way, and pretty mischievous. They were a mighty bad lot, those Camorristi. Personally I'm rather surprised that you heard no more of them. They were the sort of people who would rather any day murder three people than one, and their usual idea of revenge went a good way beyond the mere murder of the offending party; they had a way of including his wife and family, and as many relatives as possible. But at any rate *you* seem to have got off all right, though I'm inclined to call it rather a piece of luck than otherwise."

Then, as was his invariable habit, he launched into anecdote. He told me of the crimes of the Maffia, that Italian secret society, larger even and more powerful than the Camorra, and almost as criminal; tales of implacable revenge visited on father, son, and grandson in succession, till the race was extirpated. Then he talked of the methods; of the large funds at the disposal of the Camorra and the Maffia, and of the cunning patience with which their schemes were carried into execution; of the victims who had discovered too late that their most trusted servants were sworn to their destruction, and of those who had fled to remote parts of the earth and hoped to be lost and forgotten, but who had been shadowed and slain with barbarous ferocity in their most trusted hiding-places. Wherever Italians were, there was apt to be a branch of one of the societies, and one could never tell where they might or might not turn up. The two Italian forecastle hands on board at that moment might be members, and might or might not have some business in hand not included in their signed articles.

I asked if he had ever come into personal contact with either of these societies or their doings.

"With the Camorra, no, though I know things about them that would probably surprise some of them not a little. But I have had professional dealings with the Maffia – and that without coming off second-best, too. But it was not so serious a case as your father's; one of a robbery of documents and blackmail."

"Professional dealings?" I queried.

Dorrington laughed. "Yes," he answered. "I find I've come very near to letting the cat out of the bag. I don't generally tell people who I am when I travel about, and indeed I don't always use my own name, as I am doing now. Surely you've heard the name at some time or another?"

I had to confess that I did not remember it. But I excused myself by citing my secluded life, and the fact that I had never left Australia since I was a child.

"Ah," he said, "of course we should be less heard of in Australia. But in England we're really pretty well known, my partner and I. But, come now, look me all over and consider, and I'll give you a dozen guesses and bet you a sovereign you can't tell me my trade. And it's not such an uncommon or unheard-of trade, neither."

Guessing would have been hopeless, and I said so. He did not seem the sort of man who would trouble himself about a trade at all. I gave it up.

"Well," he said, "I've no particular desire to have it known all over the ship, but I don't mind telling you – you'd find it out probably before long if you settle in the old country – that we are what is called private inquiry agents – detectives – secret service men – whatever you like to call it."

"Indeed!"

"Yes, indeed. And I think I may claim that we stand as high as any – if not a trifle higher. Of course I can't tell you, but you'd be rather astonished if you heard the names of some of our clients. We have had dealings with certain royalties, European and Asiatic, that would startle you a bit if I could tell them. Dorrington & Hicks is the name of the firm, and we are both pretty busy men, though we keep going a regiment of assistants and correspondents. I have been in Australia three months over a rather awkward and complicated matter, but I fancy I've pulled it through pretty well, and I mean to reward myself with a little holiday when I get back. There – now you know the worst of me. And D. & H. present their respectful compliments, and trust that by unfailing punctuality and a strict attention to business they may hope to receive your esteemed commands whenever you may be so unfortunate as to require their services. Family secrets extracted, cleaned, scaled, or stopped with gold. Special attention given to wholesale orders." He laughed and pulled out his cigar case. "You haven't another cigar in your pocket," he said, "or you wouldn't smoke that stump so low. Try one of these."

I took the cigar and lit it at my remainder. "Ah, then," I said, "I take it that it is the practice of your profession that has given you such a command of curious and out-of-the-way information and anecdote. Plainly you must have been in the midst of many curious affairs."

"Yes, I believe you," Dorrington replied. "But, as it happens, the most curious of my experiences I am unable to relate, since they are matters of professional confidence. Such as I *can* tell I usually tell with altered names, dates, and places. One learns discretion in such a trade as mine."

"As to your adventure with the Maffia, now. Is there any secrecy about that?"

Dorrington shrugged his shoulders. "No," he said, "none in particular. But the case was not particularly interesting. It was in Florence. The documents were the property of a wealthy American, and some of the Maffia rascals managed to steal them. It doesn't matter what the documents were – that's a private matter – but their owner would have parted with a great deal to get them back, and the Maffia held them for ransom. But they had such a fearful notion of the American's wealth, and of what he ought to pay, that, badly as he wanted the papers back, he couldn't stand their demands, and employed us to negotiate and to do our best for him. I think I might have managed to get the things stolen back again – indeed I spent some time thinking a plan over – but I decided in the end that it wouldn't pay. If the Maffia were tricked in that way they might consider it appropriate to stick somebody with a knife, and that was not an easy thing to provide against. So I took a little time and went another way to work. The details don't matter – they're quite uninteresting, and to tell you them would be to talk mere professional 'shop'; there's a deal of dull and patient work to be done in my business. Anyhow, I contrived to find out exactly in whose hands the documents lay. He wasn't altogether a blameless creature, and there were two or three little things that, properly handled, might have brought him into awkward complications with the law. So I delayed the negotiations while I got my nets effectually round this gentleman, who was the president of that particular branch of the Maffia, and when all was ready I had a friendly interview with him, and just showed him my hand of cards. They served as no other argument would have done, and in the end we concluded quite an amicable arrangement on easy terms for both parties, and my client got his property back, including all expenses, at about a fifth of the price he expected to have to pay. That's all. I learnt a deal about the Maffia while the business lasted, and at that and other times I learnt a good deal about the Camorra too."

Dorrington and I grew more intimate every day of the voyage, till he knew every detail of my uneventful little history, and I knew many of his own most curious experiences. In truth he was a man with an irresistible fascination for a dull home-bird like myself. With all his gaiety he never forgot business, and at most of our stopping places he sent off messages by cable to his partner. As the voyage drew near its end he grew anxious and impatient lest he should not arrive in time to enable him to get to Scotland for grouse-shooting on the twelfth of August. His one amusement, it seemed, was shooting, and the holiday he had promised himself was to be spent on a grouse-moor which he rented in Perthshire. It would be a great nuisance to miss the twelfth, he said, but it would apparently be a near-shave. He thought, however, that in any case it might be done by leaving the ship at Plymouth, and rushing up to London by the first train.

"Yes," he said, "I think I shall be able to do it that way, even if the boat is a couple of days late. By the way," he added suddenly, "why not come along to Scotland with me? You haven't any particular business in hand, and I can promise you a week or two of good fun."

The invitation pleased me. "It's very good of you," I said, "and as a matter of fact I haven't any very urgent business in London. I must see those solicitors I told you of, but that's not a matter of hurry; indeed an hour or two on my way through London would be enough. But as I don't know any of your party and—"

"Pooh, pooh, my dear fellow," answered Dorrington, with a snap of his fingers, "that's all right. I shan't have a party. There won't be time to get it together. One or two might come down a little later, but if they do they'll be capital fellows, delighted to make your acquaintance, I'm sure. Indeed you'll do me a great favour if you'll come, else I shall be all alone, without a soul to say a word to. Anyway, I *won't* miss the twelfth, if it's to be done by any possibility. You'll really have to come, you know – you've no excuse. I can lend you guns and anything you want, though I believe you've such things with you. Who is your London solicitor, by the way?"

"Mowbray, of Lincoln's Inn Fields."

"Oh, Mowbray? We know him well; his partner died last year. When I say *we* know him well, I mean as a firm. I have never met him personally, though my partner (who does the office work) has regular dealings with him. He's an excellent man, but his managing clerk's frightful; I wonder Mowbray keeps him. Don't you let him do anything for you on his own hook; he makes the most disastrous messes, and I rather fancy he drinks. Deal with Mowbray himself; there's nobody better in London. And by the way, now I think of it, it's lucky you've nothing urgent for him, for he's sure to be off out of town for the twelfth; he's a rare old gunner, and never misses a season. So that now you haven't a shade of an excuse for leaving me in the lurch, and we'll consider the thing settled."

Settled accordingly it was, and the voyage ended uneventfully. But the steamer was late, and we left it at Plymouth and rushed up to town on the tenth. We had three or four hours to prepare before leaving Euston by the night train. Dorrington's moor was a long drive from Crieff station, and he calculated that at best we could not arrive there before the early evening of the following day, which would, however, give us comfortable time for a good long night's rest before the morning's sport opened. Fortunately I had plenty of loose cash with me, so that there was nothing to delay us in that regard. We made ready in Dorrington's rooms (he was a bachelor) in Conduit Street, and got off comfortably by the ten o'clock train from Euston.

Then followed a most delightful eight days. The weather was fine, the birds were plentiful, and my first taste of grouse-shooting was a complete success. I resolved for the future to come out of my shell and mix in the world that contained such charming fellows as Dorrington, and such delightful sports as that I was then enjoying. But on the eighth day Dorrington received a telegram calling him instantly to London.

"It's a shocking nuisance," he said; "here's my holiday either knocked on the head altogether or cut in two, and I fear it's the first rather than the second. It's just the way in such an uncertain profession as mine. There's no possible help for it, however; I must go, as you'd understand at once if you knew the case. But what chiefly annoys me is leaving you all alone."

I reassured him on this point, and pointed out that I had for a long time been used to a good deal of my own company. Though indeed, with Dorrington away, life at the shooting-lodge threatened to be less pleasant than it had been.

"But you'll be bored to death here," Dorrington said, his thoughts jumping with my own. "But on the other hand it won't be much good going up to town yet. Everybody's out of town, and Mowbray among them. There's a little business of ours that's waiting for him at this moment – my partner mentioned it in his letter yesterday. Why not put in the time with a little tour round? Or you might work up to London by irregular stages, and look about you. As an artist you'd like to see a few of the old towns – probably, Edinburgh, Chester, Warwick, and so on. It isn't a great programme, perhaps, but I hardly know what else to suggest. As for myself I must be off as I am by the first train I can get."

I begged him not to trouble about me, but to attend to his business. As a matter of fact, I was disposed to get to London and take chambers, at any rate for a little while. But Chester was a place I much wanted to see – a real old town, with walls round it – and I was not indisposed to take a day at Warwick. So in the end I resolved to pack up and make for Chester the following day, and from there to take train for Warwick. And in half an hour Dorrington was gone.

Chester was all delight to me. My recollections of the trip to Europe in my childhood were vivid enough as to the misfortunes that followed my father, but of the ancient buildings we visited I remembered little. Now in Chester I found the mediaeval town I had so often read of. I wandered for hours together in the quaint old 'Rows', and walked on the city wall. The evening after my arrival was fine and moonlight, and I was tempted from my hotel. I took a stroll about the town and finished by a walk along the wall from the Watergate toward the cathedral. The moon, flecked over now and again by scraps of cloud, and at times obscured for half a minute together, lighted up all the Roodee in the intervals, and touched with silver the river beyond. But as I walked I presently grew aware of a quiet shuffling footstep some little way behind me. I took little heed of it at first, though I could see nobody near me from whom the sound might come. But soon I perceived that when I stopped, as I did from time to time to gaze over the parapet, the mysterious footsteps stopped also, and when I resumed my walk the quiet shuffling tread began again. At first I thought it might be an echo; but a moment's reflection dispelled that idea. Mine was an even, distinct walk, and this which followed was a soft, quick, shuffling step – a mere scuffle. Moreover, when, by way of test, I took a few silent steps on tip-toe, the shuffle still persisted. I was being followed.

Now I do not know whether or not it may sound like a childish fancy, but I confess I thought of my father. When last I had been in England, as a child, my father's violent death had been preceded by just such followings. And now after all these years, on my return, on the very first night I walked abroad alone, there were strange footsteps in my track. The walk was narrow, and nobody could possibly pass me unseen. I turned suddenly, therefore, and hastened back. At once I saw a dark figure rise from the shadow of the parapet and run. I ran too, but I could not gain on the figure, which receded farther and more indistinctly before me. One reason was that I felt doubtful of my footing on the unfamiliar track. I ceased my chase, and continued my stroll. It might easily have been some vagrant thief, I thought, who had a notion to rush, at a convenient opportunity, and snatch my watch. But here I was far past the spot where I had turned there was the shuffling footstep behind me again. For a little while I feigned not to notice it; then, swinging round as swiftly as I could, I made a quick rush. Useless again, for there in the distance scuttled that same indistinct figure, more rapidly than I could run. What did it mean? I liked the affair so little that I left the walls and walked toward my hotel.

The streets were quiet. I had traversed two, and was about emerging into one of the two main streets, where the Rows are, when, from the farther part of the dark street behind me, there came once more the sound of the now unmistakable footstep. I stopped; the footsteps stopped also. I turned and walked back a few steps, and as I did it the sounds went scuffling away at the far end of the street.

It could not be fancy. It could not be chance. For a single incident perhaps such an explanation might serve, but not for this persistent recurrence. I hurried away to my hotel, resolved, since I could not come at my pursuer, to turn back no more. But before I reached the hotel there were the shuffling footsteps again, and not far behind.

It would not be true to say that I was alarmed at this stage of the adventure, but I was troubled to know what it all might mean, and altogether puzzled to account for it. I thought a great deal, but I went to bed and rose in the morning no wiser than ever.

Whether or not it was a mere fancy induced by the last night's experience I cannot say, but I went about that day with a haunting feeling that I was watched, and to me the impression was very real indeed. I listened often, but in the bustle of the day, even in quiet old Chester, the individual characters of different footsteps were not easily recognisable. Once, however, as I descended a flight of steps from the Rows, I fancied I heard the quick shuffle in the curious old gallery I had just quitted. I turned up the steps again and looked. There was a shabby sort of man looking in one of the windows, and leaning so far as to hide his head behind the heavy oaken pilaster that supported the building above. It might have been his footstep, or it might have been my fancy. At any rate I would have a look at him. I mounted the top stair, but as I turned in his direction the man ran off, with his face averted and his head ducked, and vanished down another stair. I made all speed after him, but when I reached the street he was nowhere to be seen.

What *could* it all mean? The man was rather above the middle height, and he wore one of those soft felt hats familiar on the head of the London organ-grinder. Also his hair was black and bushy, and protruded over the back of his coat-collar. Surely *this* was no delusion; surely I was not imagining an Italian aspect for this man simply because of the recollection of my father's fate?

Perhaps I was foolish, but I took no more pleasure in Chester. The embarrassment was a novel one for me, and I could not forget it. I went back to my hotel, paid my bill, sent my bag to the railway station, and took train for Warwick by way of Crewe.

It was dark when I arrived, but the night was near as fine as last night had been at Chester. I took a very little late dinner at my hotel, and fell into a doubt what to do with myself. One rather fat and very sleepy commercial traveller was the only other customer visible, and the billiard room was empty. There seemed to be nothing to do but to light a cigar and take a walk.

I could just see enough of the old town to give me good hopes of tomorrow's sight-seeing. There was nothing visible of quite such an interesting character as one might meet in Chester, but there were a good few fine old sixteenth-century houses, and there were the two gates with the chapels above them. But of course the castle was the great show-place, and that I should visit on the morrow, if there were no difficulties as to permission. There were some very fine pictures there, if I remembered aright what I had read. I was walking down the incline from one of the gates, trying to remember who the painters of these pictures were, besides Van Dyck and Holbein, when – that shuffling step was behind me again!

I admit that it cost me an effort, this time, to turn on my pursuer. There was something uncanny in that persistent, elusive footstep, and indeed there was something alarming in my circumstances, dogged thus from place to place, and unable to shake off my enemy, or to understand his movements or his motive. Turn I did, however, and straightway the shuffling step went off at a hastened pace in the shadow of the gate. This time I made no more than half-a-dozen steps back. I turned again, and pushed my way to the hotel. And as I went the shuffling step came after.

The thing was serious. There must be some object in this unceasing watching, and the object could bode no good to me. Plainly some unseen eye had been on me the whole of that day, had noted my goings and comings and my journey from Chester. Again, and irresistibly, the watchings that preceded my father's death came to mind, and I could not forget them. I could have no doubt now that I had been closely watched from the moment I had set foot at Plymouth.

But who could have been waiting to watch me at Plymouth, when indeed I had only decided to land at the last moment? Then I thought of the two Italian forecastle hands on the steamer – the very men whom Dorrington had used to illustrate in what unexpected quarters members of the terrible Italian secret societies might be found. And the Camorra was not satisfied with single revenge; it destroyed the son after the father, and it waited for many years, with infinite patience and cunning.

Dogged by the steps, I reached the hotel and went to bed. I slept but fitfully at first, though better rest came as the night wore on. In the early morning I woke with a sudden shock, and with an indefinite sense of being disturbed by somebody about me. The window was directly opposite the foot of the bed, and there, as I looked, was the face of a man, dark, evil, and grinning, with a bush of black hair about his uncovered head, and small rings in his ears.

It was but a flash, and the face vanished. I was struck by the terror that one so often feels on a sudden and violent awakening from sleep, and it was some seconds ere I could leave my bed and get to the window. My room was on the first floor, and the window looked down on a stable-yard. I had a momentary glimpse of a human figure leaving the gate of the yard, and it was the figure that had fled before me in the Rows, at Chester. A ladder belonging to the yard stood under the window, and that was all.

I rose and dressed; I could stand this sort of thing no longer. If it were only something tangible, if there were only somebody I could take hold of, and fight with if necessary, it would not have been so bad. But I was surrounded by some mysterious machination, persistent, unexplainable, that it was altogether impossible to tackle or to face. To complain to the police would have been absurd – they would take me for a lunatic. They are indeed just such complaints that lunatics so often make to the police – complaints of being followed by indefinite enemies, and of being besieged by faces that look in at windows. Even if they did not set me down a lunatic, what could the police of a provincial town do for me in a case like this? No, I must go and consult Dorrington.

I had my breakfast, and then decided that I would at any rate try the castle before leaving. Try it I did accordingly, and was allowed to go over it. But through the whole morning I was oppressed by the horrible sense of being watched by malignant eyes. Clearly there was no comfort for me while this lasted; so after lunch I caught a train which brought me to Euston soon after half-past six.

I took a cab straight to Dorrington's rooms, but he was out, and was not expected home till late. So I drove to a large hotel near Charing Cross – I avoid mentioning its name for reasons which will presently be understood – sent in my bag, and dined.

I had not the smallest doubt but that I was still under the observation of the man or the men who had so far pursued me; I had, indeed, no hope of eluding them, except by the contrivance of Dorrington's expert brain. So as I had no desire to hear that shuffling footstep again – indeed it had seemed, at Warwick, to have a physically painful effect on my nerves – I stayed within and got to bed early.

I had no fear of waking face to face with a grinning Italian here. My window was four floors up, out of reach of anything but a fire-escape. And, in fact, I woke comfortably and naturally, and saw nothing from my window but the bright sky, the buildings opposite, and the traffic below. But as I turned to close my door behind me as I emerged into the corridor, there, on the muntin of the frame, just below the bedroom number, was a little round paper label, perhaps a trifle smaller than a sixpence, and on the label, drawn awkwardly in ink, was a device of two crossed knives of curious, crooked shape. The sign of the Camorra!

I will not attempt to describe the effect of this sign upon me. It may best be imagined, in view of what I have said of the incidents preceding the murder of my father. It was the sign of an inexorable fate, creeping nearer step by step, implacable, inevitable, and mysterious. In little more than twelve hours after seeing that sign my father had been a mangled corpse. One of the hotel servants passed as I stood by the door, and I made shift to ask him if he knew anything of the label. He looked at the paper, and then, more curiously, at me, but he could offer no explanation. I spent little time over breakfast, and then went by cab to Conduit Street. I paid my bill and took my bag with me.

Dorrington had gone to his office, but he had left a message that if I called I was to follow him; and the office was in Bedford Street, Covent Garden. I turned the cab in that direction forthwith.

"Why," said Dorrington as we shook hands, "I believe you look a bit out of sorts! Doesn't England agree with you?"

"Well," I answered, "it has proved rather trying so far." And then I described, in exact detail, my adventures as I have set them down here.

Dorrington looked grave. "It's really extraordinary," he said, "most extraordinary; and it isn't often that I call a thing extraordinary neither, with my experience. But it's plain something must be done – something to gain time at any rate. We're in the dark at present, of course, and I expect I shall have to fish about a little before I get at anything to go on. In the meantime I think you must disappear as artfully as we can manage it." He sat silent for a little while, thoughtfully tapping his forehead with his fingertips. "I wonder," he said presently, "whether or not those Italian fellows on the steamer *are* in it or not. I suppose you haven't made yourself known anywhere, have you?"

"Nowhere. As you know, you've been with me all the time till you left the moor, and since then I have been with nobody and called on nobody."

"Now there's no doubt it's the Camorra," Dorrington said – "that's pretty plain. I think I told you on the steamer that it was rather wonderful that you had heard nothing of them after your father's death. What has caused them all this delay there's no telling – they know best themselves; it's been lucky for you, anyway, so far. What I'd like to find out now is how they have identified you, and got on your track so promptly. There's no guessing where these fellows get their information – it's just wonderful; but if we can find out, then perhaps we can stop the supply, or turn on something that will lead them into a pit. If you had called anywhere on business and declared yourself – as you might have done, for instance, at Mowbray's – I might be inclined to suspect that they got the tip in some crooked way from there. But you haven't. Of course, if those Italian chaps on the steamer *are* in it, you're probably identified pretty certainly; but if they're not, they may only have made a guess. We two landed together, and kept together, till a day or two ago; as far as any outsider would know, I might be Rigby and you might be Dorrington. Come, we'll work on those lines. I think I smell a plan. Are you staying anywhere?"

"No. I paid my bill at the hotel and came along here with my bag."

"Very well. Now there's a house at Highgate kept by a very trustworthy man, whom I know very well, where a man might be pretty comfortable for a few days, or even for a week, if he doesn't mind staying indoors, and keeping himself out of sight. I expect your friends of the Camorra are watching in the street outside at this moment; but I think it will be fairly easy to get you away to Highgate without letting them into the secret, if you don't mind secluding yourself for a bit. In the circumstances, I take it you won't object at all?"

"Object? I should think not."

"Very well, that's settled. You can call yourself Dorrington or not, as you please, though perhaps it will be safest not to shout 'Rigby' too loud. But as for myself, for a day or two at least I'm going to be Mr. James Rigby. Have you your card-case handy?"

"Yes, here it is. But then, as to taking my name, won't you run serious risk?"

Dorrington winked merrily. "I've run a risk or two before now," he said, "in course of my business. And if *I* don't mind the risk, you needn't grumble, for I warn you I shall charge for risk when I send you my bill. And I think I can take care of myself fairly well, even with the Camorra about. I shall take you to this place at Highgate, and then you won't see me for a few days. It won't do for me, in the character of Mr. James Rigby, to go dragging a trail up and down between this place and your retreat. You've got some other identifying papers, haven't you?"

"Yes, I have." I produced the letter from my Sydney lawyers to Mowbray, and the deeds of the South Australian property from my bag.

"Ah," said Dorrington, "I'll just give you a formal receipt for these, since they're valuable; it's a matter of business, and we'll do it in a business-like way. I may want something solid like this to support any bluff I may have to make. A mere case of cards won't always act, you know. It's a pity old Mowbray's out of town, for there's a way in which he might give a little help, I fancy. But never mind – leave it all to me. There's your receipt. Keep it snug away somewhere, where inquisitive people can't read it."

He handed me the receipt, and then took me to his partner's room and introduced me. Mr. Hicks was a small, wrinkled man, older than Dorrington, I should think, by fifteen or twenty years, and with all the aspect and manner of a quiet old professional man.

Dorrington left the room, and presently returned with his hat in his hand. "Yes," he said, "there's a charming dark gentleman with a head like a mop, and rings in his ears, skulking about at the next corner. If it was he who looked in at your window, I don't wonder you were startled. His dress suggests the organ-grinding interest, but he looks as though cutting a throat would be more in his line than grinding a tune; and no doubt he has friends as engaging as himself close at call. If you'll come with me now I think we shall give him the slip. I have a growler ready for you – a hansom's a bit too glassy and public. Pull down the blinds and sit back when you get inside."

He led me to a yard at the back of the building wherein the office stood, from which a short flight of steps led to a basement. We followed a passage in this basement till we reached another flight, and ascending these, we emerged into the corridor of another building. Out at the door at the end of this, and we passed a large block of model dwellings, and were in Bedfordbury. Here a four-wheeler was waiting, and I shut myself in it without delay.

I was to proceed as far as King's Cross in this cab, Dorrington had arranged, and there he would overtake me in a swift hansom. It fell out as he had settled, and, dismissing the hansom, he came the rest of the journey with me in the four-wheeler.

We stopped at length before one of a row of houses, apparently recently built – houses of the over-ornamented, gabled and tiled sort that abound in the suburbs.

"Crofting is the man's name," Dorrington said, as we alighted. "He's rather an odd sort of customer, but quite decent in the main, and his wife makes coffee such as money won't buy in most places."

A woman answered Dorrington's ring – a woman of most extreme thinness. Dorrington greeted her as Mrs. Crofting, and we entered.

"We've just lost our servant again, Mr. Dorrington," the woman said in a shrill voice, "and Mr. Crofting ain't at home. But I'm expecting him before long."

"I don't think I need wait to see him, Mrs. Crofting," Dorrington answered. "I'm sure I can't leave my friend in better hands than yours. I hope you've a vacant room?"

"Well, for a friend of yours, Mr. Dorrington, no doubt we can find room."

"That's right. My friend Mr.—" Dorrington gave me a meaning look, "—Mr. Phelps, would like to stay here for a few days. He wants to be quite quiet for a little – do you understand?"

"Oh, yes, Mr. Dorrington, I understand."

"Very well, then, make him as comfortable as you can, and give him some of your very best coffee. I believe you've got quite a little library of books, and Mr. Phelps will be glad of them. Have you got any cigars?" Dorrington added, turning to me.

"Yes; there are some in my bag."

"Then I think you'll be pretty comfortable now. Goodbye. I expect you'll see me in a few days – or at any rate you'll get a message. Meantime be as happy as you can."

Dorrington left, and the woman showed me to a room upstairs, where I placed my bag. In front, on the same floor, was a sitting room, with, I suppose, some two or three hundred books, mostly novels, on shelves. The furniture of the place was of the sort one expects to find in an ordinary lodging house – horsehair sofas, loo tables, lustres, and so forth. Mrs. Crofting explained to me that the customary dinner hour was two, but that I might dine when I liked. I elected, however, to follow the custom of the house, and sat down to a cigar and a book.

At two o'clock the dinner came, and I was agreeably surprised to find it a very good one, much above what the appointments of the house had led me to expect. Plainly Mrs. Crofting was a capital cook. There was no soup, but there was a very excellent sole, and some well-done cutlets with peas, and an omelet; also a bottle of Bass. Come, I felt that I should not do so badly in this place after all. I trusted that Dorrington would be as comfortable in his half of the transaction, bearing my responsibilities and troubles. I had heard a heavy, blundering tread on the floor below, and judged from this that Mr. Crofting had returned.

After dinner I lit a cigar, and Mrs. Crofting brought her coffee. Truly it was excellent coffee, and brewed as I like it – strong and black, and plenty of it. It had a flavour of its own too, novel, but not unpleasing. I took one cupful, and brought another to my side as I lay on the sofa with my book. I had not read six lines before I was asleep.

I woke with a sensation of numbing cold in my right side, a terrible stiffness in my limbs, and a sound of loud splashing in my ears. All was pitch dark, and – what was this? Water! Water all about me. I was lying in six inches of cold water, and more was pouring down upon me from above. My head was afflicted with a splitting ache. But where was I? Why was it dark? And whence all the water? I staggered to my feet, and instantly struck my head against a hard roof above me. I raised my hand; there was the roof or whatever place it was, hard, smooth and cold, and little more than five feet from the floor, so that I bent as I stood. I spread my hand to the side; that was hard, smooth and cold too. And then the conviction struck me like a blow – I was in a covered iron tank, and the water was pouring in to drown me!

I dashed my hands frantically against the lid, and strove to raise it. It would not move. I shouted at the top of my voice, and turned about to feel the extent of my prison. One way I could touch the opposite sides at once easily with my hands, the other way it was wider – perhaps a little more than six feet altogether. What was this? Was this to be my fearful end, cooped in this tank while the water rose by inches to choke me? Already the water was a foot deep. I flung myself at the sides, I beat the pitiless iron with fists, face and head, I screamed and implored. Then it struck me that I might at least stop the inlet of water. I put out my hand and felt the falling stream, then found the inlet and stopped it with my fingers. But water still poured in with a resounding splash; there was another opening at the opposite end, which I could not reach without releasing the one I now held! I was but prolonging my agony. Oh, the devilish cunning that had devised those two inlets, so far apart! Again I beat the sides, broke my nails with tearing at the corners, screamed and entreated in my agony. I was mad, but with no dulling of the senses, for the horrors of my awful, helpless state overwhelmed my brain, keen and perceptive to every ripple of the unceasing water.

In the height of my frenzy I held my breath, for I heard a sound from outside. I shouted again – implored some quicker death. Then there was a scraping on the lid above me, and it was raised at one edge, and let in the light of a candle. I sprang from my knees and forced the lid back, and the candle flame danced before me. The candle was held by a dusty man, a workman apparently, who stared at me with scared eyes, and said nothing but, "Goo' lor'!"

Overhead were the rafters of a gabled roof, and tilted against them was the thick beam which, jammed across from one sloping rafter to another, had held the tank-lid fast. "Help me!" I gasped. "Help me out!"

The man took me by the armpits and hauled me, dripping and half dead, over the edge of the tank, into which the water still poured, making a noise in the hollow iron that half drowned our voices. The man had been at work on the cistern of a neighbouring house, and hearing an uncommon noise, he had climbed through the spaces left in the party walls to give passage along under the roofs to the builders' men. Among the joists at our feet was the trap-door through which, drugged and insensible, I had been carried, to be flung into that horrible cistern.

With the help of my friend the workman I made shift to climb through by the way he had come. We got back to the house where he had been at work, and there the people gave me brandy and lent me dry clothes. I made haste to send for the police, but when they arrived Mrs. Crofting and her respectable spouse had gone. Some unusual noise in the roof must have warned them. And when the police, following my directions further, got to the offices of Dorrington and Hicks, those acute professional men had gone too, but in such haste that the contents of the office, papers and everything else, had been left just as they stood.

The plot was clear now. The followings, the footsteps, the face at the window, the label on the door – all were a mere humbug arranged by Dorrington for his own purpose, which was to drive me into his power and get my papers from me. Armed with these, and with his consummate address and knowledge of affairs, he could go to Mr. Mowbray in the character of Mr. James Rigby, sell my land in South Australia, and have the whole of my property transferred to himself from Sydney. The rest of my baggage was at his rooms; if any further proof were required it might be found there. He had taken good care that I should not meet Mr. Mowbray – who, by the way, I afterwards found had not left his office, and had never fired a gun in his life. At first I wondered that Dorrington had not made some murderous attempt on me at the shooting place in Scotland. But a little thought convinced me that that would have been bad policy for him. The disposal of the body would be difficult, and he would have to account somehow for my sudden disappearance. Whereas, by the use of his Italian assistant and his murder apparatus at Highgate I was made to efface my own trail, and could be got rid of in the end with little trouble; for my body, stripped of everything that might identify me, would be simply that of a drowned man unknown, whom nobody could identify. The whole plot was contrived upon the information I myself had afforded Dorrington during the voyage home. And it all sprang from his remembering the report of my father's death. When the papers in the office came to be examined, there each step in the operations was plainly revealed. There was a code telegram from Suez directing Hicks to hire a grouse moor. There were telegrams and letters from Scotland giving directions as to the later movements; indeed the thing was displayed completely. The business of Dorrington and Hicks had really been that of private inquiry agents, and they had done much *bona fide* business; but many of their operations had been of a more than questionable sort. And among their papers were found complete sets, neatly arranged in dockets, each containing in skeleton a complete history of a case. Many of these cases were of a most interesting character, and I have been enabled to piece together, out of the material thus supplied, the narratives which will follow this. As to my own case, it only remains to say that as yet neither Dorrington, Hicks, nor the Croftings have been caught. They played in the end for a high stake (they might have made six figures of me if they had killed me, and the first figure would not have been a one) and they lost by a mere accident. But I have often wondered how many of the bodies which the coroners' juries of London have returned to be 'Found Drowned' were drowned, not where they were picked up, but in that horrible tank at Highgate. What the drug was that gave Mrs. Crofting's coffee its value in Dorrington's eyes I do not know, but plainly it had not been sufficient in my case to keep me unconscious against the shock of cold water till I could be drowned altogether. Months have passed since my adventure, but even now I sweat at the sight of an iron tank.

Death Alley

Frederick Nebel

Chapter I
Death Ride

MAX SAUL, humming 'The St. Louis Blues', prodded the catch base of the Mauser's butt, drew out the magazine, slipped in eight nickel-cased bullets, jammed the magazine back into the butt and jacked a shell into the chamber.

Cardigan said, "Now for God's sake, Max, watch your step. Last week Pat O'Hara was one of us and tonight he's pushing up daisies. This client Ludwig Hartz is a nice enough old guy but he's got that going-places-and-doing-things complex. Even at a time like this."

Saul slid the flat automatic into his hip pocket.

"Once a yama-yama girl told me I'd live to a ripe old age. She said I had wonderful eyes too."

Cardigan ignored the humor, went on in a deep, blunt voice.

"If I thought Brodski was behind that kill, it would be all right. But I don't. I don't think this mill strike has a thing to do with it. Bush fell on Brodski because the dumb Polack instigated the strike and once made a crack that he'd blow Hartz's head off – and because Brodski has no alibi. But that's not enough, Max."

Saul chuckled.

"I know, I know, Jack. You've got Mrs. Hartz on the brain. And that nice-faced lounge lizard Everett."

Cardigan swore. He strode to one of the windows – a big man, a hard party, rangy in the framework and good-looking in a rough, male way. The St. Louis summer night sky was overcast. Motor cars whirred past on Lindell Boulevard.

Cardigan pivoted.

"Why the hell shouldn't I have her on the brain?" he demanded. "She's twenty years younger than Hartz. The night after Pat was killed she and Everett told Hartz they were going to see *The Mikado*. On a hunch – I was all worked up about Pat's death – I tailed them. They went out to Sherick's gambling joint, the Ritz, in the county. They were known there. And I saw Clara Hartz cornered by a big guy who frightened her. He faded when Everett appeared. She got a look at me but I made believe I didn't see her."

"Why didn't you tell papa Hartz?"

"I'm no snitch – unless it gets me somewhere. Hartz is dead against gambling and if he knew she went out there it would be just too bad for her. She's worried. She'll come to me. And it's damned lucky for her she wasn't out there a night later – when that machine-gun mob raided the place and got away with a hundred thousand."

Saul said, "And damned lucky, for you – the way you used a fake police badge to get in there," Saul put on his straw hat. "Well, toodle-oo, Jack."

"Watch yourself, Max."

"You know what that yama-yama girl said."

Saul went out.

Pat O'Hara was dead. Dead and shoving up daisies. He'd taken unto himself six slugs from a super .45. He must have had a flash of intuition in the limousine carrying him and Ludwig Hartz, the milk magnate, through Forest Park, that unholy night. He'd thrown Hartz to the floor of the car, yanked at his gun – and then taken the lead smack in the chest as the mystery car sped past. Brunner, the chauffeur, had jammed on brakes, smashed a mudguard against a tree – and fainted. Hartz had roared for help.

Detective-sergeant Bush had nailed Brodski, leader of the milk strike. Everybody blamed it on the strike. Everybody but Cardigan – and he was only toying with a vague idea. The Cosmos Agency had sent out Max Saul from New York to replace O'Hara, as assistant to Cardigan, the regional head. Either Cardigan or Saul had been with Hartz at all times since the murder.

Cardigan was pouring a pony of Bourbon when the telephone rang. He finished pouring, downed the drink neat and crossed the room rasping his throat.

"Hello," he said into the mouthpiece. "Oh, hello, Mrs. Hartz… No, nothing particular… Yes, I could. When?… All right. The northwest corner of the Hotel Case lounge. I'll walk right over."

The thumb of the hand that held the instrument pushed the hook down slowly. Cardigan replaced the receiver and chuckled grimly to himself.

A self-operated elevator took him down six floors to the lobby of the apartment house. He passed out onto a tiled terrace, strode down broad flags to the sidewalk and turned west on Lindell Boulevard.

He had gone perhaps a dozen yards when a stocky man stepped from beside one of the trees and fell in step beside him. The stocky man's right hand was in his pocket and the pocket bulged.

"Just keep walkin', sweetheart," he said.

"Where?"

"You'll see."

Cardigan's hands doubled but he kept walking. The hair stood up on the nape of his neck. Two girls and a man passed him going east. They didn't notice. The stocky man was in step with Cardigan, but a bit to the rear and to the left of him.

Ten feet further on a lank man stepped from the shadow of a parked sedan.

The stocky man muttered, "Get in that bus."

"Look here—" Cardigan began.

"Get in, get in," snarled the lank man, motionless. "You've got a date."

Cardigan looked down at the stocky man. It was a face he had seen before but for the present he couldn't place it. He was shoved into the rear of the sedan. He dropped down beside a man in shadow who smoked a cigar. The stocky man got in front beside the motionless chauffeur. The lank man climbed in beside Cardigan.

The red cigar-end moved. "Oke, Bunt."

The gear lever clicked. The big sedan moved away from the curb, swung into west-bound traffic, crossed Kings highway and hummed out along Forest Park.

"Well," said the man behind the red cigar end, "we had a long wait, *wisenheimer.*"

The stocky man in the front seat turned around.

"That's him, Gus. That's him all right."

Cardigan said, "I've seen you before."

"Honest?" mocked the stocky man. "Have you now?"

The man behind the red cigar and his lank companion suddenly frisked Cardigan of his gun. The lank man grinned.

"Why don't you try to get out of this with your police badge?"

Cardigan started. Then he leaned back.

"Oh," he said slowly. "I see." Then his voice rushed on. "What the hell's the idea of this party?"

The lank man jabbed a gun in his ribs. "The night before that raid at the Ritz you muscled your way in on a fake cop's shield! You were a scout for that mob! Tom Sherick remembered the shield number. You went home in a taxi. The guy drove you home remembered the address. And you paid your fare. Did a cop ever pay taxi fare? Yah! And we found out there was no such shield number on the cops!"

The car turned right into Union. Cardigan looked around at the shadowed faces.

"So help me, I had nothing to do with that." The stocky man in the front seat was the one who had let him in the Ritz. He remembered now.

"That was a fast one all right," the lank man said. "But this is gonna be a faster one."

"Ride?" Cardigan asked.

"What do you think?"

Cardigan began to perspire.

"I think," he said, "you guys are off your nut. O.K., I used a fake badge. But I'm a private dick. I was on a tail. It was the only chance I had of getting in, so I used it."

"You think up fast ones, don't you?" the lank man slurred.

The man behind the cigar laughed out loud. The man at the wheel giggled. The lank man rasped a harsh chuckle from his throat. The car sped on. It turned left into Delmar, weaved through traffic; past street cars, past traffic cops. While a gun kept pressing into Cardigan's ribs.

"Listen," said Cardigan, "I'm on the up and up. Take me to Sherick. Let me talk to him. I can square myself. I'm getting a raw deal here."

"And right in the belly," the lank man said.

Cardigan heaved in the seat. The man behind the red cigar-end moved, struck Cardigan across the head with a gun-butt. Cardigan groaned and slumped back in the seat. Through glazed eyes he saw store windows streak by. He heard the honking of the horns, the shrill blast of traffic whistles.

Then the store windows were left behind. Sounds of the city petered out. There were occasional houses, then fewer and farther apart. The warm night wind blew against his hot face. Fields began to flow past. The big car droned on complacently, doing fifty-five on an undulating ribbon of cement. It boomed through a small settlement, left that behind in two minutes; swept past fields again and patches of dark woods.

"What is it?" Cardigan muttered. "A pitch from the St. Charles Bridge?"

"You'll see," the land man said.

"Listen," Cardigan urged. "For God's sake, listen! Give me a break. I tell you—"

"You can't tell us anything," the lank man said.

The man at the wheel, leaning out, said, "It won't be long now. Right around that bend."

There was a dark forest on the left of the wide bend, and the wind carried a dank smell of marshes.

"That path's right up here, ain't it?" the driver asked.

"Yeah," the stocky man said. "I'll say when."

Cardigan said in a thick voice, "For God's sake—"

"Lay off!" the lank man snarled; then in a quiet tone, "You and Abe go with him, Louie. We'll drive on and turn around and pick you up in ten minutes."

The car was slowing down. Presently it stopped.

"Hop out, Louie," the lank man said.

"Right," said the stocky man swinging from the front seat.

The man with the cigar threw it away and opened the rear door. Louie ran around the back and waited. The lank man prodded Cardigan with his gun and Louie and Abe hauled him out and rushed him across the road, down a path that bored into the dark, matted forest.

"So it's lights out," said Cardigan, bitterly.

Louie said, "For you, sweetheart."

They moved along the edge of a black pool on damp, soggy earth. Cardigan dragged his feet, tussled between the two. But they held him up, saying nothing, hauled him deeper and deeper into the woods.

Cardigan fell between them, dragging his knees on the wet earth. They could not walk with him that way, and they stopped. Louie cursed and struck Cardigan with his gun.

"Get up!" he snarled.

Cardigan hung a dead weight between them, breathed hoarsely, muttered, "If you heels want to give it to me, go ahead!"

Louie nodded. "Let's, Abe."

"We oughter go in further."

They redoubled their efforts, dragged Cardigan on the muddy path. His legs were straight behind him, his hands clawing at the mud.

Louie cried in a low voice. "Look out, Abe! That's water! We go left here – ain't it?"

Cardigan suddenly heaved his weight and twisted violently between them, breaking from Abe's grasp. He fell to the right, dragging Louie with him. They shot down the muddy bank, plunged into black water, while Abe clawed for a footing and Louie cried, "Help!" in a frightened voice that a mouthful of water promptly smothered.

Cardigan kicked out into the black water. He did not see Louie. He did not see Abe. It was black as pitch in those woods.

Louie cried, "Ugh – don't shoot, Abe!"

"Where the hell are you?" Abe snapped.

"Here – I'm here – gimme a hand—"

Through the black water swam Cardigan, getting rid of his coat. The voices of Louie and Abe grew fainter. Cardigan swam into gnarled roots. He grasped them, drew himself beneath them, felt his feet touch bottom. He clawed up a muddy bank and burrowed into thickets.

He did not wait to listen, but stumbled on his way, sometimes on solid ground, sometimes in knee-deep bogs. He fell and rose again and kept putting distance between himself and the two gunmen. He kept on fiercely, blindly, slushing through mud, spitting mud from his lips, choking and hacking and grunting and cursing.

He did not know it, but an hour passed before he fell headlong on a dry hump of earth. He lay gasping for breath, mud from head to foot, his brain almost bursting from the exertion. Then something inside him snapped and he relaxed with a sigh.

Gray daylight was breaking when he stumbled out on the state highway. An eastbound produce truck pulled up and gave him a lift.

The driver looked at him curiously. "You're messed up a bit, ain't you, bud?"

"I was on a wild party," Cardigan said. "I'd appreciate a butt, brother."

Chapter II
The Widow Talks

CARDIGAN ducked into the apartment house through the service entrance and reached his apartment without being seen. Muddy and bruised, he looked a ruin. He scuffled an envelope that had been slid under the door, picked it up and threw it on a console. He went to the bathroom and soaked himself in a hot tub. Dressed, he looked better.

He went to the console for a cigarette, lit up and then picked up the letter he had dropped there. It was apartment house stationery. A note was inside.

A Mr. Bush of police headquarters called at 10:30 and left word you should come right down. Adams.

That was the night porter.

Cardigan scowled thoughtfully and took a drag at his butt on the way across to the telephone. He rang headquarters.

"Bush. Give me Bush if he's there... Hello, Bush. Cardigan. I... What!... Sweet cripes!... I'll be right down."

He dived into a coat, grabbed a hat and went downstairs. He taxied to Twelfth and Clark. Bush, leaning over a flat-topped desk, looked sidewise over his right shoulder as he barged in. "Oh, you," he said.

"What the hell, Bush?"

Bush shuffled four lead slugs in the palm of his hand, then threw them dicelike on the desk and snapped thumb against forefinger. He was a short, compact bald man. His tie was unloosed. He looked haggard from long hours.

Cardigan picked up one of the four slugs, turned it round and round, then dropped it back among the others. His wide mouth was tight, his heavy brows bent over his staring dark eyes.

Bush sighed. "Them guys sure meant business this time."

"How – how is Max Saul?"

"Was unconscious the last I seen him – three this morning."

Cardigan made a fist, looked at it narrow-eyed.

"And poor old Hartz—"

"Back of his nut all smashed in. Three times in the back of the nut. Saul took one. Brunner, the chauffeur, got one through the heart and the car smashed. They were coming home from Hamburg Hall. It happened on South Grand, near Longfellow. Why the hell couldn't you get down here before this?"

"I had a date."

"All night?"

Cardigan's lip curled.

"Keep your wisecracks under your jaw, Bush."

"Don't get hot."

"I suppose you're blaming this on Brodski too."

"Quit the razzberry. I'm going to bust this case, Cardigan. Hartz threatened to chuck every striker out of a job. In hard times like this that's a wild statement. Look here, Cardigan." He got up and shoved his pug nose almost against Cardigan's chin. "Ever since the O'Hara kill you've been giving me the razz. What the hell have you got on your mind?"

Cardigan turned and walked to the door.

"What hospital is Max Saul in?"

"You listen to me, Cardigan." Bush tramped after him, faced him again. "You get this. You've been jazzing around ever since O'Hara got bumped off. You've been acting superior and horse-laughing me every chance you got. And I don't like it. I've got more law in my little finger than you have in both hands, and if you slop around here much longer I'll fix you so you get shoved out of the city."

"What hospital—"

"You're just a wisecracking Mick that thinks the bureau's made up of a lot of hicks. I'm just as clever as you are, kid, and I'm backed up by authority. Last night Hartz and his chauffeur were rubbed out and your partner's in the hospital. It's damned funny that you shouldn't have been with Hartz on the two times he was fired at."

Cardigan darkened.

"We worked in shifts, fat-head. On alternate nights."

"That's funny, ain't it?"

"It'd be funnier if I pushed you in the mouth."

Bush glowered.

"You stay the hell out of here, Cardigan. I'll handle this case – in my way."

"O'Hara was murdered, Bush. Don't forget that Pat was the best friend I ever had. I'll get the guy that did it. I'll get him, Bush, and I'll give you the pinch – and make you like it."

A wily light came into Bush's eyes. His tone changed.

"Be a good guy, Cardigan. You've got something up your sleeve. What the hell is it? Remember, it pays to stand in good with the bureau."

"I stand in good with the bureau. I don't stand in good with you. And look at me weep over that."

"Be smart, be smart!"

"Nuts for you," Cardigan said, and went out.

At the desk downstairs he found what hospital Saul had been sent to. He taxied out, a tight feeling in his throat. Trouble was piling on his head. First O'Hara. Then Hartz and the chauffeur. And Max in the hospital.

Saul's face was pale; dark circles were under his eyes. Cardigan sat down on a chair beside the bed, laid his big brown hand on Saul's, pressed it once.

"How's it, kid?"

"I feel – you know – sort of lousy."

"Yeah."

They looked at each other.

Cardigan said, "I feel rotten about this, Max."

"Don't be a goof. I'll get over it. Let me feel rotten. It happened so fast. Six shots – and then we swerved. The car passed so close we almost scraped mudguards. We had both spotlights on. One of them swung around when we swerved. I saw a guy's face in the other car, Jack. It wasn't six feet away. He was grinning. A gold tooth flashed."

Cardigan looked at his hands. He didn't want to tell Saul about the ride. The nurse came in and told him he couldn't stay any longer.

"Let me know if you want anything, Max?" Cardigan said.

He went downtown and spent three-quarters of an hour eating breakfast and reading the morning paper. Then he walked to his office in Olive Street and found Miss Gilligan, his secretary, sorting mail. She was a pop-eyed, gum-chewing girl with no looks but a great amount of vitality.

"My God!" she said. "The papers! Did you see—"

"Like a nice girl, get the boss on long distance."

He spoke with Hammerhorn in New York.

"Well, since you read it in the papers there I don't have to explain... Max ought to pull through, the doctor said, but he'll be on his back for weeks... Where was I? On a date... Now don't ask foolish questions, George... What?" He scowled at the instrument, then growled. "You're the second guy today made a crack like that. I was with Hartz night before last. Last night was Max's night… Well, you get this, George. I don't have to take talk like that from you. Make another pass like that and you and your job can go to hell. Despite which I'll get the guy that killed my pal O'Hara… I'm not getting hot-headed, but don't you think you can handle the St. Louis end better than I can, pull your pants out of that plush chair and come out… Oh, well, all right, all right… Sure, George. Goodbye."

He banged the receiver into the hook and shoved away the mail Miss Gilligan had placed on his desk. He was sore. He had to admit that it looked crummy, his having been off the scene on the two occasions of murder. The ride still simmered in his brain, but he had no intention of reporting it to the police. He handled his own troubles. Besides, bigger things weighed him down. Hartz was dead. Max was out of commission. The papers were roaring with headlines.

He called a county telephone number.

"Is this you, Mr. Sherick?… Well, my name is Cardigan, the St. Louis head of the Cosmos Detective Agency. I'm the guy your sweet young things took for a ride last night. I'm back in town and O.K. Use your head, Sherick. If I wasn't a swell guy I'd turn you up. Only take a dose of something to clear your brain, look up my reputation and think over what a boner you pulled. And thank your stars I'm a swell guy. Goodbye."

He hung up, felt a little better, took his hat and went out. He taxied to Longfellow Boulevard and Clara Hartz's house.

Mrs. Schmidt let him in. She had been long with the Hartz menage, as housekeeper. She steered him into the large Teutonic living room. She tried to say something but began crying instead and went out.

In a few minutes Clara Hartz came downstairs. She wore a black jacket over black pajamas. Her face was pale, angular, with a strange cool beauty. Cardigan didn't move from the shadows of the living room. His low voice said, "I'm very sorry, Mrs. Hartz."

She lifted her chin and lowered it again without saying anything.

Cardigan went on. "I'm sorry I didn't show up last night."

"I waited two hours."

"You said over the telephone it was important."

She remained statuesque – cool, remote. "It was – about the Ritz the other night. I was worried. I wanted to ask you not to tell Ludwig. Or anybody. The suspense – knowing you knew – and your not saying anything—"

He crossed suddenly to her, his big brown jaw grim.

"Who do you think murdered your husband?"

She had greenish eyes, large – slightly Oriental, cool as ice.

"I wish I knew," she said in her flat voice.

"Do you think the strike caused it?"

"I don't know."

Cardigan's gray eyes glittered. Beside her smooth cool beauty he looked immense, shaggy, threatening. But her eyes never wavered.

"Remember," he muttered, "my friend Pat O'Hara was murdered first. That hits me deep and way down. I'm going to get the murderer – even if I have to cause a lot of heartache."

One of her arched eyebrows rose slightly, but otherwise not a feature changed. For some vague unknown reason Cardigan suddenly hated her. She was so cool, so collected. He was a man of blood and fire, bitter against circumstances, and her attitude touched him like a bar of ice.

"I don't suppose," she said, "that your telling anybody about Mr. Everett and me at the Ritz will gain you anything."

Cardigan scowled. "I'm not a scandal-monger."

The doorbell rang and a minute later Ralph Everett came in. He was a tall, slim man of thirty, with silky blond hair, girlish blue eyes and pink cheeks.

"Oh, hello, Cardigan."

Cardigan grunted.

Everett said, "Dreadful – murder," and lit a cigarette. "Sorry about Saul, Cardigan."

It was an uneasy meeting. Cardigan saw no remorse here. The death of poor old Hartz did not seem to stir them. A year and a half ago Clara had married the fifty-year-old milk magnate. And for the past year Everett had been welcome in Hartz's household. Hartz had never shown any suspicion.

"Have the police got anything out of Brodski?" Everett asked.

"No. And they won't," Cardigan said bluntly. "I don't believe this strike has anything to do with it. The strike merely proved convenient for somebody else to try murder, and have it blamed on the strike."

"But Detective-sergeant Bush—"

"I know Bush," Cardigan cut in.

Everett shrugged and looked at his watch, nodded at Clara. "I have to catch a train for Cleveland."

"I wouldn't," Cardigan said.

Everett looked at him, startled. "Why not?"

"I just wouldn't. The best thing for you to do is stay right here in town."

Everett bristled. "Why?"

"Because I'm telling you. And I'm being frank with you – both of you. Stay here in town. The press is aching for news and if you pull up your stakes I'll give them a little."

Everett came closer.

"You mean about the other night?"

"Judge for yourself. And maybe if I work back I can find out about other nights."

Everett gritted, "You would like to break a scandal, wouldn't you?"

"Not unless you force me to. And don't stick your nose in the air, either, Everett."

"You as much as insinuate," Everett snapped, "that I had something to do with Mr. Hartz's death!"

Cardigan wagged a finger.

"Just stick around St. Louis."

Clara Hartz turned away, swivelling slowly on one heel. She walked out of the room and went upstairs.

Everett muttered, "You've a nerve coming here and humiliating her!"

"And you've got a nerve leaving her and trying to go to Cleveland." Cardigan picked up his hat, touched Everett's arm. "But don't," he said.

Everett paled, clenching his hands. "You're a louse – like all private detectives," he choked.

"Like Pat O'Hara, I suppose. Like O'Hara, who got in the way of a lead party to save Hartz! You lily-livered nice boy! Hartz thought you were a swell guy – the old fool! Why, you—"

He gave it up suddenly. He strode out of the room, through the large foyer, into the street, his cheeks burning. He didn't like wavy-haired nice boys and he didn't like Oriental-eyed icebergs. He had let emotion get the better of him. He felt he had acted a fool.

Chapter III
Written Evidence

NO FUNERAL PARLOR for Ludwig Hartz, since he had not wished it that way. He lay in state in the great living room of the great brick house. Mourners came and went. Clerks, stenographers, even some of the strikers. Relatives sat about in hushed groups. Clara Hartz was in the drawing room, stunning in black, looking tragic in a cool, icy way.

Cardigan was there, standing in the foyer, a dark, shaggy-headed man, watchful though in the background.

Bush came in, his hard bald head shining. He went to the coffin, looked grim, then said some condolences to Clara and elbowed his way back toward the door. He spied Cardigan and came over.

"What are you doing here?" he grumbled.

"No law against it. I see you had to let Brodski go. You certainly paraded a lot of guys through the shadow-box this morning. Good copy, Bush."

"Be funny!"

"Any new clues?"

"You?"

"Here's a promise, Bush. I'll get you a pinch – a real, honest-to-God one. You've been nosing it around that as a dick, I'm last year's summer cold. So I'm going to get you a pinch and make you swallow those words, right on the front page."

"Baloney!"

"You're a nice guy, Bush, only you're a sorehead."

Bush swore and went out, jamming on his hat.

Everett, passing through the foyer a couple of minutes later, stopped and said tensely, "Don't you think it would be the decent thing if you went somewhere else?"

Cardigan said, "I see you didn't go to Cleveland."

Everett's lips twitched. He turned and went off stiffly.

A messenger boy appeared in the front doorway. A man-servant signed for a letter, carried it through the crowd to Clara Hartz. A minute later Clara appeared in the foyer. Cardigan saw the letter in her hand, the white look on her face. He watched her go upstairs.

His eyes narrowed. He looked around cautiously, backed up toward the stairway. He looked up, saw Clara's heels disappearing around the curve above. He turned and climbed quickly, quietly. He reached the top in time to see Clara standing in a doorway at the front of the upper hall, her back to him. Her head was bent. She was reading something. Then he heard the sudden crackle of paper as she went into the room.

He darted into the bathroom, closed the door, listened. A few minutes later he heard footsteps come down the corridor, descend the stairs. He left the bathroom, walked quickly to the front of the corridor, entered a large bedroom. He crossed to a writing-table, ran his eyes over an assortment of cards, letters, telegrams; touched nothing. There was an ivory-colored metal waste-basket beside the desk. He knelt down, saw bits of torn paper, collected them quickly, held them in his closed hand and returned to the bathroom.

On black-and-white tiles he pieced together a message written on plain white linen paper. The writing was heavy, black, oblique. It said:

Dear Mrs. Hartz:

My sincere sympathy. But as I said at the Ritz last Wednesday night, don't let this tragedy make you forget your obligation to me, in case you decide to leave St. Louis. D.D. McKimm.

Cardigan remained on one knee for a long minute, frowning at the letter. Then he gathered up the pieces, shoved them in his pocket and went downstairs.

The undertaker was closing the casket.

Cardigan went downtown in a taxi, strode into his office and said to Miss Gilligan, "Darling, call County 0606. Ask for Mr. Sherick."

He went on into his office, slapped his hat on a hook and sat down at his desk. A minute later Miss Gilligan chirped, "All right."

Cardigan pulled his telephone across the desk.

"Hello, that you, Sherick?… This is Cardigan… Oh, I'm feeling great, but outside of that I want to see you… No, I'm not going out there. I can't spare the taxi fare and besides I don't like that scatter of yours. I'm naming the place, Sherick, and you're going to meet me… Now don't talk that way. Your sweet young things took me for a ride and you'll play ball with me or I'll throw you to the cops… Never mind what I want to see you about. You come right in here and see. You know my apartment on Lindell and I'll expect you there at eight tonight – sharp… Never mind, Sherick. You heard me. You did a dumb thing by sending your hoods after me and you'll come in or else—"

He hung up and stared hard at the telephone. He took out the bits of paper, pasted them in order to a letterhead. He read the message over and over.

"H'm," he murmured. "Obligation."

At a quarter to eight that night he stood in the center of his living room holding a gun in either hand and looking around the room with keen speculative eyes. The gun in his left hand was a Colt automatic. The gun in his right was a special Colt revolver with an abbreviated two-inch barrel.

His eyes settled on a dull-colored mohair easy-chair and he strode toward it, sat down and shoved the revolver down between the arm and the cushion until it was concealed. With an easy upward motion of his hand the gun appeared. He shoved it back again, grunted with satisfaction and stood up. He slipped the automatic into his coat pocket.

He took a drink of Bourbon and looked at the little folding clock on the secretary. At eight o'clock he heard the elevator down the hall open, and a minute later there was a knock on his door.

Tom Sherick was a mountain of a man beneath a wide-brimmed Panama. The man beside him was small, thin, pale-faced, and he carried his hands in his pockets. They stood in the doorway.

Cardigan said, "I didn't expect the wet-nurse."

"Willie goes where I go," Sherick said heavily, his little eyes quivering with suspicion.

Cardigan stepped back and Sherick and the pale-faced man trooped in. Sherick went all the way across the room, but his companion closed the door with a kick of his heel and remained in front of it, his big wet eyes sinister.

Sherick stopped, turned, mopped his neck and face with a handkerchief. His pale eyes had fire smouldering in their depths. He gestured with his handkerchief.

"What the hell, Cardigan, what the hell? I had every reason to believe you was a scout for that mob. What do you want? Cripes, what do you want?"

Cardigan sat down on the arm of a mohair easy-chair. "Never mind the apologies. And damper down your loud mouth. I expected you alone. You had to bring along this snot and complicate things."

"Willie goes where—"

"O.K., he's here now. And you're here. And you're the guy I want to have a talk with."

"Well, talk!"

Willie drew in his lower lip and then let it fall out again, where it hung wet and shiny.

Cardigan said, "I want the lowdown on a bird named McKimm."

"Mc – who?"

"McKimm. He hung out around your place and he was known there. What's his racket?"

Sherick stopped mopping his big face. His little eyes narrowed.

"How should I know? Hell, is that what you got me in here for?"

"Just that."

Willie made spitting sounds with his lips and Cardigan looked at him. "Cut out spitting on my carpet."

Sherick started tramping up and down the room, mopping his face again.

"This is funny," he said. "This is funny as hell, Cardigan."

"Says you!" bit off Cardigan. "Don't stall around when you know you've got to come across. You spring, Sherick, or by God I'll throw you to the cops for that ride!"

Willie took three forward steps from the door. His coat pockets moved and as he stood with his head down between his narrow shoulders, a sullen glassy look was in his eyes.

Sherick threw an apprehensive look at him, licked his lips with a rapid motion of his tongue, jerked his pale harried eyes at Cardigan. Cardigan's eyes were flickering from Willie to Sherick, and the skin tightened on his jaw so that little muscles bulged beneath it.

Sherick rasped, "What the hell are you tailing McKimm for?"

"That's my business, Sherick, not yours. Yours is to tell me what his racket is and where I can call on him. I want to know that and the cheap snot over there with the two rods doesn't make me change my mind!"

Willie snarled, "For two cents—" His pale face rose, showing dark circles beneath his killer's eyes.

"Be quiet, Willie," Sherick said; then he snapped at Cardigan, "This is all a lot of crap!"

"Remember, Sherick, I was taken for a ride in the city of St. Louis. Not in the county, where you have the big shots smeared to lay off you. You'll tell me what I want to know—"

"Damn it, Tom!" rasped Willie feverishly. "This guy is askin' for a bellyache!" A sudden look of frenzy leaped into his eyes and his two guns came out of his pockets.

"Willie!" cried Sherick.

Willie panted, "The horse's neck's got it comin' to him!"

"Willie, put away those rods!"

A moan came from Willie's throat and he stood shaking and opening and closing his mouth slowly. Inch by inch his guns lowered until they hung at his sides.

Cardigan said, "Hell, Sherick, you're dumb to carry that hophead around with you."

"For God's sake, shut up!" cried Sherick.

Cardigan ran a hand across his forehead spreading cold sweat that had appeared there in shining beads.

"But you've got to tell, Sherick," he said, grimly. "I've got to know. And I want the truth – and then I want you to go out of here and keep your mouth shut."

Sherick began coughing into his handkerchief. His face was red and streaked with sweat. He looked harassed and cornered, and his jowels shook. He glared at Cardigan with hate and venom but with fear also. While Willie stood quivering like a bird dog held back, his lips wet and his eyes shining as though filled with tears.

Sherick stammered, "He – he gambles some. He used to be the silent owner of that gambling joint in East St. Louis – The Gold Casino. He went broke. Clean broke. I gave him a job, but he didn't keep it long. I don't know what he's doing. He used to come out sometimes and hang around."

"Alone?"

"Well, with a couple of pals sometimes."

"Who are they?"

Sherick groaned.

"What's it about, Cardigan? Gee, what's it about?"

"Who are the guys?"

"Oh, hell. Jack Gos and Billy Dessig."

"O.K. Now where does McKimm hang out?"

Sherick almost choked, but he got it out. "He's staying in a room over Lou Abatti's speak – down by the river. And damn your soul, Cardigan!"

Willie cried, "Tom – Tom, for cryin' out loud, let me give this punk a bellyache! You hear, Tom!"

Sherick jumped, grabbed Willie's arm.

"Willie, don't!"

He tussled with Willie, hurled him against the wall, took away the guns and thrust them in his own pocket. He held on to Willie, rushing him to the door. Willie cursed and moaned, and Cardigan opened the door.

"Remember, Sherick," he said. "Keep your mouth shut."

When he had closed the door he said, "Whew!" and stood wiping perspiration from his forehead.

Chapter IV
Killer's Street

CARDIGAN climbed out of a taxi at Marion and Broadway and headed toward the Mississippi. A warm river mist hung pendant in the dark streets, and infrequent street lights had needle-pointed auras of wet radiance. Cardigan's footfalls were loud, purposeful, clean-cut in the dark alleys through which he strode.

He passed a run-down billiard parlor where the curt click of balls could be heard, and the heavy voices of men. There was a boat horn braying on Old Man River somewhere beyond the house-tops. Cardigan turned a corner, passed a cigar store where a radio bleated. He turned another corner and followed a cobbled street that went slightly downgrade. Halfway down he lingered. An alley dead-ended here into the cobbled street. Fifty yards up the alley crouched a two-story red brick house with a drop light outside a door flush with a broken flag walk. Some cars were in a parking space this side of the building, and back of it was the Mississippi. Insistent was the muffled beat of a jazz band's drum.

Cardigan entered the alley. Under the drop light was a sign – black ungainly letters on white:

THE HONKYTONK

He pushed open an old wooden door painted a nightmare green. He went down worn wooden steps to a foyer where a slash-mouthed girl took his hat and gave him a check. The place was damp and hot. The old building throbbed with the beat of the jazz band. Up two steps was the dance floor. The bar was in the basement. It was a French bar – small and narrow with stools in front of it.

Cardigan pushed in. There were no bottles in sight. He ordered Bourbon straight and the barman produced it from underneath the bar. Three drunks were in a huddle arguing about the Browns and the Cardinals. The lights hanging from the ceiling quivered with the beat of the jazz band.

Cardigan drank, looking around. The Bourbon was thrice-cut. He felt his arm prodded and he turned around and looked at Sergeant Bush. The Metropolitan dick was sucking a homemade cigarette. His hard straw hat was tilted over thinned-downed eyes.

"Hello, sarge," the barman said.

"Gin," said Bush, still looking hard at Cardigan.

"You getting collegiate?" Cardigan asked.

Bush downed gin straight without taking his eyes off Cardigan. He said, "You're doing a hell of a lot of running around, Cardigan. What's on your mind?"

"Right now – a certain nosey shamus named Bush."

"Be funny!"

"Go to hell!"

Bush lowered his voice grimly.

"Listen, you. I seen Tom Sherick come out of your apartment house before. Tom and a punk of his named Willie Martin."

Cardigan scowled.

"Haven't you anything else to do but watch my place?"

"What's between you and Sherick?"

"I never saw Sherick."

"You're a liar! I was parked down the hall and saw him and the hood come out of your apartment."

Cardigan cursed under his breath. He faced Bush squarely. "You dirty flatfoot," he ground out. "Have you been tapping my wire?"

"Never mind, never mind—"

"Why the hell didn't you stop Sherick? Hadn't the guts, eh? Nah! He had his hood with him – that hophead. That's why! Bush, you're a dirty sneak. You're a disgrace to an otherwise fine detective bureau. With swell guys like Holmes and Murfee, I don't know why you were put in charge of this case."

Bush reddened and his jaw hardened.

"What did you want with Sherick, Cardigan? You better tell me, because if you don't I take a squad and go out and find out myself!"

Cardigan's lip twitched.

"You stay away from Sherick, Bush! If you go out there he'll get the idea I welched. And I've never welched on any guy."

"You got something on Sherick," Bush muttered.

"I haven't. That's just another of your weak-minded ideas."

"You got something on him and you made him come across about somebody else." Bush nodded passed Cardigan's shoulder. "Hello, McKimm."

"Hello, Bush."

Cardigan looked in the mirror back of the bar and saw the reflected image of a tall, stony-faced man who smoked a cigar. It was the man who had cornered, frightened, Clara Hartz that night at the Ritz. He went to the bar and brooded darkly over a drink.

Cardigan threw a half-dollar on the bar. He whistled, left the bar, got his hat and went outside. Bush was at his heels. Cardigan opened the door of a waiting taxi and Bush said, "I'll go with you."

Cardigan turned a withering look on him.

"Not on my money, Bush!" He climbed in and slammed the door. "Broadway," he said to the driver.

The cab swung around and got out of the alley. Looking back, Cardigan saw Bush climb in another. Cardigan leaned forward.

"Here's a two-dollar bill, kid. Drop me off up the street and then take a ride out to the north end. There's a tail back here I want to drop."

"Jake."

Cardigan looked back and saw another cab following.

"Swing left at the next street," he said. "Don't stop. I'll jump and walk to Broadway. You keep going."

"Jake."

The cab swung left sharply. Cardigan leaped off and slammed the door. He darted into an alley. He saw the second taxi shoot past, with Bush sitting on the edge of the seat.

Cardigan retraced his steps and entered the Honkytonk. He did not check his hat. He reentered the bar and saw McKimm still standing there, a felt hat yanked down over his eyes, his hands toying with an empty glass. The bar was crowded now with jabbering drunks, and the jazz band pounded. Cardigan ordered a drink and paid for it on the spot. Under his hat-brim he watched McKimm in the mirror back of the bar.

Five minutes later McKimm threw a couple of bills on the bar, waited for change. Cardigan turned and went into the foyer. The hat-check girl had her back to him. She was talking on the telephone. There was nobody else in the foyer. It was noisy with the sound of the music.

The swing-door from the bar opened and McKimm came out. Cardigan lifted his coat pocket. McKimm's eyes narrowed and his lips tightened hard on his cigar. Cardigan nodded toward the exit. McKimm hesitated, stony-faced. Cardigan moved his lips and went closer.

McKimm turned and went up the stairs. Cardigan crowded him outside.

There was no taxi.

"Walk fast," Cardigan said.

He drew his gun and pressed it in the small of McKimm's back.

"What's this?" McKimm growled.

"Get."

They walked through the black alley, turned up the cobbled street. Cardigan flattened McKimm against a house-wall, made him raise his hands. He frisked him, took a gun from an armpit holster while his own gun pressed hard into McKimm's stomach.

"Now walk again," Cardigan said. "Put your hands in your pockets and keep them there."

"Didn't I see you with Bush?"

"Get along, get along."

Their footfalls echoed in the quiet dark street. Four blocks further on Cardigan stopped a taxi and crowded McKimm in. Cardigan gave his address to Lindell.

McKimm started.

"What the hell's this?"

"Shut up."

They struck Broadway, turned left into Olive and bowled through the darkened business district, past the *Post-Dispatch* Building, across Twelfth Boulevard and up the hill. At Channing they left the car tracks, hit Lindell and went over the hump past the University.

Cardigan spoke to the driver.

"When you reach the address, a driveway swings through the basement garage. Take it."

McKimm sat in stony silence, his breath audible in his nostrils, his lips clamped on his cigar.

In the basement garage Cardigan backed out, covered McKimm. He thrust a couple of bills into the driver's hand. He motioned McKimm out and took him up in the service elevator.

"Listen, who the hell are you?" McKimm muttered.

"Get out," Cardigan said at the sixth floor.

He marched McKimm down the corridor, unlocked the door.

"Get in."

He followed McKimm into the apartment, which he had left lighted, and kicked shut the door.

McKimm turned and looked at him stonily. "Who the hell are you?" he asked again.

"Pat O'Hara's partner."

McKimm remained stony.

"What is that supposed to mean?"

"Sit down in the straight-backed chair, honeybunch. We're going to play school. I'm the teacher and you're the pupil."

McKimm sat down, said, "The floor is yours."

Keeping his gun and eyes trained on McKimm, Cardigan fished in a vest pocket, drew out a folded piece of paper.

"Catch it," he said.

He threw and McKimm caught it.

"Read it," Cardigan said.

McKimm unfolded the paper, squinted his eyes. Not a muscle in his face twitched. He looked up with his stony expressionless eyes and said nothing.

"Now what about it?" Cardigan said.

"What about what?"

"In your notes, there, what the hell do you mean by the word 'obligation', McKimm?"

McKimm looked at the note again, folded it, tossed it to the open secretary.

"I don't know what you're talking about."

"I'm in a lousy mood tonight, McKimm, and I don't want wisecracks for answers. I saw you accost Mrs. Hartz at the Ritz the night before it was raided and you didn't look pleasant. And she looked scared. I'm on your tail tight as a tick."

"And you can go to hell."

Cardigan hefted his gun.

"What was the obligation?"

"Just what it said. Maybe I should have used 'debt'. A little debt. That's all."

"Debt for what?"

McKimm stood up, his lips still tight on his cigar, barely moving when he spoke.

"To hell with you!"

"Sit down!" Cardigan took three steps and punched McKimm in the chest.

McKimm sat down, his eyes hard as marbles.

Cardigan backed across the room, got hold of the telephone with one hand. He gave a number. He got a connection and asked for Mrs. Hartz.

"Hello, Mrs. Hartz. Cardigan. I want you to come over to my apartment immediately… I'm sorry, but I'm giving orders. You'll do wise to come over, as fast as you can… Yes. Thank you."

He hung up.

Visibly McKimm's lips didn't move, but they must have, because he was saying, "What the hell kind of a merry-go-round are you on anyway?"

"I'm reaching for the gold ring."

McKimm's eyes remained round and hard and inscrutable.

When the brass knocker on the outside of the door sounded, Cardigan did not move. He called, "Mrs. Hartz?"

"Yes."

"Come in."

The door opened. Everett was there, pink-cheeked and wavy-haired. The angle of the doorway at first prohibited his seeing McKimm. He saw Cardigan, however, and the gun in Cardigan's hand.

"What's the meaning of this?" he snapped indignantly.

"I didn't expect you," Cardigan said, with a wintry smile.

"Do you think I would let Mrs. Hartz come to your place alone? Really!"

Cool and white-faced in her black cloche hat and black wrap, Clara Hartz came in first. She saw McKimm. She looked at him with her Oriental eyes, looked away. Everett closed the door. Then he saw McKimm. He seemed to grow an inch, and his white hands doubled. His blue eyes radiated sudden blue fire but he kept his mouth shut.

Cardigan said, with a touch of bitter sarcasm, "Do I have to go through with introductions?"

"What do you want?" asked Clara Hartz in her flat voice.

Cardigan pointed to the secretary. "Read that letter."

She crossed the room, picked up the piece of paper McKimm had refolded. She read the lines, shrugged, let the note slip back to the desk. One of her arched eyebrows rose.

"Well?" she said.

Everett made an exasperated sound, crossed the room, snatched up the note, read it. He flung a look at McKimm. McKimm was stony-faced, stony-eyed. Everett spun on Cardigan.

"What in God's name are you driving at?" he ripped out hotly.

Cardigan ignored him. "Mrs. Hartz, in what way are you obligated to Mr. McKimm?"

"That," she said, "is perhaps my business – and Mr. McKimm's."

"Right now it's mine too."

"On the contrary—"

"You hear!" Cardigan rasped, his face a dull red. "It's my business! It's my business to find out who murdered my partner Pat O'Hara! It's my business to know what kind of business you had with McKimm!"

"Look here, Cardigan," snapped Everett, starting toward him.

"You keep your oar out of this – and stay back!"

Everett cried, "You have no right to question Mrs. Hartz! No right at all!"

"Mrs. Hartz," said Cardigan crisply, "answer my question."

She sighed. "I suppose I'll have to. Well" – she drew in a breath— "I owe him an amount – of money. I've owed it for a little more than a year. When Mr. McKimm operated the Gold Casino, a gaming place, I played there. Rather steeply. I was foolish. He took my I.O.U.s because he knew Mr. Hartz was quite wealthy. It was unfortunate. I found out that Mr. Hartz was rigidly opposed to gambling. I never had much money to spend. Plenty of charge accounts for legitimate purchases – but no allowance. I shouldn't have, but gambling is one of my weaknesses. I couldn't get the money. The debt is still standing. That is all."

"How much?" asked Cardigan.

She let her long-held breath out. "Fifty thousand."

"What of it? What of it?" snapped Everett.

Cardigan ignored him. Cardigan's face was brown and grim with red burning beneath the brown. He was staring at McKimm. He saw the first flicker of emotion in McKimm's face. He saw McKimm's big hands gripping the sides of the chair, saw an unholy glitter growing in McKimm's eyes.

"Now I suppose," came Clara Hartz's flat, casual voice, "you'll have something else to give to the scandal sheets."

Cardigan's voice was low, ominous. "That kill's the thing, Mrs. Hartz – the murder of my partner. I tell you again I'm no scandal-monger – not just for the sake of scandal. But this goes deeper – This goes way down deep. Or I miss my bet. I miss my bet if the killer of Pat O'Hara, Ludwig Hartz and his chauffeur isn't in this room right now."

She looked at him suddenly. She saw the fierce intensity in his eyes. She followed the direction of their burning, implacable stare. Fright leaped into her eyes. She let out a stifled little cry.

McKimm raised his hand, ripped the dead cigar from his mouth. "Who the hell are you staring at, Cardigan?" he roared.

For the first time his mouth opened, his lips ripped back across his teeth. A gold eye-tooth flashed at the left corner of his mouth.

Cardigan flung at him, "I'm staring at you, McKimm! I'm staring at the guy that murdered three men and put a fourth in the hospital!"

Ignoring Clara and Everett, he took three hard steps across the carpet, his gun trained on McKimm's chest.

"Oh, my God!" breathed Clara. "No – no – no!"

"Max Saul's living, thank God," Cardigan said. "And he'll remember that gold tooth, McKimm. And you'll remember how the spotlight on Hartz's car swung around as it swerved. You used this strike as a cover-up. You're broke. You need the money. You figured to get your debt out of Hartz's legacy to his wife."

"Is this true, is this true?" cried Clara Hartz.

McKimm heaved to his feet, agony bursting on his face, guilt bare and unadorned in his eyes.

"Sit down, McKimm!" barked Cardigan.

McKimm roared, "My God, Everett—"

A gun boomed.

Cardigan felt a slam somewhere in the back and he started to pitch forward. Clara Hartz screamed. McKimm jumped and grabbed Cardigan's gun, ripped it free. He smashed Cardigan in the jaw, sent him reeling backwards and followed him, ripping his own gun from Cardigan's pocket.

Everett stood shaking and horror-stricken, a smoking automatic in his hand.

"Ralph, what have you done?" cried Clara Hartz.

Cardigan landed in the mohair easy-chair with a bang, his heels flying, his head jerking back, the chair itself tilting backwards, banging against the wall.

McKimm towered with a gun in either hand. "I'm leaving," he clipped and backed swiftly to the door.

Everett shook. "My God, McKimm, don't leave me!"

Clara Hartz pressed hands to her cheeks, stared thunderstruck at Everett. "Ralph – Ralph—"

"Shut up!" Everett screamed at her.

He shook like a man with palsy and backed up beside McKimm.

"You'll – have to take me, McKimm. I just saved – you."

Cardigan snarled, "Yellow as I always thought you were! Leaving the woman to take the rap, eh?" His face was ferocious, bitter, his shaggy hair stood on end. Pain burned in his back, but he was a hard party.

Clara's calm was gone. She was flushed, wide-eyed, gripped with terror and wild bewilderment. She saw McKimm's gun move upward. She choked and whirled and spread her body and her arms in front of Cardigan.

"No you won't!" she panted. "I see now. I see it all. You murdered Ludwig to get that money – through me later. And you, Ralph – oh, how could you! You told him of Ludwig's movements. You urged me to divorce Ludwig. I wanted to. I didn't love him. I loved you. But you didn't want me – without his money. Oh, Ralph – Ralph!" She began sobbing hysterically.

Everett looked like a lamb shorn. His dignity, his haughty manner, were gone. He shook and looked wild and desperate.

"I gambled," she cried. "I was weak. God knows I was weak! And I have no excuse. I'm a fool – a terrible fool!"

McKimm clipped to Everett, "Come on."

McKimm opened the door, stepped into the corridor, looked up and down. Doors closed elsewhere. Voices were excited – then silent.

Glassy-eyed, Everett backed through the door, confirming his guilt, leaving the woman who had loved him. She sobbed brokenly.

Cardigan had his hand on it now, on the short-barreled Colt he had planted in the mohair easy-chair before Sherick's arrival. He whipped it up. The blunt muzzle belched flame. Everett jerked and his eyes popped wide. Then he screamed and fell backward, clutched at his chest.

McKimm bolted for the staircase.

Cardigan jumped from the chair, whipped quick words into Clara Hartz's ear.

"That door over there hides an in-a-door bed. Get in there. Close the door. Hide behind the bed. Stay there."

He ran to the corridor door, looked out. A man in a dressing-gown was standing near the elevator.

"Get a doctor," Cardigan said, indicating Everett.

He started down the staircase. Doors were opening and closing, and far below someone was blowing a police whistle. Cardigan reached the lobby as he saw McKimm bolt through the front door. He went through the door a split-second later and saw McKimm crossing Lindell.

A small crowd had gathered in front of the apartment house. Some autos had stopped. People were scattering at sight of the men with the drawn guns. McKimm began running west on Lindell. Cardigan reached the opposite sidewalk and ran after him. Pedestrians ran for shelter. McKimm looked back and fired, missed and crashed the tail light of a parked car.

Cardigan raised his gun but a darting pedestrian got in the way, yelped with fright, flung himself flat on the sidewalk. Cardigan leaped over him. McKimm turned south into Euclid, stopped, turned and waited for Cardigan to swing around the corner. His gun belched and echoes hammered.

Cardigan staggered to the curb, kept his feet, fired and saw McKimm reel but keep running. He fired again and saw McKimm swerve drunkenly. He ran after him unsteadily and McKimm turned and his gun blazed and Cardigan stopped and fell down. Half-kneeling, he raised his gun and watched McKimm jolting across the street. He fired and the bullet tumbled McKimm across the curb. But he got up and staggered on.

Cardigan got up, sweat pouring from him, pain tightening his jaw. He limped across the street. He fell down on the opposite sidewalk and saw McKimm down twenty yards further on. McKimm's gun boomed. The shot snarled against the pavement near Cardigan's head. He leaned on his elbow, looked down his gun, fired.

McKimm whipped over, tried to get up, collapsed. His gun rang as it banged down to the pavement.

Cardigan toiled to his feet, gritted his teeth, staggered toward Lindell. He drew in great breaths. He made himself walk almost steadily. He looked grim and shaggy and he could feel blood crawling beneath his clothes.

There was a crowd in front of the apartment house. He pushed through it, and people saw him and exclaimed but nobody tried to stop him. The lobby was jammed. The elevator was in use, so he took the stairway up. People were jabbering in the corridors. He barely noticed them. His feet were like gobs of lead.

He reached his floor and found a crowd there. He spotted a couple of uniformed cops. He plowed through the crowd and the cops turned and grabbed him roughly.

"Leggo," he muttered.

They tightened on him.

"You damned flatfeet, leggo!"

Bush appeared in the doorway.

"Oh, it's you, Cardigan!" Bush looked baffled and angry. "Let him go, boys."

The cops let go and Cardigan reeled into his apartment. A doctor was bending over Everett.

"I knew you were up to something tonight!" Bush growled. "Now what the hell did you do?"

"This guy on the floor shot me in the back. McKimm is lying over in Euclid near West Pine. I guess some of your cops have got him by this time."

"What'd this guy shoot you for?"

Cardigan sagged to a chair.

"McKimm killed my pal Pat O'Hara. He killed Hartz and the chauffeur. He wounded Max Saul."

"Somebody said they heard a woman scream here."

"They're nuts. It was Everett. When I cornered McKimm here Everett let me have it in the back. He was in with McKimm. He wanted to get rid of Hartz too."

"You're lying, Cardigan!"

"Go to hell, Bush! Let me alone awhile."

"There was a woman here!"

"There wasn't. I got McKimm here and then I got Everett here."

An ambulance doctor and two men with a stretcher came in. The doctor bending over Everett looked up and shook his head.

"He hasn't a chance," he said.

Cardigan, fast losing consciousness, saw the white door across the room open. He shook his head. He did not want Mrs. Hartz to come. He believed that this thing could be settled without her. He knew she had been tricked by Everett. He knew she had nothing to do with the murder of his partner. He remembered that she had put her body in front of him against the muzzles of McKimm's guns.

But she came out – statuesque and white-faced.

"So," growled Bush, with a scathing look at Cardigan.

She gasped and ran across the room. Nobody else had noticed Cardigan sagging. She reached him and put her arm around him. His eyes rolled as he looked up at her. He smiled.

"You've – got – guts," he muttered.

Cardigan came to a day later in a hospital room. He turned his head and saw Max Saul sitting in a wheelchair. He licked his lips. A nurse got up and looked at him.

Max Saul grinned, "He's O.K., nurse."

"Yeah," said Cardigan. "I feel like getting up and playing kick-the-wicket or something."

"I'm sore," Max joked. "You're getting all the headlines, Irish."

"How did Everett and McKimm make out?"

"They didn't. They brought McKimm here on a stretcher and identified him. Everett cleared his conscience before he went places. And cleared Clara Hartz too. It was Everett put the idea in McKimm's head that if Hartz should die Mrs. Hartz would come into a lot of money. Everett figured he would have, too – through marriage to the widow. I think I said once that guy was a lounge-lizard."

Cardigan closed his eyes. "It's tough on the woman, Max. She saved my life."

"She took it all standing up, Jack. And she's been telephoning every half hour about you. Bush started to yammer but Captain Bricknell dampered him down."

Another nurse came in with a vase of roses. Cardigan frowned. "Now who sent those?"

"Mrs. Hartz."

Cardigan relaxed and closed his eyes.

Max Saul said, "That's what I'd call a bed of roses, Irish."

A nurse wheeled him out of the room and on the way down the hall he hummed The St. Louis Blues.

Countdown

Jonathan Shipley

I EASED through the narrow corridor, brushing against the experimental small-leaf ivy growing on its walls to keep oxygen levels comfortable. I breathed in the heavy, earthy air in approval. The aerosphere, docked at the International Space Hub, had been generating its own atmosphere for six months now in preparation for the six-month journey to Mars. There was always the chance of the flora-based eco-system going into flight shock, but it was small. The hybrids on board were hardy genetic mods.

One of the side hatches popped open with a soft *whump*. A pinched-faced man of middle years crawled out of a cubicle. "Still feels like a coffin, but mission first, comfort second. Holding up OK, Seline?"

"As well as the moment allows, Frank." Twenty hours until separation. "How's engineering?"

"Running post-final checks on all systems…again. I keep having this feeling that I missed something."

"But you probably haven't," I pointed out. "You could join the others on last leave in the concourse, you know." I wasn't displeased that he was running redundant checks, but I was beginning to worry about Tim Ertu, our botanist. Commander, engineer, and botanist were the key positions on this mission, and the three of us were living on the aerosphere 24/7. Or at least the three of us had been. Now our botanist was somewhere on the Hub, presumably enjoying his last days of freedom. My gut wanted him back to do his share of redundancy checks, but that was just me being paranoid. Everything had been checked and double-checked.

"Don't care about the concourse," Frank shrugged. "Mission first, fun second." He shuffled off toward the engine compartment.

I stopped at the cubicle, a.k.a coffin, assigned to me and crawled in, just to check the feel of it yet again. We all kept doing that, trying to shift our perception of the space from claustrophobic to homey. If we were going to be shoe-horned into these cubicles for literally years, we desperately needed homey. But the human psyche, like gases, had a way of adjusting to the space available. Give us a couple weeks, and the coffins would feel like the 'compact staterooms' in the official description.

One of the cubicles was a double berth assigned to Anne and Grable. Since relationships were never smooth sailing, it was a calculated risk, but a couple ought to add a cohesive influence within the team. Grable had grumbled about the vasectomy, but understood. The aerosphere couldn't handle a pregnancy. Life resources had been fine-tuned for ten. There wouldn't be enough food or air for eleven, even though the addition was small.

If that wasn't sobering enough, there was a grimmer side to a deep-space pregnancy. Simulations had indicated that reduced gravity and heightened radiation would impact fetal development in a major way that we couldn't predict. No one wanted to go there, certainly not our corporate sponsor who wanted the public to see the mission as the next step to Mars colonization, not as a monster vid.

At thirty-three and thirty-six, Anne and Grable were the youngest of the team. The rest of us were older, with fading hormones. Like everything else about this mission, that was no accident. The fewer hormones the better.

A quick beep. I glanced at my wristcom where text from a surface-to-Hub transmission was scrolling. *Greetings, Commander* – It was Cavalo, CEO of Cavalier Enterprises that funded the mission. *A hiccup. Ertu is off the team, but I have this covered. Out of the office the rest of the day. Check with Becca.* The text ended.

Our all-important botanist was off the team? That was what he called a 'hiccup'? I could feel what that one word was doing to my heart rate. And Cavalo – the jerk – was passing the explanation for this catastrophe down the chain of command to the mission administrator.

I retraced my steps from the aerosphere to the cluster of temp cubicles on the Hub side where the team had office space. I plopped down behind the desk and flicked open the broadband channel hard-linked to Cavalier. "A message, Becca?"

The youngish woman who appeared on screen looked unhappy. "Yes, and I'm just the messenger. Do not explode in my direction. Dr. Ertu is off the mission team. His spot is being filled by his assistant. And know that Mr. Cavalo has already signed off on this. He worked all day yesterday to come up with this solution."

Yesterday? This happened yesterday and I was just now hearing about it? I took deep breaths, reminding myself that Becca was just the messenger. Cavalo might own the mission in a literal sense, but he had no right to make snap decisions that could lead to failure in the field. "I'm coming down," I finally said. "This needs to be resolved face to face, and I doubt Cavalo will come up to the Hub."

"You know that makes no sense, right?" Becca protested. "A day before departure you're risking de-acclimating your body for…nothing. It really is a done deal."

"It is not a done deal. We can't succeed on a botanical mission without the botanist who designed the bio-systems. I will get Tim Ertu reinstated. I have to. In fact, I'll bring Tim down with me." I was assuming he hadn't heard the news yet, even though he was at the center of it. It was how Cavalo did things.

Becca looked even less happy. "Dr. Ertu is already back on Earth," she mumbled.

"Back on – how?" He didn't have the clearance for a trip planetside. Hub Control would have passed that directly to me.

Becca hesitated. "OK, I was specifically instructed not to tell you, but this is ridiculous. Dr. Ertu is dead."

That stopped me cold. Tim dead? "How?" He'd been in a small, restricted area with the rest of us for the last month. How was a big how.

"I don't have the details – no I really don't. All I know is that his body was found in a cargo shuttle running from Hub to Earth. It looks like an accident and shouldn't affect departure. Mr. Cavalo is leaning heavily on the investigating authorities not to involve the rest of the team since you have been under constant monitoring."

That took a moment to sink in. "Is there some question whether this might be—"

"Don't even go there," Becca said tersely. "At this point, it's an accident." After a long moment of silence, she continued. "His replacement is already on the way up to the Hub after undergoing a complete physical. Please do not strangle him or her upon arrival."

I took another deep breath. "You know me too well. Wait – why is gender suddenly ambiguous? Tim Ertu's backup is Dr. Maria McCray."

"Dr. McCray accepted an unexpected job offer and is no longer available. That's why we're off-plan. This replacement is Dr. Ertu's former assistant from the university. All I have is a name. Birch."

"Birch who?"

"I don't know. All I was told was that Birch was okayed by medlab and is shuttling up."

I closed my eyes a moment. "Do you see me praying that he/she is not some oversexed college stud? That's the last thing this team needs. Group dynamics in claustrophobic conditions are fragile at best. Is medlab also appropriately dampening the libido during this examination?"

Becca shrugged. "I don't know that either. I'm just the poor, overworked administrator. I'll pass any info directly to you, Seline."

I forced a smile, though I wasn't feeling it. "Thank you, Becca." And clicked off.

I lost the smile and sank my head into the heels of my hands. Tim dead. He wasn't really a friend, but it was impossible not to feel close when working at close quarters. And so senseless. My mind skipped a step and landed in conspiracy mode. The only reason to remove a middle-aged botanogeneticist with no enemies would be to scuttle the mission, which did have enemies. And an unmanned cargo shuttle where Tim had no reason to be. He didn't even have access to cargo shuttles.

Murder. I shivered. If it was murder, that meant the murderer was up here with us – not in the aerosphere containment area where only the ten of us had access, but somewhere on the Hub. We were one of maybe two-dozen projects currently docked around the central concourse – a few hundred people total. If any one of them was a murderer, that was way too close for comfort.

I got up and walked to the boundary of the mission area to check the door log. There was a regular pattern of back and forth to the concourse by most of the team, but Tim's code didn't show up at all. I frowned, processing that. He must have slipped out when the door was opened by someone else. Or had an unknown perpetrator breached the mission area and dragged Tim away?

I played with the idea but couldn't commit to it. So I coded myself out to take a look at the shuttle bay. I recognized an element of risk in going alone, but I knew a few tricks if it came to an attack. And even if this was murder, it had been carefully staged to look like an accident. No one would believe two accidents right on top of each other. There was some safety in that.

The shuttle bay was the same gunmetal gray as all the utilitarian areas of the Hub. Only the concourse made an effort to be colorful. The air smelled flat and metallic after the flora-rich aerosphere atmosphere. The cargo side was opposite the passenger area with low-grav dollies clustered around it. There were supposedly fail-safes that stopped an auto-shuttle from sealing itself and expelling atmosphere with a living, breathing person on board, and I wasn't seeing a fail-safe override. I fiddled with the controls, looking for random anomalies. Honestly, I didn't know what I was looking for. I was just looking.

A series of beeps from the other side of the bay signaled an incoming passenger shuttle. I barely gave it a glance. When I looked up again, a young man was walking in my direction. Team coveralls, but a complete stranger. It took a second to realize this must be the assistant expedited up from the surface. The replacement. Young, male, a potential nightmare. He stood awkwardly a moment, then forced a smile. "I'm guessing we have a lot to talk about, Commander," he said cautiously.

"You've obviously been warned about me," I said.

"Mr. Cavalo said something about a temper."

I ran a disapproving eye over the assistant. Too young. Rangy build that would barely fit in his 'compact stateroom'. And glasses. His vision would have been corrected with surgery with sufficient lead time, but who had time now?

He cleared his throat. "I realize I'm being forced on you at the last minute, and it's a shock to me as well. I was called in to discuss the circumstances of Dr. Ertu's demise and suddenly Mr. Cavalo drafts me for the mission. I'm Trip Birch, by the way." He held out his hand.

I wanted to ignore it, but didn't. Getting unexpectedly drafted for a two-year mission to Mars on top of the sudden death of a colleague was bizarre enough to evoke a little sympathy. "What kind of name is Trip?"

"Short for Waltrip."

And what kind of name is Waltrip? – I wanted to ask, but I held back. "Walk with me, Trip." We started back to the mission area. "So you don't really want to be part of the team?"

"Oh, I do," he said quickly. "I just wasn't expecting it. But this Mars mission is scientific heaven. Who wouldn't kill for the chance to be part—" He stopped abruptly and grimaced. "Sorry. Wasn't thinking."

Mars as the motive for murder? Astronomically unlikely. I pushed that aside and forced myself back to business. "Please tell me you are in some way qualified to step into Tim Ertu's shoes. His re-gened Mars grass is the whole reason we're spending a year on the surface. If you can't—"

"But I can," Trip interjected. "I've been part of the Mars grass research from the start, know everything about it – a lot of the ideas are mine, in fact. I'm starting my PhD in botanical genegineering this fall."

"Apparently not," I said softly.

"Oh, right. Two-year mission. But I know every step of Dr. Ertu's plan for installing the Mars grass because I helped formulate the plan. I can do this."

We reached the mission area and I coded us in. His eye went immediately to the aerosphere docked at the outer end of the space, settling into the rapt stare of a true believer. That was good. He believed in the mission. I didn't like the fact that he was young for the team, and who knew if he was compatible with our carefully crafted artificial environment. Well…medlab had to know, actually. They weren't idiots. If they had sent him up to the Hub, he had to be compatible.

I sighed and looked him squarely in the eye. "Botanical competence is not the only issue we need to discuss. We can't afford any hormone-driven surprises in flight."

He blinked in surprise. "You're talking to a nerdy grad student, not some frat stud. Self-control has never been a problem."

"We need things a little more absolute than that, hence the vasectomy. Don't take it personally. With anyone your age, medlab would have responded in the same way."

Trip shifted awkwardly. "Uh…what vasectomy?"

"As part of your physical, didn't medlab…" I fell silent as he shook his head.

"Completely unnecessary," he shrugged. "I'm sort of…between genders at the moment."

Did that mean transgendering? If it did, I couldn't see any visual clues that he was transitioning. "So. Is 'he' not the right pronoun here?" I asked carefully. My mind was spinning a flock of new, grim scenarios. A transgender in hormonal transition at close quarters sounded like an emotional time bomb.

"Oh, yes, definitely 'he'," Trip assured me, then paused. "But I'm not actively male at the moment."

That phrase was new to me. "So you're an inactive male?" He nodded, not looking entirely sure himself. Inactive male? Between genders?

"I give up," I finally shrugged. "I have no idea what you're trying to tell me."

He shifted again. "I was hoping this wouldn't come up – not because I'm uncomfortable with my choices, but because the English language doesn't describe me very well at the moment. I was a surrogate womb last year as a way to cover my graduate tuition. That in itself isn't problematic, but I'm planning to carry another child to pay for my PhD. So after the first child, it made sense not to have the reverse procedure. That's what I mean by 'between genders'. I'm still in womb state, so to speak – but not currently pregnant."

I sat back to absorb this unexpected info dump. A surrogate womb – never saw that coming. I knew there were procedures that made males as viable as females for carrying a fetus to term, and yes, surrogacy did pay well. But genderwise?

"No, the English language doesn't cover your situation very well," I agreed. "And I probably should retract all assumptions that you're a hormonal time bomb. More hormonal limbo, I imagine."

He nodded. "Yes, limbo. Not where I want to be forever, but OK for now."

Not knowing what to say, I just nodded. "So this is all about money?" I finally said. "Seems extreme compared with a student loan."

"Well…it is," he admitted. "But it makes more sense when you're also genderqueer in search of an identity." He hesitated. "So you're OK with me on the team?"

I hesitated too, still negotiating the rapidly shifting landscape of his gender state. "It's hard to be sure…but I think so. I would say let's give it a week, but we don't have the luxury of time. So welcome aboard, Trip Birch."

"Thank you." He flashed a quick smile. "It's an honor. For me, this mission is definitely about following my passion."

I was thinking furiously as I nodded politely. "Frank Zump, our engineer is currently on board the aerosphere. He can give you the grand tour and direct you to your stateroom – or coffin, as he calls it."

I kept smiling until he was on his way into the aerosphere, then headed for my office. I faded to a scowl and sat thinking in silence. Trip himself seemed OK, a good replacement, but the circumstances for his being here felt a little too convenient. Finally, I put through a call to Becca down below. "Has the medical examiner released anything on Tim Ertu's death?" I asked.

"Well…yes," she said. "A prelim report just came through citing mechanical malfunction on the cargo shuttle. The death has been ruled accidental."

"Of course it has," I muttered. "I daresay Cavalo was pushing very hard for that, but I don't buy it. I looked over the shuttle systems, and nothing looked tampered with. And considering the fail-safes built into the system, the only way Tim could pass as cargo would be if he was already dead. That's no mechanical malfunction. That's murder."

Becca's eye grew wide. "What if it this doesn't stop with Dr. Ertu? What if this is an attempt to sabotage the mission?"

I shook my head. "Overt sabotage could easily be accomplished with far less complication – simply blow up the aerosphere. I'm wondering about an attempt to infiltrate the mission."

"You mean…? She stopped and frowned. "The assistant? He's behind all this?"

"That I doubt. But he could be unwittingly manipulated. Then the question becomes by whom and for what reason. Think about it – Maria McCray gets a lucrative job offer just when she is needed for the mission. It seems that someone is willing to kill to get Trip on the team. And the bitter irony is that even if it's all true, I still need him for the mission. So here's what I need from you, Becca. A man like Cavalo has enemies—"

"Lots of enemies," she murmured.

"—so get me a shortlist of who could benefit from hijacking data or derailing the mission. Corporate competitors, personal enemies, family feuds – any of those."

I signed off and made the short trip to the aerosphere. I caught up with Trip and Frank in the hydroponics chamber where much of the in-flight food would be generated. I stared at Trip leaning over the main tank and thought, Poison the food supply and ruin the mission. And this in spite of my working theory that he was an unknowing pawn in whatever was going on. But that was the trouble with conspiracies – they made you paranoid.

"What's left on the tour?" I asked Frank.

"Just the bridge," he said gruffly. "That's your domain anyway, so I'm happy to turn the tour over to you. Mission first, convenience second, but…" He gave me a narrow look as he exited. Who the hell is this guy and why a replacement at the last minute? The unspoken words were heavily implied. He hadn't heard about Tim's death.

"He's a character," Trip noted when Frank exited.

"Just imagine his bedside manner – Frank doubles as ship medic."

"Odd combination."

"Not really. Sickbay is mainly high-tech appliances, so why not an engineer? The bridge is this way." I led the way down the ivy-covered corridor. The bridge would be a good place to talk. I settled into the flexsteel command chair while Trip investigated the banks of dormant consoles. I had checked and re-checked the nav systems earlier, then powered everything down.

"Know anything about Dr. Maria McCray?" I asked.

"I've read her articles on hyper-hydroponics, but that's about it."

"And how well do you know our patron Mr. Cavalo?" I prompted. "He seemed eager to bring you on the team."

"More desperate than eager," Trip shrugged. "I knew the name, of course, but I never met the man before this morning. He seems kind of over-the-top."

"He's very over-the-top. It's why he's a successful CEO. Have you done any other work for Cavalier Enterprises?"

He shook his head. "I'm a grad student. My only job experience was assisting Dr. Ertu in the lab. And the surrogacy, of course, although that's not really a job…just a lot of labor."

"Cute," I commented dryly.

"Come to think of it," he continued, "my scheduled upcoming pregnancy has a Cavalier connection. The woman I'll be carrying for works for the company."

"Oh?" I said with forced casualness. "Maybe it's someone I know."

"Her name is Kara Hall. Frankly, a real power-bitch, exactly the type you'd expect not to carry her own child. She just had me primed to do it for her, and I had to turn around and tell her I'm unavailable."

Already I had suspicions. I didn't know the name, but Becca probably would. "And have you found your coffin?"

"I did." He looked at me uneasily. "I'm sensing this is the end of the tour. I could go back to hydroponics, if that suits you."

"Good idea," I nodded, getting up from the command chair. Apparently I was telegraphing my impatience. "I'll see you at 1800 hours to introduce you to the rest of the team."

He left. I left. For a few minutes we were cheek-to-shoulder in the cramped corridor, then we split in different directions. I made it back to my office without actually running, but I was moving fast. "Becca, you there?" I huffed, flicking open the channel.

"Always," she nodded, appearing on the monitor. "Is everything all right? You look…intense."

"New lead. Kara Hall. What can you tell me about her?"

Becca pulled a sour face. "Not exactly a pleasant topic. Mr. Cavalo's ex, ugly divorce."

"Yet she works at Cavalier Enterprises?"

"No, she's on the Board of Directors. In fact, the divorce settlement made her the second largest shareholder on the Board."

"Power plays in the boardroom?" I guessed.

"Constantly. If she had the chance, she'd oust Mr. Cavalo and take Cavalier in a whole new direction—"

"—that doesn't include space colonization."

"Don't know about that," Becca shrugged. "But it definitely wouldn't include Mr. Cavalo."

"And a question completely out of the blue – when a male surrogate womb is 'primed', what exactly does that involve?"

She frowned. "That's the biz term for implanting an artificial placenta as the final step before actual pregnancy. What's this connected with?" Then her eyes widened. "Your newest team member?"

I nodded. "He's gender-complicated, but nothing that impacts the mission. At least I hope not. But he was being primed to carry Kara Hall's baby when he was drafted for the mission. Coincidence…or Twilight Zone?"

"Twilight Zone," Becca decided quickly. "You still think he is being used to ruin the mission?"

"Possibly, but not in any simple way. If the mission were directly sabotaged, Cavalo would just collect the sabotage insurance and mount another. But if the mission failed in a more oblique way…"

"…Mr. Cavalo would be discredited and possibly lose control of Cavalier Enterprises," Becca supplied.

"To his ex?"

"Probably."

The same ex who had just 'primed' Trip for pregnancy. It couldn't be a coincidence.

"But," Becca continued, "Ms. Hall is unlikely to risk bankrupting the company to get control of it. It doesn't make sense for her to purposefully ruin a multi-million-dollar mission when it's her money, too…unless…"

"What?" I prompted.

"There's been active trade in Cavalier stock over the last two weeks. Someone is dumping whole blocks of stock."

"But if that's Kara Hall, dumping her stock destroys any chance to control the company."

Becca mulled a moment. "She might settle for destroying the company. Especially if she's also betting against Mars grass on the commodities futures market."

I shook my head. "Not following that."

"There's a brisk futures market for Mars grass, essentially betting on its viability. If she's betting against it and the mission fails—"

"A killing," I nodded as the pieces clicked. "Both literally and figuratively. Makes sense – gotta go." I cut the link.

I reached the aerosphere at a run and headed directly for engineering. "Frank," I called to the octopus of mechanical tentacles where he was working. "Scrub up and head for sickbay. You've got your first patient."

* * *

It was a long two hours. The medical facilities in the concourse would have been better for surgery, but success also depended on secrecy. If Kara Hall had organized all this, she needed to think the mission was still on track for failure, especially with a murderer still loose in the Hub. So it was all up to Frank and sickbay.

Eventually he shuffled out of sickbay, holding a contamination canister. "You were right," he murmured. I'd never seen him so shaken.

"What is it?" I asked, not sure I wanted to know.

"Polonium-4 – a low-level radioactive isotope favored by the old KCB in the twentieth century for quiet assassinations. It was planted in the kid's extra plumbing. Would have slow-poisoned him over the next few months…and us as well with so much close physical contact. We'd all be on our last legs before we ever established Mars orbit."

And the Mars grass, the mission, and the whole team would perish in the emptiness of space. I shuddered at the cold-bloodedness of it all. "And Trip?" I asked belatedly.

"He'll be OK," Frank nodded. "At least as far as the surgery is concerned. Can't swear by the rest of him—"

"As long as he can plant grass," I interjected. "Tim's dead, you know."

"Figured when I saw the polonium. You going to the police?

Sixteen hours to departure…drawn-out police investigation. Easy call, especially when the mission's success would likely wipe the finances of the person behind the murder. For people like her, it had to be the worst punishment imaginable. "No, we stay on schedule for Hub separation. It's what Tim would want."

Frank nodded. "Mission first, murder second. Good call."

In a Cellar

Harriet Prescott Spofford

Chapter I

IT WAS the day of Madame de St. Cyr's dinner, an event I never missed; for, the mistress of a mansion in the Faubourg St. Germain, there still lingered about her the exquisite grace and good breeding peculiar to the old regime, that insensibly communicates itself to the guests till they move in an atmosphere of ease that constitutes the charm of home. One was always sure of meeting desirable and well-assorted people here, and a *contre-temps* was impossible. Moreover, the house was not at the command of all; and Madame de St. Cyr, with the daring strength which, when found in a woman at all, should, to be endurable, be combined with a sweet but firm restraint, rode rough-shod over the parvenus of the Empire, and was resolute enough to insulate herself even among the old *noblesse*, who, as all the world knows, insulate themselves from the rest of France. There were rare qualities in this woman, and were I to have selected one who with an even hand should carry a snuffy candle through a magazine of powder, my choice would have devolved upon her; and she would have done it.

I often looked, and not unsuccessfully, to discern what heritage her daughter had in these little affairs. Indeed, to one like myself, Delphine presented the worthier study. She wanted the airy charm of manner, the suavity and tenderness of her mother, a deficiency easily to be pardoned in one of such delicate and extraordinary beauty. And perhaps her face was the truest index of her mind; not that it ever transparently displayed a genuine emotion, Delphine was too well bred for that, but the outline of her features had a keen regular precision, as if cut in a gem. Her exquisite color seldom varied, her eyes were like blue steel, she was statue-like and stony. But had one paused there, pronouncing her hard and impassive, he had committed an error. She had no great capability for passion, but she was not to be deceived; one metallic flash of her eye would cut like a sword through the whole mesh of entanglements with which you had surrounded her; and frequently, when alone with her, you perceived cool recesses in her nature, sparkling and pleasant, which jealously guarded themselves from a nearer approach. She was infinitely *spirituelle*; compared to her, Madame herself was heavy.

At the first, I had seen that Delphine must be the wife of a diplomate. What diplomate? For a time asking myself the question seriously, I decided in the negative, which did not, however, prevent Delphine from fulfilling her destiny, since there were others. She was, after all, like a draught of rich old wine, all fire and sweetness. These things were not generally seen in her; I was more favored than many; and I looked at her with pitiless perspicacious eyes. Nevertheless, I had not the least advantage; it was, in fact, between us, diamond cut diamond, which, oddly enough, brings me back to my story.

Some years previously, I had been sent on a special mission to the government at Paris, and having finally executed it, I resigned the post, and resolved to make my residence there, since it is the only place on earth where one can live. Every morning I half expect to see the country, beyond the city, white with an encampment of the nations, who, having peacefully flocked there overnight, wait till the Rue St. Honore shall run out and greet them. It surprises me, sometimes, that those pretending to civilization are content to remain at a distance. What experience have they of life, not to mention gaiety and pleasure, but of the great purpose of life, society? Man evidently is gregarious; Fourier's fables are founded on fact; we are nothing without our opposites, our fellows, our lights and shadows, colors, relations, combinations, our *point d'appui*, and our angle of sight. An isolated man is immensurable; he is also unpicturesque, unnatural, untrue. He is no longer the lord of Nature, animal and vegetable, but Nature is the lord of him; the trees, skies, flowers, predominate, and he is in as bad taste as green and blue, or as an oyster in a vase of roses. The race swings naturally to clusters. It being admitted, then, that society is our normal state, where is it to be obtained in such perfection as at Paris? Show me the urbanity, the generosity in trifles, better than sacrifice, the incuriousness and freedom, the grace, and wit, and honor, that will equal such as I find here. Morality, we were not speaking of it, the intrusion is unnecessary; must that word with Anglo-Saxon pertinacity dog us round the world? A hollow mask, which Vice now and then lifts for a breath of air, I grant you this state may be called; but since I find the vice elsewhere, countenance my preference for the accompanying mask. But even this is vanishing; such drawing rooms as Mme. de St. Cyr's are less and less frequent. Yet, though the delightful spell of the last century daily dissipates itself, and we are not now what we were twenty years ago, still Paris is, and will be to the end of time, for a cosmopolitan, the pivot on which the world revolves.

It was, then, as I have said, the day of Mme. de St. Cyr's dinner. Punctually at the hour, I presented myself, for I have always esteemed it the least courtesy which a guest can render, that he should not cool his hostess's dinner.

The usual choice company waited. There was the Marquis of G., the ambassador from home; Col. Leigh, an *attaché* of that embassy; the Spanish and Belgian ministers; all of whom, with myself, completed a diplomatic circle. There were also wits and artists, but no ladies whose beauty exceeded that of the St. Cyrs. With nearly all of this assemblage I held certain relations, so that I was immediately at ease. G. was the only one whom, perhaps, I would rather not have met, although we were the best of friends. They awaited but one, the Baron Stahl. Meanwhile Delphine stood coolly taking the measurement of the Marquis of G., while her mother entertained one and another guest with a low-toned flattery, gentle interest, or lively narration, as the case might demand.

In a country where a *coup d'etat* was as easily given as a box on the ear, we all attentively watched for the arrival of one who had been sent from a neighboring empire to negotiate a loan for the tottering throne of this. Nor was expectation kept long on guard. In a moment, "His Excellency, the Baron Stahl!" was announced.

The exaggeration of his low bow to Mme. de St. Cyr, the gleam askance of his black eye, the absurd simplicity of his dress, did not particularly please me. A low forehead, straight black brows, a beardless cheek with a fine color which gave him a fictitiously youthful appearance, were the most striking traits of his face; his person was not to be found fault with; but he boldly evinced his admiration for Delphine, and with a wicked eye.

As we were introduced, he assured me, in pure English, that he had pleasure in making the acquaintance of a gentleman whose services were so distinguished.

I, in turn, assured him of my pleasure in meeting a gentleman who appreciated them.

I had arrived at the house of Mme. de St. Cyr with a load on my mind, which for four weeks had weighed there; but before I thus spoke, it was lifted and gone. I had seen the Baron Stahl before, although not previously aware of it; and now, as he bowed, talked my native tongue so smoothly, drew a glove over the handsome hand upon whose first finger shone the only incongruity of his attire, a broad gold ring, holding a gaudy red stone – as he stood smiling and expectant before me, a sudden chain of events flashed through my mind, an instantaneous heat, like lightning, welded them into logic. A great problem was resolved. For a second, the breath seemed snatched from my lips; the next, a lighter, freer man never trod in diplomatic shoes.

I really beg your pardon – but perhaps from long usage, it has become impossible for me to tell a straight story. It is absolutely necessary to inform you of events already transpired.

In the first place, then, I, at this time, possessed a valet, the pink of valets, an Englishman, and not the less valuable to me in a foreign capital, that, notwithstanding his long residence, he was utterly unable to speak one word of French intelligibly. Reading and writing it readily, his thick tongue could master scarcely a syllable. The adroitness and perfection with which he performed the duties of his place were unsurpassable. To a certain extent I was obliged to admit him into my confidence; I was not at all in his. In dexterity and despatch he equalled the advertisements. He never condescended to don my cast-off apparel, but, disposing of it, always arrayed himself in plain but gentlemanly garments. These do not complete the list of Hay's capabilities. He speculated. Respectable tenements in London called him landlord; in the funds certain sums lay subject to his order; to a profitable farm in Hants he contemplated future retirement; and passing upon the Bourse, I have received a grave bow, and have left him in conversation with an eminent capitalist respecting consols, drafts, exchange, and other erudite mysteries, where I yet find myself in the ABC. Thus not only was my valet a free-born Briton, but a landed proprietor. If the Rothschilds blacked your boots or shaved your chin, your emotions might be akin to mine. When this man, who had an interest in the India traders, brought the hot water into my dressing room, of a morning, the Antipodes were tributary to me. To what extent might any little irascibility of mine drive a depression in the market! And I knew, as he brushed my hat, whether stocks rose or fell. In one respect, I was essentially like our Saxon ancestors, my servant was a villain. If I had been merely a civilian, in any purely private capacity, having leisure to attend to personal concerns in the midst of the delicate specialties entrusted to me from the cabinet at home, the possession of so inestimable a valet might have bullied me beyond endurance. As it was, I found it rather agreeable than otherwise. He was tacitly my secretary of finance.

Several years ago, a diamond of wonderful size and beauty, having wandered from the East, fell into certain imperial coffers among our Continental neighbors; and at the same time some extraordinary intelligence, essential to the existence, so to speak, of that government, reached a person there who fixed as its price this diamond. After a while he obtained it, but, judging that prudence lay in departure, took it to England, where it was purchased for an enormous sum by the Duke of —— – as he will remain an unknown quantity, let us say X. There are probably not a dozen such diamonds in the world, certainly not three in England. It rejoiced in such flowery appellatives as the Sea of Splendor, the Moon of Milk; and, of course, those who had but parted with it under protest, as it were, determined to obtain it again at all hazards; they were never famous for scrupulosity. The Duke of X. was aware of this, and, for a time, the gem had lain idle, its glory muffled in a casket; but finally, on some grand occasion, a few months prior to the period of which I have spoken above, it was determined to set it in the Duchess's coronet. Accordingly, one day, it was given by her son, the Marquis of G., into the hands of their solicitor, who should deliver it to her Grace's jeweller. It lay in a small shagreen case, and before the Marquis left, the solicitor placed the case in a flat leathern box, where lay a chain of most singular workmanship, the clasp of which was deranged. This chain was very broad, of a style known as the brickwork, but every brick was a tiny gem, set in a delicate filagree linked with the next, and the whole rainbowed lustrousness moving at your will, like the scales of some gorgeous Egyptian serpent; the solicitor was to take this also to the jeweller. Having laid the box in his private desk, Ulster, his confidential clerk, locked it, while he bowed the Marquis down. Returning immediately, the solicitor took the flat box and drove to the jeweller's. He found the latter so crowded with customers, it being the fashionable hour, as to be unable to attend to him; he, however, took the solicitor into his inner room, a dark fireproof place, and there quickly deposited the box within a safe, which stood inside another, like a Japanese puzzle, and the solicitor, seeing the doors double-locked and secured, departed; the other promising to attend to the matter on the morrow.

Early the next morning, the jeweller entered his dark room, and proceeded to unlock the safe. This being concluded, and the inner one also thrown open, he found the box in a last and entirely, as he had always believed, secret compartment. Anxious to see this wonder, this Eye of Morning, and Heart of Day, he eagerly loosened the band and unclosed the box. It was empty. There was no chain there; the diamond was missing. The sweat streamed from his forehead, his clothes were saturated, he believed himself the victim of a delusion. Calling an assistant, every article and nook in the dark room was examined. At last, in an extremity of despair, he sent for the solicitor, who arrived in a breath. The jeweller's alarm hardly equalled that of the other. In his sudden dismay, he at first forgot the circumstances and dates relating to the affair; afterward was doubtful. The Marquis of G. was summoned, the police called in, the jeweller given into custody. Every breath the solicitor continued to draw only built up his ruin. He swallowed laudanum, but, by making it an overdose, frustrated his own design. He was assured, on his recovery, that no suspicion attached to him. The jeweller now asseverated that the diamond had never been given to him; but though the jeweller had committed perjury, this was, nevertheless, strictly true. Of course, whoever had the stone would not attempt to dispose of it at present, and, though communications were opened with the general European police, there was very little to work upon. But by means of this last step the former possessors became aware of its loss, and I make no doubt had their agents abroad immediately.

Meanwhile, the case hung here, complicated and tantalizing, when one morning I woke in London. No sooner had G. heard of my arrival than he called, and, relating the affair, requested my assistance. I confess myself to have been interested – foolishly so, I thought afterward; but we all have our weaknesses, and diamonds were mine. In company with the Marquis, I waited upon the solicitor, who entered into the few details minutely, calling frequently upon Ulster, a young, fresh-looking man, for corroboration. We then drove to the jeweller's new quarters, took him, under charge of the officers, to his place of business, where he nervously showed me every point that could bear upon the subject, and ended by exclaiming, that he was ruined, and all for a stone he had never seen. I sat quietly for a few moments. It stood, then, thus: G. had given the thing to the solicitor, seen it put into the box, seen the box put into the desk; but while the confidential clerk, Ulster, locked the desk, the solicitor waited on the Marquis to the door – returning, took the box, without opening it again, to the jeweller, who, in the hurry, shut it up in his safe, also without opening it. The case was perfectly clear. These mysterious things are always so simple! You know now, as well as I, who took the diamond.

I did not choose to volunteer, but assented, on being desired. The police and I were old friends; they had so often assisted me, that I was not afraid to pay them in kind, and accordingly agreed to take charge of the case, still retaining their aid, should I require it. The jeweller was now restored to his occupation, although still subjected to a rigid surveillance, and I instituted inquiries into the recent movements of the young man Ulster. The case seemed to me to have been very blindly conducted. But, though all that was brought to light concerning him in London was perfectly fair and above board, it was discovered that, not long since, he had visited Paris – on the solicitor's business, of course, but gaining thereby an opportunity to transact any little affairs of his own. This was fortunate; for if anyone could do anything in Paris, it was myself.

It is not often that I act as a detective. But one homogeneous to every situation could hardly play a pleasanter part for once. I have thought that our great masters in theory and practice, Machiavel and Talleyrand, were hardly more, on a large scale.

I was about to return to Paris, but resolved to call previously on the solicitor again. He welcomed me warmly, although my suspicions had not been imparted to him, and, with a more cheerful heart than had lately been habitual to him, entered into an animated conversation respecting the great case of Biter v. Bit, then absorbing so much of the public attention, frequently addressing Ulster, whose remarks were always pertinent, brief, and clear. As I sat actively discussing the topic, feeling no more interest in it than in the end of that cigar I just cut off, and noting exactly every look and motion of the unfortunate youth, I recollect the curious sentiment that filled me regarding him. What injury had he done me, that I should pursue him with punishment? Me? I am, and every individual is, integral with the commonwealth. It was the commonwealth he had injured. Yet, even then, why was I the one to administer justice? Why not continue with my coffee in the morning, my kings and cabinets and national chess at noon, my opera at night, and let the poor devil go? Why, but that justice is brought home to every member of society – that naked duty requires no shirking of such responsibility, that, had I failed here, the crime might, with reason, lie at my door and multiply, the criminal increase himself?

Very possibly you will not unite with me; but these little catechisms are, once in a while, indispensable, to vindicate one's course to one's self.

This Ulster was a handsome youth; the rogues have generally all the good looks. There was nothing else remarkable about him but his quickness; he was perpetually on the alert; by constant activity, the rust was never allowed to collect on his faculties; his sharpness was distressing – he appeared subject to a tense strain. Now his quill scratched over the paper unconcernedly, while he could join as easily in his master's conversation: nothing seemed to preoccupy him, or he held a mind open at every point. It is pitiful to remember him that morning, sitting quiet, unconscious, and free, utterly in the hands of that mighty Inquisition, the Metropolitan Police, with its countless arms, its cells and myrmidons in the remotest corners of the Continent – at the mercy of so merciless a monster, and momently closer involved, like some poor prey round which a spider spins its bewildering web. It was also curious to observe the sudden suspicion that darkened his face at some innocent remark – the quick shrinking and entrenched retirement, the manifest sting and rancor, as I touched his wound with a swift flash of my slander weapon and sheathed it again, and, after the thrust, the espionage, and the relief at believing it accidental. He had many threads to gather up and hold; little electric warnings along them must have been constantly shocking him. He did that part well enough; it was a mistake, to begin with; he needed prudence. At that time I owed this Ulster nothing; now, however, I owe him a grudge, for some of the most harassing hours of my life were occasioned me by him. But I shall not cherish enmity on that account. With so promising a beginning, he will graduate and take his degree from the loftiest altitude in his line. Hemp is a narcotic; let it bring me forgetfulness.

In Paris I found it not difficult to trace such a person, since he was both foreign and unaccustomed. It was ascertained that he had posted several letters. A person of his description had been seen to drop a letter, the superscription of which had been read by one who picked it up for him. This superscription was the address of the very person who was likely to be the agent of the former possessors of the diamond, and had attracted attention. After all – you know the Secret Force – it was not so impossible to imagine what this letter contained, despite of its cipher. Such a person also had been met among the Jews, and at certain shops whose reputation was not of the clearest. He had called once or twice on Mme. de St. Cyr, on business relative to a vineyard adjoining her chateau in the Gironde, which she had sold to a wine merchant of England. I found a zest in the affair, as I pursued it.

We were now fairly at sea, but before long I found we were likely to remain there; in fact, nothing of consequence eventuated. I began to regret having taken the affair from the hands in which I had found it, and one day, it being a gala or some insatiable saint's day, I was riding, perplexed with that and other matters, and paying small attention to the passing crowd. I was vexed and mortified, and had fully decided to throw up the whole – on such hairs do things hang – when, suddenly turning a corner, my bridle-reins became entangled in the snaffle of another rider. I loosened them abstractedly, and not till it was necessary to bow to my strange antagonist, on parting, did I glance up. The person before me was evidently not accustomed to play the dandy; he wore his clothes ill, sat his horse worse, and was uneasy in the saddle. The unmistakable air of the *gamin* was apparent beneath the superficies of the gentleman. Conspicuous on his costume, and wound like an order of merit upon his breast, glittered a chain, *the* chain – each tiny brick-like gem spiked with a hundred sparks, and building a fabric of sturdy probabilities with the celerity of the genii in constructing Aladdin's palace. There, a cable to haul up the treasure, was the chain; where was the diamond? I need not tell you how I followed this young friend, with what assiduity I kept him in sight, up and down, all day long, till, weary at last of his fine sport, as I certainly was of mine, he left his steed in stall and fared on his way afoot. Still pursuing, now I threaded quay and square, street and alley, till he disappeared in a small shop, in one of those dark crowded lanes leading eastward from the Pont Neuf, in the city. It was the sign of a *marchand des armures*, and having provided myself with those persuasive arguments, a *sergent-de-ville* and a *gendarme*, I entered.

A place more characteristic it would be impossible to find. Here were piled bows of every material, ash, and horn, and tougher fibres, with slackened strings, and among them peered a rusty clarion and battle-axe, while the quivers that should have accompanied lay in a distant corner, their arrows serving to pin long, dusty, torn banners to the wall. Opposite the entrance, an archer in bronze hung on tiptoe, and levelled a steel bow, whose piercing *flèche* seemed sparkling with impatience to spring from his finger and flesh itself in the heart of the intruder. The hauberk and halberd, lance and casque, arquebuse and sword, were suspended in friendly congeries; and fragments of costly stuff swept from ceiling to floor, crushed and soiled by the heaps of rusty firelocks, cutlasses, and gauntlets thrown upon them. In one place, a little antique bust was half hid in the folds of some pennon, still dyed with battle-stains; in another, scattered treasures of Dresden and Sevres brought the drawing room into the campaign; and all around bivouacked rifles, whose polished barrels glittered full of death, pistols, variously mounted, for an insurgent at the barricades, or for a lost millionnaire at the gaming-table, foils, with but toned bluntness, and rapiers whose even edges were viewless as if filed into air. Destruction lay everywhere, at the command of the owner of this place, and, had he possessed a particle of vivacity, it would have been hazardous to bow beneath his doorway. It did not, I must say, look like a place where I should find a diamond. As the owner came forward, I determined on my plan of action.

"You have, sir," I said, handing him a bit of paper, on which were scrawled some numbers, "a diamond in your possession, of such and so many carats, size, and value, belonging to the Duke of X., and left with you by an Englishman, Mr. Arthur Ulster. You will deliver it to me, if you please."

"Monsieur!" exclaimed the man, lifting his hands, and surveying me with the widest eyes I ever saw. "A diamond! In my possession! So immense a thing! It is impossible. I have not even seen one of the kind. It is a mistake. Jacques Noailles, the vender of jewels *en gros*, second door below, must be the man. One should perceive that my business is with arms, not diamonds. I have it not; it would ruin me."

Here he paused for a reply, but, meeting none, resumed. "M. Arthur Ulster! I have heard of no such person. I never spoke with an Englishman. Bah! I detest them! I have no dealings with them. I repeat, I have not your jewel. Do you wish anything more of me?"

His vehemence only convinced me of the truth of my suspicions.

"These heroics are out of place," I answered. "I demand the article in question."

"Monsieur doubts me?" he asked, with a rueful face – "Questions my word, which is incontrovertible?" Here he clapped his hand upon a *couteau-de-chasse* lying near, but, appearing to think better of it, drew himself up, and, with a shower of nods flung at me, added, "I deny your accusation!" I had not accused him.

"You are at too much pains to convict yourself. I charge you with nothing," I said. "But this diamond must be surrendered."

"Monsieur is mad!" he exclaimed, "Mad! He dreams! Do I look like one who possesses such a trophy? Does my shop resemble a mine? Look about! See! All that is here would not bring a hundredth part of its price. I beseech Monsieur to believe me; he has mistaken the number, or has been misinformed."

"We waste words. I know this diamond is here, as well as a costly chain—"

"On my soul, on my life, on my honor," he cried, clasping his hands and turning up his eyes, "there is here nothing of the kind. I do not deal in gems. A little silk, a few weapons, a curiosity, a nicknack, comprise my stock. I have not the diamond. I do not know the thing. I am poor. I am honest. Suspicion destroys me!"

"As you will find, should I be longer troubled by your denials."

He was inflexible, and, having exhausted every artifice of innocence, wiped the tears from his eyes – oh, these French! life is their theatre – and remained quiet. It was getting dark. There was no gas in the place; but in the pause a distant street lamp swung its light dimly round.

"Unless one desires to purchase, allow me to say that it is my hour for closing," he remarked, blandly, rubbing his black-bearded chin.

"My time is valuable," I returned. "It is late and dark. When your shop-boy lights up—"

"Pardon – we do not light."

"Permit me, then, to perform that office for you. In this blaze you may perceive my companions, whom you have not appeared to recognize."

So saying, I scratched a match upon the floor, and, as the *sergent-de-ville* and the *gendarme* advanced, threw the light of the blue spirt of sulphurous flame upon them. In a moment more the match went out, and we remained in the demi-twilight of the distant lantern. The *marchand des armures* stood petrified and aghast. Had he seen the imps of Satan in that instant, it could have had no greater effect.

"You have seen them?" I asked. "I regret to inconvenience you; but unless this diamond is produced at once, my friends will put their seal on your goods, your property will be confiscated, yourself in a dungeon. In other words, I allow you five minutes; at the close of that time you will have chosen between restitution and ruin."

He remained apparently lost in thought. He was a big, stout man, and with one blow of his powerful fist could easily have settled me. It was the last thing in his mind. At length he lifted his head – "Rosalie!" he called.

At the word, a light foot pattered along a stone floor within, and in a moment a little woman stood in an arch raised by two steps from our own level. Carrying a candle, she descended and tripped toward him. She was not pretty, but sprightly and keen, as the perpetual attrition of life must needs make her, and wore the everlasting grisette costume, which displays the neatest of ankles, and whose cap is more becoming than wreaths of garden millinery. I am too minute, I see, but it is second nature. The two commenced a vigorous whispering amid sundry gestures and glances. Suddenly the woman turned, and, laying the prettiest of little hands on my sleeve, said, with a winning smile – "Is it a crime of *lèse-majesté?*"

This was a new idea, but might be useful.

"Not yet," I said; "two minutes more, and I will not answer for the consequence."

Other whispers ensued.

"Monsieur," said the man, leaning on one arm over the counter, and looking up in my face, with the most engaging frankness, "It is true that I have such a diamond; but it is not mine. It is left with me to be delivered to the Baron Stahl, who comes as an agent from his court for its purchase."

"Yes, I know."

"He was to have paid me half a million francs – not half its worth – in trust for the person who left it, who is not M. Arthur Ulster, but Mme. de St. Cyr."

Madame de St. Cyr! How under the sun – No, it could not be possible. The case stood as it stood before. The rogue was in deeper water than I had thought; he had merely employed Mme. de St. Cyr. I ran this over in my mind, while I said, "Yes."

"Now, sir," I continued, "you will state the terms of this transaction."

"With pleasure. For my trouble I was myself to receive patronage and five thousand francs. The Baron is to be here directly, on other and public business. *Reine du ciel*, Monsieur! How shall I meet him?"

"He is powerless in Paris; your fear is idle."

"True. There were no other terms."

"Nor papers?"

"The lady thought it safest to be without them. She took merely my receipt, which the Baron Stahl will bring to me from her before receiving this."

"I will trouble you for it now."

He bowed and shuffled away. At a glance from me, the *gendarme* slipped to the rear of the building, where three others were stationed at the two exits in that direction, to caution them of the critical moment, and returned. Ten minutes passed – the merchant did not appear. If, after all, he had made off with it! There had been the click of a bolt, the half-stifled rattle of arms, as if a door had been opened and rapidly closed again, but nothing more.

"I will see what detains my friend," said Mademoiselle, the little woman.

We suffered her to withdraw. In a moment more a quick expostulation was to be heard.

"They are there, the *gendarmes*, my little one! I should have run, but they caught me, the villains! and replaced me in the house. *Oh, sacre!*" – and rolling this word between his teeth, he came down and laid a little box on the counter. I opened it. There was within a large, glittering, curiously-cut piece of glass. I threw it aside.

"The diamond!" I exclaimed.

"Monsieur had it," he replied, stooping to pick up the glass with every appearance of surprise and care.

"Do you mean to say you endeavored to escape with that bawble? Produce the diamond instantly, or you shall hang as high as Haman!" I roared.

Whether he knew the individual in question or not, the threat was efficient; he trembled and hesitated, and finally drew the identical shagreen case from his bosom.

"I but jested," he said. "Monsieur will witness that I relinquish it with reluctance."

"I will witness that you receive stolen goods! " I cried, in wrath.

He placed it in my hands.

"Oh!" he groaned, from the bottom of his heart, hanging his head, and laying both hands on the counter before him, "It pains, it grieves me to part with it! "

"And the chain," I said.

"Monsieur did not demand that!"

"I demand it now."

In a moment, the chain also was given me.

"And now will Monsieur do me a favor? Will he inform me by what means he ascertained these facts?"

I glanced at the *garçon*, who had probably supplied himself with his master's finery illicitly – he was the means; we have some generosity – I thought I should prefer doing him the favor, and declined.

I unclasped the shagreen case; the *sergent-de-ville* and the gendarme stole up and looked over my shoulder; the garçon drew near with round eyes; the little woman peeped across; the merchant, with tears streaming over his face, gazed as if it had been a loadstone; finally, I looked myself. There it lay, the glowing, resplendent thing! Flashing in affluence of splendor, throbbing and palpitant with life, drawing all the light from the little woman's candle, from the sparkling armor around, from the steel barbs, and the distant lantern, into its bosom. It was scarcely so large as I had expected to see it, but more brilliant than anything I could conceive of. I do not believe there is another such in the world. One saw clearly that the Oriental superstition of the sex of stones was no fable; this was essentially the female of diamonds, the queen herself, the principle of life, the rejoicing receptive force. It was not radiant, as the term literally taken implies; it seemed rather to retain its wealth, instead of emitting its glorious rays, to curl them back like the fringe of a madrepore, and lie there with redoubled quivering scintillations, a mass of white magnificence, not prismatic, but a vast milky lustre. I closed the case; on reopening it, I could scarcely believe that the beautiful sleepless eye would again flash upon me. I did not comprehend how it could afford such perpetual richness, such sheets of lustre.

At last we compelled ourselves to be satisfied. I left the shop, dismissed my attendants, and, fresh from the contemplation of this miracle, again trod the dirty, reeking streets, crossed the bridge, with its lights, its warehouses midway, its living torrents who poured on unconscious of the beauty within their reach. The thought of their ignorance of the treasure, not a dozen yards distant, has often made me question if we all are not equally unaware of other and greater processes of life, of more perfect, sublimed, and, as it were, spiritual crystallizations going on invisibly about us. But had these been told of the thing clutched in the hand of a passer, how many of them would have known where to turn? And we – are we any better?

Chapter II

FOR A FEW DAYS I carried the diamond about my person, and did not mention its recovery even to my valet, who knew that I sought it, but communicated only with the Marquis of G., who replied, that he would be in Paris on a certain day, when I could safely deliver it to him.

It was now generally rumored that the neighboring government was about to send us the Baron Stahl, ambassador concerning arrangements for a loan to maintain the sinking monarchy in supremacy at Paris, the usual synecdoche for France.

The weather being fine, I proceeded to call on Mme. de St. Cyr. She received me in her boudoir, and on my way thither I could not but observe the perfect quiet and cloistered seclusion that pervaded the whole house – the house itself seeming only an adjunct of the still and sunny garden, of which one caught a glimpse through the long open hall-windows beyond. This boudoir did not differ from others to which I have been admitted: the same delicate shades; all the dainty appliances of Art for beauty; the lavish profusion of *bijouterie*; and the usual statuettes of innocence, to indicate, perhaps, the presence of that commodity which might not be guessed at otherwise; and burning in a silver cup, a rich perfume loaded the air with voluptuous sweetness. Through a half-open door an inner boudoir was to be seen, which must have been Delphine's; it looked like her; the prevailing hue was a soft purple, or gray; a *prie-dieu*, a bookshelf, and desk, of a dark West Indian wood, were just visible. There was but one picture – a sad-eyed, beautiful Fate. It was the type of her nation. I think she worshipped it. And how apt is misfortune to degenerate into Fate! Not that the girl had ever experienced the former, but, dissatisfied with life, and seeing no outlet, she accepted it stoically and waited till it should be over. She needed to be aroused; the station of an *ambassadrice*, which I desired for her, might kindle the spark. There were no flowers, no perfumes, no busts, in this ascetic place. Delphine herself, in some faint rosy gauze, her fair hair streaming round her, as she lay on a white-draped couch, half-risen on one arm, while she read the morning's *feuilleton*, was the most perfect statuary of which a room could boast – illumined, as I saw her, by the gay beams that entered at the loftily-arched window, broken only by the flickering of the vine-leaves that clustered the curiously-latticed panes without. She resembled in kind a Nymph, just bursting from the sea; so Pallas might have posed for Aphrodite, Madame de St. Cyr received me with *empressement*, and, so doing, closed the door of this shrine. We spoke of various things – of the court, the theatre, the weather, the world – skating lightly round the slender edges of her secret, till finally she invited me to lunch with her in the garden. Here, on a rustic table, stood wine and a few delicacies – while, by extending a hand, we could grasp the hanging pears and nectarines, still warm to the lip and luscious with sunshine, as we disputed possession with the envious wasp who had established a priority of claim.

"It is to be hoped," I said, sipping the *Haul-Brion*, whose fine and brittle smack contrasted rarely with the delicious juiciness of the fruit, "that you have laid in a supply of this treasure that neither moth nor rust doth corrupt, before parting with that little gem in the Gironde."

"Ah? You know, then, that I have sold it?"

"Yes," I replied. "I have the pleasure of Mr. Ulster's acquaintance."

"He arranged the terms for me," she said, with restraint, adding – "I could almost wish now that it had not been."

This was probably true; for the sum which she hoped to receive from Ulster for standing sponsor to his jewel was possibly equal to the price of her vineyard.

"It was indispensable at the time, this sale; I thought best to hazard it on one more season. If, after such advantages, Delphine will not marry, why – it remains to retire into the country and end our days with the barbarians!" she continued, shrugging her shoulders; "I have a house there."

"But you will not be obliged to throw us all into despair by such a step now," I replied.

She looked quickly, as if to see how nearly I had approached her citadel – then, finding in my face no expression but a complimentary one, "No," she said, "I hope that my affairs have brightened a little. One never knows what is in store."

Before long I had assured myself that Mme. de St. Cyr was not a party to the theft, but had merely been hired by Ulster, who, discovering the state of her affairs, had not, therefore, revealed his own – and this without in the least implying any knowledge on my part of the transaction. Ulster must have seen the necessity of leaving the business in the hands of a competent person, and Mme. de St. Cyr's financial talent was patent. There were few ladies in Paris who would have rejected the opportunity. Of these things I felt a tolerable certainty.

"We throng with foreigners," said Madame, archly, as I reached this point. "Diplomates, too. The Baron Stahl arrives in a day."

"I have heard," I responded. "You are acquainted?"

"Alas! no," she said. "I knew his father well, though he himself is not young. Indeed, the families thought once of intermarriage. But nothing has been said on the subject for many years. His Excellency, I hear, will strengthen himself at home by an alliance with the young Countess, the natural daughter of the Emperor."

"He surely will never be so imprudent as to rivet his chain by such a link!"

"It is impossible to compute the dice in those despotic countries," she rejoined – which was pretty well, considering the freedom enjoyed by France at that period.

"It may be," I suggested, "that the Baron hopes to open this delicate subject with you yourself, Madame."

"It is unlikely," she said, sighing. "And for Delphine, should I tell her his Excellency preferred scarlet, she would infallibly wear blue. Imagine her, Monsieur, in fine scarlet, with a scarf of gold gauze, and rustling grasses in that unruly gold hair of hers! She would be divine!"

The maternal instinct as we have it here at Paris confounds me. I do not comprehend it. Here was a mother who did not particularly love her child, who would not be inconsolable at her loss, would not ruin her own complexion by care of her during illness, would send her through fire and water and every torture to secure or maintain a desirable rank, who yet would entangle herself deeply in intrigue, would not hesitate to tarnish her own reputation, and would, in fact, raise heaven and earth to endow this child with a brilliant match. And Mme. de St. Cyr seemed to regard Delphine, still further, as a cool matter of Art.

These little confidences, moreover, are provoking. They put you yourself so entirely out of the question.

"Mlle. de St. Cyr's beauty is peerless," I said, slightly chagrined, and at a loss. "If hearts were trumps, instead of diamonds!"

"We are poor," resumed Madame, pathetically. "Delphine is not an heiress. Delphine is proud. She will not stoop to charm. Her coquetry is that of an Amazon. Her kisses are arrows. She is Medusa!" And Madame, her mother, shivered.

Here, with her hair knotted up and secured by a tiny dagger, her gauzy drapery gathered in her arm, Delphine floated down the green alley toward us, as if in a rosy cloud. But this soft aspect never could have been more widely contradicted than by the stony repose and cutting calm of her beautiful face. "The Marquis of G.," said her mother, "he also arrives ambassador. Has he talent? Is he brilliant? Wealthy, of course – but *gauche*?"

Therewith I sketched for them the Marquis and his surroundings.

"It is charming," said Madame. "Delphine, do you attend?"

"And why?" asked Delphine, half concealing a yawn with her dazzling hand. "It is wearisome; it matters not to me."

"But he will not go to marry himself in France," said her mother. "Oh, these English," she added, with a laugh, "yourself, Monsieur, being proof of it, will not mingle blood, lest the Channel should still flow between the little red globules! You will go? But to return shortly? You will dine with me soon? *Au revoir!*" and she gave me her hand graciously, while Delphine bowed as if I were already gone, threw herself into a garden-chair, and commenced pouring the wine on a stone for a little tame snake which came out and lapped it.

Such women as Mme. de St. Cyr have a species of magnetism about them. It is difficult to retain one's self-respect before them – for no other reason than that one is, at the moment, absorbed into their individuality, and thinks and acts with them. Delphine must have had a strong will, and perpetual antagonism did not weaken it. As for me, Madame had, doubtless, reasons of her own for tearing aside these customary bands of reserve – reasons which, if you do not perceive, I shall not enumerate.

* * *

"Have you met with anything further in your search, sir?" asked my valet, next morning.

"Oh, yes, Hay," I returned, in a very good humor – "with great success. You have assisted me so much, that I am sure I owe it to you to say that I have found the diamond."

"Indeed, sir, you are very kind. I have been interested, but my assistance is not worth mentioning. I thought likely it might be, you appeared so quiet." – The cunning dog! – "How did you find it, sir, may I ask?"

I briefly related the leading facts, since he had been aware of the progress of the case to that point – without, however, mentioning Mme. de St. Cyr's name.

"And Monsieur did not inform me!" a French valet would have cried.

"You were prudent not to mention it, sir," said Hay. "These walls must have better ears than ordinary; for a family has moved in on the first floor recently, whose actions are extremely suspicious. But is this precious affair to be seen?"

I took it from an inner pocket and displayed it, having discarded the shagreen case as inconvenient.

"His Excellency must return as he came," said I.

Hay's eyes sparkled.

"And do you carry it there, sir?" he asked, with surprise, as I restored it to my waistcoat-pocket.

"I shall take it to the bank," I said. "I do not like the responsibility."

"It is very unsafe," was the warning of this cautious fellow. "Why, sir! Any of these swells, these pickpockets, might meet you, run against you – so!" said Hay, suiting the action to the word, "and, with the little sharp knife concealed in just such a ring as this I wear, give a light tap, and there's a slit in your vest, sir, but no diamond!" – and instantly resuming his former respectful deportment, Hay handed me my gloves and stick, and smoothed my hat.

"Nonsense!" I replied, drawing on the gloves, "I should like to see the man who could be too quick for me. Any news from India, Hay?"

"None of consequence, sir. The indigo crop is said to have failed, which advances the figure of that on hand, so that one or two fortunes will be made today. Your hat, sir? – your lunettes? Here they are, sir."

"Good morning, Hay."

"Good morning, sir."

I descended the stairs, buttoning my gloves, paused a moment at the door to look about, and proceeded down the street, which was not more than usually thronged. At the bank I paused to assure myself that the diamond was safe. My fingers caught in a singular slit. I started. As Hay had prophesied, there was a fine longitudinal cut in my waistcoat, but the pocket was empty. My God! the thing was gone. I never can forget the blank nihility of all existence that dreadful moment when I stood fumbling for what was not. Calm as I sit here and tell of it, I vow to you a shiver courses through me at the very thought. I had circumvented Stahl only to destroy myself. The diamond was lost again. My mind flew like lightning over every chance, and a thousand started up like steel spikes to snatch the bolt. For a moment I was stunned, but, never being very subject to despair, on my recovery, which was almost at once, took every measure that could be devised. Who had touched me? Whom had I met? Through what streets had I come? In ten minutes the Prefect had the matter in hand. My injunctions were strict privacy. I sincerely hoped the mishap would not reach England; and if the diamond were not recovered before the Marquis of G. arrived – why, there was the Seine. It is all very well to talk – yet suicide is so French an affair, that an Englishman does not take to it naturally, and, except in November, the Seine is too cold and damp for comfort, but during that month I suppose it does not greatly differ in these respects from our own atmosphere.

A preternatural activity now possessed me. I slept none, ate little, worked immoderately. I spared no efforts, for everything was at stake. In the midst of all, G. arrived. Hay also exerted himself to the utmost; I promised him a hundred pounds, if I found it. He never told me that he said how it would be, never intruded the state of the market, never resented my irritating conduct, but watched me with narrow yet kind solicitude, and frequently offered valuable suggestions, which, however, as everything else did, led to nothing. I did not call on G., but in a week or so his card was brought up one morning to me. "Deny me," I groaned. It yet wanted a week of the day on which I had promised to deliver him the diamond. Meanwhile the Baron Stahl had reached Paris, but he still remained in private – few had seen him.

The police were forever on the wrong track. Today they stopped the old Comtesse du Quesne and her jewels, at the Barrière; tomorrow, with their long needles, they riddled a package of lace destined for the Duchess of X. herself; the Secret Service was doubled; and to crown all, a splendid new star of the testy Prince de Ligne was examined and proclaimed to be paste – the Prince swearing vengeance, if he could discover the cause – while half Paris must have been under arrest. My own hotel was ransacked thoroughly – Hay begging that his traps might be included, but nothing resulted – and I expected nothing, for, of course, I could swear that the stone was in my pocket when I stepped into the street. I confess I never was nearer madness – every word and gesture stung me like asps – I walked on burning coals. Enduring all this torment, I must yet meet my daily comrades, eat ices at Tortoni's, stroll on the Boulevard, call on my acquaintance, with the same equanimity as before. I believe I was equal to it. Only by contrast with that blessed time when Ulster and diamonds were unknown, could I imagine my past happiness, my present wretchedness. Rather than suffer it again, I would be stretched on the rack till every bone in my skin were broken. I cursed Mr. Arthur Ulster every hour in the day; myself, as well; and even now the word diamond sends a cold blast to my heart. I often met my friend the *marchand des armures*. It was his turn to triumph; I fancied there must be a hang-dog kind of air about me, as about every sharp man who has been outwitted. It wanted finally but two days of that on which I was to deliver the diamond.

One midnight, armed with a dark lantern and a cloak, I was traversing the streets alone, unsuccessful, as usual, just now solitary, and almost in despair. As I turned a corner, two men were but scarcely visible a step before me. It was a badly-lighted part of the town. Unseen and noiseless I followed. They spoke in low tones, almost whispers; or rather, one spoke, the other seemed to nod assent.

"On the day but one after tomorrow," I heard spoken in English. Great Heavens! Was it possible? Had I arrived at a clue? That was the day of days for me. "You have given it, you say, in this billet, I wish to be exact, you see," continued the voice, "to prevent detection, you gave it, ten minutes after it came into your hands, to the butler of Madame ——," (here the speaker stumbled on the rough pavement, and I lost the name,) "who," he continued, "will put it in the ——" (a second stumble acted like a hiccough) "cellar."

"Wine-cellar," I thought; and what then?

"In the ——." A third stumble was followed by a round German oath. How easy it is for me now to fill up the little blanks which that unhappy pavement caused!

"You share your receipts with this butler. On the day I obtain it," he added, and I now perceived his foreign accent, "I hand you one hundred thousand francs; afterward, monthly payments till you have received the stipulated sum. But how will this butler know me, in season to prevent a mistake? Hem! He might give it to the other!"

My hearing had been trained to such a degree that I would have promised to catch any given dialogue of the spirits themselves, but the whisper that answered him eluded me. I caught nothing but a faint sibillation. "Your ring?" was the rejoinder. "He shall be instructed to recognize it? Very well. It is too large – no, that will do, it fits the first finger. There is nothing more. I am under infinite obligations, sir; they shall be remembered. Adieu!"

The two parted; which should I pursue? In desperation I turned my lantern upon one, and illumined a face fresh with color, whose black eyes sparkled askance after the retreating figure, under straight black brows. In a moment more he was lost in a false *cul-de-sac*, and I found it impossible to trace the other.

I was scarcely better off than before; but it seemed to me that I had obtained something, and that now it was wisest to work this vein. "The butler of Madame ——."

There were hundreds of thousands of Madames in town. I might call on all, and be as old as the Wandering Jew at the last call. The cellar. Wine-cellar, of course – that came by a natural connection with butler – but whose? There was one under my own abode; certainly I would explore it. Meanwhile, let us see the entertainments for Wednesday. The Prefect had a list of these. For some I found I had cards; I determined to allot a fraction of time to as many as possible; my friends in the Secret Service would divide the labor. Among others, Madame de St. Cyr gave a dinner, and, as she had been in the affair, I determined not to neglect her on this occasion, although having no definite idea of what had been, or plan of what should be done. I decided not to speak of this occurrence to Hay, since it might only bring him off some trail that he had struck.

Having been provided with keys, early on the following evening I entered the wine-cellar, and, concealed in an empty cask that would have held a dozen of me, waited for something to turn up. Really, when I think of myself, a diplomate, a courtier, a man-about-town, curled in a dusty, musty wine-barrel, I am moved with vexation and laughter. Nothing, however, turned up – and at length I retired baffled. The next night came – no news, no identification of my black-browed man, no success; but I felt certain that something must transpire in that cellar. I don't know why I had pitched upon that one in particular, but, at an earlier hour than on the previous night, I again donned the cask. A long time must have elapsed; dead silence filled the spacious vaults, except where now and then some Sillery cracked the air with a quick explosion, or some newer wine bubbled round the bung of its barrel with a faint effervescence. I had no intention of leaving this place till morning, but it suddenly appeared like the most woeful waste of time. The master of this tremendous affair should be abroad and active; who knew what his keen eyes might detect; what loss his absence might occasion in this nick of time? And here he was, shut up and locked in a wine-cellar! I began to be very nervous; I had already, with aid, searched every crevice of the cellar; and now I thought it would be some consolation to discover the thief, if I never regained the diamond. A distant clock tolled midnight. There was a faint noise – a mouse? – no, it was too prolonged – nor did it sound like the fizz of Champagne – a great iron door was turning on its hinges; a man with a lantern was entering; another followed, and another. They seated themselves. In a few moments, appearing one by one and at intervals, some thirty people were in the cellar. "Were they all to share in the proceeds of the diamond? With what jaundiced eyes we behold things! I myself saw all that was only through the lens of this diamond, of which not one of these men had ever heard. As the lantern threw its feeble glimmer on this group, and I surveyed them through my loophole, I thought I had never seen so wild and savage a picture, such enormous shadows, such bold outline, such a startling flash on the face of their leader, such light retreating up the threatening arches. More resolute brows, more determined words, more unshrinking hearts, I had not met. In fact, I found myself in the centre of a conspiracy, a society as vindictive as the Jacobins, as unknown and terrible as the Marianne of today. I was thunderstruck, too, at the countenances on which the light fell, men the loyalest in estimation, ministers and senators, millionnaires who had no reason for discontent, dandies whose reason was supposed to be devoted to their tailors, poets and artists of generous aspiration and suspected tendencies, and one woman, Delphine de St. Cyr. Their plans were brave, their determination lofty, their conclave serious and fine; yet as slowly they shut up their hopes and fears in the black masks, one man bent toward the lantern to adjust his. When he lifted his face before concealing it, I recognized him also. I had met him frequently at the Bureau of Police; he was, I believe, Secretary of the Secret Service.

I had no sympathy with these people. I had sufficient liberty myself, I was well enough satisfied with the world, I did not care to revolutionize France; but my heart rebelled at the mockery, as this traitor and spy, this creature of a system by which I gained my fame, showed his revolting face and veiled it again. And Delphine, what had she to do with them? One by one, as they entered, they withdrew, and I was left alone again. But all this was not my diamond.

Another hour elapsed. Again the door opened, and remained ajar. Someone entered, whom I could not see. There was a pause – then a rustle – the door creaked ever so little. "Art thou there?" lisped a shrill whisper – a woman, as I could guess.

"My angel, it is I," was returned, a semitone lower. She approached, he advanced, and the consequence was a salute resonant as the smack with which a Dutch burgomaster may be supposed to set down his mug. I was prepared for anything. Ye gods! If it should be Delphine! But the base suspicion was birth-strangled as they spoke again. The conversation which now ensued between these lovers under difficulties was tender and affecting beyond expression. I had felt guilty enough when an unwilling auditor of the conspirators – since, though one employs spies, one does not therefore act that part one's self, but on emergencies – an unwillingness which would not, however, prevent my turning to advantage the information gained; but here, to listen to this rehearsal of woes and blisses, this *ah mon Fernand*, this aria in an area, growing momently more fervent, was too much. I overturned the cask, scrambled upon my feet, and fled from the cellar, leaving the astounded lovers to follow, while, agreeably to my instincts, and regardless of the diamond, I escaped the embarrassing predicament.

At length it grew to be noon of the appointed day. Nothing had transpired; all our labor was idle. I felt, nevertheless, more buoyant than usual – whether because I was now to put my fate to the test, or that today was the one of which my black-browed man had spoken, and I therefore entertained a presentiment of good for tune, I cannot say. But when, in unexceptionable toilet, I stood on Mme. de St. Cyr's steps, my heart sunk. G. was doubtless already within, and I thought of the *marchand des armures'* exclamation, "Queen of Heaven, Monsieur! how shall I meet him!" I was plunged at once into the profoundest gloom. Why had I undertaken the business at all? This interference, this good-humor, this readiness to oblige – it would ruin me yet! I forswore it, as Falstaff forswore honor. Why needed I to meddle in the *mêlée*? Why – But I was no catechumen. Questions were useless now. My emotions are not chronicled on my face, I flatter myself; and with my usual repose I saluted our hostess. Greeting G. without any allusion to the diamond, the absence of which allusion he received as a point of etiquette, I was conversing with Mrs. Leigh, when the Baron Stahl was announced. I turned to look at his Excellency. A glance electrified me. There was my dark-browed man of the midnight streets. It must, then, have been concerning the diamond that I had heard him speak. His countenance, his eager glittering eye, told that today was as eventful to him as to me. If he were here, I could well afford to be. As he addressed me in English, my certainty was confirmed; and the instant in which I observed the ring, gaudy and coarse, upon his finger, made confirmation doubly sure. I own I was surprised that anything could induce the Baron to wear such an ornament. Here he was actually risking his reputation as a man of taste, as an exquisite, a leader of *haut ton*, a gentleman, by the detestable vulgarity of this ring. But why do I speak so of the trinket? Do I not owe it a thrill of as fine joy as I ever knew? Faith! It was not unfamiliar to me. It had been a daily sight for years. In meeting the Baron Stahl I had found the diamond.

The Baron Stahl was, then, the thief? Not at all. My valet, as of course you have been all along aware, was the thief.

My valet, moreover, was my instructor; he taught me not again to scour Cathay for what might be lying under my hand at home. Nor have I since been so acute as to overreach myself. Yet I can explain such intolerable stupidity only by remembering that when one has been in the habit of pointing his telescope at the stars, he is not apt to turn it upon pebbles at his feet.

The Marquis of G. took down Mme. de St. Cyr; Stahl preceded me, with Delphine. As we sat at table, G. was at the right, I at the left of our hostess. Next G. sat Delphine; below her, the Baron; so that we were nearly *vis-a-vis*. I was now as fully convinced that Mme. de St. Cyr's cellar was the one, as the day before I had been that the other was; I longed to reach it. Hay had given the stone to a butler – doubtless this – the moment of its theft; but, not being aware of Mme. de St. Cyr's previous share in the adventure, had probably not afforded her another. And thus I concluded her to be ignorant of the game we were about to play; and I imagined, with the interest that one carries into a romance, the little preliminary scene between the Baron and Madame that must have already taken place, being charmed by the cheerfulness with which she endured the loss of the promised reward.

As the Baron entered the dining room, I saw him withdraw his glove, and move the jewelled hand across his hair while passing the solemn butler, who gave it a quick recognition; the next moment we were seated. There were only wines on the table, clustered around a central ornament – a bunch of tall silver rushes and flag-leaves, on whose airy tip danced *fleurs-de-lis* of frosted silver, a design of Delphine's – the dishes being on side-tables, from which the guests were served as they signified their choice of the variety on their cards. Our number not being large, and the custom so informal, rendered it pleasant.

I had just finished my oysters and was pouring out a glass of Chablis, when another plate was set before the Baron.

"His Excellency has no salt," murmured the butler – at the same time placing one beside him. A glance, at entrance, had taught me that most of the service was uniform; this dainty little *salière* I had noticed on the buffet, solitary, and unlike the others. What a fool had I been! Those gaps in the Baron's remarks caused by the paving-stones, how easily were they to be supplied!

"Madame?"

Madame de St. Cyr.

"The cellar?"

A salt-cellar.

How quick the flash that enlightened me while I surveyed the *salière*!

"It is exquisite! Am I never to sit at your table but some new device charms me?" I exclaimed. "Is it your design, Mademoiselle?" I said, turning to Delphine.

Delphine, who had been ice to all the Baron's advances, only curled her lip. *"Des babioles!"* she said.

"Yes, indeed!" cried Mme. de St. Cyr, extending her hand for it. " But none the less her taste. Is it not a fairy thing? A Cellini! Observe this curve, these lines! But one man could have drawn them!" – and she held it for our scrutiny. It was a tiny hand and arm of ivory, parting the foam of a wave and holding a golden shell, in which the salt seemed to have crusted itself as if in some secretest ocean-hollow. I looked at the Baron a moment; his eyes were fastened upon the *salière*, and all the color had forsaken his cheeks – his face counted his years. The diamond was in that little shell. But how to obtain it? I had no novice to deal with; nothing but *finesse* would answer.

"Permit me to examine it?" I said. She passed it to her left hand for me to take. The butler made a step forward.

"Meanwhile, Madame," said the Baron, smiling, "I have no salt."

The instinct of hospitality prevailed; she was about to return it. Might I do an awkward thing? Unhesitatingly. Reversing my glass, I gave my arm a wider sweep than necessary, and, as it met her hand with violence, the *salière* fell. Before it touched the floor I caught it. There was still a pinch of salt left – nothing more.

"A thousand pardons!" I said, and restored it to the Baron.

His Excellency beheld it with dismay; it was rare to see him bend over and scrutinize it with starting eyes.

"Do you find there what Count Arnaldos begs in the song," asked Delphine – "the secret of the sea, Monsieur?"

He handed it to the butler, observing, "I find here no—"

"Salt, Monsieur?" replied the man, who did not doubt but all had gone right, and replenished it.

Had one told me in the morning that no intricate manoeuvres, but a simple blunder, would effect this, I might have met him in the Bois de Boulogne.

"We will not quarrel," said my neighbor, lightly, with reference to the popular superstition.

"Rather propitiate the offended deities by a crumb tossed over the shoulder," added I.

"Over the left?" asked the Baron, to intimate his knowledge of another idiom, together with a reproof for my *gaucherie*.

"A gauche – quelquefois c'est justement à droit" I replied.

"Salt in any pottage," said Madame, a little uneasily, "is like surprise in an individual; it brings out the flavor of every ingredient, so my cook tells me."

"It is a preventive of palsy," I remarked, as the slight trembling of my adversary's finger caught my eye.

"And I have noticed that a taste for it is peculiar to those who trace their blood," continued Madame.

"Let us, therefore, elect a deputation to those mines near Cracow," said Delphine.

"To our cousins, the slaves there?" laughed her mother.

"I must vote to lay your bill on the table, Mademoiselle," I rejoined.

"But with a *boule blanche*, Monsieur?"

"As the salt has been laid on the floor," said the Baron.

Meanwhile, as this light skirmishing proceeded, my sleeve and Mme. de St. Cyr's dress were slightly powdered, but I had not seen the diamond. The Baron, bolder than I, looked under the table, but made no discovery. I was on the point of dropping my napkin to accomplish a similar movement, when my accommodating neighbor dropped hers. To restore it, I stooped. There it lay, large and glowing, the Sea of Splendor, the Moon of Milk, the Torment of my Life, on the carpet, within half an inch of a lady's slipper. Mademoiselle de St. Cyr's foot had prevented the Baron from seeing it; now it moved and unconsciously covered it. All was as I wished. I hastily restored the napkin, and looked steadily at Delphine – so steadily, that she perceived some meaning, as she had already suspected a game. By my sign she understood me, pressed her foot upon the stone and drew it nearer. In France we do not remain at table until unfit for a lady's society – we rise with them. Delphine needed to drop neither napkin nor handkerchief; she composedly stooped and picked up the stone, so quickly that no one saw what it was.

"And the diamond?" said the Baron to the butler, rapidly, as he passed.

"It was in the *salière*!" whispered the astonished creature.

* * *

In the drawing room I sought the Marquis.

"Today I was to surrender you your property," I said; "it is here."

"Do you know," he replied, "I thought I must have been mistaken?"

"Any of our volatile friends here might have been," I resumed; "for us it is impossible. Concerning this, when you return to France, I will relate the incidents; at present, there are those who will not hesitate to take life to obtain its possession. A conveyance leaves in twenty minutes; and if I owned the diamond, it should not leave me behind. Moreover, who knows what a day may bring forth? Tomorrow there may be an *émeute*. Let me restore the thing as you withdraw."

The Marquis, who is not, after all, the Lion of England, pausing a moment to transmit my words from his ear to his brain, did not afterward delay to make inquiries or adieux, but went to seek Mme. de St. Cyr and wish her good night, on his departure from Paris. As I awaited his return, which I knew would not be immediate, Delphine left the Baron and joined me.

"You beckoned me?" she asked.

"No, I did not."

"Nevertheless, I come by your desire, I am sure."

"Mademoiselle," I said, "I am not in the custom of doing favors; I have forsworn them. But before you return me my jewel, I risk my head and render one last one, and to you."

"Do not, Monsieur, at such price," she responded, with a slight mocking motion of her hand.

"Delphine! Those resolves, last night, in the cellar, were daring, they were noble, yet they were useless."

She had not started, but a slight tremor ran over her person and vanished while I spoke.

"They will be allowed to proceed no farther – the axe is sharpened; for the last man who adjusted his mask was a spy – was the Secretary of the Secret Service."

Delphine could not have grown paler than was usual with her of late. She flashed her eye upon me.

"He was, it may be, Monsieur himself," she said.

"I do not claim the honor of that post."

"But you were there, nevertheless – a spy!"

"Hush, Delphine! It would be absurd to quarrel. I was there for the recovery of this stone, having heard that it was in a cellar – which, stupidly enough, I had insisted should be a wine-cellar."

"It was, then—"

"In a salt-cellar – a blunder which, as you do not speak English, you cannot comprehend. I never mix with treason, and did not wish to assist at your pastimes. I speak now, that you may escape."

"If Monsieur betrays his friends, the police, why should I expect a kinder fate?"

"When I use the police, they are my servants, not my friends. I simply warn you, that, before sunrise, you will be safer travelling than sleeping – safer next week in Vienna than in Paris."

"Thank you! And the intelligence is the price of the diamond? If I had not chanced to pick it up, my throat," and she clasped it with her fingers, "had been no slenderer than the others?"

"Delphine, will you remember, should you have occasion to do so in Vienna, that it is just possible for an Englishman to have affections, and sentiments, and, in fact, sensations? That, with him, friendship can be inviolate, and to betray it an impossibility? And even were it not, I, Mademoiselle, have not the pleasure to be classed by you as a friend."

"You err. I esteem Monsieur highly."

I was impressed by her coolness.

"Let me see if you comprehend the matter," I demanded.

"Perfectly. The arrest will be used tonight, the guillotine tomorrow."

"You will take immediate measures for flight?"

"No – I do not see that life has value. I shall be the debtor of him who takes it."

"A large debt. Delphine, I exact a promise of you. I do not care to have endangered myself for nothing. It is not worthwhile to make your mother unhappy. Life is not yours to throw away. I appeal to your magnanimity."

"'Affections, sentiments, sensations!'" she quoted. "Your own danger for the affection – it is an affair of the heart! Mme. de St. Cyr's unhappiness, there is the sentiment. You are angry, Monsieur – that must be the sensation."

"Delphine, I am waiting."

"Ah, well. You have mentioned Vienna – and why? Liberals are countenanced there?"

"Not in the least. But Madame l'Ambassadrice will be countenanced."

"I do not know her."

"We are not apt to know ourselves."

"Monsieur, how idle are these cross-purposes!" she said, folding her fan.

"Delphine," I continued, taking the fan, "tell me frankly which of these two men you prefer – the Marquis or his Excellency."

"The Marquis? He is antiphlogistic – he is ice. Why should I freeze myself? I am frozen now – I need fire!"

Her eyes burned as she spoke, and a faint red flushed her cheek.

"Mademoiselle, you demonstrate to me that life has yet a value to you."

"I find no fire," she said, as the flush fell away.

"The Baron?"

"I do not affect him."

"You will conquer your prejudice in Vienna."

"I do not comprehend you, Monsieur; you speak in riddles, which I do not like."

"I will speak plainer. But first let me ask you for the diamond."

"The diamond? It is yours? How am I certified of it? I find it on the floor; you say it was in my mother's *salière*; it is her affair, not mine. No, Monsieur, I do not see that the thing is yours."

Certainly there was nothing to be done but to relate the story, which I did, carefully omitting the Baron's name. At its conclusion, she placed the prize in my hand.

"Pardon, Monsieur," she said; "without doubt you should receive it. And this agent of the government – one could turn him like hot iron in this vice – who was he?"

"The Baron Stahl." All this time G. had been waiting on thorns, and, leaving her now, I approached him, displayed for an instant the treasure on my palm, and slipped it into his. It was done. I bade farewell to this Eye of Morning and Heart of Day, this thing that had caused me such pain and perplexity and pleasure, with less envy and more joy than I thought myself capable of. The relief and buoyancy that seized me, as his hand closed upon it, I shall not attempt to portray. An abdicated king was not freer.

The Marquis departed, and I, wandering round the *salon*, was next stranded upon the Baron. He was yet hardly sure of himself. We talked indifferently for a few moments, and then I ventured on the great loan. He was, as became him, not communicative, but scarcely thought it would be arranged. I then spoke of Delphine.

"She is superb!" said the Baron, staring at her boldly.

She stood opposite, and, in her white attire on the background of the blue curtain, appeared like an impersonation of Greek genius relieved upon the blue of an Athenian heaven. Her severe and classic outline, her pallor, her downcast lids, her absorbed look, only heightened the resemblance. Her reverie seemed to end abruptly, the same red stained her cheek again, her lips curved in a proud smile, she raised her glowing eyes and observed us regarding her. At too great distance to hear our words, she quietly repaid our glances in the strength of her new decision, and then, turning, began to entertain those next to her with an unwonted spirit.

"She has needed," I replied to the Baron, "but one thing – to be aroused, to be kindled. See, it is done! I have thought that a life of cabinets and policy might achieve this, for her talent is second not even to her beauty."

"It is unhappy that both should be wasted," said the Baron. "She, of course, will never marry."

"Why not?"

"For various reasons."

"One?"

"She is poor."

"Which will not signify to your Excellency. Another?"

"She is too beautiful. One would fall in love with her. And to love one's own wife – it is ridiculous!"

"Who should know?" I asked.

"All the world would suspect and laugh."

"Let those laugh that win."

"No – she would never do as a wife; but then as—"

"But then in France we do not insult hospitality!"

The Baron transferred his gaze to me for a moment, then tapped his snuff-box, and approached the circle round Delphine.

It was odd that we, the arch enemies of the hour, could speak without the intervention of seconds; but I hoped that the Baron's conversation might be diverting – the Baron hoped that mine might be didactic.

They were very gay with Delphine. He leaned on the back of a chair and listened. One spoke of the new gallery of the Tuileries, and the five pavilions – a remark which led us to architecture.

"We all build our own houses," said Delphine, at last, "and then complain that they cramp us here, and the wind blows in there, while the fault is not in the order, but in us, who increase here and shrink there without reason."

"You speak in metaphors," said the Baron.

"Precisely. A truth is often more visible veiled than nude."

"We should soon exhaust the orders," I interposed; "for who builds like his neighbor?"

"Slight variations, Monsieur! Though we take such pains to conceal the style, it is not difficult to tell the order of architecture chosen by the builders in this room. My mother, for instance – you perceive that her pavilion would be the florid Gothic."

"Mademoiselle's is the Doric," I said.

"Has been," she murmured, with a quick glance.

"And mine, Mademoiselle?" asked the Baron, indifferently.

"Ah, Monsieur," she returned, looking serenely upon him, "when one has all the winning cards in hand and yet loses the stake, we allot him *un pavilion chinois*," – which was the polite way of dubbing him Court Fool.

The Baron's eyes fell. Vexation and alarm were visible on his contracted brow. He stood in meditation for some time. It must have been evident to him that Delphine knew of the recent occurrences – that here in Paris she could denounce him as the agent of a felony, the participant of a theft. What might prevent it? Plainly but one thing: no woman would denounce her husband. He had scarcely contemplated this step on arrival.

The guests were again scattered in groups round the room. I examined an engraving on an adjacent table. Delphine reclined as lazily in a *fauteuil* as if her life did not hang in the balance. The Baron drew near.

"Mademoiselle," said he, "you allotted me just now a cap and bells. If two should wear it? – if I should invite another into my *pavilion chinois?* – if I should propose to complete an alliance, desired by my father, with the ancient family of St. Cyr? If, in short, Mademoiselle, I should request you to become my wife?"

"*Eh, bien, Monsieur* – and if you should?" I heard her coolly reply.

But it was no longer any business of mine. I rose and sought Mme. de St. Cyr, who, I thought, was slightly uneasy, perceiving some mystery to be afloat. After a few words, I retired.

Archimedes, as perhaps you have never heard, needed only a lever to move the world. Such a lever I had put into the hands of Delphine, with which she might move, not indeed the grand globe, with its multiplied attractions, relations, and affinities, but the lesser world of circumstances, of friends and enemies, the circle of hopes, fears, ambitions. There is no woman, as I believe, but could have used it.

* * *

The next day was scarcely so quiet in the city as usual. The great loan had not been negotiated. Both the Baron Stahl and the English minister had left Paris – and there was a *coup d' état*.

But the Baron did not travel alone. There had been a ceremony at midnight in the Church of St. Sulpice, and her Excellency the Baroness Stahl, *née* de St. Cyr, accompanied him.

It is a good many years since. I have seen the diamond in the Duchess of X.'s coronet, once, when a young queen put on her royalty – but I have never seen Delphine. The Marquis begged me to retain the chain, and I gave myself the pleasure of presenting it, through her mother, to the Baroness Stahl. I hear, that, whenever she desires to effect any cherished object which the Baron opposes, she has only to wear this chain, and effect it. It appears to possess a magical power, and its potent spell enslaves the Baron as the lamp and ring of Eastern tales enslaved the Afrites. The life she leads has aroused her. She is no longer the impassive Silence; she has found her fire. I hear of her as the charm of a brilliant court, as the soul of a nation of intrigue. Of her beauty one does not speak, but her talent is called prodigious. What impels me to ask the idle question, If it were well to save her life for this? Undoubtedly she fills a station which, in that empire, must be the summit of a woman's ambition. Delphine's Liberty was not a principle, but a dissatisfaction. The Baroness Stahl is vehement, is Imperialist, is successful. While she lives, it is on the top of the wave; when she dies – ah! what business has Death in such a world?

As I said, I have never seen Delphine since her marriage. The beautiful statuesque girl occupies a niche into which the blazing and magnificent *intrigante* cannot crowd. I do not wish to be disillusioned. She has read me a riddle – Delphine is my Sphinx.

* * *

As for Mr. Hay – I once said the Antipodes were tributary to me, not thinking that I should ever become tributary to the Antipodes. But such is the case; since, partly through my instrumentality, that enterprising individual has been located in their vicinity, where diamonds are not to be had for the asking, and the greatest rogue is not a Baron.

The Disappearance of Jeremy Meredith

Cameron Trost

IT WAS a dreary November evening, shortly after our return from Australia to my wife's hometown in Brittany. Louise was having dinner at her sister's house in Le Pouliguen, the boys in tow, and I was wrapping up a case of no real interest at all, except for the considerable and much-needed financial recompense. Changing countries is inevitably both a tiring and costly affair, even when you've already done it once or twice before, and it was reassuring to have found a case so soon. Private investigators rely on an established reputation and a solid client base in order to make a living from their craft, neither of which I had here. Louise had managed to land herself a job with a local shipping company before even setting foot in the country, thus taking a good deal of stress out of the move, and permitting us to rent a charming townhouse close to the beach. I didn't have a sea view from my study, but when the window was open, salty air and the cries of gulls reminded me just how close we were. That evening, however, the window was shut tight. Cold Atlantic wind was driving rain against the pane and howling as it exposed gaps in the slate roof. I almost didn't hear the knock at the front door, but as soon as it had registered, I quickly navigated my way down the narrow and uneven staircase, my right hand acting as a rudder and the banister as the channel.

I opened the door to find that the brave visitor was a young woman in a yellow fisherman's coat. Her pale face told of confusion, and her eyes asked a hundred questions.

She parted her lips to speak, but I hastened to usher her in and push the door closed against the relentless wind.

"Thank you," she whispered, slipping her hood back to reveal a curtain of curly red hair.

"English?" I asked, noticing her thanks hadn't been offered in French, and that her intonation sent my mind wandering towards the West Country.

She smiled faintly. "Yes, from Dorset originally. What about you, Mr. Tremont?"

"I'm Australian."

"I'd assumed you were British. You're a long way from home."

"I am indeed, although I feel at home here most of the time."

She allowed herself a more confident smile, and it was clear that we understood each other.

"I must apologise for coming unannounced."

"No, you really must not," I assured her. "Nobody would venture out in this weather without good reason. I'll stoke the fire and pour you a glass. What would you like? I don't have any Pimm's, I'm afraid."

She smiled again, almost laughed, despite whatever was bothering her, and I silently congratulated myself.

"I've been in France for several years now and have readily adopted the drinking habits this side of *la Manche*. Would a Kir Breton be too much to ask?"

"Not at all."

I put another log on the fire and told her to make herself comfortable, before preparing her Kir and pouring myself a double whisky.

"Cheers," we said, raising our glasses and looking each other in the eye. She was a charmer, the kind of woman you could just contemplate distractedly and lose track of time, but what occupied my mind was the mystery she contained. Make no mistake about it, nothing is more stimulating than a good puzzle.

"Tell me everything," I instructed her.

She sipped her Kir, flicked a twist of hair off her face, and began.

"My name is Harriet Meredith and I need help solving the disappearance of my father. Three years ago, he vanished while walking along the coast just west of here. You mustn't think I'm naïve. I accept that he must no longer be with us. He was a loving father, and as solid as a rock, not the kind of man who'd run off to some tropical island with a young mistress. I'm sure he either put a foot wrong and fell into the sea that night or met with foul play, and, to be frank with you, the latter is far more plausible, because he knew the coastline here better than any stretch of land in the world, even the Jurassic Coast of his own Dorset. Do you remember hearing about my father's disappearance, Mister Tremont?"

"I do not. You see, I wasn't in the country three years ago, but I will bring myself up to speed if I decide to accept your case. Please, go on."

She seemed a little taken aback, but she sipped her Kir and continued.

"No trace of him has ever been found. The entire coastline was searched, even the sea caves where smugglers used to hide their ill-gotten wares, but nothing showed up. I haven't stopped looking for him, nor will I, not until I solve the mystery of his disappearance. I owe it to him, and I owe it to my poor mother, who is the shadow of the woman I once knew.

"You'll want to know what brings me here so urgently tonight. Well, I've just had the strangest encounter with an old mariner down at *Le Café du Port*. The bar was crowded and everybody was shouting, but this old fellow must have heard one of my friends use my name and recognised me as the daughter of Jeremy Meredith. He'd had a few too many Ricards, but I managed to understand that he'd once overheard a couple of men discussing what had happened to my father, right there in a corner of the bar. It was several months ago, he told me, and he didn't know them, but he remembered one of them saying there was a man who knew Jeremy Meredith's fate. Augustin Maillot was the name. One of them had said that only Augustin Maillot held the key to the Englishman's disappearance, and then he'd fallen silent and grown sullen. His companion had asked him who the devil he meant, but the only reply he made was to say he'd had too much to drink and he ought to get himself home, just in case his wife was there waiting for him."

"Augustin Maillot," I repeated. "Does the name mean anything to you?"

"I'm afraid not. I told him so, and he must have seen that I was unsettled. He shrugged and frowned apologetically, and I thanked him for letting me know. At that point, I got online and tried to find out who this Maillot was, but nothing relevant came up, then I did a search for private investigators and found you, an English-speaking sleuth right on my doorstep. I hope you agree it was right of me to come straight away."

"Absolutely, and I would be pleased to accept the job."

With that, I poured another round of drinks.

Experience has taught me that time is of the essence when it comes to missing persons cases, so a delay of three years was a serious setback. It was perhaps that very fact, along with the peculiar nature of the assignment, which made it so difficult to refuse.

Miss Meredith went on to provide me with a thorough description of her father, and I was able to imagine an Englishman of comfortable means who had taken early retirement and moved to Brittany, accompanied by his wife and daughter. He enjoyed duck hunting, collecting antiques, sharing a glass of brandy with neighbours, and walking coastal paths. Somewhat of an avid walker myself, I decided that, in the morning, I would follow the stretch of coast he had frequented, not because I expected the police had missed any clues three years ago, but out of a hope that the undertaking would put me in the poor devil's skin.

"I ought to be going now, Mister Tremont."

"Are you ready to brave the storm again? You're more than welcome to wait it out."

She gave me a quizzical look, prompting me to clarify.

"My wife will be home shortly. I could drive you home."

She smiled, evidently somewhat amused. Her green eyes were as enigmatic as the sea.

"I'm not afraid of the storm. There's no safer weather for a woman to walk alone at night, and, when I get home, I'll take a long warm bath."

I helped her into her coat and opened the door, releasing her into the elements, watching as she disappeared.

* * *

The sun was timid the next morning, climbing listlessly into an unwelcoming sky scarred with wispy clouds. The wind had died down and the rain had ceased, but sodden soil and fallen twigs along the coastal path bore witness to the storm's passage. I had walked this stretch of the coast before, I was certain of that, but not in many years. The path hugged the clifftops like a faithful lover, allowing me to look down onto the empty beaches below, where the mouths of sea caves were immune to the ashen light of the dawning day, and limp seaweed lay on the coarse sand.

The rhythmic squelching of my hiking boots and the murmur of the waves accompanied me, and salty air filled my nostrils and nipped at my cheeks. As I walked, my eyes scanned the landscape, registering every detail, while every conceivable scenario went through my mind.

Jeremy Meredith knew his way along this path, and, from the picture his daughter had painted of him, he wasn't likely to have slipped over the edge like a drunken teenager or cocky Parisian holidaymaker.

What then?

I kept walking, step after step, recalling the dark motivations I had unearthed in the hearts of men over the years, trying to imagine which might have been behind his disappearance.

The path veered inland, continuing through a gloomy grove, while, to the left, a staircase hewn into the cliff face led down to a tiny beach. Harriet had told me that this was where her father always turned back.

Always? I wondered.

I descended the stairs into that intimate pocket nestled between land and sea and wasn't yet halfway down when I looked up to behold a magnificent manor crouched atop the headland at the opposite end of the beach, which was a mere matter of feet away. Another set of stairs, this one with an old iron gate to which a *propriété privée* sign was affixed, connected the beach to a neglected rose garden that filled the tight space between the cliff and the manor.

Don't ask me to put my finger on it. I would if I could. Suffice to say that reason and logic are not the be-all and end-all of the investigator's toolkit. Instinct has a role to play, and from time to time, that role is the lead.

How long I stood there, I can't say for sure, but that building had caught my attention. I raised my binoculars to study it more closely. It was a stately home of grey stone with red shutters, all of which were closed, and red gable trims. Although by no means in a state of disrepair, there were some signs of neglect. For instance, vines and lichen had been allowed freer rein than would be conventionally considered acceptable.

Walking in Jeremy Meredith's footsteps became somewhat of a ritual for me. Whenever I needed to be alone and to think the facts of a case through, I would return to that stretch of the coast. With each rise and fall of the rocky land, and each twist and turn of the path as it negotiated monoliths, chasms, and copses of stubborn trees, my imagination grew bolder and my mind more acute. In this way, the mystery of the Englishman's disappearance helped me solve a dozen other puzzles, some with which, no doubt, you are already familiar.

I didn't abandon the case of Jeremy Meredith, not only because his widow and daughter were counting on me, but also due to my unyielding urge to know. The prospect of never fathoming so murky a mystery bothered me immensely, and any armchair psychologist would immediately comprehend the personal nature of my obsession.

A new angle of attack or the shadow of a doubt occurred to me from time to time, and I would invite Harriet Meredith over to re-examine the facts while we took our *apéritif.* But it never led anywhere. I simply couldn't drag myself out of the mental quagmire. Despite all my efforts, the name of Augustin Maillot and the fate of Jeremy Meredith endured as reminders of my limits, taunting me during those quiet moments when there wasn't a sound to be heard, like the whispering of a ghost on a lonely night.

* * *

As so often is the case when evidence is scarce, it was a chance meeting that delivered the breakthrough, but not until six years after Harriet Meredith had first come to me for help.

It happened one winter's afternoon, after walking the coastal path with my sons. We had reached the small beach, and, undeterred by the merciless buffeting of the bitterly cold wind, the boys were running about and taking turns at hurling a tennis ball at each other. A misjudged throw, a particularly virulent gust of wind, a well-timed dodge; they all coincided to cause the ball to miss its mark and hit the only other person on the beach. The elderly man had his back to us and his gaze was drawn to the turbulent sea.

I jogged over to him and apologised.

"Not at all,' he replied, picking the ball up and tossing it to me.

"It's a magnificent manor perched up there, isn't it?" I ventured, nodding towards the headland and wearing an expression of admiration that wasn't completely unauthentic. My previous attempts at gleaning information out of local residents had always met with failure.

"Yes, I suppose so. It's the Lozac'h home." He studied my face, evidently waiting to see if I reacted to that name. When I didn't, he continued. "It's indeed a fine old manor, but it's a dark place. The custodian is a right devil of a man."

"It's inhabited?"

"No, it doesn't seem to be. Rumour has it Old Lozac'h lives abroad these days, and his children never set foot on the grounds. It wouldn't surprise me to find it on the market before long." He looked me up and down. "It might be beyond your means, I suspect."

"No doubt. In any case, I'm a superstitious man," I lied.

He turned to the house and scowled.

"She was an angel," he muttered to the wind.

Then, turning back to me, he asked, "You're not from around here are you?"

"I'm Australian."

He raised his eyebrows. "I don't think I've ever met an Australian before. I thought I could detect a slight accent, if you don't mind my saying so. At any rate, your French is excellent."

"Thank you. I endeavour to do Molière's tongue the justice it deserves. Can I ask what happened? My wife tells me an Englishman went missing in these parts several years ago."

That got him thinking.

"Quite so. The fellow just disappeared, no doubt lost his footing at the cliff edge and was claimed by the sea."

"That has nothing to do with the manor," I reminded him.

"No, that incident doesn't. I was thinking of the lady of the manor."

"Claimed by the sea as well?"

"Claimed by the devil, I say. He used to beat her, always behind closed doors, but you can tell when a woman's being abused, even if she does her utmost to hide it. No trace of her was ever found, so the convenient conclusion was drawn." He stared at the sea, and the wind howled. "She's an unforgiving mistress, the sea, and has taken her share of lives, but she shouldn't be used to conceal the darkness in the hearts of men."

I knew what the answer to my next question would be and was able to fill in the gaps in the story, all except for one essential detail.

"When did this happen?"

"A good few years ago now, perhaps eight or nine. In fact, it would have been around the same time as the Englishman vanished."

He gazed at the manor and nodded thoughtfully, and I got the impression he would have preferred it if I hadn't dragged those dark memories back to the surface, but I also suspected he spared a thought for Madame Lozac'h on a regular basis.

I didn't bother asking him about Augustin Maillot, because I was now certain the name would mean nothing to him, and that the incongruous question would only serve to make him suspicious of my motives. I had already pushed my luck, and there was no point drawing further attention to myself.

"It looks like rain. I'd better get the boys home."

He pursed his lips and bid farewell with a curt gesture somewhere between a wave and a salute.

We hurried back home, and along the way, except for during one short phone call, I chatted casually with the boys.

"There's no longer a shadow of a doubt," I told Louise as I stepped through the front door. I helped the boys out of their coats while I waited for her to catch my drift.

"The manor?" she asked almost immediately.

"That's right. I'll tell you more when we have a minute to ourselves."

She promptly secured that minute with the aid of four mugs of hot chocolate. We let the boys drink theirs in front of the television, and we stayed in the kitchen like scullery maids in a costume drama. I told her what I had learned at the beach.

"That does seem to confirm your suspicions," she admitted. "But it also means that your main suspect may have escaped justice."

"The suspect may be beyond my grasp, but not the mystery, which is what matters the most."

There must have been a mischievous twinkle in my eye, or maybe it was just that years of sharing my work with me had enabled her to predict my course of action.

"I take it you want my permission to break your promise?"

"I do, *ma chérie*. If you decide not to give it, I'll try my utmost to concoct another way, or I'll let the mystery remain unsolved, as it has been these past years, however difficult that may prove for both Harriet and myself."

She tilted her head to one side and held my gaze. "Emotional blackmail, Oscar. That hardly suits your style."

"Well, this is an emotional case, on several levels."

She didn't reply at first. Of course, she understood perfectly. This was second only to *the* mystery.

"You're out of practice, and you don't have the necessary tools," she warned.

"I know, but I've been going through the motions in my head for months, and that was based on the more problematic premise that the manor was occupied."

"Harriet's going with you, isn't she?" Her question was followed by a knowing smirk.

I raised my eyebrows as I sipped hot chocolate.

"There's more?" She read my silence. "It's all set for tonight, isn't it?"

"You know me so well."

"You have my permission to break your promise just this once, but be careful, and keep it professional."

"Thank you," I whispered. "What exactly do you mean by *keep it professional*?"

She gave me a blank stare.

"She's a lovely woman, but I've never given you cause to question my faithfulness, have I?"

"No, you haven't. It's just that, I don't know, you've never had a client like her before. I know there's a little spark between the two of you, and I don't want it flaring up with the case coming to a head."

"That will not happen," I promised her. "You know why I asked her along, don't you?"

"For an extra dash of romanticism in your nocturnal escapade?"

"I like the sound of that, but no. It's for a far more practical reason. I might need her to provide a positive identification of her father, circumstances permitting."

"Oh, I see," Louise said, staring into her mug.

* * *

We sat in my black Peugeot 406, parked along the coastal road, not too close but not too far from the manor. We were dressed in dark clothes, and, in much the same way as smugglers of yore, we were to follow the coastal path down to the beach. It would take us about five minutes at a leisurely, inconspicuous pace.

Despite Louise's warning about providing the spark with fuel, I asked Harriet to agree to hold my hand once we started along the path. I also told her we ought to hold each other and kiss passionately if we were interrupted by any passers-by; an unlikely occurrence.

She nodded, and a lock of red hair slipped out of her navy blue hood.

"Are you ready to hear my take on what happened?"

"I'm ready. Whatever happened, knowing has to be better than the haze I've endured for so many years."

I stared past her, out to the ocean. Only the foam of breakers on the furthest reef was visible in the darkness. The wind was still blowing a gale and whistling as it buffeted the car.

"I believe your father died trying to be a hero."

She smiled faintly. "That wouldn't surprise me."

"There are detectives who claim there are no coincidences, but I know that's not true. Coincidences do happen from time to time. In the case of your father, however, it's just too convenient. The lady of the manor went missing, presumably drowned, around the same time as your father vanished. Her husband was reportedly a violent man, *a devil of a man* were the exact words used."

"Domestic violence?"

"Precisely. It's just a guess, as I have no evidence at all, but I'm willing to bet that your father witnessed one of these instances of violence. He would have been on the beach, alone, and perhaps saw the commotion through one of the manor's windows. He may very well have witnessed her murder."

"I see," Harriet said quietly. "My father was a gentle man, not at all confrontational, yet he despised men who disrespected women. He would have acted, I'm sure."

"This is where the mystery of Augustin Maillot comes into play."

"How?"

"I think Augustin Maillot does indeed hold the key to your father's disappearance and that all will be revealed inside the manor."

Harriet looked horrified. "You told me it was unoccupied."

"I'm certain it is."

"Where is Augustin Maillot if he's not in the manor?"

"He's in there all right."

"You're not making sense," she complained, and I suppose she was right.

"You'll see what I mean. Let's go and put an end to this! Ready?"

By way of answer, she opened her door, pushing against the wind, and jumped out of the car.

We bowed our heads and strode along the path, hand in hand. We descended the stairs, crossed the beach, and went up the stairs leading to the manor. It wasn't until we were right up against the heavy wooden door that I switched a small torch on. I got Harriet to hold it up to the keyhole and shield it with her hands.

She watched in admiration as I picked the lock. It was a stubborn old piece of work, but eventually, it clicked in surrender.

It was both thrilling and daunting to be inside such a grand old manor, and I reminded myself to appreciate the sensation to the fullest, for, in theory, it was to be my last infraction.

I took the torch and led Harriet upstairs. After checking that the shutters were closed, I switched another torch on and passed it to her so we could scan our surroundings together.

We were in a dining hall, complete with a long table which was bare except for two silver candelabras. There were also empty cabinets against the walls, and a dark, yawning fireplace. A thick layer of dust had settled everywhere.

But it wasn't the furniture that drew my attention. There were paintings on the walls. I counted four in all.

"We're here to steal art?" Harriet asked, and I think she may have been serious.

"Not tonight."

Each painting was a portrait. There were three of men, and one of a woman. Three of them dated from the eighteenth century, and one was from the nineteenth. It was the more recent oeuvre that I decided to inspect more closely. There was a signature in the bottom right corner.

"What is it?"

"Augustin Maillot," I replied. No doubt, I was grinning intolerably.

"He was an artist?"

"No, I don't think so. The paint around the signature seems to be damaged, as though it has been scratched away, clumsily retouched, and the signature added."

I took a step back and pointed my torch at the tableau. "In my opinion, whoever painted it was quite talented. It's a remarkable portrait. The man is dressed in expensive clothes and wears exotic jewels of incredible value. It's probably a portrait inspired by a story from a previous century, for the subject and the artist did not live during the same age. Look at his face. Despite all his finery, the wrinkles and scars bear witness to a life of hardship and violence. Behind him, we look down on tiny fortified islands, as though he is standing on ramparts designed to protect an important port."

"Do you know where it is?"

"I do. Don't you? It looks very much the same today."

Harriet frowned. I'm sure the city's name was on the tip of her tongue.

"Augustin Maillot," I reminded her.

She just looked at me blankly.

I studied the portrait more closely, and ran my fingertips over it. I felt the frame, applying pressure at various points. Finally, I slid the painting to one side, but the wall behind it was untouched.

"What are you doing?"

"I'm trying to convince the pirate to reveal his secrets."

"I see," she replied.

"No such luck," I had to admit. "His secrets aren't here."

I stepped back and looked around, trying to hide my disappointment.

Neither of us spoke for several seconds.

"Let's try the library," I said, pointing my torch in the direction of a door at the end of the dining hall. "Follow me."

There was a bay window at the far end of the small library, which presumably offered a splendid view of the ocean when the shutters were open. The wall to the right was bare, except for an old leather armchair, but the wall to the left was covered in floor-to-ceiling bookshelves.

"Read the titles out to me, please."

We scoured the shelves, starting at opposite ends, and I listened to the titles she read out.

"*La Légende de la ville d'Ys.*"

"*Le Comte de Monte-Cristo.*"

"*Monsieur Vénus.*"

"*Les Soirées de Médan.*"

"*Arsène Lupin, gentleman cambrioleur.*"

"*Boucaille sur Douarnenez.*"

"*Les Pirates de Saint-Malo.*"

"*Les Rats de Montsouris.*"

"What did you say?"

"*Les Rats de Montsouris.*"

"No, before that."

"*Les Pirates de Saint-Malo.*"

"Yes, yes, that's it!" I almost yelled.

"That's what exactly?"

I breathed a sigh of relief, and what a sigh it was. Six years of mediocrity had finally come to an end.

"Think about it, Harriet. We've finally found Augustin Maillot. The rough-faced subject of the portrait, standing proudly on the ramparts of Saint-Malo, undoubtedly made his fortune through piracy."

"Augustin Maillot was a pirate?"

"No, he never existed. Augustin Maillot is a place."

"I get it now! *Augustin* hides *Saint*, and *Maillot* hides *Malo*."

"Precisely. It was just a false name used as a key. *Augustin Maillot holds the key.* You will notice that the remaining letters are *u, g, u, i, l, t.*"

"*You* and *guilt*," she gasped. "That has to be mere coincidence."

"Surely," I agreed, walking over to where Harriet stood. "Coincidences exist. But it's apt all the same, it would appear. The man your old seadog overheard that night at *Le Café du Port* must have been Monsieur Lozac'h making a cryptic confession."

I placed two fingers at the top of the spine of *Les Pirates de Saint-Malo* and tilted the book. The loud click of a simple mechanism echoed through the library, and a section of bookshelf swung ever so slightly ajar.

A faint gasp escaped Harriet's lips and she aimed her torch at the gap in the shelves.

"How did you know?"

"I didn't know," I assured her. "It was only a guess. The possibility of a hidden room occurred to me some time ago. After all, they're not uncommon in grand old homes. It was only today, after the conversation on the beach, that I realised Augustin Maillot was not, and probably never had been, a living person. From there, it was a matter of logic. If the name didn't belong to a person, it had to be connected to a *thing* or a *place*; a thing bound to open a door or a place lying beyond a door."

"The door to a tomb," she whispered, and I'll never forget how far away she sounded at that moment.

"Can you go through with it?"

She nodded. "After you, Oscar."

I pulled the door open, surprised at its willingness, and found myself at the top of a steep staircase. My shoulders, although not a great deal broader than those of most men, brushed the stone walls of the passage as I descended. The ceiling also constrained my movements, making me bow my head as though entering hallowed ground. If I hadn't been wearing my woollen flat cap, my scalp would have come off second-best as it exposed the imperfections in the rough masonry.

Harriet stayed close behind, learning from my mistakes and enjoying the advantages afforded by her slighter build. The suspense must have been so much more terrible for her than it was for me, and to this day I remain in awe of the dignity and poise she commanded during our descent.

Neither of us articulated what precisely we were expecting to find down there, but I turned to look at her once we had entered the room and saw an expression that could only be described as one of tentatively pleasant surprise. As it turned out, we had arrived in a cellar which was roughly of the same dimensions as the library above. The longer wall opposite the staircase and the shorter wall to our left bore dusty wine racks, and it took me no more than the sweep of my torch and a cursory glance to discover that a number of liquid treasures of considerable value lay within my grasp. There were also bottles of whisky, but, ever the professional, I was determined to put work before pleasure. I turned my attention to the alcove to our right, separated from the rest of the cellar by a wall with a narrow arch.

Harriet shone her torch in the same direction as mine. Her hand started to shake as the dreadful scene registered, giving the impression that the skeletons were trembling. They were splayed on a divan, the ensemble veiled with cobwebs. One wore a soiled dress, the original colour of which was difficult to guess, and the other was dressed in a loose white shirt and grey trousers. Two pairs of slippers lay among what appeared to be the remains of countless thorny flower stems on the cobbled floor.

I laid a reassuring hand on Harriet's shoulder.

"I'll take a closer look," I whispered, unsure what else to say.

A wine barrel stood between the divan and a large teak sea chest. It held an open bottle of Château Rouget, a glass, and a phial. The shells of dead insects lay in and around the glass and phial.

The scene wasn't difficult to read. Lozac'h had had a heart after all. Distraught by what he'd done, the old fellow had created a shrine to his wife and descended to offer her flowers and beg her forgiveness. It had continued for years, until the absurdity of the ritual had dawned on him. Unable to go on without her, he'd eventually accepted that there was only one way to be with her again.

"Is it *him*?" Harriet asked. Her voice trembled as she pronounced that three-lettered pronoun, and there was no mistaking the fact it referred to the man she always had and always would love more than any other.

"No, Harriet. It's not your father, I'm afraid. Here lie the lord and lady of the manor."

"Oh, I see," she replied numbly. "He decided to join her."

"The man at the bar remembered hearing Lozac'h say he had to go back home in case his wife, who was missing, had returned."

"That's what he told me, but it looks like it was an act. Lozac'h knew precisely where she was all along."

"She was where he'd left her. It was either a devious act, or he'd turned delusional."

"Where's my father, Oscar? We still don't know."

She must have followed my gaze because she took a tentative step towards the sea chest but stopped when I lay a hand on her shoulder.

"Open it," she told me, nodding her consent.

I walked over to the chest and knelt. There was no lock, just a latch. The hinges groaned mournfully as I lifted the lid. Reaching inside, I searched slowly and carefully, and succeeded in finding what I was after.

"Stay there, Harriet. I'll bring it over."

Together, we opened the wallet and she saw the photograph on the identity card. I held her as she cried tears of both grief and relief. There would be no more not knowing for Harriet Meredith.

Volatile Memory

Marie Vibbert

HEIGHTENED security measures at the port put Sandra in a long, slow line for anyone with specialized implants. Her Free Media card didn't get her past it, and she was embarrassed by the guard's smirk when she tried.

Andrei examined his nails. "Too bad you aren't me, darling. Celebrities don't wait in lines."

Trying not to move her lips, she replied, "You were never a celebrity."

"Liar. Just look at me!" He gestured down his fit torso. He wore what he'd had on when he died. Andrei had been dressed for the camera: a low-cut cantaloupe shirt and iridescent slacks, his blond curls artfully tousled. She should have stuck his avatar in a grey suit to annoy him.

She should say something like that. He would laugh. She wasn't sure how to word it, though.

The line was not moving. Sandra checked the time.

That was when the explosion hit. Sensors implanted along Sandra's arm felt the air retreat, a motion her human skin couldn't feel. An alert appeared in her vision, which she turned toward instinctively. She pushed into the pressure wave like a diver into a pool, swimming through fleeing bodies. Her conscious mind caught up well after she was running.

Andrei loped at her side, passing unseen through people and rubble. "I told you there was a pattern!" Andrei had guessed that this would be the next place hit. He would never let her hear the end of it.

Did he want her to push back or agree? How were people supposed to react, when they had time to react?

Sandra kept running, her fingers twitching and eyes flicking through zoom and scan commands, using all her implanted recorders. She found the center of the blast and slowed. Here nothing moved. She paced an outward spiral from the scorched star that marked the bomb's location. Like the others, it was set out in the open in a busy thoroughfare, perhaps disguised as a piece of luggage. The security cameras were always wiped. The device always disintegrated, made entirely of some combustible material rather than a more deadly, shrapnel-creating case.

Whoever did this cared more about hiding their evidence than creating damage. Why?

Guards, medical workers and the concerned rushed into the blast zone, pulling away survivors. A knot loosened in her stomach.

Sandra examined the debris for unexpected compounds. Andrei pointed across her field of view. "Footprint!"

Her eye display outlined a near-invisible depression in the carpet – a heart-shape with five tiny toe-prints in front of it. A strange shoe or an artificial foot. Sandra's sight clouded with lines of trajectory that collapsed into tighter probabilities. As soon as one was thicker than the others, she sprinted in its direction, Andrei a trailing kite in her peripheral vision.

She should have thanked him for pointing it out.

The gates had come down on the loading platforms automatically after the explosion, sealing the spaceport against leaks, but one had been torn open, titanium and steel hanging like shredded cloth.

Andrei said, "Gee, you think she went that way?"

The projected trajectory led straight to the hole. Sandra turned it off. She ran through security guards as though she didn't see them. They returned the favor. Their heads-up displays would mark her as Free Media, and therefore more trouble to save than worth it.

"There are three ships docked on this arm," Andrei said, using his direct link to Sandra's data feed. "One is powering up. Left ramp."

Sure enough, the loading gantry was closing on Gate C-4. Sandra slid headfirst under the bulkhead, and then rolled to her feet. The artificial gravity was weak on the gantry and she nearly hit the ceiling on the upward bound.

"Wait! They're already powering up," Andrei said.

The ship's door was closed. Sandra's fingertips burst into wire flowers and she slipped them into the door's mechanism.

Andrei fidgeted at her side. "Leave it and get out of here before they undock and we're spaced." He stepped in front of her, his face and hands protruding from the bulkhead. "No story is worth dying for. We have enough evidence. We can track the ship."

Sandra's focus was on the wireframe of the lock mechanism her vision system projected. She found the lock's ear and fed it an algorithm designed with this model in mind. A flutter, a click, and the airlock halted its cycle and started opening again.

Sandra allowed herself a smile of self-congratulation.

Andrei threw up his arms. "Yes, great. You're a master thief. The dock is still unclamping!"

She squeezed through the bulkhead as soon as there was enough room and slammed it shut behind her. Andrei scowled as he turned and stepped out of it. "Try to remember that I live in your head now and destroying it destroys me?"

The airlock held two bodies, their faces caved in. The walls were an expensive leather texture, splattered with blood.

Sandra dropped to one knee while the lock cycled, every sensor in forensic mode. "Andrei?"

"Already contacting every local security AI and patching a connection to the Free Media," he said. "Or trying to. I'm not – Sandra. Go back to the left. There."

On the wall, four parallel slashes, spaced like fingers but cutting through metal and plastic like knives. Sandra chewed her lip. "It's really her."

Andrei's killer. Neither of them said those words; they were superstitious about mentioning Andrei's death, but they both thought it.

Before she bought the personality simulator, Sandra had watched Andrei's final moments many times. He hadn't been recording but his personal camera came on automatically at his death, saving the last few minutes. A woman's laugh, tinkling like chimes, and then the finger-shaped knives punched through his chest from behind, each tapered with a stylized nail, dripping blood.

Sandra stepped around the bodies as the inner door opened, aware that every system console on the ship would declare that undocking had been delayed by airlock activity, and the killer was still on the ship.

"I can't contact anyone." Andrei whispered in his panic.

Sandra's audio scanner picked up someone sobbing. She followed the sound to the nearest passenger compartment. A room full of people turned as the door opened. A steward stood at the front in his sailor uniform, nametag askew, uncertainly holding a serving fork like a weapon.

The passengers all spoke at once. "What is…no one…tell us…who was…I demand a…"

The steward said, "We've been in here since the explosion. The captain's not responding. Are you station security?"

"Free Media Camera." Sandra could see that wasn't reassuring. "Stay here." She made a task memo: save these people.

As the bulkhead closed, Andrei said, "Oh you charmer, you."

"Shut up."

"Why? The killer robot can't hear me. Let's check the other compartments."

Sandra kept low and slow as she advanced down the corridor, scanning as far ahead as she could. "She won't be with the passengers. She hasn't killed them, so she must not see them as a threat."

"Oh goody. I was a threat."

As Sandra started up the stairs, leaving the last of the passenger compartments un-checked, Andrei sighed. "You don't have to do this. We could be safe on New Jefferson. You could pet your cat."

Some men, Sandra thought, would be happy their partner was more concerned with avenging them than their personal safety, but she didn't say that. Andrei was just being Andrei.

There was another body outside the door to the control room.

Andrei shifted from foot to foot. "So that's it? You're going to barge in there and go mano-a-mano with psychobot?"

Sandra had to admit it wasn't the best plan. She shifted resources to find a network signal.

"This is one of those times," Andrei craned his head, "when being able to look behind you would be really convenient. Get a rear-facing camera, Sandra. As soon as we survive this."

She saved another task memo for that. She got into the internal network. The ship had cleared dock, but there was no flight plan – their enemy was flying it manually. Probably to avoid someone (like Sandra) finding out where she was taking it. Outside communications were dead, power-out dead, which couldn't be right, even with the explosion nearby. The silver woman must have set up a firewall.

"You'd better get a Stonk Award for this." Andrei said. He kept anxiously looking behind Sandra, though he couldn't 'see' and craning his non-existent head wasn't going to help. "Use the publicity shot of me from last year, in front of the palm trees. My hair looks great in that one."

"Almost in," Sandra said. "Be ready to look when I turn."

"I've been ready since we got here. You have no idea how unnerving it is not to be able to move your own eyes."

Sandra activated the bulkhead for the control room.

They had both seen the killer's fingers, and Sandra had gotten a shot once with her long-range lens of a silver ankle retreating behind a door, but they'd never seen her completely.

The bulkhead slid back to reveal a handsome man in a dark suit. He looked at Sandra. He had olive skin and odd, amber eyes. He was not what they were expecting.

Then a glint of metal tilted; an art deco statue of a woman was seated at the console behind him. She turned slightly, not quite enough to see them – to see Sandra – over her shoulder. Her statue's lips curled. "Oh. At last we meet, *et cetera*."

"Don't," the man said, putting a hand on the robot's shoulder.

Sandra said, "I've disabled your navigational control."

The robot poured out of her chair like a model in a negligee ad. Her eyes were the same inhuman amber as the man's. "Look at that, Kent. It talks. Have you made yourself difficult, little breakable human?" Her voice was resonant, like chimes.

Andrei said, "Sandra, say something sarcastic! Don't let our side down!"

But Sandra could say nothing. She recorded, and saved what she could to the backup drive in her hip. She was likely going to die, but the mysterious robot – she would be identified, might be caught by others. This was the sort of death Sandra expected, when she became a Camera.

"Celeste," the man called Kent said. "Stand down. We can use her."

"You're no fun." The robot pouted a moment, then charged at Sandra, her pointed fingertips like steak knives glinting in the low light of the control room.

Andrei covered his face. Sandra stood stoic. At the last second, a black-wool-clad arm interceded. Metal impacted softness. Kent had absorbed her attack. He was inhuman. No blood came from the slashes in his suit.

Celeste threw up her hands. "Idiot! She's a Camera! Step aside and let me melt her in the ship's reactor."

That would destroy her data. Destroy Andrei. Sandra inched toward the door, hoping to use Kent's distraction to escape.

Celeste lunged at her. Kent again interposed himself. "Not again," he said.

"Fine. You can burn, too." Celeste abruptly disengaged and darted out the door, a streak of silver.

Sandra tried to follow her, but Kent was in her way, now.

"I apologize," he said, "for my sister."

"Who is he?" Andrei demanded.

"Who are you?" Sandra asked.

Kent's face was uncanny in close inspection. Too precise in its imperfections. "There's not much time. I'm afraid Celeste intends to destroy the ship's engine."

"Celeste is on this ship," Sandra said. "Why would she blow it up?"

"She'll survive in vacuum."

"Why are you helping us?"

Kent turned left and right, looking for another person. Sandra said, "Me. Why are you helping me?"

"To prevent the loss of life. I can track Celeste. She is heading for the engine compartment. Will you help me defuse the bombs?"

"Tell me who you work for and why you're blowing up spaceports."

Robots had excellent poker faces. "Would you put your story over the lives of the people on this ship? Above your own life?"

Andrei said, "He obviously doesn't know you."

This was about saving more than the people on one ship. "You don't want to kill people, but you're helping her. Why? What are you trying to accomplish? Did it all start in New Jefferson or has this been going on before that? What do you mean by calling her your sister?"

Andrei said, "Drop it. Save people. Stories are just stories."

Andrei didn't talk that way before he died. Kent said nothing. Sandra felt the time slipping away. She relented. "Show me the way."

The robot took off running down the corridor.

The ship had a Pulsar Drive – as misnamed a piece of technology as any that had passed through a marketing department's hands. It had nothing to do with Pulsars, but it did have a core that created mass to fuel the warp field. The mass was plasma, kept in place by a magnetic lattice. It was beautiful; shimmering in patterns like butterfly wings, and cruise ships always had a viewing platform despite the danger. Detective stories frequently had some poor bastard being thrown into a Pulsar Drive. Sandra hated that her epitaph might be a cliché.

Kent led them to the first explosive and knelt down. "Watch carefully as I deactivate this one. The others are the same design."

"Celeste is his 'sister'?" Andrei looked Kent up and down. "Don't see the resemblance."

"We're fraternal twins," Kent said. He paused and glanced at Sandra. "That is a joke."

Sandra checked her biological meters for hallucinogens. None found. "You heard Andrei."

Kent kept working on the bomb. "You have a personality simulation running in your volatile memory. I've accessed it."

Andrei coughed. "That's… I feel uncomfortable. Sandra, stop him from doing that."

Sandra made a task memo to check her internal firewall.

Kent stood. "I'll head clockwise, you go counter. There were six explosive devices, if she used them all."

"What if we run into her?"

"I don't think it's healthy, keeping a simulation of the dead. You know it's not him." He ran off, his suit and hair still impeccable.

Sandra turned her back and paced the curving gantry – counter-clockwise around the cylindrical room. Three decks ringed the open space, one above and one below. She scanned and found the next bomb. She felt a prick at the edges of her eyes. Andrei stepped into her vision. "Hey," he said, like he thought she was going to cry. She wasn't going to cry. "I'm me," he said.

Sandra released a shaky breath and nodded. Andrei was Andrei. He noticed things she didn't. That proved he was real. Autonomous.

When she'd disarmed two bombs and Andrei reported Kent had gotten the others, Sandra felt muscles relax in her back that she hadn't known she was clenching. She straightened. A clear, metallic voice echoed overhead. "Shame."

Sandra looked up to see Celeste crouching on the ceiling, her metal talons dug into the plating to hold her. The robot smirked. "Guess I'll have to kill you first. Work, work, work."

Sandra rolled for cover without thinking. She looked up in time to see a bulkhead door sailing straight for her.

It passed through Andrei's projected form and hit next to her with a deafening clang. Andrei had his hands deep in his blond curls. "We're going to die, and I can't help. I can't even *banter*."

Sandra got behind the fallen bulkhead – it was thick and probably her best cover. She looked back up. Sharp clumps of metal rained down. Celeste tore pieces of the railing in front of her like she was throwing breadcrumbs, oblivious to Kent behind her with a pipe.

Metal impacted metal. Celeste plunged toward the engine core. As she fell, she reached out, sharp talons, straight for Andrei, who leaned over the railing, watching. She was going to take him with her. Sandra grabbed the nearest object at hand – the bulkhead door Celeste had flung at her.

It was almost more than Sandra could lift. She felt the strain in her lower back, her hip, as she twisted and threw. The edge scored her hand on leaving, but the metal landed right where she aimed, wedged between the gangway and a pipe. Celeste hit it hard, clattered and skidded to a stop, one hand behind her dragging furrows in the metal.

Sandra found herself looking straight into the depthless jewels of Celeste's eyes, and remembered that Andrei couldn't fall. Andrei was already dead. She'd just saved a killer robot to protect a holographic projection.

Before Sandra could finish sucking in a breath, she was in Celeste's merciless metal hands, slammed against the curving wall behind her.

"You saved me," Celeste said, her voice amused, untouched by exertion. Her fingertips adjusted, giving Sandra some air.

Andrei said, "Idiot!"

"I always save my stories," Sandra said. She'd finally made a quip. Andre would be proud.

Celeste's lips curled. Then there was pain, too huge to locate at first, melting down to her stomach. Kent hit Celeste from behind. Sandra felt the impact through Celeste's talons into her bones. There was a sucking, wet sound. Sandra dropped to the floor and struggled to get up, but her body felt ripped in half. Large sections of her vision flashed with warnings. All she could do was watch chrome feet and leather shoes dancing back and forth and getting blurrier. Andrei shouted in her mind until he, too, faded.

* * *

Andrei sat on the edge of her hospital bed, filing his nails. He smiled and stood, tucking the file in his pocket. "Idiot," he said.

"So I'm told." Sandra licked dry lips.

Andrei looked at the water on the bedside table longingly. "Well, the good news is, it was a non-fatal wound. Miss Murder-nails managed to miss every major organ. Maybe that means she likes you."

Sandra laughed. It hurt in a good way. She reached for the water, and Andrei's ghost hand followed hers, so he could share the illusion of handing it to her. "Thanks."

Another shape moved behind Andrei. Kent wore the same suit, holding a bouquet. "I'm afraid she got away," he said. "She has rather a habit of that."

Sandra felt for her recording equipment and found it set to hospital privacy mode. Annoying. She had to think through turning it on. "What was she trying to do?"

"Her job," he said, and smiled slightly. "Badly. These are for you." He thrust the bouquet forward. "Our employer's interests are threatened by the Free Media. Our first priority, you understand, was to discredit and confuse, not kill. I did my best to minimize the deaths."

Sandra didn't have the energy for how angry she felt. Instead of a shout, her words came out calm. "Minimize? You're murderers."

"You were close to discovering our employer. We were sent to prevent that from happening. I'm afraid the explosions were the most certain way to attract your attention and bring you to us."

He laid the bouquet awkwardly across her chest. Sandra asked, "And now?"

"I'm here to stop your information from getting out. I think the most pleasant way is to offer you a position with our organization. You've eluded my sister twice, now. Few can say that."

Sandra coughed. It hurt. "Will I have the right to upload content to the Free Media as I see fit?"

If robots could blanche, it would look like Kent's face at that moment, a sudden complete stillness. "I'm afraid that…is not possible. We are a secret organization."

"Then no, thank you."

Andrei rucked his hair up on the top of his head. "Sandra, you almost died for this. It's what we've been chasing for years. Even if you can't report it, we'll finally *know*. Take the job."

"No," Sandra said.

"That's unfortunate." Kent hesitated. His eyes flicked to Andrei. "We could restore your partner to you: a facsimile, similar to myself, with the memories you store."

Andrei was nodding violently. "No," said Sandra, feeling a wet weight of sadness. Had Kent been someone else, once? Had Celeste?

"I don't want to kill you. Will you consent to delete your files and allow me to access your storage to confirm this?"

Kent stood over her, hands clasped, waiting.

"Destroy data? Sandra? That's not likely." Andrei weightlessly fell on the bed, a hand she couldn't feel on her shoulder. "Sandra – think about this. You'll end us both."

Sandra closed her eyes, and turned Andrei off. For the first time in months, she was alone in her mind. The silence rang.

She said, "I save stories. It's what I do."

She kicked Kent, the hospital blanket billowing up with her leg. She knew where the metal stabilizer inside her shin was hardest. It clanged against his back and the shock ran up her body. Kent didn't move.

Sandra liked to think that Kent paused, as his sister had paused, because he liked her. She twisted and flipped out of the bed, the blanket catching on his head and pulling free of her.

She ran into the corridor. She felt a hard, plastic hand close on her ankle. She fell forward, abdomen stretching. Something tore inside her. She screamed. She crawled forward as Kent ripped into her flesh. The metal reinforcing her foot squealed against his fingertips, but she got into the corridor.

A hospital technician came running. And then another, and another. Kent let go.

Sandra twisted in place. Kent was gone. The hospital blanket lay in an arc on the floor, and the foot of the bed was crushed, as though a safe had fallen on it from a great height.

So it was that secret, Kent's existence. He'd left her rather than be seen.

Sandra felt a needle. "No!" She flopped like a fish, keeping out of the hospital worker's hands. "No. No medication. I need…"

She squirmed out of arms trying to lift her and hit the floor hard. Black specks swam over the edges of the data retrieval menu. Why wasn't there a simple one-movement command to upload all files? She ignored the hands lifting her, the drug entering her. Willing her veins to still. She just needed to select 'Upload All'. Public access was the default. She needed to blink confirm. She felt the hospital firewall and unconsciousness closing in.

* * *

Sandra awoke aware of the empty place in her thoughts where Andrei should be. Everything hurt. She checked her files. They were uploaded. All public. She'd shown the universe the face of Andrei's killer. Her inbox was bursting with notifications.

Take that, robot death twins.

That was a good line. Andrei would need to hear it. Her eye hovered over the command to re-activate him.

And then left it. She moved Andrei out of active memory and into storage. It was a step.

Alone in her mind, she slept.

Water Bees

Desmond White

[Translator's Note: Henri Moreau's autobiography was published posthumously by his grandson in 1901. I've done my best to keep Moreau's vinegary, poetic tone from the original French.]

En 1888, dans la ville d'Arles

MY LIFE has become a flutter of paperwork as if clouds of moths flap and flitter on my desk. If only these papers shared the moth's predilection for leaping into the flame, I would have more fuel for my fire and more desk. But this is my punishment for ambition; for wanting '*en chef*' beside '*inspecteur*'. Now I have an office overlooking the Rhône, where I can work above the clatter, where I can interview my agents over a slow pipe and wine. I have never been unhappier.

Plus, there is that damned portrait on the wall. In the eternity of paint, I stand in a blue coat with my hand in my pocket, not like Napoleon, but a man with a hand in his pocket. My silver buttons, short-brimmed cap, and collar wrapped in laurel impress my high office, while my gray cloak and beard white as webs remind the viewer that retirement, maybe death, is my next promotion. I've been told the painting is done in the style of Carolus-Duran, but its oily glaze, highlighted wrinkles, and love for shadows reminds me of a Rembrandt. There I am, Walt Whitman civilized. A hero at his end. But who put it beside a mirror? Why must my decay be compared to my glorious old age? There is the expiration date, and there's rot.

Now I think I would have retired gracefully into the life of an old bastard, enjoying my garden and books and women, if it hadn't been for that English trouble-sower Charles Robert Darwin. Some fifty years I fought the criminal mind, and for most of it, I found the culprits a profound evil. I am not a religious man but it gave me solace knowing there was a higher order. Maybe man was touched with a little madness but he was above the bugs. He was not a system of instincts and mechanics bound by carapace. But then – *La descendance de l'homme et la sélection sexuelle*. It was on the suggestion of my wife that I read the book for my *éclaircissement*. I still remember the volume – green with gold print on the spine. And within, the suggestion that man evolved from worms! That as our respiratory organs sophisticated, we began to draw more oxygen to the blood, to grow in size, to complicate. The more I thought about it, the more the idea made sense. Like worms, we're two mouths connected by tubes. In it goes, out it goes. And we have skin that comes in browns and reds, pearls and buffs.

The Ancient Greeks envisioned mythical animals. Bears, lions, cats, dogs. If only we lived in a world as wondrous. Instead, we have been born into this mechanical, rational order of insects. And now, by Darwin's Law, we may not even be the beekeepers, but the bees themselves! But I have a theory. I think maybe we do have a bit of Divine Chaos in our minds. That our maggot flesh closed around some wild principle – that there was some mismanagement of evolution which gave us Freedom. And this Freedom has given us strange adventures.

My tragic sense disagrees – it suspects we operate under the insectoid masters of pain and pleasure, from which all morality derives. Darwin merely noticed our origins – we insects pretending to be men.

Well, there you have it. I stay in my occupation in my late years because I fear that if I were to retire these thoughts might bother me like flies.

It was this very discussion I was reading in *Le Petit Journal* over a quick breakfast. It had begun with an opinion by M. Huguet, the Great Entomologist, that 'man is as mechanical and predictable as the dung beetle.' In response, M. Tréville – Huguet's famous opponent in the sciences, and a Catholic – split the process of the brain from the soul-stuffed echelon of the mind. 'The mind is our gift by God, granting us Free Will,' concluded the professor. 'Unless you are suggesting God has man's mind, only magnified?' It was a few days before the heretical reply by M. Huguet – the very reply I read now: 'Yes, perhaps God has no Free Will. Perhaps he *must* create, he *must* love, he *must* be good – that he is bound by Principles, and cannot conceive or pursue any other. Perhaps if a scientist were to bring a microscope to *paradis* – after some time, this scientist might map the dimensions of God, predict His every action, every thought.'

But this morning, I was not rattled by this thesis, for I was tired – not yet used to sleeping at conventional hours. I would have preferred to roam the night's streets with my agents and irregulars, but it was expected in my high office that I be available to entertain city officials and go, when called, to the prefecture in Paris.

My valet informed me that a boy was waiting in the foyer. He said it without disdain this time – Arpin was new but he adapted quickly to the irregulars I employ as my eyes. (Orphans, mostly, since they appear in such frequency and work hard for their wages.)

Looking about with a bit of wonder – I believe it is these orphans' desire to one day take my job – stood a boy about waist's height, pale beneath the grime.

"Mabeuf? Are you here to waste my morning?" I said, but the boy interrupted: "It is M. Huguet. He is gone!" The boy had no information other than this message, so I sent him to alert my groomsmen.

M. Huguet! What a strange turn. Here, I had only now been reading his proclamations against the heavens to find he'd disappeared as quickly and mysterious as a lightning bolt. Had he ever done this before? I thought back to my history with the professor – for we had some history, M. Huguet being a man with some forensic skill. I could recall nothing.

My cab took me swiftly to *l'hôtel de police*. I have always hated the place – it is as hideous as a Van Gogh, with pale orange stones and blue shutters and blue doors. There is not even distance between the station and its neighbors – the building's face is a long stretch of stone which stands like a wall along the river (separated only by the road and floodwall). Have you ever been to Charleville-Mezieres? Their station is surrounded by black fencing like spears and has a respectable white-and-gray face in the style of a chateau. Arles, meanwhile, is incredibly ugly for a city once the pride of the Romans.

Inside, I found my agents strained and dirty with eyes rimmed by the black traveling bags of fatigue. I took one aside and said, "Renoir, what is this about?"

"M. Huguet, sir. He is missing. His valet reported this morning, maybe two o'clock." said the agent. "We are hoping this is a mistake. And yet—"

"And yet?"

"He has not turned up. Please, Chief Inspector. I have to interview the head cook."

"Why was I not told?" I asked, but I knew the answer. It was in my office in the mirror by my portrait. A face – my face – weathered as a ship put to sea. They had probably said aloud, "let the old man sleep."

Renoir gave me a look, and tucked away whatever he wanted to say. Instead: "If you are looking for Inspector Brochard, she is with Huguet's sister in the Closet. We have sent agents to the house and university, and they are speaking to his colleagues, including his opponent from the papers."

"I will speak to Mme. Pouget," I said.

Renoir hesitated. "I should not say this but Brochard has made it clear she does not want your involvement."

"Brochard is not Chief Inspector," I said, and he nodded dismally.

I went to the interview. The youthful hesitation of Brochard and the plain-spokenness of Huguet's sister drifted through the door.

The Closet was the size of a restroom, barely able to stomach a table and chairs. The only lights were sucked in from the barred window or vomited from a dying lamp on a hook. Inspector Brochard, as dirty and stone-faced as the walls, sat on one side of the table. I scanned her quickly – she still wore her night cloak, and a slight tremble revealed her fatigue, or perhaps the energy of coffee.

On the other side was the lovely Mme. Anne Madeline Pouget, who seemed to flow from the black exclamation of her hair (wrapped over her head like a beehive), down past the white of her face and chest to a red-and-green dress with a golden sash. Her hands were united in her lap like a priest in prayer.

"Henri," she said as I entered. "Have you come to fetch me from the boring inspector?"

We were not as familiar as first names, and she only knew me through M. Huguet, but this was the way the young women spoke in Arles.

Brochard turned and gave me a red glare. "Chief Inspector," said the lesser inspector. "There are letters from the *maire* and the Duchess of Bigaud awaiting attention."

"M. Huguet was a good friend of mine," I replied not altogether honestly. "And a good friend of the department. It will be expected the Chief Inspector be involved." That last bit was true – M. Huguet had been something of the amateur forensic generalist. His expertise in the life cycles of flying insects had helped us pinpoint the hours of death in the odd corpse, and once he had surmised a woman had been kept in a cooler for two days by the bracken of eggs in her nostrils.

"Insp. Brochard, I am tired of discussing my brother," interrupted Mme Pouget. "It has been a long night. You have my statement. Several, in fact. I would like to retire."

It was not the line I wanted – I had hoped to interview the Madame, but now I noticed the darkness around her eyes not totally concealed by the paint.

"Of course," said Brochard. She stood – inviting Mme Pouget to do the same. "Refresh yourself but be available."

I knocked at the door and the guard opened it. Mme. Pouget passed by me and smiled – she thought I had come to rescue her. I closed the door and turned to Brochard.

"Inspector," I said. "If I were younger, I would bloody your face."

"If you were younger," said Brochard, "I'd have no reservation."

"Let me be of some help," I said, trying a different tactic. "At least, by review, you might discover some strange tangent. What were the circumstances of M. Huguet's disappearance?"

Brochard sighed wearily. "Coffee first."

We retired to my office. Her eyes stayed too long at my portrait – that grisly reminder of entropy. I will speak only briefly about Brochard in a positive way – most of my thoughts about her are poison. She was the most ambitious woman I ever met. It was not a time for women in the police – at best, a prostitute might entice a culprit and there were women in the irregulars. But Brochard had come recommended by the *Prefecture* in Paris, who could not take her on because, again, she was a woman. Nor could she serve in the rural towns, which are protected by the *Gendarmerie* – those old soldiers are even more entrenched in masculinity. But in a dull post like Arles there was some place for her. Especially with an unconventional Chief Inspector like myself, who'd spent his early years under the employ of one M. Vidocq.

But Arles *was* a dull post separated by long epochs of tediousness. The city left her short-tempered and restless. And I, with my wizard's beard and ponderous way of speaking, must have been the exemplar of ennui.

"So," I said, over coffee and some little breads. "The circumstances."

"We are not sure," she said. Her body was exhausted, but the coffee was perking her up. "Right as he went to bed, he vanished."

"M. Huguet is a man of habit," I said. "You have his schedule?"

"He was a man of *complete* and *utter* habit," said Brochard. She pulled out a notebook. "Every day, he is woken by his valet, M. Blier, a veteran, precisely at 4:00 a.m. The soldier is under order to be tenacious. Huguet has his tobacco, prepares his lectures at the university. These lectures begin at 8:00 a.m. and last until 12:00 a.m. Afterward, he walks to the terrace and has lunch at *café coléoptère* on Rue des Carmes. Alone, he walks through a nearby park to digest. In the afternoon, he visits his stations. These are experiments commissioned by *la société centrale d'apiculture*, and approved by the city council, which are set around the city. They are something to do with water bees – observation of their life habits, I think. The tour takes hours, and at 5:00 p.m. he returns to his home to continue his academic work in the study. At 9:00 p.m., he retires to bed and reads until – and this is reported by the valet – he falls asleep with his book-in-hand around midnight. The valet enters the bedroom a minute after midnight, puts the book away, blows out the lamps, and leaves the good lecturer in the darkness of dreams. Only, this morning, Huguet was gone."

"At 4 a.m., when the valet came to wake him?"

"No, at midnight. His bed was empty," said Brochard. "But Huguet had been in his study earlier. At some point between his scholarship and sleep, he was abducted."

"Or left by his own accord."

"Or was killed by the valet," theorized Brochard. "The police were not notified for two hours."

"It is probable Blier woke the other servants and conducted a search of the grounds. That would take some time," I said. She nodded. That was what the valet had reported. "And his sister?"

"She hadn't heard anything from him in two weeks. 'The closest thing to mail are his opinions in the paper,' she said to me. From what I can surmise, this is all unusual. Huguet would announce any intention of breaking his habits to his servants. He was a man who liked his private life to be as outlined and underlined as his student's textbooks. To be—" She considered her words carefully, "—predictable."

"You have examined the household?" I asked.

"With scientific precision. We took the entire building – the furniture, the walls, the floorboards, the ceiling. Every surface, every crevice, every secret, every particle."

"The papers?" I asked.

"The jargon of a scientist," she said. "We looked for codes, but there is nothing there – only observations."

"And the usual suspects?" I asked.

"All of Christendom," said Brochard, looking at her notebook. "But we have narrowed it down to any society of Anarchists, Socialists, or Catholics, and to his Students, Colleagues, and Family."

"How *very* narrow," I said. "So, of his family?"

"You were acquainted with him enough to know there is no wife or children. There is only Mme. Anne Madeline Pouget – his sister – who stands to inherit the estate. She is married to M. Rémille Pouget."

"The judge?" I had never made the connection between the lady and Judge Pouget, that old beetle of justice who wears the black robes of the Grim Reaper, whose wig runs down the sides of his face like a string of scrolls, who has been the bane of many an urchin and petty criminal. "But she has such…joy."

"He must be a kinder man behind closed doors," said Brochard. "They have two daughters – Claire and Camille."

She looked in her notebook, adding: "One dachshund named Daki."

"And you suspect her?"

"It seems likely. I have heard M. Pouget inherited the debts of his father. The Huguet estate would be compelling."

"And she would know the contents of her brother's will," I said. "Is that all?"

Brochard looked to her notes and nodded.

"Well, then." I took my coat. "I hope our review was helpful."

I could see it was not – Brochard still had a grimace, but at least it was not from me. Her eyes were still scanning her notebook. "I will leave you to your investigation."

"And where are you going?" snapped Brochard.

"On a walk," I said and left her to my office.

I stopped first at the library and asked the clerk for a bibliography of M. Huguet. He seemed rather astounded to see an officer of the law, but was more than helpful, and soon we discovered a tome of interest – a book red as murder, with faux silver embroidery and two interesting names printed on the spine: Huguet & Tréville. Under supervision of the clerk, I sat on an armchair and opened *Encyclopédie de la morphologie de l'abeille* to the article on Water Bees:

"*Apis aqua* (superfamily Apoidea). You can find their galleries on driftwood and the hulls of boats or anything weathered, forgotten. We have heard it was they who built the hive between the lion's ribs [*Editor: Judges 14:8*]. But the bees prefer a tree dipped in a lake because of their peculiar ability – the water bee is amphibious. Each bug is an aeroplane, carriage, and submarine pushed into a small blue pill with wings and fins. They feast on crab and fish, and are eaten in return. They produce a honey that induces vomiting, used by doctors and midwives, and perhaps Samson on a hungry day."

How interesting, I thought, looking again to the name of Tréville. To think, the two opponents had produced an encyclopedia.

"Do you know the reputation of M. Huguet?" I asked the clerk, and he smiled with a condescending approval.

"A bestseller, Inspector."

"And M. Georges Tréville?"

"Not so much," said the clerk. "The encyclopedia was their last collaboration. Afterward, there was contention – well, you have seen the papers? And there was the affair of Tréville's poetry. A dreadful anthology – sort of a Rudyard Kipling with too much onomatopoeia. 'The bee goes bizz bizz.' That sort of thing."

I thanked him for his assistance, and took my cab to a tobacco shop on Rue des Lices, and then to the apartment of M. Pouget. The *maître* brought me to her salon, a room of luxurious laziness – cushioned chairs, tables too small to carry a book, a predilection for olive green and the bright blot of blood. The room was quiet. In an armchair sat the lovely Mme. Pouget. On her lap was a scarab beetle about the size of a purse. She was stroking its chin, and it purred with a mechanical whirr.

"Henri," she said with that confusing familiarity. I had only met her a handful of times. It must have energized her to see my discomfort. Or perhaps – and here an old man pretends – she was *happy* to see me.

I addressed her courteously, and asked her to accompany me on a tour of the city.

"Have you come to court me, Henri?" she said.

I laughed. "Today, you can be my granddaughter."

"You want to retrace my brother's steps," she said.

"Don't you?"

"No," she said. "But you expect me to."

"Yes," I said.

"To catch his killer."

"Who says he is dead, Madame?"

She looked at me fiercely. The beetle had stopped purring and clacked its mandibles impatiently. "And what if the killer is me? What if I killed the famous atheist? Would you hang your granddaughter?"

I was very uncomfortable. Finally, I said: "The noose would not pair with your eyes."

She laughed at the poor humor, and placed the beetle on the ground. It scurried after a ball of yarn.

I waited in the foyer while Mme. Pouget prepared herself, and then we went to the university to walk its halls. She showed me his lecture room – a chamber worthy of the *Convention nationale*. We found his office unlocked and full of police, and I heard nothing new in the several hours since my breakfast with Brochard. As I surveyed the writing table, none of them noticed me take a booklet, flip it open, and pocket it in my coat. Or perhaps they noticed and said nothing.

Mme. Pouget looked tiredly at the blue uniforms and silver buttons, so we refreshed ourselves at *café coléoptère*. What is Arles's obsession with the beetle? The conceit of the *café* was to imitate the green mint of shells on all of the interior decorating, and the servers brought us *beignets* shaped into dungballs. We talked mostly about the courts, I from my position in police, and her from the wife of a judge. We avoided M. Huguet as effectively as he avoided us.

Coffee rejuvenated her spirits, and she held my hand and chatted amiably about gruesome murders while we walked the *parterre* near Rue de Rejeune. I had never noticed before how the paths coil like millipedes, but I had bugs on the mind, and their predictable patterns, and the last words of Monsieur Gérard Huguet. If there are to be last words, best to have them published – I thought. Improvisation is risky. Prose lets one revise and edit and steal with citation.

But perhaps those words should not be blasphemy. Especially an irony like the boast of mapping God's feet while not noticing the footpath to destruction.

He could be alive, I countered.

I could see why Huguet enjoyed the park. Here, in the middle of this glowing city were green palisades of grass and avenues of trees laced by smooth white stone rivers. In the distance, I could see the basin of a manmade lake reflecting leaves and sky, its waves like poorly-concealed brushstrokes on oil canvas. A lake's reflection must have been the inspiration of the Impressionists (paired with failing eyesight). Nearby were couples walking in the avenues, and on the grass were men tossing sticks to their crickets.

"I've heard crickets make a highly sociable pet, only their feet kick in their sleep and make an infuriating noise in the night," said Mme. Pouget, and I felt, for a moment, that little stir of desire. It had been too long since a woman clung to me. On the pavement ahead, some children were drawing crude aphids and ladybugs with chalk.

The notebook I'd taken from M. Huguet's office led us onward to the Stations. There were eleven of them situated at points around the city, all along the riverfront, each the location of a beehive discovered, documented, and defended by an iron fence and yellow signs. Fortunately, there are few locks in Arles that can outduel my pick.

The hives were built in the hulls of boat husks and planks of driftwood and one was in the wall of an abandoned kiosk and one in a rotten desk. Each was labeled in red paint – Station 1, 2, 3, *et cetera*.

Finally, we approached Station 11, wary of bugs and weary from having achieved nothing for our labor. Wedged into the coastal rocks that comprise the floodwall, a log pointed back to the city like a cannon. The log moved with the waves as if soldiers were readjusting trajectories, and around its barrel was a haze of bees – their metallic blue bodies also flicking about in the water lapping the rocks. The muzzle had been stoppered by a wood barrel on which was printed 'Station 11' – the words were also painted on the cannonside.

"He could have fallen in," said Mme. Pouget adventurously, looking down the embankment. "Or been pushed." I looked to the Rhône and wondered. It was a slow-looking river, but fast and cold and it could drag a body swiftly into the obscure vegetation of Camargue. But I could not decipher from the rock's assortment if there had been some recent tumble. (Nor would I be filling in prints with cement *à la* Vidocq.)

"And if he had – he would be dead," I said.

"I would not grace him a single tear," Pouget replied, looking at me haughtily. "If I have my debts right, he owed me several."

"You were not close to your brother," I said stupidly.

She watched the streaks of bees beneath the water. "After this station, he goes back to his study – to write his essays."

The home of M. Gérard Huguet was built in imitation of the *Petit Trianon* in Versailles, although the *maison* is reduced and *sans* the palace gardens. What the house of Huguet offered that Arles did not was space – space between the blue-gold fence and the orange face of the house, space between the heads of its inhabitants and a distant ceiling. This space lingered exotically in the laboratory of M. Huguet, which I had never visited, having dealt with him sometimes in my office, sometimes in the courthouse, but mostly through correspondence. The lab was decorated like a Cabinet of Curiosities with glass panels pressed against the walls and coating the desks, beneath which rested columns of *Arthropoda* carefully preserved, pinned, and labeled.

Renoir was here, sleeping in an armchair, and I left him undisturbed. Who knew what orders Inspector Brochard had given him?

The valet was a man in his forties with black-gray hair and a mustache thick as a candle. He stood straight but walked with a limp from a stray musketball that'd prevented a military career. I suspected he kept his uniform pressed sharply in his *armoire* but never found opportunity to wear it.

I asked him about the master's punctuality and it was the same itinerary as Brochard's. The valet added that at 5:00 p.m. he would leave a cup of tea at the desk, and he had done so last night. Had it been sipped? Finished completely, as was usual for M. Huguet. And, the valet said, the master did complete his notes – leaving his books on the desk. Otherwise, he had not seen M. Huguet until – well, he had not seen him at all. Not unusual, either, except for the midnight appointment.

"M. Huguet was a man of mind, and that type likes solitude. They're never lonely when they're alone," said the valet in a serious manner. He was a man, I thought, with wisdom in this area.

So, M. Huguet *had* returned in the evening and been taken in his own home.

Or he left by his own free will (I thought this with a bite of humor).

Or the assailant wanted to distract us from an early abduction – or murder, I thought, recalling Mme. Pouget's theory about the river – by impersonating his later movements.

Public habits were one thing, but the habits of one's private life were an intimate sort. That last option would reduce my list of suspects incredibly. And, to be honest with myself, my intuition – that terribly unreliable tool in this rationalist age – told me the doctor had never returned to his office.

I opened a notebook on the desk – it was labeled *Station Onze* – to find page after page of identical graphs and boxes embroidered by the careful little handwriting of M. Huguet. Here was the industry of the bees of Station 11 in a language technical and tedious and absurd – footnotes on footnotes and citations to *scientific obscura*; measurements of boreholes and bee abdomens and wings; measurements of hive growth thickness, and weight; Fig. 1; Fig. 2, *etc.*; estimates of the number of bees in the hive (an incredible amount in summer, an appallingly low number in winter); estimates of the number of eggs produced per day; a fifteen-minute count of the number of bees exiting the log's underwater aperture; a fifteen-minute count from the open barrel at the top; the viscosity and volume of combe samples; sketches of the internal diaphragm of the log; articulated drawings of the bee and its organs.

Other notebooks were devoted to the rest of the stations.

In fact, there were cabinets full of these books.

An archive of headache.

"Have you heard of psychology, Inspector?" asked Mme. Pouget.

"Only in its application to the mind of the criminal," I said, drawing open the notebook for Station 10. "I have a colleague who claims there are psychic structures in our minds that determine our criminology sometime in the womb. If we could screen for those structures, we might save the justices a lot of time in deciding who to hang and who to free."

"I hope not," said Mme. Pouget. "It would take all the mystery out of murder."

I flipped through the notebook as Mme. Pouget took a seat near me, her dress obscuring the chair. "Psychology was Gérard's pastime," she said to me, opening a kit to reapply powder. "You know there is a wasp who plants her eggs in a caterpillar and then buries it in the ground. Not long after, the larvae eat their way out of the living bug – you don't want to feed the babies stale caterpillar, do you? In fact, the wasp's venom boosts the constitution of the caterpillar while paralyzing it horribly – it cannot run away, but it is very, very healthy until the eggs break open.

"My brother did an experiment with this wasp. He put it in a box and granted it a caterpillar, but as the wasp was preparing its hole, he moved the caterpillar away. The wasp came out of the hole, moved the bug back, went back into the hole. My brother moved it again, and again, and again. The wasp repeated itself – coming out, moving the bug, going back in. Over and over. You see, at first the wasp appeared clever, but it wasn't really thinking – it was following its design."

Mme. Pouget snapped her kit shut, then stood and opened a cabinet. She slid a shelf out of the furniture and dumped a stockpile of scholarship on the desk. "Some of these are notes on hornets, but some—" She picked out a booklet and gave it to me. "—some are far more disgusting."

I took a booklet and reviewed another slew of observations as monotonous as the last.

Only—

The subject was not a bug at all.

On each page, in the right corner, was the name: *Anne.*

"Eventually, he got the idea he could apply the parable of the wasp to people," said Mme. Pouget, a woman who once went by Anne Madeline Huguet.

"What kinds of experiments did he conduct?" I asked.

"I am not sure the extent. Knowing I was being tested would ruin the purity of the data. Still, he liked to gloat about my...predictability," said Mme. Pouget. She sighed (almost theatrically) and sat down again on the chair, using a loose parchment of notes as a fan. "Creeping little things, Inspector. Stimuli, to see what I would do. Comments, usually. Suggestions. Sometimes he would reorder things. Paint a chair a different color. He would pay careful attention to my pupils. My hands. To see my reaction. He would have measured my heartbeat if I let him. And not just me. My husband. My daughters. His 'friends'. He was so disappointed when I did not have twins," she added. "Can you imagine?"

"Why interact with him at all?" I asked.

"Because – because my husband is not a rich man." She looked at me with desperation. "And I hoped someday we might inherit the estate."

"And so," I summarized. "You are not sad that he is dead."

"No," she said. "No, I am not."

She stood up. "Henri," – there was my first name again! – "I want to show you something. It's something I did not show Inspector Brochard." She looked to Renoir, as cozy as a tick and whistling like a cicada. "I did not – I do not want this in the papers. They will publish anything once the public hears of the disappearance. And my reputation..."

"What is it?" I asked.

"Look at the back of the book."

I did. On the final page, in the right corner, was *Anne.* Beside it was the word *Prediction.*

Below:

'Sister. *Method*: Analysis of data and carrying capacity (or lack thereof) shows that her method would be by medication. Make it a suicide. Leave me to be found. *Motive*: My inheritance – royalties, incomplete manuscripts, letters, *etc. Alternative*: Perhaps she might find some discrete way in public – a passing cart on the street ("Oh, he tripped!") or a gentle nudge into the Rhône?'

I picked up another booklet and opened it to the last page: 'M. Pouget, by Duel.'

And another: 'Chief Inspector Henri Moreau. *Method*: Task one of his agents, perhaps Renoir or Tharaud. It would be easy for the man to obtain my routines and stage a mugging. A pistol would draw too much attention – the assassin will use a knife. Moreau can control the investigation, examine the body, *etc.*, and obfuscate all evidence. *Motive*: Unknown.' I pulled back the pages to find more data than I had expected. The doctor had been observing me carefully in each encounter, each letter, even my appearances or quotes in the newspapers. And he had delivered me several tests incognito.

"These are all booklets of this type?" I said, collecting them together. There they were – all the incriminating evidence a court would need to hang any one of us: Moreau, Brochard,

Renoir, M. & Mme. Pouget, even little Camille. Blier. Three servants – Riva, Jouillerot, and Monroc. Two colleagues – M. Guillaume Dessay and M. Mathias Beautier.

"Every one," she said.

"And these are all the booklets?"

"Every one," she said again. "God knows why I didn't burn them this morning."

"I am glad you did not," I said.

I kicked the chair leg of Renoir, and he snorted awake. "Renoir, summon three irregulars and hurry to the house of M. Georges Tréville. You will arrest him for the murder of M. Gérard Huguet."

"What?" said Renoir sleepily.

"Go!" I shouted, pulling him out of his chair and sending him running. Then I turned to the supplies of M. Huguet – helping myself to a canister of gas, a lantern, a mask, and other objects.

Mme. Pouget was watching all of this with a puzzled smile.

"But M. Tréville is not observed by my brother," she said.

"Not in this pile," I replied.

"Where will you be?" asked Renoir by the door. He had the wild look of a fruit fly on sap. I shouted the direction, and he looked as bewildered as Mme. Pouget.

"And where should I be?" said Mme. Pouget.

"Here," I said. "To show Brochard the books."

Outside, Mabeuf sat with my driver on the box seat. I told the driver the address and the cab rumbled into the lane. Quickly, I informed Mabeuf to reach Inspector Brochard at *l'hôtel de police* and inform her of the crime. We dropped Mabeuf near Pont Royal and drove on. I was finally having some shake of fear. If I was wrong, I would do more than embarrass a Catholic entomologist. Brochard would feed me to the press, and worse, might usher in my retirement. That little office on the Rhône did not seem so bad compared to a shameful toss into the private life.

I did not have time to pick the lock, so the driver struck it with a shovel. Into the pavilion I strove, quartered by fencing menacing as spears, and down onto moss-encrusted boulders that acted a net, keeping my boots above the scum life that scuttled on the waterfront. Green crabs clipped in false confidence at my soles before returning to flies and the silver rot of river ticks. Finally, I encountered the slanting timber employed by the Water Bees of Station 11.

I must have seemed some alien creature in my gray uniform and visor – a uniform in appearance like a fencer. I pulled the rings on the canisters and dropped them around the log, spilling gray smoke into the air. The canisters provided a diligent smokescreen, something like a heavy fog in concentrate, and pushed the blue guardians underwater where they coursed about angrily – some on the occasion shooting out like gunshot to encounter the confusion of the smoke and dive back in. This gave the floodwall the impression of a battlefield – the bees and smoke like whizzing bullets and the smog of artillery.

I took a saw to the log like the mortician to a cadaver, then used my hands to split open its chest. More bees spilled from the aperture. I felt their stingers prodding my jacket like so many tapping fingertips. I cracked a fresh canister on my belt without removing it and the fumes spilled over me, driving the regiment away. Blinded, barely able to trace the outline of my hands, I waited for the smoke to recede and the chocolate umber of the log to appear, and inside it, the purple-gold cake of the hive.

There – in the heartwood – I found what I feared.

A skeleton plated in amber scales, and drilled precisely, uniformly, with rows and rows of boreholes – something like sweat pores magnified, although not even pores are as evenly distributed. The boreholes had been drilled directly into the skeleton as naturally as if those bones had grown that away.

The air smelled sickly of bee-stench and old meat, and I noted with growing unease how some of the holes were filled with the purpling grease of bee-combe, and others with white wiggling larvae. I examined the corpse's chest but could find no sign of organs or musculature, only a thick padding of wax with virulent colors.

The bees had made quick work of the corpse of M. Huguet. But that is their reputation. So complete was their craftsmanship that I could have taken a section of skull and offered it to you as a meal – a wonderful pallet of yellow perforated bone dripping with honey.

Renoir and his patrol waited by my cab – they had watched the twisting storm of bees in horror.

"Tréville was not at home, but we caught him at the docks boarding a ship for Québec," said Renoir, and I could see that his private deductions had not determined my means of solution. "Tréville was not surprised to see us and confessed immediately. He gave me a 'gift' for 'the Inspector's collection.'"

Renoir entrusted me with a brown notebook. I disrobed and gave the agent the beekeeper uniform, and Renoir investigated the corpse of M. Huguet. When he returned, his face shone more with excitement than dread. In that interim I had glanced at the notebook, but only in amazement at the calculations of Huguet – not in surprise.

"But how did you know it was M. Tréville?" said Renoir.

"Some other time. Set up the perimeter. This is your scene, agent. I will inform Inspector Brochard."

"*You* are the Chief Inspector," said Renoir, but I waved my hand dismissively.

"Not forever. Not for long."

I took the cab to *l'hôtel* and drank some wine in my office, wanting something sour that did not have the energy of coffee. I stared distantly for a while, with the notebook of Huguet residing in the pocket of my coat. Then I howled as a pain shot through me – hot and focused as an inoculation. I pulled off my coat, rolled up my sleeve, and discovered a splinter among the hairs of my arm – straight and crooked as the tower in Pisa. A pustule of blue grime was wrapped around its hilt, and I discovered its bearer – a blue bee the size of a horsefly – by the feet of my chair. In my distraction, I had not noticed Inspector Brochard enter my office, but now she spoke from my portrait, where she was examining her uniform in the mirror: "How did you know M. Huguet was in Station 11?"

I placed the bee on my desk. What an annoying fellow he had been today.

"The hive was clogged by a barrel top," I said. "In the doctor's note, it was unstoppered – in fact, bees were counted coming in and out of the open hollow. The doctor was a meticulous man. I realized someone had closed it without his notice – because he was already inside."

"And M. Tréville?" she said quietly, her eyes on me – or more accurately, my reflected caricature. Her hands continued to caress the wrinkles on her collar.

"Someone had come to the office after the tour of the Stations. Someone had the tea and lay in bed and finished the notes, even if it all was done in haste. Someone intimate. And it was probably a scientist, for who else would think to check and mark and calculate the observations in the journal, even if they are probably fabricated numbers? Who a better culprit than a slighted rival and once-companion? Someone who might profit from the loss of competition, and the sudden attention to entomology, who might be called upon to review the late documents of M. Huguet?

"But finally – of all Huguet's experiments into human psychology – I am sure Mme. Pouget showed you the other notebooks – the only one missing was for M. Tréville. Why would Huguet observe me and not his colleague and intimate? But he had. The book was missing only because M. Tréville, while in the study, had taken it. He must have known about the social experiments, but not the extent the doctor had gone to predict his own murder. Yes, I am sure, Tréville did not know about the prediction until he stood in the study of M. Huguet and, like the little narcissist, read the most astounding conclusions about himself."

I gave the Inspector the notebook and told her to read aloud the last page.
She read:

> "*M. Tréville*, Prediction.
>
> "*Based on my constant attention to my rival (see preceding pages), I can generalize the procedure by which he would undertake my death. As to Motive, on General Principle, any quibbles of 'moral conscience' will be circumvented by jealousy initiated in our college days exacerbated by the publication of the encyclopedia. As my name was alphabetically secured first on the publication, I have received more credit for its erudition (a common mistake by critics).*
>
> "*Oh, and there was our dual publications expounding the same theory later in the year, long after our 'divorce', of which I received attention and he only accusations of plagiarism. I find my death highly profitable to my old friend – if he can avoid justice. As a similar expert, he will be called in on matters of posthumous publication, etc., and will be able to draw from the endless wellspring of my mind.*
>
> "*Again, all is fortified by evidence from my 'pressures' and 'stimuli' (see preceding pages).*
>
> "Probability: *Very high, and I wonder if I should submit this journal (even if I will be laughed at by the dull Moreau) to the Sûreté.*
>
> "Method: *Most ingenious, I think, from an opponent who is a scientist and poet. But, I think, as it was the Water Bee which made me most famous, it is by the Water Bee he will seek my destruction. The tearing of my helmet and stirring of the bees is too simple.*
>
> "*It will be barbaric and total. Nothing less but my submersion and metamorphosis into the hive will suffice for this predictably violent academic.*"

I would have retired years ago but I am afraid of the dark conclusions I will make in the solicitude of simplicity. The bridge between men and the lower-orders is wide and engulfing.

Instead, the active life keeps me searching for some other way. Some other truth. At best, distracted.

Or maybe it is not my choice at all. Maybe I am bound like the bee to its flower.

The Affair of the German Dispatch-Box

Victor L. Whitechurch

THORPE HAZELL often said afterwards that the most daring case which he ever undertook was that of the German Dispatch-Box. It was an affair of international importance at the time, and, for obvious reasons, remained shrouded in mystery. Now, however, when it may be relegated to the region of obsolete diplomatic crises, there is no reason why it should not, to a certain extent, be made public.

Hazell was only half through his breakfast one morning at his house in Netherton, when a telegram arrived for him with this message:

> *Am coming by next train. Wish to consult you on important question.*
> *Mostyn Cotterell.*

"Cotterell, Cotterell," said Hazell to himself. "Oh, yes, I remember – he was on the same staircase with myself at St. Philip's. A reading man in those days. I haven't seen him for years. Surely he's something in the Government now. Let me see."

He got his Whitaker and consulted its pages. Presently he found what he wanted.

"Under-Secretary for Foreign Affairs – Mostyn Cotterell."

As soon as he had finished his breakfast, including his pint of lemonade, he produced a 'Book of Exercises', and carefully went through the following directions:

"Stand in correct position, commence to inhale, and at the same time commence to tense the muscles of the arms, and raise them to an extended front horizontal position; leave the hands to drop limp from the wrists. While doing this change the weight of the body from the full foot on to the toes; in this position hold the breath and make rigid and extended the muscles of the arms, sides, neck, abdomen, and legs. Repeat this fifteen times."

Half-an-hour or so later Mostyn Cotterell was ushered into his room. He was a tall, thin man, with a black moustache that made his naturally pale face look almost white. There was a haggard look about him, and certain dark lines under his eyes showed pretty plainly that he was suffering from want of sleep.

"It's a good many years since we met, Hazell," he began, "and you have gained quite a reputation since the old college days."

"Ah, I see you have read my monograph on 'Nerve Culture and Rational Food'," replied Hazell.

"Never heard of it," said Cotterell. "No, I mean your reputation as a railway expert, my dear fellow."

"Oh, railways!" exclaimed Hazell in a disappointed tone of voice. "They're just a hobby of mine, that's all. Is that why you've come?"

"Exactly. I called at your flat in town, but was told you were here. I want to consult you on a delicate matter, Hazell; one in which your knowledge of railways may prove of great value. Of course, it is understood that what I am going to say is quite private."

"Certainly."

"Well, let me put a case. Suppose a man was travelling, say, from London to the Continent by the ordinary boat train; and suppose that it was desirable to prevent that man from getting to his destination, would it – well – would it be possible to prevent him doing so?"

Hazell smiled.

"Your enigma is a difficult one to answer," he said. "It would all depend upon the means you cared to employ. I daresay it could be done, but you would probably have to resort to force."

"That would hardly be politic. I want you to suggest some plan by which he could be got into a wrong train, or got out of the right one, so that, let us say, something he was carrying would be lost, or, at least, delayed in transit."

"You are not very clear, Cotterell. First you speak of the man being frustrated, and then of something he is carrying. What do you mean? Which is of the greater importance – the man or his property?"

"His property."

"That puts a different aspect on it. I take it this is some intrigue of your profession. Why not place confidence in me, and tell me the whole thing? I never like to work on supposition. Once some fellows tried to draw me on a supposed case of wrecking a train. I could have told them half-a-dozen theories of my own invention, but I held my tongue, and lucky it was that I did so, for I found out afterwards they belonged to an American train robber gang. I don't accuse you of any nefarious purposes, but if you want my advice, tell me the exact circumstances. Only, I warn you beforehand, Cotterell, that I won't give you any tips that would either compromise me or be of danger to any railway company."

"Very well," replied the Under-Secretary, "I will tell you the leading facts without betraying any State secrets, except to mention that there is a great stake involved. To cut matters short, a very important document has been stolen from our office. We pretty well know the culprit, only we have no proof. But we are certain of one thing and that is that this document is at present in the hands of the German Ambassador. You will understand that the ways of diplomacy are very subtle and that it is a case which makes action very difficult. If we were to demand the surrender of this paper we should be met, I have no doubt, with a bland denial that it is in the Ambassador's possession.

"Of course we have our secret agents, and they have told us that Colonel Von Kriegen, one of the messengers of the German Embassy, has been ordered to start at midday with dispatches to Berlin. It is more than likely – in fact it is a dead certainty – that this particular document will be included in his dispatches. Now, if it once gets into the possession of the German Chancellery, there will be a bad international trouble which might even land us in a Continental war. If you can devise any means of obstructing or preventing the transit of this dispatch you would be rendering the country a real service."

Hazell thought for a moment.

"Do you think this Colonel Von Kriegen knows of the document he is carrying?" he asked presently.

"I shouldn't think so, its contents are of far too much importance to trust even to a regular messenger. No, he will probably be told to exercise the greatest care, and his journey will be watched and himself guarded by the German secret police."

"How is he likely to carry the document?"

"In his dispatch-box, together with other papers."

"And he will probably travel with secret police. My dear fellow, you have given me a hard nut to crack. Let me think a bit."

He lit a cigarette and smoked hard for a few minutes. Presently he asked Cotterell if the dispatch-box had a handle to it.

"Yes – of course," replied the Under-Secretary; "a leather handle."

"I wish I knew exactly what it was like."

"I can easily tell you. All the dispatch-boxes of the German Embassy are of the same pattern. It is our business to know the smallest details. It would be about a foot long, eight inches broad, and about five inches deep, with a handle on the top – a dark green box."

Hazell's face lit up with sudden interest.

"You haven't one exactly like it?" he asked.

"Yes, we have. At my office."

"Will the key be with the Colonel?"

"Of course not. The Ambassador here will lock it, and it will not be opened till it is in the hands of the Chancellor in Berlin."

Hazell jumped to his feet and began to stride up and down the room.

"Cotterell!" he exclaimed, "there's just one plan that occurs to me. It's a very desperate one, and even if it succeeds it will land me in prison."

"In England?" asked the other.

"Rather. I'm not going to play any tricks on the Continent, I can tell you. Now, suppose I'm able to carry out this plan and am imprisoned – say at Dovehaven – what would happen?"

He stopped abruptly in his walk and looked at Cotterell. A grin broke over the latter's face, and he said, quietly:

"Oh – you'd escape, Hazell."

"Very good. I shall want help. *You'd* better not come. Have you got a knowing fellow whom you can trust? He must be a sharp chap, mind."

"Yes, I have. One of our private men, named Bartlett."

"Good. There are just two hours before the Continental train starts, and a quarter of an hour before you get a train back to town. You wire Bartlett from Netherton to meet you, and I'll write out instructions for you to give him. He'll have an hour in which to carry them out."

He wrote rapidly for five minutes upon a sheet of paper, and then handed it over to the Under-Secretary.

"Mind you," he said, "the chances are terribly against us, and I can only promise to do my best. I shall follow you to town by another train that will give me just time to catch the boat express. What is this Von Kriegen like?"

Cotterell described him.

"Good – now you must be off!"

Three-quarters of an hour later Hazell came out of his house, somewhat changed in appearance. He had put on the same dark wig which he wore in the affair of Crane's cigars, and was dressed in a black serge suit and straw hat. A clerical collar completed the deception of a clergyman in semi-mufti.

* * *

A stiffly-upright, military-looking man, with the ends of his fair moustache strongly waxed, dressed in a frock coat suit and tall hat, and carrying a dispatch-box, walked down the platform beside the boat train, the guard, who knew him well by sight – as he knew many who travelled on that line with their precious dispatches – giving him a salute as he passed.

Two men walked closely, but unobtrusively behind the Colonel; two men whose eyes and ears were on the alert, and who scrutinised everyone carefully as they passed along. Of their presence the Special Messenger took not the slightest notice, though he was well aware of their companionship. He selected a first-class compartment, and got in. The two men followed him into the carriage, but without saying a word. One of them posted himself by the window, and kept a steady look out on to the platform.

The train was just about to start, and the guard had just put his whistle to his mouth, when a man came running down the platform, a small bag in one hand, a bundle of papers and an umbrella in the other. It was only a clergyman, and the man at the window gave a smile as he saw him.

With a rush, the clergyman made for the compartment, seizing the handle of the door and opening it. Frantically he threw his bag, umbrella, and papers into the carriage. The train had just begun to move.

The man near the window had retreated at the onslaught. He was just about to resent the intrusion with the words that the compartment was engaged, when a porter, running up behind the clergyman, pushed him in and slammed the door.

"I thought I'd lost it!" exclaimed the intruder, taking off his hat and wiping the perspiration from his forehead, for it was a very hot day, and he had been hurrying. "It was a close shave! Oh, thank you, thank you!" he added, as one of the men rather ungraciously picked up his bag and papers from the floor, at the same time eyeing him closely.

But Hazell, in his disguise, was perfectly proof against any suspicion. He sat down and opened the *Guardian* with an easy air, just looking round at each of his three companions in such a naturally inquisitive manner as to thoroughly disarm them from the outset. The Colonel had lighted a cigar and said, half apologetically, as he took it from his lips:

"I hope you don't mind smoking?"

"Oh, not at all. I do it myself occasionally," returned the clergyman with an amiable smile.

The train was now fairly under way, and Hazell was beginning, as he read his paper, to take mental stock of his surroundings and the positions in which the other three were seated.

He, himself, was facing the engine on the left-hand side of the compartment, close to the window. Immediately opposite to him sat Colonel von Kriegen, watchful and alert, although he seemed to smoke so complacently. Beside the Colonel, on the seat on his left, was the precious dispatch-box; and the Colonel's hand, as it dangled negligently over the arm-rest, touched it ever and anon. On the next seat, guarding the dispatch-box on that side, sat one of the secret police agents, while the other had placed himself next to Hazell and, consequently, opposite the box, which was thus thoroughly guarded at all points.

It was this dispatch-box that Hazell was studying as he apparently read his paper, noting its exact position and distance from him. As he had told Morton Cotterell, the chances of carrying out his plan were very much against him, and he felt that this was more than ever the case now. He had really hoped to secure a seat beside the box. But this was out of the question.

After a bit he put down his paper, leant forward, and looked out of the window, watching the country as they sped through it. Once, just as they were passing through a station, he stood up and leant his head out of the window for a minute. The three men exchanged glances now that his back was turned, but the Colonel only smiled and shook his head slightly.

Then Hazell sat down once more, yawned, gathered up his paper, and made another apparent attempt to read it. After a bit, he drew a cigarette case from his pocket, took out a cigarette, and placed it in his mouth. Then he leant forward, in a very natural attitude, and began feeling in his waistcoat pocket for a match.

The German Colonel watched him, carelessly flicking the ash from his cigar as he did so. Then, as it was apparent that the clergyman could find no matches, his politeness came to the front.

"You want a light, sir," he said in very good English, "can I offer you one?"

"Oh, thanks!" replied Hazell, shifting to the edge of his seat, and leaning still more forward, "perhaps I may take one from your cigar?"

Every action that followed had been most carefully thought out beforehand. As he leant over towards the German he turned his back slightly on the man who sat beside him. He held the cigarette with the first and second fingers of his right hand and with the end of it in his mouth. He kept his eyes fixed on the Colonel's. Meanwhile his left hand went out through the open window, dropped over the sill, remained there a moment, then came back, and crossed over the front of his body stealthily with the palm downwards.

It was all over in a second, before either of the three had time to grasp what was happening. He had his face close up to the Colonel's, and had taken a puff at the cigarette, when suddenly his left hand swooped down on the handle of the dispatch-box, his right hand flew forward into the Colonel's face, instantly coming round with a quick sweep to his left hand, and, before the Colonel could recover or either of the others take action, he had tossed the dispatch-box out of the window.

They were on him at once. He sprang up, back to the window, and made a little struggle, but the Colonel and one of the others had him on the seat in no time. Meanwhile the third man had pulled the electric safety signal, and had dashed to the window. Thrusting his head out, he looked back along the level bit of line on which they were running.

"I can see it!" he cried triumphantly, as his eye caught a dark object beside the track. The whole affair had taken place so suddenly that the train began to pull up within fifteen or twenty seconds of the throwing out of the dispatch case. There was a shrill whistle, a grinding of brakes, and the train came to a standstill.

The guard was out of his van in an instant, running along beside the train.

"What is it?" he asked, as he came up to the carriage.

The police agent, who still kept his eyes fixed back on the track, beckoned him to come up. Heads were out of windows, and this matter was a private one. So the guard climbed on to the footboard.

"A dispatch-box has been thrown out of the carriage," whispered the police agent; "we have the man here. But we must get the case. It's only a little way back. We pulled the signal at once – in fact, I could see it lying beside the track before we stopped."

"Very good, sir," replied the guard quietly, commencing to wave an arm towards the rear of the train. The signal was seen on the engine, and the train began to reverse. Very soon a small, dark object could be seen alongside the rails. As they drew close, the guard held out his hand motionless, the train stopped, and he jumped off.

"Is this it?" he asked, as he handed in the dispatch-box.

"Yes!" exclaimed the Colonel, "it's all right. Thank you, guard. Here's something for your trouble. We'll hand over the fellow to the police at Dovehaven. It was a clumsy trick."

Colonel Von Kriegen lit another cigar as the train went on, and looked at Hazell, who sat between the two police agents. There was a half smile on the Colonel's lips as he said:

"I'm afraid you did not quite succeed, sir! It was a sharp thing to do, but it didn't go quite far enough. You might have been sure that in broad daylight, and with the means of stopping the train, that it was impossible. Who put you on to this?"

"I accept the entire responsibility myself," replied Hazell – "failure and all. I have only one favour to ask you. Will you allow me to eat my lunch?"

"Oh, certainly," replied the Colonel grimly – "especially as you won't have a chance of doing so when we arrive at Dovehaven. I should like you to travel all the way with us, but the exigencies of international law prevent that."

Hazell bowed, and the next moment was placidly consuming Plasmon biscuits and drinking sterilised milk, expatiating at intervals on "natural food."

"Try a diet of macaroni and Dutch cheese," were his last words to the Colonel. "They both help to build up the grey brain material. Useful in your position!"

When the train arrived at Dovehaven, Hazell was given into the charge of the police there, and marched off to the station. Here the superintendent looked at him curiously. Hazell met his gaze, but nothing was said. It was strange, however, that he was not locked up in an ordinary cell, but in a small room.

It was also strange that the bar of the window was very loose, and that no one was about when he dropped out of it that night. The German police, when they heard about it, smiled. Diplomatic affairs are peculiar, and they knew that this particular "criminal" would never be caught.

Meanwhile, the Colonel journeyed on to Berlin, with the full assurance in his mind that the papers in his dispatch-box were intact. He duly handed the latter over in person to the Chancellor, who, as the result of a cypher telegram, was eagerly expecting it.

Somehow, his key did not fit the lock of the dispatch-box. After trying it for a few moments, he exclaimed:

"Colonel, how is this? This is not one of our boxes, surely?"

The Colonel's face turned pale, and he hesitated to reply. Snatching up a knife, the Chancellor forced open the box, a cry of dismay issuing from his lips as he drew out the contents – the current number of *Punch*, in which he figured in a cartoon, and a copy of the *Standard*, containing an article, carefully marked, on the foreign policy of the Government. Insult to injury, if you like.

German oaths never look well in print, and, anyhow, it is needless to record the ensuing conversation between the Chancellor and Colonel Von Kriegen. At about the time it was taking place the German Ambassador in London received by post the original dispatch-box and its contents, minus the incriminating document, which now reposed safely in the custody of the Foreign Office, thanks to the ingenuity of Thorpe Hazell.

* * *

"How was it done?" said Hazell afterwards, when telling the story to a companion. "Oh, it was a pure trick, and I hardly expected to be able to bring it off. Fortunately, Bartlett was a 'cute chap, and followed out all my instructions to the letter. Those instructions were very simple. I told him to wear an Inverness cloak, to provide himself with the duplicate dispatch-box, a few yards of very strong fishing twine, a fair-sized snap-hook, and a light walking-stick with a forked bit of wire stuck in the end of it. The only difficulty about his job was the presence of other travellers in his compartment, but, as it happened, there were only two maiden ladies, who thought him mad on fresh air.

"Of course, I told him how to use his various articles, and also that on no account was he to communicate with me either by word or look, but that he was to get into the compartment next to that in which the Colonel was travelling, and to be ready to command either window by reserving a seat with a bag on one side and seating himself on the other.

"The cloak served for a double purpose – to hide the dispatch-box and to conceal his movements from the occupants of his carriage when the time for action came. Fortunately, both his companions sat with their backs to the engine, so that he was easily able to command either window.

"I was to let him know which side of the train was the sphere of action by putting out my head as we ran through Eastwood. He would then look out of both windows and get to work accordingly.

"What he did was this. He had the snap-hook tied tightly to the end of the fishing-line. By leaning out of the window and slinging this hook on the fork of his walking-stick he was able to reach it along the side of the carriage – holding his stick at the other end – and slip the hook over the handle outside my door, where it hung by its cord.

"He then dropped the stick and held the cord loosely in his right hand, the slack end ready to run out. This, you will observe, kept the hook hanging on my handle. With his left hand he drew the dispatch-box from under his cloak and held it outside the carriage, ready to drop it instantly.

"Of course he was standing all the time, with his head and shoulders out of the window.

"When I leant forward to light my cigarette at the Colonel's cigar, I slipped my left hand out of the window, easily found the hook hanging there, grasped it, and kept it open with one finger. Bartlett, who was watching, got ready. You can easily guess the rest. I swung my left hand suddenly over to the dispatch-box, Bartlett allowing the line to run through his hand, snapped the hook over the handle before they could see what I was about, and pitched it out of the window as lightly as possible.

"The same instant Bartlett dropped the duplicate box from the train, grasped the line tightly as the real dispatch-box flew out, and hauled it in, hand over hand. He very soon had the dispatch-box safely stowed under his cloak, and, on reaching Dovehaven, took the next train back to town, to the no small satisfaction of his chief.

"Unluckily, I quite forgot to ask Cotterell to mention in the wire I knew he would be sending to the police at Dovehaven to have a dish of lentils ready for me in my brief imprisonment. It was very awkward. But they made me an exceedingly well-cooked tapioca pudding."

Biographies & Sources

Cleve F. Adams
Flowers for Violet
(Originally Published in *Clues Detective Stories*, 1936)
Born in Chicago, pulp fiction writer Cleve F. Adams (1884–1949) lived an adventurous life, working variously as a copper miner, movie studio art director, life insurance salesman, soda jerk, life insurance executive and even as a private detective. He began writing fiction in the 1930s and soon started selling his raucous stories to pulp magazines, including *Clues*, *Dime Detective* and *Black Mask*. He also wrote under the pseudonyms John Spain and Franklin Charles. His most notable creation was the first hard-boiled woman detective, Violet McDade. A former circus fat lady, Violet is big, brawny, and as tough as any of her male counterparts.

B. Morris Allen
Parameters of Social Dispersion in Domestic Lawn Populations
(First Publication)
B. Morris Allen is a biochemist-turned-activist-turned-lawyer-turned-foreign-aid-consultant, and frequently wonders whether it's time for a new career. He's been traveling since birth, and has lived on five of seven continents, but the best place he's found is the Oregon coast. When he can, he makes his home there. In between journeys, he works on his own speculative stories of love and disaster. His dark fantasy novel *Susurrus* came out in 2017 and his short stories have featured in a number of venues. Find out more at www.BMorrisAllen.com.

Donald J. Bingle
Patience
(Originally Published in *Sol's Children*, 2002)
Donald J. Bingle is the author of six books and more than fifty shorter works in the mystery, thriller, horror, science fiction, fantasy, steampunk, romance, comedy, and memoir genres, including *Frame Shop*, a murder mystery set in a suburban writers' group, two spy thrillers (*Net Impact* and *Wet Work*), and (with Jean Rabe) *The Love-Haight Case Files*, a paranormal urban fantasy mystery thriller about two lawyers who represent the legal rights of supernatural creatures in a magic-filled San Francisco. Don resides in Illinois. More on his writing can be found at www.donaldjbingle.com.

Guy Boothby
An Imperial Finale
(Originally Published in *Pearson's Magazine*, 1897)
Best known for his sensational fiction, writer and novelist Guy Boothby (1867–1905) was born in Adelaide, South Australia, but spent most of his life in England. He initially tried his hand at theatre, writing and performing in light operas in Adelaide before deciding to seek his fortune in London. He eventually reached his destination in the early 1890s, publishing an account of his travels in 1894. This was followed by his first novel, *In Strange Company*, later that year. He continued to write prolifically across a wide range of genres, including detective fiction, completing over 53 novels by the time of his death.

Ernest Bramah

The Game Played in the Dark

(Originally Published in *News of the World,* 1913)

Little is known about Ernest Bramah (1868–1942), due to his reclusive nature. The English writer began his adult life as a farmer, but gave it up after three years, pursuing instead a writing career at a London newspaper. 'The Game Played in the Dark' features the blind detective Max Carrados, who deftly solves cases using his heightened skills of perception. Like Bramah, Carrados is remarkably precise and witty. The Max Carrados stories existed alongside the Sherlock Holmes tales in *The Strand Magazine*, and enjoyed equal success at the time.

John Buchan

Dr. Lartius

(Originally Published in *The Runagates Club*, 1928)

John Buchan (1875–1940) was born in Scotland and throughout his life worked as a novelist, journalist, historian, politician and soldier. After graduating from Oxford he spent much of his time writing, while exploring a career as a barrister and then as private secretary to the High Commissioner for South Africa. Buchan carried out the role of war correspondent for *The Times* during the First World War until he joined the army. His most famous novel *The Thirty-Nine Steps* was published in 1915 and follows Richard Hannay who protects Britain from German spies whilst following the notes of a murdered secret agent. The novel is still hugely successful and has been made into various film adaptations. Buchan continued writing a number of adventure and thriller novels, producing over one hundred works throughout his life, making him popular in the UK and Scotland in particular, as well as internationally.

G.K. Chesterton

The Vanishing Prince

(Originally Published in *Harper's Monthly Magazine*, 1920)

Gilbert Keith Chesterton (1874–1936) is best known for his creation of the worldly priest-detective Father Brown. The Edwardian writer's literary output was immense: around two hundred short stories, nearly one hundred novels and about four thousand essays, as well as weekly columns for multiple newspapers. Chesterton was a valued literary critic, and his own authoritative works included biographies of Charles Dickens and Thomas Aquinas, and the theological book *The Everlasting Man*. Chesterton debated with such notable figures as George Bernard Shaw and Bertrand Russell, and even broadcasted radio talks. His detective stories were essentially moral; Father Brown is an empathetic force for good, battling crime while defending the vulnerable.

Carroll John Daly

Under Cover

© 2020 Estate of Carroll John Daly. All rights reserved.

(Originally Published in *Black Mask*, 1925–26)

Best known as the author of the first piece of hard-boiled fiction, 'The False Burton Combs' (1922), New York-born author Carroll John Daly's (1889–1958) work continues to influence the genre today. A prolific writer of pulp fiction, his stories were regular features in *Black Mask* and *Dime Detective*. At one point, Carroll's name alone could make sales rocket. His most famous character, Race Williams, was hugely popular with readers, and became the tough, cynical blueprint for the countless hard-talking private eyes that have come after him.

Norbert Davis

Don't Give Your Right Name

(Originally Published in *Dime Detective*, 1941)

Born in Morrison, Illinois, Norbert Davis (1909–49) moved to California to study law at Stanford, before putting his studies aside to pursue his literary ambitions. He soon became a writer for *Black Mask* and *Dime Detective*, gaining a reputation for his witty, inventive stories that combined comedy with hard-boiled crime. Most remembered for his crime and detective fiction, Davis also wrote a variety of other stories, including westerns and romance tales, war and adventure – not to mention five novels. Although his life was tragically cut short when he died by suicide at the age of forty, he left behind a legacy as one of the most original voices in pulp.

Richard Harding Davis

The Frame-Up

(Originally Collected in *Somewhere in France*, 1915)

One of the most celebrated journalists of his time, Richard Harding Davis's (1864–1916) dashing looks and daring exploits as a war reporter made him something of a celebrity and national hero, with many men at the turn of the century emulating his appearance. He published his first book of short stories, *The Adventures of My Freshman*, in 1884, while at university. His appointment to managing editor at *Harper's Weekly* in 1890 was followed by another foray into fiction. Davis's short stories were met with swift success, and he went on to publish numerous short stories, novels, and plays, many of which were adapted into films.

Ramon Decolta

Diamonds of Death

(Originally Published in *Black Mask*, 1931)

Raoul Falconia Whitfield (1896–1945), who wrote under the pseudonyms Ramon Decolta, and Temple Field, is best known for his hard-boiled stories about Jo Gar, a Filipino detective in interwar Manila. New York-born Whitfield was no doubt influenced by the time he spent there in his youth with his father, a civil servant. A silent film actor and World War I pilot, Whitfield started submitting stories to pulp magazines in 1924, and would become a regular name in *Black Mask* and a host of other pulp magazines.

Arthur Conan Doyle

The Adventure of the Bruce-Partington Plans

(Originally Published in *The Strand Magazine*, 1908)

The Final Problem

(Originally Published in *The Strand Magazine*, 1893)

Arthur Conan Doyle (1859–1930) was born in Edinburgh, Scotland. As a medical student he was so impressed by his professor's powers of deduction that he was inspired to create the illustrious and much-loved figure Sherlock Holmes. Holmes is known for his keen power of observation and logical reasoning, which often astounds his companion Dr. Watson. Whatever the subject or character, Doyle's vibrant and remarkable writing has breathed life into all of his stories, engaging readers throughout the decades.

Mignon G. Eberhart

The Man Who Was Missing

Copyright © 1934 by Mignon G. Eberhart. Renewed 1961. From *The Cases of Susan Dare* (Mysterious Press/Open Road Media, 2012). Used by permission. All rights reserved. (Originally Published in *The Delineator*, 1934)

With a career that spanned from the 1920s to the 1980s, Mignon Good Eberhart's (1899–1996) success was almost unparalleled among her contemporaries. Eberhart first took up writing as a teenager, and later returned to it after she married in 1923. Her first novel, *The Patient in Room 18* (1929), introduced Nurse Sarah Keate, one of Eberhart's many female protagonists and among the most popular mystery characters of the era. Within the next decade, Eberhart was America's leading female crime novelist, thanks in no small part to her prolific output.

Tom English

The Deadly Sin of Sherlock Holmes

(Originally Published in *Gaslight Arcanum: Uncanny Tales of Sherlock Holmes*, 2011)

Tom English is an environmental chemist who loves watching old movies, reading vintage comic books, and writing strange tales of the supernatural. His stories have appeared in *Weirdbook* and *Black Infinity Magazine*, and several anthologies, including *Re-Haunt*, *Challenger Unbound*, *Dead Souls*, and Flame Tree Publishing's *Haunted House Short Stories*. Tom also edited *Bound for Evil: Curious Tales of Books Gone Bad*, a 2008 Shirley Jackson Award finalist for best anthology; and has written four inspirational books with his wife, Wilma Espaillat English. He resides with Wilma, surrounded by books and beasts, deep in the woods of New Kent, Virginia.

T.Y. Euliano

Gator Bait

(First Publication)

T.Y. Euliano's writing is inspired by her day job as a physician, researcher and educator. A tenured professor at University of Florida, she's received numerous teaching awards, approximately 100,000 views of her YouTube teaching videos, and was featured in a calendar of women inventors. Her short fiction has been recognized by *Glimmer Train*, *Bards and Sages*, and the Faulkner Society. Unlike most doctors, she dispenses medical advice for free – as long as the patient is fictional. Her blog teuliano.wordpress.com helps writers get the medical details right, because nothing ruins a scene quite like having a character on a ventilator carry on a conversation.

Robert Eustace

The Mystery of the Circular Chamber (with L.T. Meade)

(Originally Collected in *The Master of Mysteries*, 1898)

Madame Sara (with L.T. Meade)

(Originally Published in *The Strand Magazine*, 1902)

Working under the pseudonyms Robert Eustace and Eustace Robert Rawlings, English doctor Eustace Robert Barton (1854–1943) authored several works of mystery and crime fiction. His scientific and medical expertise often informed his work, both thematically (his stories are known for their preoccupation with scientific innovation) and in terms of key plot components. He frequently collaborated with other authors, including L.T. Meade, Edgar Jepson, and Dorothy L. Sayers, supplying them with necessary supporting medical and scientific information.

Tracy Fahey
Down We Go Together
(First Publication)
Tracy Fahey is an Irish writer of Gothic fiction. In 2017, her debut collection *The Unheimlich Manoeuvre* was shortlisted for a British Fantasy Award for Best Collection. Her first novel, *The Girl in the Fort*, was published in 2017 by Fox Spirit Press, and her second collection, *New Music for Old Rituals* was released in 2018 by Black Shuck Books. She is published in over twenty-five Irish, US and UK anthologies. Her PhD is on the Gothic in visual arts, and her non-fiction writing on arts practice has been published in edited collections and journals. She has been awarded residencies in Ireland and Greece.

R. Austin Freeman
The Echo of a Mutiny
(Originally Published in *Pearson's Magazine*, 1911)
London-born R. Austin Freeman (1862–1943) was at the forefront of Edwardian detective fiction, along with his contemporary G.K. Chesterton. Freeman trained as a physician, working as a colonial surgeon in West Africa until illness sent him back to England. He continued to practise medicine, producing in his spare time a crime series centred on the character Dr. Thorndyke. An early forensic scientist, Thorndyke uses a precise scientific approach to analyse data in his laboratory. Beginning with *The Singing Bone* (1912), Freeman is credited as being the first to develop the inverted detective story, where the focus rests not on the culprit – who can be known from the start – but on the process of solving the case.

Anna Katharine Green
The Grotto Spectre
(Originally Collected in *The Golden Slipper and Other Problems for Violet Strange*, 1915)
Mother of detective fiction Anna Katharine Green (1846–1935) was born in Brooklyn, New York. A poet even at a young age, she later turned her hand to detective novels, perhaps partly inspired by stories from her lawyer father. She enjoyed immediate success with *The Leavenworth Case*, the first outing for the amiable but eccentric Inspector Ebenezer Gryce. Having found a successful formula, but always coming up with original and intriguing plots, Green went on to write around thirty novels as well as several short stories. She created interesting detective heroes and established several conventions of the genre, her name becoming synonymous with popular, original and well-written detective fiction.

Auguste Groner, and Grace Isabel Colbron (translator)
The Case of the Golden Bullet
(Originally Published in 1892)
Austrian writer Auguste Groner (1850–1929) is known internationally for her contribution to detective fiction. Born Auguste Kopallik in Vienna, she first studied painting at the Museum of Applied Arts, before training as a teacher. Over the course of her life, Groner worked as a teacher and was on the staff of several magazines. She first took up writing in 1882, and in 1890 introduced Joseph Müller in *The Case of the Pocket Diary Found in the Snow*, creating the first serial detective in German fiction. By 1893 Groner's renown had grown so great that she was recognized at the Chicago World's Fair, and Müller would appear in her work

for decades to come. Her stories have been translated into English by New York author and translator Grace Isabel Colbron (1869–1948).

Lee Horsley
Foreword: Detective Thrillers Short Stories
Lee Horsley is a retired Reader in Literature and Culture at Lancaster University. She has written books on twentieth-century politics and literature, including *Fictions of Power in English Literature 1900-1950* (1995). During the last couple of decades she has written numerous articles and books about crime and detective fiction. Her publications include *The Noir Thriller* (2001; 2009), *Twentieth-Century Crime Fiction* (2005), and (as co-editor) *The Blackwell Companion to Crime Fiction* (2010; paperback reissue 2020). Her strongest interest is in the hard-boiled and noir writing which came to dominate pulp publishing in the 1920s and which has, over the whole of the last century, continued to exert a hugely important and varied influence on both film and fiction.

Tina L. Jens
A Case of Purloined Lager
(Originally Published in *Tales from the Red Lion*, 2007)
Tina L. Jens' novel, *The Blues Ain't Nothin': Tales of the Lonesome Blues Pub*, won the National Federation of Press Women Best Novel award and was a Final Nominee for the Horror Writers and International Horror Guild awards. She's had more than seventy short stories and twelve poems published in SF/F/H/M markets. She served as Editor for Twilight Tales small press for ten years. For the past decade, she's taught the fantasy writing courses at Columbia College. Jens received the 2017 Rubin Family Fellowship artist residency at Ragdale Foundation. She lives in Chicago, IL, with her husband and guinea pig.

William Le Queux
The Woman with a Blemish
(Originally Collected in *Stolen Souls*, 1895)
Anglo-French writer and journalist William Tufnell Le Queux (1864–1927) led a storied life. Born in London and educated in Europe, he grew up to become a diplomat, explorer, pilot, and an early adopter of radio technology, broadcasting from his own station before most homes even had radios. He worked as a journalist throughout the 1880s, editing *Gossip* and *Piccadilly*, before turning his attention to literature. Much of his work dealt with matters of international intrigue: sensationalist tales of spies and invasion which pitted Britain against a series of foreign threats, as in his bestseller *The Invasion of 1910* (1906).

Murray Leinster
Murderer's Encore
© 2020 Steeger Properties, LLC. All rights reserved.
(Originally Published in *Dime Detective*, 1953)
Murray Leinster was the pseudonym of American author William Fitzgerald Jenkins (1896–1975). An enormously prolific writer, he published his first story in 1916 at the age of nineteen, and wrote one thousand five hundred stories over the course of his career, continuing to publish work well into the 1960s. Though best known for his science fiction, he also turned his hand to detective fiction, horror, romance, and westerns, as well as novels and scripts for film, television and radio.

Tom Mead
Heatwave
(First Publication)
Tom Mead is a UK-based author and playwright. He has previously written for *Litro Online*, *Flash: the International Short-Short Story Magazine*, *Glassworks*, *Lighthouse*, *Ellery Queen Mystery Magazine*, *THAT Literary Review* and *Alfred Hitchcock Mystery Magazine*, amongst others. His work also appears in the Flame Tree Publishing anthologies *Cosy Crime Short Stories* and *Detective Mysteries*. His one-act play *Persons Unknown* was produced at London's Canal Café Theatre in September 2018. He has recently completed his first novel, a macabre locked-room mystery called *Occam's Razor*.

L.T. Meade
The Mystery of the Circular Chamber (with Robert Eustace)
(Originally Collected in *The Master of Mysteries*, 1898)
Madame Sara (with Robert Eustace)
(Originally Published in *The Strand Magazine*, 1902)
Elizabeth Thomasina Meade Smith (1844–1914), writing under the pen name L.T. Meade, was an enormously prolific English author – so much so that eleven out of her approximate three hundred works were published posthumously. Recognized today as an early feminist, she belonged to the progressive Pioneer Club and the founder and editor of *Atalanta*, a monthly periodical for girls. Smith wrote across numerous genres, occasionally collaborating with other authors, such as Robert Eustace. Her and Eustace's partnership also yielded some notable female villains, including Madame Koluchy, criminal mastermind and leader of the 'Brotherhood of the Seven Kings'.

Arthur Morrison
The Narrative of Mr. James Rigby
(Originally Collected in *The Dorrington Deed Box*, 1897)
Arthur Morrison (1863–1945) was born in the East End of London. He later became a writer for *The Globe* newspaper and showed a keen interest in relating the real and bleak plight of those living in London slums. When Arthur Conan Doyle killed off Sherlock Holmes in 1893, a vacuum opened up for detective heroes. In the wake Morrison created Martin Hewitt, publishing stories about him in *The Strand Magazine*, which had also first published Sherlock Holmes. Though a man with genius deductive skill, Morrison's Hewitt character was the polar opposite to Holmes: genial and helpful to the police. He was perhaps the most popular and successful of these new investigator fiction heroes.

Frederick Nebel
Death Alley
(Originally Published in *Dime Detective*, 1931)
Staten Island-born Louis Frederick Nebel (1903–67) dropped out of high school at 15, working variously as a dockworker and valet before moving to Canada to work as a farmhand. His experience of the Canadian wilderness inspired his earliest works, a number of adventure stories which appeared in the magazine *Northwest Stories*. He soon started selling detective stories to *Black Mask*, and became a regular contributor under editor (and mentor) Joseph Shaw. Nebel's stories appeared in a number of other pulp magazines

of the era, before he eventually moved on to 'slick' magazines such as *Collier's* and *Cosmopolitan* in 1937.

Jonathan Shipley
Countdown
(First Publication)
Jonathan Shipley is a Fort Worth writer of fantasy, science fiction, and horror whose writing ranges from traditional fantasy to vampires to futuristic space opera. Although he self-identifies as a novelist, it is short fiction where he has enjoyed success, with sales of over a hundred stories. He was a contributing author to the *After Death* anthology that won the 2014 Bram Stoker award, and last December he was a speaker at the 2018 World Building Conference in Graz, Austra, which opened up his writing to an international audience.

Harriet Prescott Spofford
In a Cellar
(Originally Published in *Atlantic Monthly*, 1859)
Harriet Prescott Spofford (1835–1921) was born in Maine, with the family moving to Massachusetts during her early life. From the age of seventeen she supported her family with her early published stories: her mother was an invalid and her father, one of the California Gold Rush Pioneers and a founder of Oregon City, suffered from paralysis. Spofford published over one hundred stories in the next few years, but it was her 1858 publication of 'In a Cellar' in *The Atlantic Monthly* that elevated her reputation and secured her future as a widely successful author.

Cameron Trost
The Disappearance of Jeremy Meredith
(First Publication)
Cameron Trost is a writer of strange, mysterious, and creepy tales about people just like you. He is the author of *Hoffman's Creeper and Other Disturbing Tales* and *The Tunnel Runner*, and is the creator of Oscar Tremont, Investigator of the Strange and Inexplicable. Like Oscar, he hails from Australia but now lives on the rugged coast of Brittany, and they both love castles, forests, storms, and a dram of fine whisky.

Marie Vibbert
Volatile Memory
(First Publication)
Besides selling forty-odd short stories, twenty-some poems and a few comics and interactive fictions, Marie Vibbert has been a medieval (SCA) squire, ridden seventeen per cent of the roller coasters in the United States and has played for the Cleveland Fusion women's tackle football team. Her work has been called '...the embodiment of what science fiction should be...' by *The Oxford Culture Review*. Follow her @mareasie on Twitter or learn more at marievibbert.com.

Desmond White
Water Bees
(First Publication)
Desmond White is a speculative writer and English teacher. He is the editor-in-chief of *Rune Bear*, assistant editor of *Coffin Bell*, and has prose and poetry published in *HeartWood*,

The Tishman Review, *Kasma Magazine*, *Ghost Parachute*, *Rue Scribe*, and others. In 2018, Desmond's short story 'House Divided' was included in Z Publishing's *America's Emerging Writers*. Now for a fun fact: Desmond White has lived in Indonesia, China, and Venezuela. Currently, however, he resides in Denver, Colorado, with his wife and her cats and the two thousand strays she feeds by the door.

Victor L. Whitechurch
The Affair of the German Dispatch-Box
(Originally Collected in *Thrilling Stories of the Railway* 1912)
Victor Lorenzo Whitechurch (1868–1933) was a clergyman, educated at Chichester Theological College in England. He was also a fiction writer, best known for characters such as the vegetarian, fitness fanatic and detective Thorpe Hazell; and spy Ivan Koravitch. Whitechurch wrote several stories inspired by his clerical vocation, however he was also a railway enthusiast, as evidenced by his many railway mysteries featuring the detective Godfrey Page and later better developed with his Thorpe Hazell stories. The eccentric nature of Hazell was intended as a contrast to Sherlock Holmes.